The
MX Book
of
New
Sherlock
Holmes
Stories
Part XXXVII – 2023 Annual
(1875-1889)

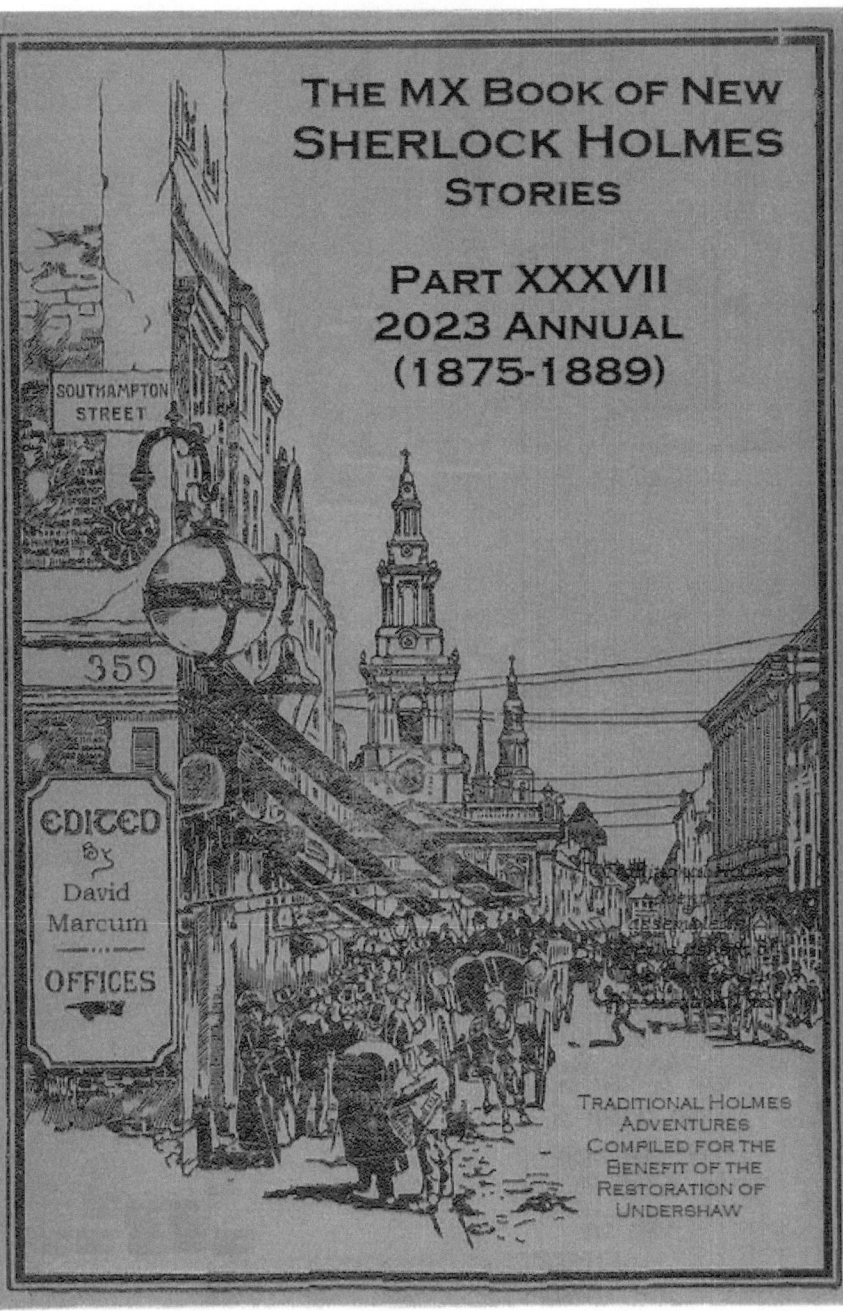

THE MX BOOK OF NEW SHERLOCK HOLMES STORIES

STORIES

PART XXXVII
2023 ANNUAL
(1875-1889)

SOUTHAMPTON STREET

359

EDITED BY
David Marcum

OFFICES

TRADITIONAL HOLMES
ADVENTURES
COMPILED FOR THE
BENEFIT OF THE
RESTORATION OF
UNDERSHAW

ISBN Hardback 978-1-80424-221-6
ISBN Paperback 978-1-80424-222-3
AUK ePub ISBN 978-1-80424-223-0
AUK PDF ISBN 978-1-80424-224-7

Published in the UK by
MX Publishing
335 Princess Park Manor, Royal Drive,
London, N11 3GX
www.mxpublishing.co.uk

David Marcum can be reached at:
thepapersofsherlockholmes@gmail.com

Cover design by Brian Belanger
www.belangerbooks.com and *www.redbubble.com/people/zhahadun*

Internal Illustrations by Sidney Paget

CONTENTS

Forewords

Adventures

(Continued on the next page . . . .)

(Continued on the next page . . . .)

(Continued on the next page . . . .)

(Continued on the next page . . . .)

(Continued on the next page . . . .)

PART V – Christmas Adventures

(Continued on the next page . . . .)

(Continued on the next page . . . .)

The Unwelcome Client – Keith Hann
The Tempest of Lyme – David Ruffle
The Problem of the Holy Oil – David Marcum
A Scandal in Serbia – Thomas A. Turley
The Curious Case of Mr. Marconi – Jan Edwards
Mr. Holmes and Dr. Watson Learn to Fly – C. Edward Davis
Die Weisse Frau – Tim Symonds
A Case of Mistaken Identity – Daniel D. Victor

PART VII – Eliminate the Impossible: 1880-1891
Foreword – Lee Child
Foreword – Rand B. Lee
Foreword – Michael Cox
Foreword – Roger Johnson
Foreword – Melissa Farnham
Foreword – David Marcum
No Ghosts Need Apply (A Poem) – Jacquelynn Morris
The Melancholy Methodist – Mark Mower
The Curious Case of the Sweated Horse – Jan Edwards
The Adventure of the Second William Wilson – Daniel D. Victor
The Adventure of the Marchindale Stiletto – James Lovegrove
The Case of the Cursed Clock – Gayle Lange Puhl
The Tranquility of the Morning – Mike Hogan
A Ghost from Christmas Past – Thomas A. Turley
The Blank Photograph – James Moffett
The Adventure of A Rat. – Adrian Middleton
The Adventure of Vanaprastha – Hugh Ashton
The Ghost of Lincoln – Geri Schear
The Manor House Ghost – S. Subramanian
The Case of the Unquiet Grave – John Hall
The Adventure of the Mortal Combat – Jayantika Ganguly
The Last Encore of Quentin Carol – S.F. Bennett
The Case of the Petty Curses – Steven Philip Jones
The Tuttman Gallery – Jim French
The Second Life of Jabez Salt – John Linwood Grant
The Mystery of the Scarab Earrings – Thomas Fortenberry
The Adventure of the Haunted Room – Mike Chinn
The Pharaoh's Curse – Robert V. Stapleton
The Vampire of the Lyceum – Charles Veley and Anna Elliott
The Adventure of the Mind's Eye – Shane Simmons

PART VIII – Eliminate the Impossible: 1892-1905
Foreword – Lee Child
Foreword – Rand B. Lee
Foreword – Michael Cox
Foreword – Roger Johnson
Foreword – Melissa Farnham

(Continued on the next page . . . .)

Part IX – 2018 Annual (1879-1895)

(Continued on the next page . . . .)

(Continued on the next page . . . .)

(Continued on the next page . . . .)

PART XIV: 2019 Annual (1891 -1897)

(Continued on the next page . . . .)

(Continued on the next page . . . .)

(Continued on the next page . . . .)

Part XIX: 2020 Annual (1882-1890)

(Continued on the next page . . . .)

(Continued on the next page . . . .)

Part XXII: Some More Untold Cases (1877-1887)

(Continued on the next page . . . .)

The Dundas Separation Case – Kevin P. Thornton
The Broken Glass – Denis O. Smith

Part XXIII: Some More Untold Cases (1888-1894)
Foreword – Otto Penzler
Foreword – Roger Johnson
Foreword – Steve Emecz
Foreword – Jacqueline Silver
Foreword – David Marcum
The Housekeeper (*A Poem*) – John Linwood Grant
The Uncanny Adventure of the Hammersmith Wonder – Will Murray
Mrs. Forrester's Domestic Complication– Tim Gambrell
The Adventure of the Abducted Bard – I.A. Watson
The Adventure of the Loring Riddle – Craig Janacek
To the Manor Bound – Jane Rubino
The Crimes of John Clay – Paul Hiscock
The Adventure of the Nonpareil Club – Hugh Ashton
The Adventure of the Singular Worm – Mike Chinn
The Adventure of the Forgotten Brolly – Shane Simmons
The Adventure of the Tired Captain – Dacre Stoker and Leverett Butts
The Rhayader Legacy – David Marcum
The Adventure of the Tired Captain – Matthew J. Elliott
The Secret of Colonel Warburton's Insanity – Paul D. Gilbert
The Adventure of Merridew of Abominable Memory – Tracy J. Revels
The Affair of the Hellingstone Rubies – Margaret Walsh
The Adventure of the Drewhampton Poisoner – Arthur Hall
The Incident of the Dual Intrusions – Barry Clay
The Case of the Un-Paralleled Adventures – Steven Philip Jones
The Affair of the Friesland – Jan van Koningsveld
The Forgetful Detective – Marcia Wilson
The Smith-Mortimer Succession – Tim Gambrell
The Repulsive Matter of the Bloodless Banker – Will Murray

Part XXIV: Some More Untold Cases (1895-1903)
Foreword – Otto Penzler
Foreword – Roger Johnson
Foreword – Steve Emecz
Foreword – Jacqueline Silver
Foreword – David Marcum
Sherlock Holmes and the Return of the Missing Rhyme (*A Poem*) – Joseph W. Svec III
The Comet Wine's Funeral – Marcia Wilson
The Case of the Accused Cook – Brenda Seabrooke
The Case of Vanderbilt and the Yeggman – Stephen Herczeg

(Continued on the next page . . . .)

Part XXV: 2021 Annual (1881-1888)

(Continued on the next page . . . .)

The Switched String – Chris Chan
The Case of the Secret Samaritan – Jane Rubino
The Bishopsgate Jewel Case – Stephen Gaspar

Part XXVI: 2021 Annual (1889-1897)
Foreword – Peter Lovesey
Foreword – Roger Johnson
Foreword – Steve Emecz
Foreword – Jacqueline Silver
Foreword – David Marcum
221b Baker Street (*A Poem*) – Kevin Patrick McCann
The Burglary Season – Marcia Wilson
The Lamplighter at Rosebery Avenue – James Moffett
The Disfigured Hand – Peter Coe Verbica
The Adventure of the Bloody Duck – Margaret Walsh
The Tragedy at Longpool – James Gelter
The Case of the Viscount's Daughter – Naching T. Kassa
The Key in the Snuffbox – DJ Tyrer
The Race for the Gleghorn Estate – Ian Ableson
The Isa Bird Befuddlement – Kevin P. Thornton
The Cliddesden Questions – David Marcum
Death in Verbier – Adrian Middleton
The King's Cross Road Somnambulist – Dick Gillman
The Magic Bullet – Peter Coe Verbica
The Petulant Patient – Geri Schear
The Mystery of the Groaning Stone – Mark Mower
The Strange Case of the Pale Boy – Susan Knight
The Adventure of the Zande Dagger – Frank Schildiner
The Adventure of the Vengeful Daughter – Arthur Hall
Do the Needful – Harry DeMaio
The Count, the Banker, the Thief, and the Seven Half-sovereigns – Mike Hogan
The Adventure of the Unsprung Mousetrap – Anthony Gurney
The Confectioner's Captives – I.A. Watson

Part XXVII: 2021 Annual (1898-1928)
Foreword – Peter Lovesey
Foreword – Roger Johnson
Foreword – Steve Emecz
Foreword – Jacqueline Silver
Foreword – David Marcum
Sherlock Holmes Returns: The Missing Rhyme (*A Poem*) – Joseph W. Svec, III
The Adventure of the Hero's Heir – Tracy J. Revels
The Curious Case of the Soldier's Letter – John Davis
The Case of the Norwegian Daredevil – John Lawrence
The Case of the Borneo Tribesman – Stephen Herczeg
The Adventure of the White Roses – Tracy J. Revels

(Continued on the next page . . . .)

Part XXVIII: More Christmas Adventures (1869-1888)

(Continued on the next page . . . .)

Part XXIX: More Christmas Adventures (1889-1896)

Part XXX: More Christmas Adventures (1897-1928)

(Continued on the next page . . . .)

The Adventure of the Chained Phantom – J.S. Rowlinson
Santa's Little Elves – Kevin Thornton
The Case of the Holly-Sprig Pudding – Naching T. Kassa
The Canterbury Manifesto – David Marcum
The Case of the Disappearing Beaune – J. Lawrence Matthews
A Price Above Rubies – Jane Rubino
The Intrigue of the Red Christmas – Shane Simmons
The Bitter Gravestones – Chris Chan
The Midnight Mass Murder – Paul Hiscock

Part XXXI: 2022 Annual (1875-1887)

Foreword – Jeffrey Hatcher
Foreword – Roger Johnson
Foreword – Steve Emecz
Foreword – Emma West
Foreword – David Marcum
The Nemesis of Sherlock Holmes (A Poem) – Kelvin I. Jones
The Unsettling Incident of the History Professor's Wife – Sean M. Wright
The Princess Alice Tragedy – John Lawrence
The Adventure of the Amorous Balloonist – I.A. Watson
The Pilkington Case – Kevin Patrick McCann
The Adventure of the Disappointed Lover – Arthur Hall
The Case of the Impressionist Painting – Tim Symonds
The Adventure of the Old Explorer – Tracy J. Revels
Dr. Watson's Dilemma – Susan Knight
The Colonial Exhibition – Hal Glatzer
The Adventure of the Drunken Teetotaler – Thomas A. Burns, Jr.
The Curse of Hollyhock House – Geri Schear
The Sethian Messiah – David Marcum
Dead Man's Hand – Robert Stapleton
The Case of the Wary Maid – Gordon Linzner
The Adventure of the Alexandrian Scroll – David MacGregor
The Case of the Woman at Margate – Terry Golledge
A Question of Innocence – DJ Tyrer
The Grosvenor Square Furniture Van – Terry Golledge
The Adventure of the Veiled Man – Tracy J. Revels
The Disappearance of Dr. Markey – Stephen Herczeg
The Case of the Irish Demonstration – Dan Rowley

Part XXXII: 2022 Annual (1888-1895)

Foreword – Jeffrey Hatcher
Foreword – Roger Johnson
Foreword – Steve Emecz

(Continued on the next page . . . .)

Part XXXIII: 2022 Annual (1896-1919)

(Continued on the next page . . . .)

Part XXXIV: "However Improbable . . . ." (1878-1888)

Part XXXV: "However Improbable . . . ." (1889-1896)

(Continued on the next page . . . .)

Part XXXVI: "However Improbable . . . ." (1897-1919)

The following contributors appear
in the companion volumes:
The MX Book of New Sherlock Holmes Stories
Part XXXVIII – 2023 Annual (1890-1896)
Part XXXIX – 2023 Annual (1897-1823)

Editor's Foreword:
The Sherlockian Reformation
by David Marcum

We are in a Golden Age of Sherlock Holmes, and have been since 1974. The demarcation is quite defined. Before that fateful year, Holmes was known the world over, and even then he was indisputably the greatest detective of all time – despite what a few other Great Detectives might have declared about themselves – but before 1974, finding ways to enter and enjoy The World of Holmes were severely limited. There were editions of The Canon – but not nearly so many as today. There were a few pastiches, but for most people, they might as well have never existed. These might be published in some magazine that would rotate off the newsstands after a month, never to be seen or found again by the common person. A scholarly work or occasional pastiche might be written for those within the tightly controlled Sherlockian community, with no intention to ever share it outside that circle.

This went on for decades – until 1974, when the modern-day Sherlockian equivalent of Martin Luther, Nicholas Meyer, nailed a new Holmes adventure to the church door, *The Seven-Per-Cent Solution*, his version of Luther's *Ninety-five Theses*, and gave Holmes to the masses, starting the Sherlockian Reformation.

And thank God he did.

The years when The Canon initially appeared, between 1887 and 1927, seem like a long stretch of time – three whole decades – but when one considers that just a pitifully few sixty stories were published during that time, what readers were able to learn about Holmes and Watson over the course of that span was actually severely limited. Sixty stories over thirty years – that averages just two stories per year. A starvation diet! And in truth, the appearances of the original stories were even more irregular.

A Study in Scarlet was published in November 1887, and *The Sign of the Four* in 1890 – and neither made a ripple. It was only in June 1891, just a month after Holmes's supposed death at the Reichenbach Falls, that Watson – wishing to spread the word about his recently deceased friend – published "A Scandal in Bohemia" in a new magazine, *The Strand*. The results were electrifying – and one wonders if *The Strand* would have gone on to such great heights without the infusion of Holmes's adventures during its early days.

1

Between June 1891 and December 1893, Watson, with the assistance of the First Literary Agent, published twenty-four shorter narratives. This run of two-dozen tales came to an end for several reasons. Watson, already grief-stricken due to Holmes's death, was further rocked by the death of his wife Mary, most likely in 1893. No doubt his enthusiasm for life – and writing – was severely damaged during this bleak period. His Literary Agent, a doctor named Arthur Conan Doyle who had notions of becoming the next Sir Walter Scott with his dense historical novels, was tired of being identified with Holmes's adventures, and wanted to disassociate himself from the project. And finally, Colonel James Moriarty, the brother of Professor James Moriarty, began to attack the memory of Sherlock Holmes by way of letters, leaving Watson no choice but to respond by laying forth the true facts of Holmes's fateful Swiss encounter with the Professor. When "The Final Problem" was published in December 1893, Watson likely felt that writing other posthumous adventures was unnecessary.

At that time, much of the world was shocked to learn that Holmes had apparently died over two years earlier, on May 4th, 1891. While those who had known Holmes had been aware of it at the time, he was generally unknown to the public – particularly due to his insistence that others take the credit for his work – so his 1891 passing went largely unremarked. The announcement in 1893 rocked the world.

After Watson wrote and published "The Final Problem", his Literary Agent moved on to other things, and Watson apparently lost the will to continue producing new stories. One wonders what might have happened to him, a widower living alone in Kensington, working at a practice that likely left him quite uninspired, and eking out his days, one after another *ad infinitum*, in a dull routine of existence.

Then came a dramatic moment of fate – specifically on April 5th, 1894 – when Watson re-encountered Sherlock Holmes, not dead at all, but rather working in the shadows for nearly three years, carrying out missions in foreign lands and awaiting the opportunity to return to London and finish up the Moriarty affair. After a quick bit of business that same night in an empty house in Baker Street, Holmes was once again free to devote his life to examining those interesting little problems which the complex life of London so plentifully presented.

But this did not include allowing any more of his adventures to be published in *The Strand*.

This probably suited Watson, at least for a while. He sold his practice and returned to Baker Street, and appears to have taken a much-greater interest in Holmes's cases throughout the rest of the nineties and early 1900's – until his remarriage in Fall 1902.

For this period, The Proto-Canon consisted of twenty-six stories – two longer adventures and the twenty-four shorter tales that had appeared in *The Strand*, and later collected – with one exception – in *The Adventures of Sherlock Holmes* and *The Memoirs of Sherlock Holmes*. From August 1901 to April 1902, just one other story, another longer tale, appeared serially, *The Hound of the Baskervilles*, and when it was finished, the story count rose to twenty-seven – not very many published adventures over a fifteen-year period, and very little indeed for those early admirers of Mr. Holmes to explore and enjoy.

In Fall 1903, Holmes "retired" – ostensibly to Sussex to be a hermit apiarist, but actually to carry out various important chores for this brother Mycroft, laying the groundwork for England's defense against the ever-increasing German aggressions, and the inevitable war which was certainly coming. It was then that Watson was released to publish another set of cases – all clearly set before Holmes's publicized "retirement". These thirteen narratives, appearing from October 1903 to December 1904 and later collected as *The Return of Sherlock Holmes*, raised the Canonical count to forty.

And after that, they were published in a scattered run over the next twenty-three years. Between 1908 and 1917, Watson published eight stories, One of these, *The Valley of Fear*, was a longer case, and Watson was certainly prompted to publish it in 1915, as it told of Pinkerton agent Birdy Edwards' infiltration of The Scowrers – much like Holmes had recently done from 1912 to 1914 when, as Altamont, he infiltrated the German spy network in the years leading up to the War.

His Last Bow (including "The Cardboard Box", originally published in 1892 but not collected in *The Memoirs*) was published in 1917. And then – nothing for four more years. Eventually, another set of irregular adventures began to appear, a dozen of them from October 1921 to March 1927. There was one each for 1921, 1922, and 1923, three in 1924, four in 1926, and two in 1927. And that was it. The Canon was complete. These final twelve of sixty were collected and published in 1927 as *The Case-Book of Sherlock Holmes* – and that was the end. Sixty tales and no more.

Or so it was believed. And as so many to this day would try to enforce.

But in 1974, a pastiche was nailed to the church door, and the Sherlockian Reformation began, and there was no going back.

Thank God.

The years between 1927 and 1974 must have been bleak times for many Sherlockians. As mentioned, there were editions of The Canon, but if someone wanted to know more about Holmes beyond that, then he or she was mostly out of luck. There were some very obscure and esoteric scholarly works published, but most people probably didn't know about them and couldn't easily obtain them. A few local Sherlockian organizations were formed throughout the United States, but attendance was usually by strict invitation only (and then only if you were male and knew someone on the inside – no common Sherlockian riff-raff need apply.) And even if one was interested, most of these organizations met in locations that were far out of reach for the majority of Americans in different parts of the country. (In contrast, the much-more-welcoming and democratic Sherlock Holmes Society of London was founded in 1951, following the amazing success of the Holmes display in Baker Street during the Festival of London. American Sherlockian fellowship remained much more . . . exclusive.)

Like esoteric Sherlockian scholarship of this period between 1927 and 1974, new Holmes adventures were also a rare thing. There had been numerous parodies of Holmes since the early days of original Canonical publication, but these unsatisfying and un-clever drabs don't count. William Gillette's 1899 play, *Sherlock Holmes*, was possibly the first legitimate extra-Canonical adventure – and also the first example of someone foisting his or her own incorrect ideas onto Watson's notes. A romance with Alice Faulkner? Professor *Robert* Moriarty? *Pfui!*

In the years before and after the last Canonical story was published in 1927, a few additional new cases appeared for those who needed more – even if they weren't exactly correct. In print was Vincent Starrett's "The Unique *Hamlet*" (1920). There were a few pastiche films, such as John Barrymore's *Sherlock Holmes* (1922). Radio dramas were mightily important in the 1930's and 1940's, and Edith Meiser had the brilliant idea of adapting The Canon to radio – the two went together perfectly. But after a few years of repeating the same Canonical stories, Meiser began broadcasting extra-Canonical cases as well – and that door would never be shut again.

Further pastiche films followed starring actors who looked like Holmes – Arthur Wontner and Basil Rathbone. The occasional obscure pastiche appeared in print, such as Arthur Whitaker's curious "The Case of the Man Who Was Wanted" (1948). For a short while in the late 1920's, and then resuming in the mid-1940's, August Derleth brought forth Solar Pons adventures – *The Sherlock Holmes of Praed Street* – but like Sherlockian scholarship, these ended up being known to only a few people inside the circle, and they were almost a secret for decades – until the post-1974 world when the Sherlockian Reformation began.

1954 saw the publication of *The Exploits of Sherlock Holmes* by Adrian Conan Doyle and John Dickson Carr. This is a good set of stories, but it was viciously attacked at the time, particularly by The Baker Street

Irregulars, in part because of Adrian Conan Doyle's previous attacks on everyone else who had an interest in Holmes – for he felt that all roads to Holmes must lead through him. Ironically, there were others who felt that they were Holmes's Keepers, and that their own legitimacy was being challenged.

That all changed in 1974, when Nicholas Meyer published *The Seven-Per-Cent Solution*. It was a runaway best-seller, and made into a very successful film the following year. The pastiche had been nailed to the door of the restrictive established Church of Holmes, and people realized that they didn't have to kiss someone's ring to be a Sherlockian.

There was now a different path that bypassed this restrictive route. Numerous pastiches followed, and they have only grown exponentially.

And thank God.

As mentioned, the Solar Pons stories were published for the masses for the first time in the mid-1970's. Other mainstream pastiches followed by the likes of Nicholas Utechin and Sean Wright and John Gardner. Nicholas Meyer found more of Watson's hidden manuscripts. This was the same period when other fandoms began to exert similar influence. For example, the fires of *Star Trek*'s popularity were kept burning throughout the 1970's – from the cancellation of the original show in 1969 to the first film in 1979 – by amateurs who created fan fiction, self-publishing and distributing it by way of very amateur-looking home-made documents. The same was happening with Sherlockian pastiches. There were a number of little self-printed volumes produced during this period. Some were excellent stories (and some not-so-excellent), typed and copied by the authors, folded and assembled and stapled by the authors, and sold by the authors. These are now expensive and rare collector's items – and it's quite amusing that they are now so valued, in spite of their terrible formatting errors and typos, by the same people who treat modern Sherlockian publishing, with its same earnest sincerity, with a gibe and a sneer.

Before his unfortunate passing in 2018, Sherlockian Phil Jones had assembled and maintained a database of Sherlockian pastiches. It began to get away from him in his final years, but that was understandable, because there were so many more pastiches appearing every day. (Thank God.) Phil's Excel spreadsheet had grown to over 10,000 entries. Of course, a sizeable amount of these weren't traditional Canonical pastiches, but still, that's a lot of post-Canonical adventures. If Phil were still alive and maintaining the database, there would be many more entries, and I'm very proud that the stories in *The MX Book of New Sherlock Holmes Stories* would occupy a very sizable percentage of all known Sherlockian pastiches.

Consider: If non-traditional and non-Canonical pastiches were trimmed off of Phil's database, reducing it to an arbitrary 8,000 entries, then the MX anthologies would be over *10%* of that. With the publication of these new volumes, Parts XXXVII, XXXVIII, and XXXIX, we've now reached over *800* Sherlock Holmes adventures! In actuality, the traditional pastiches on Phil's very complete list were probably quite a bit less than 8,000, so the MX books likely occupy an even greater percentage of all the traditional Canonical pastiches that have ever been written.

The idea for these books occurred in 2015, as a push-back against the idea of a modernized broken Holmes that was infiltrating the traditional pastiches that I collect and read. Even authors who should have known better, and who were supposedly writing about the True Holmes in the correct era, were slipping in references to Holmes's *"mind palace"*, or that he was a *"high-functioning sociopath"*, and including *"Mike"* Stamford, *"Greg"* Lestrade, and Molly Hooper. It was becoming the new baseline that Watson's wound was psychosomatic, and that Mary Watson was a secret government assassin, Irene Adler a shady dominatrix, and Mrs. Hudson the widow of a drug dealer. It needed to be re-established that Holmes was a *hero*, born in the 1850's, and not a broken obnoxious creep born in the 1970's. And apparently this was appreciated, because these MX collections have since become the biggest and bestselling Holmes anthology of all time, thirty-nine massive volumes (so far) with more in the works from over 200 worldwide contributors. And along the way, the authors' generously contributed royalties have raised over *$110,000* (so far) – that's *One-Hundred-and-Ten Thousand Dollars!* – for the Undershaw school for special needs children at one of Sir Arthur Conan Doyle's former homes.

But as a Sherlockian, the best part of all of this to me is the new adventures. As a child, I discovered Holmes at age ten in 1975, one year after the Sherlockian Reformation began. (Luckily I was unaware of all of those bleak years between 1927 and 1974.) Even then, in those early days, there were very few extra-Canonical adventures once the pitifully few Sixty were read (and re-read and re-read . . . .) I *starved* for more Holmes. And now there is more, and I'm no longer going hungry . . . and thank God *. . . but there still aren't enough Holmes adventures.*

Holmes abhorred *"the dull routine of existence"*. Imagine how he would have felt to have his career defined by only sixty cases. Even adding the 140+ "Untold Cases" mentioned in the Canon only brings it to around two-hundred – which Holmes would have certainly called a *"dull routine"* if that's all there was.

Instead, new extra-Canonical adventures bring us *"the dramatic moment of fate"*, as described by Holmes, *"when you hear a step upon the stair which is walking into your life, and you know not whether for good or ill.*" As the lucky editor of these books, as well as a number of similar True Holmes anthologies published by Belanger Books, I now receive new Holmes adventures *nearly every day*! Before I start to read these new submissions, each is undefined and, as Holmes once said, presents "*infinite possibilities*". The new story might be tragic or comic. Gothic horror or police procedural. Country settings or in town. Early in Holmes and Watson's friendship, or late. The thrill of receiving and reading new Holmes stories *never gets old*. It's an addiction – and I know that it's shared by many others, the very faithful supporters of these books.

For those, like me, who need more traditional Canonical Holmes adventures, consider what it was like in a pre-1974 world, with very few Holmes adventures beyond the very-much re-read Canon. The new publishing paradigm that now immediately connects authors to readers didn't exist. Instead, getting anything published at all in those days was nearly impossible, and when (or if) it finally was, many readers would never know about it, or have the chance to read it. And except for a select few, being a Sherlockian was severely limited by those who desperately kept access restricted and the church door locked. They still would, if they could, but now it's far too late.

In 1974, a pastiche was nailed to the church door, and the Sherlockian Reformation began, and there's no going back.

Thank God.

* * * * *

"Of course, I could only stammer out my thanks."
– The unhappy John Hector McFarlane, "The Norwood Builder"

As always when one of these collections is finished, I want to thank with all my heart my incredible, patient, brilliant, kind, and beautiful wife of almost thirty-five years, Rebecca – Every day I'm more stunned at how lucky I am than the day before! – and our amazing, funny, creative, and wonderful son, and my friend, Dan. I love you both, and you are everything to me!

With each new set of the MX anthologies, some things get easier, and there are also new challenges. For several years, the stresses of real life have been much greater than when this series started. Through all of this, the amazing contributors have once again pulled some amazing works from the Tin Dispatch Box. I'm more grateful than I can express to every contributor who has donated both time and royalties to this ongoing project. It's amazing what we've accomplished. I also want to give special

7

recognition to the multiple contributors of this set: Arthur Hall, Sonya Kudei, Tracy Revels, Dan Rowley and Don Baxter, Tom Turley, and Peter Coe Verbica. Finally, I cannot express how thankful I am to all of those who keep buying these books and making them the largest and most popular Sherlockian anthology ever.

I'm so glad to have gotten to know so many of you through this process. It's an undeniable fact that Sherlock Holmes authors are the *best* people!

I wish especially thank the following:

- *Michael Sims* – I'm thrilled that Mr. Sims is participating in these books. He has written a wonderful biography of the Literary Agent, *Arthur and Sherlock*, and additionally, I've enjoyed reading his posts on social media for years. I was thrilled to discover that he is originally from Crossville, Tennessee, a small town about an hour west of where I live, and where my wife and I were married. Michael: I can't thank you enough for your support and participation!

- *Steve Emecz* – From my first association with MX in 2013, I saw that MX (under Steve Emecz's leadership) was *the* fast-rising superstar of the Sherlockian publishing world. Connecting with MX and Steve Emecz was personally an amazing life-changing event for me, as it has been for countless other Sherlockian authors. It has led me to write many more stories, and then to edit books, along with unexpected additional Holmes Pilgrimages to England – none of which might have happened otherwise. By way of my first email with Steve, I've had the chance to make some incredible Sherlockian friends and play in the Holmesian Sandbox in ways that I would have never dreamed possible.

  Through it all, Steve has been one of the most positive and supportive people that I've ever known.

  From the beginning, Steve has let me explore various Sherlockian projects and open up my own personal possibilities in ways that otherwise would have never happened. Thank you, Steve, for every opportunity!

- *Roger Johnson* – From his immediate support at the time of the first volumes in this series to the present, I can't imagine Roger not being part of these books. His Sherlockian knowledge is exceptional, as is the work that he does to further the cause of The Master. But even more than that, both Roger

8

and his wife, Jean Upton, are simply the finest and best of people, and I'm very lucky to know both of them – even though I don't get to see them nearly as often as I'd like. I look forward to getting back over to the Holmesland sooner rather than later and visiting with them again, but in the meantime, many thanks for being part of this.

- *Brian Belanger* –I initially became acquainted with Brian when he took over the duties of creating the covers for MX Books, and I found him to be a great collaborator, and wonderfully creative too. I've worked with him on many projects with MX and Belanger Books, which he co-founded with his brother Derrick Belanger, also a good friend. Along with MX Publishing, Derrick and Brian have absolutely locked up the Sherlockian publishing field with a vast amount of amazing material. The old dinosaurs must be trembling to see every new and worthy Sherlockian project, one after another after another, that these two companies create. Luckily MX and Belanger Books work closely with one another, and I'm thrilled to be associated with both of them. Many thanks to Brian for all he does for both publishers, and for all he's done for me personally.

And finally, last but certainly *not* least, thanks to **Sir Arthur Conan Doyle**: Author, doctor, adventurer, and the Founder of the Sherlockian Feast. Honored, and present in spirit.

As I always note when putting together an anthology of Holmes stories, the effort has been a labor of love. These adventures are just more tiny threads woven into the ongoing Great Holmes Tapestry, continuing to grow and grow, for there can *never* be enough stories about the man whom Watson described as *"the best and wisest . . . whom I have ever known."*

David Marcum
April 5th, 2023
The 129th Anniversary of
Holmes's Return from
The Great Hiatus

Questions, comments, or story submissions
may be addressed to David Marcum at
thepapersofsherlockholmes@gmail.com

Dark Lantern
by Michael Sims

It was the day before Halloween 1993 and I was prowling the book shelves at the Nashville Goodwill store. Past a thicket of musty shirts and jeans, beyond a junkyard of orphaned kitchen utensils, I was digging for treasure at a dollar a book. I was scanning the bookshelves, left to right, top to bottom, when I felt the hair stand up on the back of my neck.

I had felt a ghost nearby – myself as a young boy.

What my eyes noticed and my instinct recognized before alerting my conscious mind was a fat textbook whose nerdy bulk shouldered aside jacketless volumes gold-stamped *Danielle Steele* and *Dean Koontz*. I saw not a grimy old book but a teenage boy in a wheelchair by a window in a ramshackle house two hours to the east, on the Cumberland Plateau. Late afternoon, with an autumn sunset gilding even the cheap, mismatched bookshelves. I was born in this house in 1958, grew up in it, learned to read in it. The window showed a rocky backyard garden. On a small hill beyond, oak-and-hickory woodland crowded the mown grass. The room held a small bed, bookcases, and a lamp on a rickety table absurdly made from the leaf of a Formica kitchen table.

That boy in memory was reading the same middle-school-level book I had just found on the Goodwill shelves – *Outlooks through Literature*, whose spine bore the names Pooley, Stuart, White, and Cline. On its cover was a drab sepia photograph of men and women silhouetted within the arches of what appeared to be a two-story bridge. Seated in a wheelchair at fourteen, standing in a thrift store at thirty-five, I turned familiar-feeling pages to a Contents list whose items inspired affection that ran like a herald before a montage of memories:

> Unit One, *The Short Story*
> Unit Two, *Biography and Autobiography*
> Unit Three, *A Book of Poetry*
> Unit Four, *Romeo and Juliet*
> Unit Five, *Classical Heritage*
> Unit Six, *A Tale of Two Cities*
> Unit Seven, *At Random*

Unit One opened with "The Adventure of the Speckled Band" by Arthur Conan Doyle, which I now know was among the first Holmes short stories after two novels. It was also the beginning of my own fascination with Victorian fiction. "*It is fear, Mr. Holmes. It is terror,*'" I read at the top of the page. "*These words were enough to challenge the Master Detective, Sherlock Holmes, to an immediate investigation, some rapid deductions, and a brilliant solution.*" Facing it on the left, a colorful full-page illustration portrayed a woman in what appeared to be stages of collapse.

I think this was my first encounter with Sherlock Holmes as a character in a book rather than as distilled mannerisms in a TV movie. This story was the wardrobe that opened into Narnia, the tornado that whirled me to Oz. It drew me into the Holmes stories, and thence into the larger world of Dickens and Eliot, Austen and Darwin. Standing in Goodwill, I felt my cheeks tug into a smile as I perused the footnotes illuminating terms likely to baffle U.S. students: *dogcart, Waterloo, Bengal Artillery.* It was fun to see again the note for *dark lantern* – a lamp that has a movable panel to hide its light, an invention that has always struck me as confusingly metaphorical. I may have met Holmes earlier, thanks to my lepidopteran instinct to sniff every book in the garden, but if so it must have been on a page lacking the scented lure of illustrations and footnotes.

Even scanning quickly that day in 1993, I recalled this uninviting typeface, the antique illustrations, a bulk of 754 pages supposedly meant to be traversed during a school year. The endpapers bore a rubber-stamped *JOHN GLENN HIGH SCHOOL* and a Michigan address. I love about used books' archaeological clues to other lives – shards such as *Merry Christmas, David, from Aunt Iva* or a *Cats* ticket stub marking the last campsite toward the summit before a reader gave up and started back downhill.

Browsing these pages in Goodwill, I found a distinctive aspect of *Outlooks through Literature* that I had forgotten: Extra flourishes around the author bio at the end. Obsessed – almost from birth, it seems now – with how books were created, I had always read author and illustrator biographies, "*By the Same Author*" pages, acknowledgments, and source notes. In revisiting this book I found, beginning an inch below Holmes's explanation to Watson of how he had nudged Dr. Roylott to his grisly death, a section entitled "*Could This Really Have Happened?*"

There I found the results of a careful study by W.T. Williams, "*a British naturalist,*" who determined that there was no such snake as the swamp adder of the story, and that many of its antics no snake could perform. Then came questions under "*What Do You Say?*" and "*Author's Craft,*" a note about prefixes under "*Know Your Words,*" and a paragraph about Conan Doyle. These extras were like windows on the rear of a house, showing tantalizing glimpses of the building through whose back door I

11

had just emerged. It seems to me now, thirty years after rediscovering this book in Goodwill, that I spend most days peering through windows into the pantries and tool sheds of stories to see how they are made.

In late 1971, halfway through the eighth grade, I dropped out of regular school and began studying with "homebound" teachers who came to the house three afternoons a week. I suffered from increasing leg and back and joint pain, later diagnosed as juvenile rheumatic arthritis, blamed on a bout of rheumatic fever. Pain earned me my own room – in the back, overlooking garden and woods. My bed was no more than ten feet above the cellar, with its dusty Mason jars, its spider-webbed wooden shelves fitted into soil walls. Beneath my dreams, frogs declaimed from standing water. So many memories wafted from this volume.

About the same time as my original encounter with this textbook, I spent a stormy night at Erlanger Hospital in Chattanooga. I was scheduled for a spinal tap for early the next morning – the most horrific experience of my life up to then and still a milestone of agony that makes me cringe.

I was in a ward with three old men. At some point one of them was shaved with a dry scraping noise. Suddenly in the darkness after midnight, machines exclaimed and lights were on. One man had died. The only TV on that floor was in a waiting room down the hall. During a fierce thunderstorm someone pushed my wheelchair down there, where we watched *The Hound of the Baskervilles* – Stewart Granger as a pallid sixtyish Sherlock Holmes and William Shatner, of all people, as George Stapleton. Omniscient Google tells me that this version first aired on ABC in February 1972, the month I turned fourteen, but it must have run again later because my memory takes place during a summer thunderstorm. And of course you can always trust memory. Have I merged two hospital visits?

"My dear Mr. Sims," Holmes would murmur, "I must say I find you a most disappointing witness."

During the broadcast, a close flash of lightning was followed by a power outage. Soon, no doubt, the power returned, but my memory stops with the lightning and the demise of the TV screen. I don't recall getting to see the rest of the movie before going back to my room, where soon I woke to a nurse's discovery of the old man's death. I do remember lying in that bed, staring at the ceiling after they wheeled him out, feeling my own pulse ticking like a bomb, thinking about my father's heart attack at thirty-eight, when I was three.

Because I note on its flyleaf the date on which a book enters my life, I see that the year after Erlanger, on 16 December, 1973, I received the two fat volumes of William S. Baring-Gould's *The Annotated Sherlock Holmes* from the mail-order Mystery Guild that enabled me to survive my isolation. They contained the species of footnotes and sidebars found

12

in *Outlooks through Literature*, but these glosses blossomed into a tropical profusion of research and speculation: Illustrations of hansom cabs, meditations on the super-villain snake of "The Speckled Band", biographies of illustrators. Uncomfortable, as usual, in my now private room at home, I stayed up all night after these books arrived in the mail.

As I stood before those Goodwill bookshelves in 1993, I was still two years away from my first publishing deal, for a book of days called *Darwin's Orchestra: An Almanac of Nature in History and the Arts*. In its index I find nine entries on *"Holmes, Sherlock (fictional character)."* Twenty-seven years and sixteen books down the road, I see that the Sherlock Holmes stories were more important to me than I had realized even as the textbook stirred memories of their discovery. They helped enchant literature for me, and gossip about their origin opened a window into formerly opaque history. Doyle and Holmes introduced me to a number of perennial interests I found so entertaining that ultimately I built a career around them.

I have edited eight anthologies of Victorian fiction – including, to show the legacy of that textbook, *The Penguin Book of Murder Mysteries*. Again and again, as I wrote my nonfiction book *Arthur and Sherlock: Conan Doyle and the Creation of Holmes*, I found myself in the emotional terrain of that first encounter and in the nerdy landscape of literary research that the book's footnotes and illustrations inspired.

In the way that literature and life distill experience into essence, this fictional turf has become a site for discovery and adventure, not a place of pain or fear or loss. Those aspects of my childhood have seeped into its soil and perhaps nourish it, but they no longer flower. In waking my imagination and curiosity, Holmes and Watson gave me the possibility of growing up to live in a larger world – a world I first explored amid London's mythic cobblestones and fog, which could be navigated even from a wheelchair.

Michael Sims
March 2023

"What Is It That We Love in Sherlock Holmes?"

by Roger Johnson

Edgar W. Smith, as you may or may not know, was the founder and first editor of *The Baker Street Journal*. His editorial in the second issue of that august and ever-lively organ, dated April 1946, opened with the question above.

"The Implicit Holmes", as he titled it, is not a long piece – only 624 words – but the answers that Smith offers are thoughtful and remarkably comprehensive. They were certainly coloured by the writer's memories of the recent global war, but they remain valid nearly eighty years on.

"We love the times in which he lived, of course: the half-remembered, half-forgotten times of snug Victorian illusion, of gaslit comfort and contentment, of perfect dignity and grace . . . ." Many of his readers would indeed have remembered those times, and would have appreciated the way they are depicted by the detective's faithful amanuensis.

"And we love the place in which the master moved and had his being: the England of those times, fat with the fruits of her achievements, but strong and daring still with the spirit of imperial adventure . . . ." When Smith wrote that, of course, he was very conscious of the devastating changes that England – and notably London – had suffered as a result of enemy action in, not one, but *two* world wars. Since then, political shifts and the neophiliac fervour of the 1960's and '70s have caused yet more drastic and often lamentable alteration, but much of Holmes's England is still there, and the search for it can be very rewarding.

"But there is more than time and space and the yearning for things gone by to account for what we feel toward Sherlock Holmes. Not only there and then, but here and now, he stands before us as a symbol – a symbol, if you please, of all that we are not, but ever would be." One of the most appealing aspects of Sherlock Holmes, it seems to me, is that he is *not* a "super-hero": He can't fly, see through a brick wall – or punch a hole in a brick wall. He can't melt steel with heat-rays from his eyes, or move faster than a speeding bullet, nor will such a bullet bounce harmlessly off him. Sherlock Holmes is one of us – a human being, and his powers are human. You and I could never be like Superman or Captain Marvel, and the chances that we could ever rival Batman are effectively non-existent. But we *could*, perhaps, be like Sherlock Holmes.

"*For it is not Sherlock Holmes who sits in Baker Street, comfortable, competent and self-assured; it is we ourselves who are there, full of a tremendous capacity for wisdom, complacent in the presence of our humble Watson, conscious of a warm wellbeing and a timeless, imperishable content.*" Few of us, I think – and none, I dare say, who read this – would disagree with that statement.

Brief though it is, the whole article is well worth reading, and it doesn't require access to that fabulously rare early issue of *The Baker Street Journal*. You can find it online at:

https://mseffie.com/assignments/sherlock/articles/The%20Implicit%20Holmes.pdf

Read it, and take note of the final sentence: "*That is the Sherlock Holmes we love – the Holmes implicit and eternal in ourselves.*"

And, I would add, that is the Holmes we look for, and thankfully often find, in the stories that the ever-industrious David Marcum has collected and edited for our delight in this wonderful series.

Roger Johnson
BSI, ASH
Commissioning Editor: *The Sherlock Holmes Journal*
February 2023

An Ongoing Legacy
for Sherlock Holmes
by Steve Emecz

Undershaw
Circa 1900

*T*he *MX Book of New Sherlock Holmes Stories* continues to be one of the projects we are most proud of. The total raised for Undershaw school for children with learning disabilities has now passed $110,000.

There are a record 23 positive reviews from *Publishers Weekly* for the collection:

https://bit.ly/MXBookPW

In addition to Undershaw, we also support Happy Life Mission (a baby rescue project in Kenya), The World Food Programme (which won the Nobel Peace Prize in 2020), and iHeart (who support mental health in young people).

Our support for our projects is possible through the publishing of Sherlock Holmes books, which we have now been doing fifteen years. You can find links to all our projects on our website:

https://mxpublishing.com/pages/about-us

We're already looking forward to the autumn and more volumes.

Steve Emecz
March 2023
Twitter: *@mxpublishing*

The Doyle Room at Undershaw
Partially funded through royalties from
The MX Book of New Sherlock Holmes Stories

A Word from Undershaw
by Emma West

Undershaw
September 9, 2016
Grand Opening of the Stepping Stones School
(Now *Undershaw*)
(Photograph courtesy of Roger Johnson)

For this latest instalment of news from Undershaw, you find us waiting with bated breath for the first signs of Spring, but already there is life bursting through every corner of our school. Last week saw our exciting programme of events to mark National Careers Week, during which every student found themselves immersed in presentations, talks, workshops, and challenges themed around various skills and careers. As a school we have so many roles, whether it is to solidify learning, excite our students with new experiences of culture, or simply to listen, understand, and champion each young person. It's all in a day's work here. Our Careers Week was no different. We are passionate about exposing the students to the sheer wealth of possibilities before them as they begin to lay claim to their futures. The qualifications available to the students are just one part of their journey and, as we all know, it's what they choose to do with this academic landscape that will count for so much as they take the long-awaited leaps into their independent lives.

Undershaw is building a unique place for itself amidst a community of corporates, passionate charities, and some trailblazing organisations that all work towards a diverse, equitable, and inclusive world. Lately, we have been approached to provide insights into reports for government which will hopefully provide the bedrock of the workplaces of the future. We educate and inspire other schools on their Special Educational Needs provision, and we have more students than ever on roll and awaiting a place at Undershaw. Without a doubt, it is such a dynamic place, both inside and outside the school gates, but we continue to take each pillar of our provision and challenge ourselves to be the best we can be. Undershaw is so much more than the sum of our parts.

Our Careers Week has been such a highlight of our year so far, and it illustrates the point perfectly that in amongst our qualifications and the latest iterations of our employment record, we all started with drive, ambition, aspiration, and self-belief. This is what we do. Undershaw stands alongside students as they weave their own tapestry of interest, passion, and accomplishment. We are furnishing them with the hard and soft skills required to be successful in the workplaces of the future. What a wholesome endeavor, and one of which we shall never tire.

My heartfelt thanks as ever for joining us on our journey. Our school is something of which you can all feel very proud. It's easy to see where your generosity goes, and with friends like MX Publishing, we all feel we have a passionate band of supporters behind us. I hope you keep up with our news on our website and, if you are ever passing, please do come and see us.

Until next time…

Emma West
Headteacher
March 2023

"Undershaw," Hindhead, Conan Doyle's House.

Editor's *Caveats*

When these anthologies first began back in 2015, I noted that the authors were from all over the world – and thus, there would be British spelling and American spelling. As I explained then, I didn't want to take the responsibility of changing American spelling to British and vice-versa. I would undoubtedly miss something, leading to inconsistencies, or I'd change something incorrectly.

Some readers are bothered by this, made nervous and irate when encountering American spelling as written by Watson, and in stories set in England. However, here in America, the versions of The Canon that we read have long-ago has their spelling Americanized, so it isn't quite as shocking for us.

Additionally, I offer my apologies up front for any typographical errors that have slipped through. As a print-on-demand publisher, MX does not have squadrons of editors as some readers believe. The business consists of three part-time people who also have busy lives elsewhere – Steve Emecz, Sharon Emecz, and Timi Emecz – so the editing effort largely falls on the contributors. Some readers and consumers out there in the world are unhappy with this – apparently forgetting about all of those self-produced Holmes stories and volumes from decades ago (typed and Xeroxed) with awkward self-published formatting and loads of errors that are now prized as very expensive collector's items.

I'm personally mortified when errors slip through – ironically, there will probably be errors in these *caveats* – and I apologize now, but without a regiment of professional full-time editors looking over my shoulder, this is as good as it gets. Real life is more important than writing and editing – even in such a good cause as promoting the True and Traditional Canonical Holmes – and only so much time can be spent preparing these books before they're released into the wild. I hope that you can look past any errors, small or huge, and simply enjoy these stories, and appreciate the efforts of everyone involved, and the sincere desire to add to The Great Holmes Tapestry.

And in spite of any errors here, there are more Sherlock Holmes stories in the world than there were before, and that's a good thing.

David Marcum
Editor

Sherlock Holmes (1854-1957) was born in Yorkshire, England, on 6 January, 1854. In the mid-1870's, he moved to 24 Montague Street, London, where he established himself as the world's first Consulting Detective. After meeting Dr. John H. Watson in early 1881, he and Watson moved to rooms at 221b Baker Street, where his reputation as the world's greatest detective grew for several decades. He was presumed to have died battling noted criminal Professor James Moriarty on 4 May, 1891, but he returned to London on 5 April, 1894, resuming his consulting practice in Baker Street. Retiring to the Sussex coast near Beachy Head in October 1903, he continued to be associated in various private and government investigations while giving the impression of being a reclusive apiarist. He was very involved in the events encompassing World War I, and to a lesser degree those of World War II. He passed away peacefully upon the cliffs above his Sussex home on his 103rd birthday, 6 January, 1957.

Dr. John Hamish Watson (1852-1929) was born in Stranraer, Scotland on 7 August, 1852. In 1878, he took his Doctor of Medicine Degree from the University of London, and later joined the army as a surgeon. Wounded at the Battle of Maiwand in Afghanistan (27 July, 1880), he returned to London late that same year. On New Year's Day, 1881, he was introduced to Sherlock Holmes in the chemical laboratory at Barts. Agreeing to share rooms with Holmes in Baker Street, Watson became invaluable to Holmes's consulting detective practice. Watson was married and widowed three times, and from the late 1880's onward, in addition to his participation in Holmes's investigations and his medical practice, he chronicled Holmes's adventures, with the assistance of his literary agent, Sir Arthur Conan Doyle, in a series of popular narratives, most of which were first published in *The Strand* magazine. Watson's later years were spent preparing a vast number of his notes of Holmes's cases for future publication. Following a final important investigation with Holmes, Watson contracted pneumonia and passed away on 24 July, 1929.

Photos of Sherlock Holmes and Dr. John H. Watson courtesy of Roger Johnson

The
MX Book
of
New

Sherlock

Holmes

Stories

Part XXXVII – 2023 Annual
(1875-1889)

Moriarty
by Kevin Patrick McCann

"My horror at his crimes was lost in my admiration at his skill."

I sense his presence everywhere
Spreading like a tumour,
In quaysides slopped out by the Thames,
Whisperings and rumour.

From Limehouse up to Whitechapel,
Deceptive as a fog,
His puppets strike without pity,
Each one's a soulless cog.

He is my dark *Doppelgänger*,
My mind's demented twin,
I detest him for this craving,
He fills my need for sin.

The Adventure of the
Improbable American
by Will Murray

"Nomenclature," remarked Sherlock Holmes one autumn evening before a crackling fire, "may be one of the most under-appreciated minor branches of knowledge."

I looked up from my magazine. "I beg your pardon?"

"Knowing the proper names for things," replied Holmes, "is not merely the mark of an informed and educated person, but it may at times prove to be essential."

"As a doctor," I returned, "I know this to be true."

"As a physician," said Holmes, "I imagine you know the correct name for the space between the eyes."

"Yes, of course. It is called the *gabela*."

"And the vertical indentation below the human nose?"

"The *philtrum*."

"What about the thin wall of cartilage that separates the nostrils?"

"It is the *septum*."

"Very good. Now can you name the fleshly part of the nose directly beneath the septum?"

Here, I hesitated. My memory couldn't conjure the proper word – or any word. I was baffled. "I confess to being stumped," I informed my friend. "I believe I once knew the term. Alas, it presently escapes me."

"Permit me to recover it for you then. *Columella nasi* is the name that eludes you."

"Oh, yes. I recall hearing of a patient who suffered such a severe injury to his nose that both septum and *columella nasi* had to be surgically removed, giving him rather the appearance of a man cursed with the flat nose of an ape."

"Before I met you, an early problem that I sought to solve revolved around proper nomenclature."

"Is that so?"

"I can say, with confidence, that a man's life, or rather the preservation of same, was the direct result of knowing the correct term for something."

"Singular," I exclaimed. "Would you do me the kindness of relating the story?"

"The mystery itself appeared rather trifling when first presented to me, but as I fell into it, it grew and grew until it became so enlarged that it threatened the life and limb of a close friend. It initially involved the recondite meanings of obscure American words and progressed from there."

"Go on," I encouraged. "You know that I am constantly fascinated by your doings."

Holmes paused to relight his black clay pipe, which had gone out. Once satisfied that the bowl was properly fuming, he resumed speech.

"As I was saying, my dear Watson, these doings took place when I was quite young and first living in Montague Street, beside the British Museum, where I spent a great deal of my leisure time when not contending with clients. As I recall, the year was 1875.

"It was in the spring of that year, when I made the acquaintance of a ginger-haired American named Garrett. I chanced upon him at a public house one evening and remarked that I could see that he had recently traveled by train, and quite some distance, and further that he hadn't traveled as a passenger. Therefore he was a brakeman."

"He neither denied my deduction, nor confirmed it. Eying me speculatively, he asked, 'How do you come by that proposition?'

"'Your boots are coated in a residue of cinders and coal dust of a type and composition that could only from frequent association with moving trains, particularly goods and coal trains. From this, I would assume that you work for the London and North Western Railway. You don't have the wind-burned and grimy countenance of an engineer, so that is out. Therefore, I conclude that you must be a train guard.'

"He laughed, and clapped me on the back, saying, 'Well done!'

"'Furthermore,' I continued, 'although your accent suggests that you were raised in the East End of London, possibly in Shoreditch, in recent years you have lived in America.'

"This took him aback. 'I'll not deny it,' he stated, 'but since we are strangers, I must insist that you explain yourself.'

"'The pocket watch dangling from your vest is of American manufacture,' I told him. 'You employed the word 'proposition', where a lifelong Englishman would have used 'supposition'. 'Proposition' is an Americanism.'

"Smiling broadly, the man returned, 'For that, friend, I insist upon buying you a pint.'

"And so commenced my friendship with the singular and improbable Mr. James Garrett.

"I found him to be rather eccentric, and no doubt he thought the same of me. We became friends after a fashion. He was the first American who had ever befriended me, and I was anxious to learn about life in the corner colonies from a man who had dwelt in that country. But he proved to be strangely elusive, if not niggardly, with facts, often avoiding substantive conversational turns.

"Garrett claimed to be an inveterate reader, but when I questioned him as to his preferred authors, he laughed and told me I would probably not know them since they were American writers whose works were never published in England. He was an impudent sort, prone to giving nicknames to people that were often obscure, if not impenetrable.

"I hadn't known Garrett long when he commenced calling me Zeus. When I asked him why, he said it was because of my lofty brow and Olympian ambitions. I took this as a compliment at first, but frankly admit that the habit began to rankle me after increasingly frequent use.

"Now he hailed from Philadelphia, and was a railroad man – his term for it – who had traveled all over the United States of America before coming to England to care for his aging mother. At the time I knew the fellow, his father had passed away and his mother was failing – hence his abandonment of America for his natal city.

"Garrett worked as a train guard only upon occasion, the necessity of tending to his surviving mother's needs mandating this indulgence in seeming indolence. Since my time was also often free, we shared many meals during our leisure hours.

"You are no doubt," Holmes asked me, "familiar with the practice of Cockney rhyming slang."

"I am."

"Mr. Garrett seems to have coined his own version of it. Where the Cockney idler might say 'box of toys' to signify 'noise', and 'bees and honey' to suggest 'money', this American was partial to words that rhymed with *goose*."

"That suggests a rather limited vocabulary," I ventured, "if not a peculiar turn of mind."

"While it does," agreed Holmes, "the man was highly inventive, if not ingenious in his extemporaneous coinings. I will give an example. The first time I heard him speak thus, we were in a public house on a very rainy day and in walked a rather large man who was notably hirsute. His ears practically sprouted fur.

"'What ho, Zeus!' Garrett said to me, referring to me by that name for the first time. ''Take a gander at the hulking moose who just sauntered in as big as you please from the juice sluice.'

"I looked over to the entrance door and beheld this rather enormous fellow that I have just described. I gathered that I was somehow Zeus to friend Garrett, but I had never before heard the word 'moose'. The 'juice sluice' referred to the downpour from which the patron was attempting to escape.

"'What on earth is a 'moose'?' I inquired. 'I am unfamiliar with the term.'

"Garrett studied me a moment and seemed to suppress a smile. I gathered that he was amused by my ignorance – I, who had regaled him with accounts of some of my early exploits.

"'Since you are fond of spending so much time at the British Museum,' he suggested to me, 'why don't you look up the word?'

"This I attempted to do, but I will confess that I got nowhere. I couldn't find the word in any British dictionary or any other work I consulted.

"When next I saw Garrett, I raised the question again.

"'Small wonder, Zeus,' he said. 'The word comes from an Indian term, *wampoose*.'

"'Thank you for that morsel,' I replied. 'My original question stands yet unanswered.'

"'A moose is something which, when encountered, motivates smart men to vamoose,' Garrett stated in his jocular way.

"Here I paused to consider this new term. 'I am unfamiliar with the term "vamoose",' I allowed.

"'Well,' he said politely, 'it isn't to be confused with the Indian term, for it is Spanish.'

"'How do you spell this word?' I asked him.

"Garrett spelled out the word as v-a-m-o-o-s-e. But I recognized from my Spanish that it was an American corruption of the word *vamos*, meaning to run away from something.

"'I take it that a "moose" is something fearful, if not frightful,' I suggested.

"'That, Lord Zeus, depends upon the moose.' And that was all he would say about it. I grew rather frustrated, because even in those days I was an inveterate seeker of knowledge and there was no information too minute or obscure to consider unworthy of absorbing.

"When next I ran into Garrett, I told him that I had consulted certain knowledgeable savants of my acquaintance, but all were baffled by the nonsensical word, 'moose'.

"This time, he laughed. That I was confounded seemed to have amused him.

"'A word can have many meanings, of course,' he pointed out. 'But not all of these can be found in the dictionary.'

"'"Moose" is a slang word then,' I suggested to him.

"Garrett shook his shaggy head, saying, 'No, you'll find "moose" in American dictionaries. But I imagine the British Museum harbors no such tome.'

"'There,' I replied, 'you are mistaken. For I did consult an American dictionary, but I didn't encounter the word.'

"'Oh, it mustn't have been much of a dictionary then,' he responded, 'for it is a perfectly ordinary word in America.'

"'Apparently it is all but unknown here.'

"Garrett smiled. 'Not to me. But certainly to you.'

"'Is it too much to ask that you unburden me from my confusion?' I pressed.

"He looked at me steadily with his rather devil-may-care eyes and said, 'Since you have set your sights on being a consulting detective, I think you would appreciate having to work out your own solutions.'

"'Unquestionably,' I replied crisply. 'But here I am unable to progress.'

"'Don't get tangled in your loose burnoose,' he stated. 'The solution is simple. You haven't resolved it yet. That is all. I'm sure that if you keep your eyes and ears peeled, the opportunity will arise.'

"Seeing that he would be no help, I let the matter drop. But it vexed me. Apparently, Garrett enjoyed my frustration, because he dropped other such difficult words at odd moments during our occasional meetings. For example, we were walking along one evening and he complained that the cobbles beneath our feet were as hard as a goose.

"I glanced towards him and said, 'I don't know of any goose which could be described as hard as stone.'

"'A tailor's goose would certainly fill with bill,' he responded.

"'You have me, then,' I replied with good humor. 'Yes, the stones are as hard as an iron. But fortunately not as angular.'

"'There you have it, Zeus,' he crowed. 'That's the spirit!'

"'I've come to a tentative conclusion about the word "moose",' I ventured to say.

"'Excellent! Let me hear it then.'

"'Since you applied the word to a rather large individual and you have admitted that it is an Indian word, I believe it is a term for a particularly fearsome Red Indian warrior.'

"'That is a clever guess,' he replied gravely, 'but altogether erroneous.'

"'Well, the apparent facts appeared to fit the word,' I returned defensively.

"'Appearances, as you know, can be quite deceptive,' he replied mildly.

"'I cannot argue against that well-worn phrase,' I told him.

"In those days, I was more high-spirited than I am now. And the longer I was subject to this man's whimsical approach to life and to our friendship, the more irritated I became.

"I can well imagine," I offered.

"On one occasion, I asked Garrett whether he had another clue as to the meaning of the impossible word 'moose'?

"He thought about that a minute and said, 'It isn't to be confused with another Indian word, "papoose". Nor should it be mixed up with "caboose", though all these words share a common rhyme.'

"'I take it these are also Indian words?'

"'I wouldn't assume that,' he returned in that irritatingly elusive manner of his. 'What do you suppose, Lord Zeus?'

"'"Wampoose", "papoose", and "caboose' all have the same root. It would seem that they collectively belong to the same language.'

"'So,' he replied imprudently, 'look them up. If you are able.'

"That night, I visited the British Museum and got nowhere. None of these terms were in any dictionary of the English language. I had begun to suspect Garrett of making up words, although which words were the product of his imagination and which were factual, I could only guess. I assumed 'moose' to be a word known in America. But I had my doubts about the other two."

"The man was obviously trifling with you," I answered.

"Garrett had a whimsical side to him, and he was difficult to bear at times. But he challenged me in a way that I found difficult to ignore. In those days, I had few friends, as in fact is the case these days, and my chief occupation was in exercising my mind and adding oddities to my little brain attic. American or American Indian words might never be of practical use to me, but I desired a certain command of them. Even if I forgot them, I was sure that I could recall them if it were ever necessary to do so.

"Our association went on for several months and it was alternately convivial and exasperating. From time to time, I saw nothing of Garrett. He was off on the rails doing his duty.

"I thought little of his absences, since I had become accustomed to them. But there came a time when I didn't see him for two weeks, and then three weeks and finally a month came and went without sight of him.

"This unprecedented silence didn't penetrate my consciousness until the end of the aforesaid month because I was caught up in a case which took me to Northumberland.

"Upon my return, I looked for Garrett in our usual haunts and didn't find him. Inquiring about, I learned that he hadn't been seen in some time.

"I had never been to Garrett's home, but I knew the address, for letters passed between us from time to time, so I resolved to go there in order to see what was what.

"Upon arriving, I learned from the landlord that Garrett's mother had passed away whilst he was elsewhere. He had returned for the funeral and then gone away again, presumably to resume his professional duties.

"Since Garrett had been known to write me from the hinterlands, I waited for a letter, and before long it came. I can recite it to you from memory, for it was brief:

My dear Zeus,

I regret that you will not set eyes upon me again. Without my mum, I am bereft. Don't look for me. But if you do, you will find me hanging loose like a goose from a noose in the caboose.

Yours sincerely,
James Garrett

"There was a postscript. It said simply: *I couldn't depart on my final journey without providing you with a last clue. It is* 'elk'."

"My word!" I exclaimed. "Suicide! Was his body ever found?"

"I am coming to that. Unavoidably, I read this note with alarm. And also with a cold resignation. It had taken two days to arrive and I feared that this was two days too late.

"Nevertheless, I went to the offices of the London and North Western Railway Company with the note and presented it to the superintendent, explaining the circumstances surrounding James Garrett's farewell missive.

"Reading it, the official said, 'It sounds like he intended to hang himself, but I don't know this word "caboose".'

"'I believe it to be an American Indian name. But its meaning eludes me.'

"'Thank you for this information, Mr. Holmes. I will look into the matter.'

"The man said this with the same resignation that I felt, but I also harbored a sense of urgency as if it might not yet be too late. So I told the fellow, 'It is possible that Garrett hasn't committed the act as yet. It may be possible to forestall this tragedy, if only swift action is undertaken.'

"Like so many who dwell in comfortable offices, the official was slow to accept the pressure of my urgings. But finally he relented and

41

summoned a subordinate, who agreed to telegraph all stations on the line Garrett normally worked.

"'Thank you,' I told the man. 'Now I must undertake to understand the significance of the word "caboose".'

"'Good luck to you, sir.'

"I went immediately to the British Museum and threw myself into intense study. But only one thing did I learn. Upon looking up the word 'elk', I discovered that the European elk and the American elk are two entirely different but related animals. Our elk has a counterpart in North America that is known by another name: 'Moose'.'"

"Ah!" I said. "You found the answer to the original question."

"Yes, but little good it did me then and much less was the satisfaction than otherwise, for I had wrongly assumed elk pointed to the impossible word 'caboose'. In actuality, the animal in question is known by that unlikely name to citizens of both the United States and our brethren in Canada, but here the term is so obscure it was subsumed under the rubric of elk. And so I learned a valuable lesson that sometimes the correct information can only be winnowed out by attacking a question indirectly.

"Having failed to learn the meaning of the word 'caboose', I went back to Garrett's flat and spoke with the landlord, again explaining the situation in detail and asking to be let in in order to pursue further clues, if any such existed.

"The man was initially reluctant, but I prevailed upon him by the expedient of letting him peruse Garrett's farewell letter. I was subsequently allowed into the empty quarters.

"It was a sad and forlorn place, for the man made meager money, especially since he worked so infrequently. But I found something that caught my eye."

Here Holmes paused. A look came into his eyes that made me think that his mind was casting back to that exact moment and seeing precisely what he had observed then. I couldn't imagine what he was about to divulge. But when he spoke, it took me by surprise, even though I was partially prepared for it.

"James Garrett brought with him from America what amounted to his personal library. These books were what we call 'penny dreadfuls'. I don't know what the Americans call the wretched things, but they were sensationalist paper-covered novels, written by largely anonymous hacks.

"I imagined that they were things he took with him to work and read during the monotonous stretches between railroad stations – for James Garrett was a brakeman and spent much of his time in the guard's van with little to do when the train is in motion and between station stops.

"Looking at this shelf of tattered ephemera, I realized that these were all printed in America and might contain a clue to the word 'caboose'."

"Surely, you didn't sit down and read a shelf-full of novels."

"I did not. Of course I did not. There was little enough time, and the hope of success was at best thin. But I was grasping any straws and these were the only reeds at hand.

"Fortunately, I had learned during my afternoons at the British Museum to skim rapidly for certain words and phrases in my delvings. Otherwise, I would have wasted a great deal of time reading books word for word in the hope of stumbling across what I sought."

"I see," said I. "You trained yourself to search for words that were key."

"Exactly," Holmes replied. "I've become quite adept at it. And it was a fantastic time-saver once I had become skilled enough to be proficient at the practice. I sat down and began skimming these pathetic stories in search of the word 'caboose'.

"Which might or might not be present in any of them," I pointed out.

"Correct. I chose novels that were set in the frontier of America, for it was my suspicion that, like 'wampoose' and 'papoose', 'caboose' was a word common among certain American Indian bands.

"The first novel I raced through failed to disgorge that word, but I did discover the word 'papoose', which gave me hope. I couldn't tell from the context, but it appeared to refer to an American Indian infant, or possibly the carrier in which the mother used to pack the child around. For I was watching for any word that ended in *o-o-s-e*."

"Remarkable!"

"The second novel was of no value. And I cast it aside before finishing it, for I felt that I was wasting my time. A third work concerned American railroads and, although my suspicion was it wouldn't necessarily contain any American Indian terms, due to the subject matter, I decided to stay with it.

"And I was richly rewarded for doing so. The word appeared often in this particular novel. Initially, I struggled to understand its significance, for it seemed to refer not to anything concerning any American aboriginal tribe, but to a particular type of railroad car apparently common in American trains. I struggled to understand to what the word 'caboose' applied, for it was used casually and written for an audience that apparently was familiar with the word and didn't require further explication.

"Sitting there, anxious to act upon my discovery but paralyzed by my failure to completely understand the term, it suddenly hit me that the answer was obvious: James Garrett was a brakeman and spent his time in

43

the last car in a train set. Here in England, that car is referred to as the 'guard's van' or 'brake van'. But apparently in America, it has somehow been designated as the 'caboose'. I have no idea how the term originated, but when I made the now-obvious connection, I leapt from my chair and rushed by cab to the offices of the London and North Western Railway Company at Euston station.

"Pushing my way into the office of the superintendent, I explained that they must look for James Garrett – or his body – in a guard's van.

"Scores of trains were traversing Great Britain at that time, and exploring every one of them was a task that seemed to me to be daunting. But the superintendent made it clear that James Garrett wasn't likely to be in any guard's van on any moving train. He hadn't been on the schedule for that duty for days.

"Horror, I confess, stopped me cold.

"After some thought, I realized the obvious. Had James Garrett committed suicide on a moving train, the body would have been discovered by that time.

"Addressing the superintendent, I explained my observation and asked, 'We must seek Garrett in a guard's van that isn't presently in service.'

"The man replied that there were many such, but agreed that this was a much more finite task and could be undertaken without delay.

"Telegraphs became busy and train yards all over Great Britain were informed of the possibility that a man had hanged himself in an idle guard's van."

Holmes paused again. It was clear to me that the memory of that time was still strong in his mind. Never a terribly expressive personality, his emotions are kept largely in check. He had become, during the years I knew him, something of a mental machine, which toiled along lines that didn't permit excess emotion to distract him.

Yet I could detect emotion touching his spare features.

"As I waited in the man's office for telegraphic responses," he resumed, "it occurred to me that I had assumed from the fact that Garrett's letter to me bore a London postmark that he had mailed it before departing the city on a final run with the intention of doing away with himself somewhere along the line.

"However, it came to me quite suddenly that, despite his many eccentricities, Garrett took his position as brakeman quite seriously. I began to conceive that it was unlikely he would do away with himself on a moving train and leave the engineer to his own meagre devices in the event of an emergency.

"If I was correct, I reasoned, Garrett might not have left London at all, and the guard's van might not be very far away.

"I expressed my opinion to the superintendent, who summoned his underlings and asked if there was an idle guard's van on a siding in the area of London.

"The answer wasn't long in coming. There was such a car. It was in the railway's train yard.

"To this we departed making all haste.

"Arriving, we wended our way through sidings, all of which ended in that most forlorn of sights. The buffer at the end of a spur marking the terminus of the track, and designed to prevent a car from going off the rails and into the dirt. This particular guard's van had been shunted there for repairs.

"Approaching it, we steeled ourselves from what we might find. The superintendent himself climbed up and threw open the door at the rear veranda.

"He stepped in and I heard him gasp, and then he all but stumbled out the back door.

"'It is him!' he cried out, clutching the veranda's rail. 'Garrett! I am afraid he has done the worst.'

"Hearing these words, I climbed the footplate, pushed past the man, and entered the cramped compartment within.

"There was sufficient light from the side duckets to reveal James Garrett sprawled rather awkwardly beside a tool chest built into one wall, a heavy rope around his neck and looking as if he had departed this world.

"Glancing upward, I perceived an iron hook hanging from one rafter which I later learned existed for the purpose of hanging the guard's wet clothes to dry – but I failed to see the rope attached to it. And so dropped to one knee before the man's body. I hesitated ever so slightly, but when I touched the man's body, it was still warm.

"Only then did my sense of smell shake off the shock of paralysis of this discovery. I smelled whisky. There was a bottle beside him and it was all but empty. It was clear that Garrett had decided to drink himself into near oblivion before taking the final plunge, as it were.

"However, his plan went awry, for he had drunk himself into a stupor from which he was unable to muster up the strength and resolve to affix the heavy rope to the ceiling in such a way that he could step off a guard's seat to his doom.

"With my clasp knife, I cut the rope from his neck and massaged his throat. He seemed to breathe without effort, although his breath was ragged. Lifting his eyelids, one after the other, I saw that his gaze wasn't focused, which I attributed to inebriation.

45

"Leaping back to my feet, I turned and stuck my head out the back of the car and exclaimed, 'Garrett lives! He failed, owing to an excess of whisky. We must convey him to hospital at once.'

"An ambulance came in due course and James Garrett was given over to the staff of St. Mary's Hospital. He wasn't safe yet, for his efforts to blot out his pain hadn't done his brain and liver any good.

"I visited him once, and he wasn't quite himself. I imagined that the grief over the passing of his mother and the prospect of being an orphan, although one of emancipated years, had depressed his spirits.

"During this visit, I revealed how I had deciphered the word 'caboose' by pouring over his little library.

"Garrett laughed a little raggedly, but said nothing. I suspected that the fellow wished that he had burned those books before leaving his home. I detected in his manner a feeling that he was sorry that he had failed to do away with himself, and thus no expression of gratitude was due me. For I received none.

"In an effort to cheer him up, I informed Garrett that I had at last solved the mystery of the word 'moose'.

"Here, his laugh was more genuine and he looked at me without equivocation. 'I knew that you would come through, Zeus. You had only to persevere.'

"'You, too, must learn the value of perseverance. You have received a setback in life, but it isn't an unusual one. Most children sooner or later bury their parents. Once you are released, you must pick up the pieces of your life and soldier on.'

"'If I do,' he murmured, 'I will not do so here, but back in America. Where they know the same words that I do.'

"I thought that comment was on the pathetic side, but said nothing. Other than to remark, 'Of course, that is your decision to make. But if you leave England, I will surely miss your company.'

"Garrett nodded sympathetically. I noted that the spirited conversation that formerly marked his personality was entirely absent. Patting him on the shoulder, I bade him farewell for the moment.

"Strangely, I never heard from him again. He was released from the hospital and cleared out his belongings and sailed for America

"I confess I was disappointed when I realized that he had departed our shores without saying goodbye. This confirmed my suspicion that he blamed me for saving his life. I will admit to feeling hurt and even bewildered. But I was young in those days and not as wise as I am now.

"I don't know whatever became of James Garrett, but from the perspective of today, I suspect we would have grown apart without the intercession of the events I have just related."

I stated, "The poor fellow sounds like a depressive personality. One who masks his moods with flippancy and an assumed air of superiority."

"So I later surmised, when I became sufficiently knowledgeable to comprehend the vagaries of the human personality. I subsequently realized that Garrett's irreverent manner was the cloak of a grieving man who had lost one parent and expected to lose the other, and endeavored to deny the impending loss by adopting a personality that enabled him to cope with his lot in life."

"I congratulate you. That is as accurate a summation of the psychological complexion of a troubled personality as I have ever heard. It is unfortunate that the friendship ended as a result of saving the poor fellow's life."

Puffing on his pipe, Holmes nodded gravely. "I imagine that as my consultancy grew and my fame expanded, Garrett may have felt less comfortable passing the time with me, for he had no ambitions other than to be a railway man. Of course, he had returned to England only to care for his mother. Even under the best of circumstances, it appears clear that he would have returned to America ultimately. But I would like to know that he is well, if only to satisfy my mind that he is no longer of a morbid turn of mind."

"Such are the loose ends of life," I pointed out.

"Yes," stated Holmes. "Life is full of loose ends. Personally, I detest them. Perhaps that is one reason why I like to solve my little mysteries and clear up the problems of others. I prefer to live in a world where there are fewer loose ends, and those stubborn strands that remain to dangle distractingly before our eyes, are less and less significant."

At those words, he tilted back his head and stared up at the ceiling with a dreamy expression suggesting thoughts into which I didn't care to further delve.

I will only add that on a later occasion, I brought up the other loose end of his narrative.

"Did you ever discover the derivation of the word 'caboose'?"

"I did. And it surprised me. For, despite all suggestions to the contrary, it wasn't a product of Red Indian tongues, but derived from the Low German word *kabuse*, meaning a ship's galley. The winding road through which *kabuse* became 'caboose' is too convoluted to recount, other than to point out that working brakemen cooked their food in the guard's van stove. But that revelation, too, taught me a valuable lesson on not assuming connections between elements, even which circumstantial evidence pointed strongly towards a seemingly probable conclusion."

"It would appear to me that James Garrett provided you with quite a number of valuable lessons during your young life," I observed.

47

"No doubt. And I would thank him if only I could, even if he could not see his way clear to expressing gratitude for my efforts on his behalf."

With that, Sherlock Holmes lapsed into another of his pensive silences.

The Return of
Spring-Heeled Jack
by Brenda Seabrooke

As I accustomed myself to sharing rooms with Sherlock Holmes, a mystery initially arose as to his occupation. I'd noticed in the first two weeks of our acquaintance that strange visitors dropped in at odd hours. At those times, he always asked me politely if I would give them privacy. Of course I always accommodated him and took my reading material up to my room, but I wondered who these people could be that I only saw glimpses of in passing. Sometimes they appeared exotic, as if from a foreign land, or perhaps they were connected with the theater. Once I met a man so wizened I didn't see how he could possibly walk by himself, even with the aid of a cane. He gave me an enigmatic smile as he drifted by on his way down the stairs. To my amazement, Holmes was absent when I opened the door to our sitting room. Nor was he, apparently, in his bedroom, though I didn't open it to check. I did, however, listen carefully, but heard nothing to indicate he was in there. I retired at eleven, and the next morning Holmes was at the breakfast table when I joined him.

He often missed meals provided by our landlady, Mrs. Hudson, a widow who fussed about his health every time he went without. She seemed less concerned with my health as I gained steadily from her regular meals, and my face soon lost its hollowed look. My wound from the Maiwand battle had not yet healed, stymied as it was by the bout of enteric fever which almost killed me and left me weakened and using a cane and, most seriously, lacking in my previous energy. I was invalided out of the army, a surgeon with no practice, on a small stipend which would end in a few months. I needed to walk every day to regain my stamina, but until recently I hadn't felt up to anything more strenuous than visiting the nearby tobacconist. The steps up to our rooms slowly became less of a challenge as I pushed myself every day to go down them and back up, even if I only stayed in the house. I attributed any progress to Mrs. Hudson's excellent meals and vowed to walk more each day, weather permitting.

On one of these walks, on a particularly foggy evening, I met a man in front of the building. He halted to allow me to go ahead of him. As I stepped up to the door and inserted my key, I recognized him.

"Inspector Lestrade! What a terrible night to be out."

I had only known who he was for a few weeks. Before Holmes revealed to me that he was a "consulting detective", as he called it, Lestrade had been just one of the many visitors who stopped in, often requiring me to withdraw to my upstairs bedroom while Holmes used the sitting room to meet with his "clients". Only a couple of weeks before had I learned Holmes's true profession, when invited to accompany him during his investigation of a murder in Lauriston Gardens. There I had been formally introduced to Lestrade, an inspector with Scotland Yard.

He was thin with a narrow face and sallow complexion which might signal illness in some, but seemed not to be the case with him. He had a cagey look, reminding me somewhat of a ferret, and a sense of coiled energy which hid his native suspicion of the human condition – that neither larceny nor homicide was ever far from many a man's or woman's soul.

"It certainly is, Doctor."

"You have business with Holmes?" I asked, before instantly realizing that it was unlikely he'd visit for any other reason. I was curious, as those were early days, and there was still much about Sherlock Holmes that I didn't know. I hoped to learn more of my flatmate's occupation, and what he did during his irregular hours.

"Possibly," was Lestrade's tight-lipped reply.

By now the door was open and I pushed it back, bidding him enter ahead of me. "Go on up. I daresay you'll be quicker than I am."

And he was. He put me in mind of a greyhound as he all but galloped up the stairs. I made my way up behind him. He waited at the door for me to enter, noting my halting progress. I knocked – and suddenly I realized it was somewhat strange to knock on one's own door, but I had no way of knowing if Holmes was entertaining one of his strange visitors.

He was not. "Come in," came the reply.

I ushered Lestrade in and followed slowly. "You have a visitor," I managed as I removed my coat, scarf, gloves, and hat. Lestrade was occupied at doing the same. I hung our coats on the rack by the door and turned to observe.

"Inspector!" Holmes said proffering the chair to the left side of his, facing the fireplace. "I wondered when you might drop in."

"Indeed. I was laid up with a case of grippe or I would've come sooner."

Lestrade took the chair. Holmes didn't ask me to leave, so I moved to my fireside chair, sinking into it carefully and trying not to make any noise. I picked up a newspaper from the floor and pretended to read it. I hoped they would forget about me and I could determine more about my new friend and his affairs.

"What can I do for you?" asked Holmes after offering Lestrade some refreshments.

"You've heard of Spring-Heeled Jack?"

"Indeed I have. He was a rough prankster who first turned up in the outer areas of London – in 1837, I believe. Periodically he has appeared in villages and other cities, but these sightings have usually been attributed to mass hysteria. He attacked women, springing at them and with claw-like hands and ripping their clothing. Women began wearing gloves with claws built into them to protect themselves, though I know of no instances where that happened. Perhaps Jack noted their defensive gloves and left them alone."

"That's about what it was. This latest outbreak – you've read of it in the press – seems to be the return of Spring-Heeled Jack to central London. He leaps down from a gate post, a plinth, some form of height, or materializes out of the thick fog and tears at feminine clothing. Like the first Jack, his face is covered, and he hides under a dark cloak."

"As I recall," Holmes said, "the earlier Jack was said to leap from rooftop to rooftop breathing fire."

"I doubt that. Merely stories, each telling becoming more exaggerated. This Jack doesn't do that. He possibly leaps off lower ledges and walls, but more likely he springs at his victims from the fog and they add the notion of heights."

"Maybe the current Jack doesn't know how the original breathed fire. Easy enough to spit folded flames of fabric from one's mouth while leaping down, and this Jack may not be able to leap from that height. He was said to be a devil, a demon, terrifying the ladies of the land."

"He did that." Lestrade nodded. "And now women all over London are afraid to go out in this thick fog for fear Jack will leap on them. He snatched kisses in the past, but doesn't seem to be doing that now. Yet the ladies remain fearful he will."

"What do you wish from me?"

"I was hoping you could help us with the case, you being a consulting detective. The Metropolitan Police thinks it's Jack returned to terrorize London after years in the shires."

"But you don't subscribe to this." It was not a question.

Lestrade shook his head.

"There are other non-police detectives in London," Holmes said.

"You work somewhat differently." The two regarded each other.

Holmes waved his hand. "Indeed?"

"That's right. You've shown that the most obvious is often not the solution."

51

"Nor do I leap to a conclusion based on a whim. Some may think that the original Spring-Heeled Jack is back, but I suspect that isn't the case, and I've heard no facts to support such a conclusion."

"That's what I told my colleagues you would say," Lestrade said, "but why do you think thus?"

"For one, too much time has elapsed since the first appearance of Jack in 1837 – that's forty-four years. Assuming the original Jack was at least twenty years of age, he would now be over sixty-four, and probably more – not the age to leap off ledges and walls, or even plinths, unless he's a circus acrobat. And certainly not from rooftops."

"He seems to have dispensed with the fire-breathing as well," Lestrade said.

"Hmm," was all Holmes said.

"Have you been keeping up with the reports in the newspapers?"

"I have. Three attacks, all of them not far from here. I can't see that three ripped garments would necessitate a Scotland Yard detective to seek outside help. What do you wish from me?"

"This has been kept quiet, but last night another attack was made in this filthy fog, and the young woman's throat was slashed. We have no clues except that it again appears to be Spring-Heeled Jack's return. Will you take the case? I'll see to your remuneration."

Holmes steepled his fingers. I'd noticed he often did this when he was thinking. "The murder entirely changes the complexion of the case. I will need the details and to see the body."

"I'll arrange it with the morgue. The victim appeared to have fainted, but when she was turned over, the method became obvious. The police at first thought it was a regular murder, understandable in the heavy fog, but later in the morgue, the rips on her clothing were visible."

"No doubt made *post mortem*," Holmes said, "to tie it to the attacks, but what you have here is a case of something entirely different – a Claw Man, I would call him, rather than Spring-Heeled Jack."

Lestrade winced. "I hope the newspapers don't get wind of that. A *Claw Man* indeed."

"They will have to know of the murder. They will find their way to it on their own."

"Will you take the case?" Lestrade repeated.

"I will, but understand I work alone unless I find it necessary to utilize the Force. I'll need to interview the young ladies attacked by the perpetrator."

"That won't be immediately possible in two of the cases. The two maids have returned to the country houses to escape this wretched fog. The milliner's assistant is the only one currently available."

"She will have to suffice, then. Can you have her at the Yard this afternoon?"

Lestrade nodded and held out his hand. Holmes hesitated a moment, then reached across and clasped it. "Watson will see you out."

At the downstairs door, Lestrade wound a scarf around his neck, covering his mouth, and then he jammed his hat on until it almost covered his ears. "Will you accompany him to the morgue?" he said to me softly. "You could be helpful on this case."

"Don't you have a trained coroner?"

"We do, but you've had experience with injuries to the human body. Another pair of eyes never hurts."

I agreed to go and closed the door quickly to keep the pea soup out of the house as much as possible. I walked slowly back up the stairs. What had just happened? Had I been invited to join Holmes on another of his cases?

"Lestrade asked me to accompany you," I said on entering.

Holmes was reading. Had he heard me? I took my customary chair by the fire. The clock ticked and the fire purred, making me sleepy until Holmes suddenly slammed the book closed with a loud pop. I almost jumped under the table as memories of the battlefield assailed me. I managed to contain myself, but startled visibly. In those days, any sharp loud noise did that to me. Holmes looked at me. He must have noticed my involuntary movement.

"Like that, is it?" he said and I thought he understood what made me react so.

"Yes. Not always, but most of the time."

He nodded as if I had confirmed something. "My apologies." I could see that he meant it.

By now I was beginning to get used to Holmes's knack of reaching conclusions through his perceptive observations. I remembered Dr. Joseph Bell, a professor under whom I'd studied for a while in Edinburgh. He taught his students to look for clues about his patients on their person, their behavior, their speech, their dress. Ink-stained fingers pointed to a clerk. Drops of marmalade on a cravat showed a fondness for sweetness, that sort of thing.

"What do you think of Lestrade's problem?" I asked.

Instead of replying directly, Holmes countered, "What do you know of Spring-Heeled Jack?"

"I remember that in my childhood, children were told to behave or Spring-Heeled Jack would come for them."

"Even in Scotland. Did it work?"

"No. We always wanted to see him leap over buildings. That's how we thought of him then. Children take what they want from stories. Strangely enough, he was something of a hero to some of us – rather like Robin Hood. We wanted someone who could get away from adults by super-human feats. We ignored the clawing of clothing. If questioned about the matter, we probably would've denied our hero would do such a thing as claw ladies. Or kiss them – until we reached a certain age, of course. A lot of boys had sore legs from all that jumping but, of course, we never made the connection." I remembered my mother heating water to soak my aching ankles and sprinkling it with mustard powder to relieve the pain.

"This Jack cannot be the original, as I told Lestrade, but that doesn't mean others haven't taken up the role. They wouldn't be as old as the first Jack. For what it's worth, I also believe the original was either part of a group doing the attacks, or there were imitators, even then. The culprits may have been a group of wealthy young men or a club with such stunts required for their initiation process. No, this is something else entirely, done under the smokescreen of the persistent fog."

"How do you propose to solve the murder?"

"We shall gather information. Come, Watson – we're off to the morgue."

I was not bothered by the visit to the morgue. I'd spent much time in them, and much time with dead bodies – some killed in front of me in battle, some dying in hospitals. It was the fog that bothered me today. Breathing became a chore. I tied my scarf over my nose and mouth as we hailed a cab in Baker Street.

The driver could have been a highwayman behind the scarf covering his face. He also wore a most-unusual set of spectacles which interested me. I enquired of him if they were for bad eyesight.

"No sir. These be plain glass. Per'tecks me eyes sommat from this fog."

"Very clever."

"Where to, Guv'nor?"

Holmes told him.

I sat back and tried to take shallow breaths. This stuff was brown today, but sometimes yellow or green – hence the descriptive "pea soup" name – and it wasn't good for our lungs, as it could cause choking fits and even death in some cases.

At the morgue, we found that Lestrade had left a number of documents related to the case – investigatory notes, as well as information about the three previous women who had been attacked, along with

54

transcripts of the interviews carried out with all three. Holmes spent several moments reviewing them and, although he read quickly, I knew that he would retain what he had seen.

We also confirmed that Lestrade had arranged for us to view the fourth victim, who had not survived. She awaited us, laid out on a slab.

She wasn't like the descriptions in the notes of the previous three victims who lived to tell about it. She appeared to be from a higher societal class. The reports had indicated the first victim was a lady's maid, the second worked in a millinery shop, and the third was also a maid at a great house in the area where she'd been attacked. All three provided the same description of the attacker: He was wearing a dark gray cloak, and a mask covering his head and face.

They were lucky the slasher had been interrupted, sparing their lives. This girl, however, hadn't been so fortunate.

"Tell me, Watson, what do you see?"

The autopsy had already been performed, leaving the ghastly seams mostly covered by a sheet. Her clothing had been left on a nearby table. The young lady was lying with her eyes closed, hands beside her body. Her light brown hair had been well-coiffed, but now was somewhat disheveled in her journey after death. I drew upon what I remembered of Dr. Bell's methods and described what I saw, starting with the nearby clothing. "Her gloves are rather expensive leather, as is the case with her white fur muff. Her peacock velvet dress has a fine lace collar. Her warm cape of white wool is trimmed with white fur – ermine no doubt. That, and her muff, mark her as coming from a prosperous background. Her hat is missing, perhaps stolen before she was discovered." I turned my attention to the body.

"She's young, not much more than twenty. Her hands prove to be soft and uncalloused. Therefore she doesn't work with them – not as a cook, seamstress, or scullery maid. She was healthy, well-nourished, and may have had a rosy complexion, if not for exsanguination. I don't know what she was doing out in this filthy air, but it probably wasn't an errand of necessity."

"Quite right," Holmes replied. He examined a loose thread that he'd picked off her dress, placing it in a small envelope he took from his pocket. Then he gave the same attention to the mud on her shoes. I thought it strange. "As you say, her clothing tells us she was from a wealthy family, unlike the previous victims. She has been well-cared for, both in her background and her personal grooming. What do you make of the wound?"

I leaned forward. The slash on her throat had already been neatly stitched up, but I could tell that the killing stroke had been made from her

55

left to her right. "The killer is right-handed and most probably slashed her from behind. The slashes to her clothing may have been done *post mortem*, or while she was dying, to make it look like Jack."

"Very good, Watson. You have a keen eye."

"A surgeon on a battlefield must make quick decisions. One learns to be fast."

He nodded once. "Indeed." He pulled out a magnifying glass and again examined the young lady's shoe soles. "Do you see anything here?"

I looked through the glass. "A small bit of mud."

He took out a pocketknife and scraped a bit onto a paper, which he twisted and returned to his pocket along with the knife. Next he turned the magnifying glass onto the slashes in the dress. The velvet had been torn, but the slits were fairly even.

"I have seen animal clawings in India," I offered. "Tigers, especially. These look more like they were done by a sharp knife than a claw."

"No doubt the murderer will be disappointed you weren't fooled," Holmes said, "but tell me how you know that."

"A claw would chew the cloth more. These are clean slashes that run down the warp in a straight line, as if carefully done."

Holmes smiled. "Very good, Watson. You'll do admirably."

Any praise from Holmes, as I was to learn, was high praise indeed. "Thank you. I think. Who would do such to this young lady?"

"Any number of miscreants lurking about London, but I suspect most of them would have done more to her. That wasn't done in this case and we must find out why. Why kill a young woman and mutilate her clothing after death? Why this young woman? Was it a crime of opportunity? Design? Random or targeted? When we find the answer to these questions, we will find the killer. For now, we need her identity."

"Surely her family will have reported her missing by now."

"One would think so."

The coroner's assistant, a thin, pale young man, brought us the autopsy report. Holmes and I scanned it. "See anything we didn't already know?" he asked.

"No," I said. "A healthy young lady, no evident diseases. Death caused by severing the carotid arteries, most likely from behind."

"We found this in her muff," the assistant said. He handed Holmes a folded note on thick paper. Written on it in sepia ink was an invitation to early tea from *C.B.*

"So this was her destination," I said.

"Indeed. Let's have a look at the sites of the attacks." He kept the invitation after signing for it.

We boarded the nearest Underground and made our way to the farthest site of the attacks. As we exited at Notting Hill Gate, I hoped the fog would have lessened in that part of London, but enough of it still swirled around us to necessitate the wearing of scarves. We walked to the site of the Claw Man's first appearance. According to the information we'd received, the attacker had evidently lain in wait in a nearby mews and slashed at the clothing of the first victim, Lucy Blank, a nearby parlor maid. He caused two slits before she managed to pull away from her attacker and run for help. The attacker ran away as well, and the attending constable found nothing at the site. The attacker was described as tall, though not excessively, and he'd worn a black cape, and a black mask over face and hair. He had hissed like a wild animal, and she thought he growled, too.

The second attack came a few days later, again during heavy fog. The site was off Bayswater Road on the edge of Hyde Park. Millie Pinson, a milliner's assistant on her way home, was pulled into some bushes and her clothing slashed. She described the attack identically to the first one. She confirmed the hissing, but not the growl.

The third attack on Judy Henkins, a lady's maid, occurred on the north end of the Edgware Road toward Maida Vale. The fog was so thick that Miss Henkins couldn't see much, but she remembered that the attacker made the same sounds heard by the previous victims. She had indicated that he was taller than Lestrade, but not much taller.

"A tall, animal-sounding man in a cape with a black head mask who makes an even number of slits with his claw hand." Holmes summed up the meager information.

"Not much help there," I remarked.

"On the contrary, there's more information than meets the eye."

I waited for him to explain, but he sat back on the seat of our cab and closed his eyes until we arrived. The cab let us out into the street, just around the corner from the site of the murder, now rather hard to find in the darkening foggy mews. I looked about but saw no one – no constables and no horsemen, though an army could have been ten feet away and only the stamping hooves and jingling bridles would have revealed them. "The murderer knew what he was doing in this cursed fog," I said.

"Indeed he did." Holmes lit a Lucifer and examined the cobblestones by its meager light. A dark brown stain was all that remained of that poor young lady. What was she doing out in this dreadful fog?

"The murderer no doubt knew she would be coming this way and lay in wait. Or he may have engineered the meeting. Would you think there should've been more blood here?"

"Hard to say," I answered. "Her shawl was stiff with blood, but her dress barely touched with it."

He lit another Lucifer, moving it about as he searched for evidence of blood. "A-ha! Just as I thought. Look at this."

I followed the light and saw small brown smudges on the cobbles. They went around the corner into a street that ran near Berkeley Square, a prestigious location. There, on the edge of the pavement, we found more blood. "The constables didn't look far afield," I said. "It appears that she was killed here and dragged into the mews where she might not be found straightaway."

"It does. This isn't a well-traveled roadway, but some carts and other vehicles have been along here since last night and may have obliterated any other blood spatters." He lit more Lucifers, but we found no more blood droplets.

"I was hoping to find evidence of the direction the murderer might have taken. However, he may have been smart enough to carry a rag to wipe his boots before leaving a trail. The sample of bloodstained mud that I took from the victim's soles must have adhered as she was being dragged."

We walked back to Baker Street by lamplight and glowing window light. Mrs. Hudson admonished us for missing luncheon and tea, but prepared a substantial meal for us and, after our journey, we were ready for it. After dinner, I poured myself a brandy. Holmes asked for one as well as he settled in his chair on one side of the fireplace. He busied himself filling one of his pipes, the cherry-wood, and lit the bowl. The pungent aroma of black shag filled the room.

We sipped our brandies in the quiet broken only by the sounds of the fire. I lit a cigar and perused the evening paper I'd picked up on the way back. I found the article for which I was looking and read it quickly. "Still no identification of the young woman."

"That should be done soon," Holmes said. "She was too much of a lady not to be missed by now. I shouldn't be surprised if she lived somewhere near Berkeley Square."

"How would a murderer entice young lady of those establishments to go out in this fog?"

"Murderers are often ingenious. They delight in fooling Scotland Yard, outwitting decent society. I shouldn't be surprised if they aren't born that way, though no doubt some evil might be learned."

The fog mercifully lifted somewhat during the night. By morning, a thin light came in the windows. After breakfast, Holmes proposed that we revisit the scene of the murder when the light was more propitious. I must admit the walk was far more enjoyable when we could safely breathe the air. Holmes was correct in his conjecture. We found what appeared to be a faint track of blood stains leading away from the mews, around the corner, and then alongside Berkeley Square where they eventually disappeared. Holmes studied these and made notes in a small book he took from his pocket. Then he put it away. "Let us pay a visit to Scotland Yard."

We hailed a hansom and rode in comfort. Holmes enquired of the duty constable for Inspector Lestrade.

"He's just in, not two minutes ago." He directed us to the inspector's office where a young man sat with a stunned look on his face. Lestrade was surprised to see us, but invited us to sit in the chairs before his desk. "This is Mr. Gerald Fenton. He has just identified his sister, Persephone, as the victim."

Holmes and I made suitable sympathetic comments which Mr. Fenton barely acknowledged. He was a nicely dressed young man in his early twenties, sandy hair, pale blue eyes, and a chin that wasn't as strong as it might need to be during his lifetime, despite the thin moustache he had likely grown for compensation. A goatee might have been of more use, but perhaps he could not yet manage it. "I – I thank you," he said barely above a whisper, but that could be attributed to his shock.

"Tea would be helpful," I said to Lestrade. "Four sugars." He arose and attended to it, and shortly a cup was brought by a constable. Mr. Fenton gulped it down as if his life were being saved. Perhaps it was. I have often observed the efficacy of hot sweet tea in shocking circumstances.

"Was your sister accustomed to going out alone in the severe fog?" Holmes asked.

"No, but she might if she wasn't going far. She might have been going to visit my inten – a young lady I've been courting."

"Who is this young lady." Holmes asked, "and where does she live?"

"The Honourable Clarinda Bellamy. Her father is the baron, Sir Bertram. They live in Berkeley Square. We are a scant two streets away. They are friends, and her brother has – *had* – a *tendresse* for my sister."

Tears gathered in his eyes and spilled over. He pulled out a snowy handkerchief and wiped them away. "I don't know how I shall tell my parents."

"That's our job," Lestrade said, which soon resulted in all of us climbing into a police brougham. Lestrade and I were left sitting in the pull-down seats in the corners. Though not the most comfortable conveyance when crowded so, it allowed for swifter travel in the streets and roadways.

The Fenton home was a red-brick attached house, Georgian style, to which had been added a turret on the corner which jutted out into the street, and a fence that heavily featured acanthus leaves. A proper butler whom Fenton called Marchmon took our hats and coats. Fenton led us into a drawing room, its proportions disguised with rose-printed wallpaper covered with a profusion of gold-framed classical paintings and ornate furniture in dark woods with red velvet upholstery. Mrs. Fenton was resplendent in gold brocade trimmed with black beads, and an incongruous black feather in her brown hair. Her eyes were pale blue like her son's. She seemed startled to see him in the company of so many unknown men. "Gerald, who are these – ?" She hesitated and swept us with another glance. " – these *gentlemen*?"

"Mrs. Fenton, I'm Inspector Lestrade of Scotland Yard." He didn't introduce Holmes or me. "I have some bad news about your daughter."

"She isn't in trouble, is she?" Her eyes went from one of us to the other, clearly wondering who Holmes and I were.

"No, Mama." Gerald took out his handkerchief and wiped his watery eyes again.

"I am sorry to inform you that your daughter is the victim of a crime," Lestrade said.

"She's been murdered, Mama," Gerald said.

"Murdered?" Mrs. Fenton, who had half-risen from her chair, fell back into a sprawl. "Murdered?" she screamed.

"Yes," Lestrade replied. "She was found yesterday, not far from here. She had no identification on her person. We didn't know her identity until your son enquired at Scotland Yard."

Holmes had the presence of mind to ring for the butler while I fanned her paper-white face. Her husband was summoned from his study, and a maid came with a *sal volatile* which I used to revive the lady, as she was half-fainting now, uttering little mewing sounds.

Mr. Fenton, upon being informed of his daughter's demise, was as distraught as his wife. Faced with their reaction, young Gerald began sobbing. I led him to a chair and in a low voice told him someone in the family had to take charge. He didn't look like he wanted that someone to be himself, but he wiped his eyes again and went to his father, who took his hand as if it were a lifeline and said, "So much depended on Persephone. Whatever will we do now?"

"We'll go on, Papa," Gerald said bravely, and I saw his Adam's apple bob above his cravat, which seemed limp now as if some of his tears had made their way onto it. Marchmon was almost in the same state. Holmes went to a tray on a table and poured a generous amount of brandy into a glass, which he then pressed into Mr. Fenton's hand. I sent Marchmon to summon tea for Mrs. Fenton. Upon his return, Holmes took the butler into the hall question him. I could do little to assuage the family's grief other than pour brandy into their hot sweet tea and instruct the maid to stay with her mistress. After a while, I was able to join Holmes in the hall, while Lestrade asked the family some further questions.

I reached Holmes and the butler in time to hear the latter say that on the morning of the girl's death, she received a note inviting her to early tea.

"By early tea, do you mean at two in the afternoon?"

"Well, sir, it were more like half-two. It were an odd time for tea, but Miss Persephone were pleased with the invite, so I didn't say anything. I did suggest she not go, since the fog were so bad, but she laughed and said she was just going a few streets away and she could walk it with her eyes closed if need be."

"Do you know where she was going?" Holmes asked.

"I do not, but t'were any great distance, she would've used the carriage."

"Could the invitation have been from the Bellamys?"

"I couldn't say, sir, but it's possible."

"Do you know the names of any of her friends?"

"Well, sir," he lowered his voice, "the Fentons haven't lived here long. She knows the Bellamy daughter and her brother Billy, who seems to have – " His voice caught. " – *had* eyes for Miss Persephone."

"Watson, if you could get that address, please. We'll need to talk to them. I'll inform the inspector."

"It isn't far, sir. Just one street to the west."

Berkeley Square was near Albemarle Street, where the Fentons resided, but in social class it was worlds away. We soon covered the distance to where Sir Bertram Bellamy lived, on the northeast corner of the Square. As we approached the house, an imposing carriage bearing a crest turned in front of us.

"High horses here indeed," Holmes remarked. "If I'm not mistaken, that was the crest of the Earl of Oxleigh. Before you joined us," he continued, "Marchmon mentioned that the Earl lives on the Square. He intimated the Fentons would like to make their acquaintance. They may live close to the Phipps, which is the Earl's family name, but unless Gerald were to save the life of the Queen or some other daring deed, Marchmon fears that may never happen. Fenton is, I believe, a speculator in commodities. Unless the Earl were in need of a large sum of money, the Phippses will never even know that the Fentons exist. The Earl's family is solid with diversified interests in shipping, as well as inherited land and wealth. The Fentons are barking up the wrong tree."

The Bellamy's town house was, as to be expected of a baron, twice the size of the Fentons. It, too, was Georgian, but with every appointment in perfect order. The door opened almost before Holmes's hand left the handsome knocker, itself in the shape of a hand. The butler was more imposing than Marchmon, and no doubt less chatty, but then his household wasn't in the chaos of grief.

"Yes," the solid man said, peering down his nose. The act involved drawing the upper body back in order to look at us in that fashion.

Holmes handed him a card. "Sherlock Holmes and Dr. Watson to see the Honourable Clarinda Bellamy and her brother." I hastily dug out my card.

"What might this matter concern?"

"That shall remain private." Holmes gave him an icy smile that said, "No butler will quell me," and I wondered, not for the first time, about his family history. He hadn't mentioned any in the short time I'd known him.

The butler returned shortly and ushered us into a morning room, where a young lady was seated with a book. I couldn't tell if she were reading it, or had just picked it up to give herself something to do while she awaited the two strangers at her door. Her dark hair was drawn back from her pale face. She had strong features, dark brows, a wide mouth, and rather prominent nose.

Holmes introduced us. "We were hoping to speak to your brother as well."

"He has gone out." She didn't invite us to sit, so we stood. "What did you want to speak to us about?"

"Miss Persephone Fenton."

"You do know her," I said when she winced almost imperceptibly.

"I know of her. I have met her a few times."

"Her brother Gerald has been courting you, I believe," Holmes said.

"I don't call it 'courting'. I went driving with him on a few autumn afternoons last year when the weather was fine and this beastly fog wasn't around."

"He seems to think it was more than a few drives," I said.

"Then he is mistaken. What is this about? You surely didn't come here to discuss the courting habits of Gerald Fenton."

"No, we came to ask you what you might know of Miss Fenton," Holmes said. "We are helping Scotland Yard with a case."

"As I said, I hardly know who she is. What is she to do with me? And what case?"

"She was found murdered yesterday," Holmes said. "Not far from here,"

"Oh?" She looked down at her book, suddenly shocked. "That – that's *dreadful*! Where did it happen?" She looked up.

Holmes told her.

"Why was she out in that fog?"

"Her brother believed she was coming to tea with you."

"Oh no! Why would she tell him that? I went to my sewing circle."

Holmes raised his eyebrows at her venturing out in the beastly fog herself. She seemed to understand. "It was just across the Square at Olivia's – the Countess of Oxleigh."

Was it my imagination, or did she take pride in speaking of her destination? "Wasn't it difficult to maneuver in the fog?" I asked.

"Not for me. I walked straight across to the Square fence and followed it around to the left. The Earl's house is across on that far corner."

"Miss Fenton wasn't on the way to the sewing circle?" Holmes asked.

"No. It's just a few of Olivia's friends and some of the other neighbors."

"I see," Holmes said. I saw also. Miss Fenton wasn't ranked high enough on the social scale to join the sewing circle – no doubt organized for poor children in Africa when London had its own share of poor children needing warm clothing.

A clamor sounded in the hall and a handsome young man joined us. "Clarinda, I've just heard about Persephone Fenton's murder from Deavers! And to think it could've been you, just a few streets away."

"Oh Billy!" she replied. "I shudder to think so!"

"You are, I believe, from Scotland Yard," he said to Holmes.

Holmes introduced us without bothering to correct his assumption.

Billy Bellamy was about my height, with thick dark hair and a long thin nose that gave him a supercilious look. I wouldn't have thought him upper-class enough for that look. "I'm William Bellamy," he said. "What has this to do with my sister?"

"It was our understanding you'd been seeing Miss Fenton, the victim," Holmes said.

"Our acquaintance hadn't progressed that far. I found her an agreeable young lady, but I'd no intentions in that direction, if that's what you mean."

"And where were you yesterday at two in the afternoon?" Holmes asked.

"I was at my club." He named a popular sporting establishment. "From noon until late."

"How late?"

"Very late."

"I didn't even hear your return," Clarinda said. "I read late," she explained.

"The lamplighters were turning off the gas when I arrived," Billy added.

"Do you live here with your father?" Holmes asked.

"Yes," Billy said. "Our mother died three years ago."

"Our father isn't well. I hope you won't bother him with your questions?" Clarinda had paused before her question, as if she'd been about to preface it with something silly, but thought better of it under the circumstances.

"What happened to Miss Fenton?" Billy asked. He'd been standing, but now he sank into a velvet chair.

Holmes explained.

Clarinda put her hand over her eyes and shuddered.

"Oh good God!" Billy cried out. He seemed more upset than his sister. Perhaps the social standing wasn't as important to the future baron as it was to the Honourable Miss Bellamy.

Holmes took out the note from his coat pocket and handed it to Clarinda. "Did you send this note to Miss Fenton? It was found with her."

She glanced at it, but made no move to take it for a closer look. "Certainly not. That isn't my handwriting. And I never sign anything with a *CB*. I write out *The Honourable Clarinda Bellamy*. Someone must've been playing a trick on the poor girl."

Holmes asked a few more questions. Deavers was in the house when Clarinda left for the sewing circle and when she returned several hours later. Billy's club could vouch for him if need be. Their father was bedridden with a chest catarrh.

"Do either of you know who could have sent the note to the victim?" was Holmes's last question as he returned the note to his pocket.

They both replied adamantly they didn't send it, nor had they any idea who might have.

We took our leave. "Except to see the British class system at work," I said as the door closed behind us, "that wasn't very helpful."

Holmes smiled. "Indeed," was all he would say.

We next called at the Earl's townhouse, the most imposing on the Square. His Countess was at home and would see us. She was formal with us, but did invite us to sit when Holmes told her the reason for our visit. "Oh dear. The poor girl! No, I don't know her, but I've heard of her. Someone mentioned inviting her to join us in the sewing circle, but others said not quite yet."

I wondered what they were waiting for – Her father to buy the Square and build a house in the middle of it, perhaps? – but I kept quiet. What did I know – a Scottish boy, a doctor from Barts, and then an army surgeon in Afghanistan?

The Countess had nothing to add to our store of information. Holmes clarified the situation after we took our leave. "Persephone's father made money in commodities, but owns no land except his London house which, though worth a bit of change, isn't the echelon to which the family aspires. Marchmon indicated that he started as a grocer's clerk. A future baron for a son-in-law would be a long step up for the family. An 'honourable' for a daughter-in-law would open doors for them. The Bellamy family pockets aren't to let yet, but with Billy gambling his nights away at his club, that could be in the near future. The Fentons may have been willing to wait for that to happen."

"Sounds contractual to me."

"Oh it is. And stultifying. Most of the population is larcenous and criminal and venal – else I wouldn't have a job," Holmes said, "but the upper class is the worst. Tell me, Watson: Do you think Clarinda is a tiny woman?"

I thought of what I could see of her, seated in the parlour. "She never stood up, and her voluminous skirt hid her legs." I refused to politely call them limbs. I'd seen too many blown off and I'd surgically removed too many myself not to call body parts what they are. "Judging from her arms as she held the book when we entered, I'd say no, she isn't tiny. She may be almost as tall as I am. Why do you want to know?"

He gave me an enigmatic look just as Lestrade hailed us from the nearby police conveyance. "I sent a constable to fetch Millie Pinson, the milliner's assistant, as you asked, Mr. Holmes. She should be at the Yard now."

Miss Mollie Pinson sipped tea in Lestrade's office as we entered. She was fetchingly dressed in chocolate velvet with matching toque on her dark brown hair, and a cinnamon chiffon veil thrown back to reveal her heart-shaped face. Lestrade introduced us. "Mr. Holmes wishes to ask you some questions about your attack."

She took a moment to set down the teacup then turned to Holmes. "I'm ready."

Holmes regarded her without speaking. As the silence grew, I said, "I see you're attired in a colour to defeat the fog." I nodded at her ensemble. "Even in this lighter fog, one needs to guard oneself from its noxious qualities."

She smiled. "Thank you. Most people don't understand the reasons for wearing certain colours, fabrics, or even hemlines. I wear my skirts shorter because I don't care to sweep up the filth of London's streets."

"Very sensible," Holmes said, finally speaking.

"I'm one of ten, seven of us girls. We learned early to safeguard everything we have. Including our clothing."

"Tell us about the attack."

She took another sip of tea and this time held on to the teacup. "I was on my way home after the shop closed when suddenly a tall figure leaped in front of me. He came out of the fog."

"You had no sense of anyone there before you saw him?"

"No, nothing. His claws ripped down my skirt in two places, and then, as quick he'd come, he left. I didn't even have time to scream."

"Did you see the claws?" Holmes asked.

"No, but his hand came toward me and I felt a tug on my skirt. Twice."

"Did you notice any smells?"

"You mean the odour of brimstone?"

Holmes smiled.

"No, I didn't," she answered.

"What about scent?" I asked. "Mendicants? Perfumes?"

"Nothing for certain. Maybe something that reminded me of hothouse flowers."

"How are they different from other flowers?" Holmes asked.

"The scent seems more cloying."

Holmes nodded as if in agreement. "Did he speak?"

"No, it all happened in silence. I didn't even have time to scream."

"Did you hear anything at all? A whistle? Throat-clearing? A cough? A foot scraping?"

She finished her tea and set the cup down. "Well, as you know, the fog muffles everything, but at the same time you can hear more clearly. He did make hissing sounds."

"The other young ladies mentioned that hissing," Lestrade said. "They also mentioned growling sounds."

"No, I didn't hear any growls. The hissing could have come from his mouth, but it was more of a swishing sound. I work with cloth, and I know the different sounds that can make. Crinkles and rubbing sounds. Swishing."

"And you heard swishing?" Lestrade asked.

"Yes. Swishing."

"If it were cloth," Holmes asked, "do you know what it would be?"

"It wasn't taffeta or satin, velvet or linen or cotton. More like silk, but hushed. I suppose the fog could muffle it."

"Were you wearing a cape?" I asked.

"No, I wore a short coat over a woolen dress. Wool is very quiet."

"That will be all, Miss Pinson," Holmes said. "I have no more questions. Thank you for coming down. You've been very helpful."

She looked dubious, but nodded.

66

Lestrade summoned an officer to take her home. "If you think of anything else, please inform a constable."

When we were alone, he added, "Very kind of you to tell her she was helpful, but I can't think in what way."

"Can't you?" Holmes asked, raising an eyebrow.

Lestrade looked at me as if I might have a clue, but I shrugged slightly. "She seems to like outdoor flowers better than hothouse ones."

"I believe the fog may be worsening," Holmes said. "It wouldn't be amiss to station a constable in Berkeley Square for the night."

"You think another attack might be imminent? On the Honourable Clarinda?"

"Not with a constable on station."

By the time the police vehicle delivered us back to Baker Street, I realized again we hadn't eaten since breakfast. I was ravenous and fell on Mrs. Hudson's excellent roast chicken dinner, followed by plum cake. Brandy and a cigar by the fire and I was as comfortable as a recovering invalid could be. Holmes declined the cigar. "I think this might be another one-pipe night, but I'm prepared to extend to a second one if need be."

"A one or two-pipe case?"

"Helps me get all the strings in order."

"You know who the killer is?"

"I'm reasonably sure. but reasonably sure isn't enough."

"Do you think the killer will strike again tonight?"

"Not with a constable to keep the Square safe. The killer will not appear again as long as people are wary. In a week or so will be time for care."

He did indeed smoke a second pipe, but before its time was up, I had retired upstairs for the night with a book. I hadn't turned the page once before I fell asleep. Later I awakened, put the book on the night table, and turned down the light. I couldn't remember the last time I was this tired, I thought as I fell into sleep again.

The newspapers were initially filled with stories of the Claw Man killer in the fog, but no further were reported, and the story quickly lost prominence.

The fog went away, but returned two days later. Holmes had been in and out, pursuing his own investigation. Finally, he sent a note to the countess and paced the sitting room until he received a reply. It read: "*The invitation has been sent and accepted.*"

"The game is now afoot, Watson," he said as he grabbed his coat and scarf and stick. I did the same and followed him out the door.

We were fortunate to find a hansom at the door. I learned later Holmes had paid the driver to wait there until he was needed. We hurried to Scotland Yard to see Lestrade. Holmes had a plan, it seems. He dropped no clues on the way, but insisted I accompany him.

"You're sure of this?" Lestrade asked after Holmes laid it all out for him and for my benefit as well. "I don't want to be made a fool of in those exalted circles."

"I am sure. The note was delivered at half-two. It's now half-three. Half-four is tea time."

I had to admit the plan was simple, but devious and not without risk. Lestrade spoke to a constable, explaining the danger, but the young man was eager to do it for advancement. We collected supplies and left for the Earl's house on Berkeley Square. The streets were fairly empty. Fog kept most Londoners inside. Holmes and I, along with Lestrade and the constable, exited the vehicle on the side of the Earl's house. We entered through the tradesman's door, but these were mere precautions. No one could even see across the street by now. Silence fell on the Square with the weight of stone.

Holmes explained his plan to the Earl.

"Will it work, do you think?" the Countess asked with trepidation.

"Indeed," Holmes replied. Moments later, he, Lestrade, and I had stationed ourselves in the shrubbery close to the front of the house. A door closed somewhere nearby.

I peered through the choking darkness, my mouth and nose covered by my brown scarf, but my eyes stung and I wished that I had special eyeglasses to protect against the fog, as had been worn by the hansom driver we'd encountered a few days before. I vowed to have some made up for me when I had any extra money.

In a few minutes, the front door of the Earl's house opened. Footsteps sounded on the steps behind us. A cloaked figure passed near us – the Countess – but didn't acknowledge our presence. I hoped she would walk slower. We didn't want her to advance too far from safety.

The figure hesitated and rearranged the scarf over her face. Beside me, Holmes exhaled. She took a few more steps toward the street, crossed it, and turned left to walk along the side of the fenced enclosure. A figure glided out of the fog behind the lady. It was the Claw Man! I could almost see a glint off the knife as he raised it to slash the Countess's throat from behind her, and for a moment, I thought that Holmes's plan had gone amiss. Before any of us could move, however, the Countess turned and grabbed the Claw Man's right hand and twisted it behind him.

The Claw Man screamed in high-pitched anger and fought back, but Holmes materialized to grab the other arm and Lestrade leaped out with handcuffs. A light bloomed at the door of the Earl's house, and he and the butler rushed out. Holmes reached up and removed a black mask that covered the face and hair of the Claw Man, revealing his true identity.

As expected, the Claw Man, based on what Holmes had revealed to us, was the Honourable Clarinda Bellamy. Even in manacles, she continued to kick and scream with rage. I have scarcely seen anyone so angry. Her identity was discovered, her plan was foiled. Lestrade summoned the police wagon and sent her to the yard with the strictest instructions: "Do not let her out of your sight. Do not listen to her entreaties. She is the vilest murderess, and we apprehended her in the middle of trying to kill again. She is no better than a common criminal, no matter what she says."

The Countess and Earl invited us into the house. The constable, whose name was John Stevens, was asked to join us as well. He had been chosen to portray the Countess because of his average height. He was happy to remove his disguise and restore his uniform while we discussed the case.

"How did you know it was Clarinda?" the Earl asked Holmes.

"She didn't stand when we were at her house, which, while not proof, was indicative. She didn't want us to know she was tall enough to be taken for a man, and also that her skirt, being silk, hissed and might remind us that the Claw Man hissed under his cloak. She smelt faintly of flowers as Miss Pinson noted. It was not a common scent, with more gardenia than jasmine used. Gardenia is a heavier more powerful floral scent than any I've encountered and more memorable, but Clarinda didn't think about that. It wouldn't be enough to convict her, but it was enough to put her under my suspicion.

"I considered the Fenton's situation. Their dearest wish was to advance in the social hierarchy of London. This could only be achieved in their case by marriage, or perhaps saving the Queen's life.

"The Fentons played a long game. Gerald and Persephone both hoped to marry Baron Bellamy's daughter and son to raise the family's social position – but Clarinda's eye was on a higher prize than Gerald Fenton's. She wanted the Earl of Oxleigh."

"But I'm married!" he exclaimed, taking his wife's hand. "And I don't even know her."

"She comes here with the sewing circle," his wife said. "And you've seen her walking in the Square when the weather is fine." She turned to Holmes. "She really thought my husband would marry her if I were dead?"

"Her mother is dead. She lives with her father and brother, and I observed her to be a determined person. She thought she could arrange the marriage by eliminating the Countess. She would console the Earl and a marriage would ensue. This is how some people think – people who put themselves above all things, including the laws of man."

"But how did you know?"

"When I visited the places where the three slashing attacks occurred, I realized they were in order if one rode the Underground, starting with the most distant one, and working back. The attacks all happened near stations. She took a big chance with her plans for the second attack so near the first, but the fog was thick enough to warrant success. Each attack placed the Claw Man closer to the Square, which was her plan. She thought the police would think the Claw Man was playing his tricks again but had become more dangerous, moving from assaults to murder. Poor Persephone was simply a pawn. Miss Bellamy thought no one would ever suspect a woman."

"How did you know the Claw Man could be a woman?" I asked.

"I was alerted when the victims said the Claw Man wasn't unduly tall and I thought why couldn't *he* be a *woman*, and why would a woman kill another woman? The answer led me to Clarinda Bellamy – a woman who wanted something and would do anything to get it.

"In the hall as we left the Bellamy's house on the first day of the case, I saw a woolen cape. It was dark grey, but I twitched the hem and saw it was red on the other side. A woman could commit the crime, disappear into the fog while removing her face mask and turning her cape inside out. She could hide the mask in a sewing basket, or her muff along with the knife and no one would suspect her. The police would be looking for a man."

"How did you know to look for the reverse of the cape?" the Earl asked.

"At the morgue, I'd seen a red thread on the clothing of the victim." He pulled an envelope out of his waistcoat pocket. "Here it is. If you compare it to the reverse of her grey cape, you'll find it's a perfect match in color. That wouldn't be enough to convict her in court – hence tonight's charade to catch her repeating her crime – but victimless this time, of course. When her invitation arrived, asking the Countess around to tea, I knew she was ready to commit her next crime, and I put my plan into place. Constable Stevens played his part to perfection. I hope that will be in your report," he said to Lestrade.

Lestrade took the envelope. "Indeed it will."

"In the fog with the scarf over her face, the murderer couldn't tell that the figure wasn't the Countess," I said. "You used the opposite of Clarinda's trick – a man disguised as a woman."

"Brilliant," the Earl said.

"That was an exciting evening's work," I said after we were back by our fire with brandy to warm us after dinner. Holmes lit a cigar, but I passed.

"This was a case of people wanting what they can't have, though with time, I think the Fentons could've achieved their marital desires. The Bellamys would've needed money after Billy gambled all of theirs away, but Clarinda wanted more than mere money – She wanted to be a Countess."

"I suspect she didn't want to be sister-in-law to Miss Fenton either," I said.

I could see why Holmes preferred sleuthing to arguing a case in a court of law or counting guineas or plotting in the Foreign Office. I could grow rather fond of it myself.

"One thing I'm curious about: Why did you scrape the mud off Miss Fenton's shoe in the morgue?"

"As I said, it had a red-brown tinge to it that looked like dried blood. When I applied the test of my own devising to it, I proved the presence of hemoglobin. I thought when we found the killer, I could do the same with his shoes – *her* shoes, as it turned out. But I couldn't see Clarinda's feet for her skirts, and anyway, she'd most likely changed her footwear. In the meantime, if she hadn't been an 'Honourable', I could've demanded to see her wardrobe and checked all of her shoes for red-tinged mud."

"Holmes, you think of everything."

"It is my job, Watson. I'm a consulting detective. I think for everybody."

"Indeed."

The Incident of the
Pointless Abduction
by Arthur Hall

During the years when my friend Mr. Sherlock Holmes and I shared many of his adventures as London's only consulting detective, we found ourselves confronted by a variety of crimes. Some had obvious purpose, such as the robbery of funds from a bank or the murder of someone as an act of revenge. Others at first seemed entirely without motive, which always attracted Holmes's attention, since it invariably meant that something deeper lay behind the criminal act. Always it was the unique or unexpected features of a case that inspired him to undertake it with the greatest enthusiasm.

One such affair began on a late summer morning, distinct in my mind because it marked one of the rare occasions when I was able to induce my friend to take exercise for its own sake. We had encircled much of Regent's Park when I felt a stab of pain. My wound from the Battle of Maiwand had been troubling me lately, and Holmes recognised this instantly.

"Watson, I see that you are experiencing some distress." He guided me to an unoccupied bench. "Let us rest here for a while before returning to Baker Street."

After about twenty minutes the ache abated. I was again able to move without pain, and my breathing had become regular. I was about to reassure Holmes that I had fully recovered when a man who appeared faintly familiar came by leaning heavily on a stick. He seemed to me to be in a melancholy state, as if he carried much care upon his shoulders.

I rose to confront him, noticing Holmes's concerned glance and experiencing relief that I had not suffered as a result of the sudden movement.

"It is Arnold Skelton," I remembered. "My dear sir, do you recall me?"

For a moment he stared at me, his head held to one side and his brow furrowed. "I believe we have met somewhere."

"Maiwand!" I announced. "You were brought to me with a dislocated shoulder, and we talked at length. I am Doctor John Watson."

"Indeed!" His expression brightened somewhat. "Your ministrations were most welcome at that awful time. Weeks after our brief meeting, I was injured for a second time." He glanced towards the leg that he supported with his stick. "Half of that got blown off."

"My dear fellow, I can't begin to tell you how sorry I am." I glanced back to where Holmes waited. "Why not come and sit with us for a moment or two? If I may say so, you appear to be exhausted."

He agreed to both my suggestion and my observation, and we joined Holmes on the bench. I made the introduction, but didn't disclose his profession to my former comrade. Mr. Skelton had moved with considerable difficulty, but I sensed that his injury wasn't the cause of the confused aura, or the sadness that seemed to surround him. He enquired little of me, but soon began to talk freely about himself. He related how, because of his injury, he had experienced difficulty in finding employment since his return to London. We agreed that our army pensions alone enabled a scant existence only. He had, he told us, been on the edge of absolute poverty when his only relative, an uncle, died, leaving he and his wife with an inheritance that would carry them through their declining years if used sparingly.

Throughout his narrative, he had reverted to a sombre countenance. Holmes had observed him, as was his way, and contributed few words, but his expression told me that something within the conversation interested him. It was as my former acquaintance paused that he enquired, "Mr. Skelton, if I may be so bold, it is apparent to me that something troubles you deeply. Perhaps if you were to take Doctor Watson and myself into your confidence, some remedy might be found."

The ex-soldier stared at him silently for an instant, so that I thought he had regarded the remark as an impertinence, but then his head fell to his chest and tears appeared in his eyes.

"No one can help. My first thought was Scotland Yard, but they will kill her if I take such an action."

"But not if the assistance comes from a friend who isn't known to them."

Holmes had at once assessed the situation. Arnold Skelton's wife had been abducted.

"But what can you do?" He shook his head hopelessly.

"I am by profession a consulting detective. This situation isn't new to me."

There was a moment of silence, during which a flurry of leaves fell from an increasingly threadbare beech.

"I cannot perceive the reason for it," Mr. Skelton said. "We aren't rich, as I have explained, and they have demanded nothing from us as yet."

"Several possibilities suggest themselves. Pray tell us the circumstances of this distressing incident, omitting not the slightest detail."

"It is really very simple. I am in the habit of spending my afternoons in Hammersmith Library. My wife takes in washing locally, to get us a few extra shillings now and then. I usually return to our home at about five o'clock, by which time her work is completed and our evening meal half-cooked, but yesterday I knew something was amiss from the moment I entered."

"Because there was no aroma," I ventured, noting Holmes's nod of approval.

"That, and because the place was silent. I could hear no movement, or my wife humming to herself as she often does."

"Was there any indication to explain her absence?" Holmes enquired.

"Only this." From a pocket, he produced a piece of crumpled paper.

I altered my position so that I, too, could read the message that was scrawled in a childish hand:

> *She is safe, for now. If you are in the Pink Elephant at seven tomorrow night, you will learn more. Should the police be informed, you will never see her again.*

"This is all?" Holmes asked then.

"It is. I immediately searched all over the house, and in the street, but there was no sign of her."

"And you have heard nothing more since?"

"Nothing."

Holmes nodded. "The Pink Elephant, I recall, is a tavern frequented by all manner of thieves and pickpockets."

"It is, and it is one I constantly avoid." He glanced at his injury again. "It will be difficult to get there, but I dare not ignore the appointment."

"Allow me to be your representative," I said at once, with feeling.

"Thank you, Doctor, but I have no means of knowing if a substitute would be allowed."

"We will undertake to accompany you," Holmes offered then. "If we arrive separately, it will not be realised that there is a connection between us."

There was a still moment as several crows flew noisily overhead. The relief on Skelton's face was evident. "Thank you, gentlemen. You place me greatly in your debt."

We reassured him further, and by the time he left us, he was in better spirits. When we rose, Holmes enquired as to my ability to walk without pain, and I informed him that I was again perfectly capable.

"The ache isn't constant. It occurs at irregular times."

"Nevertheless, I'm prepared to visit the tavern alone to assist your friend if I can."

"Thank you, but I will not hear of it."

We made our way back to our lodgings and a luncheon of Mrs. Hudson's steak pie. When the meal was over Holmes insisted, unnecessarily, that I rest while he brought his index up to date. The afternoon drifted by slowly, and few words passed between us. After an excellent trout dinner, we put on our hats and coats and prepared to leave for Hammersmith.

"Are you armed?" he asked.

"My service revolver is ready, as usual."

"Excellent. I am similarly equipped."

The hansom took us through Fulham and into the outskirts of Hammersmith. The driver was familiar with The Pink Elephant and appeared surprised when Holmes instructed him to bring his horse to a halt several streets away.

"I didn't want to chance our arrival coinciding with that of Mr. Skelton," he explained as the cab rattled out of sight.

A short walk brought us to the tavern. It looked to be a building that had stood since Tudor times but had long since fallen into some disrepair. A small crowd of roughs stood drinking and guffawing loudly outside, and I noticed that our appearance attracted their attention.

"We are out of place here." I commented.

"On reflection, perhaps we should have adopted disguises."

He pushed open the door warily. We were met by a cacophony of voices, each seeming to be attempting to shout above the others. The clinking of glasses, various obscene accusations angrily phrased, and the hoarse singing of a female voice to piano accompaniment mingled in the smoke-laden air. At a nearby table, a man with a patch over one eye played cards with a brutish-looking Lascar. The heated conversation in several directions suggested that violence was about to break out.

"Not your usual sort of drinking-place, I think?" Holmes said, smiling briefly.

"I'd have preferred to meet our client in my club."

"Ah, I see that Mr. Skelton has taken a seat near the corner, so we will take the table that has just been vacated near the bar."

We took our seats and soon realised that there was no service here. Holmes approached the bar and returned with two pints of ale, his searching glance taking in every person. A tattooed boy stood up to block his path, but quickly made way when he saw that he had instilled no fear.

"A more scurvy band of rogues and vagabonds I have rarely had the misfortune to meet," he murmured as he sat opposite me. "I have observed no attempt to approach our client as yet, although the appointed time has passed."

I made what I hoped was a casual survey of the room. "In this tangle of humanity, it could easily escape our notice."

"He hasn't left my sight for an instant. I chose this chair carefully for its position."

As we drank and spoke little for ten minutes or so, the noise seemed to grow louder.

Somewhere at the far side of the room an uproar broke out. Then several unsteady customers assembled at the bar. The landlord served them and they drank quickly, before making their exit.

"A minor skirmish. Not unusual here, I would think," Holmes said as he drained his glass.

I glanced towards the bar, where a few elderly men remained. The landlord had been replaced by a stout and muscular woman, presumably his wife. As I watched, she pulled a pint of ale for a man in a flat cap who was perched precariously on a high stool. He drank it in a single gulp and got to his feet, staggering in our direction. As he approached our table he stopped and stared at us curiously.

"I haven't seen you gentlemen here before."

"We haven't been here before," I answered.

"This is the last place I shall ever be."

Holmes regarded him silently. Then: "Forgive me, sir. I don't understand."

"I have come to the end of my life. There is little left to live."

I was about to ask him to explain when a huge man rose from a nearby table.

"Come on, Sid," he said as he took the arm of the man who had spoken. "It's time you went home."

I was about to make some remark about this strange fellow when the barmaid shouted something in a loud voice. The distant songstress went quiet at once, as did the accompanying piano. The hum of conversation too, had become muted. All around us, men leaned forward in their seats to catch her words. She peered to the right and left of her, apparently uncertain as to whether she had been heard.

"Someone has left this on the bar," she repeated, holding up an envelope. "It is addressed to Mister Arnold Skelton."

"I wondered how the kidnappers would communicate with our client," Holmes whispered. "That is always their greatest risk."

Our client rose and approached the bar. As the landlord's wife surrendered the envelope, the man who had escorted our recent conversationalist from the room appeared by my side. He leaned his thick body close to me and whispered.

"Don't give him no mind, gentlemen. We call him 'Suicidal Sid', because he's always threatening to end his life. It's just his way of getting others to feel sorry for him enough to buy him a pint or two."

Holmes glanced in my direction as I replied. "I'm glad to learn that he isn't serious."

"Never!" He appeared to find the notion humorous. "Don't you worry – he'll be back with the same story tomorrow night."

He retraced his steps to the bar then, as Mr. Skelton walked past us carrying the envelope. He made straight for the exit as Holmes had instructed, and we followed when we were certain that he had no pursuit.

All but one of the customers who had congregated outside the tavern were gone. The man remaining lay curled upon the pavement, snoring loudly with an empty bottle beside him. Our client awaited us a short distance along the street, in the shadows of a tree overhanging a garden wall.

"It was as you expected, Mr. Holmes," he said, handing my friend the contents of the envelope.

Holmes held the scrap of cheap paper so that it was readable in the glow from a well-lit nearby window. I peered over his shoulder.

I await you at 17 Carmel Square.

He nodded. "I know the place. There is no need for a hansom. We can walk there in a few minutes."

I questioned that because of the limitations of our companion, but he was willing, and so we slowly set off in silence. Holmes watched constantly for followers, but there were none. Twice we turned corners and crossed to the other side of the street, finally finding ourselves in a short thoroughfare with two well-spaced houses on each side. All was in darkness as we approached the first of these, except for the single streetlamp near the tiny front garden.

"A board, proclaiming this property to be for sale, has been uprooted and thrown to one side," he observed. "From its condition, this house has long been unoccupied."

The meagre glow illuminated our way along the uneven path. The front door needed a coat of paint and opened easily at Holmes's touch.

"Keep your hand on your revolver, Watson," he advised me.

We entered a gloomy corridor cautiously. He produced his dark lantern, which revealed peeling walls and a worn carpet as we made our way past empty rooms to the back of the house. The door of a spacious parlour hung open, and we drew our weapons as we passed through it. It was empty with a dank atmosphere, and every movement echoed loudly. Holmes held up the lantern and peered into the blackness before moving to a corner and picking up an oil lamp which he lit from a vesta. We were suddenly surrounded by shadows, and I saw that the walls were adorned with posters and music hall programmes.

"This house evidently once belonged to a performer," he observed, holding up the lamp.

Mr. Skelton, who had said little, moved closer awkwardly. "I have seen some of these productions. Who in the world can be doing this?"

I turned to speak to him, but my attention was caught by something on the rear wall.

"Holmes, look!"

My friend peered in the direction I had indicated.

"It is a dummy, a doll," he said. "It is the sort of effigy used in a ventriloquism act, but it is fixed to the wall."

"It is grotesque," our client remarked.

"I cannot imagine the purpose of it," I said.

"It seems that the former owner of this house couldn't leave his profession behind him." Holmes examined some of the posters. "The dates suggest that he must have been a very elderly man."

"*Are you here, Arnold Skelton?*" A high-pitched squeak of a voice said suddenly.

In the shadows, we looked at each other in surprise. Holmes's attention was quickly on the effigy, and then I realised that its mouth had moved.

"Answer!" he whispered to our companion.

"I am," Mr. Skelton's voice wavered. "What have you done with my wife?"

After a moment's silence, the shrill tones came again as the hideous face became animated.

"*You must go, tomorrow evening at eleven o'clock precisely, to Hampstead Heath. After your carriage has passed The Tall Trees Inn, continue for half-a-mile. Then look for a lantern, hanging among the branches of an elm. If you enter the trees at that place, you will find that your wife awaits you.*"

"But what is all this about? Why have you done this? What is it that you have against me?"

78

The quality of the acoustics was suddenly different. I sensed that our client's words fell flat in the silence. Holmes had already realised that the exchange had come to an end, for he turned and ran back through the corridor to the front of the house.

"He may be in time to catch our adversary," I told Mr. Skelton. "It would be better if we leave this awful place now."

I assisted him as best I could, back into the street. After a short while Holmes reappeared, a little breathless.

"There was never a chance of apprehending him," he admitted. "At the back of the house I forced the door and entered. The interior has the appearance of a boiler room, but the place was deserted. By the light of my dark lantern, I was able to see the back of the effigy, and that it had been recently plastered into the wall. Beneath it was a trap door. A rope ladder led into the depths, but our enemy had long made use of it."

"But where does this leave us?" Our client asked.

"With an appointment for tomorrow night." He turned to me abruptly. "Watson, there is something that may require your attention. Mr. Skelton, kindly remain there for a few minutes, after which we will return to you."

Without waiting for a reply, Holmes hurried me away. Around the corner, the way I had presumed him to have taken to the rear of the property, a body lay prone upon the pavement. It was obvious to me that there was no hope for the man, for his shirt was bloody and a long knife hung from his chest. Carefully, I turned him over.

"It is the man from the tavern!" I exclaimed. "The one who was described as 'Suicidal Sid'."

"He was here as I ran past before. I saw at once that he was beyond help."

"Do you believe that our adversary did this?"

"I would think it a certainty. As you know, I don't believe in coincidences."

"This man was following us?"

"Doubtless, probably hoping to induce us to give him money for more drink. Instead, he saw our ventriloquist friend and recognised him, and so he couldn't be allowed to live." He peered around us. "The tunnel, therefore, surfaces not far away."

"We must see that this poor fellow is taken to the mortuary."

"Indeed. If we can find a telegraph office that is open at this hour, we will send a message to Lestrade."

Soon after, we were fortunate enough to discover a cab in the High Street. We roused the sleeping driver and left Mr. Skelton a short distance away, near his home. Holmes dispatched a telegram to Inspector Lestrade, and we were soon seated back in our sitting room. I was astonished to discover that it was almost the midnight hour.

"You realise, of course, that this escapade was planned well in advance," he said as we sipped brandy before retiring. "That dummy was installed some time ago, most likely for this specific purpose. As I mentioned previously, the greatest risk to a kidnapper is when the ransom is paid or when there is a meeting between him and those representing his victim. Here, our adversary overcame that difficulty successfully."

"We still haven't discovered his purpose. It cannot be gain, surely. Mr. Skelton, as he himself has mentioned, isn't a rich man."

"More likely revenge, I think. But we may discover the truth of it tomorrow. I noticed also that, although the dummy was made to speak, which indicates a theatrical background, its operator couldn't hear us."

I considered. "He didn't answer Mr. Skelton's question directly."

"Quite so. Also, he would certainly have commented, had he known that our client was accompanied."

"Then he will be surprised tomorrow. I am curious as to who owns that house."

"I have a mind to visit the agency in charge of its sale after breakfast. But for now, I will bid you goodnight."

With that, he disappeared into his room. I replaced my empty glass on the tray, as he had, and went up to my bed.

Holmes had already left when I sat down to breakfast. The absence of anything but a half-full coffee pot told me that his morning repast had been meagre. I hurried through my bacon, eggs, and toast and drank my coffee quickly, because this morning I had early appointments with several patients. The time passed swiftly, as I saw one followed after another. In the early afternoon I returned to Baker Street in time for a delayed luncheon.

I drank the last of my tea and had barely settled myself in my armchair when Holmes entered the room with a flourish.

"All is discovered." He hung up his hat and coat. "I now know who the owner of that house is. Apparently, he decided to suspend advertising that it's for sale while he torments our client – hence the discarded sales board. From the description furnished by the agent, I am almost certain who our adversary is. His reason for all this, however, will doubtless be revealed this evening."

He said no more, and I knew it would be futile to enquire, for my friend's custom was to reveal that which he wished me to know at his chosen time. He then called for more tea, and we spent the afternoon in both conversation and companionable silence. By the time dinner was served, we had reviewed several old cases and smoked to the extent that a heavy fog hung over our sitting room. Our good landlady threw open the window in disgust as we sat down to eat.

Shortly after the table was cleared, the doorbell rang. Mrs. Hudson showed in Mr. Lawson Ketching, who appeared deeply troubled. It was soon apparent that he had no connection with our current enquiries, and I expected Holmes to suggest an appointment for another time, but on hearing the nature of this new problem my friend gave the gentleman some advice that sent him on his way much relieved.

"A trifling matter," he explained when we were alone again. "I saw at once that it wouldn't occupy sufficient time to spoil our plans." He glanced at his pocket watch. "But I see that it is time to ready ourselves. Come, Watson, let us see if we can bring our client some relief and enlightenment this night."

The Tall Trees Inn was in darkness. We passed beneath a row of thick pines meeting overhead to form an arch that blotted out the sky and alternated with open fields over which a faint mist swirled. There had been little conversation since we boarded the carriage. Mr. Skelton had been waiting for us outside his home as instructed, and his anticipation of the reunion with his wife was evident in his restless manner.

"We must have travelled half-a-mile past the inn by now," I said, breaking the silence.

Holmes peered into the darkness. "There is the lantern, in the tree near the milestone. Driver, pray stop here and wait for us."

The light shone out of the darkness a little way ahead. We drew our weapons and advanced along a narrow track with our client limping behind us. As we neared the illumination, Holmes raised an arm and we came to a halt. We found ourselves surrounded by an eerie silence, broken only by the occasional cry of an owl. My friend led us into the trees, the utter blackness relieved only by the meagre glow provided by our adversary.

Holmes gestured to indicate that I should tread carefully and Mr. Skelton should remain. I advanced with him until the lantern hung in branches directly above us. Another light suddenly flared, and a woman of mature years became visible, tied by one arm to the trunk of a sturdy elm. With her was a figure clothed in the manner of a monk, his long robe and cowl concealing both his build and his features.

Holmes was about to whisper something to me, probably an instruction on how we should proceed, when Mr. Skelton rushed past us at a speed at which I wouldn't have thought him capable, throwing caution to the winds.

"Margaret! Margaret! Has he harmed you?"

81

He approached his wife and embraced her, and the hooded figure retreated slightly to allow this.

"Linger with your touch, so that she will remember," he said in a curiously toneless voice. "For she will never grace your sight again."

Mr. Skelton turned to him. "Who are you? You promised to release her!"

"Indeed, I did, and I will. I made no such pledge regarding you, however."

It struck me then that our enemy believed his victim to be alone, since we stood outside the circle of light cast by the lantern.

Our client, his arms around his wife, replied in a voice that shook. "What have you against me? Until now, I have never laid eyes on you."

"Oh, but you have! I suppose I shouldn't have expected you to remember. It will add to the discomfort of your last moments, if you are unaware of the reason for your punishment." From beneath his robe, he produced a shotgun, which he aimed at Mr. Skelton. "If you wish to preserve your wife's life, I suggest that you stand away from her."

Mrs. Skelton screamed as her husband obeyed, and Holmes stepped from the shadows.

"Put down your firearm – Instantly!"

Our adversary hesitated but a moment, before turning lightning-fast and discharging his weapon. My friend threw himself behind a thick elm as the blast ripped into it. I stepped into view and fired my service revolver at once, aiming at the centre of the man's body. He cried out as the shotgun spun in the air and dropped at his feet, shouting a foul oath as he fled into the trees and out of our sight.

I immediately made to give chase, but was halted by a shout from Holmes.

"Let him go, Watson. Mrs. Skelton is safe now."

"But Holmes – he'll escape!"

"That is of no consequence," he said in a quieter tone. "I'm now aware of his identity. We'll deal with him another day."

We then ensured that Mrs. Skelton had survived her ordeal well. She was, not unexpectedly, overcome with relief, and her husband with gratitude.

Holmes went very still for a moment, listening.

"As I thought – there is another track near to this one. Someone on horseback has just passed along it at considerable speed. Our enemy is returning home with his purpose unfulfilled, I think."

"Your supposition was correct," I reminded him. "From the beginning, you believed his actions were those of vengeance."

"I could imagine none other since profit was clearly not the objective here. The details I expect to learn soon, at our subsequent encounter. But now, let us re-join our driver and transport these people to their home. I'll make arrangements to have them guarded and, in the morning, I'll send a message to Lestrade and bring this affair to its close."

Later, we were in our sitting room enjoying a brandy, positioned as always on either side of a dying fire. Between sips, Holmes examined the shotgun which he had retrieved from the forest floor.

"You really are an excellent shot with that service revolver of yours. You struck this weapon from the abductor's hand with little more damage to it than a split stock."

"I aimed at his middle. He moved quickly."

"He did indeed. Otherwise you would have permanently ensured that he commit no more crimes. That situation will still be achieved nevertheless, since he will certainly face the hangman for the murder of 'Suicidal Sid'. Once again, old friend, you probably saved my life with your quick action, for I hardly managed to conceal myself in time." He crossed to the coatrack and indicated several small holes in his ulster. "But now it would be as well to retire, for I anticipate a busy day ahead of us."

We then separated, I with a feeling of warm satisfaction at my friend's words.

The next morning, I rose later than is my usual custom to discover that Holmes had been out before we sat down to breakfast.

"You have sent the telegram you mentioned to the Yard." I ventured.

"Quite so. I included a brief description of what transpired last night, and it wouldn't surprise me to receive a reply within the hour."

"I should remind you that I have a few patients to attend to this morning."

"Then pray do so quickly. It would reduce my satisfaction at seeing this man brought to book considerably, were you not there to witness it."

As it happened, I returned to Baker Street before mid-day. Sadly, one of my appointments had been cancelled with the passing of the patient during the night.

Holmes was sprawled lazily in his chair, a steady stream of smoke curling upwards from his cherry-wood pipe. His eyes glittered with anticipation.

"Ah, Watson. In good time, I see."

"You have heard from Lestrade, then?"

"His telegram arrived not long after you left. I have asked Mrs. Hudson to serve luncheon early, and I believe I hear her on the stairs at this moment."

We enjoyed lamb cutlets, which he attacked with unusual relish. This I had long noticed was typical of Holmes's behaviour when the end of a case was in sight. He refused dessert but contended himself with two cups of strong coffee.

"Are we to leave soon?" I enquired.

"As soon as our friends from Scotland Yard have had sufficient time to prepare themselves."

The noise of a heavy cart passing along Baker Street reached us before I asked, "Where are we to meet them?"

"Why, The Pink Elephant, of course. It is curiously fitting that this affair should reach its conclusion there."

He would say nothing more lest he reduce the dramatic effect. I knew his ways of old.

Less than an hour elapsed before we boarded a hansom that conveniently passed our lodgings as we emerged. Holmes spoke little during the journey to Hammersmith, but I sensed in him the air of a magician who enjoys revealing his cleverness to a mystified audience.

The smoke-filled atmosphere of the tavern seemed no less dense than before. I recognised some of the men who sat drinking from our previous visit. They looked as if they hadn't moved since then and gave us the same evil look. There were also, I noticed, two or three new faces whose expressions were no less unfriendly.

Holmes paused, his eyes everywhere.

"Which of these is the man who escaped us last night?" I asked him.

"None of them."

"Are we expecting him then?"

He shook his head, smiling faintly at my confusion. "He is already here."

"But – "

"Come, Watson. Soon all will be clear to you."

We approached the bar and he ordered drinks. The landlord leaned towards us because Holmes had spoken in a whisper. Immediately my friend produced a pair of police handcuffs, which he snapped onto the man's wrists. The landlord roared with anger and surprise and attempted to escape by the door behind the bar, but three of his new customers were there at once to hold him fast. He then gave vent to a succession of the foulest oaths but subsided as he realised that escape was hopeless.

"Excellent!" Holmes said to the landlord's captors. "Allow me to introduce Inspectors Crayforth, Merrill, and Stark. Lestrade informs me that they are new at the Yard and show great promise." With that he took a police whistle from his pocket and blew a single blast. Moments later, the Good Inspector himself joined us.

"Good afternoon, Lestrade," said Holmes. "I really must congratulate you. Both your choice of men to assist us and their disguises were most effective. Here we have the fellow I described to you in my telegram. I am confident that I can prove murder and kidnapping to your satisfaction, and doubtless other crimes will present themselves as we proceed."

The inspector looked the landlord up and down with a critical eye. "Thank you, Mr. Holmes. I think we should all adjourn to the Yard." He looked around him at the mixed expressions of the other customers and the seedy appearance of their drinking place. "It will be easier there to get to the bottom of this business."

The three disguised officers bustled the landlord from the tavern to a waiting police coach, with Lestrade, Holmes, and me following in another. On arriving at our destination, Lestrade quickly conducted our prisoner to a cell before dismissing his three subordinates.

"Now, m'lad," he began as soon as the door had clanged shut behind us. "What's all this about?"

"It's a mistake, that's what it is."

"Hardly that," Holmes retorted. "Your faint lisp that I noticed previously was clearly evident last night, as was your missing index finger of your left hand. You wore gloves, but it was apparent nevertheless because they were tight-fitting."

Our prisoner glared at my friend fiercely. "You will never prove anything."

"Much to the contrary, I think. You have abducted Mr. Arnold Skelton's wife with the purpose of luring him to a place where you intended to end his life. During this, you killed a man known as 'Suicidal Sid' because he witnessed your flight and could identify you. We don't know the reason for your actions, but doubtless they will come to light when your victim confronts you." He glanced at Lestrade, who nodded.

"A telegram will bring Mr. Skelton here in an hour or so."

At this, the landlord's face took on an expression of disgust. "Don't bring that man here, gentlemen, I implore you. My hatred for him is more than for anything in this world."

"But why?" I intervened, "I knew him slightly at Maiwand. He struck me as a stout and reliable fellow."

The prisoner stared at the stone floor, shaking his head. "I see that you have too much against me. I know I am for the hangman. Very well, I will tell you all."

Holmes, Lestrade, and I moved closer, waiting for the man's revelation. Presently he sat more erect, with his back against the stone wall.

"My name is – or *was* – Matthew Wakeman," he began. "My mother died while I was still young, and so there was just my father and me. He was a music hall performer, what is termed a ventriloquist, and was quite famous in his day. The only thing he ever did for me as a child was to teach me his art and others, all of which I practiced for a while, and we lived together in that house not far away, where I spoke to Arnold Skelton two nights ago by means of an effigy which I had installed."

I wondered if Holmes would indicate that we also had been present, but he did not.

"I grew to manhood and became engaged to a girl I loved dearly, whose name was Priscilla Beecham. We were six months away from the wedding date when I discovered that she had betrayed me. In my anguish, I threw away my prospects for a career in the theatre and joined the army." He gave me a quick empty stare. "So you see, Doctor, I, too, was at Maiwand. Sometime before the battle, I realised how valuable some of the deceptive practices that my father had taught me could now prove to be, if adapted carefully. Since my betrothal ended, I cared nothing for honour or my fellow man. I joined the gambling circle that my comrades had established, and quickly accumulated a considerable sum, deliberately losing on occasion to avert their suspicions. Then Arnold Skelton and another man, Luke Chambers, joined the group. These two must have been smarter than the rest, or familiar with cheating methods, for I was quickly exposed. It was then discovered that I had planned a strategy to defraud the regiment by causing deliveries of rations to be intercepted and resold later. All was lost. I was court-martialled."

"Did you say, 'Luke Chambers'?" Lestrade interrupted. "I seem to remember that the Yard has an unsolved murder of a victim of that name who also lived in the area." He stared harshly at Wakeman. "Are you also responsible for that?"

"There is nothing to be gained by a denial now, I imagine. After leaving the army, I returned to Hammersmith, as it was the only place I had ever lived. However hard I tried, securing employment proved impossible, and I gradually came to realise that my efforts were somehow being deliberately frustrated by, I suspected, the very men who had caused the end of my army career. I left the district and reverted to my original profession, constantly moving from town to town appearing in local music halls. Eventually I returned to the capital. By now I had met my wife, who knows nothing of my past, and time had altered my appearance. To enhance this, I shaved off the thick beard I had tended for years. I had long since changed my name. When I became landlord of The Pink Elephant, it was as Adam Redvers."

Lestrade looked down on his prisoner, shifting his position as Holmes asked, "At what point did you kill Luke Chambers?"

"You could say it happened by chance or, as I considered, that it was a natural justice taking its course. A year or so ago, I walked along Hammersmith High Street and happened to look into the window of a barber's shop. My wife had been nagging me for weeks to get my hair cut until I could stand it no longer. I peered into the shop looking for a vacant chair. There, seated nearest to the window with his face lathered, was one of the men responsible for my downfall – none other than Luke Chambers. He had aged, of course, but I was in no doubt of his identity. I followed him as he left the shop, staying a fair distance back and using the crowd for concealment until my opportunity arose. He entered the alley that runs between Consort Street and Queen's Row, and I saw that it was otherwise empty. It occurred to me that it would be fitting that he should know of me and why I was taking revenge, so I accosted him and made all clear.

"For a moment he looked shocked, then instead of the apology or fear that I might have expected, he laughed. I tell you, gentlemen, making fun of my past was like impaling me with hot needles, and I felt the pain of it as I buried the knife that I have carried since my army days into his stomach. I turned it as I pulled it from his body, enjoying his agony as he howled like a beast and bled upon the earth. The satisfaction that settled upon me then was indescribable, as if I had found a kind of peace. It was at that moment that I knew I had to seek out that other instrument of my ruination, Arnold Skelton."

Holmes, Lestrade, and I exchanged glances. Here was a man who could do no wrong in his own eyes, devoid of compassion.

"And so," said I, "you determined to find Mr. Skelton and deal with him similarly, despite his wounded state?"

The man who now called himself Adam Redvers shrugged. "His condition isn't related to my purpose. Many of my comrades suffered wounds. Injuries and death are a part of war. Sometime after establishing myself as the landlord of The Pink Elephant, I made enquiries through some of my regular customers and discovered that Arnold Skelton also lived nearby. I followed him once or twice to the library and his other regular haunts, but soon saw that he was rarely alone for long. Always some friend or acquaintance would join him to assist his progress or help him to carry some burden or other. I therefore devised the plan of abducting his wife as a means of attracting him to a place convenient for my purpose. It was never my intention to harm her, beyond that. The meeting at the tavern was so that I could observe him first. I feared that he would have aged beyond my recognition."

"Which is when you arranged a rendezvous that was intended to culminate in his murder," Holmes concluded.

"I felt it was justified. He set my life on a different course, when I had taken my new career to heart."

"Can you not realise," I enquired then, "that all your misfortunes are of your own making? Had you not sought to profit from the deceit of your comrades and the army, you would still be enjoying that career now. Everything that has happened to you since stems from those acts because you resorted to crime."

"In this world," he said with resignation, "you takes your chances and opportunities when you can. Some people are born to be the victims of others."

"You have no regrets?"

"None."

"You may well have changed your mind by the time you meet the hangman," Lestrade retorted. "I have seldom met a villain who didn't, or as much without remorse as you are. You are for it, m'lad, and no mistake."

The prisoner then lay on his bunk and curled up as if in sleep. He turned away and would speak no more, despite several attempts at further questioning by Lestrade.

"I think this affair is concluded for Watson and myself," Holmes said as we left the cell. "What remains is strictly the province of the Yard."

"We will take care of it, Mr. Holmes," the official detective assured him. "Be in no doubt of it."

"Then we will leave you to your business. As for us, I believe a dinner of roast partridge awaits us, and I have instructed Mrs. Hudson to accompany it with a bottle of white wine of excellent vintage which I supplied earlier."

The Adventure of the Absent Crossing Sweeper
by Steven Philip Jones

Chapter I – Inspector G. Lestrade

"Now I wonder what this will be about?"

It was the twelfth day of the New Year of 1882, and something on the street suddenly attracted the attention of Sherlock Holmes as he was sorting through correspondence from the first morning post.

"Is it a client?" I asked as I perused my own correspondence at the table over a plate of rashers and eggs.

"It's Lestrade."

"Perhaps he's gotten himself in another fog."

"That is always possible, but I suspect there's something more to this visit."

"Why is that?"

"He looks more chagrined than is his wont. No matter, we shall find out presently." My friend picked a jack-knife off his desk, stepped to the fireplace, and transfixed his correspondence to the center of the mantelpiece just before Lestrade entered our sitting room. Holmes welcomed him and invited him to share our breakfast, but the policeman declined, saying he had already eaten. "Very good. Then draw your chair up to the fire and tell us what brings you here this frigid morning."

"I actually would like to speak with your Irregulars regarding some private business. I might even need to hire a couple of them for a few days."

For once Holmes appeared as taken aback as I. "I'll tell them, but may I ask what need Scotland Yard has for street-boys?"

"Not Scotland Yard." Lestrade paused, behaving more self-consciously than I would have expected after observing him over the past year. "A crossing sweeper named Sandro Capra has been absent from his corner since St. Andrew's Day. I'm hoping your cadet force may know something regarding his whereabouts. If not, then I'm hoping they can help me search for him."

My friend rummaged his memory and said, "I'm not familiar with any boy by that name. Is this Capra a friend?"

"No, but . . . ." Lestrade sighed in a frustrated way, removed his hat, and combed his fingers through his hair. "Let me tell it this way: Mr. Holmes, you know your way around London as well as a cabbie, so I presume you're familiar with the building that was completed last summer along New Oxford Street between Binniehill and Chesterton."

Holmes raised his eyebrows and leaned back in his big armchair. "The Queen Anne? I have seen it, but know nothing about its history."

"I can help with that. The owner is W.K. Reiner, a pork butcher whose shop is at the Chesterton corner and who lives on the second floor. Well, Capra carved himself out a post on the Binniehill corner when the construction started. He never misses a day, even though Reiner and the other shop owners try to discourage him – or I should say he never missed a day up to the thirtieth of November. Since then, I've done what I can to find him, and even some of the constables whose beats include that part of New Oxford Street and Seven Dials have been keeping their eyes peeled and ears open. They're doing this as a favour, so I ask that goes no further."

I asked, "Why didn't you make this an official investigation when Capra was reported missing?"

"Because no one reported him missing, and if my superiors knew what I was up to, they'd insist I drop the matter."

"Surely you've uncovered some details in six weeks."

"I have." A quick blush passed over Lestrade's lean face. "But I've reached an impasse."

Holmes placed his elbows upon the arms of his chair with his fingertips together and stretched out his legs. "Well, if you care to share what information you've collected with the doctor and me, we might notice something your diligence or concern blinded you to."

Genuine appreciation brightened our guest's features. "Thank you." He opened his official notebook to reference a page. "Let me start with the shop owners. Reiner is squat but muscular, with a sharp-nosed, alert, and ruddy face, green eyes, and a closely cropped blond beard. Henry Gundling, a cheese-monger, has the shop beside Reiner's. He's also small, but stout with a pleasant, clean-shaven face, black eyes, and long brown hair shot with grey.

"Next is Sam Leunch, a greengrocer, and finally the owner of the shop on the Binniehill corner is a baker named Moritz Hoffbeck. Leunch and Hoffbeck are a pair, both slender and tall, but Leunch has a dark, hard, decisive face with grey eyes, while Hoffbeck has a pale pinched face and cold brown eyes. All four are True Inspiration Congregationists whose families emigrated together from the former Duchy of Hadenfeldt-Stoutenberg when they were boys, and are often referred to as 'brothers' since they have always lived near one another in Kentish Town and

Camden. Or I should say they did, until Reiner moved into his building this summer. That struck me as out of character, but none of the brothers will say what prompted Reiner to distance himself. I thought it might be for privacy. Reiner is the group's sole bachelor. But Hoffbeck also lives alone, and has since his wife Iselda was expelled to an American Congregationist colony in 1861. The 'brothers' are tight-lipped about that too, but I imagine her expulsion had something to do with Inspirationist philosophy. They consider marriage a sign of spiritual weakness, discourage childbearing, and do not recognize divorce.

"Now on St. Andrew's Day, an apprentice at the milliner shop across the street noticed a young woman dressed as an upper servant talking with Capra around three o'clock. His name is Marshal Pennington, and he remembers her patronizing the building over the summer and autumn, and always tipping Capra and briefly chatting with him whenever she did. Pennington describes her as blonde, not much older than twenty, petite, attractive, and speaking with a Northern accent."

I asked, "How did he hear her accent?"

"Pennington passed by them once while making a delivery. On the day in question, however, Hoffbeck stormed out of his shop and scolded the lad, only to have her reproach him. Constable Jeavons approached to assist, but Hoffbeck tried to dismiss him. When that failed, Hoffbeck apologized for the commotion and slunk back to his bakery, by which time the woman had scuttled away so Jeavons abandoned the matter. Come day's end, Capra had departed, with no one seeing him leave his post or where he went."

Holmes stood, took his pipe from its place on the mantelpiece, and absently filled the bowl with the dottels and plugs from his previous day's smokes which had been carefully dried on the corner. "This disturbance happening on the same day that Capra vanished could just be a coincidence."

"I would like to talk with the woman just the same," replied Lestrade, "but she hasn't been back to the building. I suppose that could also be coincidence."

"Yes. Does she frequent any particular shops?"

"The butcher and the bakery. Most often she purchases lebkuchen and bratwurst."

"Do you know if she had a to-do with Hoffbeck or any other proprietor before this?"

"I've been told no."

"What did Hoffbeck tell you about their disagreement?"

"That all he did was request she stop emboldening the boy." Turning to another page, Lestrade added, "He also said, 'If that juvenile highwayman is gone, good riddance! He levelled blackmail upon the public in general and timid females in particular.'"

I commented, "He's scarcely the only Londoner to hold that opinion."

Holmes concurred and asked, "Could Hoffbeck tell you more about the young woman than Pennington?"

"No. None of the shop owners claim to know anything more about her, except she conducts her business and then is on her way."

Holmes lit his pipe and puffed some blue smoke-rings into the air. "You have interviewed the other shop owners in the neighbourhood and their employees?"

"None of them knows anything about the young woman. I should mention though that Pennington noticed Capra slipping out the Binniehill-side servant's entrance on more than one morning just before dawn. He also saw Reiner drag Capra out of the building by the collar a few mornings prior to the last day of November. I talked to Reiner, and he admitted to catching the boy sleeping in the cellar, but couldn't recall the precise day. However, he's sure that was the last time he has had any contact with Capra. By the way, there is another servant's entrance on the Chesterton side of the building, and a cellar entrance through Reiner's shop."

"You examined the cellar?"

"Of course, but the only things there are some left-over materials from the construction. There was a sack of horsehair tossed into one corner that Capra might have used for a bed. There were also sacks of quicklime and sand, along with piles of billets, bricks, and stone. It's all stacked along the east wall, except for that horsehair sack and some broken bricks piled in the opposite corner."

Holmes crossed his arms and tapped his fingers against the sleeves of his dressing gown. "Does Reiner or any of the other shop owners keep employees?"

"Each retains the usual number for their type of business."

"Does anyone else live in the building besides Reiner?"

"A gentleman on the third floor – James Stoutenberg."

I noted his last name. "And you interviewed this fellow?" Holmes asked.

"I would like to, but I can't."

I asked, "Why is that?"

"I need permission from the Foreign Office, and I doubt I would get it even if this were an official investigation."

"Who is he?"

"James Stoutenberg is the heir-presumptive and cousin of Christian Louis, current claimant of Hadenfeldt-Stoutenberg."

For the second time that morning, I was taken aback. "How is it a royal member of a former Prussian duchy is living in New Oxford Street?"

"Not only living there, Doctor, but doing so rent-free."

Holmes commented, "That is admirably charitable."

"I might call it excessive, but I have it on good authority it's due to the tolerance Louis's family extended to True Inspiration Congregationists when the family was in power. Most German-speaking duchies are far less accepting of Inspirationists."

"And on what authority did you learn this?"

"From a confidant at *The Times* who is often consulted by the FO. He also said that the cousins aren't speaking, as Stoutenberg is a bit of a black sheep. Nevertheless, Christian Louis provides him with a small allowance, but Stoutenberg isn't a remittance man – not if what he tells folks about spending the last ten years in Colorado working as a hard rock miner is true. The man is burly, in his late thirties, has dark hair and moustache, dresses like a mobsman, and claims he would still be mining if not for contracting trachoma which forces him to wear cinder glasses during daylight. According to the Guion Line, he arrived in Liverpool on the *S.S. Vandeleur* on 5 November, but I've asked the Rocky Mountain Detective Agency in Denver for whatever information they have on him and hope to receive their reply soon."

This seemed to worry Holmes. "Aren't you taking a risk?"

"I'm being careful. I have no desire to get the sack."

"As you say then. When the reply comes, I would be most interested in hearing what the Agency tells you."

"Certainly, but I have one more thing. It may have to do with Capra and it may not, but a stranger has been watching Reiner's building off and on since 28 December."

Holmes cocked his head on one side. "Can you describe him?"

Lestrade turned to a different page in his notebook. "He's described as being in his forties, ugly and bull-necked, with a weathered complexion and reddish hair, moustache, and beard. What's really interesting is he wears a flat brown or grey American-tailored wool suit with waistcoat, a thin ribbon tie, and a bowler hat." Lestrade shut his notebook. "A fellow wearing American clothes is watching the building where Stoutenberg is living after recently returning from the United States?"

"Is there a pattern to when this stranger appears?"

"There doesn't seem to be. The shop owners as well as other people in the neighbourhood have spotted him during different times of the day and night."

I asked, "Hasn't anyone ever confronted him or sent for a constable?"

93

"He ignores anyone with the gumption to speak with him, and whenever a constable is sent for, the stranger always vanishes before our man arrives."

Holmes rubbed his long hands together. "You certainly have collected a pretty bounty of curious particulars, Lestrade. Now, it's time for you to tell us about young Capra."

Lestrade laid his notebook on his lap. "His posture and speech are those of a person born and bred in a slum like Seven Dials, and I doubt he has ever attended a church school, or even a ragged school. In age, he's around ten. In height somewhat more than four feet. In appearance, he's as scrawny and dirty and ragged as you would expect. Nevertheless, Capra could be called handsome with a concave nose, mahogany hair, and hazel eyes. As for his personality, he's pleasant enough, but wary and shrewd."

"A rather typical street-boy. And what has become of his post? The number of pedestrians using that footpath during the day must make it a coveted spot."

"It is that, but Hoffbeck has been relentless in preventing another 'outlaw with a broom' from commandeering the location."

"And why you are going to such lengths to locate this crossing sweeper?"

Lestrade drummed his fingers on the notepad's cover. "The only explanation I can give you is that I pass that corner each morning and always felt the better for it after giving Capra a farthing to start his day, unless it was a holiday and then I gave him a copper." Lestrade put away his notebook. "So Mr. Holmes: What do you think?"

Holmes emptied his pipe in the hearth and placed it back upon the mantel. "It has been my experience that a confounding problem generally has a simple solution. This Capra may have been swept out by the tide while mudlarking, or a dispute for his turf may have resulted in an injury – or worse – for him or the transgressor."

"Yes, I know, but whatever the reason is, I wish to find it out."

"All right. I should like a little time to consider these facts before offering any theories."

Lestrade's shoulders slumped slightly but he said, "Yes, sir. You know how to contact me."

"I shall. And I would be surprised if a boy named Wiggins doesn't visit you before the afternoon."

"I appreciate that, Mr. Holmes." Lestrade then bid us good morning and departed.

Holmes moved to the window to watch him walk away in the direction of the Metropolitan Station. After a few moments he said, "I never knew that Lestrade could be so gracious." He turned to his desk and sat. "Even so, I believe he was being evasive."

"How so? Do you doubt his reason for wanting to find the boy?"

"What reason is that? He never gave us one." Unlocking the desk, he pulled out foolscap and began writing a letter. "I rather suspect Lestrade must dust off his sympathy whenever he takes it from the box. He has been a policeman for nearly half my life and is as tough a professional as you'll find. Detectives of his stature normally come up through the Yard's records bureau, not as constables, but Lestrade walked a beat and it's his tenacity, as well as the life he lived before joining the force, that makes him as successful as he is. It also explains why his methods run towards the conventional, but if anyone was born for his job, it's Lestrade. I'll be much mistaken if he isn't still a professional for another twenty years. All of this isn't meant so much as a compliment but an explanation why I suspect he's being evasive regarding his motive. Perhaps not with us, but certainly with himself."

As he was speaking Holmes completed his letter, placed it in an envelope, sealed it, and addressed it. After that he went to his room to exchange his dressing-gown for his frockcoat, ulster, and cravat. "I must post this directly, and then I'll deliver Lestrade's request. If anyone calls, tell them I don't expect to be back before dinner."

Chapter II – Death in Seven Dials

Holmes hadn't returned, and I had almost finished my lunch when our landlady escorted a street Arab who was no more than seven into the sitting room. "He wants to speak with Mr. Holmes."

"I expect him soon, but he isn't here."

"I know, Dr. Watson, but the lad is very persistent and wants to wait for him."

The boy said, "He tol' me to come here, sir."

"Mr. Holmes did? Oh, I see." I motioned the boy to approach the table. "What's your name?"

"Russell, sir."

"Why did Mr. Holmes tell you to come here?"

"He tol' us to tell him if we sees a man watchin' the Oxford building."

"Do you mean a building on New Oxford Street?"

"Yes, sir, vot I said."

"Are you sure Mr. Holmes didn't tell you to report to Inspector Lestrade of Scotland Yard?"

"Not if we sees this gent."

"All right. Well, since Mr. Holmes is unavailable, why don't you show this man to me?" Russell hesitated until I removed a penny from my pocket and presented it to him, with the assurance of another when we reached New Oxford Street. I instructed the landlady to hail us a cab. "And when Mr. Holmes comes back, tell him what the boy told us and that I've thrown my lot in with him."

When the cab reached our destination, I had the driver park one street away from Chesterton. That way the boy and I could blend in with the pedestrians as we approached Reiner's building, a formidable four-storey red-bricked structure with ornament and windows fortified by balustrades on the upper three stories and granite peers rooted between its street-level shops. Here and there I spotted some of Holmes's Irregulars deployed about the place so as not to draw the public's attention. I felt a pluck at my skirt and looked down at Russell, who pointed and murmured, "That's him."

Standing in front of a draper's shop across from The Queen Anne was a brutish man with leathern skin and auburn mane, beard, and moustache. The American cut of his clothes set him apart, but what truly stood out was how intensely he watched the structure, like a soldier posted against a siege. If he was aware of anything else around him, he didn't show it.

"Thank you, Russell. Here." I gave the boy his second penny and he scampered away as I commandeered a bench three doors from the draper's and sat as if waiting for someone. It struck me then that I should have asked Russell if Holmes or Lestrade had inquired about Capra, but that opportunity had passed, so I took to watching the earthly comings and goings of New Oxford Street. Eventually I found myself pondering about how folks once lined this road to taunt the condemned on their way from Newgate Prison to Tyburn Gallows. Fortunately, it had changed and was quite civilized now.

Suddenly my reverie was interrupted when I spotted an evidently angry man walking down Binniehill towards The Queen Anne. He was dressed like a labourer, but otherwise satisfied Lestrade's description of James Stoutenberg, and when he reached the servant's entrance, he entered.

I glanced towards the stranger.

He remained at his post, so I remained at mine.

Less than a minute later, a young woman who resembled the description of the pretty patron Pennington had seen appeared on Binniehill, but instead of wearing the fashion of an upper servant, she was smartly dressed in a plaid shawl, a white lace cap with her yellow hair dressed in long *crêpe* bands, lace ruffles at her wrist, and primrose-coloured kid gloves. She maintained a steady pace as she rounded the corner and entered the butcher shop.

Again, I glanced towards the stranger.

Again, he remained at his post.

Less than ten minutes later, the young woman stepped from the shop with a man who resembled Lestrade's description of Reiner. I didn't see where she was carrying any sort of purchase. Instead, they chatted briefly and congenially before she hugged him and headed up Chesterton Street in the same direction she had just come. The butcher gazed after her for a few moments before returning inside.

I debated whether to follow her, but the choice was taken out of my hands when the labourer exited the Binniehill servant's entrance and headed back the way he had just come. As for the stranger, he waited a moment and then followed the labourer, so after a brief pause, I followed them.

The labourer walked several blocks and then veered into Seven Dials Making his way through the warren, he eventually reached Ellis Road and went through a lonely zigzag before stepping into an alley off Hamilton Street.

The stranger hesitated and then carefully glanced into the alley before entering.

Half-a-minute later, I did the same and found the stranger lying face down on the flags near the rear of a bottle-and-rag shop.

Even before I approached the prone figure, I could see that the back of his head was broken in. I searched for the labourer, but he was nowhere about. All the alley doors were locked, and all the windows along the ground floor were barred. There were also no tracks because of the brick pavement. Lying beside the dead man was a riveting hammer, its well-worn handle splotched with dried plaster and acid stains. Muck on the claw bore testament that it was the murder weapon. It appeared to me that the labourer must have concealed himself in the doorway to the shop, waited for the stranger to pass, struck, and bolted out the far end of the alley. One blow would probably have been sufficient, but the dead man had been struck two or three times. I didn't touch the body, but instead blew my police whistle and, when I saw a constable coming, I abandoned the alley, made my way back out of the slum, and called a cab.

Chapter III – The Mystery Broadens

Daylight was turning to dusk when I arrived in Baker Street and heard Holmes call from the window, "Stay there, Watson! And tell the cabman to wait!" In less than two minutes, Holmes was out the door with two editions of *The Daily Telegraph* tucked under one arm and a note clutched in his hand. Climbing into the cab, he instructed the driver to proceed to Seven Dials and then said, "Your timing is marvelous, Doctor. A constable delivered this from friend Lestrade a few minutes ago. Listen to this: *'Stranger is dead. Definitely murdered, so I have dismissed your Irregulars. To see how things have progressed, please come to the alley behind Hamilton Street.'* I told the constable I would be along presently. Before we arrive, though, is there any chance you can provide me with some details about Shepherd's murder?"

"Is that the stranger's name?"

"Osgood Shepherd, formerly the Sheriff of Saguache County in Colorado."

"How did you find that out? And why did you instruct your boys to tell you and not Lestrade if they saw this Shepherd?" Holmes waved his forefinger to signal that his question took precedence, so I recounted the incidents of the afternoon. As I did, my companion leaned back and shut his eyes so that he looked to have fallen asleep. I concluded my report by explaining, "I thought if I remained with Shepherd's body that it would implicate Lestrade through my association with you, and yours to him, but it appears I did the inspector no service."

Holmes shrugged his shoulders. "You can take heart that, One: Lestrade was duty-bound to tell his superiors about his personal search for Capra eventually and, Two: If his message is any indication, he still remains on the force." Opening his eyes, Holmes handed me the newspapers, directed my attention to two articles, and requested that I read them. "Their relevance shall be made clear soon, but in the meantime, I must put you on your oath not to discuss them with anyone."

The first article, dated the third of December, reported on the miscarried robbery of Mr. Harry Emanuel, whose family has been one of London's foremost jewellers since 1802. A couple using the alias Mr. and Mrs. Hunton Dwyer had arranged for Emanuel to bring jewels for approbation to their house on Drury Lane and, when he arrived, they tried to overpower him, but Emanuel managed to escape.

The second article, dated the previous Monday, reported on a robbery of the same type, except this one was successful. Julius Mancune, an assistant at Theodore and Mark in Bond Street, delivered jewels worth £2,000 to Number 17b Regent Street, where he was cordially greeted by a couple using the alias Mr. and Mrs. Uwe Waltermire, who promptly chloroformed and bound Mancune before absconding with the gems.

The residences had been licensed from different West End agents, and both house agents, and Messrs Emanuel and Mancune, described Mrs. Waltermier-Dwyer in aggregate as in her early twenties, gregarious, dainty, with golden hair, emerald eyes, and almost angelic in appearance, while Mr. Waltermier-Dwyer was a quiet, handsome, and hardy specimen slightly past his first youth, tall and dark, with a trim handlebar moustache. The lady spoke with a cultured British accent while the gentleman spoke not at all. The one inconsistency in their descriptions came from Mr. Emanuel, who said Mr. Dwyer wore spectacles, but only when assessing the jewels.

When I finished reading, I noted that, "In many respects, these descriptions are similar to the man and woman I saw this afternoon."

Holmes glanced out the window. "We still have a minute before we arrive. Just enough time to share that on the tenth of January, I was retained through correspondence by Theodore and Mark to investigate the theft of their property. They're concerned with Scotland Yard's lack of progress in the Emanuel robbery, the conduct of which is in the hands of the fair-haired Gregson. I'm unfamiliar with any prig team matching the couple's description, so I spent the bulk of my day visiting other Westminster house agents with the goal of finding out if the Waltermiers or Dwyers called on any of them while renting the Drury Lane or Regent Street residences or possibly attempting to hire a home for a third attempt. None of them had – but Hello! We have arrived."

Chapter IV – *Objets D'intérêt*

A constable met our cab and escorted us through a crowd outside the alley to Lestrade, who was standing near Shepherd's body, jotting in his notebook. When he saw us, he assured Holmes that nothing had been moved.

"Thank you, Inspector." In a lower voice Holmes inquired about Lestrade's standing with his superiors.

"A tad dented but intact. My record with the force not only justified overlooking my 'over-enthusiasm', but putting me in charge of this mixed and somewhat delicate case."

"A prudent decision considering your familiarity with it." With that, Holmes examined the alley and the body, starting swiftly and intently, but gradually slowing as his expression grew more curious. After twice walking with measured steps to the far end of the alley and then inspecting the doorway to the shop a second time, he softly uttered, "This crime bewilders me."

"How so?" Lestrade asked.

"Its motivation. The logic of it isn't as it appears." Holmes crouched over the hammer. "This is a rather telling choice of weapon, don't you agree?"

"I do."

"Have you identified the dead man?"

"Not by name. He was carrying a room key from Cumming's Private Hotel, and I sent a man there to follow up. I do know he was a Colorado lawman."

"You found more on his body?"

"This was in his jacket along with a Colt Frontier Six-Shooter." Lestrade held out a hexagonal badge with *Saguache County Sheriff* engraved on the front. "And there were these." He presented Holmes with a reward handbill and a newspaper clipping. He read them and then handed to me. The handbill read:

$10,000 Reward!
Stage Robbed – Bethlehem Pass!
September 6th – Loss: $86,000!

$10,000 Reward for arrest and conviction
of all the Highwaymen, or proportionately for each,
and $10,000 for Recovery of the Treasure, or
proportionately for any part thereof.
Eleanor, Colorado
September 7, 1879
Nox Mining Co.

The clipping was from the *Eleanor Epitaph* and was dated September 7, 1879:

Four Killed and Three Wounded in Stage Robbery
Large Amount of Silver and Gold Taken
Robbers Remain At Large

The southbound coach of the Barlow and Sanderson Stage Company was attacked around twelve o'clock yesterday afternoon in Bethlehem Canyon, and two treasure boxes broken open. Silver bars valued at $70,000 were taken, along with four pouches of gold dust and nuggets valued at $16,000. The silver and gold was being transported from the Nox Mining Syndicate in Eleanor to the railhead at Canon City, to be delivered to the First National Bank of Denver.

During the robbery, four of the seven passengers were killed and two more passengers wounded along, with the driver, James W. Tallman. The Nox Mining Syndicate is

100

offering a reward of $10,000 for the apprehension of the robbers and the recovery of the treasure.

The robbery occurred in a narrow and rocky stretch of the canyon about eight miles north of the stage station outside Mahonville. This stretch is surrounded by brush and timber, and after Tallman drove across a small stream, he found the pass blocked by two large boulders.

Two men, well-mounted, rode out from the brush armed with Colt revolvers and a Spencer rifle, and Tallman recognized one as Jim Case, who broke out of the Saguache jail last month. Meanwhile one passenger, N. B. Brown, a faro dealer at Madam Wilding's Elysium in Eleanor, fired his revolver at the second robber and shot off the forefinger of the desperado's left hand. This robber was heard to shout, "It's a trap!" before firing his rifle repeatedly at the coach.

Tallman attempted to escape by driving through the brush, but Case shot the two lead horses and wounded Tallman, who retreated into the brush, followed by two passengers, Solomon Peckham, a saloonkeeper from Denver, and Perry Oxley, a former Nox mining engineer traveling to San Francisco to catch a steamship to Mexico to begin a new job. Oxley was also wounded.

Case disarmed his confederate to stop the shooting and shouted for the passengers in the coach to come out with their hands raised, but there was no reply and when Case looked inside, he proclaimed, "My God, they're all dead!" Those dead included Brown and Mr. and Mrs. Barthinius Wick, a Mormon couple who had been visiting family in Eleanor. 1st Lt. Luther Brewer, assigned to Camp Douglas, Utah, was sufficiently injured to be mistaken for dead, but it appears he will survive the assault.

I returned the papers to Lestrade. "This article appears to be incomplete. It quits abruptly without even giving a description of the holdup men."

Lestrade nodded. "I agree, Doctor, but I was thinking if this man was a sheriff, then the remainder of the article may have been extraneous to him, and he only clipped what was needed or wanted."

"That sounds sensible," I conceded.

"In any event, we'll get those descriptions, and when we do, it won't surprise me to learn that Jim Case could pass for James Stoutenberg's brother."

Holmes said, "So you've developed a hypothesis?"

"There is only one that makes sense: The sheriff came here hoping to finally lay his hands on the man who escaped his jail and claim the reward from the Nox Mining Company. That said, I have my doubts that it was Stoutenberg who killed this man."

This surprised me, but I remained silent as Holmes asked, "Do you have another suspect in mind?"

"No one specific yet, but *we* know his trade." A wry smile stretched the inspector's lips.

"'We'?"

"Mr. Holmes, if this were mine to wager, I would bet it that you and I are thinking the same thing right now." Lestrade took out a guinea and handed it to Holmes.

My friend carefully examined the coin, even biting it to see if it was solid gold. After a few moments he appraised, "Dated 1813, and in marvellous condition."

"I might even call it pristine."

Holmes grinned. "You've been holding back on me, Lestrade. I'm afraid I've set a bad example." He winked and gave back the coin. "I presume you dug this out of the poor fellow's pocket."

"It was with his other money, which, if you add all that up, doesn't come close to matching what this guinea is worth. I doubt a sheriff even earns twenty pounds in one month."

This exchange was leaving me confused and I asked them to explain.

Holmes said, "The murderer is very likely a counterfeiter. Riveting hammers are pets to such criminals, and the plaster and acid blemishes on this one's handle are exactly what you'd expect to find on a bit-faker's tool."

"What about the guinea?"

"It appears to be genuine, but my hunch is an expert will disagree. If it's a fake, its craftsmanship is exceptional, and there's no filling common in gold snides due to the precious metal's prohibitive expense."

Lestrade gave a short theatrical cough. "Not so prohibitive if Stoutenberg robbed that stagecoach. If he's working in tandem with a counterfeiter, then he could provide a plentiful supply of gold."

"So you intend to question Stoutenberg?"

"As soon as I have consent, and with what I've collected here, plus whatever we discover at the hotel, I hope to be granted that soon." Lestrade held up his notebook. "To set those wheels in motion, I'm sending a preliminary report to the Yard. I'm also requesting men watch Reiner's building to keep an eye on Stoutenberg's comings and goings. If you have any theories that you believe should be included, though, Mr. Holmes, I would be glad to do so."

Holmes bowed his head in a gesture of thanks. "You have performed your usual thorough job, Inspector, and I can think of nothing that I should want to add, but please let me know of anything else of interest you discover."

"That I will. Good night."

We bid Lestrade good evening and departed. I expected we would return to Baker Street but, after hailing a cab, Holmes told the driver to take us to Binniehill Street near Reiner's building. As the drive commenced, Holmes slipped an envelope into my hand that was dated from Sheriff Jeb Moses, Eleanor, Colorado, and addressed to Holmes. Enclosed were a letter and what appeared to be a complete copy of the article Lestrade found on Shepherd.

"What's this?" I asked.

"Information concerning Stoutenberg's time in America. I feel certain Lestrade's request for sentries will be approved within the next hour or two, and it's imperative that I examine some areas of the building before they arrive. In the meantime, Doctor, would you please read those."

I did as Holmes brusquely asked and the letter went as follows:

December 13, 1881

Dear Mr. Holmes,

General Dave Cook of the Rocky Mountain Detective Association asked me to reply to your request for information regarding James Stoutenberg. He was involved with a stagecoach robbery on September 6, 1879, that took place within my jurisdiction and I was charged with tracking down him and his confederates. I'm including a clipping about the hold-up from our town newspaper to provide you with details of the robbery, and what follows are details about what occurred subsequent to it.

Let me begin by informing you that Stoutenberg is the same man that the driver, Tallman, identified as Jim Case, a German emigrant who makes the Pueblo judge who signed his naturalization papers some ten years ago almost regret he ever heard of The Institutes of the Lawes of England. Case also did not break out of jail. We know now he was set free by the Saguache Sheriff Osgood Shepherd. Case and a confederate had been scheming for some time to rob one of

103

the coaches that irregularly transport Nox treasure to Canon City, and Case shared this scheme with Shepherd in exchange for his freedom, some assistance, and a percentage of the treasure. What Shepherd didn't know at the time is that Case had endeared himself to his wife, Zenya, who had confided to Case that over the previous four years she and Shepherd, a former bandit, had robbed three stages making payroll deliveries. Let me add here that Shepherd is age forty-eight, six-feet-two inches high, two-hundred pounds, with brown eyes and reddish-brown hair, mustache, and beard.

While Shepherd made a show of hunting for Case, he stopped at Villa Grove, some twenty miles northeast of Saguache, to enlist his old wheel-horse, John Schwartze – a good man with a gun but prone to being hot-tempered. Meanwhile, Case traveled nearly eighty miles further north to Eleanor to alert his confederate, a Nox mining engineer named Perry Oxley. It was Oxley who notified Case when the next shipment of treasure was scheduled to be transported to Canon City, and he was on the stage when it departed on September 5th, having presented his resignation two days before. It was Schwartze who lost his finger during the robbery and wounded Oxley by breaking the engineer's left arm with a bullet.

When Tallman reached Eleanor with news of the robbery, Mr. Paul Kirk, the current president of the Nox Mining Syndicate, issued the $10,000 reward, and I pursued the bandits.

Case has eluded me to this day.

By the time I realized Oxley was an accomplice, he had escaped to the interior of Brazil under the identity of Morris Neighbor. There he became the manager of a coffee and sugar fazenda, *only to succumb to malaria three months later. By all reports, Oxley was penniless when he arrived in South America, and was penniless when he died.*

Schwartze got himself arrested on October 4th by Sheriff Charles Shibell of Pima County in the Arizona territory for killing a man during a drinking binge. Shibell telegraphed me, but by the time I arrived, Schwartze had been sentenced to hang the next morning. Schwartze was also penniless and convinced he had been deserted, so he presented me with the following confession:

104

"Everything we stole we stashed in a played-out mine called The Great Whale near Lake City, where Case and Oxley once worked. Case told us to go our separate ways, lie low for ten months, then come back to split our haul. I went to Saguache to fill Shep in on what happened after the robbery, and that's when he told me he was going to double-cross Case. After Shep got back from Villa Grove, he found a billet-doux that Zenya wrote, and it said she'd run off with Case. Shep told me to light out for our old hideout in the Dragoon Mountains, wait two months, and then meet him in Tucson where we'd split the silver and gold. In the meantime, Shep would settle with Zenya and Case, and if Oxley ever came after his share, Shep said he would settle with him, too."

I sent a telegram to my deputy to retrieve the treasure from The Great Whale and arrest Shepherd, but by the time it arrived, the gold and silver were gone, Shepherd had vanished, and Zenya Shepherd was dead.

On October 6th, Zenya had tried to holdup a stagecoach carrying payroll from the First National Bank in Pueblo to a mine near Leadville. The schedules for these deliveries are staggered and kept secret to try to prevent such heists, but lawmen whose towns run along the stage road are notified when they occur. The October 6th attempt happened near Salida, some forty-five miles north of Saguache, and like the Shepherds' three earlier robberies, Zenya disguised herself as a man, flagged the stage down brandishing a Henry rifle, and demanded the payroll. Unlike their previous holdups. However, this one took place after summer in poor weather (during a snowfall), and Shepherd was riding on the coach. He had caught up with it near Saguache and told Peregrine White, the driver, that the Bethlehem Pass bandits were looking to pull another heist before they absquatulated. According to White:

"As soon as I stopped the horses, Shepherd shot the bandit, and me and the shotgun messenger ran with him to the body. Shepherd couldn't believe it was Zenya. He was beside himself, and when he recovered enough of his senses, he said he wasn't going to tarnish her memory by taking her home draped over a horse, so we buried Zenya near the road, and Shepherd marked her grave with a large green stone. After that, we continued on while he returned to Saguache."

Like the Nox treasure, though, Shepherd has not been seen again.

As for Case, I think it's pretty obvious he skedaddled with the treasure, but never had any intention of taking Zenya Shepherd with him.

Since then, I have wondered if Shepherd ever tracked Case down, and which one might have killed the other if he did. I know if the survivor had been captured in Colorado, the presiding judge would have gladly sentenced him to Hell if the statues only permitted it.

Sincerely yours,
J. Moses

I returned the envelope and its contents and Holmes said, "So now you know where I learned Shepherd's name."

"But the date on the letter? You must have written the agency soon after Stoutenberg arrived in England."

"Quite so. The government has been cognizant of 'Jim Case's' crimes for several months, and when Stoutenberg arrived last November, it took the precaution of recruiting me to investigate his deeds abroad and substantiate his guilt. You may well imagine my consternation then when Lestrade informed us that he also wrote the agency only a few weeks after me."

"Why wasn't Stoutenberg arrested as soon as he set foot in England? Moses is a lawman. Couldn't his letter be used as an affidavit for the holdup and whatever crime Stoutenberg was incarcerated for in Saguache?"

"Perhaps, but then the United States could demand Stoutenberg's extradition."

"I doubt very much a British court would agree to that if Stoutenberg is guilty of murder here."

"You are forgetting that Shepherd is an American citizen. That complicates matters. And we don't know if Stoutenberg did kill Shepherd."

"But who else had a reason to murder him? Besides, I know I saw a man who looked like Stoutenberg enter the alley, and I saw no one else after I followed Shepherd into it."

"The Americans have an idiom for situations such as this: 'You can't convict a man on what everybody knows. You have to have proof.' A British court will not be satisfied with an American sheriff's unsworn testimony. Neither will Christian Louis, since this will drag his family's

106

name through the mud. For the sake of diplomacy, hard evidence is needed here, and it must be collected without the official force's knowledge."

It was an exasperating situation, but I said, "If it must be that way. But Holmes, why did the government specifically reach out to you?"

A sly smile spread across his lips. "Lestrade isn't the only one with confidants. I have one in the Foreign Office – rather unique gentleman who recommended me for this mission." Before Holmes could say more, the hansom came to a halt and the cabbie announced that we had arrived. My companion exited the cab, paid the driver to wait, and we finished our journey on foot. When we reached The Queen Anne, Holmes led us inside through the servant's entrance.

After we cautiously ascended to the third floor, Holmes motioned me to wait on the narrow stairs while he crept down the unlit corridor. He stopped at each of four doors, listened within, and tried the doorknobs. Two of the doors were unlocked, but both rooms were vacant. The third door was locked but he unbolted it with a picklock, peeked inside, then waved me to join him. "This appears to be Herr Stoutenberg's *donjon*. He is away, so I shall have a look about. If you prefer not to participate, you may stay here. I should only be a minute."

"I would be less conspicuous waiting in there."

Holmes smiled and whispered, "Good man!"

We entered an apartment solely illuminated by lights from the street streaming through the windows. Each room was functionally furnished, and I watched Holmes efficiently search the place, starting with the bedroom, where a fine suit of clothes haphazardly tossed upon the bed seemed to catch his attention. Holmes didn't comment, but when he noticed an open copy of *Michael Kohlhas* in a chair in the sitting room, he said, "I think the heir-presumptive was watching Shepherd watching him. Come look." The chair had indeed been situated so that the reader had an excellent view of the draper's shop.

When satisfied there was nothing to find of further relevance, Holmes moved to the last apartment, which was cater-cornered from Stoutenberg's rooms. This suite was sparsely furnished with a few feminine articles, and dimly illuminated like the previous apartment with shadows hanging heavily in the corners, but there was also an air of long disuse. Once more Holmes efficiently searched, but the only things he found here that interested him were two photographs inside an otherwise-empty cupboard. He examined them and then handed them to me. "Look carefully at these." The first was a frayed photograph of a slim groom and pretty bride in their early twenties, and the second was a fine *carte de visite* of a clean-shaven man, also in his early twenties. "Do you recognize any of these people?"

I was actually somewhat nonplussed by what I saw – or imagined I saw. "I wouldn't say I recognize them."

"Your best surmise then."

I pointed to the card. "This could be Reiner when he was a young man and – " (I pointed to the wedding photograph.) " – this woman bears some similarities to the young lady I spotted today. But so does Reiner in the hair and eyes."

"Do you recognize the groom?"

"He is a stranger to me, but I would say he looks much like how Lestrade described Leunch and Hoffbeck."

"All right. Wait here." Holmes returned the photographs to the cupboard before motioning to follow him. "I want to see the cellar before we leave."

We quietly descended beneath the building and, with no windows, the cellar was as dark as a crypt, but Holmes had brought two candles and matches. He lit the wicks and handed me a candle. The earth-smelling place looked much like Lestrade had described, except that a bag of quicklime had been opened and there were two piles of broken bricks. "Someone was here after the inspector," I said.

There was an apprehensive cast to my friend's face to which I was unaccustomed, but instead of exploring the cellar as he had the rooms upstairs, he glanced at his watch.

"Surely it has been less than an hour," I noted.

"It has, but we can accomplish nothing further here without a warrant. Therefore, we should go outside and make certain those sentries Lestrade requested arrive. Stoutenberg cannot return here without my knowing."

Exiting the building, we secreted ourselves and then waited. After some minutes, passed Holmes muttered in a casual way, "It occurs to me that Lestrade is to be complimented."

"For what precisely?"

"For having Wiggins and his troops watch this building. I should have posted them myself to watch Stoutenberg."

"What about the government's proscriptions?"

"The Irregulars have proven themselves trustworthy more than once, Watson. They know any betrayal of confidence would irrevocably sunder our partnership."

I took this *cum grano salis* [1] but pointed out, "If Stoutenberg could spot Shepherd – a frontiersman – couldn't he have spotted your street-boys?"

"Shepherd avoided those he wished to avoid, but being out for vengeance, he wanted Stoutenberg to see – but, Hello! Here are the sentries!"

Holmes pointed to two policemen wearing plain clothes, taking up their own blinds to watch The Queen Anne. Being careful that they didn't see us, we left and returned to our cab, where Holmes instructed the driver to take us to Baker Street. He looked at his watch again and said – more to himself than me – "A quarter-after-seven." Holmes didn't speak again for a while, his silence pensive, but gradually he relaxed and commented, "All things considered, I suppose we have performed a good night's work."

"If hope so, but I still fail to see where the crimes of an annexed duchy's heir-presumptive are being treated as like a matter of high politics."

"Well, as you yourself have noted, I know nothing about politics, but there's more of concern here than just Stoutenberg's American indiscretions."

"Certainly. The jewel robbery."

"That, yes, but don't forget the guinea. If Stoutenberg and Jim Case are indeed the same man, then we know he's in possession of at least $16,000 in gold. Now let us suppose Stoutenberg hit upon a scheme to transfigure all that plunder into counterfeit coins to make disseminating it easier – perhaps even increase its aggregate value."

"If he did, it's a clever tactic."

"I daresay Lestrade might agree with you, but what happens to the public's trust in our economy if is discovered that there are thousands of fake guineas in circulation?"

The truth of what Holmes said made me catch my breath. "I should have thought of that."

"Granted we are discussing low politics, but that doesn't make it any less crucial to the government."

Holmes again fell quiet, but when we reached Baker Street and I was climbing out he said, "I must leave you here, Watson. I have just enough time for one last errand."

"Can I be of any assistance?"

"Not tonight, but I may need your co-operation tomorrow. Let us discuss it then." With that he told the driver to proceed to Pall Mall and the hansom took off.

Chapter V – One Must Have Data

When I woke the next morning, Holmes had already departed and didn't return until after dinner. He seemed somewhat disquieted as he told

109

me, "I've been in contact with Lestrade on-and-off throughout the day, and we have agreed to meet in one hour at New Oxford Street. Gregson will be there as well, since I felt it best to inform him that I had been retained by Theodore and Mark. I mentioned nothing about our visit to Reiner's building, however. Are you free to accompany me? Before you answer, I should warn you that things may turn unpleasant."

"If you need me, I'll be there. But where did you rush off last night?"

"To check in with my confidant." Holmes would say no more as he made a quick meal of some cold beef and a glass of beer. When he finished, he asked if I would mind if we walked. I had been indoors the entire day catching up on medical journals and welcomed an opportunity to stretch my legs, and as we strolled towards the Doctors' Quarter, Holmes began to recount his day's adventures.

"I spent my morning pouring through records at Her Majesty's Land Registry and the General Register Office. Like Lestrade, I thought it peculiar that Reiner moved away from his three so-called 'brothers' after so many years, so I decided to research his purchase of the property. The date of purchase was 13 August, 1861, which shows he had a good eye for real estate at an early age. He then commissioned the architect George Murdoch to design the building, but construction didn't commence until 19 November, 1879, and was completed on 16 July, 1881.

"I was unable to find an explanation for this delay, so eventually I moved on to the next peculiar event Lestrade mentioned and located a copy of Moritz and Iselda Hoffbeck's marriage certificate. It's dated 15 August, 1860, and lists Mrs. Hoffbeck's maiden name as Leunch. That prompted me to send a telegram to the justice of the peace where the brothers' families registered when they arrived in England, and he confirmed that Mrs. Hoffbeck was the sister of Sam Leunch. Next, I dispatched inquiries to the various shipping lines, but none of them have any record of Iselda Hoffbeck sailing to the United States in 1861. However, the passenger lists at Norddeutscher Lloyd do document her sailing to Bremerhaven, Germany, on 4 July, 1861, and then eight months later, she and a baby named Elisabeth Hoffbeck sailed for New York and arrived on 25 March, 1862."

This appalled me. "What kind of man sends away his pregnant wife and then his family?"

"Doubtless a man over-tender of heart. The Bremerhaven authorities haven't replied yet with details about Elisabeth Hoffbeck's birth certificate, but the New York Police Bureau has confirmed that Mrs. Hoffbeck and her daughter lived at an Inspirationist settlement in Ebenezer, New York for a year, then moved to the Haupt-Amana colony in Iowa, where Mrs. Hoffbeck died of Bright's Disease in 1878. In the meantime, the White Star Line has confirmed that Fräulein Hoffbeck arrived in Liverpool on the *S.S. Britannic* on the twenty-sixth of May, 1879, and Lestrade was able to confirm that she worked for a year as a tweeny for Mr. Eugene Young and family of Pimlico."

"Only a year? Did she secure another position?"

"Yes, as a wife. I found a marriage certificate for Fräulein Hoffbeck and Mr. William Abbe dated May 28th, 1880. I ask you to hold on to that man's name, as I'll refer to it again shortly."

"All right."

"The last thing I researched was the bottle-and-rag shop in Seven Dials. I wondered why the alley behind it was selected for Shepherd's murder."

"Couldn't it have been a random choice? The murderer realized he was being followed and reacted."

"That may be, but didn't the path the labourer took strike you in any way deliberate? In any case, the owner of the shop is Timo Auf der Maur, a Swiss emigrant from Basel-Statdt, who came to England in 1847 and has operated his business in Hamilton Street since 1849. Auf der Maur is a German name and Bael-Stadt borders Prussia, but I found nothing to indicate he has any allegiance to Stoutenberg or his family, or the Abbes, or anyone in Reiner's building. Nevertheless, Lestrade visited the shop this afternoon and there he confiscated a very shiny guinea dated 1813 from the cash box."

"Another counterfeit?"

"Well, Lestrade tried to bait Auf der Maur by telling him it was a snide, and the proprietor seemed genuinely upset, but he insisted that he couldn't recall where he got it. Lestrade had no way of proving Auf der Maur was lying, so he pressed the man on Shepherd's murder, but again Auf der Maur claimed ignorance, insisting he only knew about the crime because a policeman questioned him. 'What is one more murder in Seven Dials, after all?' He also said no one fitting Stoutenberg's description entered his shop last night, and that the alley door is always bolted. He couldn't even remember when he last opened it, or if he still had its key.

"Lestrade examined the door but couldn't tell when the entry was used last. It also had an old Dutch Elbow, a simple enough lock to open without a key if you know how. Lestrade also noticed that the shop contains more multifarious congeries than he would have thought possible for such cramped confines, including servant uniforms, so he inquired if anyone matching Mrs. Abbe's description had been a patron in the past few months. Auf der Maur said he had had several, that many maids sell him cast-offs, and that he wouldn't do half the business he does in fineries without them."

By now we reached Wigmore Street and Holmes stepped up his narrative.

"Let us return to William Abbe, who is one of London's premier counterfeiters. He recently finished serving nine years for bit-faking and now resides in the Seven Dials slums, a popular neighbourhood for coiners. This neither confirms nor refutes he's working his old trade again, but if he is, he must have had an enticing incentive, since he surely knows if he's arrested a second time the sentence will be fourteen years. I should mention that he's large in figure, in his middle thirties, and has black hair and moustache."

"So Abbe could have been the labourer I saw."

"As well as Mr. Waltermier-Dwyer. Abbe even wears spectacles on occasion due to the strain counterfeiting puts upon his eyes.

We reached New Oxford Street, where Lestrade and Gregson were waiting a block east from Reiner's building. Both had brought dark lanterns, and Lestrade's mastiff face was set like flint as he said, "They're gone. Both of them."

"Exactly as we feared," Holmes replied, then told me, "The inspector is referring to Mr. and Mrs. Abbe."

Gregson told me, "We just came from their home on Little Saint Andrew Street," and then informed Holmes, "Their neighbours say the Abbes haven't been seen since yesterday afternoon, so a search has been initiated. One neighbour also spotted a burly man with a brown moustache and beard leaving the house shortly before a commotion began on Monday night. That sounds like Shepherd, who Lestrade has learned arrived in England aboard a Cunard vessel on 26 December, and was registered at Cumming's Private Hotel by the name Alex Ely."

Lestrade said, "There was no sign of any violence in the house. There was also no riveting hammer amongst Abbe's counterfeiting tools, but we did find a guinea die in near excellent condition."

"What about any gold or silver?"

"None," to which Gregson added, "Nor any jewels."

"All right. Lestrade," Holmes said, "are the sentries are still watching the building?"

"Yes. So far, they've seen nothing noteworthy."

"And have you procured a warrant to search the building?"

"I have."

"Any restrictions regarding Stoutenberg?"

"We may search his apartment, but cannot question him unless we find something incriminating, and after we contact my superiors."

"Then let us to work."

112

Holmes, the inspectors, and I marched across the street, entered The Queen Anne through the Chesterton servant's door, and advanced to the third floor. Holmes and I waited while the inspectors investigated the four apartments after gaining entrance with a skeleton key. The discarded suit was still on Stoutenberg's bed, and Gregson examined it while Lestrade went through the closet. "Some clothes and two suitcases from a set are missing."

"He's rabbited with the jewels!" Gregson hissed. "I'll add him to the search!"

"A bird in the hand," Holmes cautioned as the inspector moved to leave.

"We can't let him slip through our fingers!"

"Why not send one of your sentries to notify the Yard?"

Gregson begrudgingly agreed and left to dispatch a man while Lestrade led the way into the cater-corner suite. He looked around and asked, "Are you sure she'll come here?"

"As sure as one can be, Inspector."

"All right. I'll just look about then." Lestrade began searching the rooms and when he was preoccupied, I quietly asked Holmes, "Who is coming here?"

"Mrs. Abbe."

"Why should she come here?"

"The lady needs refuge after bolting her home. Where better than a place she likely believes the police know nothing about?"

This made no sense to me, but before I could inquire further, Lestrade uncovered the photographs in the cupboard. "Look! These men could have been Hoffbeck and Reiner twenty years ago."

Holmes slid his eyes to glance my way as he asked, "Are you sure, Lestrade?"

"As sure as one can be. I wonder what they're doing here."

Gregson returned and told my friend, "I hope you're right, Mr. Holmes."

"Time will tell. Lestrade has found something of interest."

Gregson looked at the photographs before Lestrade replaced them in the cupboard. Meanwhile, Holmes closed the door to the suite, cautioned the policemen from lighting their lanterns, and said, "I suggest we wait in stealth so not to alert our quarry of our presence. Make yourself comfortable, gentlemen, as we may be here long into the night."

Chapter VI – The Springe

Our dark, silent vigil eclipsed one hour, then two, and then three, but at approximately thirty minutes past eleven o'clock, we heard a key in the door. We each retreated into a shadow and waited as the young woman I had seen the day before entered carrying a threadbare carpetbag. When she shut the door, Holmes turned up the lights and Lestrade dashed forward. He was ready to rush if she attempted to escape or draw a weapon, but she looked very hard at us and coolly asked, "Who are you? What are you doing in my rooms?" She spoke with something of a German accent.

Gregson curtly introduced us as he looked over Lestrade's shoulder as his colleague searched the carpetbag. All it contained were clothes and toilet items, so Lestrade placed it on the floor while Gregson went to instruct the sentries to fetch Hoffbeck, Leunch, and Gundling. At the same time, Lestrade went to Reiner's apartment, presented him with the warrant, and brought the butcher to the young woman's suite. When Reiner saw Mrs. Abbe, he haughtily asked, "What's going on here?"

Lestrade told him, "This young woman says this is her apartment."

"This is why you invaded my home?"

"Nobody invaded! You saw our warrant! Now are these her rooms?"

Reiner pursed his lips before reluctantly answering, "Yes."

Lestrade began to ask something more, but Holmes requested to speak with him and me in private. "Inspector Gregson, you won't mind staying with Mr. Reiner and Mrs. Abbe? And may I borrow your lantern?"

Gregson agreed but watched suspiciously through the door as Holmes directed Lestrade and me down the stairs.

Chapter VII – Buried Secrets

We nearly reached the bottom of the narrow staircase before Holmes told us he would like to examine the cellar.

"Is there something I missed?" Lestrade sounded concerned.

"Not from what you told me. Since we must wait, I wanted to see it for myself."

Holmes lit the candle in his lantern as Lestrade did the same. Dingy yellow illumination flickered over the chamber's walls and the inspector immediately spied the quicklime bag and the two brick piles. With an expression of the most profound gravity he said, "That bag wasn't open, and that stack was not there when I was here."

"It could be," said Holmes, "that Stoutenberg has buried his treasure here."

I'm convinced Lestrade knew better but he replied, "I pray you're right, but since we have a warrant, I'll take a look."

Trepidation hung in the air as the broken bricks were moved and our apprehensions were justified.

Beneath the first pile was the remains of a boy wrapped in a tattered blanket. None of us doubted this was Sandro Capra. A sloppy attempt had been made to dismember the corpse and burn it, a sight that gave even my hardened nerves a shudder. A quick examination revealed that the poor child had also been throttled.

Under the second pile was another body which Lestrade identified as William Abbe. His forehead had been punctured with a tool like the one used on Shepherd and quicklime had been sprinkled over the corpse, probably to try to cover the odour of decay. There were also four pouches of gold dust and nuggets, three full and one almost a quarter empty. None of the pouches were labelled, but where else could they have come except the Bethlehem Pass holdup?

Holmes asked me, "Can you tell when this man died?"

"The calcium oxide hinders things, but it's safe to say he has been dead at least three days."

Lestrade looked at Capra with a mournful glare and grumbled, "I did miss something."

"Nothing that would have saved the lad. I assure you he has been dead at least a month, likely longer, though I cannot imagine who would have done this to him or why." As I spoke, we heard the sentries arrive and lead the other shop owners upstairs. Holmes inhaled deeply, exhaled slowly, and said, "Inspector, it's time to present my theories to you and to the people collected upstairs. I only wish my evidence wasn't so slight. It's circumstantial, honestly."

Lestrade nodded. "Many men have been hanged on circumstantial evidence. I'll have a man come down here and send the other to bring a police surgeon."

"Excellent, although I recommend you give those instructions where Mrs. Abbe and the others cannot hear you."

"All right." Then, still looking at Capra, he recited in a solemn hush, "'*You tender Christians all, I pray unto these lines give ear, And of a cruel murder now you quickly shall hear.*'" [2] A scowl scarred the lean man's mouth. "We'll play it however you want, Mr. Holmes. I have my own theory on what happened here and am up for anything that lets me slap the darbies on the fiend."

As soon as Lestrade rejoined us, one of the newcomers angrily pleaded, "Will you now tell us why we were brought here?"

115

Holmes apprised the speaker. "You are Moritz Hoffbeck. The husband of Mrs. Abbe's mother." All four proprietors blustered until Holmes assured them, "I can present documents showing when Iselda Hoffbeck was sent to Bremerhaven, and when she and a baby named Elisabeth Hoffbeck sailed to America. I also can present the marriage certificate for Fräulein Hoffbeck and William Abbe."

"Have it your way then," Hoffbeck groused. "Mrs. Abbe is my daughter."

"Please, please, that will not do. Mr. Reiner is Mrs. Abbe's father."

Mrs. Abbe didn't react, but Reiner blanched as Hoffbeck stammered, "You couldn't – you're *wrong*!"

"Not according to the facts." Holmes retrieved the photographs from the cupboard. "I presume these belonged to Iselda Hoffbeck and she gave them to her daughter. I also presume she listed you as the father on Mrs. Abbe's birth certificate, even though it's plain to see that there's no resemblance between you two. Mr. Reiner, however, is short in height, blond, and has green eyes. The semblance is even more apparent in this card taken when he was clean-shaven and about Mrs. Abbe's present age, but just as revealing is the excellent condition of the card in contrast to this wedding photograph. Formality dictated that Mrs. Hoffbeck retain the latter, but this disparity demonstrates indifference towards one memento and consideration for the other. Furthermore, why would a man who banished his wife, and only admitted to the existence of their child when compelled to do so, ever arrange for this suite? No, it seems more likely that the suite was Mr. Reiner's idea."

"That is all conjecture."

"Based upon observation and dates, as is my suspicion that Reiner offered you and Messrs Gundling and Leunch – the other friends whose trust he betrayed – your own shops along what was becoming a prominent business avenue. Since he did nothing with his investment for over twenty years, you must have rejected his olive branch, but then Mrs. Abbe arrived and he resurrected his original proposal with an altered indulgence: You three were still welcome to your shops – and this time you accepted with the best location on the corner of Binniehill Street going to Mr. Hoffbeck – but this suite was proffered to Fräulein Hoffbeck in recompense for Reiner being unable to acknowledge his parenthood. How could he without shaming you and your mother, Mrs. Abbe? But you refused him by marrying a man recently released from prison, which forced Reiner to rescind his offer."

The woman didn't argue or acquiesce. She merely asked, "'As the mother, so her daughter?'"

116

"Or your pride was wounded. As considerate as Reiner's offer was, it still amounted to another rejection. Or perhaps the *Psalter-Spiel* and prayer-meetings hold no appeal for you."

She silently fixed Holmes with a wary stare. "Think of me what you will, but nothing you claim is criminal."

"Unlike assault and jewel robbery. A feigned Northern accent will not dissuade Messrs Harry Emanuel and Julius Mancune that it was *you* who attempted to rob the former with your husband on the third of December, and that you and Herr Stoutenberg robbed the latter this past Monday."

The men grew vociferous again until Gregson called an end to their objections. He then asked, "Are you positive, Mr. Holmes? William Abbe is a counterfeiter. Why should he turn to stealing?"

"Because there's less risk and penalty. Remember, if Abbe was arrested again for counterfeiting, his sentence would be considerably lengthier than the one he just finished."

"But why should Mrs. Abbe team with Stoutenberg to rob Mancune? Why couldn't it have been one or the other both times?"

"Let me answer your second question first. The aptitude exhibited in Monday's robbery indicates that a more practiced hand than Abbe's was at the rudder than on the first attempt. Then there are the different aliases. A name like Hunton Dwyer might be concocted by an Anglo-Saxon like Abbe, but Uwe Waltermier smacks of a Continental influence. Finally, there are the eyeglasses. Abbe might have had to wear spectacles when he appraised the jewels, but Stoutenberg didn't require them when indoors."

"That still leaves my first question. And why would Stoutenberg steal jewels if he had the gold?"

Before Holmes could explain, Reiner asked, "What gold?"

Lestrade told him, "Herr Stoutenberg robbed an American stagecoach of over eighty-thousand in gold and silver in 1879."

Reiner boggled. "You must be mistaken!"

"Four people were killed during that holdup, and the man you and your friends have seen watching this building was a sheriff who came to England to find Stoutenberg. The man's name was Osgood Shepherd, and he was murdered near here yesterday in Seven Dials."

"You cannot think that Herr Stoutenberg killed him! It's impossible! I never saw him leave yesterday or today. He prefers the indoors during daylight because he has trachoma."

"Do you know if Herr Stoutenberg left his rooms last night," Holmes asked, "or is there now?"

The butcher hesitated before saying, "All I know is I didn't see him if he left."

117

"And I know that Herr Stoutenberg isn't at home. I also know that the policemen who escorted Messrs Hoffbeck, Leunch, and Gundling here have been watching your building since last evening, and at no time did they see Herr Stoutenberg come or go."

With an expression of frustrated remorse, Gregson glared at Mrs. Abbe and rumbled, "And Heaven help you if he gets away with those jewels." Instead of making the woman anxious, she rebuffed the inspector with a sneer that left Gregson in a pitiful state of reaction. His lips compressed and the veins stood out like whip-cords in his neck as he strode out, proclaiming he was enlisting help in the search for Stoutenberg.

Lestrade instructed the sentries to join Gregson and then informed Mrs. Abbe, "The other inspector and I searched your house today and interviewed your neighbours. We know Shepherd visited you Monday, and that you and your husband argued after he left. What did Shepherd want, and why did you quarrel?"

Mrs. Abbe painted a blank expression on her face and said nothing.

"When was the last time you saw your husband?"

"Yesterday."

"Where was that?"

"Here. He may have had dealings with Herr Stoutenberg."

"You don't know?"

"Bill wouldn't tell me where he was going when he left yesterday, so I followed him, and he came here. I was worried he might be getting back in the yellow trade."

Holmes asked, "Was there anything in particular that made you think that?"

The young woman didn't respond.

"Perhaps I can answer that. While the inspectors were searching your home, they found a guinea die among your husband's counterfeiting tools." The woman still made no response, so Holmes looked at the men. "Herr Stoutenberg and William Abbe were partners. Herr Stoutenberg supplied the material, while Abbe supplied the skilled labour to turn the holdup gold into guineas. However, Stoutenberg was aware Shepherd was on his trail and that the sheriff might intentionally or unintentionally bring this scheme to wreck. He therefore prepared for this contingency by forming a secret partnership with Mrs. Abbe. She provided the material – the conception of a jewel robbery – while he provided the skill." Holmes trained his focus back on Mrs. Abbe. "But the vigilant Shepherd worked out your scheme and threw a spanner into the works by coming to your home and telling your husband what you two had done. You argued and, during the row, you killed your husband."

There was only the barest flutter of the young woman's eyebrows and the corners of her mouth. "What are you saying? Is Bill dead?"

Lestrade told her, "He's buried down in the cellar with the gold from the stagecoach robbery."

She crumpled into tears and cried, "No! That cannot be so!"

"He was hit in the forehead with a hammer. Shepherd was also killed with a hammer. And the funny thing is that Inspector Gregson and I failed to find a hammer among your husband's tools."

"You don't suggest I harmed Bill? I could never!"

"Even if he tried to harm you? His death wound suggests that he was moving towards his killer when he was struck. Maybe you were defending yourself?"

"None of that happened!"

Holmes took up the reins and in a callous tone said, "It would have been physically impossible for you to transport his corpse by yourself, so you enlisted Stoutenberg's help. I know it was him because the skillful method in which Abbe was buried smacks of the same adroitness exhibited in Monday's jewel robbery. He not only doused the body with quicklime, but impersonated Abbe to delay detection of your crime. It was a clever obfuscation, but Stoutenberg knew that Shepherd was too experienced a hunter to be fooled. Actually, he counted on this so Shepherd would follow him into Seven Dials, although I remain uncertain if Stoutenberg lured Shepherd away from this building to confront or subdue him."

Before Mrs. Abbe could reply, Reiner cautioned her, "Say nothing! My lawyer is at your disposal, and you should listen to his counsel before speaking further with these men."

Holmes smiled at Reiner as he told the young woman, "You would be wise to obey your father." Then, flushing up, he stared at Hoffbeck. "And if you have a lawyer, sir, you would be just as prudent to contact him."

Sweat broke out on Hoffbeck's pale brow. "Why should I?"

"Because there's a second body in the cellar – the crossing sweeper missing since the end of November."

"What is that to me?" Hoffbeck barked, even as he quivered with emotion.

"You put him there."

"His name was Sandra Capra, in case that you didn't know" Lestrade said as his eyes narrowed.

Everyone else in the room was considerably astonished and made no sound as Holmes continued, "The body has been crudely segmented and charred, which tells me almost everything I need to know about the crime. Dismemberment goes hand in hand with impulsive murders, most of which are spurred by fury, and I can only imagine the painful memories seeing Mrs. Abbe stirred up. It's also no secret that you objected her showing the sweeper kindness whenever she visited your shops, or that you confronted her about it on the day the boy vanished. Perhaps she only patronized Capra to bedevil you, the man who banished her mother and, by extension, herself, but in any case, he was swept up in your melodrama.

"We know Mr. Reiner ousted Capra from the cellar after finding the boy sleeping there sometime before St. Andrew's Day, and I suspect you caught him sleeping there again that night, which prodded you beyond your endurance and you strangled the child in a rage. Now even readers of *The Newgate Calendar* know the impulse to hew a victim into parts is so the killer can bury them helter-skelter or dump them in a river or lake. Only someone with access to a large oven would consider trying to incinerate the sections, but when that failed, you fell back on burying them as quickly as you could." Holmes looked at Lestrade and quietly asked, "Was that your theory as well, Inspector?"

"Near enough, Mr. Holmes." Lestrade glared at Hoffbeck with a dreadful anger. "Near enough."

Chapter VIII – A Retrospection

"There is a family resemblance to crimes," Sherlock Holmes said the following morning as he sat in his armchair in front of the fire. "Mankind is a habitual species, and even if you snap a person from his particular life-routine, be it by accident or necessity, he will eventually again begin following the practiced ruts in his old daily road."

Holmes and I had remained with Lestrade the night before until the police surgeon arrived and Mrs. Abbe and Hoffbeck were given into custody. After that, the inspector went to Scotland Yard, I went to Baker Street, and Holmes went off on another confidential errand. By the time my friend returned to our rooms, it was after breakfast and he looked worn and dissatisfied.

"'*Actus non facit reum nisi mens sit rea,*'" [3] he quoted as he donned his dressing-gown. "As confident as I am regarding the attendant circumstances of Capra and Abbe's murders, I fear that one would be hard-pressed to prove *mens rea* and *actus reus* for either." Holmes picked his black clay pipe off the mantelpiece, lit it, and sat.

"What of Stoutenberg?" I asked. "Any news?"

"Not yet, but I should be surprised if he's still in the country." Leaning back with a weary, heavy-lidded expression, Holmes watched the blue smoke-rings from his pipe chase each other up to the ceiling. "He sacrificed the gold he brought to England in exchange for his liberty and two-thousand pounds in jewels. 'A bird in the hand.' Fortunately, he also has $70,000 in gold and silver bars cached in Colorado."

"Wouldn't he have brought that, too?"

"Doubtful. Consider the inconvenience and risk of hauling several heavy bars, especially if they're stamped with '*Nox Mining*'. And if he did bring them, then why didn't Stoutenberg counterfeit any silver coins? They're far easier to manufacture and disseminate than bogus guineas."

"Then isn't it just as possible that he hid the treasure somewhere other than Colorado? I also keep wondering if Shepherd might not have located the gold and silver. How else could he pay for his booking to England and subsequent room and board?"

"Have you forgotten the payrolls he and his wife expropriated? No, no, I see no reason to suppose the bars are anywhere except where Stoutenberg hid them in Colorado."

"Then you should tell Sheriff Moses."

"I have. With the blessings of the Foreign Office, I mailed him a letter this morning pinpointing the location."

"Which is where?"

"Zenya Shepherd's grave."

I was shocked by the audacity of the notion. "Why in Heaven's name there?"

"Why would Shepherd or anyone else ever look there?"

"Then how did you deduce the spot?"

Holmes straightened up. "Well, in fairness, I should first admit to dabbling in a little obfuscating of my own in Mrs. Abbe's keep last night. Only instead of disguising myself, I disguised some facts while omitting others altogether. It became a taxing threading act, balancing what to reveal and not reveal so as not to expose the Foreign Office. Citing just one example, you and I know Mrs. Abbe visited her father after following her husband to The Queen Anne, but imagine the uncomfortable questions Lestrade would have asked if I challenged her on this."

"I see what you mean."

"The Foreign Office is grateful for my efforts, but my discreetness has at least temporarily thwarted the arrest of Shepherd's murderer."

"Was it Stoutenberg then?"

"No, Mrs. Abbe."

"No!" I said, considerably astonished at his words. "How that can be?"

"It's a rather tangled skein, Watson. You remember that Stoutenberg endeared himself to Zenya Shepherd and enticed the aid of her husband? Being a creature of habit, Stoutenberg repeated this tactic to get what he wanted from the Abbes. When Shepherd found out he told Abbe, who,

121

upon learning about his wife's *affaire de cœur*, tried to attack her. This also explains why the snide found its way into the sheriff's pocket."

"How does her infidelity do that?"

"Zenya Shepherd thought she was going to 'run off' with Jim Case. Herr Stoutenberg probably told Mrs. Abbe the same thing. Imagine her disheartenment upon discovering she had been deceived by a cad. I fear Stoutenberg overlooked Hafiz's cautionary against snatching a delusion from a woman, particularly one who felt she had already been betrayed by two men who should have been dear to her."

"Stoutenberg also underestimated the fury of a cuckold. Shepherd not only murdered his wife, but spent over two years tracking Stoutenberg to London."

"But what about Mrs. Abbe? She has killed her husband in self-defence and cannot go to the police, since they will insist upon knowing why her husband attacked her. Abbe's body must be disposed of, but she will need assistance. Her father certainly will not help her, so who else can she ask except the man who is planning to abandon her? But Mrs. Abbe has a plan. When she asks for Stoutenberg's aid, she mentions nothing about Shepherd's wife so he will agree to help. He also sees a way to use Abbe's death to turn the tables on Shepherd, ignorant that Mrs. Abbe's ultimate scheme is to do the same to him.

"For the next two days, Stoutenberg will visit Seven Dials wearing William Abbe's clothes. Going without his cinder glasses when outside is a necessary but effective hardship, since the people who see him will think that he's a stranger or Abbe. Then, on the afternoon of Shepherd's murder, Stoutenberg, again disguised as Abbe, walks to Reiner's building, so that it appears Abbe is calling on the heir-presumptive. Meanwhile, Mrs. Abbe has trailed Stoutenberg to the servant's entrance before visiting Reiner's shop. All she needs to do is give her father some story that involves leaving her husband or his abandoning her and that she wants to accept the suite. Reiner agrees and she leaves, but instead of returning home, she proceeds to the alley behind Hamilton.

"Stoutenberg had no reason not to share his plan, or the path he will coax Shepherd down, with Mrs. Abbe, so she knows to conceal herself in the doorway behind the bottle-and-rag shop and wait. She may have even suggested this be a part of Stoutenberg's path, or perhaps Stoutenberg chose it by coincidence. Either way, I suspect Mrs. Abbe, like many other slaveys, was familiar with this shop. In any case, she waited for Shepherd to pass and smote him three times, possibly directing some of her indignation for Stoutenberg upon the poor sheriff. Then she dropped the hammer beside the body and tucked the counterfeit guinea in a pocket.

Stoutenberg, not being in the alley, was unaware of what happened until later."

"But I was close behind. She couldn't have escaped out the far end of the alley without me seeing her."

"No, she couldn't, but she had ample time to escape through the bottle-and-rag shop, which explains how Auf der Maur got the snide Lestrade found. She may have paid him to leave the door open, or she paid him as she fled through the shop, since I think it not inconceivable that she picked the lock. It would have only been prudent for Abbe or Stoutenberg to coach her on some rudimentary criminal skills if they were going to commit a robbery together, but in any case, the door was locked from the inside before you could try it.

"By the time Auf der Maur realized a murder had been committed behind his shop, his benefactress would have been gone, but being unaware the guinea she paid him was counterfeit, he gave the police a story. After doing all this, I can believe that he was genuinely upset when told the guinea was bogus. Auf der Maur had been tricked, but could say nothing without confessing to aiding a felony."

"But you still haven't explained why Mrs. Abbe put the snide in Shepherd's pocket. If he knew about Stoutenberg and Abbe's counterfeiting plans, he could have collected one of their bogus guineas as evidence."

"From where? Abbe wouldn't have left them lying around his house in the open. What's more, the excellent condition of the die and the small amount of gold missing from the one opened Nox bag indicates Abbe had only manufactured a handful of snides. Such a small number suggests these were his initial efforts meant for trial and not circulation. That is what confounded me in the alley. The hammer and coin were obviously staged to make it appear as if someone was attempting to incriminate a counterfeiter. At the time I was stymied, but Mrs. Abbe knew when the police found her husband's body with the gold, it would become clear that Abbe was already dead when Shepherd was murdered and Stoutenberg would immediately be suspected. You said it yourself: 'Who else had a reason to murder Shepherd?'"

In an instant it was as if a veil had been pulled away and everything became clear. "My word! She really was turning the tables on him!"

"As neat a trick as any I have encountered. Even the reward flier and newspaper clipping played in her favour, although I doubt that she knew that Shepherd was carrying them. It would have made sense for him to bring them with him Monday to show Abbe as evidence for his accusations, but I fail to see how she could have anticipated he had yet to remove them from his pocket. As for Stoutenberg, I doubt it took him long once he discovered Shepherd had been murdered to realize that he had been castled. Recovering the gold from the cellar was now too risky – especially if he spotted Lestrade's sentries – and once Shepherd's counterfeit guinea was tracked back to him, the protections he was enjoying courtesy of our government would be rescinded without forewarning. His only move was to resign his king and make flight with haste."

"But Mrs. Abbe is taking a tremendous risk. If any of this is ever discovered, she will face the rope."

"I refer you once more to Hafiz. Such risk no longer matters to her."

Something about Holmes's observation saddened me more than anything else about the case, or it did until I recalled the dead boy. "So Capra's death had nothing to do with any of this?"

"No, nor its revelation – though if it did, I don't see how that would make the tragedy any more palatable."

I agreed, but then asked again how Holmes figured out where the gold and silver were hidden.

My companion took a long draw on his pipe and exhaled the smoke. "As I said, Stoutenberg repeated the tactic he used on the Shepherds with the Abbes. I therefore doubt concealing the Nox gold in Abbe's grave for safekeeping is the first time he employed this move. If I'm correct, then Stoutenberg shall return to Colorado to retrieve it and, if Moses is vigilant, than a judge there will at last have the opportunity to sentence the heir-presumptive to the Purgatory he deserves. That is the fervent wish of the Foreign Office, anyway, since it will make for less of a diplomatic headache then if he was to be arrested here."

NOTES

1. "With a grain of salt"
2. "The Murdered Boy", C. Croshaw, 1820
3. "The act is not culpable unless the mind is guilty."

The Adventure of the Disappearing Daughter
by Dan Rowley and Don Baxter

"Here is an interesting article, Holmes."

"I take it the subject is the weather. I believe there is speculation that, in addition to the thousands of deaths, the eruption of that volcano in the Dutch East Indies in August has had some effect on the atmosphere, resulting in colder temperatures."

Although I had shared quarters with Sherlock Holmes for close to three years now, his uncanny ability to deduce what I was thinking could still at times be unnerving. "Yes, the article is partly about the tragedy, but it also is about the effect of Krakatoa on the weather. How did you know that?"

"You have been remarking for several days about how windy and cold it has become. Each time you mention it seems unusual for October. Just now, while reading, you shivered and glanced out the window. That is congruent with your recent remarks. And, after looking out the window, you then glanced at the atlas on the bookshelf, I assume with the thought of looking at a map of where the volcano is located."

At that moment, there was a knock on the door of our sitting room, and our good landlady, Mrs. Hudson, came in. "There is a young gentleman here to see you, Mr. Holmes. He seems rather distraught."

"Thank you, Mrs. Hudson. Please send him up."

Shortly, a young man in his early twenties entered the room. He was tall with curly brown hair and chiseled features. His striking blue eyes quickly took in the room with its odd assortment of artifacts, including a Persian slipper filled with tobacco and a knife impaling correspondence to the mantel over the fireplace.

Holmes stood. "Hello, I am Sherlock Holmes, and this is my colleague, Doctor John Watson. How may we help you?"

"I am Sebastian Fisher. A friend of mine told me you had solved a matter for his uncle involving a forged will and an imposter posing as a relative. I came to you because my fiancé seems to have gone missing."

"That normally is a matter better handled by the police."

"Well, that's just the thing. Her father refuses to talk about it and has forbidden any of us from going to the police. He insists he sent her for a rest in the south of France. But I don't believe him."

125

"That's a different matter and may have some items of interest. Please have a seat and tell us your story. Leave nothing out, even if you believe it is trivial. I'll be the judge of what's important. Based on that, I'll decide whether to take your case. Start with a bit about yourself, and your fiancé and her family."

"As I said, I am Sebastian Fisher. Currently I am a registrar at the London Hospital. I hope to follow in the footsteps of Erasmus Wilson and become a specialist in dermatology." I looked at him closely. So he was studying to specialize at one of the finest teaching hospitals in the country. This was turning out to be the year of the doctors. Earlier, in April, the fiendish Doctor Roylott had attempted to kill his stepdaughter with a poisonous viper at Stoke Moran in Surrey. I turned my attention back to our visitor's narrative.

"I am engaged to Caroline Bainbridge. She is the daughter of Sir William Bainbridge. Doctor, you probably know of him."

"You're referring no doubt to the member of the Royal College of Physicians, I take it."

"Yes. He lectures there and also at the London Hospital. As you may know, he also is an avid researcher after having studied in Paris and Berlin. He has met such luminaries as Pasteur and Koch. Sir William and my father were roommates in public school, and our families frequently get together socially. That is how I met Caroline."

Holmes interjected. "Do you study under him?"

"No, I am not in that rarified group. I tend to rotate through wards wherever there are cases of skin disorders that require specialized treatment, even if they are the symptom of another illness."

"So he doesn't practice in your area."

"No. I am never sure exactly what he's working on, as he tends to keep that to himself."

"And when did you last see your fiancée?"

"The Bainbridges came to our house for a Sunday luncheon yesterday. I have nothing scheduled this morning, so I decided to go over to see Caroline at about half-past-ten. When I was admitted, Mrs. Bainbridge came out of the drawing room to see me. She was quite distraught and could barely speak due to her tears. Sir William just then came down the stairs prepared to leave for the day. When he saw me, before I could speak, he barked at me that he had sent Caroline to the south of France for a rest. When I tried to express my confusion, he became quite angry and refused to tell me why. He forbade me or Mrs. Bainbridge from discussing Caroline further with each other – or anyone else for that matter, as he wouldn't have anyone questioning his judgment about sending her away. He also said the wedding would be cancelled if either

126

of us disobeyed him. He then left the house without saying goodbye to me or his wife."

"Is that typical behavior for him?"

"Yes, he can be quite peremptory. Everyone at the hospital lives in fear of his wrath. I believe Mrs. Bainbridge and the servants are in the same state of mind. About the only two people who aren't so afraid are Caroline, whom he dotes upon, and her younger brother, Robert. I must admit at times he frightens me as well. That is why I shied from questioning his statement about sending her to France."

"Why would you question it?"

"All the past week she was perfectly normal, including on Sunday. If anything, she was even more vivacious than normal due to her excitement over our coming nuptials. On Sunday, that was all she, her mother, and my own mother could talk about. In fact, Sir William banished them to the drawing room because, in his words, he needed respite from their 'infernal chattering'."

"So why did you decide to come to me?"

"After he left, Mrs. Bainbridge began sobbing. When I had calmed her down sufficiently, she said we couldn't disobey Sir William, but on the other hand she said she was beside herself with worry about her daughter's unexplained departure. I told her I would try to think of something we could do without Sir William finding out. I went for a long walk to mull over my options. Suddenly I hit upon coming to see you. My friend told me you were very discreet. I decided you likely could find a way to investigate this in a way that Sir William couldn't discover."

"Do you suspect that's he's done something questionable?"

"I honestly don't know. Prior to this, I would have thought not, but his behavior is odd. He is imperious, as I said, but Caroline's sudden disappearance is driving me so mad that I'm coming to believe anything is possible."

"Who are the members of the household, and where is it?"

"Sir William, his wife Martha, and Caroline live together. Robert attends the London School of Economics and Political Science and has a small apartment near there. He wants to become a journalist like his hero, Walter Bagehot. Sir William of course doesn't approve. There also is a butler, several maids, and a cook who live there. The gardener and Sir William's driver do not. The house is on Upper Grosvenor Street between Grosvenor Square and Hyde Park."

"Well, I believe there is enough of interest here for me to take your case. Watson, are you free to join me?"

"I am."

127

"Capital. Fisher, can you accompany us, and if we go to the house now, will Sir William be there?"

"I can go along and introduce you. I obtained permission to be absent from the hospital this afternoon. Sir William will be away from home, either doing rounds in the hospital or working in his laboratory there."

"Excellent. If Mrs. Bainbridge is sworn to secrecy, I assume she will abide by it?"

"Yes, I believe so."

"Fine. We'll meet you at the house in an hour. I want to look up a few things before we go. Please write down the address." After Fisher left, Holmes turned to his bookcase to retrieve a volume that I realized was a set of short biographies of leading Londoners. He studied it intently and then turned to me. "Watson, this provides just the bare bones of Bainbridge's background. What do you know of him and the London Hospital?"

"A person like Sir William would practice there for two reasons: First, the research facilities are among the best in Europe, not to mention the high quality of the assistants. They also practice the latest methods of sterilization.

"In the second place, due to the hospital's proximity to Whitechapel and the poor unfortunates who live there, the physicians are able to see a most astonishing array of ailments, no two of which are the exactly the same. For example, the last time I visited a friend there and went on rounds with him, I saw ten patients with issues ranging from alcohol abuse, pneumonia, pleurisy, food poisoning, gangrene, consumption, and rickets. Because some of these diseases are infectious, the ward is set up so that patients can be isolated if need be. In fact, Sir William is the head of that area of the hospital."

"An excellent summary. Now let us don our overcoats so that the chill and wind you're concerned with don't affect us."

Putting on our coats, we went down to the street and hailed a cab. On the way to the Bainbridge home, Holmes was sunk in silence, his eyes staring at something far off. I knew not to interrupt his reverie. We drove to the south side of Grosvenor Square and then shortly arrived at the Bainbridge residence. Fisher was waiting for us on the street. Holmes greeted him. "You are quite sure Sir William will not be here?"

"Yes, he will be at the hospital and then likely he'll go from there to the Royal College."

"Why would he go there?" I asked.

"He's quite interested in immunization theory, as I mentioned earlier. He is fluent in several languages, and the range of his reading is quite prodigious. Tonight, he's reporting on the recent discovery by Klebs of the bacteria that causes diphtheria. Perhaps this can lead to a cure for that scourge. Sir William met Klebs when they both were in Berlin, but Klebs now works in Switzerland."

Holmes nodded, and we went up the stoop of a three-story Georgian stone house that looked like others on the street, complete with bay windows and gas lights on either side of the door.

Fisher knocked, and a solemn butler greeted us. Fisher asked if we could see Mrs. Bainbridge. The butler indicated we should wait in the drawing room. Soon a short, slightly plump woman in her late forties joined us. She had prematurely greying hair and exhibited an air of nervousness. Her eyes were red, and she was twisting a handkerchief in her hands. She was accompanied by a young man not yet in his twenties, who I assumed was Robert. He was short with delicate hands and features.

After brief introductions, Fisher explained. "I know Sir William enjoined us to stop talking about Caroline with one another or anyone else, but we're worried, and I promised myself I would find a subtle way to get to the bottom of this. Mr. Holmes is a consulting detective with much discretion and wisdom. I implore you to allow him to assist us."

Mrs. Bainbridge's face writhed with indecision. Wringing her hands, she turned to look at Robert. They stared at each other for some time. Finally he nodded and she turned back to us. "Oh, Sebastian, I am wracked with anxiety, as you know. I'm worried what will happen if this comes out! If you can assure us that William will never be the wiser, I would so much welcome any help in discovering what has become of dear Caroline."

Holmes, who at times could be abrupt, knew how to be soothing when the occasion warranted it. "Madame, I assure you that your husband need not know. May I ask some questions?"

At her meek assent, he continued. "When is the last time you saw your daughter?"

"This morning, she went for her customary walk before breakfast. I had much to do, so I merely had a cup of coffee and went upstairs to prepare to go out. William went to his study to work on a lecture he's to give at the Royal College tonight. I came down to work on some correspondence before going out to do some shopping and have lunch with a friend."

"Did you see your daughter when you came down?"

"No. I assumed she was in her room. But then William came in and told me he had sent her to the south of France for a nerve cure – but there was no need for such as that! When I tried to ask about it, he cut me off and said I wasn't to speak of it again! I was terrified, and came back in here and started to cry. Caroline is quite loving and thoughtful, and I couldn't believe she had left without leaving me a note, even a short one."

"What happened next?"

"Not long after, Sebastian came to call on her, and – "

She broke off, unable to continue. I felt much sympathy for this poor woman, who began silently crying again. Her son immediately went to her side to commiserate with her. Once she had recovered sufficiently, Holmes then questioned her in more detail about Fisher's visit, and her account was the same as his. Holmes was deep in thought for a minute. The family and our client watched him in some perplexity, but I motioned they shouldn't break his concentration, as I was accustomed to this habit of his. He abruptly continued. "Did your daughter seem tired or unhappy to you?"

Both mother and son stated she had not. They confirmed Fisher's statement that she was happy and full of energy.

"What is her daily routine?"

"Before breakfast, weather permitting, she takes a walk. She loves to go over to Hyde Park and stroll along the walkways, even on a blustery day such as this. She finds it invigorating and says that walking stimulates her ability to think and plan. Upon her return, she has a light breakfast and usually goes to her room to read or write letters. After the noon meal, many days she and I go shopping for her trousseau and to look at potential wedding presents for me to suggest to friends. Depending on Sebastian's schedule, they often go out in the evenings to the theater or a concert."

"Are any of her clothes or other personal items missing?"

"I looked after William left, and it didn't seem that anything was gone in her room. I was reluctant to ask the maids due to William's injunction that I not speak of this. I did look in the cloak closet, and her normal outdoor clothing isn't there."

"Why do you think he demanded that you not speak of this?"

She sighed. "I assumed that William is concerned about scandal if rumors start that she has succumbed to nervous prostration. William's mother was prone to that, and he is very sensitive about it. But I'm not so sure that is the correct explanation. I have had no word from her, which is very unusual. As I said, she could have left me a note, or sent a telegram before crossing the Channel. Her disappearance is so unusual that I fear something has happened to her. But if that is the case, then I'm at a loss to explain why William is acting like this."

Her son spoke up. "Nor have I heard from her. She sends me little notes several times a week. She likes to tease me about Father's disapproval of my choice of career. It is a running joke with us."

"I see. Let us go back to the outdoor clothing. What does it look like?"

130

"It is a hunter green, short-waisted jacket with a matching purse. On a day like today, she wears a hat which is also green with a red feather. Sebastian bought it for her."

She seemed about to start crying again, but Holmes forestalled that. "May we look at Sir William's study?" She hesitated, but at the urging of Fisher and young Bainbridge, she finally acquiesced.

Fisher led us across the hall to a large room at the front of the house. It was paneled in dark oak and had bookshelves from floor to ceiling on all four walls. The front and side walls had large windows that let in plenty of light, and there was a large fireplace on the inside wall. On the side of the room opposite the door in front of the fireplace was a large desk strewn with books, journals, and writing materials. Over in the back corner was a large safe. Holmes immediately began a minute inspection of the items on the desk, confirmed the safe was locked, and then he walked along the shelves to examine their contents. He also stopped for a while and peered at the fireplace. Although I wasn't sure of what he hoped to learn, I knew from experience that his keen eye and sharp mind were taking it all in and making deductions that Fisher and I couldn't fathom.

Suddenly came the sound of the front door opening and closing, and then we heard Mrs. Bainbridge leave the drawing room, saying rather loudly, "William! I thought you were going straight to your lecture."

"I forgot some notes in my study." Then a rather stout man appeared in the doorway. He was wearing an overcoat and carrying a medical bag. He immediately turned a bright red, and his gruff voice demanded, "I say, Fisher: What is the meaning of this intrusion?"

Before he could respond, I stepped forward with an outreached hand. "Sir William, it is a distinct honor to meet you. I am Doctor Watson, and this is my colleague." Luckily this was years before my friend had become familiar to my loyal readers, so Sir William didn't realize who we were. Holmes bowed slightly. "It is indeed an honor to meet you. Fisher here was telling us about your magnificent collection, and we begged him to let us see it. Any fault is ours, but I must say your erudition is overwhelming. Your mastery of foreign tongues and breadth of subject matter speak for themselves."

"This is intolerable, Fisher! You should know better! The three of you must leave immediately. Fisher, don't return unless I summon you."

Holmes again inclined his head. "We shall take our leave so that we don't disrupt you any further."

Retrieving our overcoats, the three of us went out to the sidewalk. Fisher started to say something, but Holmes spoke first, saying, "Don't concern yourself. He didn't ascertain why we were there, and I'm sure Mrs. Bainbridge and her son will not disabuse that this was merely poor judgement on your part. Once we've cleared this up, I will make things right with him. I believe a walk is in order. Follow me." He turned west on the street and walked toward Hyde Park. Near the entrance, he spied a line of cabs waiting for fares = exiting the Park. Holmes asked us to stay where we were, and he proceeded to approach the line of cabs. We couldn't hear him, but he evidently was working his way down the line, questioning the drivers. One of them pointed to another driver, Holmes gave him a coin, and then walked to the indicated driver, who appeared to be eager to talk, having seen the remuneration presented to his fellow. He and Holmes engaged in an intense conversation for several minutes. Holmes then climbed into the cab and was out of sight for quite some time. When he emerged, he had a half-smile on his face. Holmes nodded to the driver and pressed a coin into his waiting palm.

Returning to us, Holmes disregarded Fisher's attempt to question him. Instead, he said, "Watson and I will now return to Baker Street. We will contact you when we wish to see you again." Fisher was speechless as Holmes walked back toward the line of cabs and entered the first in line. I reassured Fisher. "I don't know exactly how, but be assured Sherlock Holmes will lead us in the correct direction. I'm confident he will determine what has happened, and he'll inform us in good time. You should return to your duties at the hospital. Try and put your mind to rest. You're in the best hands possible." I hurried to join my friend in the cab. He was already deep in thought. In a few minutes, he turned to me.

"Well, Watson, what do you make of all this?"

"I must admit that this is perplexing. My first thought was that Sir William might be up to something, but Fisher says he was devoted to his daughter. On the other hand, if his story is true, why was her departure so sudden, taking none of the items a young lady would want, even if on a rest cure? And I don't see her abandoning Fisher either to escape him or run away with another."

"Yes. I fear there is another, more sinister explanation."

"You believe, then, that there has been foul play. But assuming she is still alive, then why is Sir William demanding that the family not even discuss the matter and concocting a false story? If, for example, she has been kidnapped, I could possibly understand an unwillingness to go to the police. But surely he could allay their fears by explaining his plan to extricate her, and then forbid any conversation. That would be far more natural, even given his imperious ego."

"Once again, Watson, you have put your finger on the most puzzling aspect of this matter. In my experience, and based on my researches, the relatives of a missing loved one simply don't act in this manner. I have the germ of an idea, but will need to make some further inquiries. We must hurry though. Ah, here we are."

We descended from the cab and went up to our rooms. Holmes immediately went to his table of scientific apparatus and began working with his slides and microscope. He also consulted a notebook on a nearby shelf. When done, he turned to me. "I must go out. I may be back rather later this evening, but please wait up for me." I knew it was useless to try and persuade him to allow me to accompany him. He went into his bedroom, and after a short while I heard him exit by the other door from his room onto the landing and go down the stairs.

It was mid-afternoon, as windy and bleak as ever. I was relieved that Mrs. Hudson already had the fire going in the sitting room, and she thoughtfully brought me some fresh-brewed tea and her delicious shortbread biscuits. After that, although it was difficult to keep my mind off where Holmes might be, I tried to catch up on some of my medical journals, and then took a short break for the cold evening meal Mrs. Hudson had prepared. I refrained from alcoholic stimulants, anticipating I might need my wits about me for whatever Holmes had in mind when he returned.

I was relaxing with the newspaper when I heard him reenter his bedroom by the landing door. After a short time, he came into the room. "Capital, Watson. Are you prepared for some excitement?" As he was speaking, he went over to his chemical table and placed a bottle in his pocket.

"Our first priority," he explained, "is to retrieve Miss Caroline Bainbridge and take her home."

"You know where she is!"

"Of course. I believe you should take your service revolver. I've already given Mrs. Hudson a telegram to send to Fisher. Let us make haste."

I went to the desk and retrieved my revolver. We donned overcoats and went out to obtain a growler. Holmes gave instructions to the driver that I didn't hear, but I soon realized we were journeying to the warehouse district by the docks. As we alighted, a light rain had begun to fall. Holmes told the driver to wait, and added an extra emolument to the fare being the inducement. He then explained our destination and gave me some instructions about what we were going to do.

We proceeded along two streets. There was no curb, and the pavement glistened with the rain. That area of London had no streetlights, so we were barely visible in the deepening gloom. Holmes suddenly stopped and pointed to a large building ahead on our left, which we were approaching from the rear. He motioned for me to stay behind and remain

133

silent. He took the bottle out of his pocket and poured some of the contents into his handkerchief. I detected the odour of ether. Holmes then began weaving as if he were intoxicated and went around the corner, turning left toward the front of the building. He was gone for only a moment, then returned carrying a rather large man over his shoulder. I helped him with his burden, which we deposited in an alley behind the building.

He whispered, "As I expected, he was guarding the door. I stopped to ask him directions, slurring my words and grasping his arm with my left hand for balance. He never noticed my right hand with the handkerchief until it covered his nose and mouth. That has rendered him immobile for a good thirty minutes, which should be ample time to accomplish our task. Just follow me and make no sound."

We went back the way from which Holmes had come. Rounding the corner of the building, I saw double doors further along the wall. We moved that way and, upon reaching them, Holmes gripped the handle of the left-hand door and carefully opened it a few inches.

We took a moment to survey the inside of the warehouse. It was filled with stacks of crates and barrels from the front to the back. On the left side of the building was a stairway leading to a doorway several stories above the ground floor. A man was seated at the foot of the stairs, so engrossed in a penny dreadful that he didn't notice us looking in. To the right side were large bay doors, obviously where goods were loaded and unloaded into the cavernous interior. We couldn't directly walk to the foot of the stairway from our current position without the man noticing us, so Holmes sensibly indicated we would enter and move to the right, and then gradually proceeded to the left, so as to better deal with the situation by the stairway.

We slipped inside, easing the door closed. I followed Holmes as we silently moved toward the loading doors. Holmes stopped by these and made some adjustment to the opening mechanism, which I assumed was intended to render them inoperable. Then we turned down a row between the stacks of crates to our left and slowly made our way further so that we were approaching the staircase from behind it.

As we neared the end of a row, Holmes held up his hand – a signal to halt. We looked toward the foot of the staircase, where the man was still sitting. I glanced to the right and noticed a doorway in the back wall on the ground floor, leading to what obviously was another room. Light spilled out, and I could hear a raucous noise coming from inside – apparently an argument over some type of card game.

Holmes motioned for me to remain where I was. I marveled at how he approached the guard at the foot of the staircase without making a sound. When he was behind the guard, his hand shot out and once again the handkerchief covered the guard's nose and mouth. He promptly slumped over, and Holmes arranged him so that he appeared to be sleeping.

Holmes waved me over and we stealthily went up the stairs. He tested each step to ensure there was no creaking or other noise, and I carefully followed in his footsteps. At the top of the staircase, Holmes eased open the door and, ascertaining we could safely enter, went in.

In the center of the room, bound and gagged to a chair, was a young woman. In other circumstances, I would have taken the opportunity to stop and admire her beauty. This clearly was Caroline Bainbridge, a younger version of her mother. Her brown reddish-tinged hair complemented by wonderful green eyes and an upturned nose. Her expression showed that she realized we were there to rescue her. We quickly released her from her bonds, and it was clear she comprehended the need for remaining quiet.

Holmes went to the doorway and surveyed the warehouse below. He beckoned us to follow, and we went back down the stairs with the greatest care. Just as we reached the bottom, however, a brute emerged from the back door under the stairway. Startled for a moment, he gave a curse and shouted for his comrades.

"Quick, Watson – Take the young lady out the door from which we entered. Head toward the cab!"

As I hurried my charge toward the front, I looked back and saw Holmes seize an iron bar laying on the floor. He used it as a wedge to topple down several stacks of crates, effectively blocking the direct pathway to the front. Imprecations and loud shouting broke out behind the debris, and sounds of scurrying and fumbling in the relative darkness indicated that the card players were stumbling over one another in a frantic effort to get at their prey.

Miss Bainbridge and I rapidly reached the door by which we had entered, with Holmes close behind. I pushed it open, hurrying the girl outside. When Holmes joined us, he slammed it shut and rammed the iron bar through the handles of the two doors, blocking further exit. Even in our haste, I was pleased that I had correctly divined the purpose of his actions at the loading doors. As we rounded the corner, pounding and more cursing could be heard behind us from inside the warehouse.

We hurried along and jumped into the cab. Holmes directed the driver to make all haste to Upper Grosvenor Street, promising an additional reward for speed. The driver enthusiastically took off like a shot.

Miss Caroline Bainbridge finally caught her breath. "I do not know who you are, but thank Heavens you rescued me."

"I am Sherlock Holmes, and this is Doctor Watson. Your fiancé approached us to determine the circumstances of your disappearance."

135

"But how ever did you find me?"

"I believe the best course is for us to have a word with your father, and leave it to his discretion what to tell you."

She looked puzzled but, given Holmes's serious demeanor, asked no more questions.

Soon we arrived at the Bainbridge residence, where Fisher was already standing out front, where I learned that he had been told to wait for us. He and the young lady embraced and murmured to one another. Holmes went to the door, knocked, and was soon in a whispered conversation with the butler. The door closed, and a few minutes later was re-opened. Upon entering, there was a tearful reunion of mother and daughter, with Fisher standing by beaming and grasping our hands in gratitude. On hearing the joyful noise, Sir William emerged from his study. Dumbstruck upon seeing his daughter, he rushed to hug her. He then looked at Holmes and me, and cried, "What are you two doing here? Fisher, you have once again disobeyed my direct orders!"

"I am Sherlock Holmes, a consulting detective." Bainbridge began to sputter, but Holmes cut him off. "I never said I was a doctor. You as a scientist should know better than to make assumptions rather than ascertaining facts. I believe it would be preferable if you, Doctor Watson, and I retired to your study for a discussion."

We retired to the study and closed the door. Sir William still seemed shaken. "Mr. Holmes, I will overlook your antics earlier today for the moment because you have returned Caroline to us. How did you guess what happened?"

"I do not guess, but rather examined the facts and drew the correct conclusions. When Fisher came to me, I knew there were four possible explanations for your daughter's disappearance. By observing your behavior and hearing about your nature, although you are secretive and imperious – Please, do not interrupt me. I was going to say that your behavior didn't fit any pattern with which I am familiar. Let us review the possibilities.

"One was that your daughter ran away, either with another man or to escape something here, and you concocted the story to avoid scandal. That seemed highly unlikely, as everyone unanimously agreed she was very happy and excited about her upcoming nuptials.

"A second possibility would be that you were hiding her, perhaps from some danger or for a reason of your own. You might have kept silent due to lack of trust in anyone else's discretion. But had that been the case, you are smart enough to know she communicated with Fisher, her mother, and her brother almost every day they were apart. Knowing that, to avoid

136

suspicion, you would have devised a method for her to communicate with them. You did not, so I eliminated that.

"Third: She was dead, either by accident or deliberately. I didn't believe you capable of such an act, or that you would hide it because of your devotion to her. Also, I did not perceive a motive by anyone else. And why would you cover up her death by a story that eventually would be known to be false? The very fact you used the tale that she was going to France indicated you expected her return after some period of time.

"That leaves kidnapping – but why would you not attempt to assuage your family's anxiety, swear them to secrecy, pay the ransom, and procure her return? We will return to your curious behavior in a moment.

"I confirmed the kidnapping explanation in several ways. I noticed that you had burned a paper in the fireplace here in your study. A corner was uncharred, and it was common, cheap stock, not matching any of the paper here in the study and unlikely to be used in a home such as this. We had learned that your daughter was in the habit of walking to Hyde Park. I traced her likely route and found a line of cabs outside the Park. Questioning the drivers, I found one who had arrived before anyone else this morning. While at his station, a man rushed up and said his friend had fainted in the Park due to the cold and blustery weather. He said he had left two other companions with her and had the driver take him to a bench along the edge of the Park. The man and his two companions helped the unconscious girl into the cab. They gave the driver an address about one mile to the northeast. I confirmed with the driver that the young girl's clothing matched the attire your wife described. The driver dropped the four people off at the address and returned to his station at the Park.

"This afternoon I went to the address and questioned the landlady. She only has two lodgers, both single men who were at work today – one a solicitor's clerk and the other an accountant. She told me that no one had come to the door this morning, which is kept locked when she is alone. I surmised that the culprits had a carriage hidden nearby, and used this ruse to throw off any pursuit.

"They had not, however, counted on my involvement. When I got into the cab, I noticed that there were traces of mud on the floor. There also appeared to be pieces of small green matter embedded in the mud. I took a sample, and, upon return to my lodgings, I used my microscope and confirmed my original impression that the mud was from the warehouse district near the docks. I have been making an extensive study of the various soils in London, and hope to someday write a monograph on it. I was also able to verify that the green matter was coriander seed, which I confirmed against some notes I'm keeping regarding the use of plant species in detection work.

137

"It was then a simple matter to go to Lloyd's this afternoon and confirm there has only been one shipment of coriander recently to London, and to learn the warehouse where it is being stored. I went there in the early evening to ascertain there was a guard outside, which was not the case in any of the other nearby warehouses. So I then knew where your daughter was being held.

"But one thing didn't quite fit the pattern of all the facts: Let us return to your behavior. You are a wealthy man, with excellent credit. Most likely the kidnappers made their ransom demand promptly. Am I correct?"

"Yes, they notified me this morning by affixing a letter to the window near my desk in this study. You're correct that I burned it in the fireplace."

"Yes, that makes sense. So I asked myself: Why did you not immediately get the money? Why did you fabricate a story rather than confide in your wife and enjoin her silence? Once I thought through the matter, it was obvious the demand was for something other than money, and that you needed time to collect the non-monetary ransom. Had you told your wife about the kidnapping, she would have realized you could have obtained money quickly. To avoid questions, you made up the France story, confident in your ability to maintain the fiction, keep her acquiescent, and collect the ransom.

"What could such a ransom be? When I inspected your study, I noticed that the overwhelming bulk of the materials were related to bacteriology, in multiple languages. Indeed, on your desk were papers for your lecture on the bacterium that causes diphtheria, recently discovered by an old acquaintance of yours.

"That must have been a further spur to your efforts to become the English Pasteur or Koch. Doctor Watson mentioned something to me this morning which provided the clue, although I didn't realize it until later. He said the hospital treats cases of food poisoning, sometimes botulism – a Latin derivative for 'sausage', given that many cases of the disease originate from consuming contaminated cured meats. So, Sir William, have you isolated the toxin in the bacteria that causes botulism?"

The eminent doctor hung his head. "Yes, I have. I am trying to study the botulism toxin so as to create a cure. The fiends that took Caroline demanded I give them the toxin in exchange for her. I didn't want to arouse the suspicions of my assistant, so I was planning on only bringing small amounts home each day until I could accumulate enough. The kidnappers gave me one week to collect the toxin. You are correct that I was trying to forestall questions about the nature of the ransom. I must admit I had a rare moment of panic and came up with the story that she'd suddenly gone to France. I was distressed about my darling girl and wasn't thinking clearly for once."

"Yes, that's understandable. Fisher told us you are normally secretive about your work, which in itself isn't suspicious. However, while disconcerted over the disappearance of your daughter, you fell back on your normal posture of secrecy and domination, without fully thinking through the possible consequences. I'm sure that, under calmer circumstances, you might have taken a different approach. I also assume it would have been difficult for the kidnappers to have stolen the toxin from your laboratory, and that is why they resorted to their kidnapping scheme."

"Yes, it would have been next to impossible. My laboratory is immediately adjacent to a ward that is manned by nurses and doctors twenty-four hours a day, so no one can enter without risk of being seen. Also, there are security guards patrolling from closing until morning, which increases the danger of detection. And I have many vials in the laboratory, so that a thief might mistakenly purloin the wrong one."

"As I had thought. To continue: When you arrived home while we were here, you claimed you had forgotten some notes. I thought that odd, given a man of your intellectual caliber. Instead, you were dropping off the toxin, which you had in your medical bag. I trust you keep it locked in that safe over there."

"Yes, it is very virulent. My tests on laboratory animals show it is extremely powerful and dangerous to handle. I believe, based on my research, that a small amount contaminating the water supply would kill hundreds of people."

"I surmised that to be the case. Sir William, I implore you, as a knight of the realm and a gentleman, to cease your researches and destroy all samples of the toxin. This episode demonstrates its danger should it fall into the wrong hands. Apply your intellect to something less perilous, but still beneficial to humanity."

"Mr. Holmes, I will take that under consideration. I will be forever grateful to you and Doctor Watson for saving Caroline. May I pay your fee?"

"My only fee is that you comply with my request. I leave it to you how to deal with your family, but would recommend the truth."

I spoke up. "And frankly, Sir William, I would have more faith in the judgment and discretion of your wife and future son-in-law. In my experience, trying to control people in this manner rarely leads to a pleasant result. You are fortunate that they saw through your story, even if they didn't divine the rationale. As a consequence, they came to Sherlock Holmes, and your daughter is safe once again. While your desperation was perhaps understandable, it's usually preferable to rely on someone whose expertise is germane – unlike your own."

With that, Holmes stood up and we left the study. We were greeted in the hallway by the tearful mother and daughter and a protective but obviously happy Fisher. After our goodbyes were concluded, we went outside, procured a cab, and returned to Baker Street and our respective beds.

The next morning, ensconced in front of a hearty fire with cups of coffee, I looked up from my newspaper. "Holmes, I am reading an article that mentions the arrest of a gang of hoodlums at a warehouse but says nothing about a kidnapping. Is that our matter?"

"It is. After we returned here, I sent a telegram to the Yard, informing them where they could find a group of criminals, and I was confident there would be ample evidence of some sort of illegal activity there. I wanted to avoid any questions about the toxin, and that the men we caught wouldn't want to add to their list of offenses by admitting to kidnapping. As always, the Yard can be relied upon to be unimaginative and focus only on what is in front of them."

I nodded. "Your travels to the false address, Lloyd's, and the warehouse couldn't have taken as long as you were gone. What else did you do?"

His visage was grim as he explained. "Watson, my methods are clearly influencing you. I disguised myself and affected a Serbian accent, and visited haunts that I know harbor criminal elements."

"Why Serbian?"

"Despite the Congress in Berlin four years ago, the Balkans really haven't settled down. Last year's alliance of Germany, Austria-Hungary, and Italy have further disturbed the region, because the latter two have Balkan aspirations, Russia and Turkey aren't happy with the results of the Congress, and an independent Bulgaria unsettles Greece and Serbia. I deduced that such a volatile situation would make a prime market for a poisonous toxin. When I visited the criminal lairs, I feigned interest in purchasing such a toxin. My reward was to uncover that there is an active auction being held among the powers in that region."

"Good Heavens! Do you mean to tell me that someone really would use such a toxin as a weapon? Based on what Sir William told us, such an act would be barbaric."

"Unfortunately, not everyone has your sense that warfare should be governed by humane rules. I fear we may be entering an era when not only the actual combatants will be at risk. Sadly, civilians may be targets as well."

"Are the Bainbridges safe?"

"I also send a note to someone that I know within the Government to provide discreet protection for the family."

"But how could those thugs at the warehouse manage such a dastardly scheme?"

"They are but puppets, Watson. I believe they didn't send the ransom demand, but had only been promised money. Indeed, they likely weren't even aware of the purpose behind the enterprise. For some time, I have sensed the machinations of a criminal genius at work here in this country. He is probably behind this. I don't as yet know his identity, but I shall not rest until I uncover him and thwart his evil deeds . . . ."

The Abridge Disappearance
by David Marcum

"Mr. Holmes, they won't take me seriously! They're doing nothing!"

Lucas Harlaw was perched on the edge of his chair, and I expected that he would rise to his feet, the third time since his arrival, as his agitation and frustration grew.

Those feelings had not been caused by my friend, Sherlock Holmes, who had listened to the man's urgent appeal with sympathy and compassion. Rather, it was due to the fact that Harlaw's son had now been missing for three days, and he couldn't interest anyone into instituting a sincere search.

Holmes glanced my way, and I rose to pour a brandy for the unnerved father. He had refused the offer when first arriving, but this time I insisted. When I approached him with the glass outstretched in his direction, his head turned sharply, as if he were surprised. He had been gazing into the distance, and I could only imagine what tragedy he had been picturing.

While he took a drink, and then another, I recalled his unexpected entrance, not five minutes earlier.

I had come down late that morning, having been away the previous day to attend the funeral of a friend who, like me, had survived Maiwand three years before. For him, the thousand or so days since then had not been kind. Although I hadn't felt so at the time, with my initial wounds and subsequent wasting bout of enteric fever, I had been far luckier than Bob Chapleton – deprived of both legs, blinded in both eyes from wounds inflicted by the savage Ghazis who likely thought they were mutilating his corpse, and left without the use of his right arm. He'd been salvaged and treated and sent home to a horrified family who did the best that they could, but Bob had slowly retreated into himself until a rainy morning in late October when he mercifully slipped free of his bodily bonds.

It had been a grim gathering, not one of those funerals where people celebrate a long, well-lived, and happy life while carrying on a reunion with old friends and family. I was glad to be back in Baker Street. The rains that had followed me down from Weedon Bec in Northamptonshire were just as heavy that morning, and the hearty breakfast provided by Mrs. Hudson didn't lighten my mood. Holmes, sensing that I was feeling withdrawn when I made my appearance, simply said good morning and remained at his chemical bench, where he was examining some curious properties of a fungus he'd obtained on an ancient gravestone during our recent trip to Dunfermline.

The ring of the doorbell occurred just as I had poured my second cup of coffee and moved to my chair, carrying several of the morning's newspapers. Holmes glanced my way, and we both recognized that the insistent ringing that the caller was in some distress.

In a moment, quick steps on the stairs ended with a knock on the landing door. Holmes bade the caller to enter, and a tall man stepped in, looking from one to the other of us, wide-eyed and grim, before deciding that Holmes was who he needed to see.

"Mr. Holmes," he said, stepping across the short distance to where we sat. "My name is Lucas Harlaw. My son, Michael, has disappeared, and I can't convince anyone to help me!"

As I rose to direct Harlaw to the basket chair, Mrs. Hudson followed him in, asking if she should bring more coffee. Our visitor looked around at her, seemingly surprised that she was there. "None for me, thank you," he stammered.

"Something stronger, perhaps?" I asked. "A brandy? I know it's early, but – "

"No, nothing, Doctor . . . Watson, isn't it?"

I nodded.

"I've heard of you – both of you, actually. From Horace Wenlock, when you found his lost periapt last spring."

"A trivial affair," said Holmes, seating himself in his usual chair, his voice steady in order to bring some calm to the agitated man.

"Not so trivial to Horace," said Harlaw. "Finding it before the date named in the will meant nothing less than saving his inheritance and making sure there was enough money for his sister's surgery. He assured me that otherwise, she would be dead by now, so indirectly, you saved her life." He had settled into the basket chair, but immediately slid forward again so that he was perched upon the edge. "It was Horace who suggested that I seek your help, Mr. Holmes. My son – no one will listen."

"Calm yourself, sir, and tell us what has happened, and we'll see what we might be able to do for you. Please – explain fully, and leave nothing out."

Harlaw nodded and moved back into the chair, although he didn't relax, sitting perfectly upright as if stretched by a tight wire.

"I'm an attorney with chambers in Paddington," he began. "My work is often involved with legal documents related to construction. My wife and I have one child, a son. Michael is nineteen and attends The College of Mary, about five miles out of Abridge, in Essex. It's a Wesleyan school, built around fifty years ago by a minister named Anderson." As he related the story and set the scene, Harlaw calmed himself, but it was only temporary. "Abridge was on the coaching route from London to Chipping Ongar, and Anderson initially ministered there. He started a preparatory school for the locals, and within a few years it had grown into the college. Since then, they've been rather successful. A number of wealthy alumni have provided for upkeep and modernizations.

"The campus is around two-hundred acres, but the major portion of that is forest, cut up with trails and paths. There are a dozen or so buildings for around two-hundred students, including four dormitories, a library, a science building, a gymnasium, a chapel, a dining hall, a music building with an auditorium, the steam plant, the college president's house, and the main building, Anderson Hall, which holds classrooms and administrative offices.

"Michael heard about the school through our church, and when it was time for him to go to college, this was really his only choice. He's studying music – not a career that I would recommend for a comfortable life, but it seems to call him. From all that I've heard, Michael is having a wonderful time – he has maintained a scholarship and a good group of friends. He's now in his sophomore year, and all has seemed well – until this weekend.

"Michael is a very conscientious young fellow. My wife and I have often joked that even as a child, he seemed to be like a thirty-year-old man, not taking foolish chances, making responsible choices, keeping us informed about anything we need to know. That's why this past weekend has been so upsetting – although we can't get anyone to take us serious!"

Suddenly Harlaw's emotions surged and he unexpectedly stood, his hands clenched. Clearly whatever had happened, even something that was being negated by others, was strongly upsetting the man.

"Please sit," said Holmes, "and continue your tale. The scene is set. Now – what has happened?"

Harlaw nodded and recomposed himself.

"Michael was due to come home on Friday evening. It isn't a far trip by train, and he usually stays with us in Paddington every weekend, unless he lets us know otherwise. His return this Friday was confirmed, because Saturday, the third, was his mother's birthday. It's only a journey of an hour or so, and he returns to school on Sunday afternoons. There's rarely anything happening at the school on the weekends – even the meals are rather scanty – so letting the students who are able to return home do so isn't discouraged by the administration.

"When Michael didn't arrive on time, we thought he'd missed his train – it has happened a few times – but then he didn't show up that night at all, and we received no word from him. By Saturday morning we were getting frantic. The school doesn't have a telephone, so I sent several

144

wires, but apparently, since the offices were closed for the weekend, they went unanswered. I went down to Abridge on Saturday evening, but no one at the nearby Loughton Station, which is the closest terminus, remembered Michael boarding the train there on Friday, and at the college, none of his friends who were there remembered him leaving.

"I rousted several of the administrators, right up to the college president himself, but no one can offer any clue as to where he might be. I went to the police, but they had no inclination to take my fears seriously. They said that he hadn't been missing for very long, and that every spirited young man of nineteen sometimes slips the leash. Then he implied that my wife and I were being overprotective!"

He then stood up again, his body coiled with energy, as if he'd explained enough, and that we should join him in dashing to catch the next train. Holmes raised a calming hand, and after a moment and a couple of deep breaths, Harlaw again resettled into the chair.

"The attitude of the police wasn't entirely unreasonable," said Holmes. "At the time you spoke to them, your son had only been missing for twenty-four hours."

"Yes, but now it's Monday morning, and there's still no word. I returned to London Saturday night and waited for a while with my wife – she was becoming quite unwell – thinking that Michael might still arrive, but we heard nothing. Subsequent wires to the school went unanswered. Sunday we both went there, asking further questions of Michael's friends and at again the station. We spoke once more to the police as well, but their attitude is clearly that we are overreacting, and they have been much less than helpful. Finally, we recalled what you accomplished for Horace Wenlock, and I came back here to seek your help. My wife has remained at the school, trying to find some lead as to where Michael might be." His eyes shut and his fists clenched, and he cried, "Mr. Holmes, they won't take us seriously! They're doing nothing!"

I rose before he did and convinced him to have some brandy. Meanwhile, Holmes tapped his finger several times on the arm of his chair before nodding.

"I hope that this truly is nothing more than a young man thoughtlessly going about his own business, but it does sound out of character from the way that you've described your son. We can accomplish nothing here in London. Watson, will you accompany us to the school?"

I had no demands on my time that Monday morning, although venturing out into the rain was not very appealing. In minutes, bundled against the raw weather of early November, we joined Harlaw in the growler which he'd told to wait upon his arrival. On the drive across London, he clearly wanted to speculate regarding where his son might be,

145

and what sort of trouble he might be in, but Holmes raised a hand to silence him.

"I need facts, Mr. Harlow – anything else at this point is a distraction." And he settled into a rumination, leaving the father and me in awkward silence – for in fact, there was nothing else that we could really discuss. I asked him once about his practice, but the answer was short, as if he too had no response for anything that was unrelated to his missing son. It was the same within the train from Liverpool Street Station, ach of us weighted under our own thoughts, and only when we arrived at our destination did the sense of urgency reawaken.

We disembarked at the Loughton Station, a mile or so west of Abridge. Harlaw explained that the school was located north of Abridge, not far from the road leading to the upper reaches of Epping Forest. As he went to secure a cab, Holmes sought out the station master, who reacted a bit warily.

"I saw you with Mr. Harlaw," he said. "He's been in and out of here a half-dozen times in the last few days, along with his wife, asking questions, as if we'll suddenly remember something. I can tell you now, gentlemen, I don't remember his son. None of us do. Friday nights are especially crowded, and anyway, we wouldn't know the lad if we saw him."

"How did Mr. Harlaw describe his son?" Holmes asked.

The station master glanced at the returning father. "Tall and slim, like him. Said they look quite alike, and that the lad wears a long wool coat in cold weather – something like you're wearing, sir. An Inverness."

Harlaw joined us just then and confirmed his son's description. "I fear that if he wasn't noticed here at the station, it's because he never came here."

"It's very possible, sir," said the station master, "but then again, there's simply no way to tell. As I mentioned before, Friday evenings, with everyone getting away to London, are simply too busy to remember one lad among so many – and if you recall, Friday was dark and rainy and cold, like today. People were huddled up and moving quickly, and it wasn't too easy to see anything."

Holmes thanked the man, and when he'd stepped away, said, "I believe that he's right. If we don't find anything at the school, we can always return and do more excavating here – although that would be a tedious business that would require a lot of luck with very little chance of success."

Harlaw led us outside to the cab, and soon we were rattling east, out of Loughton and toward Abridge. Conversation was limited due to the rain thundering on the cab roof, and I very much pitied the poor driver and

146

horse, and anyone else who had to be out working in the cold autumn torrent.

We passed through Abridge, and looking out through water-streaked windows, I could barely see the medieval buildings of the small town center. Then we turned north and, not long after, we were entering the grounds of the modest College of Mary which, Harlaw informed us, had recently celebrated its semi-centennial. All of the buildings seemed to be clustered together, and to the south, I could just make out the modest forest, in a low spot separated from the main campus by a series of athletic fields. As we traveled along the circular drive that ran by all of the buildings, I observed a number of people walking in the direction of the woods, most carrying umbrellas, and nearly all of them in waterproof coats. As we stopped at Anderson Hall, a large red-brick building surmounted by a high white tower, a man left the building to walk toward us. Harlaw reacted with surprise.

"Mr. Holmes, Doctor," explained Harlaw, "this is John Clark, the president of the college." He looked urgently toward the older man. "Dr. Clark, is there any news?"

Clark, who had an umbrella of his own, stepped forward to greet us. He was a heavy-set man in his fifties, dressed well against the weather. In the limited light, I could tell that he would normally be a good-natured fellow, but his expression that morning was grim.

Ignoring the anxious father's questions, Clark instead replied, "Mr. Harlaw. Gentlemen. Let us get inside."

He led us into the sudden warmth of the Hall, where we divested ourselves of our wet coats and hung them on a rack just inside the door. As we did so, a small woman came out of a side room to our right and ran up to Harlow, who turned and gave her a quick hug. She was followed by a small man in his thirties wearing *pince-nez*,

"Lydia!" cried Harlaw. "Any luck? What is happening?"

She shook her head, and Clark said, "Your wife has been very persuasive, Mr. Harlaw. She convinced us to conduct a more thorough search. You may have seen the people – students and staff – who are now heading toward the College Woods. We have suspended classes for the morning, and they intend to make a thorough sweep – not only the easy locations like the trails, the amphitheatre, the lodge, and the spring house, but also the areas below the ridge – along the stream, for instance, and the rough areas where someone might be if he . . . if he left the trails."

"Additionally," the man with *pince-nez* informed us, "they intend to search around the two sinkholes and the small cave."

Mrs. Harlaw gave a small gasp, and Clark frowned. "This is the Assistant Dean," he explained, "Martin Carlyle."

147

Mrs. Harlaw stepped away from her husband and grasped the smaller man's arm. "Sinkholes?" she said, a rawness suddenly in her tone. "A *cave*?" There was a rising note of panic in her voice.

Carlyle was suddenly speechless, as if he were a deer that had been surprised in the forest and was now unsure which way to bolt. "My wife," Harlaw explained, taking her gently by the shoulders and pulling her back to his side, "has a . . . *fear* of sinkholes. When she was a girl, one of the men who worked on her father's farm was fatally swallowed by one when it unexpectedly opened beneath him."

"They aren't unknown in this area," Clark explained. He lowered his voice and spoke to Mr. Harlaw, as if his wife wasn't also right there. "When speaking with your son's roommate, we found that he has had an interest in the sinkholes and the cave . . . and has been known to explore around them." He then glanced at Mrs. Harlaw, adding, "It would only be prudent to look there, considering the lad's fascination for such places."

Holmes said, "Would it be possible to speak to the roommate? Is he involved in the search?"

Clark shook his head. "No, he's resting in their room. He has a small touch of something and is running a slight fever, so it was thought best to excuse him. But wouldn't you like to visit the woods while the search is taking place?"

"Not yet," Holmes replied plainly. "I'm sure that your search will be most effective on its own, without our help. It looked as if you had more than a hundred people venturing forth. Our time will be better spent trying to determine where young Mr. Harlaw might have gone."

Mrs. Harlaw stepped forward. "You're Mr. Holmes," she said.

Holmes nodded, and Harlaw apologized. "I'm sorry, my dear – I should have introduced Mr. Holmes and Dr. Watson as soon as we arrived."

She ignored him, her gaze fixed firmly on my friend. "I've heard that you're a miracle worker, Mr. Holmes. I have a feeling – I sense that we'll need a miracle. Please – find my son."

Holmes started to reply, and knowing him so well by then, I knew that it would be something about probability and false hope, but then he caught himself and said simply, "We can but try, Mrs. Harlaw." Then he turned and reached for his coat, as did I.

Harlaw also started to put his on as well, but Holmes shook his head. "Stay here with your wife, Mr. Harlaw, and help coordinate the search. Watson and I can be more effective on our own."

Harlaw started to object, but Holmes added, cutting him off abruptly, "President Clark can show us the way, and introduce us when necessary."

He looked at Mrs. Harlaw, as if to seek her assistance in letting us work without her husband's presence. She nodded.

We stepped back into the driving rain, each taking a step apart from one another and pausing to raise our umbrellas. Then Clark led us to the right, around the building, and down a series of walkways through the center of the campus, pointing out features as we went, his voice raised to overcome the steady drumming of the rain. "There is the Center for Campus Ministry – our little chapel. It's one of the oldest buildings on campus. And over there is Pearson Hall, with the dining room and upper-class apartments." He gestured behind us and to the left. "Across from Anderson are the science and music buildings. We'll pass the library, and then we'll reach the dormitory where young Harlaw lives."

On the stretch between the chapel and the library, I noticed several round metal lids in the ground near the walkways, each about two feet across, rather like the covers to London's sewer manholes. There were strong jets of steam escaping from each one, and depending on the wind as we reached them, we had to detour to avoid walking right through the hot mist. When I asked the president about them, he proudly explained that they were access points to the buried steam pipes. "Our third president, Dr. Gambill, had the foresight to install steam heating in all of the buildings. The steam plant is at the far north side of the grounds, behind the music building, and the pipes run underground in every direction."

Holmes nodded, but he was looking left and right as he studied the layout of the various buildings. Then we reached a rather modern-looking structure of mud-yellow bricks, four stories, square and plain, without much character. "This dormitory, Copeland, along with the others of similar appearance, was constructed in the sixties," the president explained. Then, rather apologetically, he added, "One of the alumni provided the funds. His son was the architect – and his vision was, um, rather . . . uninspired. I'm afraid that explains the somewhat . . . ugly presentation, as compared to our other older buildings."

Clark held the door for us, allowing us to enter first. The lobby was plain, with a couple of unmarked wooden doors and an unmanned desk opposite the entry. Clark led us through a doorway on the right which opened into a narrow and dark stairwell. We went up one flight and then through a heavy door into a short hallway, where we were met by five closed doors. I knew in relation to where we had entered that we were in the corner located at the front right of the building. Clark passed two doors and then, at the center door, he knocked, and a weak voice inside bade us to enter.

It was the corner room, not very large. It had two windows, one looking back toward the central part of the college from whence we had just walked, and the other, on the adjacent wall, facing the nearby gymnasium. The walls were painted a dull bluish-gray, only adding to the cold damp feeling of that November day. There was a built-in closet with two doors, and there were also two desks, two small bookshelves, and two narrow beds. Nearer the front wall was the empty one, and the shelves and desk nearby were stacked with books and papers, displaying the same untidiness that I lived with every day in Baker Street. Clearly, Michael Harlaw had Holmes's same enthusiasm, and also his haphazard filing system.

In addition to textbooks, there were sliding mounds of sheet music, leaning towers of popular novels, and also several larger and heavier textbooks poking out from underneath scattered papers. Grouped together on the top shelf of the bookcase was a handsome set of the works of Edgar Allan Poe, as well as a number of novels by Collins and Dickens.

The bed across the room held a young man of nineteen or twenty, covered to the chin with a couple of blankets. There was much less clutter on his side, but one also had the impression that he had much less in his life that interested him. There was a cricket bat propped against one wall, and several textbooks stacked upon the desk. There was nothing on the bookshelf except a pair of dirty spiked shoes on the bottom shelf, almost certainly used when playing sports. There was also a half-filled bottle of clear liquid and a glass on the table beside the bed.

Clark introduced us. "Mr. Sykes, this is Sherlock Holmes and Dr. Watson. Mr. Holmes is a detective who was asked to come up from London by Mr. and Mrs. Harlaw to look for Michael." Then he looked at us. "This is Simon Sykes. He has been Michael's roommate since they began attending the college. They are in the same year." Returning his attention to Sykes, he said, "Please answer their questions." Then he stepped back, as if to cede the floor to Holmes.

"How are you feeling?" asked Holmes. I could see why he was concerned, as the young fellow didn't look too well at all. He was quite pale, with damp-looking skin and hair lying in lanky locks across his brow. There were red spots on both cheeks the size of shillings. Without waiting for an answer, I stepped forward for a closer look, touching his forehead with the back of my hand while explaining that I was a doctor. His fever was present, but fortunately very slight. However, I knew that it might rise as the day progressed, as was typical.

"How long have you felt this way?"

"Almost a week," he explained. "Since waking up on Tuesday morning. I've been to the infirmary twice – it's located over the library – and they've given me a tonic." He indicated the bottle. I picked it up, seeing that it was a willow bark concoction containing salicylic acid.

"Any signs of cough or wheezing when you breathe?" I asked, and he shook his head. "Does your fever climb at night?"

"It does, but not too badly. I just take another spoonful of the tonic prescribed by the nurse and then sleep straight through."

I nodded. "You should be fine if you don't stress yourself, or become too active before the fever breaks. Make sure to drink plenty of liquids." I looked around. "You have nothing here but the tonic. You need water."

"It's available down hallway," said the boy.

"You should keep some here. Drink it regularly – as much as you can take."

"I'll make sure of it, Doctor," said Clark. I nodded, stepped back, and deferred to Holmes.

"I'm sure you've been asked this before," he said, "but did Michael Harlaw give any indication that his plans last Friday had changed? That he wouldn't be returning to London at the normal time?"

"Not at all – but I actually didn't see him on Friday. He didn't sleep here on Thursday night, and our paths never crossed on either of those days." He pointed toward the shared closet. "His bag and clothes are still there – he didn't pack to take anything with him."

"Not since Thursday night?" asked Clark, frowning. "That's even longer than we believed. Why didn't you tell us?"

Sykes' eyes widened, and the accusatory tone in the president's voice made him suddenly look much younger than his years. "No one asked me specifically, sir. I just thought that since Michael was missing, everyone knew *when* he went missing."

Clark nodded and waved a hand, as if there was no blame attached.

"And you have no idea where he would have gone?" continued Holmes. "Does he have any friends with whom he might have impulsively traveled?"

Sykes shook his head to both questions, and he had no additional information to offer as Holmes continued to question him about Harlaw's activities and habits. Then he queried about the College Woods, and specifically Michael's interest in sinkholes and the cave.

"He's interested in everything around here, sir – the woods, the buildings, the secret history." He looked at Clark as if debating whether to continue, and then added, "He has keys to all the different buildings – so that he can explore after hours. He sometimes goes up onto the rooftops as well."

"What?" Clark asked, as if suddenly picturing Michael Harlaw in a new light – more than just a good student who had so far avoided attention. "*How* does he have keys?"

151

"From the older students," explained Sykes, now possibly regretting his frankness, perhaps due to his illness lowering his guard. "The graduates. There are lots of sets of keys to be found. The older students have them, and when they graduate, they pass them on to certain of the younger students. It's something of a tradition. But they never cause any problems!" Sykes hastened to add. "To do anything destructive would ruin it for everyone else. It's just that sometimes the students who have keys like to visit the secret parts of the campus – the tower in Anderson Hall, for instance, or into the basement of the dining hall, where one of the school's ghosts can be found."

"Ghosts?" I asked, wanting to know more before Holmes, for whom such aspects were irrelevant, could change the subject.

Sykes nodded, while Clark puffed in disgust. "There are several of them," the lad added. I wondered if he would have been so forthcoming had he not been ill. His eyes brightened as his enthusiasm for the topic made him sit a little straighter. "There's the ghost in the music building, who puts out lights in the auditorium. He died from too much opium. And the dining hall ghost – a student who hanged himself a generation ago." He became more energetic as each one was recalled. "Then there's the old lady who died in the lodge down in the woods – they say she doesn't know she's dead, and if the lights are put out in the house, she relights them as soon as you leave the building. And there's the 'Good Evening' ghost – a dead policeman who will speak on certain nights from a tree above the fountain where he was once killed.

"There's the one-legged ghost," the lad continued, further warming to the subject, "who was ambushed on the spot where Anderson Hall was built, back during the Civil War. After he lost his leg, the doctors tried to save him, but he died there, and has been looking for his leg ever since. At night, you can hear him hopping around in Anderson, moaning and calling for his missing limb. And there is the couple that wasn't allowed to marry – a local girl and a boy from the college. They killed themselves, and they can be seen in the summer moonlight on the old stone steps, on the town side."

Clark was suddenly irritated. "This is all humbug!" he cried – quite possibly the first time I'd heard that phrase used aloud and outside a book. "I assure you, gentlemen – I've heard none of these stories, and none of this is true! Mrs. Walker was a fine lady – she does not haunt the lodge house! A young man did die of an opium overdose, but it was while he was at home, recovering from an unexpected surgery. Why would he haunt the auditorium? And a boy and girl killing themselves and then lurking around the stone steps after death – ? Impossible! Such a story would be well-known everywhere, and this is the first I've heard of it!"

152

Holmes continued to look at Simon Sykes. "You indicated that Mr. Harlaw has an interest in 'secret' aspects of the college's history. What form does this take?"

"What?" asked Sykes, still looking at the college president and realizing that he'd perhaps been indiscreet. "Hmm, it's nothing bad. He does research." He nodded toward Harlaw's desk and the teetering piles of books and papers. "He's read both of the college histories written by past professors, and he spends a lot of his spare time at the local newspaper office, looking at the old issues for any news about the college from years ago. It fascinates him. He's always trying to tell the rest of us about it – when this or that happened, or when someone famous visited – and he arranges tours for those that he can get interested."

"Tours? Tell us more about that."

"He . . . Michael finds out the history of the college, and then plans nighttime walks. He keeps them secret and mysterious. It's more fun that way. He only invites a few people at a time. I've been on several of them. We . . . ." He looked at Clark, who was looking ever more intently back at him. "We go into the woods and the basements, and sometimes onto the roofs. There's a secret room in the chapel – stairs that go up to a room in the wall – and we've sat on the Anderson tower at night underneath the flagpole, watching people walk below who have no idea we're up there."

"When was Michael's most recent tour?" Holmes asked.

Sykes pointed to the desk. "I'm not sure. I know that he had found something new he wanted to share, but he wasn't finished doing his research . . . ."

He trailed off as Holmes had already pivoted to the desk, pulled out the chair, sat down, and started sorting through the stacked papers. It didn't take long until he found a sheet near the top that interested him.

He quickly scanned it, read it again more carefully, and then turned to Clark, a hint of urgency now in his voice. "Does Guy Fawkes have any association with this area?"

The college president was obviously puzzled – as was I. "Why, not that I've ever heard," he said. "I believe that Fawkes was originally from York before he ended up in London. I've never heard that he was in this part of Essex. Why"

Holmes vaguely waved the sheet back and forth and then continued to search the missing boy's desk. He finished shifting through the remaining papers and books without finding anything else of apparent interest. Then he systematically went through the drawers, pausing only once to hold up a ring of a dozen or so old-looking keys. "I suspect these fit all the doors of the various college buildings," he said. "It's of interest that Master Harlaw didn't take them with him when he went missing."

"Of interest how?" demanded Clark, whose previous basic good nature, though worried, was now becoming impatient.

"Because where he was going this time, he didn't need them." Holmes then countered with another cryptic question. "Do you have a man who oversees the campus – someone in charge of the grounds and the buildings?"

"That would be Fielding. He'll most likely be at the steam plant."

"Take us there." Holmes's tone was suddenly urgent. "Immediately." He folded the sheet that he'd found and shoved it into his pocket. Then, with a look toward Sykes, a short thank you, and a curt wish that he feel better soon, Holmes was quickly out the door, suddenly hard upon a scent that none of the rest of us could even perceive.

"We'll speak later," said Clark grimly to the sick young man. I simply nodded in his direction. Outside, as Clark and I hurried downstairs to meet the now-fretful Holmes waiting in the lobby, the president asked softly, "Guy Fawkes?"

I shook my head. "Have patience. We'll know soon enough."

Outside, the rain had markedly diminished, which was a fortunate thing, but there was still a cold damp wind blowing from the north, causing a man to put a hurry in his step. Holmes was ahead of us by five or ten feet, walking north and going back the way we had come just a quarter-hour earlier. As we passed the library, Clark increased his pace to catch up. As they walked together, the president made comments that I couldn't hear while pointing straight ahead, indicating that we should continue in that direction to reach the steam plant. Holmes nodded, still deep in thought, but looking from here to there all around is in every direction. As we progressed, the walkway back to Anderson Hall veered away to our left and we approached what had been identified as the dining hall immediately on the right. Then just past it, with Anderson now far to our left across an open field and the science building now at our right, Holmes stopped, asking, "What is that?"

He was pointing to the field, and more specifically, to a set of stone and brick steps that stood in the middle, apparently rising to nowhere.

"Those are the old stairs to Memorial Hall. It was one of the original dormitories, before it was torn down twenty years ago. The building was constructed of wood, but the stairs were more permanent. While also originally scheduled for removal, they were left in place long enough that they became something of a permanent feature of the college landscape. Now we use them. Sometimes the choir will stand on them to give a concert, and in the spring, we have each class stand on them to record their photograph."

154

Holmes continued looking at the steps and Anderson Hall beyond them, and then he looked back toward the dormitory we'd just visited, and in several other directions as well. He nodded to himself and resumed walking briskly toward the steam plant, now obvious to us, at possibly at a faster pace than before.

We came to the proper edge of main campus and crossed a narrow paved access road. Beyond was a solid red-brick building, dwarfed by a pair of high smokestacks, constructed of the same material. They must have each reached a hundred feet or more in the air, and I could see that near their top, just before visibility was lost in the mist, that a pair of decorative letters had been worked into each structure using contrasting yellow brick. As seen from the campus, the left stack had the letter *C*, while the right had an *M*: *College of Mary*. Smoke was coming from each, both stacks high enough for the soot to be carried away by the winds without settling on the college below.

We walked carefully down a muddy gravel drive and around to the opposite side of the building, where Clark led us through a heavy door and into the clattering plant. The abrupt change from the dreary wet November day to the hot steamy room was jarring. One had the sense of overall hidden heights and depths inside, but views in every direction were occluded by a mass of criss-crossing pipes, partial walls ending at eye or knee level, and areas of dark shadows.

The noise wasn't deafening in the short term, but it would cause permanent damage after just a short while. I had treated men who had worked in the bowels of steamships for detrimental hearing loss, and I knew that whomever spent much time in this place would suffer the same disabilities. There was a constant roar of a flame somewhere out of sight, and a regular clanking within the pipes all around us. These ran along the floors and hung all around at differing heights, supported by heavy metal straps attached to the ceiling. They constantly shook and knocked, and there were numerous shrill hisses and whistles as steam was vented regularly all around us, without any set pattern. The air inside the building was wet, and my face was already damp. I wiped it with my handkerchief, thinking that if any of us had worn glasses, we wouldn't have been able to see past the sudden condensation – the same running dripping film that coated the interiors of all the windows.

Clark called for Fielding several times with no response, his voice lost in the din, and then with a shrug, he led us deeper into the hellish maze. Or so it seemed, but in less than fifty feet, with several turns that made me doubt that I could easily find my way back out, we were at the doorway of a snug little office, built against one corner of the building. Why it was so far from the outer door, I didn't know. It had a pair of internal windows

155

looking out upon the plant and the door had a window as well. These showed that the office was lit, but the accumulating water running across the glass meant that nothing inside could be seen.

The door was apparently warped, but Clark gave it a hard pull on his initial attempt – he seemed to know that would be necessary – and let us go in first. He followed and pulled the door shut, and I felt as if the noise level had been drastically muffled and the temperature dropped by twenty degrees.

Fielding was hunched over his desk, copying entries from one sheet to another. He looked up without surprise, recognized Clark, and then pulled a couple of twists of cloth out of each ear. "Mr. Clark," he said, glancing questioningly at Holmes and me. "What can I do for you?"

Clark started to explain about the missing young man, and who we were, but Holmes interrupted him. "Do you have a map of the campus?" he asked, the exigency quite apparent in his voice.

Fielding rose and looked curiously at Holmes. Then he glanced at the college president and, apparently deciding that authority to Holmes had been granted and that the matter was urgent, he turned to a cabinet, pulling open the top drawer and withdrawing a yellowed and folded sheet. He laid it on the desk and then flipped it open to reveal a map about two-feet-square, with the major points roughly reproduced here:

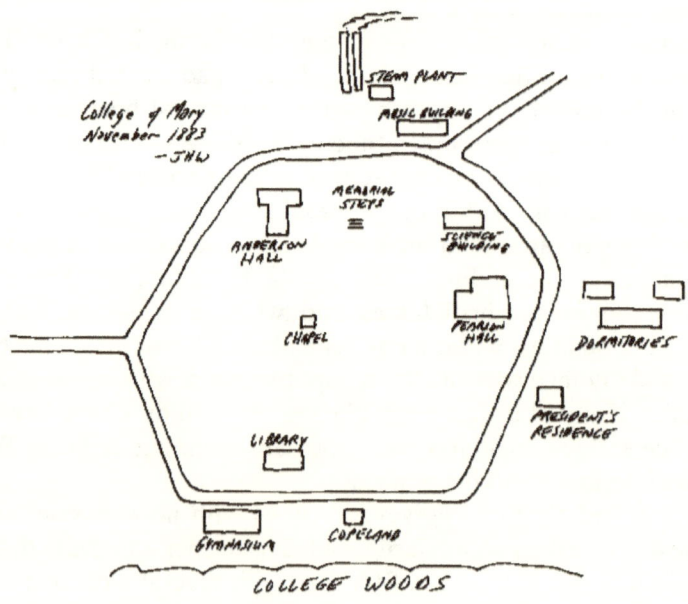

Without comment, Holmes leaned over, tracing his finger along lines from building to building, outlining a network of steam that ran underground to each building's heating system. I could imagine the larger pipes running up to smaller pipes inside walls and floors, and thence to metal radiators, where the heat would spread into the rooms. Meanwhile, as the heat was lost to the buildings, the steam inside the radiators would cool and condense back into water, running down through a series of return lines, carrying it again to the steam plant to be reheated and recirculated once again – something like a circulatory system, wherein the water was the blood, receiving heat energy in the same way that the lungs provided oxygen.

"Here," said Holmes, pointing on the map where Memorial Hall had once stood. "Would this building have been connected to the steam plant?"

Fielding nodded. "It would have." He was clearly curious as to what was going on, but he could tell that Holmes had no time for extraneous questions.

Holmes glanced at Clark. "The venting steam – I saw it coming from the access points in all directions as we walked here from the dormitory."

"That's right. There is an ingress point to the pipes – and sometimes two or three – at some point near every building."

"And at these points – Are the pipes simply buried in the ground, or can they be reached by way of *tunnels*?"

He looked at Fielding then, who nodded, beginning to comprehend Holmes's theory – as was I. "That's right. Brick tunnels, constructed underneath the grounds. There's enough space for men to enter and make repairs as needed."

"And there would have once been such a tunnel to Memorial Hall as well. Would it have been destroyed when the building was torn down? Or simply abandoned in place?"

Fielding rubbed his unshaven jaw. "Probably left in place – in case a new building was ever to be constructed there."

Holmes nodded, but Clark still didn't understand. "Why – Why are you asking about tunnels?" Then he caught up as well. "Do you think that Michael Harlaw – ?"

"The missing boy?" Fielding interrupted. "Do you think he's in one of the tunnels? He wouldn't last five minutes with the steam on – and it's been on continuous for several months, since the weather turned cold. There are big pipes running along the tunnel bottoms – iron pipes, some a foot or more across! – and they would burn whatever touched them. And the steam you see venting from the access points fills the tunnels as well – it leaks from the pipes. Anyone in there would be boiled alive."

Holmes looked grim. "But what about in an abandoned tunnel – the one that runs from Anderson Hall to where Memorial used to stand?"

Fielding nodded. "It might be safe – at least from steam. The live steam pipe running into Anderson enters on the other side of the building, and it would have been cut off from the one abandoned on the old Memorial side."

"Which is why," Holmes added, "there was no steam venting from the old access point in the field near the Memorial steps – as I observed when we walked by, and as shown here on the map."

"But Mr. Holmes," said Clark, raising his hands, "clearly you think that Michael is in a steam pipe tunnel – and if he is, pray God it's the one that doesn't have any steam. But what led you to this conclusion?"

"This paper from his desk," Holmes said, fishing it from his pocket and unfolding it upon the desk:

Guy Fawkes Tour!
Join the Latest Secret Tour of
The College of Mary and
Celebrate the 278th Anniversary
of The Gunpowder Plot!

"That anniversary," said Holmes, "is today – November 5th. In 1605, Fawkes and his friends were caught after trying to put explosives in tunnels underneath Parliament. *Tunnels*," he emphasized.

"But there was no evidence that tunnels were actually used in the Gunpowder Plot," protested Clark.

"It doesn't matter," said Holmes. "It's the popular perception. And the idea of tunnels – supposedly under Parliament and also on this campus – combined with today's date and Michael's fascination with history and the college's secret sites, suggest that he has been exploring the tunnels – and that he might still be down there."

"But sir – !" protested Fielding.

"Yes," said Holmes, raising a hand, "I know. He would be dead – cooked alive. But it was also cold last week when he went missing – when he likely decided to explore the tunnels on his own before leading a group on his 'official tour'. The steam would have been up then as now, and the pipes hot then too, so if he found a way in, he would have used the only tunnel that was cool enough to enter – the one between Memorial Hall and Anderson. Or so I've reasoned." He squared his shoulders. "And there's only one way to find out." He reached and folded the map. "Can you show us where the old tunnel terminates in Anderson's basement? I assume that there is a basement of some sort – I noticed small ventilation openings in the ground-level bricks as we walked by."

Holmes jammed the map into his pocket. Then we went back outside into the frigid cold, Fielding with us, and settled into a near-run across the narrow road and back onto the campus proper. We were motivated by our desire to locate the missing boy, and also due to the terrible bodily shock we'd taken when we stepped from the humid steam plant, which felt much like a tropical greenhouse, and into the bitter November midday. As we passed the field where Memorial Hall had stood, now marked only by its old stone staircase, I looked for some sign that the young man might be out there, just feet away, but of course there was nothing. Upon reaching Anderson, Clark led us to a side door of the old brick building, and I was glad to see that it was on the opposite side of building and the hallway where we had recently left Mr. and Mrs. Harlaw.

Just inside, we came upon a steep stairway leading up to the first floor. Clark veered left around it, and then just behind to a nondescript white-painted door leading back underneath the stairs. He pulled a key from his pocket and unlocked the door.

"Wait," said Holmes. "Is this door always kept locked?"

Clark affirmed it. Holmes frowned.

"Michael may have brought the specific keys with him to this building and this door, and left the rest of his key collection behind, and then someone could have found this door unlocked and relocked it on Friday or today, but I fear that since this door *was* locked just now, it means that he didn't come this way to enter the tunnel." He looked around. "Is there any way to verify if this door was found unlocked after Thursday night?"

Clark nodded and pointed to a doorway just across the narrow hall. "Mrs. Jenks would know."

He ushered us into her office, a tiny room littered with all sorts of knitted decorations, many involving cats in various ridiculous poses, and an overwhelming smell of cinnamon. The room was already crowded with just the lady, and Clark, Holmes, and I completely finished filling it. Fielding remained in the hallway, but he listened through the open door.

Clark explained to the fragile elderly lady behind a small desk that we were going to the basement, and he wondered if that door had been found unlocked since Thursday. "The basement – and the records we keep down there – falls under Mrs. Jenks' purview," he explained to us.

She was a short and thin little woman who had to be at least seventy, and she seemed as if she must be a permanent feature of the college – as if she had been seventy when the school opened, and she'd still be there, seventy years old, a hundred or more years in the future. She nodded sagely and said, "That door has *not* been left unlocked." She said it firmly, as if quoting one of the inviolable Biblical Commandments, her mouth tight. "I've had to go down there two times since Thursday – once on Friday morning, and again today. It was securely locked both times, and I relocked when I was finished. Had it been found unlocked, I would have reported it!"

Then she leaned forward and lowered her voice, her grim mien suddenly bright with curiosity as she looked from Holmes to me and back again. "Are you the men here to certify our ghost? I've written to London three times, in order to get on the Registry."

"Ghost?" asked Clark, a bit shocked. "What ghost? Surely you don't mean – ?"

"The one-legged ghost," she said knowingly, leaning back with a satisfied sigh, as if she'd been holding her breath about it for years and could now relax. "The records say that his name was Litton. Oh, I know that you don't *believe* in him, President, but he's *real*! Those of us who have spent any time here in Anderson Hall know it. We hear him hopping around, and crying out from the pain of his wound. Sometimes, if it's a very *still* day, and the sunlight isn't too *bright* – like today – we *see* him. I've been here since the building was built, and he never stops, year-in, year-out. His *pain* never stops, you see. Why, just this morning, I've heard him, again crying and knocking. I – "

"You *heard* him?" asked Holmes, speaking to the old woman for the first time. "Here – in your office?"

"No, just an hour ago, when I had to return some records to the basement. I wasn't scared, you know. I have no reason to fear *him* – or *any* of the dead who wander the College. We have a small vault downstairs where we keep the more important – "

"And did you hear him any last week?" Holmes pressed. "When you also went to the basement on Friday as well?"

She pursed her lips, and then smiled and nodded. "I *did*! He seemed especially active then. I didn't know what might be agitating him. Perhaps it was the anniversary of the day he *died*. I have often thought – "

But we didn't wait to hear what she thought. I don't know if Clark thanked her or not, but Holmes was already through the basement door and starting down the stairs into the darkness, with Fielding and me following, and Clark right behind.

At the bottom, Holmes lit a match, and for a moment I wondered if Clark would protest in fear that the place might accidentally catch fire. But Holmes quickly located where a lantern stood on a side table, and in seconds it was lit. He picked it up and stepped into the wider basement.

It was low, with even lower beams that made us duck our heads. It was clean enough, as clean as it could be, with no hanging cobwebs or piles of trash, often found in claggy basements where objects are hidden away because there is nowhere else to put them. There were shelves around the walls piled with documents, but I could only wonder how they hadn't already been ruined by the dampness down here. In the flickering light, the spaces behind the papers seemed to move, and I wasn't sure if it was just shifting shadows, or some sort of dank-dwelling insects or secretive rodents.

There was a terrible smell of rot and mildew, and cold was seeping up through the floor, which seemed to be a mixture of old broken cement, interspersed with numerous spots of bare soil. Some sort of room with a heavy open door was to our right – perhaps the vault which had been mentioned by Mrs. Jenks. Just past it, coming in low to the floor, was a big iron pipe, six inches in diameter. Just after it entered the exterior wall, it turned up and branched into a pair of smaller pipes, half the diameter of the larger, that went up through the basement ceiling. From where I stood, I could feel the heat emanating from the main pipe. This, then, was the incoming pipe from the steam plant. Beside it, returning through the ceiling and then out through the same wall near the floor, was a smaller pipe, which was likely the cold-water return.

Seeing it, Holmes turned the other way, where a similar set of pipes ran out through the basement wall in the direction of the old Memorial Hall. He walked up to them and then placed his hand upon the bigger one. He didn't flinch – for there was no steam in that pipe.

He knelt on the ground where the pipes entered, and I could see that there were several small ventilation holes set in the brickwork – holes opening to somewhere else: The abandoned steam tunnel. He leaned closer and called urgently, "Michael! Michael Harlaw! Can you hear me?"

There was no response.

He tried it again, and then another time. We all yelled together, and then we were silent, listening intently.

Nothing.

Holmes cursed. "She said she heard him just this morning! Just an hour or so ago!" He looked at Fielding. "Can you break down this wall to access the tunnel?"

"I can, but that wall is three feet thick. I'll have to go get some tools and some men."

"Stay with us instead. This isn't how Michael got into the tunnel. The door upstairs was locked, and there's no way through here. He entered from outside – by way of the Memorial Hall access point. Where is it?"

161

Fielding shook his head, looking abashed. "I don't know. Somewhere in the field between here and the science building, but I've never seen it. They tore down Memorial before my time, and must have covered it over."

"Then somehow Michael found it," said Holmes, "and he's left it disguised so that it wouldn't be easily noticed, giving him sole access. Let us pray that he didn't hide it too well!"

Holmes then repeated that Fielding would be more useful helping us search the field than trying to break through the wall – "At least for now," he added. In just a moment we were back upstairs and then outside, and this time the wet cold didn't seem to matter at all. Holmes paced off the approximate direction from where the pipe left the building, and we fanned out about twenty feet on either side of it. I saw our goal first – a spot about three-feet square, two-thirds of the way across the field to the science building, where the grass appeared to be more dead than that around it.

Holmes nodded. "That fits with where the access is sketched on the old map."

On approaching it, we found that it was a big piece of iron plating, covered with a thin layer of root-bound soil in which grass managed to grow. The grass and dirt along three edges showed where the lid had been pried up and lifted, with the fourth edge, its grass undamaged, serving as something of a hinge. Together, Fielding and I heaved and threw the entire thing back. I wondered that a single young man could have lifted and then replaced it so carefully, and I half-expected that we would find him immediately inside the access point, having been trapped at that spot because he couldn't lift the lid to effect his escape.

But he wasn't there.

We had exposed a square well about four feet deep, with walls constructed of what looked like rotting brick. Even as we were peering down and Clark was fruitlessly calling Michael's name, the door to Anderson Hall opened, and Mr. and Mrs. Harlaw, accompanied by the Assistant Dean, Martin Carlyle, came running our way.

"Oh my God!" cried Michael's mother. "Have you found him? Is he in that hole?"

"We suspect so," said Holmes, tearing off his Inverness and tossing it onto the wet ground. Then he pulled me aside, instructing me to send Fielding for seek additional help, and to bring back digging tools. Then he added in a low voice, "If the rest of the brick is in as bad shape as this access passage, there could very well be a cave-in. I'll work my way along the tunnel and see if I can find Michael – or," he said, lowering his voice even more, "determine where we need to dig down to make a recovery." Then, while he dropped to his knees and crawled over backward across the lip of the hole, I turned and immediately sent Fielding on his grim errand. He headed toward the steam plant at a run.

I stepped back to the brick box's edge and peered down. Holmes was kneeling at the bottom and looking along a second tunnel which ran away from Anderson, toward the science building. "This one is caved in after only a few feet," he said. "Just past the opening to this box – just a couple of feet across – the tunnel opens up. It's a brick arch, about three feet high. The cave-in on this side looks to be old – not from the last few days." He shifted and looked back in the tunnel running to Anderson, which we had just crossed during our search. "This tunnel is clear – as far as I can see, anyway. I'm going to make my way."

"Holmes," I called. "Wait – I'll go back to the basement and fetch the lantern."

"No time," he said, and then he was gone.

I suppose that he'd been crawling for about half-a-minute when I wondered why I was still up there, simply waiting. Fielding had his instructions, and I could do nothing for the terrified couple or the fretting college representatives trying to comfort them. Meanwhile, employees and students who hadn't joined the ongoing search in the woods were starting to drift our way from adjacent buildings, but hanging back, as if sensing a tragedy in the offing. Soon I would be surrounded by a few dozen men and women who would be as useless as I felt.

I turned and clambered down backwards into the pit.

Kneeling on the muddy soil, I looked down the tunnel and saw a flicker of light somewhere in the narrow distance. Just how far was impossible to tell. "Holmes!" I called. "Can you see him?"

There was some response – possibly he said, "A moment, Watson!" but I wasn't sure. Then I heard him exclaim. I couldn't understand the words and whether they promised good or ill, but the served as the impetus to move me forward. I began to crawl into the hole, worming my way through the small opening into the larger passage and wishing that I'd had the sense to leave my coat behind as well.

The light quickly faded, blocked as it was by my body. What little of it that there was where Holmes had reached was likely considerably diminished by my added presence, but I kept going nonetheless. I knew from walking the distance above that it was just a few hundred feet, but here, crawling every brutal inch, it seemed as if it might go on forever.

As Holmes had said, the tunnel itself was constructed of brick, arched above with enough room for my back to move without scraping. But the cement between the bricks was rotten, crumbling and protruding in spots, and completely missing in others. Often the bricks were sagging or pushing into the tunnel, and in places they had fallen out entirely, leaving

163

bare soil or ominous black voids behind them. Several times I leaned into the wall, or just barely brushed against it, and felt the brick-work move, as if I were pushing against a hanging drape. I gently moved back, hoping that my movement wouldn't bring down hundreds of pounds of brick and dirt onto my back. At other times, my passage seemed to cause crumbles of masonry to shower around me, without me having made any actual contact with the walls at all. I was terrified that I would cause it to collapse around me, leading to a substantial cave-in stretching far in both directions. I was no more than four or five feet below the surface, but soil is heavy, and wet soil heavier, and what was contained in that depth was more than enough to crush and suffocate me – as well as block the passage for Holmes's return.

Hanging from the roof of the tunnel were countless roots of varying thickness, grown deep from the grass above. Some were as thick as my wrist, but others were like threads, brushing along my face like wet spider webs. All of them were dripping with water that had saturated the ground above from the steady rains. While I mourned my ruined coat and suit, I was glad for my hat, which kept the wet twisted tendrils from dragging through my hair.

Perhaps worst of all was the constant and ever-seething population of *rhaphidophoridae*, popularly known as *cave crickets* or *spider crickets*. Bigger and lighter than the small, black, and friendly crickets one found in civilized places, these creatures were substantial. *Meaty*. It may have been my imagination, but I felt that they were radiating a vinegary odor which made my eyes burn. There were thousands of them, and as I approached and my eyes adjusted to the dim light, I could see that even as I watched them, they were watching me.

These creatures were possibly what I had seen behind the shelves in the Anderson basement, but then they were at a distance. Now they were all around me. Waves of them rolled away from me as I crawled, moving down the tunnel toward Holmes as my movements herded them forward, jumping frantically about with their thick grass-hopper legs as they were disturbed, sometimes hitting my face, and on several occasions landing on my bare neck. In a couple of cases, I felt them creeping further beneath my collar, pulled back by my movements, and underneath my shirt. Once one landed in my open panting mouth. I gave a grunt of disgust and spit the thing out, but I kept going. They were only crickets, and I would be able to rid myself of them later. For now, my help was needed.

The floor of the tunnel was plain soil – mud actually, as there was quite a bit of standing water. It was hard to find traction to push forward. Several times my hand slipped and I cried out. Traversing the tunnel was made worse by the presence of the old iron steam pipe, left abandoned in place. As I crawled I had to straddle it, at least eight inches in diameter, and I regularly barked my hands and wrists against the widened bell joints where the pieces of pipe had been pushed together. I began to worry about picking up some dread disease by way of muddy wounds that I might open on the ragged rusty pipe.

There was nowhere to go but forward, and I awkwardly thrust one knee ahead and then the other, matching the abbreviated stride with similar arm motions. I found that I was looking down, my breathing heavy, simply forcing myself to move, inch after inch, knowing that there was a finality in front of me, one way or another. Then, to my surprise, I heard a voice directly in in my path.

"Watson," said Sherlock Holmes softly. "He's alive – but we have to dig."

I looked up then and saw that Holmes had lit a match to let me see what he'd found – a young man, so similar in visage to his father, unconscious but breathing, his right leg buried under a cave-in of brick and stone and mud. Beside it was a mound of material that the young man must have previously removed, but without any measurable success. Apparently, the more he'd shifted, the more fresh material he'd loosened.

"Should I go back for help?" I said. "We can measure off the distance, and then excavate from above."

"I don't think that we can wait for that," he said softly. "In any case, it would probably bring down the entire ceiling onto us. With your help, I believe I can free him – but for God's sake be careful, or the whole structure will fall and engulf us!"

I have no sense if it was ten minutes or an hour. Time ceased to having meaning as we slowly freed Michael Harlaw from what would have been his unknown tomb. One brick at a time, one stone, pulled gingerly loose by Holmes and handed to me. One scoop of viscous soil after another, drawn away and collected behind me so as to not block our way when we eventually departed. I would turn and place it carefully along the tunnel wall. I didn't want to simply toss it, possibly dislodging more of the brickwork, and I also didn't want to inadvertently build a second randomly constructed wall behind us that we'd have to force across when bringing out the injured boy.

And boy he was, despite his age. He seemed too young for the situation in which he'd found himself – but then again, that had been true of so many tragedies that I'd witnessed, even before a similarly aged army had been slaughtered at Maiwand. So different had that day been – hellish heat, choking dust, and blinding sunlight that made seeing impossible, aching thirst beyond comprehension, and the sounds of killing artillery and dying screams. Here was cold and wet and dark, with the only noises coming from the scraping of stone and mud, and the dripping of water into what might be our graves, and the small grunts of effort, more and more frequent, as the next brick was pulled loose and moved aside, and the next and the next . . . .

But every task is completed one small piece at a time, and I was in the act of moving yet another brick, the last one it turned out, when Holmes murmured, "I have him. He's free. Let is bring him out of this Hell-hole."

It wasn't that simple. First, I carefully fought my way out of my overcoat, and then we wrapped it around the young man's lower body so that any injury to his legs wouldn't be worsened as we pulled him out. After tying the sleeves in place, we commenced our return.

The journey back to the daylight and the grass above was in some ways much worse than the trip in, but in the same way we had un-buried the boy, we accomplished it in small stages, crawling one foot or just one inch after another. When we were near the entryway, I saw that two men were down in the brick access hole – Clark and the boy's father. They had been calling to us the entire time, but Holmes and I had no awareness of it. Above us stood Fielding with a crew of men, all carrying shovels, picks, and long iron bars to use as leverage – now thankfully unnecessary. When we were out and the boy had been lifted into the dim rainy daylight, what there was of it, Clark ordered them to weld up the lid for good.

Meanwhile, Mrs. Harlaw had fallen to her knees beside her son, and it was her sobs that seemed to rouse him. With a feeble smile, he reached for her hand before again lapsing back into unconsciousness. It would be the next day, in the small facility that served as Abridge's only hospital, that he would awaken completely. With the strength of youth, he would quickly recover – and his parents wisely waited several days before sharing with him all the concern and anguish that he had inadvertently caused. It was a lesson he would long remember.

It was toward the end of November when the Harlaws visited us in Baker Street. The boy seemed to have no lasting ill effects – just a limp, which I recognized would vanish in time. He gladly accepted our offer of tea and biscuits. His parents were less relaxed, both of them sitting with a tense awareness of their son, as if he were still in danger, even in our safe sitting room. I knew that it would be a long time before they would be able to forget what had happened, or to allow themselves to trust their son as they had before. Although the young man didn't seem to have been greatly affected, a lesson about life's fragility had left his parents both shaken and nervous.

166

After a moment of enjoying his refreshments, Michael confirmed what Holmes had been able to piece together.

"I've learned quite a bit about the school," he said without any false modesty. His father watched him with a studied frown, but with something like pride showing far back in his eyes. "That kind of thing has always interested me – doing research about places where others don't know to look. Learning forgotten facts. Putting together the pieces. I believe that I know more about the College of Mary than most of the professors.

"Every few years, the graduating students bestow on a lucky few the keys that they've accumulated. An even greater secret – known to just a few students – has been the existence of the old tunnels. Last year, one of the senior fellows showed me how to find the tunnel between Anderson Hall and the old Memorial dormitory. I learned where all the other entrances are as well – quite a few besides the obvious places where the steam vents – but the rest of them are impassible once the heating system is activated each fall.

"I'd waited too late to explore the other tunnels – I planned to get into them in the spring – but I knew how to enter the one where you found me. I'd originally planned a tunnel tour for my friends on Guy Fawkes Day, in honor of his use of tunnels. I decided to examine its condition beforehand, so I entered on Thursday night. I believe that the rain weakened the brickwork. Before I knew it, there was a cave-in. I turned to jump back the way I'd just crawled, but my leg was trapped.

"I did my best to work myself loose, but it was impossible, and I was afraid that too much digging would finish burying me. My lantern had been buried under the mud and bricks. I yelled over and over, but no one heard me, and I lost track of how long I was down there. I thought . . . I thought . . . ."

He didn't weep, but he was clearly shaken then with emotion at the realization of how close he'd come to death. I hoped – as I'm sure his parents did as well – that he'd learned a lesson. But that day I suspected that he would continue exploring his fascination with uncovering unknown knowledge and finding out things that others didn't, even when it meant disregarding his own safety.

I was right. Soon after our meeting, Michael Harlaw decided that his study of music wasn't how he wanted to spend his time and energy. He transferred to the University of London to pursue a career in archaeology – a field in which he's now quite well known.

On that November day in 1883, before Michael had found his true path, I glanced from the young man of nineteen to Sherlock Holmes, himself just twenty-nine. I knew where I'd previously seen Michael's disregard for personal safety when weighed against *finding out*. I recognized the trait in the young man because I'd come to know it so well in Sherlock Holmes. My friend was just such a person. I could imagine Holmes at that age, deciding to explore a lost tunnel on his own, regardless of the consequences. On that day in 1883, when Holmes was just weeks from turning thirty, he still had the same quality. It was part of what made him so tenacious at determining the truth and serving as an advocate for those who weren't able to solve their own mysteries.

And even as Holmes would continue to push to understand and to know, and edge himself into danger, because it was what he did best, I would balance out these tendencies and ward him when I could.

For that was what I did best.

NOTE

Curiously, the college where I received my first degree in the 1980's had similar haunted buildings with ghosts very much like the ones described here. I also inherited keys to most of the buildings from former students, and wearing my deerstalker (which has been my only hat, all year long, since I was nineteen years old to the present), I would often visit these buildings by night, exploring roofs and basements, towers and attics and forgotten chambers, either giving guiding tours or on solo expeditions.

This campus also had old steam tunnels, just as described here, some still very much active, and others abandoned. (I still live less than a mile from that school, taking walks there on a regular basis, and the tunnels are still there, as are the secret openings – if one knows where to look.) As a student, I would visit these tunnels, leading secret expeditions with other students or alone. Often, one could crawl through the crickets for quite a distance along the brick-arched tunnels, only to encounter a complete cave-in, with no visible signs on the surface to indicate where it had occurred, as the old rotten bricks had given away at some point long past.

It only occurred to me in later years how such a cave-in might trap or kill unwary visitors, and how it might be years – or never – before what happened was discovered and the bodies finally found.

I was really stupid back then.

– DM

The Adventure of the
Green Horse
by Hugh Ashton

"Y ou must help us, Mr. Holmes!"

It would be a heart of stone that could resist such a plea, coming as it did from the mouth of one in such obvious distress. The name on the card that had been sent up to us was "*Mrs. Frederick Lomax*", and the bearer proved to be a young woman of about twenty-five years of age, fashionably dressed.

"Pray, calm yourself, Mrs. Lomax," Holmes reassured her. "Please take a seat here. Perhaps, Watson, you could arrange for Mrs. Hudson to bring us some tea?"

I hastened to obey as Mrs. Lomax settled herself into the chair in which Holmes's clients typically unburdened themselves of their worries, and indeed, when I returned from my errand, she appeared more composed as she addressed Holmes.

"It is my sister, Mary," she began. "I call her my sister, but in truth she is my step-sister, the child of my step-father's first marriage. Mary Draycott is a little older than I, and I fear that nature has not favoured her in the matter of looks, nor the law in the matter of inheritance – her mother's estate was willed entirely to her brother, who now lives in Canada. She remains unmarried, and makes her living by acting as a nurse-companion to elderly gentlefolk in their last months of life. There is an agency which specialises in providing such services – I can provide you with the name if you wish."

"Later, later," Holmes murmured. "Please continue."

"As I say, she has been practising this profession for some years now without incident, until last week. The last patient she attended – that is to say, before her current post – died a month ago."

"The name of this patient?"

"A Lady Fiona Pugsley, an elderly lady who lived in Portman Square, the widow of General Sir Archibald Pugsley. After Lady Pugsley's demise, the relatives came to settle the estate, and it was noticed that a valuable item was missing."

At that moment, the tea arrived, and the conversation ceased momentarily. When Mrs. Hudson had left, and the door closed behind her, Mrs. Lomax resumed her story.

"The item in question was a small jade carving in the shape of a horse, which had always stood beside Lady Pugsley's bed. It had supposedly been brought back from China by the General, and was said to be very valuable.

"Upon the servants being questioned, all denied any knowledge of the horse's whereabouts, and suspicion then fell on my sister Mary. When asked about the horse, she immediately produced it, saying that she had been presented with it by Lady Pugsley as a gift in recognition of her services as a nurse and companion."

"Then it is merely a question of her word," said Holmes. "I confess that I am unsure of the problem facing you."

"If it were this alone," replied Mrs. Lomax, "I would agree with you. However, the relatives referred the matter to the police, and it was discovered that in six cases previously, some trinkets or small items, none as valuable as this jade carving, had been discovered as missing from the estates of the elderly patients for whom Mary had been caring. They confronted Mary with this, and she denied any knowledge of these pieces. Even so, they do not believe poor Mary, and she lives in constant fear of arrest of crimes that she denies, and I know in my heart that she did not commit."

"And you wish me to establish her innocence?"

"Precisely that, Mr. Holmes."

"Very well. There would appear to be some elements to this case which provide interest. The name of the agency that employs your step-sister?"

"The Barnet Nursing Agency has offices in Chipping Barnet. The establishment employs about half-a-dozen nurse-companions in the same manner as they employ Mary."

"Indeed. Do you know the name of the police officer who is in charge of this case?"

"Inspector Williamson of Scotland Yard, I believe."

"A name I have heard, but I have yet to have the pleasure of making his acquaintance. However, that will soon be remedied."

"One last question, Mr. Holmes. Your fee?"

"We will discuss that when the time comes. Trust me, it will not be more than you can afford." Holmes smiled easily as he rose to his feet and extended his hand. "Thank you, Mrs. Lomax. I have your address on your card and will contact you as soon as any matter of import arises."

She seemed somewhat surprised at this rather abrupt dismissal, but rose and took Holmes's hand. "Thank you, Mr. Holmes. Goodbye to you, and to you, Dr. Watson."

"And what do you make of our Mrs. Lomax?" Holmes asked me, after we had watched from the window as she took a cab.

"If I were to deduce anything from her style of dress, which was fashionable, but not of the highest quality, I would hazard that Mr. and Mrs. Lomax aren't in as favourable financial circumstances as they would like themselves to be."

"I agree. Excellent observation on your part. Did you notice her wedding ring?"

"I confess that I did not."

"Perhaps I should rephrase that. Did you notice the *absence* of her wedding ring? Perhaps its absence will prove significant." He paused, as if in thought. "I regret that you were here today to meet Mrs. Lomax."

"What can you mean?"

"If Mrs. Lomax hadn't met you, I would be sending you round to Chipping Barnet now to enquire about the possibility of hiring a companion for your elderly Aunt Amelia. I have a feeling about this. Since she now knows your name and face, that is impossible. Never mind. We'll pay a visit to the Registrar of Companies, and then proceed to Inspector Williamson."

The police officer turned out to be a lean, almost-cadaverous individual of gloomy aspect.

"I confess to you, sir, that we don't have a lot to go on here," he admitted when we introduced ourselves and explained our mission. "Miss Draycott seemed all-too-keen to show us the little gee-gee when we asked her about it, but we only have her word for it that it was a gift."

"Do you have the horse here?" asked Holmes.

"That I do, sir." Williamson opened his desk drawer and extracted a small object, which he passed to Holmes.

"Good Heavens, Watson!" my friend exclaimed, letting out a low whistle. "Look at this!"

The carving, not more than two or three inches in length, was exquisitely worked in Oriental fashion. The material was a pale green stone, which almost seemed to shine with its own light as it lay in Holmes's palm.

"Inspector," Holmes said severely, "your desk drawer is no place for this. Its rightful place is the British Museum, or, failing that, your office safe."

"It is valuable, then?"

"Almost priceless, I would say. It is fashioned from nephrite jade, the most prized and precious kind, and the workmanship is exquisite. I believe this dates from the Han dynasty, nearly two-thousand years ago."

"Good Lord!" exclaimed Williamson

"If it were to be offered for sale – and I am no expert in these matters, you understand – I would estimate a price of fifteen-thousand pounds to be not unreasonable."

"Good Lord!" Williamson repeated. "I shall follow your suggestion as to the safe immediately, sir."

"And the other items listed as having been stolen from her other patients. Where are they?"

The inspector spread his hands. "We searched Miss Draycott's lodgings, and a policewoman searched her person. There was no trace of them, nor any evidence, such as pawnbroker's receipts, of their ever having been in her possession."

"I see. Do you have a list of these items listed as missing from the other occasions and their descriptions?" Holmes asked.

"Here you are, sir."

"Excellent," remarked Holmes, scanning the paper. "On the face of it, these would appear to be mere trinkets by comparison with our friend here," indicating the green horse, "worth perhaps fifty pounds or so each at the very most."

"Still a tidy sum, sir," Williamson pointed out.

"Indeed, but in a different class entirely. May I take a copy of this list?"

"I will have one made for you." He pressed an electric bell and instructed the constable accordingly.

"Have there been any similar complaints from other clients of the agency employing Miss Draycott?"

"Not to my knowledge, sir. Mary Draycott is the only one of which I have any knowledge."

"You have talked with her, have you not? How did she strike you?"

"I have to confess that her appearance did not strike me very favourably. She does, however, have a pleasant voice, and a manner which I am sure her patients find relaxing and calming." He paused for a moment. "When she told me the details of how this here," indicating the jade horse, "was given to her by Lady Pugsley, I felt that she was telling the truth. I don't know if you ever have such a feeling, sir, but in my experience, the truth makes itself known through little things, such as posture, and tone of voice."

"Indeed it does, Inspector. And her denials of the other items?"

"Again, it seemed sincere, but since she professed no knowledge of these items, other than to admit that she had noticed some of them while at work in the houses from which they were missing, there was no specific event or events to be verified or disproved."

"Excellent, Inspector. You have grasped the truth that absence of proof of innocence isn't the same as proof of absence of innocence. Would that all juries could think the same. Where is she now?"

"You may find her caring for Lady Beddesley in her house on Brompton Street."

"I may pay her a visit at some point. But while we wait for your constable, perhaps you can tell me something about the Barnet Nursing Agency."

"Not a lot to say, sir. Its offices are just one room on the High Street, above the fishmonger's, and the only employee, other than the nurses that it sends out, appear to be Mr. Lomax."

"You are aware, are you not, that Mr. Lomax appears to be married to Mary Draycott's step-sister? Before visiting you, Watson and I paid a visit to the Registrar of Companies and discovered that a Mr. Frederick Lomax is the proprietor of the agency. The card of my visitor to Baker Street earlier today gave her name as Mrs. Frederick Lomax. I feel that there is more than a little coincidence here."

Williamson gave a visible start. "No sir, I did not know this. Why do you say that she 'appears' to be married to Mr. Lomax?"

"When she visited us, I noticed that she had been wearing several rings, including her wedding ring. The marks were still on her fingers."

"I believe all this puts a fresh complexion on the case."

"It does indeed," Holmes smiled. "But as yet, I'm unsure exactly what turn events will take. I take it that you would have no objection to our visiting Mr. Lomax in Barnet?"

"None at all. To be frank with you, sir, I am pleased to have your opinions on the matter. Ah," as the constable re-entered, bearing papers. "Here is the list of items you requested. May I simply ask that you keep me informed of any developments as they occur?"

"Naturally, Inspector. A very good day to you."

In the cab from Scotland Yard, I asked Holmes about his thoughts regarding the case.

"I have a theory," he answered me. "A theory which as yet lacks the foundation of a set of data to prove it. Ah, here we are." The cab had deposited us outside a house in Portman Square.

We descended the area steps and knocked on the kitchen door, which was opened by a girl in maid's uniform.

"If it's Mrs. Wallace the cook you're looking for, she left when her Ladyship died. There's just me and Mrs. Finch, the housekeeper, left here to look after the place all on our own."

"Excellent," Holmes smiled. "If you could answer a few questions for me, I'd be most grateful. Do you remember a Mary Draycott who nursed Lady Pugsley?"

"Course I do. Not much in the way of looks, poor dear, but a good heart for all that. I couldn't believe it when they said she'd taken that little thing from her Ladyship's table without asking."

"Do you think her Ladyship might have given it to her, then?"

"I'm sure she would, sir." The answer was given in firm unhesitating tones. "Mary Draycott is a good kind person, and Lady P, as she liked us to call her, knew that as well as anyone. I do believe she could have asked for anything she wanted from Lady P, and she'd have had it."

"I see. Were there ever any visitors from the agency who sent Mary Draycott?"

"A Mr. Lomax came to call before Mary came to join us. And he called again about a week before Lady P passed away. Came in happy enough, I seem to recall, but he left as if he'd just had a thundercloud sit on him. I only met him those two times, but I can't put my hand on my heart and tell you I cared for him one bit."

"And anyone else?"

The maid shook her head. "Not that I can remember, unless they called on my day off. I'd be the one who'd let them in, see?"

Holmes thanked her for her trouble. "And here's half-a-crown for your trouble."

"Why, thank you, sir."

"Where next?" I asked Holmes. "Barnet, or Brompton Street?"

"Neither," he said. "Ah, here we are." We had halted outside a handsome townhouse, the ground and upper storeys of which appeared to be empty. "This is one of the houses from which an item was reported as missing – a silver spoon, to be precise." Again, we descended the area steps and knocked on the door. This time, it appeared to be the cook who answered.

Holmes introduced himself.

"I've read of you, sir," our interlocutor protested, "but I haven't done nothing."

"My dear lady, no one is accusing you of anything. I simply want to ask you a few questions if I may. Do you remember a Mary Draycott, who cared for Mr. Hammersley during his last illness?"

"Mary? I do indeed. Such a comfort to the poor gentleman, she was. Nice as pie to us all."

"And do you remember something about a missing spoon?"

"I do that. It was a silver rat-tailed spoon from the time of King James, they said. It was the one that Mr. Hammersley used to take his medicine. It went missing after his death."

"And do you think Mary Draycott might have taken it?"

She shook her head emphatically. "No, sir, I do not. Mary Draycott was an honest, good person."

"Thank you. One last question: Did anyone from the agency who sent Mary Draycott ever visit here?"

"Yes, there was a Mr – Lucas? No, Lomax – that was his name. He came to see if Mary Draycott was doing her job properly. That would have been a few days before Mr. Hammersley passed away. No," correcting herself. "I tell a lie. It was the day before he died. I remember Jane, the parlourmaid, took him upstairs to the sickroom so that he could see that all was being done proper. Jane told me that he didn't behave towards her like a gentleman should. I'll leave you, sir, to guess what she meant by that."

Again Holmes presented a half-crown, along with his thanks.

"And what does all this mean?" I asked. "How many more houses are we going to visit?"

"To answer your last question first, I don't think it will be worth visiting any more. We have visited the last two where Mary Draycott worked, and the trail will have gone cold. The servants who worked with her will all have gone to other positions, and the houses will have passed into other hands. There is no more that we can do today in this regard. So let us take ourselves to the wilds of Chipping Barnet."

Once we had reached our destination, Holmes pointed to a fishmonger's shop. "Above there, if I am not mistaken, are the offices of the Barnet Nursing Agency." However, it was to a pawnbroker's establishment that we took ourselves.

"I am interested," Holmes said to the shopkeeper, "to know if you have for sale any silver spoons of the time of King George II or earlier."

"I'd have to check the books, sir, but I think I have one or two here." After consultation, he arranged three spoons on the counter in front of us and held one up. "This one might be a bit early for you, sir. James the First, I believe."

"As you say, a little earlier than I was expecting, but the rat-tail design is exceptionally fine. The price?"

"A guinea, sir."

"And while I am here, I am of the fancy that an amber-headed scarf-pin would be an excellent addition to my wardrobe."

"I know that I have just the thing for you here, sir. However, there is an insect trapped in the amber. I trust you have no objection to that."

The pin's head was as large as a walnut, and as described, the amber contained a perfectly preserved fly.

"Perfect," said Holmes. "The fly adds interest." He cocked his head enquiringly.

"I was going to ask fifteen shillings, but if you take this along with the spoon, I will sell this for twelve-and-sixpence."

"Excellent. One-pound-thirteen-and-sixpence, then, for the pair?"

"That's right, sir."

"I know that you have your professional secrets, but I would like to ask you if this spoon and this pin were brought in by the same person."

The shopkeeper looked at Holmes in amazement. "You're right, sir, but how in the world would you possibly know that? Yes, it's the same woman, and there are quite a few others that she has brought in from time to time."

"I won't pry further, other than to ask if she has brought in any rings recently?"

"Now, sir, I believe you are a true magician. You frighten me, sir. I refuse to answer that question."

"And your refusal provides me with that answer. Thank you. Thirty-three-shillings-and-sixpence, we said? Here you are."

"Thank you, sir."

Holmes chuckled as we left the shop. "A moment, if you would, Watson." He paused to adjust his newly acquired scarf-pin in a prominent position. "And now for the Barnet Nursing Agency."

Mr. Frederick Lomax was a small man whose round face was framed by black bushy side-whiskers. His clothes had once been of good quality, but were now sadly worn and threadbare in some places.

As Holmes and I entered, he rose to greet us, and gave a visible start as he beheld the amber pin at Holmes's throat.

"What – ?" he stammered. "How may I help you gentlemen?"

"I believe that you supply nurses – companions, if you will – to provide comfort to those about to depart this life," Holmes said.

"That is so," the other acknowledged.

"Your agency comes recommended by the heirs of Mr. Augustus Barnstable, who passed away some two years ago. You supplied a nurse by the name of Mary Draycott, I seem to recall, who took care of him in his last hours."

Lomax's face had drained of colour as Holmes delivered his speech, and his eyes glared at us from an almost perfectly white visage as he replied through bloodless lips. "I don't know who you are, but I must tell you that Miss Draycott is unavailable. Indeed, at present we are unable to undertake any more engagements, and I must therefore bid you both a good day."

Holmes stood his ground. "May I trouble you for the answer to one more question?"

"If you must." The permission was given grudgingly.

"Where is the jade horse?"

I didn't think it was possible for a face to grow any paler, but Lomax was by now literally as white as a sheet. "I have no idea what you are talking about," he told us defiantly.

"Then I will tell you. A nephrite jade horse of the Han dynasty is now in the possession of the Metropolitan Police. It is there because one of your nurses, Miss Mary Draycott, is under suspicion of having stolen it from her charge, Lady Pugsley."

"Haven't they arrested her yet?"

"So you do know about it, then?" Holmes answered smoothly.

"Damn your eyes!" the other exploded. He bent and extracted a revolver from his desk drawer. "Unless you leave within five seconds, I shall fire."

"I wouldn't do that if I were you. Watson here is a dead shot with the revolver you can make out in his coat pocket – yes, the one in which he currently has his hand – he is left-handed, you see. If I go down, you too will certainly fall, and Watson here will not shoot to kill. He will save you for the hangman."

The pistol dropped from Lomax's hand as he sank into the chair and broke into hysterical sobs. "I believe you know it all."

"Nearly all."

"It was Tabitha's idea to employ her."

"Your wife?"

Lomax nodded. "Mary is a sweet and innocent soul, handicapped by her looks. Her mother's money was left to her brother in Canada. What Tabitha knows, and Mary doesn't, is that her brother is dying of consumption, and has left a considerable fortune to Mary in his will."

"And if Mary were to be no longer in circulation, under arrest or worse, your wife would then inherit as next of kin?"

Lomax nodded again. "That was the idea. I had lost money on 'Change, more than I could afford, and this Agency," he waved his hand around the room, "by now had but one nurse on its books – Mary. By visiting the homes of the patients where she worked, I was able to abstract certain small but valuable items that, as you seem to have discovered, I took to the local pawnbroker's in exchange for cash. How much did he ask for that scarf-pin, if I may ask?"

"Twelve-shillings-and -sixpence."

"Oh, the rogue!" Lomax exclaimed with a bitter laugh. "I only received seven shillings for it. Of course, there was no proof that Mary had taken these things, but they were small enough to be overlooked, but large enough to be noticed if a detailed inventory was ever taken. They would act as circumstantial evidence if Mary were ever to be suspected. But when I visited Lady Pugsley before placing Mary there, I caught sight of that little green horse that you referred to earlier. I don't have a detailed knowledge of such things, but I knew this was valuable. Its loss would prompt an enquiry. My aim was to remove the horse and place it among Mary's things so that it would be discovered there so that she would be arrested, charged, and sent to prison. How was I to know that it would form a gift from patient to nurse before my arrival, and Mary would be proud to acknowledge its possession?" He broke off. "Have you any objection to my taking my medicine? My heart," he offered by way of explanation.

Holmes shook his head, and Lomax extracted a glass into which he poured what appeared to be water from a bottle, adding some drops from a small phial that he extracted from his waistcoat pocket before draining the draught.

"Quick, Watson!" Holmes shouted to me as Lomax slumped forward.

There was a smell of bitter almonds as I raised the unconscious body, feeling for his pulse. "Prussic acid, I fear," I said to Holmes. "We have lost him."

"I don't think it is the first time this phial has been used," Holmes said. "If we investigate, I am sure that many of Mary Draycott's patients died very soon after Lomax paid a visit."

"You don't suspect her of anything?"

"I do not. But we must make haste to take the widow before she, too, escapes us." He opened the window onto the street and blew three loud blasts upon his police whistle. A uniformed constable was with us within a matter of a few minutes, to whom Holmes explained the situation.

"If you wait here, sir, I'll bring my sergeant to go with you to find Mrs. Lomax, and I will stay here while you find her."

"If you're going to the station, please telephone Scotland Yard, and ask Inspector Williamson to join us at the station."

As the constable left us, I turned to Holmes.

"What in the world did you mean by saying I had my revolver with me, let alone saying that I am left-handed and could drop him firing left-handed from the hip? You know very well that I don't carry my revolver with me unless specifically requested by you to do so."

Holmes laughed easily. "He was a nervous man and could easily have pulled the trigger of his own gun before being fully aware of any

179

consequences. I had to provide him with a good reason why he shouldn't do so."

It was only five minutes before the constable reappeared, together with another policeman who introduced himself as Sergeant Jennings.

"I'll come with you, sir. What charges should I bring against her when I arrest her?"

"I think, Sergeant, that we should simply ask her to accompany us to the station, and await Inspector Williamson's judgment on the matter."

"Very good, sir."

We set off for the Lomax residence, which was known to Sergeant Jennings, and which proved to be a rather mean terraced house in a side-street. Tabitha Lomax's face brightened at the sight of Holmes and me, but her expression changed when informed of her husband's death and Jennings's request to accompany us to the station.

Once there and joined by Inspector Williamson, she corroborated her husband's story, and confirmed Holmes's suspicions that some of Mary Draycott's patients had experienced unnaturally early deaths as the result of poison being added to their medicine by Lomax on his visits when he took the small articles.

When shown the list of articles that had been reported as missing, she laughed heartily. "This list," she said, "represents a mere fraction of the items that Fred took from Mary's houses. One spoon?" She laughed. "He took at least six spoons and a cream jug. That jug alone paid the coal man for a week with what we got from that miser of a pawnbroker."

"Tabitha Lomax, I hereby arrest you on the charge of conspiracy to pervert the course of justice, and of being an accessory after the fact to numerous acts of theft," Williamson told her after she had made a full statement. "We'll also take in that pawnbroker. He is certain to have known that he was receiving stolen goods."

"And now, if you have no objection, Inspector," Holmes added, "Watson and I would like to accompany you to Scotland Yard where I can collect the jade and return it to Mary Draycott."

"Certainly."

An hour or two later, we were knocking at the door of the room occupied by Mary Draycott in the Brompton Street house where she was currently acting as a nurse.

The door was opened by a woman who, as we had been told, was less-than-attractive in her appearance. A large port-wine birthmark covered one side of her face, and the poor creature also suffered from a severe squint. However, there was a feeling of sincerity to her smile, and she invited us into the room which was neatly and comfortably furnished.

"Mr. Sherlock Holmes and Dr. Watson," she said in a soft melodious voice. "I am honoured. No doubt you were sent here by Sister Tabitha?"

"Indirectly, I suppose that may be true," said Holmes, and proceeded to relate the events of the day that had passed.

To our surprise, Mary Draycott burst out laughing. "I suppose that it is no laughing matter, really. I certainly believed that Fred was responsible for the deaths of some of my patients, but I couldn't prove anything, any more than he could prove that I stole any of the objects whose disappearance he wished to lay at my door. None of it would have worked, you realise. I could never be found guilty by a jury."

Holmes smiled. "You are right, you know. A jury would have to be satisfied beyond all reasonable doubt that you had stolen those things, and any advocate worth his salt could have implanted that doubt in their minds. They would be duty bound to declare you innocent, even if they felt you were guilty."

"The only evidence, such as it is, is this." She indicated the jade horse.

"Have you any idea what this is worth?" asked Holmes.

"Han dynasty, nephrite jade. Probably carved for a member of the Imperial court. I think somewhere between fifteen- and twenty-thousand pounds."

I looked at her in astonishment. "How on earth – ?"

"A hobby of mine, Doctor. Look." On the shelf above her bed was a row of volumes pertaining to antiquities, including some volumes on Chinese jade.

Holmes chuckled.

"I may not be a pretty face, Mr. Holmes, but the Lord gave me a good power of understanding. I always knew what Tabitha was doing and what Fred was doing at her bidding."

"But why would she call in Holmes to establish your innocence?" I asked.

"Oh, that was never her intention. She believed that the evidence against me was strong enough to secure my conviction. And if even the great Sherlock Holmes couldn't save me, then . . . ." She shrugged. "She always pretended to pity me, but actually despised me, and envied me for the fortune that will come my way when Gerald dies – Oh yes, I know all about it, and I believe it is now only a matter of months now. And Fred?" She laughed. "Fred's preposterous little Agency. He had no head for business. If it wasn't for me, that couple would have been bankrupted long ago – I acquired a good reputation and he was able to charge good money for my services."

"You were indeed good at what you did," Holmes told her. "All the servants with whom we spoke had nothing but praise for you and your character."

"It was work that I enjoyed doing, and I flatter myself that I did it well. I felt loved and appreciated, not just by my patients, but by the other servants whose lives I was easing by caring for their masters and mistresses."

"And so after all these years, you felt that you deserved – this?" said Holmes, indicating the horse.

She said nothing, but looked Holmes in the eye and nodded.

"Holmes," I said. "What are you saying?"

"I say nothing now, and I shall not say anything in the future about this."

Mary Draycott looked at Holmes, at the jade horse, and back again at my friend.

"Come, Watson. We are done here," said Sherlock Holmes.

"God bless you, Mr. Holmes," Mary Draycott said to us as we closed the door on this extraordinary woman and her green horse.

The Adventure of
Woodgate Manor
by Sonya Kudei

It was an unusually dark April morning in the year 1884, as dark as midwinter, and I awoke almost two hours later than I was normally accustomed, having been deceived by the overcast sky into believing the hour to be much earlier than it actually was. When I at last descended the stairs and entered the sitting room of the Baker Street quarters I shared with Sherlock Holmes, feeling somewhat dismayed by my tardiness, I found my friend standing between the parted curtains, peering down at something in the street below.

"Ah, Watson," he said without looking up, "you have elected to rise at just the right time. I do believe we are about to meet a new client very shortly. Come and take a look."

Ignoring the slight gibe, I went up to where he stood by the window and looked over his shoulder. In the grey street outside, made even more dull by the muted light, there stood a young woman in a steel-blue dress and fur-lined jacket whose plain but not-unattractive features, partly concealed by her brown bonnet but still visible as she glanced nervously up at our windows, clearly showed the pallor and haggardness of distress. Wringing her gloved hands, the lady hovered uncertainly on the edge of the pavement. Her gaze lingered on the *221* above our front door as if she sought reassurance that she was at the right place, while at the same time her inner sight appeared to be absorbed in some private recollection.

"I see no reason not to agree with your view," I said, "as it should be evident even to someone as unobservant as myself that the young lady in the street, although seemingly distraught, does indeed have every appearance of someone wishing to seek your counsel. I wonder what might be keeping her from taking the final step."

"Isolation," said Holmes without delay. In the gloom of that strange morning, the word had an ominous ring.

"Not the social kind, of course," he added. "The fine brocade jacket and the expensive leather boots speak of a lady from a well-to-do family. No, this is a more insidious kind of isolation. Notice the lady's pitifully agitated state and the way she appears to be having an inner debate with herself. This is clearly a matter of great personal importance to her, yet one in which she is forced to partake by herself. How so? It could be a

183

matter of being faced with a situation that, despite manifesting unsettling surface appearances, may not have any overt aspects of wrongdoing that one might be able to put one's finger on. Or it may be something more sinister, something that she is unwilling or unable to share with anyone else. Either way, I have no doubt that we will find out soon enough."

No sooner had Holmes uttered the last word of his preliminary assessment than the lady, as if on cue, visibly pulled herself together, turned resolutely towards our front door, and crossed the street with a few brisk, determined steps. The next moment there was a knock on the door. A murmur of voices downstairs told us that the uniformed boy had answered the door, and a few moments later he knocked and popped into our sitting room to announce a Miss Meredith Pearson.

"Excellent," said Holmes. "Show the lady in, Billy."

The distressed young woman appeared in the doorway. She had evidently exerted a conscious effort to regain the outward appearance of composure, and had done so with no small amount of skill. The turmoil we had witnessed only a few minutes before was not entirely gone, however, for her eyes still betrayed a panic-stricken, haunted look.

"I must apologise, Mr. Holmes," said our visitor, "for coming here without prior notice, but something very distressing has happened and I don't know where else I can turn. I fear that unless something is done urgently, they will send me to a madhouse!"

"We shall be happy to assist you in any way we can, but I must first beg that you will present us with any relevant information that may aid us in finding a solution to your problem. Pray take a seat, Miss Pearson. This is my colleague Dr. Watson, before whom you can speak as freely as before myself. "

The lady seated herself on the sofa and took off her delicate gloves with cautious, measured movements, as if not trusting herself to perform this simple action properly. Meanwhile, I had taken a seat in my armchair while Holmes moved to stand in front of the fireplace, his expression keen and attentive.

"I fear," she said, "that I find myself at a loss as to where to begin, for the matter is such an unusual one that it borders on the fantastic. And yet, there is no one, save myself, who can attest to its veracity, as the one other person in whom I can confide is far away and shall not return for a while."

"Rest assured, Madam, that we do not doubt that your problem is a serious one, for only a matter of some gravity could have brought you here with such haste."

The lady looked bewildered at my friend's casual deduction. "How did you divine that, Mr. Holmes?"

"Your gloves, Madam, although both of a distinct shade of rose, differ in style. The left glove is unadorned, apart from a single button on the side, while the other has a fine lace lining. I'm convinced that a lady of such a refined fashion sense could hardly be compelled to go out in public with mismatched attire unless confronted with a matter of some urgency."

Miss Pearson blanched as she looked down at the gloves resting on her lap. It was obvious that she hadn't been aware of the mismatch until my friend had pointed it out to her.

"Your reasoning is correct, Mr. Holmes," said the lady in a low voice. "Something terrible happened last night that has nearly driven me mad with fear and worry.

Holmes calmed the lady with a few reassuring words and then begged her to inform us what it was that was troubling her.

"Pray start from the commencement," he added.

Miss Pearson hesitated for a moment, and then began to speak.

"I am the only daughter of Sir Richard Pearson, a classical philologist of some renown. My mother died when I was a child, and since then my father and I have lived a quiet life at our family's ancestral seat in Woodgate Manor, near Arundel, sharing the ancient manor house with just a handful of servants.

"Tell me about these servants," said Holmes.

"There is the old butler, Mr. Trenton, and the cook, Mrs. Giles, who took over after Mrs. Trenton passed away last year, and Amy, the maid who joined the household not long after, and Mr. Jameson, the coachman." The lady's brow creased in thought. "Oh, and there is also the groom, Geoffrey."

"Thank you," said Holmes. "Pray proceed with your narrative."

"About half-a-year ago, my father travelled to Somerset for the purpose of staying at a medicinal resort near Bath for three weeks, as he is wont to do every autumn, when his arthritic symptoms worsen with the weather. You can imagine my surprise, Mr. Holmes, when my dear father, who is now an old and ailing man, returned to Woodgate with a new wife – Sarah, a lady scarcely five years my senior. Since my mother's death, my father had been fully immersed in his studies, never showing the slightest inclination to remarry. And so it was no small shock to me that he should have done so in such an impetuous manner, and that his new wife should be such a young lady. Apparently, however, my father had become so taken with Sarah within days of meeting her that all rational considerations had been forsaken. He didn't even have the presence of mind to wire me the news of his impending marriage in advance. And as the whole affair happened so fast, my father and Sarah had no time to

185

arrange a formal wedding, choosing instead to have a small ceremony in St. Michael's Church in Bath.

"Despite the suddenness of it all, I didn't hesitate to show my father that I was happy for him and I went to great lengths to get along with Sarah. This last hasn't always been easy. For although my new stepmother is clearly devoted to my father and has barely left his side since her arrival, she is rather aloof with me. And it is as if her aloofness has passed on to my father, who hasn't been himself ever since Sarah came to live with us. Whereas previously he used to be the most doting of all fathers, he now barely has any time for me at all, devoting instead all of his attention to Sarah. I barely have the words to express how alone this sudden change in my father has made me feel and, indeed, had it not been for my childhood friend James Hartford, whose occasional visits were my only comfort during those difficult times, I do believe my life would have been unbearable. Alas, he was called away some time after Christmas to take up a new administrative post in India, but not before asking my hand in marriage. We are set to marry after his return in the autumn. I hope I am not digressing too much by mentioning these things, Mr. Holmes."

"On the contrary," said Holmes, "your narrative has been most informative. Pray continue."

"The events that I am about to relate," said Miss Pearson, "are of such outlandish and even preposterous nature that I scarcely know where to begin. But I will start with the departure of Mr. Hartford, for it was shortly after my friend left that some very odd things started happening around me. It began as a series of strange noises and fleeting impressions of shadows moving in dark corners behind me. As the days went by, the disturbances began more persistent. At first I dismissed these incidents as the products of fancy of a nervous woman who had been through a trying time, as echoes of childhood fears. Woodgate Manor is an old building, parts of it incorporating ancient structures that were used as watchtowers in Jacobean times. When I was a child growing up in such a lonely old building with few companions, I didn't like to linger in dark corners by myself for I feared there might be some ghost from ancient times lurking there. But I had never seen a ghost until a few months ago.

"It was a chilly morning in early February, and I was in the morning room after breakfast, busying myself with some light embroidery. There was no one else in the room apart from Amy, the maid, who was clearing out some dishes and tea things, quietly and almost imperceptibly as is her wont. My solitary diversion was interrupted by a sudden eerie sound, like a throaty moaning. Startled, I instinctively sprang to my feet and, looking up in the direction of the large mirror above the mantelpiece, I saw a terrifying figure reflected there. It had a most grotesque visage with leathery withered skin and horrific bulging eyes. Oh, Mr. Holmes, I was so frightened I nearly fainted from shock!

"I turned around, expecting to see an intruder, but there was no one. Only Amy, standing there with her duster in hand, looking as stunned as I felt.

"'Did you see it too?' I asked Amy.

"'See what, Madam?'

"'The thing in the mirror,' said I.

"'I saw nothing, Madam.'

"'Why do you look frightened then?'

"'Why, I am frightened of *you*, Miss Meredith!' said Amy.

"I need not tell you, Mr. Holmes," said our visitor, "that I lost no time in relating the story of the incident to my father and Sarah. To my dismay, however, neither of them appeared to be convinced by my account of the ghost. In fact, both of them seemed to put more credence in the version of the story told by Amy, who insisted on not having seen anything other than myself jumping at imaginary shadows. Amy's account appeared to give my stepmother the impression that I was under a considerable amount of mental strain, and that what I needed above all things was rest. Indeed, for a few days after the incident, my stepmother nursed me as if I were a stricken child, frequently voicing grave concern for my well-being.

"Following my convalescence, I tried to put the memory of the frightening incident behind me, but little did I suspect at the time that this was only the beginning of my troubles – for it didn't take long before disturbing things started happening around me again, things that only I seemed to be able to see or hear. Oh, it would have made anyone start to doubt one's own sanity! I tried to convey my anxieties to my father, as I knew he would have done everything in his power to soothe me and set things right had he been his old self. But the strange transformation that has come over him ever since Sarah took up residence in Woodgate Manor has rendered my appeals futile. Indeed, my only solace has come in the form of letters from Mr. Hartford, who has done his best to put my mind at ease, assuring me that all will be well once he returns and we are married. And for a while it looked as if things were turning for the better, when suddenly I experienced another shock.

"This was about three weeks after the incident in the morning room. One evening I sat by myself in the library, engrossed in a book, when a sudden movement that I saw from the corner of my eye, accompanied by a loud crash, made me leap to my feet. In an instant I saw what had been the cause of the noise. In a far corner by the antique books section, an expensive Grecian vase that was normally displayed on a stand now lay in pieces on the floor. But this wasn't the worst of it, for as my gaze followed the trail of scattered fragments, I beheld a dark figure standing in the shadows between two bookcases. As it stepped out, I could see what it was – a ghastly ghoul in a black cloak with dreadful glassy eyes that stared at me unblinkingly. The terrible sight made me scream with terror and, vision darkening, I fell into a swoon.

"When I came to, I was lying down, and my father and stepmother, as well as a smiling man I had never seen before, were by my bedside. This man introduced himself to me as Dr. Edward Thorpe, explaining that my stepmother, anxious about my mental equilibrium, had called him in. Dr. Thorpe proceeded to ask me a series of questions about the events in the library which seemed mystifying to me until I learned that, unbeknownst to me, Amy had also been present at the time of the incident, tidying up some shelves at the back of the library in her silent and unobtrusive way. And it seems that Amy's account of what had happened once again contradicted mine. According to Dr. Thorpe, when asked to recount the incident in the library, Amy swore that she had seen no mysterious figure in black and that it had been *I* who had broken the vase. To make matters worse, my father believes Amy's version of the story and seems to think that my own account is nothing but a product of an overstimulated fancy. Oh, I shall never forget the expression on his face as he gazed down upon me lying there like some poor delusional invalid."

This last remark seemed to throw Miss Pearson into a most pitiable state of distress, and we had to impart more than a few calming words before the lady was able to go on with her story.

"Since then," she said, "Dr. Thorpe has become a frequent visitor at Woodgate, attending to me on an almost daily basis. In fact, he has been around so often that he has practically become a friend of the family, and has even dined with us on several occasions. Despite my protestations to the contrary, he is insistent in his view that the incidents I have described to you have been mere products of my mind. His preferred remedy for this has been to prescribe even more rest. Oh, Mr. Holmes, I have been confined to my bed for such long periods of time in recent weeks that I have often felt like a prisoner. It is only due to my father and stepmother's having gone to Eastbourne for the day that I have managed to come to London at all."

"I see," said Holmes, but there was no way of telling what he saw. His face was like a mask. "Can you describe this Dr. Thorpe for me? Pray be precise as to the details."

"He is a man of middle age, with graying hair and a well-manicured beard. He is always impeccably dressed, with a tailored suit and a watch chain of gold. In his demeanor he is the perfect gentleman, although his manner can be rather histrionic at times. Underneath this affable veneer,

188

however, there is something about him that gives me pause, something that I cannot quite articulate. I have only caught the briefest glimpses of it on a few occasions – a cold, steely gaze here or an awkward silence there. This sinister air is accentuated by a curious scar on his face. It is long and thin, starting just under the corner of his eye and extending all the way down the cheek, where it is partly concealed by his beard."

"Thank you, Miss Pearson. Pray continue with your narrative, for I suspect it isn't yet complete."

"Indeed you are correct, Mr. Holmes, for I am yet to touch upon the dreadful matter that has driven me here with so much urgency. The event I refer to happened last night and, although trivial enough in itself, it has inadvertently brought to my awareness the true purpose of Dr. Thorpe's visits. It was about an hour after dinner, and I had been sitting in the drawing room with my father and stepmother before retiring to my room. As I got upstairs to my chamber and began to get ready to turn in, I realised that, as I still felt rather wakeful, I might prolong my evening and occupy myself with needlework for a while yet. Remembering, however, that I had left the small basket where I keep my embroidery things in the drawing room, I went downstairs to retrieve it.

"As I reached the closed double door of the drawing room, I could hear the voices of my father and stepmother coming from inside. There was something about their tone that made me pause outside the door. My stepmother was telling my father something in a hushed, urgent voice. As I stood there, overcome with a surging sense of dread that made me unable to move, I realised that they were talking about me.

"'It would be for her own safety,' I heard my stepmother say.

"'I do confess to be in agreement with your views, Sarah,' said my father, 'but perhaps it is too soon to make a final decision.'

"'Dr. Thorpe says that we must act now, lest she come to harm. Oh, Richard, you know Meredith better than anyone. How can you go on pretending that there is nothing wrong, when she is clearly not herself anymore? Inventing fanciful tales to attract attention, accusing poor Amy of telling lies, smashing things around the house. Who knows what she might do next? She may well harm herself!'

"'I have no doubt that you are right, my dear. I am still, however, not wholly convinced that she is mad.'

"'What other proof do you need, Richard? You wouldn't want something terrible to happen to her, would you?'

"'Of course not, my dear.'

"'We should heed Dr. Thorpe's advice then. He is a respected alienist, and has seen many cases of this kind. We should trust him then when he says that confinement in a special institution is the only thing that can possibly save her. And he has been kind enough to find a spot for her in Thornton Asylum. I hear that it is a very charming, rustic place with sea views. And it is only an hour's train journey from here. We would be able to visit often. Think about it, darling. This would be for Meredith's own good.'

"As you can imagine, Mr. Holmes," said our visitor, "upon hearing all this, I was left in a state of considerable agitation. Barely able to suppress a wave of nausea, I rushed back to my room, where I stayed up all night trying to find any way to end this plight. It was nearly dawn when I remembered Mr. Hartford telling me on one occasion of an outstanding detective in London who had been able to help people with the most unusual problems. I had no difficulties recalling your name, for Mr. Hartford had uttered it more than a few times, always with a sense of admiration. And so I knew that I had to come and see you the very next day, that you might be the one person who might be able to help me in my hour of need. Mr. Hartford would have done everything in his powers to help me, were he but here, but alas, he is unable to do anything from halfway across the globe. And by the time he comes back – Oh, I dread to even think! By then it may be too late. Once they put me into an asylum, they might keep me from seeing James, and I might never be allowed to leave the confines of Thornton again. Oh, will you help me, Mr. Holmes? I assure you that I am not mad, and everything I have told you is the truth!"

"My dear Madam, pray have no fear, for I do believe you," said Holmes in an earnest voice. "I don't doubt your sanity in the slightest. And you have acted wisely in coming to see me."

"Oh, Mr. Holmes, what is the meaning of this disturbing situation? And what am I to do?"

"It's too early to tell with any level of certainty as to what lies at the root of this business. There are still a number of things I should like to know before I'm able to form an opinion on the matter. What is certain, however, is that this is a deeply complex, troubling problem, and that the solution may not be an easy one. You have provided us with sufficient data to get started with an investigation, but there is one further detail that may be of use to us. You have said that Dr. Thorpe has been a frequent visitor at Woodgate Manor as of late. Has the esteemed physician by any chance been invited to dine at the manor again?"

"As a matter of fact, he has, Mr. Holmes. He will be dining with us again tomorrow evening."

"Excellent!" The keen look in my friend's eyes suggested that he had already formed some sort of plan. "Now, Miss Pearson, I have reason to believe that whatever it is that has been causing you trepidation in recent weeks may well show its face again tomorrow evening. It is imperative that you stay calm regardless of what happens. You need not fear for your safety, for Dr. Watson and myself will be on hand somewhere out of sight to ensure that you don't come to harm. Until then, I strongly suggest that you return to Woodgate without further ado to avoid arousing anyone's suspicions as to the true purpose of your coming to London."

"I do not understand the meaning of anything that has been happening recently, Mr. Holmes, but I will do as you say."

My friend assured our client that we would do everything in our powers to help her find a way out of her predicament. The equanimity of his tone seemed to visibly set the lady's mind at ease. Miss Pearson bade us good morning and bustled out of the room, while Holmes stood looking at the vacant space she had left behind with a sharp yet inscrutable gaze.

Baffled by the strange tale Miss Pearson had told us, I couldn't help interrupting his meditation. "By Jove, Holmes," said I, "this seems to me a most sinister and mystifying business. I must admit that I am completely at a loss as to what might be behind this case. Why should Miss Pearson suddenly start seeing phantoms?"

"Pshaw, Watson!" said Holmes, snapping out of his reverie. "Those are no phantoms that Miss Pearson spoke of. There is some foul play at work here, of that I have no doubt. Someone is trying to make this poor lady think that she has gone mad in order to have her committed. The questions are who, and to what end?"

"Have you already formed an opinion as to the answer to either of those questions?"

Holmes leaned against the mantelpiece with one elbow propped on top. "If we combine the elements of Miss Pearson's impending marriage to Mr. Hartford," he said, "and the latter's prolonged absence, this posits the prevention of their union as the foundation of the possible motive behind the sudden onset of the harassment of our client. The concurrent appearance of this Dr. Thorpe and his vocal advocacy of institutionalising Miss Pearson as the only viable cure for the lady's recent nervous outburst suggests that he may have a hand in the affair. In what way, however, might he profit from getting Miss Pearson out of the way and preventing her marriage? This question, along with several other outstanding ones, must be answered if we are to understand the nature of our client's predicament."

With that, Holmes sprang into action and headed for the door.

"Where are you going?" I asked.

"I have some inquiries to make," he said. "I should be back before supper."

191

When Holmes returned that evening, I could see by glancing at his strained face that his investigation hadn't been as fruitful as he may have hoped. Ignoring my expectant look, he flung himself into the armchair across from me and sat brooding for a few minutes in morose silence.

"Well, Watson," he said at last, "this business truly is maddening in more ways than one."

"Does this mean that you haven't found any answers?"

"I fear that the few answers I have unearthed only serve to beget more questions. Troubling ones. I do believe that this case may be even more sinister than I initially suspected."

Lighting a pipe, which had an immediate restorative effect on his mood, he began to relate what he had discovered.

"As my investigation," he said, "is based on the assumption that the doctor may have some hidden interest in committing Miss Pearson to an asylum for the mentally unsound, my starting point was to gather any data on Dr. Thorpe that might help me form a clear picture as to his involvement in the matter. There are, however, no existing records of any practicing physicians that go by the name Dr. Edward Thorpe. We can therefore conclude that Dr. Thorpe is a false identity assumed by someone who in all likelihood isn't a real doctor.

"Since the name has proved to be a false lead, my next step was to attempt to trace the man by the detailed description provided by Miss Pearson. The good lady's reference to Dr. Thorpe's unique scar immediately struck me as a point of interest, for it brought to mind the trial of Xavier Zeldt, the hypnotist. Have you any recollection of the case?"

"I cannot say that I do."

"Xavier Yves Zeldt was a former illusionist who later embarked upon a career as a hypnotist. He started off by performing mesmerism tricks on stage as a crowd-pleasing novelty act, but soon moved on to providing private sessions as a form of medical treatment. This proved to be a rather successful venture until one of his patients, a young widow by the name of Elizabeth Stowe, attacked him with a penknife during one of their sessions, slashing his cheek, only to die within a few hours of unexplained causes. Zeldt was put on trial for murder but acquitted due to insufficient evidence.

"It was only a short trial and didn't generate much publicity. I had to go to Scotland Yard to find out anything beyond the most basic facts. The information that I did obtain as to Zeldt's physical appearance is very much in line with the physical description provided by Miss Pearson. Moreover, for a skillful manipulator and impersonator like Zeldt, who once already made an effortless leap from being an illusionist to being a hypnotist, shifting his occupation to that of an alienist may be a logical next step. And as there have been no conclusive records as to his whereabouts since the trial, which took place some three years ago, one is tempted to consider the possibility that Xavier Yves Zeldt and Dr. Edward Thorpe might in fact be the same person."

"Good Lord! What could this possibly mean for Miss Pearson?"

"It means that the poor lady is being preyed on by a subtle yet dangerous villain. And she may not be the only one."

Before I had a chance to ask Holmes to explain the meaning of this cryptic remark, there was a soft, hesitant knock on our door, followed by a louder, more determined one. The next instant a young, plainly dressed woman stepped hesitantly into our sitting room. She was unwholesomely thin and her pale, prematurely aged face spoke of years of vice and ill use. Nevertheless, there was a quiet, self-possessed air about her.

"I'm sorry for troubling you, gentlemen," she said to us, looking from one to the other as if unsure whom to address. "But I need to speak to Mr. Holmes. The lady who was here this morning may have mentioned me. I am Amy Briggs, Miss Pearson's housemaid."

"Indeed." Holmes gave the girl an acute searching look. "And might I inquire as to the chain of events that led Miss Pearson to divulge information regarding her visit to you?"

"She didn't, sir," said the girl. "That is to say, she didn't divulge anything to me. A lady like Miss Meredith would never have told someone like me about her plans. I know I have no right to be here, sir, and I never would have come, if I hadn't found out by chance that she was coming to London to see you. You see, this morning, as I was sweeping her room, I saw a note with your name and address written on it. The poor innocent had left it there on her bedside table, never suspecting for one moment that someone else might see it while she was out. So when I saw her going out, I knew this could only be in order to seek you out, sir. And I knew right there and then that I had to pay you a visit myself."

"And for what reason?" asked Holmes.

"Well, sir, I have no way of knowing what precise things Miss Meredith may have related to you, but I can tell you right away that whatever it was she might have told you, I know more about the matter than she does. I have been suspecting for a while that Miss Meredith might be catching on to what has been brewing around her, for even someone as innocent as her is bound to wise up sooner or later. Oh, if only she knew the whole story! Whatever she may think is going on, I assure you the truth is even worse. I should know, as I have been a part of the evil scheme being plotted around her from the start. But I will have no part in it anymore, so I decided to come to you right away and tell you whatever you need to know to help this poor lady. I didn't wish to arouse Sir

193

Richard's suspicions by following Miss Meredith directly and so, as I have the afternoon off, I waited until the end of my shift and then I came straight to you."

"You have our attention, Miss Briggs," said Holmes without taking his eyes off the girl. "Pray take a seat. I am Sherlock Holmes, and this is my colleague Dr. Watson. We would be glad to listen to your account."

The girl took a seat on the far end of the sofa and began to speak.

"Well, Mr. Holmes, it's like this: I'll be the first to admit I'm nobody's idea of a Good Samaritan, and if you're having doubts as to my true reasons for being here, I don't blame you for it. My life has not always been an unhappy one, but circumstances have made me do things that anyone would be ashamed of. I wasn't always so. My childhood was a happy one, and I received a decent enough education. But then it all fell apart when my father was thrown into debtor's prison, leaving my mother and me reduced to the streets. My poor mother didn't last long in such miserable circumstances, and I soon found myself having to do certain things to make ends meet. But I assure you that whatever evil things I may have done, they pale in comparison to the misdeeds of this so-called Dr. Thorpe. It takes a sinner to know a sinner, and I was there from the start, back in those days when he was still known as Xavier Yves Zeldt.

"He began his career as an illusionist, performing parlour tricks for and taking part in variety shows in the West End. I was his stage assistant in those days, handing out leaflets, selling refreshments, lying down in a box to be sawn in half, or doing any other thing that had to be done to run the show. It was hard work, but still better than some of the things I was doing when I first met him." She briefly averted her gaze to the floor, before continuing with her narrative.

"Xavier," she said, "started using mesmerism to enliven his acts, but he soon discovered that this dark art had other uses too. He'd always had a way with women, using his charms to make them do his will, and he soon found women to be easy prey for his hypnotism tricks. They were the perfect subjects for his experiments in hypnosis, and before long he had established himself as a practicing hypnotist. With his wily ways, he had no difficulties getting himself invited to the homes of well-off ladies who had nothing to do and sought any kind of diversion. He claimed to be able to use hypnosis to cure minor ailments, but in reality he was learning how to play with the minds of unsuspecting women, using his home visits to single out those that might be of use to him for his own evil purposes.

"One of these special ladies was a young widow called Edith Peters, and another a clerk's daughter by the name of Elizabeth Stowe. Both of them fell under his spell and became passionately enamoured of him. Poor fools! Their devotion, however, suited Xavier just fine, and he played them both like fiddles, biding his time until he was certain as to how to best make use of them. I was now his maidservant, as his mesmerism practice had by now enabled him to live in comfort in a sizable town house in Hampstead. This meant that I was able to witness the events as they unfolded.

"Trouble began when each woman learned about the existence of the other. If you ask me, Xavier allowed this to happen on purpose, just to be able to see their reactions, for he is a cruel and heartless devil. Whether he expected this or not, this sent both women into a jealous fury. The younger of them, Elizabeth Stowe, was particularly affected. The poor thing seemed unable to bear the thought that Xavier had been deceiving her. The next time he came round to her house, she was seized by a fit of rage and slashed his face with a pen knife. On the evening of the same day she died. She had taken a large dose of laudanum that no one knew how she had come by. There was police business over it, and as Xavier was an obvious suspect, having visited her house on the day of her death, he was put on trial for murder. In the end, however, he was acquitted, as they couldn't prove it was him who had made her take the fatal dose. There had been no sign of struggle or coercion of any kind.

"Now I have no way of proving this, Mr. Holmes, and even if I did, who would listen to someone as lowly as myself? But I'm sure that he did it! I know this the way I know night follows day. He murdered Elizabeth Stowe. Whether he tricked her into drinking a large dose somehow, or whether he played some mind trick that made her take the drug herself, he murdered her all the same."

"One moment," interrupted Holmes. "Were there any witnesses present at the time of this incident who could shed some more light on his involvement? Did the police question anyone?"

"No, Mr. Holmes," said Miss Briggs. "The Stowes were trusting enough to leave that poor girl alone with him. There was an old female servant present in the house at the time, but she was in the kitchen and had heard nothing."

"Thank you, Miss Briggs. Pray continue."

"Well," said the girl, "I might be many things, but the one thing I'm not is a fool. I knew right away that something was off. And I told him as much.

"'And what do you know about this business, little Amy?' asked Xavier in his cloying voice.

"'Only what is plain for anyone with a pair of eyes to see – that it's very strange that this young creature, who had her whole life ahead of her, should take her own life after starting hypnotherapy with you.'

"His answer to this was an icy stare that would have chilled you to the bone.

"'Little Amy,' he murmured, 'how bold you are now – so unlike that person you were when I first met you. Remember what you were like back then, little Amy?'

"I said I didn't wish to.

"'Just a frightened little thing in the street,' he answered in my stead. 'I am the one who took you off the streets, and I am the one who can put you back there. Would you like that to happen, little Amy?'

"I told him I wouldn't.

"'In that case, little Amy would do well to not say a word about this ever again.'

"So I kept my mouth shut and continued being his servant. Meanwhile, he had married Edith Peters for her late husband's money, but this soon proved to be insufficient to fund his ever-increasing cravings for luxurious living. Being a cunning fiend, Xavier soon realised that his talent for manipulating the minds of gullible women could give him access to ladies of an even higher standing, and thus greater financial opportunities. And so, after the end of the trial, he and Edith moved out of London and he began calling himself 'Dr. Edward Thorpe, Alienist'. He put all his acting talents into presenting himself as a respected practitioner in the field, discovering that people were easily deceived by a respectable outward appearance and a smooth, educated voice.

"Xavier's new line of work brought him new clients in high places. It also gave him the power to diagnose someone as insane. This gave him some new ideas. It didn't take long for someone as cunning as Xavier to put these things together and come up with a scheme that would bring him the sort of riches he desired once. But in order to put his plans into effect, it was necessary to find the right victim.

"As he still had me in his thrall, he began using me as something of a scout. He would write glowing letters of recommendation for me designed to make any wealthy gentleman looking for a housemaid wish to hire me on the spot. My mission was to become familiar with each household I entered and to report to him every single detail that would help him make an assessment. If he decided that the situation didn't suit his plans, I'd make some kind of excuse and leave, before being dispatched to the next place.

"After a few false starts, last spring I was hired as a housemaid in Woodgate Manor. After reading the initial reports I had sent to him, Xavier became convinced that Woodgate might be just the opportunity he had been looking for. The setup looked ideal – a feeble old man practically on his deathbed with a single daughter, a wonderfully weak-willed one, sitting all by themselves on a pile of money in the midst of the Sussex countryside. All this would eventually pass on to the daughter – that is to say, Miss Meredith – unless Xavier found a way to relieve her of her inheritance. Marriage wasn't an option, as the lady already had a fiancé to whom she was devoted. And so Xavier devised an elaborate scheme to make Miss Meredith appear insane and have her committed to an asylum.

"As Sir Richard himself was deemed unlikely to agree to commit his only daughter to an asylum on his own initiative, Xavier decided to bring to the scene another one of the women he had under his spell, one whom he would use as his agent to manipulate Sir Richard into bringing about the outcome he desired. For this purpose he chose Sarah, another one of his old hypnotherapy patients, and after instructing her how to act and what to say, he arranged for her to be present in Bath, under the guise of a well-off lady of leisure, at the same time as Sir Richard, who sojourns there for medicinal reasons every year in the autumn."

"Pardon my interruption," said Holmes, "but is this the whole truth?"

Miss Briggs paused her narrative and looked down at her hands for a moment.

"Or are you shielding someone? Edith Peters perhaps?"

"You've guessed right, Mr. Holmes," said the girl after another moment's hesitation. "I wanted to keep Edith's name out of it, as she's just another poor fool that's being used, but you've guessed it yourself, sir. I suppose there never was a chance of keeping this concealed if the whole matter ever came to light. Yes, this person posing as Sarah, the one who married Sir Richard, is no other than Xavier's own wife, Edith."

"Quite so," said Holmes.

I was quite appalled by this revelation, but did my best not to show it. My friend, however, didn't appear to be affected in the least.

"In fact, Mr. Holmes," continued Miss Briggs, "when Xavier decided he needed another accomplice to enact his scheme, Edith was his first choice, as she is as malleable as bread dough and willing to follow any command. He thought nothing of having his own wife marry someone else under a false name, as to him women are nothing but tools to be used for his own purposes. Her protests were short-lived, as he has complete control over her mind and can make her do whatever he demands.

"Edith was adept at applying Xavier's mind manipulation tricks on Sir Richard, and had him under her thumb in a matter of days. By the end of his residence in Bath, they were already married. The old senile fool, if you'll pardon me for using those words, sir, was so infatuated that he never questioned for one moment why an attractive young lady such as Edith should suddenly fall at an old man's feet, renouncing all desire to do anything other than be at his side at all times. This was precisely where

Xavier wanted her, in order for her to be able to act as a constant channel of his own will.

"After Sir Richard returned to Woodgate with his new wife, my own duties were extended. Now I was no longer just a spy, but a resident ghost as well. Xavier didn't wish to leave anything to chance. When he was inevitably called to the scene as Dr. Thorpe, his diagnosis of Miss Meredith's insanity had to look convincing. Therefore Miss Meredith shouldn't only *appear* to be mad – Rather, she should actually be *driven* mad. As my own probing into her past revealed childhood fears of ghosts, Xavier chose to use fear at the means of driving the poor lady insane – fear of Woodgate ghosts. And so he sent me detailed instructions as to what I had to do to terrify the girl, even going so far as to provide me with a special mask. That horrible ugly thing! I have no idea where he found it. I suppose he had it custom made.

"As things turned out, I played my part all too well. And how would I not – to someone who was once an illusionist's assistant, playing out the tricks that Xavier came up with wasn't a problem at all. That poor girl – I nearly drove her out of her mind with terror! As soon as her nervous state became apparent, Sir Richard's devoted wife advised him to call in a doctor that she claimed was known to have helped people with nervous disorders in the past – the eminent alienist Dr. Edward Thorpe. Sir Richard, who had by now become entirely dependent on his new wife, believing every word she said, consented. And Xavier played the part from the moment he stepped onto the scene, awing Sir Richard with his learned talk while making poor Miss Meredith doubt her own sanity.

"The next stage of Xavier's game was to go after Miss Meredith's money. And so as soon as the poor lady started jumping at shadows, Xavier put Edith – as Sarah – to work to talk Sir Richard into changing his will. Miss Meredith was Sir Richard's only heir, and the entire estate would have gone to her after his death, but Sarah, as I'll continue to call her, talked the old man into thinking that this was a terrible idea, considering the girl's fragile mental state. And how she talked! Sarah talked and talked incessantly, sitting by his side without ever leaving him alone for so much as a minute. She was constantly telling him all those things Xavier taught her to say, over and over again. And she succeeded!

"Sir Richard gave in and made a change to his will. Poor Miss Meredith doesn't even know yet, for Sir Richard hadn't the heart to tell her. The old fool, if you'll pardon me for saying that, thinks things will just work out for the best in their own time. According to the new provisions, should Miss Meredith become incapacitated, Sarah will inherit the entire fortune. This, of course, means Xavier. Sir Richard isn't expected to live long. And after he is gone, Xavier won't waste time making it look as if the old man's widow has sought consolation by getting married again – to Dr. Thorpe, of course, the gallant doctor who was always there for her when she was in need.

"And he's getting very close, Mr. Holmes! There's only one thing that remains to be done, and that is to convince Sir Richard that Miss Meredith really has gone mad. Sarah has been working on him tirelessly, filling his mind with all kinds of deceit, and she's already nearly succeeded in turning him against his own daughter, making him believe that she has to be removed for everyone's sake. But there is still some of the old Sir Richard left in him, and it's only this that has been shielding Miss Meredith from a terrible fate. So Xavier must remove this final obstacle, and he wants this to be done quickly too, as he wants Miss Meredith out of the way before her young fellow comes back from overseas.

"This he intends to achieve by making another move tomorrow night, when he will be dining with the Pearsons again. He has devised another scare for Miss Meredith – his check-mate move – and wants me to help him stage it. But unlike the previous times, when there was no one else around besides Miss Meredith and myself, this time I am to do this performance in the presence of Sir Richard and the others, during dinner. Xavier has given me detailed instructions as to what tricks I need to use and where exactly I need to stand in order to make sure that it is only Miss Meredith who sees the ghastly spectacle and is driven into another terrified reaction. I am to stand behind Sir Richard, you see, in a very particular spot that Xavier has chosen for best effect. But that isn't all, Mr. Holmes. Xavier has also given me a vial of laudanum that he wants me to slip into poor Miss Meredith's tea before dinner, to make sure she isn't herself when she gets her little scare. This time, he really does want the poor thing to be driven out of her mind!

"Well, sir, it was this request that made me decide that I've had enough of it. I don't want to do this anymore. All this has the makings of another Elizabeth Stowe scenario, and I want no part in it. At first I didn't know what to do or whom to ask for help. But when I learned of Miss Meredith intention to consult a private detective, one that even Xavier himself has sometimes spoken of, and always with a sense of awe, I knew what I had to do. I decided that if Miss Meredith was going to ask for your help, then I may as well do whatever I can in my humble way to help you save her. Even if confessing to have been Xavier's accomplice puts the law on me, this is still a small price to pay just to be free of him. And that is my entire sad story, sir, for what it's worth."

"Thank you, Miss Briggs," said Holmes, who had been listening to the girl's story with a rapt expression. "Your timely and edifying account has certainly given me a number of things to meditate upon. May I just ask why it is that you haven't gone to the police instead of seeing me? It does appear as if you already possess enough material evidence to have Xavier Zeldt put under investigation. At the very least, your knowledge of Sarah's true identity and the fact that she was already married at the time of her marrying Sir Richard would be a solid enough basis to annul their union. This would immediately bring Xavier Zeldt's entire house of cards down."

"Oh, no, sir!" The girl shifted uncomfortably in her seat. "I wouldn't go to the police. If you'll permit my saying so, I don't believe they would be any match for him. He would find a way to outwit them, of this I have no doubt. And besides," she added, looking away to the floor, "I very much doubt that they would believe someone like me."

The untold tale of a sordid, sinful past that lay behind the girl's implication made me look away with embarrassment for a moment. Holmes, as ever, was unfazed.

"That is perfectly understandable, Miss Briggs," he said. "And you have done a great service to Miss Pearson by coming to see us. Have you a safe or a drawer with a lock and key in your room?

"Only a small one under the bedside table."

"Then I suggest you put the vial that Zeldt gave you there and save it as evidence. Apart from that, don't do anything out of the ordinary until Zeldt has been apprehended."

"But what about tomorrow evening, sir? I really don't want to play another trick on that poor girl."

"If all goes well, you will not have to. But promise me, Miss Briggs, that you will not do anything that would give Zeldt a reason to become suspicious."

The girl promised that she wouldn't and with that, Holmes thanked her again and showed her out.

"Well, Watson," he said once we were alone again, "what do you make of this curious tale?"

"Very curious indeed," said I. "It certainly is a most peculiar and sinister case. To think that a woman should be persuaded to marry an old man she has never met by her own husband for profit is a detail that struck me as being particularly reprehensible."

"Indeed. It has, however, confirmed my suspicion that Zeldt must have had an ally on the inside from the start. That this person should be Sir Richard's new wife was a logical inference, as was the necessary conclusion that she had to be someone close to Zeldt. As the records of the Zeldt trial pointed to there being no women in his inner circle other than his wife, Edith Zeldt, this immediately led me to the improbable yet logical conclusion that Edith Zeldt and the woman posing as Sir Richard's wife were in fact one and the same person. Miss Briggs' account has corroborated my theory. This, however, hasn't made the solution easier."

"What do you mean?"

"Only that the fact of Mrs. Pearson's true identity places yet another fine layer of complexity upon the already intricate web that surrounds our client. So far we've had not only phantoms and fleeting impressions to contend with, but also the tragedy of a manipulated father and the presence of an elusive villain who can easily choose to disappear. Now, on top of it all, we have got the added weight of a sham marriage which, if exposed, may yet further the old man's mental deterioration."

"But Holmes," said I, "isn't the fact of this sham marriage the very thing that could be employed to effect the quickest solution for removing the threat facing Miss Pearson? Once this fact has been brought to light, the darkness that has been clouding Sir Richard's judgement will no doubt disperse, compelling him to put an end to any idea of committing his only daughter to an insane asylum."

"Your views aren't without merit, Watson. Alas, their validity extends only to a certain degree. For this potential quick solution to expose Zeldt's scheme may just as quickly become a double-edged sword. This whole affair has been built upon subjective impressions and the control thereof by means of various manipulative tactics. Facts, meanwhile, have been of little value. Were we to inform Sir Richard of the mere facts while neglecting the many impressions he has been manipulated to adopt, the Zeldts may well find a way to manoeuvre this to their advantage, perhaps by making 'Sarah' look like a victim of false accusations. To someone who has been as entrenched in the Zeldts' web of lies as Sir Richard, any shocking revelations about his wife may compel him, in his addled state, to perceive this as a personal attack against her. This may inadvertently lead to his fully siding with Sarah, which would, in turn, make his attitude to Miss Pearson even more hostile."

"What do you propose to do then?" I asked.

"To present the revelation of the truth in such a way as to make Mrs. Pearson show her true allegiance at the same time."

"My dear Holmes, I must confess that your meaning entirely eludes me."

"Watson, think about it: Mrs. Pearson has been rigorously trained by her true husband, Zeldt, to perform the role of Sir Richard's wife to perfection. Her act, however, is confined to the boundaries of the predictable monotony of life in Woodgate Manor. If, however, the lady is confronted with something as unexpected as being called out for what she truly is by an unannounced visitor during such a social occasion, the mask of her stage persona is bound to slip. She is bound to turn to Zeldt for guidance, thus giving herself away. By thus exposing the Zeldt's scheme, we should be able to bring Sir Richard to reason, and thereby help our client escape the fate that awaits her unless we intervene."

"But by making that kind of shock appearance, we would be putting ourselves at a considerable amount of risk."

"Quite so. It is precisely for this reason that while I was out, I took the liberty to wire the Sussex County Constabulary in Lewes. One of their officers will be on standby in the Woodgate area tomorrow afternoon. I presume you aren't averse to a short trip to Sussex?"

"Not at all."

"Excellent! Look up the trains then. Something around three in the afternoon would be ideal. We don't want to arrive there too early."

I was already leafing through my *Bradshaw*. "There is a train at half-past-two, departing from London Bridge."

"Well done, Watson. That's settled then," said Holmes and began to refill his pipe. He didn't bring up the strange case of Woodgate Manor for the rest of the evening.

When we set out for Arundel around two o'clock the next day, the muddy grey clouds that had darkened my mood since the previous day still lingered in patches above us. As the train chugged along the tracks, passing through the countryside that emerged around us as soon as we had left the outskirts of London behind, the clouds became more dispersed, but the sun still failed to show itself. Against such a subdued backdrop, even the many sheep and cows that dotted the rolling hills looked downcast.

At Arundel Station, we hired a trap that carried us down the five miles of country lanes leading to Woodgate Manor. Just outside the gate we were met by Samuel Braddon of the Sussex County Constabulary. He was an amiable fellow of about thirty who held my friend's accomplishments in high esteem. Having surveyed the premises prior to our arrival, he was now able to escort us down a side where we were least likely to be seen. As we approached Woodgate Manor, an oddly fortress-like building whose crumbling turrets towered high above the grounds, I was struck by the thought that such stealth was unnecessary, for the whole place appeared utterly lifeless. Not a soul stirred, not a sound could be heard apart from the buzzing of insects, and I was instantly reminded of those fairy tales where the inhabitants of an entire castle are put under a sleeping spell. The highest of the turrets, whose coarse limestone walls and large windows near the top made it stand out from the rest of the building, was evidently the ancient watchtower of which Miss Pearson had spoken.

Holmes instructed Constable Braddon to wait for us by the decorative shrubs to the side of the main entrance, and then the two of us set off in the direction of the side door.

"Be on your guard, Watson," Holmes said. "Something is amiss here."

My friend's forecast was confirmed as we went past the windows of the ground floor dining room gallery, for therein no formal dinner was in progress. We soon found a side door that had been left open as promised. Once inside, we found ourselves in a deserted corridor with a high vaulted ceiling and a row of stained-glass windows on one side that didn't let in much light. The air had the still, oppressive atmosphere of a place that doesn't see much activity, and the house was silent apart from our footsteps. As we trod cautiously further on through the semi-darkness, we came upon a deep recess on the right which, upon closer inspection, was revealed to be the foot of a winding stairwell, no doubt going up to the ancient watchtower, for the masonry was much older than the rest of the house.

Holmes paused and pricked up his ears, as if sensing some movement above. After a few moments, I too was able to discern a faint scuffling sound.

And then, a woman's voice screamed, "Mr. Holmes!"

"It's Miss Pearson!" I exclaimed. But Holmes had already bolted up the stairs. I followed, nearly tripping up the steep steps in my haste.

At the top of the stairs we found the remains of the ancient lookout, which was now filled with large heaps of clutter, including an old church organ, the back of which loomed on the left and a large six-panel walnut folding screen on the right. In the midst of it all stood an elegantly dressed middle-aged man whose impeccably groomed features left no doubt that this was the false doctor whose real name was Xavier Zeldt.

"Ah, Mr. Holmes." Zeldt's voice was as serene as his face, but his eyes were icy. "I have been expecting you. And might this be your colleague, Dr. Watson? Welcome, welcome, gentlemen! I am very pleased to make your acquaintance. I believe you already know who I am. My patient, Miss Pearson, may have spoken to you about me. The young lady thought that she was being discreet, but it is a doctor's business to know his patients' secrets. Wouldn't you agree, Mr. Holmes?"

"Where is Miss Pearson?" asked Holmes, ignoring the tone of Zeldt's strangely mesmerising monologue.

"You would like to see her?" asked Zeldt with the same calming voice, his eyes strangely unblinking. "I am afraid I cannot permit that at this moment. You see, Mr. Holmes, Miss Pearson isn't feeling well, and I have had no choice but to have her sedated. Her father, upset by the sudden

203

worsening of his daughter's health, has fallen ill himself and is now being watched over by his devoted wife. It saddens me to say that the dinner that was meant to take place in my honour this evening has been called off. The lady of the house has been good enough to let the house staff have the evening off, so I do believe we are on our own here.

"What have you done to Miss Pearson?" Holmes took a step towards Zeldt. The ancient wooden floor boards creaked under his feet. "And where is Miss Briggs?"

Zeldt took a small step back, his form framed between the side of the church organ and the outer edge of folding screen. The two objects stood on either side of him like parts of a grotesque theatre set.

"Ah, yes, Miss Briggs," said Zeldt. "She too has been to see you recently? Oh dear, how reckless of the girl. You see, Mr. Holmes, I must know what these two ladies have told you about me. I fear that both are currently suffering from an imbalanced state of mind, the kind that is liable to make afflicted young ladies invent fanciful tales, even untruths about persons associated with them, including their own physician. And a respected professional would be unwise to allow his reputation to be so mischievously tarnished. Wouldn't you agree, Mr. Holmes?"

A soft whimpering moan sounded from behind the high Gothic panel of the church organ.

"Miss Pearson is somewhere at the back of this room," said Holmes in a sharp tone. "You will either let us pass or we will remove you."

"As you wish, Mr. Holmes." Zeldt stepped aside, revealing a shocking tableau behind him. On the opposite side, Miss Pearson leaned wanly on the edge of one of the tower's many large paneless windows, looking as if about to plunge down to the ground any moment.

"Good Lord!" I gasped.

"Watson, wait!" Holmes gripped my forearm as I was about to jump to Miss Pearson's rescue. "This is a trick."

"Is that really what you believe?" said Zeldt in his strange lilting voice from where he now stood behind us. "Is this the reason why you will abandon this lady to her fate?"

Holmes slowly turned back to look at Zeldt, and I could tell by his hard stare that my friend had had enough of the soft-spoken self-proclaimed alienist. It was then that an apparition stepped out from behind the folds of the screen on the right. It was a ghostly pale woman with long red hair dressed in a flowing lavender gown.

"Xavier, why did you kill me?" whispered the spectre in an eerie voice. Zeldt, startled, turned in the direction of the voice, and in an instant the figure of the calm doctor was transformed into a blanched, frightened wreck. Letting out a piercing shriek of pure terror, he reflexively took a step back and stumbled at the top of the stairwell. Unable to keep balance, he keeled backwards and tumbled down the winding flight of steep limestone steps. I rushed down to where Zeldt now lay at the bottom of the stairs, only to discover that he had broken his neck in the fall and died instantly.

My friend hadn't bothered to follow. When I came back up to the lookout, informing him of Zeldt's fate, he was supporting a semi-conscious Miss Pearson, with the apparition, who, on closer inspection, was revealed to be Miss Briggs in disguise, hovering anxiously nearby. They were, however, not where I had expected them to be, by the window on the opposite side where we had last seen Miss Pearson, but standing in front of the church organ. At the spot where Miss Pearson had been leaning over the edge of the window, there was now only a tall mirror.

"It was an illusionist's trick, Watson," explained Holmes. "Miss Pearson was never on that side. She was here all along, leaning against the keyboard of the church organ, and it was her reflection that we saw in front of the window, expertly set up so that it looked exactly as intended. It was a clever ploy indeed, and Zeldt had thought of every detail but one – the direction of the shadows in the reflected image."

"I'm afraid, Holmes, that I don't see what you mean."

"You see, Watson, but you do not observe. Take a look at the mirror over there. Notice that we can see the sun through the window behind the mirror and that the light is reflected off our faces? Someone standing on the other side in the position Miss Pearson was in when we initially saw her, her back to the window, would have had her face in a shadow as the sun would have been coming from behind. And yet there was direct sunlight on Miss Pearson's face. This could only mean that the lady was in fact positioned on *this* side, facing the window, whereas it was her reflection that was visible on the opposite side. It was this detail that made me realise that what we were looking at was an illusion."

My friend's methodical, unaffected explanation of this brilliant display of dazzling mental power made me feel almost overcome with a sense of awe. There was still, however, one detail that I was unable to understand.

"But Holmes," I said, "to what end would Zeldt arrange such an elaborate trick?" Deciding, as I spoke, to see if I could find clues as to this mystery myself, I took a step towards the mirror. Holmes immediately pulled me back.

"Don't, Watson," he said, "unless you want to end up like our friend Zeldt. I suspected that parts of this ancient wooden floor have crumbled off over the years, and there is now a large hole in the centre of the floor that has been covered up by a rug. Underneath it there is a sheer drop five storeys high. Had we rushed in to help Miss Pearson, we would have plunged to our deaths."

"Good Heavens!" I cried. "But why would he have gone out of his way to kill us?"

"Quite possibly because he was none-too-pleased that a detective should have been informed of his scheme. He had gone so far with the Pearsons that he didn't want to lose it all, now that he was on the threshold of victory. Presumably after we had fallen to our deaths, he and Mrs. Pearson would have cleared out the bodies and thrown them into a nearby pond, and that would have been the end of it."

"That is right, Mr. Holmes," said Amy Briggs, who had been standing by. "After I returned to Arundel last night, Xavier was waiting for me at the station. As it turned out, he has informants posted there, and after he was told that both Miss Pearson and I had gone to London on the same day, he became suspicious and had me followed from the moment I arrived in the city. From that point, it wasn't hard for him to put the pieces together and to reach the conclusion that both of us had gone to see you. Oh, Mr. Holmes, he was beastly to me! He said that he would make me pay for my betrayal unless I helped him set the stage for his showdown with the detective, as he called it.

"Out of despair, I came up with the idea of disguising myself as Elizabeth Stowe in order to distract him, if he really did come after you, sir. Knowing as I do how he felt about her death, I thought the sight of her might throw him off track. I must admit that I never expected my idea to be as effective as it proved itself to be. I only ever saw Elizabeth a few times, but she had a rather striking appearance that was easy enough to replicate. And fortunately, the late Mrs. Pearson had many fancy dresses and fine wigs that I was able to use to effect Elizabeth's likeness. As for the rest – Well, sir, I suppose you might say I have a few acting talents of my own."

"Indeed," said Holmes, regarding the girl with an appreciative look. "I must say that you have shown real ingenuity, and if it hadn't been for your surprise intervention, we might have had a difficult time rescuing Miss Pearson."

"Why, thank you, sir." The girl looked genuinely moved by my friend's approbation.

While Holmes was still engaged in conversing with Miss Briggs, I went to check on the other lady, who still leaned in a half-daze against the church organ. The poor girl had evidently been given morphium by Zeldt after being brought to the top of the tower. She quickly came to, however, after I administered some smelling salts, and was already herself again by the time we helped her downstairs, where we were soon rejoined by

206

Constable Braddon. After fully recovering her senses, Miss Pearson was so grateful for being saved from the clutches of the rogue alienist that she offered to pay Holmes a substantial reward out of her personal savings. My friend gallantly refused the generous offer, consenting to accept only a standard fixed fee.

By a wry twist of fate, upon hearing of the hypnotist's death, Edith Zeldt, alias Sarah Pearson, who had played such an instrumental part in convincing Sir Richard that his daughter had gone mad, went mad herself, and was committed to the same asylum that she and her real husband Xavier Zeldt had intended for Miss Pearson. Sir Richard, already ailing and senile, was shaken to the core by the shocking revelations about his wife, and died of a seizure within a month of the events at the tower. Mr. James Hartford, upon receiving the news of Miss Pearson's ordeal, returned from India early, and the two were soon married in a small private ceremony, whereupon the former Miss Pearson, now Mrs. Hartford, went away with her husband to join him at his outpost. Meanwhile, by a stroke of good fortune, Miss Briggs found a suitable new position with a vicar's family in Hertfordshire, where she remained for many years. Thus was concluded the bizarre affair of Woodgate Manor.

The Incident of the
Mangled Rose Bushes
by Barry Clay

In my long association with my friend, Sherlock Holmes, the famous consulting detective, I had known many cases to begin with trivial incidents, only to discover later as we investigated that there were dire machinations at play, perhaps involving theft, danger, and even murder. Some few cases, however, began mysteriously and ominously, only to be found, when all was said and done, to be more innocent and benign than they had first appeared. Even fewer cases could be found to begin and end harmlessly, and a few – a very few – could even be called, if one had a mind to do so, *comical*. The Incident of the Mangled Rose Bushes, even though a serious crime was afoot, was a case that certainly fell in the last category.

I had been relaxing with Holmes in our shared lodgings when our landlady, Mrs. Hudson, ascended the stairs to inform us that we had two visitors, a Mrs. Russell and a Mrs. Brooks. Holmes asked her to show them up, and thus began one of the oddest – almost ludicrous – incidents my friend had every investigated.

As we listened to the trio ascend the stairs, Holmes said to me, "Would you care for a wager, Watson?"

"A wager?"

"I will wager you a dinner at Clarendon's that the age of the two ladies we are about to meet, if added together, will exceed one-hundred and twenty, and possibly one-hundred-and-forty." His eyes were alight with humor.

"I don't see how you can know that."

"Is it a wager?

I decided against it. "Even if you are right, it would be exceedingly impolite to settle it by asking them their ages. It just isn't done."

It took an unusually long time for Mrs. Hudson to escort our guests to our lodgings, and when she introduced them, I could see why. They were of advanced age, and one of them was using a cane for support. Looking at them, I decided Holmes was correct, and I was glad I hadn't taken his wager. If either was less than sixty-years-old, I would have been surprised. I could see that both of them were a little out of breath from the climb, and I went to assist them. I attempted to take the arm of the lady nearest to me.

"If I can – "

But she swatted at me with her hand! "Young man, I may be seventy-three, but I am quite capable of going up a flight of stairs without having a coronary or needing an assistant!" Startled, I stepped back. She had spoken with a slight accent that I recognized as American, and I wondered at it.

The other said, "Be that as it may, Alvera, that settee looks mighty inviting, don't you think?" She was the one with the cane, and perhaps the stairs had been harder on her than her companion.

Mrs. Hudson was trying not to smile at them behind their backs. She nodded at me and withdrew discreetly, shutting the door behind her.

Holmes had risen and in a gentleman-like way said, "Ladies, please, take a seat." I could tell that he found the two of them as amusing as Mrs. Hudson had.

Having been rebuked by one of them, I offered no more assistance. I watched them make their way – not quite unsteadily, but not quite steadily either – to the settee. I only regained my seat when they took theirs.

Holmes did the same. "I am Sherlock Holmes, and this is my associate, Dr. Watson."

"What a polite young man you are," said the lady I had attempted to help, with a sideways glance to me that spoke volumes about how I measured up in comparison. "I am Mrs. John Russell. This is my close friend, Mrs. Theodore Brooks."

Mrs. Russell was a short, thin woman with iron gray hair interspersed with only a few strands of black in it to indicate its original colour. She wore wire spectacles, and she was dressed in a dark purple dress that was nearly black and which had gone out of fashion at least thirty years ago. Her companion, Mrs. Brooks, was stouter, and her outfit a dark green though, like Mrs. Russell's attire, of a cut I hadn't seen worn in decades. Both wore hats and gloves, for they obviously had come to call on Holmes to a business matter, and ladies of that generation didn't leave one's house to conduct business in anything less than one's finest. Mrs. Russell had decorated her hat with a trio of striking white roses.

"I see you are a gardener, Mrs. Russell," stated Holmes.

She looked at him shrewdly. "Now, how did you know that?"

"You have fresh flowers on your hat, and of a shade not often hawked by the flower sellers one finds along the street. You are wearing a dress that has been mended – expertly I might add – several times. It is barely detectable, but it tells me you are a frugal woman who wouldn't buy roses when she can grow her own."

209

"Oh!" she said. "Then it was nothing! You were just paying attention."

Holmes smiled. "I have often told others so, but I am rarely believed. To continue, I also know that you are here on business that is important to you, but didn't meet with sufficient attention from the local constabulary."

Mrs. Brooks exclaimed, "You're like a stage magician! How did you know we have been the police?"

"Because the police are generally the first recourse of anyone who has a problem for which I'm needed, and knowing that your companion is of a frugal nature, she wouldn't come all this way to engage my services if she had found satisfaction from her local police force, nor would she pay for services if it were unimportant to her."

"How do you know she came from some distance?"

"Because she stated that she has a space large enough to grow roses, which you will not find anywhere close to Baker Street, save for a few very large houses well beyond her financial reach."

"Well, if that don't take all!"

Holmes smiled. "May I ask what brings you ladies to engage London's only consulting detective?"

"It was Dorothea's idea," Mrs. Russell told him primly, as if she still didn't quite approve of it.

"I convinced her she had to hire private help," explained Mrs. Brooks. "I read about you in the newspaper." I had wondered how the ladies had chanced upon Holmes.

"I admit, I took some convincing, but when it happened again, I decided Dorothea was right. I had to go for help. But lands! The cost of the cab! Who knew it had gone up so high? Highway robbery, it was! Highway robbery!"

Patiently, Holmes asked, "What, precisely, happened?"

"Someone dug up one of my rose bushes, Mr. Holmes!" she said indignantly. "Again!"

"The same bush?"

"No, another one."

"Can you provide details?"

"Of course I can provide details! I'm not senile, you know. Not yet. Not like Mildred Shaw. Half the time she can't even tell you what day it is!"

"Then we should be glad that we can have the story from you and not from her. When was the first occurrence of this indignity?"

"Three weeks ago. Wednesday. I had gone to meeting. Dorothea and I go together, every Wednesday from seven to eight. It's good, I think, to attend midweek services. Don't you agree?"

Holmes was no more religiously observant than I am, but he said, without committing himself, "I would consider that a fine, upstanding practice."

"But when we returned, there was one of my rose bushes, massacred, dug up, a hole where it had been deep enough that it was half way to China! Roses everywhere. The stems and roots destroyed. It's criminal! Do you know how long it took me to raise that bush?"

Mrs. Brooks interjected, "Everyone admires them."

Mrs. Russell continued as if her friend hadn't spoken. "When Mr. Russell proposed and brought me here from the States after our marriage, we lived in a walkup hardly big enough for the two of us. After many years, with him and me scrimping and saving, he bought that house. When we took possession, there was only one, scraggly-looking rose bush along the fence. It was a shame, a shame! I'm only happy John wasn't there to see it." What she said gave me a start, but then I realized that she had suddenly gone from the past to the present desecration of her roses and was speaking of her late husband. "The hoodlums who did it should be happy that Mr. Russell has gone to his reward, because if he'd been there, he's have filled their behinds with buckshot, that's what he'd have done!"

"Let me assure myself that I fully understand you. Thirty years ago, Mr. Russell, who was your husband, bought the house in which you now live?"

"Well, it might be thirty-one now. Got it for a song, he did. No one wanted a house that had been owned by a crook, did they?"

I could see this interested Holmes. "Who owned the house before you?"

"My lands! That was so long ago. But it was in the papers. Give me a minute." And she squeezed her eyes shut. "It had something to do with flour." And then, triumphantly, she said, *Miller!* Caleb Miller was the name. Some say he bought the house with ill-gotten gains, but the law caught up with him, it did. But back then, the law was something. None of this, 'Are you sure, Madam, that you didn't imagine this?' Thirty years ago, the local bobby would have taken me seriously, rather than winking and smiling with the other constables."

"That must have been most disturbing for you," remarked Holmes.

"Not in the least," she retorted. "Who cares what those young whipper-snappers think?"

Holmes was undisturbed by the sharpness of her reply. "A very healthy attitude, I would think. But to return to the rose bush: What did you do?"

"Well, that late at night, what could I do? But the next day, I met Dorothea and we went to the station and reported the vandalism."

"You left everything as it was?"

"I wanted them to see it!" She nearly quivered with indignation.

"An attitude worthy of praise. If only Scotland Yard made a practice of leaving the area around a crime equally undisturbed, they would solve more crimes."

"But they never came!"

"Indeed? What did the policeman at the desk do when you reported the incident?"

"Pretended to write it all down, but I could tell he didn't take it seriously. He says to me, 'Probably just some young boys out for a lark.' Any fool could see it was more than that! Dug halfway to China, that hole was, with a mound of soil beside it like Mount Everest, but he couldn't even be bothered to walk down and take a look. 'I'm sure it looked very deep to you, Ma'am,' he said, when I told him."

"But he wasn't at all rude, Alvera," Mrs. Brooks said.

"No, he wasn't rude, not like the next one."

"So it happened again?"

"The next week. I had set things to right and had the florist plant another bush, but when Dorothea and I got back from meeting, there was *another* bush uprooted and massacred like an Indian had scalped it."

"But not the newly planted bush?"

"No. Another bush. The one beside it."

"May I ask how many bushes you have?"

"Forty-two," she said, proudly. "I have all different colours and kinds." She pointed to the roses in her hat. "These here are Alfred de Dalmas roses."

"What colour were the roses from the first bush?"

"They were *Zephirine Drouhin,*" she said without hesitation.

"Which would be?"

"Pink, of course!"

"And the second bush?"

She stopped to look at him. "It was another *Zephirine Drouhin.*"

"Also pink?"

"They only come in one colour."

"And when you went back to the station with news of this second incident?"

"The constable at the desk didn't look old enough to have a drink at a pub without his mother taking him by the ear. He told me that it was probably a dog got in past my fence. A dog! A dog with a shovel, maybe! And then he had the effrontery to ask me if I might be exaggerating a little. I was fit to be tied."

I could well imagine it.

212

"What did you do then?"

"Went back and filled in the hole." I was aghast. This elderly lady, seventy-three years old, shoveling dirt into a hole by herself. It couldn't have been good for her health. But I restrained myself from saying anything. "I decided not have another bush planted until I was sure it wasn't going to happen again."

"That was when I suggested Alvera hire you, Mr. Holmes," Mrs. Brooks supplied. She told her friend, "You really should have listened to me then, Alvera. You might still have your *La Reine Victoria*."

Holmes continued, "So it happened a third time, this past Wednesday night – two days ago, I presume – when you were at meeting?"

"You presume right," Mrs. Russell informed him. "Another bush uprooted, a hole longer than your arm, but this time, the poor bush was chopped up like onion for a soup! Petals all over the yard!"

"And I assume the roses on that bush were also pink?"

The look she gave him was one of appreciation. "You're a sharp one, Mr. Holmes. I never even thought of that. They were all pink bushes. Do you think it important?"

"I theorize that it is critical. Did you report this latest invasion of your garden to the station house?"

"For all the good it did me! Even though it was the third time, they *still* wouldn't even consider looking at it. That's when I decided I had to bite the bullet and hire you."

"I am gratified that you did. This is a pretty problem, and I'm disappointed in the local constabulary, who should have at least had the courtesy of examining the damage, for I'm confident that they would have found even a cursory examination enlightening. Did you fill up this third hole?"

"Of course. Can't have my garden looking like it has moles the size of elephants running rampant through it."

"Naturally not. I would like to see your garden. May I have your address?"

She rattled it off.

I made note of it, and Holmes said, "Today is Friday. We shall be down at your house this afternoon, probably late, as I have some inquiries I want to make first. Will you be in?"

"I am almost always in," she informed him.

"I thought as much."

Mrs. Russell straightened her back and seemed to be preparing herself to do something unpleasant. "How much will I owe you?"

"Now? Nothing. But if I solve your problem, and I think I will, I would expect payment."

"Naturally!" she retorted. "That's why I asked."

Holmes looked amused. Instead of naming an amount, he said, "Let me ask you what fee you would consider reasonable."

"Well, I mean, the police are free."

"That they are," Holmes agreed, "but I must make a living, and the police, as you pointed out, haven't given your problem the attention it deserves. If I don't resolve your problem, you need not pay me at all."

She took a breath. "I'll pay five pounds," she said as if she were saying she would cut off her right arm, and then declared, "And not a farthing more! But it will be worth it to have this bother over and done with." It was so far from Holmes's customary fee that it rather took me by surprise. And then she shook her finger at him. "I won't have you taking advantage of me!" she warned him.

His face a mask of seriousness, my friend said, "I wouldn't dream of it, Mrs. Russell. The amount you named should be sufficient, and very generous of you."

Generous was not the word I would have used, but I reminded myself that the good woman probably had no idea of the going price of first-class detective work and was no doubt forced to live a frugal life. Five pounds might be a sizeable portion of her income, and she certainly appeared to consider the amount more than adequate, which was confirmed by her next words.

"Well, Mr. Russell always said that if one wants good work, one must pay what it's worth for it."

"I can see Mr. Russell was a shrewd man," Holmes said.

"A good husband, but the good die young, they say."

I couldn't help but wonder what she thought it meant that she was seventy-three years of age, but, of course, I said nothing.

"You should go home and try not to worry about this," Holmes told her. "Dr. Watson and I will be out later today, in the afternoon, to examine your garden and see what we can glean from any clues the perpetrator of this inconsiderate deed may have left behind. I might have a word or two with the head of your local station when I'm in the area. Don't trouble yourself about this any further. You can consider that the two of us are on the case. Your rose bushes have nothing more to fear."

She thanked us and they rose to leave. "Watson, would you be so kind as to show our two guests to the front door and hail them a cab?"

"I would be delighted," I told him, and I was. The walk down the stairs was a long one, with both ladies holding tightly to the railing and planting their feet carefully at each step. Once on the pavement, I hailed a cab, ensured the dear ladies were safely on their way, and returned to our lodgings.

214

Holmes was looking through one of his scrapbooks when I returned upstairs. "I have no record of a Caleb Miller in my clippings, but then it was a good thirty years ago – and perhaps thirty-one or more – if Mrs. Russell's memory serves us. A trifle before our time, I fear."

"Do you think it is important that he once owned the house?"

"In all likelihood. Criminal activity breed criminal activity."

"How did you know our clients were older before you saw them?"

"Did you not notice how long it took for them to ascend the stairs? I could hear the hesitancy in their tread and the sound of a cane. They were announced as two married ladies, but their husbands didn't accompany them. Given these two facts, I assumed both had outlived their husbands, suggesting that they were at least in their sixties."

"How are you going to proceed?"

"As I promised them, we will examine Mrs. Russell's garden. No doubt, any traces of the depredations she calls a 'massacre' will have been put to right, but it would be less than diligent not to examine the scene, and it might yet turn up something of note. But first, I think a trip to the local archives, and then the newspapers, might be in order. I want to know more about this Caleb Miller."

The trip to the local archives was unexpectedly quick. I accompanied Holmes, who gave the address of Mrs. Russell's home and received back the information that Mr. John Russell had purchased the home in June of 1853 from Mr. Caleb Miller. From there, we preceded to offices of *The Local Ledger*. Holmes explained his reasoning.

"Mrs. Russell stated that Caleb Miller was in the newspapers. I want to know exactly what he did that earned him such notoriety."

The visit to *The Ledger* took far longer. After inquiry, we were sent to a Mr. Holcomb in the lower level of the building, where a small, rabbit-faced man with a precisely trimmed mustache made much of us. "I hardly ever get visitors here," he informed us. "How may I help you?"

"My associate and I are researching a crime we believe occurred in 1852 or 1853. We would like to see any copies of newspapers you would have from that time period."

"Oh, my! How exciting! Well, take your seats, and I'll bring them to you." He was as good as his word, returning in a short time with a box in which as a large number of papers. "Here's the first of them," he told us. "Do be careful. They are very old." He was right. The pages were yellowed and brittle from age. He went to bring us more and was to make several trips before he was done.

"What are we looking for, Holmes?"

"Any mention of Caleb Miller, of course, but I would think any report of a large robbery, perhaps a bank or a jewelry store. Finding one will probably lead to the other."

At that point, Holmes's theory was obvious. "You think there is money or jewelry buried under one of the rose bushes."

"Precisely, though we will most likely find it to be jewelry, as paper currency would probably have disintegrated after an internment of thirty years."

We concentrated mainly on the crime pages, but even then, it took several hours. Holcomb watched us from his desk with interest. I was the first to find mention of Caleb Miller. "Here it is." I read:

> *Local landowner Caleb Miller, along with George Lark and Steven Rendell of no fixed addresses, were arraigned before the bar and found guilty of criminal enterprise in the robbery of several London jewelry stores and the willful murder of Edward Oakes.*

I checked the date of the paper. "November 12, 1853. That was after Mr. Russell bought the house from Miller."

"No doubt he was forced to sell the house to pay for his legal expenses." Holmes set down the paper through which he was looking and rifled among several others. "Ah, here it is." I waited while he read the article, which he then summarized. "It would appear Miller, Lark, and Rendell were all engaged in the systematic robbery of jewelry stores over several months, always late at night after they were closed. They broke into Engraves and Oakes, not realizing that Mr. Oakes was on the premises, working late. He raised the alarm and paid for it with his life. The three were apprehended when they attempted to flee." He asked me, "Was their sentence mentioned in your article?"

I looked. "Yes. They were transported to Australia." I looked up. "I'm surprised they didn't get the gallows. It *was* murder, after all."

"It doesn't specifically state it here, but I infer that the death of Mr. Oakes wasn't intentional."

"So the three could still be alive?"

"Possibly. Is there any mention of whether or not all the stolen property was recovered?"

I skimmed the rest of the article. "No, not all of it. Apparently, there were some gems and jewelry that never turned up."

Holcomb approached and asked, "Have you gentlemen found what you were looking for?"

"We have," Holmes assured him. "Thank you for your help."

216

"Oh, it was my pleasure. This is the most excitement I have had here since I started. Do not trouble yourselves putting everything back. I will ensure it is all replaced in order."

We stopped at a pub for lunch, then took a cab to Mrs. Russell's address. As expected, her garden was a profusion of roses from yellow to white to pink, and even deep red. She had variegated varieties as well. The house itself was a little worse for wear, and I perceived it hadn't been cared for quite as well as the garden. It was a one-storey house, though rather large for all that. Some of the paint along the edges of its trim was beginning to flake. We followed the walk, ascended the steps to the wide, wooden porch on the front of the house, rang the bell, and waited for Mrs. Russell to make her way to the door.

She was dressed in her everyday clothes, and she seemed less severe because of that. She greeted us, and Holmes asked if he could examine the garden. "I assume that space along the fence is where the two most recently uprooted rose bushes were?"

"Yes." She looked at the spot sadly. She seemed far less cantankerous than when we had first met her, and I wondered if the expensive ride to Baker Street in conjunction with her current trial had exhausted her patience by the time we first met her. Holmes withdrew his magnifying glass from his pocket and left us to examine the area she had indicated. She stepped out from her house onto the porch to get a closer look at him, and I knew better than to offer her my arm.

"What is he doing?" she asked me.

"He is examining the area for clues."

She looked at me. "Aren't you going to help him?"

I shook my head. "I would only get in his way."

The look she gave me was disturbingly penetrating. "You seem a very humble man, Dr. Watson."

I was a little taken aback. "I hope to be, Madam."

She turned her gaze back to Holmes, who was now on his hands and knees, still using the glass. "A very unusual man, your Mr. Holmes."

"I have known no one else of with his observational skills and powers of deduction."

We watched companionably until Holmes was done. He returned to the porch. "I can say without doubt," he told Mrs. Russell, "that no dog has ever been in your garden. Nor were young boys, unless one of them was unusually large for his age. Have there been any men in your garden in the last three weeks?"

"Men? No. Not since Mr. Russell passed on."

"Not even a tradesman, perhaps?"

The question jogged her memory. "The florist who planted the rosebush."

"Can you describe him?"

"Certainly. He was a very short, very thin man of perhaps forty years of age, balding at the top, but he wore a hat to cover it up. Why do you ask?"

"I found signs of a man's footprints. Based on the stride and depth of the prints, I would say he was about Dr. Watson's height, but heavier. They couldn't have been left by your florist, who would have certainly not left such a deep impression. No tradesman or delivery boy would have cause to leave the walk, unless they wished to examine the rose bushes closer, which strikes me as unlikely. No, they are undoubtedly the footprints of your vandal."

"Can you catch him, Mr. Holmes?"

"If he returns again, without doubt."

She seemed a little anxious when she asked, "Do you think he will?"

"I think it likely," he told her. "He has been here three times. He is looking for something he believes is buried underneath your rose bushes – or, I should say, under one bush in particular. To judge from your description of the most recent wreckage, he became angry when he didn't find what he was looking for and took his frustration out on the bush. Did you say that when your husband bought the house, there was only one rose bush along the fence?"

"What a good memory you have! Yes, I did say that."

"Do you remember what bush that was?"

"Oh, Mr. Holmes, that bush is long gone! It was sickly when we bought the house."

"Perhaps that was because someone had dug it up to bury something under it, and he didn't know how to replace it properly."

"Do you think so?"

"I do. I can account for the vandalism in no other way. Do you remember where that bush was?"

"Yes. Let me show you." She made her way down the steps and into the garden, stopping before one of the rose bushes, this one sporting white roses. "It was right here."

"Do I correctly assume that the bush you replaced bore pink roses?"

"Why, I believe you are right! How did you know that?"

"Because your vandal believes that something is buried under a pink rose bush, but he isn't certain where along the fence it is." Drily, he added, "No doubt, he was quite dismayed to find so many pink rose bushes here when he only expected one."

"Are . . . are you going to dig up my Alfred de Dalmas?"

"Not right now, Mrs. Russell, but I fear we will have to do so at some point."

"Oh, dear!"

"But I am confident you will be able to nurse it back to health. And if not, I suspect you will be able to replace it with the latest variety from the findings we may discover under it."

"What do you think is there?"

"Jewelry. Gems, perhaps. We won't know for sure until we find them."

"Oh, dear! My poor Alfred de Dalmas!"

Comfortingly, Holmes said, "When we dig it up, we will be careful. But for now, don't pay special attention to this bush. We will leave it undisturbed. We don't want our vandal to think anything more but that he must try again. We must be careful. No one in the neighborhood must know what we plan. You must not even tell Mrs. Brooks, for she might say something to someone else by accident. It will be our secret for now."

Mrs. Russell objected, "Dorothea is my closest friend! She befriended me, a poor homesick bride from America who knew nobody in London."

"It will only be until Thursday. You will go to meeting with Mrs. Brooks this Wednesday as always, and Dr. Watson and I will watch your house. I repeat that you must tell no one. We don't want to alert your trespasser that we're interested in the case."

"Can I tell Dorothea on the way to meeting?"

Holmes smiled. "I think that would be acceptable, though I advise you to wait until you are out of sight of your home."

"Very well, Mr. Holmes. Mr. Russell always said, when you hire experts, listen to what they tell you."

"That," Holmes replied, "is exceptionally good advice."

We made our way from Mrs. Russell's house to the local police station, which was only a short walk away. In this quiet neighborhood, there was no need for a large station, and in total there were probably only a few constables. Perhaps they had few men to spare, and that accounted for their lack of interest in Mrs. Russell's complaint. Holmes introduced us to the constable at the desk and asked if we could speak with the officer in charge.

"That would be Sergeant Scower," he told us. "This way."

He took us to an office where the name *Sergeant Stephen Scower* was stenciled upon the door. The constable knocked, opened the door, and announced, "A Mr. Sherlock Holmes and Dr. Watson to see you, sir."

Scower was an older man with a round face, white whiskers, and deep wrinkles lining his forehead. I was reminded a little of the drawings of

219

Father Christmas one sees in the papers, though his beard wasn't nearly as long as in those depictions. He greeted us. "Sherlock Holmes. Even here, I've heard of you. What brings you to the quietest precinct in London?"

"I have been hired by Mrs. John Russell to investigate the vandalism of her rose bushes every Wednesday night when she goes to her religious gathering."

"Ah! Mrs. Russell has been giving the sharp side of her tongue to my constables."

"If they have been ignoring her," Holmes pointed out, "then perhaps they deserve it."

He looked at Holmes keenly. "I'm surprised you're interested in this. My boys rather thought she was overreacting to a dog trespassing in her garden, or perhaps some boys looking for a little trouble."

"So she told us. Are you aware that her house was once owned by Caleb Miller?"

"Who?"

"Caleb Miller."

"Can't say I knew that." He squinted his eyes. "Why would I care?"

"Mr. Miller, along with two other men, was convicted of murder and burglary, specifically of jewelry shops, in November of 1853, and subsequently sent to Australia. Apparently the authorities never recovered everything that was stolen."

Understanding showed on his face, followed by mild remorse. "Well, that does put this in a different light."

"I believe Mr. Miller hid the unrecovered jewels under a rose bush."

"And he's now returned? After all this time?"

"Him, or someone who knew him. More than thirty years have passed, and he might conceivably be only in his fifties. He might even have become an upstanding citizen in the colony, with no one the wiser of his past. He might be here alone or with his confederates, or perhaps it isn't him at all but someone else who knows that under one of the rose bushes is a fortune. And that is why we're here."

"This coming Wednesday," Holmes continued, "Dr. Watson and I intend to watch Mrs. Russell's house while she leaves it unattended to attend a religious meeting. While I saw the footprints of only one man in her garden, I cannot be certain there aren't several individuals involved, especially since a trio of men was convicted of the thefts. It would help to have several stout young constables in attendance."

"But what if Miller doesn't come back?"

"I consider that unlikely. After the third attempt, the vandal lost his temper, wrecking more havoc on the third rose bush than the previous two, indicating he is frustrated. There is too much at stake for him not to return if he is able."

"And if he isn't able?"

"Then we will need to keep watch on Mrs. Russell's house until we are certain he has lost interest."

"I don't have a lot of men here," he cautioned us.

"One or two men will suffice."

Scower considered. "Very well," he said at last. "We'll give it a try."

That following Wednesday found us dressed in dark clothing, standing under a tree along the street within sight of Mrs. Russell's home. Two young constables, Everett and Blish, were on the other side of the street under the shadow of another tree some distance from the house. I couldn't see them, but I knew they were there.

"I still think it's a dog," Constable Blish had told Everett as they had walked to their post, thinking they were far enough away that we couldn't hear him.

Holmes murmured to me, "Let us hope he isn't correct. It would be exceedingly embarrassing to have a dog make its way into the garden. Should Lestrade learn of it, I would never hear the end of it."

But he wasn't really serious.

A little before seven, as the sky was darkening to black, Mrs. Brooks appeared, cane in hand and walking in a slow but steady pace. She approached the house, opened the gate, and made her way by the walk to the porch. She knocked on the door, and Mrs. Russell opened it and admitted her. Shortly after that, the two elderly ladies exited the house and made their way together down the street. They were the only pedestrians in this quiet neighborhood, in which lights could be seen in the windows of the houses, but nothing heard.

We had waited perhaps a quarter-of-an-hour when three men, one of whom was carrying a shovel over his shoulder, approached. "Ah," remarked Holmes quietly. "Here they are."

But instead of stopping at the house, they walked past it. Had they seen us? Or had Holmes been mistaken? But no, they stopped a short way later, looked around, then returned and opened the gate. Once in the garden, they appeared to discuss something – rather heatedly, I thought. Eventually the discussion ended, and the three approached one of the bushes. The man with a shovel began digging around it. As previously arranged, Holmes and I left the concealment of the tree, and so did the two constables. Holmes had warned us not to move too quickly and call notice to ourselves, and I was pleased to see that the constables were following his instructions.

Still, it was only a matter of time before one of the men noticed us nearing the house. Perhaps because they were in uniform, the constables were spied first. Looking up and catching sight of them, one of the men yelled, "Coppers! Run for it!" The man who was working the shovel dropped it, and the three men ran in separate directions. The two constables began chasing them, and I could see they were splitting up after two of the men who went around the house and no doubt hoping to lose the law by escaping through adjoining properties. The third man had leaped the fence and began running in our direction, swerving only when he saw us. I sprinted after him. His change of direction had caused him to lose speed, and I was on him in an instant. I tackled him around the legs and brought him down. He attempted to resist, but Holmes was there and had him in his iron grip.

"Here now!" he bluffed. "What is all this? I've done nothing wrong!"

"The owner of this house would disagree," announced Holmes, "and this is what one gets when one massacres an old lady's rose bushes." Then he added sternly, "You should be ashamed of yourself."

A short time later, all three men were at the station house, and a shiftier lot I had rarely seen. Unshaven, ill-groomed, and not a little worse for wear from digging and running, they looked the part of petty crooks, though I suppose they were far from petty. To my surprise, while George Lark and Steven Rendell were among the three men we had captured, Caleb Miller was not. Instead, another man, younger than these two felons, was the third. He sullenly gave his name as Johnny Richardson. While he was somewhat younger than the other two, he turned out to be the ring leader, and a face that might have been called handsome by some women was marred by a countenance I could only describe as evasive.

"We should have paid you no mind," said Lark to Richardson.

Richardson shot back, "Then you would have found nothing!"

Rendell said, "Ain't that what we got, except we got collared."

They were not bosom friends. The story wasn't long in the telling.

Miller, Lark, and Rendell had been sentenced to Australia. Following the initial robbery, Miller had hidden some of the gems, but he refused to tell Lark and Rendell where they were secreted. After serving their sentences, and unwilling to let Miller out of their sight, Lark and Rendell had formed a partnership with Miller. The three had actually made a respectable living importing goods from England and selling them to their fellow colonists in Sidney. They might have continued to make a living like this, for Lark and Rendell now had families, but the memory of the hidden gems gnawed at them.

"But Miller was canny," Lark informed us. "He wouldn't say where he had hidden them, only that they were safe from all but the earthworms."

"So we knew they were buried," admitted Rendell, "but we didn't know where."

Johnny Richardson had been sent to Australia for a violent burglary of an older couple in their homes. He had arrived later than the other three by several years, and he had been employed by Miller in their shop. Miller had remained unmarried, and when he took ill, it was Richardson who had nursed him, since he, too, was unattached. "It was on his death bed that he told me where the gems were buried, under his pink rose bush. He made me swear to dig them up."

"And you came here to fulfill his dying wish, all out of the goodness of your heart, I suppose," said Sergeant Scower, sarcastically.

Richardson was in a quandary. He knew that the gems were buried under a rose bush in Miller's old home, but Miller had neglected to provide the address of his home before he died. He was forced to bring Lark and Rendell into his confidence.

"I should have just stayed in Sidney," Rendell confessed. "I have a wife and two boys going to be men soon. But I couldn't leave all that loot in the ground."

Lark agreed with him. "The second worst decision of my life," he told us.

"The first being?" asked Holmes.

"Robbing those jewelry stores in the first place," he said viciously. "It got be sent down under, didn't it? Made my poor mother sick."

And so the three had manufactured a need to return to England to arrange imports with new export houses. They booked travel under assumed names in case the authorities might recognize their real ones, rented rooms, and then made their plans, realizing with shock that things had changed.

Richardson explained. "There were so many rose bushes I could barely count them all! Miller had said there was only one. The only thing I could remember was that it was pink."

"We had to figure out when we could dig in the garden," said Rendell.

"But the old lady never left it during the night!" complained Lark. "And we couldn't start digging up her rose bushes during the day."

"Finally, we realized she left her home every Wednesday night for an hour."

"But it was so dark by then, we couldn't tell the colour of the bushes for sure."

"So we would walk by the house from time to time during the day and take note."

"But then it was hard to remember which bush was which."

It was an argument over which bush they should uproot next that we had witnessed before their capture.

I think Holmes found their recital almost as amusing as he had found the ladies Russell and Brooks, perhaps more so. The three men could hardly be described as criminal masterminds.

"What am I going to tell my April?" said Lark.

"Your April? My Constance, more like. I promised her my criminal days were over. She's liable to kill me."

The constables put them in the only cell in the station house. When we were alone with the sergeant, he said, "What am I going to do with that lot?"

"I should send them back to Australia," said Holmes. "They appear to have become upstanding citizens until tempted by their past. Warn them that a return to England will find the law less merciful." He added, "I should make it clear to them that we will unearth the gems and return them to their rightful owners, so they will have no cause to return."

"As to that," began Scower, "after we talked last week, I did some research. Seven stores were robbed by this crew. Five had their jewels back. The two that didn't get their stolen goods back no longer exist. It's been thirty years, after all. As far as I can tell, there isn't anyone left who has a valid claim to them."

"Then it sounds as if Mrs. Russell may become a rich woman."

"Well, it only serves her right, I guess. We never paid her the mind she deserved. If it hadn't been for you, Mr. Holmes, I suppose these men would have found their gems eventually, and we'd have been none the wiser."

"Might I suggest," offered Holmes, "that there is one other way you could make amends for ignoring her complaint?"

The next day found us at Mrs. Russell's home with the two constables from the previous night, both of whom apologized to the elderly woman for not taking her seriously. Scower did the same. "They both told me about it, and I thought it was nothing. I beg your pardon, Madam. You can thank Mr. Holmes for setting this right."

Mrs. Russell was delighted with the apology, forgiving them all graciously, saying, "Forgive others as you have been forgiven." But she was less happy when she had to watch her Alfred de Dalmas dug up. She understood it needed to be done, and the two constables handled the work as gently as they could. Still, I could tell it was hard on the good woman. Mrs. Brooks was in attendance, leaning on her cane and commiserating with her friend.

224

Eventually, a box was found in which was a small bag. Mrs. Russell poured out a handful of gems from it. "My goodness! Is this what it was all about?"

"It is," affirmed Holmes.

"Whose are they?"

Holmes glanced at the sergeant, who said, "After thirty years and all this trouble they caused you, they are yours, Madam."

"What will I do with them?"

Holmes said, "Whatever you want."

"Well," she said. "At my age, the best thing I can do with a treasure like this is give it to charity. I have all I need for this life. And the Good Book says to store up treasures in Heaven. You cannot take it with you, no matter how pretty they are." She put the gems in the box, then seemed to have second thoughts before she closed the lid. She reached in to pick one of the gems up with her fingers. She handed it to Holmes. "Would you be willing to take this in addition to your five pounds?"

"I would gladly take this *instead* of my five pounds, Mrs. Russell, and consider myself greatly overpaid."

And, in truth, once it was appraised, we learned that it was the most that Holmes had been compensated for any of his cases up to that time, including those for royalty or the very wealthy. Never has five pounds accrued to so much in so little time as it had that day.

The Sandwich Murder
by DJ Tyrer

"You appear flustered," observed my good friend, Sherlock Holmes, as I entered our rooms at 221b Baker Street.

"I came in a hurry," I said in response as I sat down opposite and paused for a moment to catch my breath. "I have a case for you. A murder."

"Really?"

It wasn't often that I was the one to present him with a mystery, but on occasion, my medical career would lead me to chance upon one, and those were often some of the most baffling.

"Yes," I told him. "You remember I was called away yesterday to attend a sick man."

Holmes nodded. "Gibbons, I believe the name was."

"That's right. Henry Gibbons, a clerk in the offices of a dry goods company."

"You had better tell me what happened."

"Well, you remember that the boy-in-buttons came in with a note for me? It was from one of my patients, a Mr. Holdstock, a manager at the dry goods company, summoning me urgently to assist a sick employee. I took a hansom, but though I arrived promptly at their office, Mr. Gibbons was already dead when I entered.

"As Holdstock explained it, he'd been summoned from his office by the sudden cries of concern of his clerks and found Gibbons collapsed beside his desk in pain, apparently suffering from an acute stomach illness. The fool wasted precious time attempting to revive the man from his partial swoon with a damp flannel, and then pulling off his jacket to 'make him comfortable'. Even though the man was clearly quite ill and Holdstock was happy to lecture me on the likelihood of his having suffered burst appendix, the manager, as he put it himself, 'didn't wish to disturb a doctor for nothing.

"When I was eventually summoned, death was already nigh, taking him with surprising swiftness.

"Having ascertained that there was nothing I could do to revive him, I quickly questioned his colleagues as to what had happened. It seemed that, shortly after returning from an early lunch, Gibbons had begun to complain of a stomach ache. He resumed his duties, despite the ache rapidly blossoming into pain, and over the course of the next couple of hours, he complained that the pain was growing worse and that he felt dizzy. He spoke of leaving early for the day. He rose from his seat, whether with the intention of leaving or of seeking medical assistance, nobody could say, only to collapse to the floor, vomiting and clasping his stomach. This was when the manager entered and sent for me. Gibbons, then, began to convulse and, a short while later, died."

"What was your initial suspicion?" asked Holmes as I paused.

"Well, despite what Holdstock thought, a ruptured appendix seemed unlikely, as the pain appeared to have remained centered in the belly and not migrated to the side as happens with appendicitis. An infection by some bacillus seemed probable, although most, such as Typhoid Fever, have a more gradual onset – days not hours – than the seemingly quite-sudden decline that Gibbons suffered."

"Poison," said Holmes.

"That was where my thoughts began to stray, although it was not until I was able to perform a *necropsia* on his corpse this morning that I knew for certain.

"The stomach was inflamed and contained traces of a powder that I identified as arsenic, as well as the remains of a jam sandwich, which was both his last meal and the means by which he was poisoned."

"What is it that has sent you rushing back here to tell me all this?" Holmes asked as I finished.

"Lestrade," said I.

"Ah, yes," said my friend with a hint of a smile, "the good inspector can have that effect on a man. But what exactly has he done that has made you . . . *concerned*."

"Well, having discovered that Gibbons died by poison, I naturally called Lestrade."

"Naturally."

"Well, he made the obvious assumption that if the man died from eating the sandwich that he had brought in from home, then the man's wife must be the guilty party – the murderess. He has gone round to their home to arrest her."

"As you say," said Holmes, "the obvious assumption. But you have your doubts."

"I believe," said I, "that Lestrade is about to make an egregious error."

"Strong doubts," Holmes almost purred the words. "Your reasons?"

"Well, although it does seem obvious at first thought, a little consideration tells me that it is quite unlikely. Surely, with access to her husband's meals, Mrs. Gibbons would poison him slowly over time, hoping to make his death seem like the result of a general decline, something most would accept without demure, not by providing a singular lethal dose that would cause him to die suddenly – suspiciously."

227

"I concur," said Holmes, and I felt a surge of relief at the simple words. "As you say, she had plenty of time to kill him in a manner that wouldn't attract attention. Such a sudden poisoning would indicate either an act of sudden rage or a moment of opportunity otherwise denied that the killer took advantage of, and as a sudden rage more generally results in the use of a weapon than a subtle act such as this, I would lean towards the latter."

Holmes looked at me intently then. "You are correct to be concerned. Lestrade is almost certainly about to arrest an innocent woman."

"Hence I came to you," I finished. "Lestrade needs to be shown the real guilty party. But to convince him, we need more than suppositions and sound logic – we need hard proof."

Holmes nodded. "And I suspect he'll hardly be inclined to have us interrupting his own interrogation in what he perceives to be a straightforward case with contradictory theories, no matter how sound. If we can present him with the guilty party, Lestrade will not cry foul at our interference."

"So," I asked Holmes," where do we begin?"

"With the man's co-workers. He died at work and, if his wife is innocent as we believe, it seems unlikely there was any place other that the poison might have been added to his sandwich between his home and there. If none of his co-workers is the guilty party, they may, at least, be able to lead us to the killer."

And with that, we set off to the office where Henry Gibbons had died.

Although we arrived at the office fully certain of our theory, I rapidly began to wonder if I had been mistaken, and even Holmes, inscrutable though his face was, seemed quieter as each person we questioned in turn denied seeing anything suspicious and offered no suggestion of any enemies who might have wanted to kill Gibbons.

"The man might as well have been a saint," I commented in frustration once we had questioned over half the people who had worked with him.

Holmes shook his head. "No man is a saint through every second of the day, no matter how pure his general disposition. Even the best man has the potential to cause offence and enmity, even if entirely by accident or through no fault of his own."

"But if Gibbons did," I said, "it seems no one saw it."

But it seemed someone had, although they didn't know the significance of what they knew.

It was as we were questioning a man named Andrews that we discovered the information we needed to end our impasse.

228

"Cor lummy!" he exclaimed as we explained why we were questioning him. "He died of poison? You sure?" I assured him that I was, and, in an even louder voice, he cried, "Well, I sure am a lucky fellow!"

"Why, whatever do you mean?" I asked.

"Well, if it weren't for him, I would've eaten those sandwiches, wouldn't I?"

It took us a few minutes of questioning, Andrews being a somewhat flighty fellow, before we fully understood his meaning.

It transpired that the jam sandwiches Gibbons has eaten weren't his own, but had been brought in by Andrews for his lunch, only to be taken by Gibbons while he was still at his desk. Indeed, further questioning of Andrews and the other clerks revealed that Gibbons was suspected of being one of those petty blights upon honest workers: A food thief, stealing the meals of his fellow clerks rather than spending a penny of his own wage to feed himself.

"I'm not sure," said Holmes at last to the still rather giddy clerk, "how far I would characterise your lot as 'lucky'."

"What do you mean?" Andrews asked, blinking at him.

"Well," I contributed, "although it seems that Gibbons did, indeed, save your life and, in that particular sense, you are lucky, it must be considered that you are the target for murder."

"Me? I don't understand."

Holmes leant a little closer to him and fixed him with a piercing gaze.

"Unless," he said in a wry tone, "you wanted revenge for his thefts of food from you and your fellows and poisoned him yourself, it would appear that this poisoning was an attempt to kill *you* that failed. Until we can ascertain who wants you dead and why, your life will remain in danger."

Andrews stared back at Holmes, silent at last.

Holmes and I headed to Scotland Yard to apprise Lestrade of our discovery. The inspector wasn't in a good mood when he was called out from his interview room to speak with us.

"That woman claims that she never even made herself a sandwich," he cried as he joined us. "Says she never ever made him lunch."

"She didn't," confirmed Holmes, before proceeding to explain what we had learned.

"You mean this Gibbons wasn't even the target of the poisoner?" sputtered Lestrade when he was done.

"It would appear not. The clerk, Andrews, doesn't seem to have sufficient wits to have poisoned him and not have revealed the fact."

"A whole morning wasted," Lestrade muttered.

229

"Spent covering every possibility," I said in an attempt to mollify him.

"At least you didn't send officers to her house to turn it over," said Holmes in an affable tone that seemed to do nothing for the inspector's mood.

Lestrade snorted. "Well, if you two think you're on your way to solving this one, I might as well leave you to get on with it – I do have other cases to tackle. Let me know when you need me to arrest someone. In the meantime, I'll tell the wife she's free to go."

"Perhaps," I suggested, "don't mention that her husband was not the intended target."

The inspector rolled his eyes. "I may have taken a wrong turn, Doctor, but I'm not an imbecile. I shan't be revealing what little I do know. Now, run along before I find a drunk in need of a doctor's attention."

Upon our return to the dry goods company, we resumed our questioning of the clerks, and I couldn't help but feel a twinge of sympathy for Lestrade. It seemed this case, on the surface so simple, was nothing but dead-ends.

As with Gibbons, it appeared that no one, not even the man himself, could think of anyone who might wish to do Andrews harm. Unmarried, he made his own sandwiches, so we returned to the question, once more, of who had put the poison in the sandwich and how it might have been achieved.

"At least," I said, in a poor attempt at humour, "we can rule out Andrews himself."

It seemed that, unless the poison were in the jam already, the only place it could have been added was in the office between Andrews putting his sandwiches to one side and Gibbons stealing them.

I was dispatched by Holmes, with Andrews's permission, to the man's rooms to take inventory of anything that might contain arsenic and to secure the jar of preserves for testing. I also spoke to as many of his neighbours as were in and willing to answer a knock at their door.

Not one had anything bad to say about the clerk, nor anything much at all, and none had seen anything suspicious.

With no other source from which the arsenic might, somehow, have made its way into his sandwiches, it was just left for me to return to Baker Street and carry out a test on the strawberry preserves.

"It was negative," I told Holmes as he entered, later that evening. "The jar was clean of arsenic. I'm sorry that information isn't much use."

"No," said Holmes, "it is most useful."

230

"Really? For I'm feeling that my investigation has achieved nothing."

"Oh, Watson, remember that every point eliminated brings us closer to the truth. Now we know that the poison wasn't an accident as occurred with the Bradford sweets poisoning, nor is it the work of someone acting at random by poisoning a jar that anyone might buy, nor was it someone with access to Andrews's rooms. No, it is someone with access to the office, for that is the only place the poison could be added to the sandwich."

"But who wanted Andrews dead?" I asked. "We've found no evidence that anyone did."

"We didn't discover that Gibbons was stealing his colleagues' food until Andrews let it slip. It could be that the reason isn't an obvious one. Or . . . ."

Holmes trailed off and was silent for a moment, then made a most startling suggestion: "Unless Gibbons really *was* the intended victim all along . . . ."

"Whatever do you mean? We've established that the poison was in Andrews's sandwiches and that he must, therefore, be the target."

"Ah, but their colleagues were aware of Gibbons predilection for stealing food. If you wanted him dead, poisoning someone else's food, knowing that he would take it, would be the perfect way of killing him while, simultaneously, muddying the waters as to target and motive."

"But how could they be certain he would steal Andrews's sandwiches and not someone else's food? Had he taken something else, someone else would've been poisoned."

"Perhaps our poisoner didn't care?" said Holmes. "Or it could be that only the sandwiches were there to steal. We must check who else brought food with them and where it was kept. Possibly the killer knew Andrews would never eat the sandwiches if Gibbons didn't – "

"Whatever do you mean?" I asked.

Holmes looked at me intently. "I mean that your earlier suggestion that we could rule Andrews out as the poisoner was misplaced. If Andrews wished to be rid of Gibbons, whether purely to stop an inveterate food thief, or for some reason of which we are, as yet, unaware, poisoning his own sandwiches would've held no risk for him. If Gibbons steals and eats them, then success – he has killed the man and deflected suspicion away from himself by making it look like he was the intended victim. If Gibbons failed to live up to his usual habit, then he just tosses the sandwiches away and tries again another time, going hungry but avoiding any risk to himself."

"Goodness, I do believe you're right. It must be Andrews, for it is the only solution to the puzzle that makes any sense."

231

"And yet," said Holmes, "he didn't strike me as such a cunning man, nor one capable of concealing his guilt."

I considered his words. "It might be that he is a fine actor."

"Then he missed his true calling upon the stage." Holmes sighed. "Although it would seem improbable for him to be the killer, it isn't impossible and, with the number of alternative possibilities reducing towards zero, it would seem he is our man. Yet I cannot abandon my certainty of his innocence. And without some further clue, we have nothing upon which Lestrade could hang a case, or the man."

Once again, it seemed, we had found ourselves at a dead end.

We returned to the office the next morning to renew our investigation. I had rather hoped that Andrews or one of his fellow clerks would've absented themselves without explanation, betraying his guilt, but they all were at their desks, working, when we entered.

Some cases are readily solved by meditation upon some vital clue or the villain revealing himself in some manner, but others, such as this, can only be resolved through the tedium of careful analysis of all their aspects, regardless of their apparent connection, or lack thereof. Thus it was that Holmes and I, to the perceivable annoyance of the manager, Holdstock, began questioning the clerks again, starting with Andrews, to confirm every last detail of that morning and, most importantly, the location of the sandwiches.

The sandwiches in question had been placed in a small, cool cupboard which was allotted by the company for just such a purpose. It seemed that none of the other clerks had placed any food in it, a habit that had been established for some weeks as a result of Gibbons's thieving ways, either keeping their lunches somewhere close to their persons, or planning on buying something from some nearby street vendor. Andrews agreed that his had been the only thing in there when he placed them in the cupboard.

"It would seem," said Holmes, "that the sandwiches being bait for the victim cannot be denied, being the only food there for him to steal. But we return to the vexing question of whether it was Andrews or another who carried out the act of poisoning."

"Well," said I, "although Andrews is the obvious suspect, as the only person still leaving food there where Gibbons might take it, the fact that his habit could be observed by anyone in the office means that we cannot dismiss the possibility that another added the poison, in spite of the risk that it might kill the wrong person, had Andrews retrieved them before Gibbons.

"Which," I added, "would vindicate your feelings about Andrews, given that another being the killer remains distinctly possible."

Holmes smiled, and there was a hint of the wolf about it.

"Yes. Based on my observations, I'm inclined to declare Andrews innocent. Another here – " He swept his eyes over the ranked desks where the clerks sat. " – is the guilty party and I shall find him by the day's end."

It seemed a daring boast in the circumstances, but Holmes was never one to make such declarations lightly.

Holdstock approached us and, addressing me rather than my companion, asked, "Will you be much longer? Your presence here is proving a little, ah, disruptive to the concentration of my clerks."

"Not long now," said Holmes, and Holdstock drew back his head a little, as if offended to be addressed by him.

"Very good."

Before he could turn away, Holmes asked him, "Oh, by-the-by, do you keep any rat poison on the premises?"

The man blinked, then said, "Yes, we do. It is in the cupboard beneath the stairs to my office. We had a problem with vermin getting into our warehouse next door and, from there, entering the offices and chewing upon files and generally causing a nuisance. The cupboard is kept locked, and I'm sure the rat poison played no part in this tragedy."

Holmes thanked him for his assistance and acknowledged that he was probably right. Then, in a light and cordial tone that clearly grated with the man, said, "You may be on your way."

Holdstock snorted and stalked off to his office.

In spite of his query, Holmes didn't follow the man, but went over to the cupboard where the sandwiches had been stored and proceeded to undertake a more close-up examination of its interior.

Then, standing with a nod, he walked the short distance to the cupboard under the stairs and tried its door. It was locked, just as the manager had said.

"Do you wish me to fetch Mr. Holdstock?" I asked, glancing up the stairs to the panopticon-like office.

Holmes shook his head and knelt down beside the door, producing a thin length of wire from somewhere about his person. Without explanation, he inserted it into the lock.

At some point, during one of his forays into the nefarious corners of the underworld, my companion had picked up knowledge of the art of lock-picking, and I watched with fascination as he deployed it against the cupboard door, the simple lock of which yielded itself up to him within moments.

Crouching beside my friend, I looked into the cupboard. There on a shelf above stacked reams of paper, was a container marked with a skull and crossbones and the words "*Rat Poison*".

"Well," I said, "there it is. But what is the significance?"

He removed the container and laid it on the floor beside him, and reached out and tapped the back of the cupboard. One of the boards was loose and shook a little beneath his touch.

"As I thought," he murmured, pulling it free to reveal a space behind it.

With a start, I realised that it opened into the cupboard where the food had been stored.

"Now we know how the killer managed to place the poison in the sandwiches without being observed," I commented.

"Yes," said Holmes. "I noticed one of the boards appeared to be loose when I examined the cupboard, but I couldn't move it from that side."

"How did you guess?" I asked. "I mean, you clearly had this idea when you asked Holdstock about the rat poison."

"I did," admitted Holmes. "As I continued to ponder the seeming impossibility of anyone tampering with the food unobserved, I came to see that there was only one answer to the vexatious question, and that was that the poison had been applied while the sandwiches were in the cupboard, but without anyone opening it. If the door couldn't be opened, then surely there must be another way into it. And if there is another way in, I thought to myself, did it not make the most sense for it to be accessed from in proximity to the poison itself?

"After all, if you wish to remain unseen preparing a murder, why risk being spotted bringing the means into work with you?"

"But," I pointed out, "this cupboard is kept locked. While it may have been possible for a clerk to open the food cupboard door in order to facilitate their crime, how can he have opened this door to do so – unless you posit one of them shares your skill with locks?"

Holmes chuckled. "It is indeed possible that one might, but I do believe a far simpler explanation presents itself."

"Which is?"

"We allowed ourselves to be blinded by assumption, and you remain so."

I have to admit I was rather annoyed to be spoken to so, even if I must admit Holmes does frequently see facts that evade my observation.

"Think, Watson," he continued. "Forget about suppositions concerning the theft of food and workplace rivalries. Look beyond that and see the obvious."

"Holdstock!" I exclaimed.

"Precisely. He has a key. I am certain. After all, he is the manager, here. Or if not, he could demand it from whomever does. Too, he spoke with certainty as to its location. Had he left the problem of vermin solely to a caretaker or cleaner, he doubtless would have spoken more vaguely."

"And," I concluded for Holmes, "if he had a key, he's the only person in the office who could have placed the poison."

"Exactly," said Holmes. "And if you would recall what you told me of your summons, he was, as you put it, 'a fool' who delayed calling a doctor. Not a fool, Watson, but a cunning murderer who sought to give plentiful time for his poison to do its work."

"And his insistence it must be a burst appendix," said I. "He was clearly hoping to fix the idea in my mind so that I would give the true cause no further thought."

"And there was his biggest mistake," Holmes said with a smile as he slapped me on the shoulder. "You have an enquiring mind, not one to be beaten by repetition into parroting what someone else claims. Nor, if you failed to fall for that attempt, were you so blind as to make the assumption Lestrade did. Had he chosen some dullard of a doctor, Holdstock likely would have succeeded in his scheme, but whether out of convenience or hubris, he chose the one medical man in London guaranteed not to follow his script."

"I thank you for your praise," I told Holmes, "but even though I concur with your assertion of his guilt based upon the means by which Gibbons was dispatched, there is a question of motive. As you said, our focus had been upon the motive and not the means, leaving us fumbling, but now we appear to be reversed, certain of the means, but to my mind, unclear as to motive. We can prove nothing. Even if we find his finger marks upon the container, that can be explained as a relic of his perfectly lawful accessing of the cupboard. With no witnesses, we need more than a neat story."

Holmes nodded. "I agree. And I do believe I know *why* Holdstock murdered him . . . ."

He closed the cupboard door, jiggled the lock back into place, and then said, "Come, let us tell our suspect that we are done for the day and no nearer solving the mystery."

We did so, and Holmes concluded our audience with the manager by informing him, "We shall return in the morning to question your staff again, although the fact none have anything useful to say on the subject leads me to think the murderer must be located elsewhere."

The relief that flickered across the man's face might have been assumed to derive from the prospect of our leaving the office to resume its usual workings, but I was certain it reflected the guilt Holmes had deduced was there.

It was getting late when we arrived at the home of the late Mr. Gibbons and spoke to his wife, who greeted us with effusive thanks for having rescued her, as she put it, from Lestrade's suspicions.

"You are most welcome," said Holmes at his most charming. "Now, we hope to find the evidence that will bring your husband's murderer to justice."

That brought forth more effusive praise, until Holmes succeeded in quieting her by reminding her that the villain was not yet detained.

"How can I help?" she asked. It was a question that I also wanted answered.

"The first thing I must ask," said Holmes, looking around us, "is about the state of your home. I'm sure a fine woman such as yourself wouldn't leave it in such a mess."

She puffed up a little at his words. "No, it was the police, looking for poison."

"Of course," said my friend.

"I just haven't had the heart to do much about it," she added with a sigh.

Holmes and I exchanged a look and I recalled what he had said to Lestrade. I wasn't sure how my friend had known the inspector had sent no one to her house, but Lestrade hadn't disputed his observation. Now, it seemed someone else had paid it a visit while she was being interrogated. We said nothing to her of our suspicions, Holmes changed the subject.

"I don't wish to distress you, Madam, but I believe your husband had a . . . shall we say a penchant for pocketing items that weren't strictly his to take. Yes, I can see in your eyes that you know what I refer to.

"Well, it is my belief that he was murdered because he had taken something he shouldn't."

Mrs. Gibbons gave a loud and heaving sigh. "Oh, I told my Henry his thieving ways would get him into trouble one day. Surely, it might just be someone's lunch or a pen, but I said to him, someone is bound to take exception."

Holmes nodded. "And they did." He laid a comforting hand upon her shoulder. "It is a shame your husband didn't heed your wise words."

She gave him a weak smile and he asked her, "What did he bring home recently? Anything unusual?"

Mrs. Gibbons looked away for a moment, then said, "There were, I remember, a silver picture frame, very nice, and a pen, also silver. He sold them at the pawnshop on the corner."

Holmes looked at me. "Let us pay the pawnshop a visit."

With the offer of a shilling for his time and an assurance that he wasn't in trouble, the owner of the pawnshop was willing to oblige us in our enquiries. The pen had been sold, but he could recall its description with a facility of memory I found most impressive.

"It was relatively plain," he said, "with a rather broad nib, but had been engraved with the words 'To my darling Robert, from Amelia.'"

I looked at Holmes. "Holdstock's Christian name is Robert, and his wife's name was Amelia."

"Was?" asked Holmes. "I take it you don't mean she changed it?"

"She died, last year. I treated her during her decline."

Holmes made no comment, but turned back to the owner of the pawnshop and said, "You still have the picture frame?"

"Yes . . . ." The man went over to an overburdened shelf and rummaged through its contents and produced an empty silver frame.

"Did it have a portrait?" I asked.

He nodded. "Yes. I have a box of such portraits. There's no real value in them, but you never know when someone might want one. I shan't be a mo'," he added. "It's just on the top."

And a moment later, he had produced it for us.

"That's her," I said. "That's Amelia Holdstock."

"And there," said Holmes, "is the motive for murder, one almost forgivable: Gibbons stole objects of sentimentality from Holdstock, whose heart, doubtless, is still pained at his wife's passing."

"But," said I, "if he knew Gibbons was the thief, why not dismiss him and pass the matter to the police?"

"Indeed," said Holmes with a nod of agreement. "As much as his righteous fury is understandable, Holdstock had no need to set himself up as judge, jury, and executioner. Nor should he have risked the life of the innocent, Andrews. His actions were reckless and unnecessary. Let us summon Lestrade and allow him to redeem his pride by arresting the murderer and closing the case."

I couldn't help but feel some pity for Holdstock as I watched Lestrade lead him out of his house to the Black Maria that was waiting to receive him. The man had suffered and Gibbons had renewed that suffering as if by twisting a knife. But there had been no need for him to take the path he had chosen. Had there?

The doors closed on him and he was whisked away, the final conclusion of the case no longer in our power to decide.

The Adventure of the Wandering Stones
by Mark Wardecker

The spring of 1885 found the detective, Sherlock Holmes, enveloped in a whirlwind of activity that taxed even his prodigious stamina. In addition to such homegrown sensations as the bloody affair of the broken abacus and the disentangling of the Wheatsheaf Market disappearances, it also involved travelling to the Continent twice in as many months, where he successfully concluded the career of Zvirbulis, the Lettish mountebank, and recovered the legendary ochre amethyst, so greatly cherished by both the royalty and the people of its native land. Though my friend, when engaged in a case, could work for days on end without sleep and by nourishing himself with only black coffee and the most pungent shag tobacco, by the time he returned to England, the exhaustion was beginning to tell upon him. Though I could not convince him of the fact, his state was no doubt aggravated by his reliance on the cocaine bottle in those final weeks abroad, a practice to which he usually only resorted when beset by boredom. In fact, I believe he agreed to my suggestion that we take a holiday for his health's sake only in order to avoid another of my lectures on the debilitating effects of that drug. It did surprise me, though, that he already had a location in mind for a relaxing sojourn away from the smoke and noise of London.

On a rainy, muddy day at the end of May, we set out, looking forward to our destination: The village of Milbury in Wiltshire greeted us upon our arrival in the late afternoon with warm sunshine and dramatic, cloudy skies. I must admit this small settlement in the southwest didn't disappoint us, and we spent the next few glorious spring days taking the air by walking around and studying the famous circles of standing stones that would have been ancient when the Romans first beheld them. Walking around the remaining stones that formed the large surrounding outer ring first, we admired the glamour and mystery of the henge and observed its still clearly identifiable inner ditch and grassy bank that enclosed a part of the village that had extended into it. We then studied the two smaller inner rings, and meditated upon the possible lives of the builders of these enigmatic monuments. Given their natural majesty, it was easy to believe these were sites of religious significance and difficult not to speculate

238

further. We both discussed and argued what we knew of the Celts and Druids and their alleged sinister practices of human sacrifice and mysticism, and Holmes recounted a theory of Edward Duke's that perhaps ancient religious sites, like this one, were all constructed in geographical alignment with one another.

"It is a mystery worth exploring, is it not, Watson? Were the efforts of those mysterious, prehistoric people being somehow directed and coordinated across the land? And then there is the mystery of the Druids."

"I remember reading in *De Bello Gallico* of men being burned in an enormous wicker sculpture of a giant."

"Ah, but you can't always trust Caesar. The timing of his posting to Gaul turned out to be so fortuitous that it beggars belief. I can imagine the Gauls being as shocked by their insidious plans as his readers were in Rome," Holmes joked. "Several scholars have noted that these circles and others align with solar and lunar positions, but it is hard to believe their sole purpose was calendrical. Standing here now, I can also imagine that these stones have witnessed their share of horrors, and may have even inspired them."

In addition to these lazy perambulations and meditations, we also spent time in Milbury itself, a charming village that consists mostly of buildings that date back to the sixteenth century, and Milbury Manor is a truly fine and impressive representation of Tudor architecture. Many of the less-ostentatious buildings display the exposed beams, chalk or clay walls, and thatched roofs of the period, including the little whitewashed cottage in which we stayed that was on the outskirts of the part of the village that inhabited the outer stone circle. That description also applied to the old public house we frequented in the evening. Not surprisingly, The Dented Helm's very round, very bald, and very ruddy landlord swore to us, and the staff affirmed, that the pub was quite haunted by Roman soldiers, Roundheads, and assorted suicides from throughout the ages who appear at varying times and in various rooms. It was on our first evening in town, while Holmes was standing at the bar asking the proprietor about the stones, that we learned of the recent death of a tramp at one of the smaller circles. That he had piqued Holmes's interest was as apparent to him as it was to me, and the man became suspicious.

"But why so interested in the death of some wanderer?"

"It is my business," declared Holmes, enlivened by the emergence of a mystery, as well as the strong ale. "I am a consulting detective, and often work with the police when they are particularly challenged, which occurs with troubling frequency."

"Oh, aye! If that's the case, maybe you can help me solve the mystery of my vanishing profits!" he said loudly, raising a chorus of laughs from the crowded tables and bar.

"Perhaps a demonstration is in order, Holmes," I goaded.

Holmes nodded, stood, and looked the publican over from toe to head.

"You are good with numbers and horses and have been to sea, probably as a quartermaster in the Royal Navy. The fact that you own the most successful inn in a nationally significant tourist destination, despite your jest, is indicative of your business sense. Your rolling gate, anchor tattoo just peeking out from beneath your sleeve, and use of the phrase 'pull your finger out' a few moments ago are all indicative of your naval background. You had to learn about business somewhere, which suggests a quartermaster's role. As for the horses, well . . . ." He trailed off waving toward the man's boots. "And you obviously have a daughter in her early twenties," he said, waving laconically in the direction of the hostess.

"The family resemblance between you and the barmaid is clear. Along with your daughter, I would expect to see your wife working with you in such a small inn, but the woman I see in the kitchen wears no wedding band and looks to have never done so. That you do wear a ring and that you have worn your stable boots into your pub in such a state that no wife I've ever met would allow suggests you are a widower. That you keep a shrine of her embroidery projects on that part of the wall behind the bar is a trait common to the bereaved and confirms it. The latest one is dated four years ago."

Noticing the man's crestfallen expression and my glare, Holmes quickly added, smiling, "As for your profits, judging by the visible blood vessels on your face, the redness of your nose, free perspiring, and sizable waistline, you may want to avoid enjoying too much of your own excellent hospitality. But not today. Please let me stand you a glass of this most excellent ale, sir!" he declared, placing several coins on the bar.

"Well, I'll be Mr. Holmes. I swear you're as sharp as a tack and correct on all counts. And I thank you for the drink. Reg Heyplumb's the name."

"It is a pleasure to meet you, Mr. Heyplumb. Please, tell me more of this tramp's death."

"Now, Mr. Holmes, 'tweren't no foul play involved, and it's surely nothing to interrupt your holiday for. Just an old man, died in his sleep on his way past two weeks ago. This were at the edge of the small, western ring. Now that I think of it," he said, breaking out in a grin, "you may be interested to know there is an old legend about the stones that folk often recount when a death such as this occurs. Since probably afore words was written, there's been stories told of how the stones sometimes wander

240

down to the river to drink. 'Twere anyone unfortunate enough to witness this magic, they was instantly struck down for their impertinence. It's uncommon to find a body among the stones – it's only happened this once in my lifetime – but even if a dead animal be discovered, folk will joke about 'the stones walking once more in Milbury'."

The next few days passed lazily as I have already described, with some additional expeditions to the nearby River Kennet. Having found a spot that would be worth fishing, I determined to do just that the next morning. Holmes, not being much of a sportsman, remained behind to do some reading. When I returned later that afternoon with several rainbow trout for dinner, I was surprised to see a young, blonde-haired, and moustachioed man in a tweed suit and straw boater authoritatively marching toward the cottage with two constables. I caught him up just as Holmes was opening the weathered, creaking door to admit him.

"Ah, you must be Dr. Watson, judging by old Heyplumb's description, and you sir, must be Sherlock Holmes."

"At your service, Inspector . . . ?"

The man looked somewhat surprised, Holmes simply waved indicating the constables and then motioned us both inside.

"I'm Inspector Dandridge. You men can stay outside," he said as Holmes closed the door and gestured for him to take a seat in one of the easy chairs by the fire. After I set aside my catch and poured some brandy for us, we settled down to hear the inspector's story.

"I broke my fast at The Dented Helm this morning, and I'm glad I did. Mr. Heyplumb mentioned meeting you last night. When he did, I recalled a letter from one of my colleagues, who was recently posted to the Yard, in which he sang your praises."

Holmes leaned back abruptly, lowered his eyelids, and demanded, "Please, Inspector Dandridge, you clearly did not come here to sing my praises. Tell us your story. Start at the beginning and leave nothing out."

"Of course," he replied, clearing his throat awkwardly. "That was all by way of saying that something happened again last night that I can't explain, and I could definitely use your help. You see, if I didn't know any better, I'd probably declare that the stones are once again wandering in Milbury."

Holmes leaned back further, steepled his fingers, and said, "Ah, there has been another death then?"

"Indeed, Mr. Holmes – two deaths. A young couple: Jeremy Stimtoe and Maisy Flinders. It was like they fell asleep watching the stars and never woke up. Old Fariss, who likes to walk around the bank in the mornings when the weather allows, discovered them shortly after dawn and reported it to the station. They were found, lying side-by-side, holding hands, along the edge of one of the smaller circles near a rough looking part of the western side of the henge."

"And there were no signs of foul play?" I asked.

"No, Dr. Watson. Like I said, it was like they had just gone to sleep."

"Like the tramp who died two weeks ago?"

"Precisely, Mr. Holmes, except, in his case, we just assumed his heart had given out and left it at that. But Stimtoe and Flinders were nineteen and seventeen respectively and very well-known and liked locally. She was a housekeeper at the Manor and he was a groom. They had only recently started courting. I'll double-check, of course, but to the best of my knowledge and observation, they were both in excellent health."

"To have a second death at the site, like the tramp's, would be quite the coincidence, but a pair of them strains all credulity. Are the bodies still at the scene?"

"No. Due to the couple's popularity and the visibility of the location, I had them taken immediately to the morgue. You can view them there, of course, and I was careful about having them moved. I can show you exactly where they lay if you'd like to accompany me to the circle."

Holmes sighed impatiently and said, "Very well, we shall have to view them in the morgue. We can visit the scene of their deaths afterward."

And with that, the inspector and his two constables led us to a local mortuary. As we walked through the narrow streets, flanked with old buildings that seemed to lean toward us and shutting out much of the sunlight, I quietly reminded Holmes, "As your doctor, it would be remiss of me not to point out that the point of this trip was rest and relaxation. I can't say I entirely agree with your taking up another case before we've even settled in."

"Nonsense, Watson. Take in these surroundings. Breathe this air," he declared and inhaled dramatically. "What could be more healthy? Why, look at all this exercise we're getting. Besides, you must admit you are at least a little curious? If not, I suppose we could turn and go back to the cottage . . . ."

"All right, Holmes. You win. But do go easy."

The mortuary, which functioned as the morgue, was a large, one-story building, and after traversing a long corridor that led past empty, dimly-lit viewing rooms and an office where the undertaker was occupied with his books, we entered a large room that was cool and damp. The only two windows were covered by dark, floral-patterned curtains, but the gaslights illuminated it adequately for the usual purposes, and in this case, examinations. The coroner, Dr. William Templeton, a sturdy man with sizable white sideburns, had already come down from his practice and was sitting in his shirtsleeves by a table beneath one of the windows. We sidled past the room's other quiet occupants so the inspector could make introductions. As Dr. Templeton spoke, I drew back the sheets from Stimtoe and Flinders and began checking their temperature, rigour, lividity, and other conditions, while looking for some clue as to what had caused their deaths. Holmes stood between the two slabs, hovering over me as I worked while listening to the coroner's summation.

"I place their deaths at approximately the same time, about ten o'clock yesterday evening. We have quite a mystery before us here, gentlemen, as I have not discovered any cause of death. I've ruled out foul play, such as poisoning, completely," he noted in stentorian tones, seeing Holmes bend over and sniff around Stimtoe's mouth. "As I am also the village's general practitioner, I can attest that both of these young people were the very picture of health. Given the circumstances, their families would prefer I don't perform a *post mortem* examination."

"I must agree, Holmes. Like the inspector said, it's like they simply passed in their sleep. Have you found anything?"

He stood back up and turned from Flinders, sighed heavily, and pulled up the sheet.

"No. But it is absurd that both their hearts would decide to stop beating at almost the exact same time and at their ages. No, to find an explanation, we shall have to look elsewhere. Please lead us to where the bodies were discovered, Inspector," he said as he turned, smoothed his hair, and left the room and a rather bemused Dr. Templeton.

The humidity had risen noticeably and the sky grew overcast as we made our way out of the village in the direction of the outer circle and bank. The smaller inner-circle that was our destination loomed before us as we walked over the thick green grass, the large gray stones truly looking like a brooding gathering of giants about to perform the most solemn of rituals.

"We must hurry, Inspector," demanded Holmes who began to jog ahead in the indicated direction. "This sky threatens rain. Point me in the right direction."

When we drew up to him, he was crawling along the ground with his glass, waving at us to stay back. He then began slowly backing away from the spot while still hovering close to the ground. Inspector Dandridge and his constables were amused by this performance until I explained to them that he was now tracing the couple's footsteps as they approached their destination. Holmes then began walking all around the monument in wider circles, and then returned after reaching the ditch. He was obviously annoyed.

"What did you find, Mr. Holmes?" asked the inspector.

243

"Their resting place . . . at the spot you indicated, and the direction from which they both approached the monument . . . together. There is a lack of data here, or at least a lack of data that points toward anything other than coincidence. No, there must be something more. Now, if you'll excuse me, I must think."

And with that, he turned and began walking hurriedly back to the cottage, lighting a cigarette. I apologised to the inspector for his abruptness and assured him we would soon be in touch. I also encouraged him to let us know if any new developments arose.

Back at the cottage, I found Holmes sitting in one of the easy chairs, smoking his pipe while looking into the distance from our rain-spattered windows. A full pouch of foul-smelling tobacco was on the table next to him, and I knew I would hear nothing from him for quite some time. Though it pained me to do it, I discarded my catch from earlier in the day and made my escape to The Dented Helm when the storm subsided. By the time I had finished my supper that evening, the place was full of talk about the young couple, and a few of the punters cornered me at various times to ask if that detective I was travelling with was looking into it. I told them only that we knew Inspector Dandridge was investigating the matter and had every confidence in the man. On the walk home, I noticed the weather felt colder and more seasonal than the hot and sometimes humid spring weather we had been experiencing. Back at the cottage, Holmes had constructed a pallet out of various cushions in a corner by the fire and was sitting upon it, smoking languorously. As it grew late, it became clear that he didn't intend to retire to his room, restricting his movements to filling his pipe and raising it to his lips. Restraining the urge to remonstrate with him about overtaxing himself, I decided to leave him to it and head to my room with one of Scott's novels.

I awoke in the dark early morning to Inspector Dandridge pounding at the door, asking for Holmes. By the time I had dressed, Holmes had already admitted the man and put a kettle on.

"Ah, Watson. It's about time you awakened. Here – take this and have a seat. The inspector says we have another body on our hands."

I took the cup and saucer and made my way to an armchair. Holmes handed another to Inspector Dandridge, sat down, and said while re-igniting his pipe, "Did our friend, Fariss, make another discovery on his walk?"

"I'm afraid so, Mr. Holmes."

"Dear me. If we don't figure this out, that man may have to settle on another route to avoid future suspicion. Are we looking at the same circumstances as the other three?"

"Yes, except this man had clearly been drinking and seems to have collapsed in front of the stones."

"Ah, so it didn't look as if he had been sleeping?" I asked.

"No Dr. Watson. More like he passed out and fell face first onto the ground."

"And you could smell liquor on the man?" asked Holmes.

"Yes, and he had a flask of cheap gin in his vest."

"Is the body still there?"

"Indeed it is, Mr. Holmes. Because of the difference in attitude, I felt it necessary to let you examine the scene precisely as we found it."

"You display insight and sound judgement, Dandridge. Hang on to them, and you will no doubt rise in the force. Let's waste no further time." Holmes tapped out his pipe and drained his cup. "We can depart as soon as you finish your coffee." He then sprang from his chair to don his Inverness cloak, ear-flapped hunting cap, and scarf, as the morning still had a chill to it.

Once more, as we approached the solemn circle of rocky sentinels and the two constables we had met the day before, we found a body between the circle and the bank. It was a man who looked to be in his early forties with dark brown hair, a walrus-like moustache, and several day's beard growth. His garish, houndstooth suit was dishevelled and displayed dark stains in several places. Holmes removed his glass and dropped down beside the poor man, examining every inch of him before retracing the footsteps of the deceased, like a hound who has caught a scent. I could tell he had found some clues by several of his inarticulate exclamations and bursts of laughter. He leapt back to his feet, grinning, and scanned along the green bank, talking to himself.

"Too windy now and too warm, but on a still night, if it was cold. Low to the ground . . . .

"Watson," he continued, "I have been sluggish in mind and wanting in that mixture of imagination and reality that is the basis of my art. It puts me entirely to shame!" he announced as he walked back over to us. "Inspector, I remember the day before yesterday being unseasonably warm, but the night, it was much cooler?"

"It was, indeed, Mr. Holmes. It's rare for us to have so many hot days in the spring, but what does that have to do with – "

"And the day and night the tramp died . . . Were the conditions similar?"

"Yes, they were, Mr. Holmes," said one of the constables. "I remember stopping in at The Helm for some lemonade to try to cool myself off earlier that day, but it was chilly that next morning when I was roused from bed."

245

"And the wind?" asked Holmes.

"I believe there was a breeze, a bit stronger than now," confirmed the inspector. "But what can you tell me about the body?"

"Ah, our friend here has much to tell us that you should find interesting. Note the grease stains on the lower part of his coat and pant legs, as if he has been leaning against heavy machinery. Now look at his right boot, and those cracks in the leather right at the base of the toes. There's nothing like them on his left boot. There's more, but let's cut to the chase," said Holmes, holding up the man's right hand. "Do you see the ink stains?"

"I do, Mr. Holmes, and those cracks in his boot look like they were caused by putting weight upon a treadle. This man operates a printing press."

"Excellent, Dandridge. His clothing is also spattered, but the particles are much finer and harder to observe with the naked eye. But look more closely at his hand. Are the colours of the ink not suggestive to you?"

"I'll be d----d!" cried the inspector. "Currency! This man is a *counterfeiter*!"

"Precisely. Watson, would you please examine the body now to see if you can discover a cause of death? I must admit, I could find nothing."

As I stooped to examine the corpse, Holmes shaded his eyes with his hand and scanned the horizon once more.

"Dandridge, am I imagining it, or does that hill jutting up from the very regular line of the henge just there suggest a different kind of earthwork? It's like a crooked tooth in the regular line of the henge."

"Oh, yes. The Romans built a mine here. That is thought to be the old entrance, but as you can see, it's long been sealed off."

"Yes, even so . . . Ah, Watson. What news?"

"He died at around eleven o'clock last night. Judging by the smell of alcohol that still lingers, he must have been drunk as a lord. That would definitely explain his collapse, but I still can see no certain sign of what caused his death."

"That I may be able to supply this evening if the current weather holds. I need to do a little research. Dandridge, please remove this fellow discreetly and try to delay any word of his death getting out. It is still early enough that you may be able to pull that off. Perhaps one of you can even catch Fariss before he encounters a neighbour. Then, if you could come to the cottage tonight at ten o'clock, I think I may be able to demonstrate what killed these unfortunates and perhaps help you lay your hands upon some villains," he concluded, turning and walking swiftly back toward the village.

"And bring a revolver and some extra Darbies!" he fired over his shoulder at us.

I left Dandridge and his men to the ignominious task of hiding the body as best they could until a cart could be procured. Back at the cottage, I prepared a small lunch for myself and tried to settle in for a nap to pass the time until we could resume our investigation. When I awoke in the early evening, Holmes hadn't yet returned, so I made myself a sandwich and then sat by the fire to smoke and stare out of the windows, since I knew I couldn't bring myself to focus upon anything else in my eagerness to learn more about our counterfeiters and deadly stone circle.

He returned at just past nine-thirty and helped himself to the coffee I had brewed in order to fortify us for our night's work. As always, he wouldn't eat while involved with a case. I tried to get more details from him, but he was stubbornly vague.

"All will soon be clear, my friend. I just wanted to do a little research in town to satisfy myself upon a few points and then surveille the area around that part of the ditch and bank. We have a lively evening's entertainment before us. You remembered to bring your revolver?"

I picked up my trusty service weapon and unwrapped the grease cloth in which it was wrapped.

"Very good. And it looks like Inspector Dandridge is ready to join us," he said as three silhouettes approached our door. "Come in, Inspector! And your men. You are working overtime tonight. Help yourselves to some coffee before we depart."

Soon we were all on our way back to the familiar, yet always enigmatic, stone circle. The night was cold and my old wound ached slightly as I watched the heads of Holmes, in his hunting cap, and Dandridge, in his boater, bobbing before me, their breath hanging visibly in the air, while we walked through the thick grass outside the village. The moon was full, so we didn't need any additional illumination during the walk. Soon, Holmes put up a hand for us to halt before we arrived at the stones.

"I think that is quite far enough. I'm sure I shall have adequate time to cross to the other side, find exactly what has been causing these strange deaths, and return before succumbing myself. Whatever you do, do not light any matches until I have returned"

I looked over at the ancient mine and back at my friend.

"I don't like where this is going, Holmes. Surely there's a better way to test whatever idea you've formulated."

"There is no time. We must complete this business tonight before the counterfeiters, who are our next order of business, have flown. If anything should happen to me, you and the inspector hold your breath and run like the devil to pull me back here!" he ordered, before running through the stones to where we had found the other bodies.

When he reached that spot, he knelt and looked around him for a moment. Rising, I noticed with some nervousness that he stumbled a little before lurching over to the left and running several feet. At this point, he knelt once more and then collapsed. As he struggled to stand again, I took off at a bound with the inspector on my heels. I could sense the thinness of the atmosphere halfway before I had even reached him and was becoming seriously winded when I gasped for what air I could get and held my breath. When I reached Holmes, he pointed at the ground and gasped, "There!" He indicated a large rock jutting from the earth, no doubt a toppled stone that now rent the ground like a broken blade. At one corner of this stone, the earth had been visibly opened, the long, dark line, visible even in the moonlight. I wasted no time and, with the help of Inspector Dandridge, supported Holmes as we hurriedly staggered back to the constables. Gasping, the three of us fell to the ground and sat gulping in air until we were recovered enough to speak. I pulled a flask of brandy from my vest and passed it to Holmes.

"Gas from the mine?" I ventured as he passed the flask back to me, nodding. I took a swig and passed it to the inspector.

"Methane," replied Holmes. "Released from that fissure I pointed out to you. It is unusual for it to cause asphyxiation outdoors, but the other day, when I noticed the mine entrance, I remembered hearing about cases where both farmers and cattle had expired while working near large piles of manure. And those cases always occurred when the weather was like that of the past few days and nights. The pressure, temperature, and lack of a breeze seemingly combining forces somehow to keep it close to the ground.

"My guess is that this is the origin of the myth of the wandering stones. Something would open the ground, allowing the methane beds below the surface to vent. Something like a minor earthquake, mining activity, or perhaps the acoustic vibrations of heavy machinery."

"The noise and vibrations of a printing press!" exclaimed Inspector Dandridge.

"Precisely that."

"And suffocation *is* sometimes undiagnosable," I offered. "Remarkable. It took the first three victims in their sleep before they could even wake to figure out what was happening. The counterfeiter succumbed quickly, no doubt because he'd been drinking."

"And was keeping a nose to the ground," added Holmes. "He was very likely looking for the cause of the deaths in order to correct the situation before circumstances led the authorities to their operation.

248

Speaking of which," he said, suddenly springing to his feet, "we'd better proceed to that next order of business. Inspector, though I'm reluctant to deplete our meagre forces, I am afraid one of your men should stay behind to avoid another tragedy."

"Not to mention the risk of a fire," I added.

"Very well. Edwards, please stay here and keep an eye out," ordered Inspector Dandridge as he began walking with the rest of us toward the bank.

As we descended into the ditch outside the outer stone circle, Holmes said, "I spent some time yesterday doing a bit of research in the village. Several years ago, a local historian and enthusiastic spelunker found another ancient opening in the outer bank of the henge. This one, though, with a little digging, was still accessible. He wrote a paper about it, postulating that it was part of this Roman mine system. It's archived in the local library."

He pointed over to the mine entrance we had already identified, as we began to ascend the bank.

"At sunset, I walked over this bank and staked out a place near the alternate entrance. As I expected, as it got later, three men arrived and entered the cave. I think they are likely to be there still."

When we reached the top of the bank, Holmes warned, "Now, I think silence will be best. We shall make our way over toward those trees at the base of the bank."

We walked quietly down the slope. The four oak trees Holmes had indicated were about one-hundred-and-fifty yards along the edge of the bank. As we continued, the river was visible in the distance, thanks to the moonlight reflecting from the water. When we had reached the trees, we stopped for a few minutes, and Holmes pointed out the small opening we were about to enter. There was no one about outside, so we quietly walked another fifty feet to the cave entrance, and Holmes drew a revolver from his coat. The inspector and I did the same, and we listened. Though we heard nothing from outside the cave, once we crossed the threshold on Holmes's signal, the thrum of machinery became faintly audible. There was one passageway leading away from the entrance, with lanterns strewn along the uneven floor, providing dim lighting. It was tall and wide enough that we could walk two abreast and stand comfortably, so we proceeded cautiously. We passed other smaller, branching passages as we went, but these were dark, besides which the increasing volume of thrumming machinery clearly indicated the way. After a few minutes, the passage veered slightly to the right. The throbbing of the machinery was very loud at this point. Holmes motioned for us to stop while he stepped forward and glanced quickly around. He then motioned that the press was around the corner and held up three fingers to signify how many men he had seen.

Once again, on Holmes's signal, we all dashed at once around the turn and into a cavern that was about twenty feet in diameter with a ceiling almost as high. It was well lit with lanterns and even some torches that had been affixed to the walls with sconces. The light from these gleamed upon the metal parts of the machine that was making all the noise. It was an ingenious device, an offset printer that, though it took up much of the cavern, was considerably smaller than any commercial press I had seen. Since there was no available power supply, one member of the gang sat on a stool, steadily working a treadle with his foot, which set off a chain reaction of pumping pistons and rotating gears. At the other end, another gang member was gathering the blankets of paper as they emerged from two great spools. Along the left wall, at a long table, another villain sat, tinkering with printing plates. The pulsation and whirring of the machine could be heard echoing down other corridors exiting this space, but as I was taking in the scene, I could still hear the shrill cry of the inspector above it all, commanding, "You lot, put up your hands! You're under arrest!"

The three of us had each instinctively covered one the criminals with our pistols, and there was nothing for the counterfeiters to do but comply. We had obviously taken them by surprise, no doubt helped by the roar of the press. All three immediately stood with upraised hands, waiting for the constable to place the manacles on their wrists. As the press wound down and the noise subsided, the man who had been sitting at the table pleaded with the inspector. "Look, Guv'nor, it was just a joke – a gimmick to promote a new investment firm: '*Hernby's: It's like they give you a license to print your own money.*'"

"You're a bright one," replied the inspector. "I'm not buying it, but you're free to try it on with the judge." He then informed the men of their rights, and we all walked back along the passageway to the cave's exit.

"You may take the credit for this one, Dandridge," said Holmes as we emerged from the cave. "My name need not appear in your account,"

"Why, thank you, Mr. Holmes. That is extremely kind of you. And thank you, too, Doctor Watson."

"Don't mention it, Inspector," said Holmes. "You provided us with a most interesting case, which was just what the doctor ordered, so to speak. Why, Watson, this has been a most excellent vacation! I must say I feel truly energised."

I shook my head and grinned as we emerged back into the bright moonlit night and made our way back to the solemn stones that continued to maintain their quiet vigil over the town of Milbury.

The Charity Collection
by Paul Hiscock

The New Year was only a few days old, and festive decorations still adorned our rooms at 221b Baker Street, when Mr. and Mrs. Morton called upon us with a curious request for assistance.

"I planned to make a charitable donation," began Mr. Morton, as soon as he and his wife had been seated comfortably in front of the fire.

"That is most laudable," replied Holmes, "but I fail to see how I can assist you. After all, it isn't a crime to be generous to one's fellow men."

"It is not men I wish to help, Mr. Holmes, but children. Orphans, to be precise."

"Mr. Holmes understood what you meant, Stanley," said Mrs. Morton wearily. "I think you will find he was being humorous."

"Indeed," chuckled Holmes. Then he continued, in a more serious tone, "However, I still do not understand why you have come to us for help. I can see from your suit that you are a frugal man. Although it is smart, and was obviously expensive, it is well worn. A vainer man would have replaced it by now. Alone, it might have suggested that you were once rich and fallen on hard times, but your hat is brand new, and clearly of finest quality. Similarly, I couldn't help but notice your wife's shoes."

Mrs. Morton looked down, and then, self-consciously, drew back her feet so that they were hidden beneath her skirt.

Unperturbed by her reticence, Holmes continued. "They are expensive, but not fashionable, and do not match her outfit, a fact which wealthy women would find intolerable. Rather they are a practical choice, sturdy and hard-wearing. It is obvious that you have money, but you aren't overly concerned by appearances. Instead, you choose only to spend when it is necessary, and on items that will provide good value by outlasting cheaper options. The money you save would leave you plenty to give to charitable causes."

"You are absolutely correct, Mr. Holmes. I don't like to spend frivolously. My parents weren't rich, and taught me to be thankful for everything we had, no matter how small. I may have made my fortune, but I still try to follow the example they set. They would probably have considered this new hat to be an outrageous extravagance, and I do wonder if my old one might have served for another year. However, my wife persuaded me to accept it as a Christmas present, and promised me it wasn't too expensive. Besides, even with such an expenditure, we are still

251

lucky enough to have plenty to share with those less fortunate than ourselves."

"That old thing was falling apart," muttered Mrs. Morton. Her husband didn't reply, but reached over and patted her knee affectionately.

It was rare for Holmes not to discern the nature of a case the moment he met a client, but in this instance I could see that, despite the accuracy of his deductions, he still remained unsure why the Mortons had sought us out.

"If you would like us to find a worthy cause that you might support, we could probably make some suggestions," I said, but Mr. Morton shook his head.

"Thank you, Doctor Watson. I'm always interested to hear about charities doing good work, especially among the poor and criminal classes, and would welcome any recommendations that you gentlemen might make. However, in this instance, I was hoping that you could help me find one specific charity – or rather, the man representing it."

Holmes leaned back in his chair, and I could see from the satisfied expression on his face that he had begun to perceive the shape of the case, although I was still perplexed.

"When did you first hear about this charity?" asked Holmes.

"It was on Christmas Eve," replied Mr. Morton. "I had a few final errands to run before I could start to enjoy the festivities, and so I wasn't at home when a gentleman knocked on our door. My wife answered, and when she heard that he was collecting for charity, she received him warmly. Didn't you, my dear?"

She nodded, and Holmes asked her, "For which charitable cause was he collecting?"

Mr. Morton didn't give her a chance to respond, but instead answered the question himself.

"It was an orphanage in Southwark. This gentleman, Mr. . . . ? I'm sorry, my dear, I've forgotten his name again."

"It was Mr. Brown," she replied, and I wondered if she might take up the narrative, but her husband continued.

"That's right. Such a common name, it just keeps slipping from my mind. Yes, this Mr. Brown was collecting for an orphanage in Southwark. He and some like-minded individuals had resolved to raise funds to furnish the children with a small festive meal, and maybe even some simple toys for Christmas."

I could see that Holmes was frustrated. He would have preferred to have heard Mrs. Morton's first-hand account of the encounter. However, he held his tongue for the time being.

"Knowing that I would heartily approve of such a noble endeavour, my wife fetched the household cash box and made a generous donation. The gentleman thanked her effusively, wishing her a most merry Christmas before moving on to continue collecting elsewhere.

"When I returned home a few hours later, my wife told me what she had done. She shared some of the stories about the poor abandoned children that Mr. Brown had related, and I'm not ashamed to tell you, gentlemen, I was moved to tears by their plight. I regretted that I hadn't been there, because if I had been I could have made a far greater contribution. You see, the household funds were already depleted by our Christmas preparations, and my wife doesn't have a key to the main safe in my study.

"As we made merry over the days that followed, my thoughts often returned to those unfortunate children, whose Christmas would have been so different to our own. I started to think about my resolutions for the year ahead, and decided that one of them would be to offer more support to this orphanage and the children who live there. Now, usually my wife wholeheartedly supports my charitable decisions, but in this instance she appeared reluctant. It transpired that while she had listened to all Mr. Brown's stories, she hadn't noted the name of the orphanage. She apologised profusely, but I wasn't concerned. After all, I didn't think it would be hard to find the right place, and so the next day I travelled down to Southwark and began to make enquiries. However, the search proved more difficult than I had anticipated. Although I found a number of orphanages in the area, none of them quite matched the descriptions in the stories my wife had shared. Furthermore, the kindly individuals who ran them had never heard of Mr. Brown, nor received any charitable donation like the one he had planned."

"My husband was quite dejected when he returned home," said Mrs. Morton, finally deciding to contribute to the narrative. "However, as I told him then, maybe I was mistaken as to where the orphanage was, but why not make a donation to one of the other places that he visited? After all, the children there are in just as much need, and there is no doubt that they would appreciate his generosity. Yet he is determined to find Mr. Brown and those specific children, which is why we have come here today. Please don't judge him too harshly for wasting your time on such a trivial matter. It is foolish, but I'm sure you can see that he has only the best of intentions."

Mr. Morton turned on her angrily. "Do not call me foolish, especially in front of these gentlemen! I have told you that this is important to me, and I expect you to accept my decision."

"I'm so sorry," she murmured.

Mr, Morton calmed down immediately. "No, it is I who should apologise for losing my temper."

"Mrs. Morton," said Holmes, "I believe your husband is concerned about something more serious than just making another donation. Mr. Morton, you suspect that this might be a criminal matter."

Upon hearing Holmes's words, the blood drained from Mrs. Morton's face. She swayed in her seat, as though she was about to faint, and I rushed to her side to offer my assistance.

"I feared this might happen," said Mr. Morton. "My wife is a sensitive creature, and I knew that she would take it to heart if she realised what I suspected. However, you are quite correct, Mr. Holmes. I'm less concerned with finding the orphanage than this man, Brown."

"You believe that his story of the orphanage was an invention, intended to engender sympathy so that he could fraudulently obtain donations from generous people like you and your wife?"

"I'm afraid I do, Mr. Holmes. I did not tell my wife because I didn't want her to feel guilty at having been deceived by this rogue."

"Even if Holmes can find him," I cautioned, "I doubt you will get your money back. An opportunist like this will probably have spent it all by now."

"You misunderstand, Doctor Watson. I'm not looking for reparations, or revenge. However, I am concerned that others might fall prey to this same trick. I don't want any other kind souls to be deceived, or for any more money to be taken that otherwise might have supported deserving causes."

"A worthy goal," I said, and Holmes nodded in agreement. "I'm sure that we will be able to help you."

"My husband is a most generous and selfless man," sighed Mrs. Morton. "It is one of the reasons why I married him." She seemed a little brighter, but was obviously still discomposed by the realisation that she might have been fooled.

"Very well," said Holmes. "If we are to proceed, I will need a detailed description of this Mr. Brown from you, Mrs. Morton. Please try to remember as much as you can. Even the smallest, most inconsequential detail might hold the clue that will help me track him down."

"I will try my best," said Mrs. Morton, "but I'm not sure how helpful I will be. I'm not sure that I would recognise him if I passed him on the street. There wasn't anything very distinctive about him."

Mr. Morton patted her on the knee. "It's fine, my dear. Just try your best."

"Well, I think he was in his thirties. Not as old as us, but not young either. He had brown hair, straight, and slightly too long. His nose was quite wide and flat, as though it had been squashed. I remember thinking that it looked like he'd been hit in the face. Maybe it was by someone he'd tried to steal from before?"

"Possibly," I agreed, encouragingly. "Go on."

"He was about the same height as my husband."

"About five-feet-five, then," said Holmes."

"But quite a bit thinner than him – not just around the belly, but in his face too."

She paused, worried that she might have offended her husband, but he laughed amiably and put his hand on his stomach.

"I have put on a few pounds since we met. I admit that, when it comes to food, I find it slightly harder to be abstemious than in other parts of my life."

"Please continue, Mrs. Morton," said Holmes. "What else can you tell us? For example, what was he wearing?"

"It's hard to tell. He wasn't there long, and never unbuttoned his overcoat."

"Well, what was that like? What colour was it? Was it good quality?"

I could tell that Holmes was getting impatient. It always frustrated him how little other people noticed.

Mrs. Morton hesitated for a moment as she tried to remember. "It was black . . . no, a dark navy blue, and good quality. Better than that tatty thing my husband wore today, at any rate. It is one of the reasons I let him in. It was obvious he was a gentleman, not some beggar."

"Appearances can be deceiving," I said. "Anyone can dress the part of a gentleman."

"Looks are one thing, but sounding the part is harder," said Holmes. "How did he speak? Did he have an accent?"

"No, he just sounded normal, but now that you mention it, he sounded slightly rougher than most of my husband's gentleman friends. I didn't think anything of it at the time. After all, as my husband has already told you, he isn't from a wealthy background himself. However, maybe if I had thought about it, I might have been more cautious."

"I'm not surprised you didn't think of it until now," replied Holmes. "However, now we know he is a local man, or has lived here long enough to sound like he is."

"Is there anything else we can tell you?" asked Mr. Morton.

"No, I think I have learned everything I can from you," said Holmes. "I need to speak to your servants next. They might remember something about this man that you have forgotten."

"I don't think they will be able to help you," replied Mrs. Morton. "It was so busy that day, what with it being Christmas Eve, and we only have a small household. The servants were all either preoccupied in the kitchen, or out on errands themselves. Knowing this, when I heard the door, I shouted out that I would answer it myself, so that they could continue with their work. I regret it now, but I'm afraid that I was the only person who saw Mr. Brown."

"That is unfortunate," replied Holmes, "but it is perhaps instructive. Calling on Christmas Eve was a well-calculated decision. In addition to the likelihood that people will be more generous in the festive season, they are also busy, and likely to ask less questions, making a donation quickly so that they can return to their preparations. We should speak to your neighbours. If Mr. Brown took advantage of the Christmas distractions in your household, it is likely he called upon other families as well."

"A capital idea," said Mr. Morton. "I will hail a cab, and we can travel there together. Thank you, Mr. Holmes. Come along, my dear."

He held out his hand to help his wife to his feet, and then led her out of our rooms.

It took a few minutes for Holmes and myself to find our coats and get ready to leave. By the time we opened the front door, a cab was waiting for us, and Mrs. Morton were already sitting inside, sheltering from the cold, while her husband waited by the curb.

At the bottom of the steps, Holmes paused, pulled a piece of paper from his pocket, and held it out at waist height. A moment later a boy appeared. I didn't see where he had come from, but he took the note.

"Find out everything you can about this man, and report back to me this afternoon," said Holmes.

The boy nodded and held out his hand. He plucked the coin that Holmes flicked towards him out of the air, and then disappeared as quickly as he had appeared.

"Do you think your Irregulars will be able to find out anything about this Mr. Brown?" I asked.

"Possibly not, although that itself would be informative. A criminal with such a distinctive *modus operandi* ought to be well-known within the underworld community."

The cab dropped us in Pembroke Square, an attractive residential area in Kensington consisting of a small park surrounded by terraced houses. I could see why Mr. Brown had chosen to target the households here on Christmas Eve. The families living here were all affluent, and would have given generously if they fell for his story, as Mrs. Morton had.

We watched as our clients entered their house, and then Holmes led us to front door of their immediate neighbour on the left.

A footman opened the door when we knocked, and Holmes handed him his card.

"I will tell my master you are here," he said.

"Not yet," said Holmes. "You might be able to help us. Were you working on Christmas Eve?"

"Yes, I was here all day. The family held a party and there were people coming and going all day."

"Among all those people, did you answer the door to a man collecting for charity?"

"No. We had a couple call here before Christmas, but none that day."

"The man we're looking for was collecting for an orphanage in Southwark. He went by the name of Brown. Was he one of the men that called on one of the other days?" asked Holmes.

"No, there was no one by that name."

"He could have been using a different name and story," I suggested.

Holmes shared the description that Mrs. Morton had given us, but the footman shook his head.

"No, no one like that came here. Do you want me to fetch my master so that you can speak with him?"

"I don't think that will be necessary," said Holmes. "Thank you for your help."

The footman shrugged and closed the door.

"Are you sure we shouldn't be speaking to his master?" I asked. "He might have dealt with Mr. Brown directly, like Mrs. Morton did."

"It is possible, but unlikely," Holmes replied. "Come on, Watson. We should move along. It's a cold day, and we have a lot of houses to visit."

Over the course of the next hour-and-a-half, we called at all the houses around Pembroke Square, until we were once more standing outside the Mortons' house. Our enquiries hadn't been fruitful. In a couple of cases, nobody had been at home. At some houses we just spoke to the servants, whereas at others we questioned the master or mistress themselves, but none of them recognised the description of Mr. Brown. One man slammed the door in our faces as soon as we started speaking. Even if Brown had stopped there, it was clear that he wouldn't have received a warm welcome.

Our most promising encounter was with an elderly widow who lived on the other side of the Square. She welcomed us inside and insisted that we join her for a cup of tea while she answered our questions. However, when we finally persuaded her to tell us what she knew about Brown, it transpired that he had never visited at all. She had pretended to know something just to get us to keep her company for a little while. I probably should have been angry, but I felt sorry for her, and besides it was a pleasant and warm interlude in what was otherwise a cold and frustrating afternoon.

"I don't understand why Brown only visited this one house," I said to Holmes, as walked up to the Mortons' front door. "Not everyone we have met today would have fallen for his trick, but some of them surely would have."

"It suggests that Morton was very carefully targeted," replied Holmes. "He prides himself on his charitable giving, to an extreme degree, and it seems that our thief knew about this. If Brown came to just this house, it's because he was told that he would receive a warm reception."

"So we are looking for someone with a vendetta against Morton? Why else would someone who knew him help a criminal target him?"

As I was finishing my question, Holmes gestured for me to be silent, and a moment later, Mrs. Morton opened the door.

"Have you discovered anything?" she asked breathlessly. It appeared that she was so anxious to hear about our investigation that she had run to answer the door.

"No," I said, "it appears that Brown didn't visit any of your neighbours."

"Really? I suppose there is nothing more you can do then. We'll have to tell my husband that your investigation has been unsuccessful."

"Unsuccessful?" The sound of Mr. Morton's voice came from the other side of the hallway behind his wife. He came over to stand beside her. "Surely you aren't giving up so soon, Mr. Holmes?"

"Certainly not. As I was about to tell your wife, I have a new theory to pursue. Who knows about your charitable giving?"

"Why, everyone, Mr. Holmes. I make no secret of it, although I know that there are some gentlemen in my social circle who think that I'm foolish to give so much away."

"It is possible that someone told Mr. Brown about your charitable proclivities and that he targeted you because of them. We will need to speak to your servants after all, and then, perhaps, your employees."

"Very well," replied Mr. Morton, less enthusiastically, "but I cannot imagine any of my staff, here or in the factory, betraying me. I'm not just generous to strangers. I make sure that everyone who works for me is well provided for."

He led us through to the servants' quarters and introduced us to everyone. As Mrs. Morton had said earlier, it was a small household. Just the butler, cook, and a maid. They all seemed shocked when we told them why we were there.

258

"Who would do such a cruel thing to the missus?" asked the maid, a young girl who was obviously of a sensitive and sentimental disposition. "She told us all about those orphans, and how they were going to have a Christmas dinner after all, and now you tell us that was all a lie, and they never got fed after all? It breaks my heart, it does."

She started crying, and the cook put her arm around her shoulder to comfort her.

"No, girl," replied the butler, a ruddy-faced man, in a gruff tone that brooked no-nonsense. "They are saying that the orphans never existed."

Despite his words, the maid continued crying, making it difficult to continue our interview, but Holmes seemed unconcerned.

"Thank you, all of you. I think we've seen enough here."

"What about the servants?" I whispered to him. "Surely we should question them further."

"I studied their reaction," he replied. "They were all genuinely shocked, both that their master had been stolen from and that their mistress had been deceived. If they provided any information to Brown, it was by way of a careless conversation overheard in a shop or public house. I doubt they would even remember their mistake, or that they would be able to furnish us with any useful information. No, I don't believe they have the answer we are looking for." Then he turned to Mr. Morton. "If we might have directions to your office, and a letter of authority permitting us to interrupt work and question your staff, we will continue our investigation there."

Our client shook his head. "I will do better than that," he said. "I will take you there myself."

Morton informed us that his wife was quite overcome by the events of the day, and that she had elected to stay at home. Therefore, it was just the three of us who travelled across the river and east to Rotherhithe, where Morton's biscuit factory was located. As we travelled, Morton spoke with obvious pride about his business. He had a right to be proud. Not only had he built up the business from nothing, but he also produced a fine product. I was never disappointed when Mrs. Hudson produced one of his biscuits to accompany a cup of tea. He protested that he couldn't imagine any of his employees betraying him.

"I pay them well – more than they would get in another factory, at any rate. And they were each given a box of biscuits to take home for Christmas!" he told us, slightly defensively. However, he seemed slightly less certain of them than he had been of his household staff.

Upon our arrival, we were greeted by the foreman of works.

"Is something the matter, sir," he asked. "Only we weren't expecting to see you here today, but you can see we are all hard at work."

"There isn't anything wrong here, Michael," Morton said. "You are doing a fine job. However, Mr. Holmes here has some questions for the workers."

"Should I shut down production? Only it will cost us. I doubt we would be able to get everything up to speed again before the end of the day."

"No, no, that won't be necessary. Mr. Holmes can speak to them while they work."

The factory floor was certainly a hive of industry. Men, women, and children bustled around the large machines, feeding in ingredients and maintaining the works. The largest congregation of people was at the far end of the factory, where a large group of women gathered around a table, packing the finished biscuits into decorative tins and boxes, designed to entice customers in shops around the country. It was towards this group that Morton led us first. As we approached, I could hear them chattering and laughing. However, they fell quiet as soon as they saw us approaching.

"Good afternoon, ladies," he said to the gathered women.

"Good morning, Mr. Morton," they chanted back to him.

"I hope you can help us," said Holmes. "We are looking for a man."

"Aren't we all, love?" shouted a woman at the far end of the table. "Although I reckon I might be more to your tastes. What do you say, handsome?"

The girls all laughed.

"That's enough, Molly," said Morton. "Mr. Holmes is a detective, and here on business, not to exchange bawdy badinage with you."

I heard Molly mutter, "More's the pity," but then she held her tongue, like the rest of the girls.

"Someone stole some money from Mr. Morton's house," said Holmes.

The women looked shocked, and started muttering to each other again.

"Do any of you recognise this man?" shouted Holmes above the hubbub, and the women settled down to hear him share the description.

"Why, that sounds like Luke!" shouted one of them, and then the others started to join in, agreeing with her.

"Who is this man, Luke?" asked Holmes.

"Why, he's one of our senior engineers," said the foreman. "He keeps the machines running and the ovens burning hot. I'm not sure what you think he might have done, but I cannot imagine him getting involved with anything criminal."

"We shall see. Take us to him, and quickly. If he is guilty, and he hears we are looking for him, he might try to run."

The foreman briskly led us across the factory floor.

"There he is," he said, pointing out a man standing next to one of the industrial ovens.

It was very noisy in that part of the factory, and as a result our quarry didn't hear us approaching. He jumped in shock as Holmes placed a hand upon his shoulder.

"Will you come with us?" Holmes said.

I wondered if we had the right person, as this man in a boiler suit looked nothing like the gentleman Mrs. Morton had described. However then he turned around and looked at us, and I realised that I had been mistaken. His workers' clothes had fooled me here, just as his smart attire had fooled Mrs. Morton. However, this was undoubtedly the same man, with his long brown hair, slim face, and that distinctive squashed nose.

Luke looked confused and turned to the foreman for an explanation. The foreman advised him, "Just do as the gentleman says," and I was grateful, as I didn't relish a chase across the factory floor if he decided to flee.

Luke allowed himself to be led away from the machines by Holmes, and Morton guided us towards the office, where we could question him in peace.

Once we were there and the door was closed, it was quiet enough to proceed. There were only two chairs in the office, one each side of the desk, and unsure about who should take them, all five of us elected to stand.

"Were you in Pembroke Square on Christmas Eve?" Holmes asked.

"Where is that?" asked Luke, and Holmes frowned.

"It is where I live," said Morton.

"I don't know anything about that," said Luke. "I never go near any of your fancy houses."

"My wife says a man who looked just like you called at our house, collecting money for charity. Are you calling her a liar?"

"I'm not calling her anything!" Luke replied, indignantly. "I've never even spoken to the woman. I've only seen her when she has toured the factory with you. She must be mistaken. There are plenty of men who look like me."

"Not with a nose like that," I said. "That's a very distinctive injury. What happened to you?"

"Used to box, when I were a young man. Other man caught me a sucker punch and broke my nose. Never got set right, so I ended up like this."

261

"If you weren't in Pembroke Gardens that day," I asked, "where were you?"

"I were right here," he replied, "working on the machines."

"Now I know you are lying," said Morton. "The factory had already been shut down for Christmas. All the workers had gone home."

The foreman coughed, softly. "Begging your pardon, sir, but that isn't quite correct. It is true that we had shut down production, but there were still a few of us here. The machines needed to be switched over, ready for the new orders."

"Switched over?" I asked.

"You see, sir, before Christmas we were making a lot of, what I call, your fancy biscuits. You know, ones that gentlemen like you might put out at a party, or give as a gift. Very popular, they are, and they sell very well, before Christmas. However, come the New Year, people tend to prefer something plainer, so we have to switch over the machines to make those instead. It's fiddly work and requires a specialist hand. Luke here is our best, but even with him and a few of the other lads, it still took us all day."

"And you are certain that he never left?" I asked.

"Absolutely. None of us took a break longer than ten minutes all day."

"Then I am at a loss," I said. "How can one person be in two places at the same time? Unless he happens to have a *doppelgänger* walking around London, it would seem impossible. What do you think, Holmes? How did he do it?"

I turned to look at my friend, and saw that he was standing by the window, looking out on to the factory floor. He didn't even seem to be listening.

"Did you hear what the foreman said?" I asked. "They were here all day on Christmas Eve. How could Luke have made it to Pembroke Gardens and back without being missed?"

"You should have listened more carefully. It was clear to me immediately that he wasn't our man."

"However did you reach that conclusion? Apart from his clothes, he looks just like the man Mrs. Morton described."

"But he doesn't *sound* like him. Do you not remember what Mrs. Morton said? He had a normal accent, and to her that certainly meant London. Yet it was clear from the first time he opened his mouth that he wasn't from here, but from Yorkshire."

I cursed myself for not having noticed something so obvious.

"Maybe he faked a London accent," I said. "It can be done. I've heard you imitate all types of voice."

"That is true, but it takes a great amount of practice. I don't think this man is capable of such a deception, and even if he was, it wouldn't address the other insurmountable problems in this case."

He turned to Luke. "Thank you for your time. You are free to go now."

"Just like that? First you are accusing me of something, I'm not even sure what, and now I can just go?"

Holmes nodded, and the foreman touched Luke on the arm.

"Let's leave these gentlemen to their business," he said, and led the other man out of the office.

"Well, this is a fine mess," said Morton once they had left. "The factory is disrupted, one of my best workers is upset, and we are still no closer to finding this Mr. Brown. I admit, based on your reputation, I had expected more from you Mr. Holmes."

"I am sorry if you feel dissatisfied, Mr. Morton," said Holmes. "I can assure you that we have investigated most thoroughly, but I admit our search has led us down a blind alley. However, if you will permit us, Doctor Watson and I will return to your house. I'm certain that we'll be able to pick up the correct trail there and resolve this matter quite promptly."

"Very well, but I cannot chase around London with you any further. I must stay here and ensure that things are running smoothly again after this disruption."

"Yes," replied Holmes. "I believe that would be for the best."

"I still don't understand where we took a wrong turn," I said to Holmes as we rode in the cab back to Pembroke Gardens. "I was certain that we had our Mr. Brown."

"Watson, you are a creative man, are you not?"

I was thrown by this sudden change of subject.

"Yes, I'm a writer, so I suppose I am."

"Could you then describe someone for me?"

"Who? One of the people we have met on this case?"

"No, none of them. A fictional person. Someone you have only seen in your imagination."

I racked my brain. It was a harder task than I would have thought.

"Very well," I began. "He is tall, almost six feet. Thick black hair with mutton chop sideburns. He has a sharp chin, and an even sharper nose. Oh, and a bushy black moustache."

Holmes clapped his hands. "Congratulations, Watson, you have just described Constable Collins with the addition of a fine new moustache. I should suggest that he try growing one forthwith."

I thought back over my description and realised that was who I had been describing. We had worked with the constable on a case just before Christmas.

"It is harder than you might think, and besides, I'm not really that type of writer. All my accounts are about real people and events. I barely have to use my imagination at all."

Holmes laughed. "Don't concern yourself, Watson. You demonstrated my point perfectly. It is difficult to do. Most of us, if put on the spot, will draw upon a face that we have seen in the past, maybe add a distinctive detail to make them stand out, as you did by adding a moustache."

"That is all very well, but I don't understand what it has to do with the case."

"I gave Mrs. Morton a similar test earlier, and she struggled just as you did."

"You think her description of Mr. Brown was made up?"

"I know it was. Under pressure to provide me with a detailed description, she thought of a man she had seen once or twice while visiting her husband's factory. She probably didn't even realise that she was doing it, just as you failed to recognise that you were describing Constable Collins, but it rang false to me, especially when she described his accent. She was thinking about what I wanted to hear, and added in the detail about his rougher accent so that I would be convinced that he was a criminal."

"So there never was a Mr. Brown. Then who was it that called at their house on Christmas Eve?"

As I asked this, the cab drew to a halt.

"I think it would be better if you asked Mrs. Morton that question," replied Holmes, before he stepped out into the street.

Mrs. Morton was surprised to see us again.

"Where is my husband? Why did he not come with you?"

"He had a few matters to attend to at his factory," replied Holmes. "He will follow us in due course."

"Is everything all right there?"

"Yes. There was just a bit of a disruption when we confronted your Mr. Brown."

"Mr. Brown?" she asked, the surprise obvious on her face. "You actually found him. I never imagined . . . that is to say, I'm surprised you found him so quickly."

"It wasn't hard," said Holmes. "After all, your description was most detailed. His colleagues recognised it immediately."

"That is good news," she said, hesitantly. "Has he confessed to his crimes?"

"No, he is denying everything."

"Well, of course he would. Criminals always do." She sounded more confident now. "Still, my husband must be pleased that you found him."

"Criminals often deny committing their crimes," replied Holmes, "but then so do innocent men." Then his expression turned hard. "It was a mistake to describe a real person, Mrs. Morton. You could have doomed an innocent man. Besides, had you been more imaginative, you might have had us futilely searching London forever trying to find Mr. Brown."

"I don't know what you mean," she said, but I could see in her eyes that she knew she had been outwitted.

"Mr. Morton is a most generous man," said Holmes, suddenly changing the subject, as he had done with me in the cab.

"Yes, he gives to lots of charities and good causes."

"All his employees, both here and in the factory, seem to like him, and you yourself told us that his generosity was one of the reasons you married him."

"Indeed it was. It is a quality I find most attractive."

"However, I expect you thought that his generosity would extend to you as his wife. A wealthy man like him could afford to buy you the finest jewellery and clothes. When did you realise your mistake?"

Mrs. Morton sighed. All the fight leaving her in that moment.

"As soon as we were married. He was quite generous when we were courting. Nothing too extravagant, but enough. However, as soon as I was his wife, he expected me to act like him, wearing every outfit until it is almost rags and never buying any jewellery or other fine things. I can barely show my face in society – not that I have many opportunities to anyway. After all, meals in restaurants, visits to the theatre, and attending concerts are all unnecessary extravagances."

"So you started to steal from him."

"Just a little. It wasn't like I could buy much anyway – he would notice any expensive purchases. However, I could pay for the occasional lunch in town, to visit one of the finer salons to get my hair cut, or buy the odd secret piece of jewellery that I could wear when I was out on my own."

"When did you decide to disguise them as fake charitable donations?"

"The very first time I took anything. I hadn't realised how closely he watched the household accounts. He noticed that something was missing immediately. I panicked for a moment, then told him I had given some money to a beggar in the street. I thought he might still be cross that I had given away his money without consulting him, but instead he was delighted. After that, he encouraged me to make generous charitable donations whenever I saw an opportunity, and I realised that this could make us both happy."

"Until you became too greedy."

"I overspent the budget that he had set me for Christmas, by a considerable amount. It was foolish of me, but I had grown complacent. As soon as I worked out what I had spent, I realised that it was too much to be explained in the usual way. However, I could claim to have given a much larger sum to a gentleman if he called at the house, especially if he was collecting for a particularly worthy cause. However, as you must have realised, that was my mistake."

"Your stories of the orphanage were too convincing," I said. "Your husband was too moved by the stories you told him."

"He always was a soft-hearted fool." She could have sounded cruel, like she was mocking him, but her tone was tender. "When did you first suspect me?"

"Almost immediately," said Holmes. "You are a poor liar, and if your husband didn't love you so much, he would probably have discovered you already."

She looked confused. "Then why did you spend all that time looking for Mr. Brown if you knew he didn't exist?"

"There was a small possibility that I might have been wrong, and I wanted to verify it for myself. However, I also knew that your husband wouldn't just accept such an accusation levelled at the women he loved. He needed to see that I was conducting a full and thorough investigation."

"Have you told him yet?"

"No, and I'm not certain whether I should."

"The truth will devastate him," said Mrs. Morton.

"Yes. You don't deserve him, but revealing what you have done will not help anyone. So here is what I propose: I will tell your husband that my Irregulars tracked down Mr. Brown. He watched me as I set them the task earlier. The story will be that he heard I was looking for him and fled town, but that I have told the police about his crimes, and if he ever returns he will certainly be arrested."

"And what will you do to me?" she asked, apprehensively.

"Nothing. You will stop stealing from him, and start actually making the charitable donations you were pretending to give before. Be the wife he thinks you are, but know that I will be watching. If you start taking the donations for yourself again, I will know, and I will tell him everything."

"Thank you. I'm so grateful, and I know this is more than I deserve. I do really love him, and I promise to try to show him every day from now onwards."

266

"Very well," said Holmes. "You can tell him that I will speak to him tomorrow, when I expect to have the matter resolved to his satisfaction. However, now it's time for Watson and myself to return to Baker Street."

Mrs. Morton showed us out of the house, thanking us over and over for not revealing the truth to her husband. Once we were on the street, I turned to Holmes.

"Are you sure it is right to lie to Morton? Surely he deserves to know the truth about his wife."

"I don't believe punishing them like that would serve any good purpose. It is better to let Mrs. Morton make amends for her crimes by helping him in his charitable endeavours."

"And what about your fee? It seems wrong to take his money."

"I need to let him pay," said Holmes. "It will help convince him to believe our story. However, I do not intend to keep it. I gather there are a number of orphanages in Southwark. I'm sure that they will make good use of Morton's money."

The Catastrophic Cyclist
by Tom Turley

No doubt it would surprise his readers to discover that my late friend Watson was in some ways a very private man. It was not that he was ever less than forthright in our personal relations. Indeed, I often told the Doctor that after years of observation, I could read him like an open book. Nonetheless, there were certain corners of his life that he kept hidden, not only from the public but from me, his closest friend. Only in his last two years, for example, did my biographer write in detail of his marriage [1] – aside, of course, from his meeting with Miss Mary Morstan in The Sign of Four.

It wasn't until I retrieved Watson's tin dispatch-box from the vaults of Cox and Company (for the Doctor left his manuscripts to me, rather than to his long-time literary agent) [2] that I learned of the existence of these memoirs, neatly filed with notes of cases unrecorded when my colleague died in 1929. As his executor, I must pass over them in silence. They shall not be published for fifty years after my own death, which – at eighty-three – cannot be long delayed. [3]

This stipulation does not apply, however, to "untold" cases not relevant to Watson's personal affairs. I am at liberty to publish any I may care to, at the time that suits me best. Alas, I fear that in my hands, these cases are likely to remain untold. If I once churlishly complained that my Boswell "degraded what should have been a course of lectures into a series of tales," it was because I recognised that an account of The Science of Deduction *based solely on "severe reasoning from cause to effect" (such as the treatise I have since begun) would be of interest only to those within my chosen field. Very few members of the public are likely to investigate* The Whole Art of Detection. *It is "the colour and life" of Watson's stories that have made my name a household word. [4]*

Yet, within the Doctor's dispatch-box there is one tale that even from my pen would have substantial popular appeal. Several months ago, I heard from Stanley Hopkins (now long retired from Scotland Yard) of an elderly spinster in Hampshire who possessed what Hopkins called "a remarkable talent for deduction." The lady, even more remarkably, has gained veiled notoriety of late as a fictionalised character in a series of detective novels – much as I myself was thought to be for many years. Her name struck a distant chord of memory, and when I re-examined Watson's notes I saw that "Miss Amelia Hixon" (here I employ the nom de guerre *her own Boswell assigned her) had been a client in the early years of our detective partnership. For me to tell her story, even at so late a date, seemed then an unwarrantable liberty. I therefore elected to send Miss Hixon a copy of my friend's account, ask if I might visit her when she had read it, and allow her to decide whether her own "literary agent" should make use of the ancient, inconclusive story the Doctor had christened in his notes "The Catastrophic Cyclist".*

My one-time client set our meeting for the last day of May. Earlier that month, I had come up to London for the Coronation, and I was later present when Mycroft briefed the new Prime Minister on the *Hindenburg* disaster, the unfortunate change of government in Spain, and the recent ravings of the latest madman in Berlin. [5] My elder brother's grasp of world affairs, even at the age of ninety, had lost very little to the years.

All the same, a fortnight's reunion was quite enough for both of us. It was with mild relief, therefore, that I boarded an early-morning train at Paddington for my southwestern journey. Railways remain my preferred mode of travel. After my visit with Miss Hixon, I would enjoy a pleasant ride to Eastbourne, the South Downs, and my bees.

Meanwhile, I sat reminiscing on the rail journeys Watson and I had shared together: To King's Pyland in Dartmoor and Pett Bottom in Kent, to the Copper Beeches outside Winchester (whence I was bound today), not to mention our arduous Continental trips to visit the Crowned Heads of Europe. [6] I missed the Doctor's quiet companionship, for his invaluable gift of silence had provided me the opportunity for undistracted thought.

In order to refresh my memory, I picked up the relevant year of Watson's journal, which I had brought to supplement his case notes. Following his death, the Doctor's step-daughter had kindly sent me the volumes covering the period before he met her mother. Reading them now brings me as near to my old friend as it is possible to come. Perhaps I have grown sentimental in my dotage! The journal's entry pertaining to the Hixon case began as follows:

> *August 19, 1886: Received a letter from Constance, informing me that her father's condition is unchanged. The poor girl begins to sound a little desperate. Why won't the old scoundrel die?* [7]
>
> *Late this morning, we had an interesting client: A vicar's daughter from a village in Hampshire. She is only eighteen, rather pretty, [Trust Watson to note that!] and exhibits an appealing combination of diffidence and determination, having slipped away from home without her parents' knowledge to take an early train. She wants us to investigate what she insists was the murder of her father's curate, a young man (of course!) who died in what was presumed to be a*

269

*cycling accident. Holmes was rather severe with her for not
coming to us sooner, but we are bound for Nether Millstone
in the morning.*

Indeed, the Reverend Roger Ayles had been dead five days by the
morning we arrived in Nether Millstone. It seemed unlikely, therefore, that
a first-hand examination of the scene could be of any value. Miss Hixon
had explained her tardiness by citing the need to assist her father with his
parish obligations and with preparations for the funeral, which had been
held the afternoon before. Moreover, the Vicar was convinced by the
inquest's verdict of accidental death and gave no credence to his
daughter's suspicion that the coroner had been in error. He strictly forbade
her to pursue the matter. It was only after he was called unexpectedly to
Winchester that she dared to rise before her mother and take the early train
to London.

Here, and for the following account, I have referenced Watson's notes
to augment my faded recollection of the matter. His reworked notes were
quite voluminous, at times amounting to a narrative. So far as had been
determined by the time of our arrival, the facts of the affair were these:

Roger Ayles was twenty-six, an Oxford graduate, and by all accounts
an attractive and personable young man. He had held his position for four
months, having taken lodgings in the village with an aged widow. While
he appeared to have no deep vocation, the Curate was conscientious in his
duties and well-liked in the parish. Not surprisingly, his advent had caused
a stir among the female population, especially among the girls and young
ladies to whom he offered piano lessons. Mr. Ayles played both the piano
and the organ, and his lessons took place in the church.

On the afternoon before his death, the Curate gave their usual lessons
to two of his piano students: Miss Hixon and the baker's daughter, Betsy
Norton. He mentioned to them, as he had previously told the Vicar and his
landlady, that he intended to visit friends in Oxford the next morning. On
learning that their teacher would make an early departure, Miss Norton
had annoyed our client (as we were informed in Baker Street) by offering
to deliver a pastry for his breakfast. "Betsy was always playing up to him,"
Miss Hixon sniffed. She herself, she sulkily admitted, was an indifferent
baker. I still recall the Doctor's sympathetic smile at this display of envy.

The girl was adamant that Ayles's cycling death couldn't have been
an accident, despite its occurrence in near-darkness and a driving rain. Let
us consult Watson's notes:

*"Roger – that is, Mr. Ayles," Miss Hixon blushed, "was a
brilliant cyclist. His parents gave him one of the new Rovers*

– they're very safe, you know [8] *– and he rode it like the wind!"*
When Holmes suggested that "riding like the wind" would not
have been advisable on such a morning as she had described,
Miss Hixon amended her account. Oh, she felt quite sure that
Mr. Ayles would have been extremely *careful while riding to*
the railway station where he met his end. My friend looked
dubious but did not contradict her.

Our first task in Nether Millstone, therefore, was to determine the accuracy of our client's belief. On the advice of the stationmaster, we began by interviewing two elderly porters who had witnessed the accident. They confirmed that it was raining heavily that morning. Ayles, approaching from the High Street, had begun to descend a steep, cobble-stoned hill that led directly to the station – the same road visible from where we stood. At first, the cyclist had seemed in full control. Then he wavered suddenly and nearly fell. Righting himself, he clung to the handlebars with a virtual death grip, making no attempt to slow his progress or to avoid the brick wall fronting the rail station. He hit head-on at speed and was crushed against the bricks. "It looked like he done it deliberate," one of our informants stated, raising the possibility that it was suicide. [9]

I next visited the village constable, who had been summoned to the scene within moments of the accident. He had examined the wrecked cycle's tires and brakes, finding them to be in proper order aside from the damage resulting from the crash. He concluded that a mechanical flaw was not at fault. To my disgust, I had no opportunity to inspect the vehicle myself, for it had already been sold for scrap. Nor did an investigation of the road yield any clues. There were no defects in the cobblestones sufficient to cause a sudden swerve, and any sinister impediment in the Curate's path could easily have been removed during the days prior to our investigation. I vowed that when I saw Miss Hixon, I would remind her that she had much to answer for.

Watson, meanwhile, had gone at my request to interview the village doctor, who assured him that the Curate's injuries (which included a broken neck and fractured skull) had sufficed in themselves to bring about his instant death. However, because the porters' evidence indicated that Ayles may have been impaired before the wreck, I had asked my friend to confirm that there had been no autopsy. Dr. Forsythe replied, not unreasonably, that with the proximate cause of death so obvious, he had seen no reason to conduct one.

Even so, the possibility of poison had occurred to me. The accident took place soon after the Curate presumably had eaten breakfast. Our client had testified that Miss Norton – apparently her rival for Mr. Ayles's affections – had contributed a portion of that meal. Although I had no compelling reason to suspect the baker's daughter, it was a point to keep in mind during my next interrogation.

Here I am indebted to the Doctor, whose extensive notes preserve my conversation with the victim's landlady. He and I compared impressions of the morning during what Watson grumbled was an abysmal luncheon at the village inn.

Mrs. Crutchley was a dour and aged gentlewoman fallen on hard times. She showed me the Curate's small but tidy garret in her dilapidated house, remarking that while it was "humiliating enough to take in lodgers," she had at least "supposed a young man of the cloth to be a suitable tenant." On the contrary, Mr. Ayles had soon become "a beacon for unmarried girls". Far worse, "he seemed to relish the attention." At first, his landlady had allowed the Curate to use the piano in her parlour for his lessons – until the morning she discovered him and a student "locked in an embrace." Afterwards, Ayles's students were banished to the church, "where, beneath God's altar, he would perforce behave."

I enquired whether Mrs. Crutchley was acquainted with the pertinent young lady, but she refused to "carry tales". However, she went on to inform me that, "When the little hussy brought him cherry tarts on his last morning, I told her not to come again. Cherry tarts indeed!"

To test my hypothesis, I quickly obtained answers to the following questions:

"Did Mr. Ayles eat any of the tarts?"

"Three of them, as I recall."

"Did you partake of them yourself?"

"Certainly not. They weren't meant for *me*. Besides, I never touch sugar."

"By chance, are any of the tarts still here?"

"After five days, and with the young man dead? Why should they be?"

I couldn't restrain a groan of discomfiture. A vital piece of evidence was lost.

While seeing Mrs. Crutchley, I had asked Watson – far better equipped than I to cajole young members of the fair sex – to interview Miss Norton. The Doctor left behind a detailed record, so I shall allow him to tell the story in his inimitable way:

I called for Miss Norton at the bakery, but her father sullenly informed me that "Her Majesty" had "stayed at home". Home proved to be an ill-kept cottage adjacent to the

272

village shops. Upon knocking, I was shown into a poky room intended for a parlour, where there sat a lovely young woman dressed in black. Miss Norton, despite her humble parentage, had the appearance and deportment of a lady. She was perhaps twenty, certainly a year or two older than our client. Although small of stature, her blonde curls and graceful figure contrasted favourably with Miss Hixon's tall, dark angularity. If the two of them were indeed rivals, my hostess held by far the stronger hand.

After greeting me with no apparent curiosity, Miss Norton listened calmly as I explained my mission. "I hadn't thought that there was any question about Mr. Ayles's death," she said. "Surely, it was just a tragic accident."

"That remains to be seen," I told her, regretting the pomposity that crept into my voice. "There are still a few minor points that need investigation."

"And you and this . . . Mr. Holmes are here to resolve them. Are you acting on behalf of the police?"

"No, Mr. Holmes was asked to investigate the matter privately."

"May I enquire who is his employer?"

"He would consider that information confidential, I'm afraid."

"Of course." Her smile held the lightest touch of mockery. "Well, Dr. . . . . Watson, of course I'm willing to help in any way I can, but I know very little of the matter. What was it that you wished to ask me?"

"I understand that you were one of Mr. Ayles's piano students."

"Yes, I and half-a-dozen other girls in Nether Millstone. Do you intend to question all of us?"

"Not necessarily." Slightly nettled by the repetition of her mocking smile, I stopped fencing and came to the point. "We've been told that you supplied a pastry for the Curate's breakfast on the morning that he died."

"Oh, really? I can't imagine where you got that information." The fury in those beautiful blue eyes made it apparent that she knew precisely. "You are aware, Dr. Watson, that my family owns a bakery?"

As though in confirmation of this fact, the parlour door flew open, and a middle-aged, weary-looking slattern came into the room. "Wot're yer wastin' yer time in here for, Betsy?

You need to get on with bakin' them pies for the church social!"

"In a moment, Mother," her daughter icily replied. "This gentleman was just leaving." As the woman sighed disgustedly and left us, Miss Norton asked, "Any other questions for me, Doctor – on your way out the door?"

"Only one, Miss Norton, and I must apologise for asking it: Were you and the late Mr. Ayles on more-than-friendly terms?"

"He was my piano teacher and my pastor. Nothing more."

"And yet, I see you're dressed in mourning." With that parting shot, I turned my back on outraged beauty, regretfully convinced that a cold heart lay beneath.

As we masticated an unappetising Ploughman's Lunch, Watson and I agreed that we had found substantial – though by no means conclusive – evidence of murder. While her motive remained obscure, Miss Norton had possessed both the opportunity and (if the cherry tarts indeed were poisoned) a viable weapon. Recalling my chemistry, I asked Watson about the medical effects of a small amount of amygdalin made from ground-up cherry pits. The Doctor replied, as I expected, that although the resulting dose of cyanide wouldn't be lethal in itself, it could have been sufficiently disabling to render the Curate dizzy and disoriented as he descended the hill above the station. The problem was that our evidence was gone. Nor would an autopsy be of any use, for hydrogen cyanide would no longer be detectable in a five-day-old corpse. [10] It appeared, therefore, that any hope of confirming the possibility of murder rested with our client.

Miss Hixon had asked us not to call at the vicarage until she was able to explain the situation to her father. However, as our return journey was scheduled for late afternoon, the unpleasant confrontation could no longer be delayed. We arrived at the Hixons' cottage shortly before three o'clock.

I can recount the case's penultimate stage with few references to Watson's notes, for our contentious interview with the Reverend Horace Hixon comes readily to mind. Furious with his daughter, the Vicar insisted that we abandon the investigation. He offered to pay whatever fee Miss Hixon promised if we would simply go away. While the question of a fee had not arisen, I was adamant concerning my obligation to report the case's progress to my client. In the event, I was required to do so in her father's presence.

I began by questioning Mr. Hixon in regard to his late curate's character. The Vicar acknowledged that "Mr. Ayles had his faults, like all us mortal men," but he declined to specify what those faults were. "They were of concern," he loftily informed me, "only to myself, as his superior, and God."

Impatient with such pious nonsense, I asked my client directly whether the Curate had ever made advances to his piano students. After a terrified glance at her father, Miss Hixon replied almost inaudibly, "Oh, *no*. I'm sure poor Mr. Ayles would *never* have done anything like *that*."

This was a palpable lie, and I was not deceived by it. The Vicar, meanwhile, was enquiring hotly whether I intended to involve his daughter in a scandal. He blustered on about "slandering the reputation of a clergyman" – a gentleman whose esteemed father, Sir Desmond Ayles, Bart., also happened to be his church's patron. Rather snappishly, I expressed surprise that Mr. Hixon seemed more concerned for his late curate's reputation than for his daughter's safety. Watson was concurrently attempting to console the girl, who had begun silently to weep.

Miss Hixon's distress at last brought the Vicar to his senses. Patting her shoulder, he turned to me almost pleadingly. "Mr. Holmes, even if Mr. Ayles wasn't an ideal curate, surely the kindest thing is to leave his sins to God and put this dreadful death behind us."

More pious platitudes! "I will accept that solution, Vicar, provided you are willing to condone the sin of murder."

"Murder?" he repeated stupidly. "You really believe that Ayles was murdered?"

"I believe that possibility exists." Finally permitted to make my report, I presented the essentials of our investigation, withholding only the identity of the chief suspect and the means by which the poison could have been ingested. Although the two Hixons were equally appalled, it was obvious that our client immediately divined both omissions. Her father was more concerned with practicality.

"Can you prove it?" he asked simply.

"Considering the loss of physical evidence during the five-day delay, probably not to the satisfaction of a court of law. In order to establish the crime's motive, we would require your daughter's testimony."

"That shall not occur." The Vicar regarded us implacably. Our client hung her head.

"Then I have the honour to wish you both a very pleasant evening. Come, Watson."

The Doctor and Miss Hixon exchanged despairing glances as we turned towards the door. Then – for reasons which at the time I didn't fathom – the girl called after us, "Mr. Holmes, can you at least tell us whom you suspect?"

Her question failed to arrest our departure. I merely called across my shoulder, "The same person *you* do, I am sure."

Yet, this wasn't quite all. The Doctor recorded one last interview, so again I shall rely upon his notes.

> *As Holmes and I stood waiting for the train to London, a breathless and disheveled Miss Hixon rushed out onto the platform, having apparently run all the way from home.*
>
> *"Please, Mr. Holmes," she gasped when the detective turned to meet her. "You really must forgive me. Surely you see that I couldn't possibly admit to any impropriety with Mr. Ayles with Father standing there."*
>
> *My friend, to his discredit, is an unforgiving man when he has lost a case. "I should expect, Miss Hixon," he responded curtly, "that any impropriety was on the Curate's part, not yours."*
>
> *"Oh, indeed," our client whispered, blushing scarlet. "The fact is, you see, that on one occasion during a piano lesson, Roger did put his hand upon my knee."*
>
> *"And what was your reaction?" Holmes gelidly enquired.*
>
> *Miss Hixon gazed at him in mild astonishment. "Why, I removed it, Mr. Holmes. Quite firmly, I assure you. And I'm bound to say that Roger never bothered me again. I'm sure he was afraid that I would tell my father."*
>
> *"But you never did?" I asked her gently.*
>
> *"Oh, no, Dr. Watson. Roger would have lost his place, and I didn't really want that. After all, he was an excellent piano teacher, an adequate curate, and a nice enough young man in his own way. Not at all the kind of curate Father would have chosen after he was gone. Handsome, too," she wistfully reflected. "Of course, Mother perpetually reminds me that 'Handsome is as handsome does.'"*
>
> *Miss Hixon sighed. "I suppose it was after my rebuke that he moved on to Betsy. I'm quite sure he found her more receptive. After all, Roger's father is a baronet, and Betsy has always had ambitions far above her station."*
>
> *We would have gone on to enquire whether her rival possessed a motive for murdering the Curate, but the conversation ended abruptly with the arrival of our train. Miss Hixon started as its approaching whistle blew.*

"Good gracious, gentlemen! I must get home before Father returns from Mrs. Warren's. Otherwise, he'll surely see though my little subterfuge."

She dashed away as quickly as she'd come, and it was the last we saw of a remarkable young woman.

On our walk to the station, the Doctor had upbraided me for leaving a damsel in distress. Fortunately, I was able to convince him, by the time we had returned to London, that I simply lacked sufficient evidence to have pursued the case. His impression of Miss Norton notwithstanding, a reputed embrace on a piano bench, three suspect tarts, and a black dress and frosty manner could hardly have convinced a British jury of her guilt. "As you know very well, Watson," I reminded him, "in such a doubtful case as this, it is far better to let a murderer go free than to hang a young woman whose only crime may have been a desire to rise above her parentage." And my friend reluctantly agreed.

So ended, for the next half-century, the untold tale of "The Catastrophic Cyclist". It is strange that with the case half-written, the Doctor never returned to it in later years. No doubt he was distracted that September by the advent of his bride, and afterwards by the joys and trials of matrimony. In all events, (as his readers are aware) my friend's first story to see print was *A Study in Scarlet*, our first case together, published in 1887's *Beeton's Christmas Annual*. Although a cyclist did figure in a later tale, the lady who appeared there was Miss Violet Smith, not Miss Amelia Hixon. [11]

Why this was so I couldn't say, but Miss Hixon offered her views when I returned last month to Nether Millstone. Having read the long-abandoned manuscript, she decided that, "It wouldn't be very satisfactory for Miss Christian's readers, I'm afraid. No wonder Dr. Watson left it in the 'tin dispatch-box' you mentioned. What a kindly man he was! I'm sure he wouldn't have wanted to embarrass me. Besides, the story doesn't really have an ending, does it?"

We had sat for half-an-hour in Miss Hixon's small, beautifully preserved Victorian parlour, a veritable time capsule of our younger days.

"But what *was* the ending?" I respectfully enquired. "I have no doubt you know exactly what became of Betsy Norton."

"You would know that yourself, Mr. Holmes, had you ever lived in a place like Nether Millstone. Her neighbours began avoiding Betsy. Oh, she went on living here for several years, but the village thought they *knew*, you see, so people took no notice of her. I never said a word myself, except to Father, but old Mrs. Crutchley was *most* indiscreet. So Betsy became a pariah. Surely that does not surprise you."

"No. I knew of a similar instance once in the United States." [12]

"In the end, Betsy went to live in Portsmouth and married a man of her own class – a life assurance salesman, I believe. Her parents never spoke of her again. For a while, they tried to keep Norton's Bakery going, but very few of the village housewives went on shopping there. Father made quite sure that Mother didn't, when I identified our suspect after you and Dr. Watson left.

"The sad thing," sighed Miss Hixon, "is that I've realised in the years since then that I may have misjudged Betsy. I didn't like very her much, you know, so it might be that my suspicions amounted to no more than jealousy. Of course, once she had acquired the reputation of a murderess, the damage had been done."

I now risked an imprudent question. "Could it be," I wondered, "that Miss Norton killed the Curate because – if, in fact, she did – because, as the penny-dreadfuls put in our day, she had been 'ruined'?"

"Oh, *no*, Mr. Holmes." My hostess was by no means shocked. "Had Mr. Ayles done *that*, Betsy never would have murdered him. She would have gone to him, after a short while, and said she was with child. You see, she was naïve enough to believe he would be forced to marry her. The problem, of course, was that our curate took Betsy no more seriously than any other village girl. Oh, he might have made some provision for her and the child, but, as a baronet's son, he hadn't the slightest intention of marrying beneath his class. Mr. Ayles was really a *most* unsuitable young man to be in Holy Orders. I'm sure my father would have soon got rid of him in any case."

Miss Hixon and I agreed that "The Catastrophic Cyclist" should fall under the same interdict that Watson had prescribed for certain other untold tales: Not to be published for fifty years after my demise. "I shall be gone myself by then," she smiled, "so it won't greatly matter if people know how foolish I was as a young girl."

Just as she pronounced this verdict, the maid arrived with tea.

"Before you go, dear Mr. Holmes, you really must try this Cherry Bakewell Tart. I told my Evelyn to use the same recipe that Betsy always did. Now, *Evelyn*," she added in a hushed aside, "I *did* remind you, did I not, to leave out that last ingredient? One grows so absent-minded nowadays!"

NOTES

1. Holmes had in mind here three stories Watson wrote during 1928-1929, two of which were published in *The MX Book of New Sherlock Holmes Stories*. The Doctor's remembrance of his first wife, Constance Adams, appeared as "A Ghost from Christmas Past" in Part VII (2017), pp. 130-152, while "The Adventure of the Disgraced Captain" (Part XXVII [2021], pp. 200-222) traced the course of his final marriage to Priscilla Prescott. "The Adventure of the Tainted Canister", which Watson finished only weeks before he died, focused on the death of Mary Morstan and its aftermath. This story is available (as "Sherlock Holmes and the Adventure of the Tainted Canister", 2014) as an e-book or audiobook from MX Publishing
   https://www.amazon.com/Sherlock-Holmes-Adventure-Tainted-Canister-ebook/dp/B00J3QS5CW

2. Who was, of course, Sir Arthur Conan Doyle. In his "The Unintended Offenses" (*Steel True, Blade Straight 2022 Annual,* Manchester, NH, Belanger Books, 2022), David Marcum posits the reason for Watson's late-life decision to make Holmes, instead of Doyle, his literary executor.

3. Here, happily, Holmes was mistaken, for he would live almost another twenty years. His biographer, W.S. Baring-Gould, informs us that The Great Detective died on his 103rd birthday, January 6, 1957. See *Sherlock Holmes of Baker Street: A Life of the World's First Consulting Detective* (Avenel, NJ: Wings Books, 1995 [1962]), pp. 287-292, 319.

4. In quoting his querulous complaint to Watson, Holmes evidently reviewed "The Adventure of the Copper Beeches". It is pleasant to see here that he recanted his objections and expressed appreciation for the Doctor's contribution to his fame. If Baring-Gould may be believed (p. 287), *The Whole Art of Detection* was ready for mailing to the publisher on the very day Holmes died.

5. The coronation of King George VI took place on May 12, 1937. The "new Prime Minister" Holmes refers to was Neville Chamberlain, who succeeded the retiring Stanley Baldwin.

6. See my *Sherlock Holmes and the Crowned Heads of Europe* (London: MX Publishing, 2021).

7. Colonel Alexander Adams of San Francisco, a former Confederate officer and member of the Ku Klux Klan, had suffered a debilitating stroke the year before upon learning of Constance's engagement. Guilt-stricken, his daughter refused to join Watson in England so long as the Colonel remained alive. He died in September, and their wedding took place in London on November 1. See "A Ghost from Christmas Past".

8. Introduced only the year before by John Kemp Stanley, the Rover was one of the new "safety bicycles" that soon replaced the old "penny-farthing" models. (See the online article "Rover 'Safety' Bicycle, 1885" at:
   https://collection.sciencemuseumgroup.org.uk/objects/co25833/rover-safety-bicycle-1885-bicycle

The penny-farthings were so called because their front (penny) wheel was much larger than the rear one (farthing). Although fast, they were unstable, difficult to mount, and dangerous. By employing an efficient chain drive, the Rover and its ilk could be equipped with smaller wheels of equal size, allowing a lower center of gravity and safer driving. They were thus the forerunners of modern bikes. The Rover likewise boasted rubber tires, although the pneumatic tire was not invented (by John Dunlop) until 1888. Evidently, Dunlop's competitor Palmer had produced *his* tires in time for them to be installed on the bicycle owned by Herr Heidegger, the unfortunate German master from "The Priory School" (a case from 1901). For more information, see the Wikipedia articles "History of the Bicycle", "Bicycle Tire", and "Bicycle Brake".

9. Roger Ayles's accident bears a remarkable resemblance to that of French composer Ernest Chausson (1855-1899), who, while riding to a railway station with his daughter, also lost control of his bicycle and crashed into a wall. According to one source: "*His death silenced the most distinctive voice in French music in the generation immediately preceding Debussy's.*"
    https://www.pcmsconcerts.org/composer/ ernest-chausson/
    Gramophone lists Chausson's among "*The 10 most bizarre and tragic composer deaths*":
    https://www.gramophone.co.uk/features/article/the-10-most-bizarre-and-tragic-composer-deaths

10. Amygdalin, contained in the pits of almonds, cherries, and other stone fruits, is converted by the body into hydrogen cyanide. According to one source, "*chewing and swallowing more than a few pits may be dangerous. . . . Symptoms of acute toxicity include headache, nausea, seizures, convulsions, and difficulty breathing.*"
    https://www.healthline.com/nutrition/cherry-pits#what-to-do-if-swallowed
    As late as 2012, an article from Sam Houston State University ("Forensic Research Extends Detection Of Cyanide Poisoning") stated that "*[u]nless cyanide is found at the time of death on the mouth or nose, elevated cyanide concentration can only be found for up to two days under current toxicological testing. . . .*" Professor Chi-Chung Yu, whose research was mentioned in the article, had discovered a new biomarker that he hoped could "*extend the detection window up to weeks or even months.*"
    https://www.shsu.edu/~pin_www/T@S/2012/cyanideresearch.html#:~:text =Since%20cyanide%20salts%20are%20solid,preserved%20for%20further %20forensic%20testing

11. "The Solitary Cyclist", which Baring-Gould dates as having taken place in April 1895 (p. 310).

12. Holmes may have in mind the infamous Borden Murders in Fall River, Massachusetts. Miss Lizzie Borden was acquitted of her parents' murder and inherited their wealth, only to be shunned by Fall River society until her death in 1927. Although it occurred during the Hiatus (1892), there are several accounts of Holmes and Watson's participation in the case. See, for

example, David Ruffle's *Holmes and Watson: An American Adventure* (London: MX Publishing, 2015).

The Adventure of the Sketched Bride
by James Gelter

Sherlock Holmes had handed me the note as soon as I sat down for breakfast. He sat back and lit a cigarette as I glanced it over.

> *It is my intention to call upon you within the hour to discuss those matters which Mr. Lestrade of Scotland Yard has already communicated to you.*
>
> *Douglas P. Stillwell, Jr*

"And what has Lestrade communicated to you?" I asked.

Holmes blew a thin jet of smoke into the air.

"Not a thing. But I did find this in *The Times* this morning."

He tossed over the newspaper. At the bottom of the page was the small headline, "*A Brazen Burglary at Cranley Gardens*" – under which ran the following brief article:

> *As we go to print, we have just received word of a violent attempt at burglary at the home of Mr. Douglas P. Stillwell, the well-known cotton importer in Cranley Gardens. Mr. Stillwell's butler was apparently grievously injured in an attempt to stop the criminal or criminals. It has not been confirmed what, if any, of Mr. Stillwell's possessions had been taken. More to follow.*

"It doesn't give us much," said I.

"No," said Holmes after a long exhale, "but it is enough to pique my interest. It has been quite some time since a good burglary has come our way – not since that business at Monsieur Brisbois' chateau last year. I confess that I have kept a keen eye on the papers, local and Continental, looking for just such a case. There was an intriguing episode in Bern just a day ago, and I was tempted to board a train last night. I'm glad I chose otherwise, though I couldn't have predicted another such case to appear so soon – and in Hornsley of all places. Ah! And this, I take it, is the long-awaited epistle from Lestrade."

The boy had entered and handed a message to Holmes. He read it and passed it to me.

> *Would like you to look into Cranley Gardens robbery. Thief was violent but took nothing of import. Went over the place, found nothing in particular. Had to leave to address significant development in Lady Culver blackmail affair. Recommended Stillwell call on you.*
>
> *Lestrade*

"It seems that someone working on the Lady Culver case finally had the good sense to look at Count Von Bruener's house from the outside," said Holmes.

"And how would that bring about a major development?" I asked.

"Because they would then realize that the home of their top suspect has a fourth story, even though there is seemingly no access to it within the interior of the house. If Lestrade had invited me, I am sure I would have found the hidden entrance to this missing floor without trouble. But while Lestrade has decided to dine on that grand feast alone, he has at least sent us a sandwich to nibble on. That knock on the door must be our new client."

A few moments later, a broad and portly gentleman stood in the doorway of our sitting room. His round, clean-shaven face was bright red, the few strands of dark hair that remained atop his head were wet with perspiration, and his sloped shoulders lurched up and down with each breath he took. I thought him to be well into his thirties, but learned later that he was only twenty-five. He was dressed in a dandy fashion with a rich green morning coat, black velvet waistcoat with brass buttons, and a violet silk cravat. His bulging eyes glanced back and forth between Holmes and me as he dabbed his forehead with his handkerchief.

"You must be Mr. Douglas P. Stillwell, Jr," said Holmes in his amiable way. "Please have a seat. Watson, a cup of coffee for the gentleman."

"Just water, if you would be so kind," said the gentleman between gasping breaths. "This heat has overwhelmed me."

Holmes sat down on the sofa, his keen eyes darting over the merchant. Stillwell gulped his water as though he were a man dying of thirst. At length, his breathing slowed and the livid colour of his cheeks began to fade.

"Thank you for seeing me, Mr. Holmes," he said at length, "I believe Inspector Lestrade has told you all about the business."

"Hardly," replied Holmes. "It seems he was too busy to find time for either of us. But it is just as well. I prefer to hear directly from those involved with a case if it can be managed. Police testimony tends to focus on the most obvious facts, and thus ignore the ones of consequence. My good man, do feel free to remove your cravat and collar if they are causing you discomfort in this heat. There is no need for manners to lead to exhaustion."

"You needn't worry. Another glass of water and I will be myself again. Would you be so kind, Doctor? Thank you. I am anxious to discuss this dreadful misfortune with you, Mr. Holmes."

"Very well. Your home was burgled last night, as I understand."

"Yes, it was."

"And your butler beaten?"

"Augustus, yes. Poor fellow. He took a blow to the head."

Holmes put out his cigarette, sat back, and closed his eyes.

"Pray, start from the beginning, and leave no detail out."

"Well then," said Stillwell, "I suppose I should let you know that I inherited my home, Perfect House, last year following the death of my father, Douglas Stillwell, Sr. I claimed his bedroom for my own, but haven't had the heart to make any changes to his study, which is adjoining. It was his sanctuary. I was never permitted to enter when he was alive except when invited, a rare occurrence that usually meant I had done something to displease him and was to hear him expound upon the matter. The rule applied to all in the house and all obeyed. Indeed, the rule was so thoroughly instilled within us all that I fear my father's wrath should I break it, even after his death. The room has been kept exactly as it was when my father died. Both doors, the one leading to the hall and the one that connects to my bedroom, are always locked. I don't even permit the maids to enter the room to dust.

"Last night, about one o'clock, I awoke with a start at the sound of a loud thud coming from the study. I then heard the voice of Augustus shouting, 'Who are you? What do you – ?' His words were cut off and I heard grunts and gasps as if some scuffle was going on. I sprang from my bed and fumbled in the dark to find the key to let me into the study."

"Why not go out into the hall?" Holmes interrupted. "Obviously if the butler was already in the study, he had made his way in from there."

"In retrospect, you are right, Mr. Holmes. But I was in a panic and not thinking clearly. I was shouting hysterically, and my hands were shaking. I finally got the key in the lock, but just as I did, I heard one final shout from Augustus followed by a mighty *Thack!* I unlocked the door and entered the study. Augustus was lying on the floor, unconscious. The window was flung open. I ran over to it and looked out onto the street, but his attacker had already fled. Just then, Rodger, the footman, entered the room from the hall, followed quickly by the rest of the staff.

"I sent Rodger out to find a police officer and the hall boy to fetch a doctor for Augustus. The wound on his head didn't bleed, but had already swollen to a great size. He has been in a pitiable state ever since. He cannot seem to focus his eyes on anything and complains of the pain."

"And does he remember what happened?"

"Yes. It took some time to get him cognizant enough to speak to the police, but he is a strong soul and he managed. His room is directly below the study, you see. He is a light sleeper, and the creaking of the floor above roused him. He thought it was me walking about, which he found curious since he knows my aversion to entering the study. He threw on his trousers and dressing gown, therefore, and came upstairs to make sure everything was all right with me. The dear lad. When he entered the room, he saw a man standing before the open window, stuffing something into a small bag. He cried out and the man instantly pulled out a stick and attacked him. The two wrestled about, but the stranger proved to be the better fighter. He struck poor Augustus on the head, knocking him out cold. The next thing Augustus remembers was me pressing a brandy bottle against his lips."

Holmes looked across at Stillwell.

"Do you mean to say that when he arrived at the room, the hallway door was already unlocked?"

"Unlocked and open."

"And how do you account for that?"

"I don't know what to make of it. The door showed no sign of being forced. I have the only key, however, and it was obviously still in my possession as I used it to enter from the bedroom. Of course, the burglar could easily have opened it from the inside, having first entered from the window."

"Was the window forced?"

"No, but I have no idea if it was ever locked. I rarely went into the room, and it is on the second story, so it was never something that had worried me before."

"But it is accessible from outside?"

"Well, I certainly wouldn't have thought so, but I'm not the energetic sort. Inspector Lestrade was confident, however, that the tree beside the house could provide a way for an able-bodied man to climb up."

"Did your butler describe the man?"

"He didn't see much. There was a dark lantern that the thief must have brought with him, but it was only open a crack, and so there wasn't enough light for Augustus to clearly see the man."

"And what was taken?"

"That is the most confusing and distressing part of all, Mr. Holmes," said Stillwell as he began to turn red again. "The only thing missing was a framed sketch of my late mother in her bridal gown that had always been on my father's desk."

Up until now, Holmes had been languid in his attitude toward our client's story, but now he sat up and his eyes shone with excitement.

"This case grows interesting. A sketch, you say?"

"Yes. My mother had been good friends with Sydney Prior Hall, now an illustrator well-known for his images of the Franco-Prussian War. He was still unknown at the time of her marriage and had no money for a wedding gift. He drew this portrait of her, therefore, on the morning of her wedding. Though it wasn't more than a rough sketch, it was a remarkable likeness. Her face seemed to glow on the paper. It was always very precious to my father."

"Strange," said Holmes. "Why would so simple a thing as the drawing of a dead woman be the cause of such bold action?"

He sat in silence for a moment then sprang to his feet.

"I should like to see the scene of this remarkable crime without delay."

"My carriage is waiting outside," said Stillwell.

"Excellent. You will accompany us, Watson? Good. Just give us five minutes, Mr. Stillwell, and we will join you out front."

It was early August, and the morning air was already sweltering. The carriage was a Clarence with fixed windows, and soon the inside was like an oven. Holmes was unperturbed by the heat.

"How long has this butler, Augustus, been in your service?" he asked, as we rattled on along Finchley Road.

"Six months," replied Stillwell with sweat pouring down his flabby face. "But his father was butler before him."

"So you have known him for quite some time?"

"Not at all. His story is a rather sad and, if I may beg your confidence, scandalous one."

"You need not beg for my confidence or my colleague's. We give it to you freely. Tell me all."

"Well, I first met him last year. Butler Urwin, who had been my father's most trusted servant for decades, had become ill and was bedridden. His wife had died a few years before and he had no family to speak of – or so I thought. Then one day, this fellow, Augustus Coburn, arrived at the house asking to visit with the dying man. I saw him come and go on a few occasions and was struck by his handsome, aquiline face, his golden hair, and brilliant blue eyes. I asked Urwin about the fellow, and he told me that the lad was an old family friend, but he wouldn't share more than that. Butler Urwin passed a few weeks later, and I was shocked to learn afterward that he had bequeathed all that he owned to this Augustus fellow. Out of curiosity, I invited the lad to the house and asked him to explain his relation to Urwin.

"'It is astonishing,' said I, 'that Urwin, whom I have known my whole life, would leave all his money and possessions to a man I have never met. It is quite a generous thing to do for a family friend.'

"'I'm not a friend of his family,' replied the lad, 'I *am* his family. I am his son.' He then went on to tell me his remarkable story. I will sum it up for you as best I can.

"My father made his fortune importing cotton from the States. Hugh Urwin was the first servant he ever hired, serving as his valet. In 1860, Urwin travelled with father to America to tour the southern plantations. While there, father hired a local maidservant by the name of Lettie Coburn. Augustus has shown me her picture. She was a striking woman, with golden hair and large blue eyes. Urwin fell in love with the young woman instantly and the two began an intimate affair. Urwin, however, had a wife back home, so they kept the relationship a secret.

"My father was staying in South Carolina when it became the first state to secede from the Union. He had to make an urgent departure, for it was feared the federal government would cut off all of South Carolina's ports, and he needed to depart aboard a ship before they did so. Urwin begged my father to bring Lettie with them and allow her to continue her duties in England. She was without a family, he argued, and it would be cruel to leave her alone in a country that was about to be torn apart by war. My father had a soft spot for the young woman himself and agreed, not knowing Urwin's true motive for the request.

"Within a year of his return to England, Father had married my mother, Josephine Westphail, and purchased Perfect House, which he so named as it was exactly the type of house he had dreamed of as a child, living in unfurnished rooms by the docks. In addition to continuing on as Father's valet, Urwin became butler of the house, his wife became the cook, and Lettie Coburn stayed on as a maid. Other servants were hired to complete the staff.

"Urwin and Lettie's secret relationship continued under my father's very nose, and under Mrs. Urwin's as well. But then it became apparent that Lettie was carrying a child. Urwin, in an attempt to avoid scandal, found her another household position in a small village in Dorset. My father was loath to see her go, especially as she didn't give a reason for her departure.

"Lettie gave birth to Augustus and raised him in Dorset. She never revealed to her son who his father was, despite his pleas that she do so. She passed away sometime last year, and Augustus found letters among her possessions. It seems that she kept a regular correspondence with her former lover and the content of their missives made it clear that he was Augustus's father. Naturally, Augustus wanted to see the man in the flesh, and so made his way up to London. He came to Perfect House to call on Urwin, only to find him on death's door. I am glad that they had even a little time together. Urwin, overjoyed to meet his son at last and seeing that he had become a handsome and capable young man, sent word to his lawyer instructing him to change his will so that Augustus would be the sole inheritor of his money and possessions.

"I was moved by the lad's story and expressed curiosity at what he planned to do next.

"'I haven't thought about it,' he replied. 'It all happened so quickly, learning of my father, meeting him, and then losing him. It seems he didn't spend much of what he earned over the years and made some small but wise investments. Still, the inheritance doesn't amount to so much that I can live off it forever. I will be needing some sort of work. I served as a footman in Dorset, but I have become so taken with London, I cannot imagine going back.'

"Without further thought, I offered him his father's old position. I was quite taken with the fellow and it seemed so very natural that we should both take the positions that our fathers had held before us. He was greatly touched by the offer and accepted it without hesitation. He has since proven to be a good servant. In fact, last night wasn't the first time he has put himself at great risk for my protection."

"Really?" said Holmes, his eyebrows raised. "Something like this has happened before?"

"Not exactly. I am fond of country drives and ride through Highgate Woods every Saturday. I got in the habit of bringing Augustus with me, for he is a wonderful conversationalist. About a month or so after he joined the household, we were out on such a drive when a ruffian brandishing a gun stepped out in front of the carriage and demanded whatever money or valuables we had. Just as I handed over my purse, Augustus leapt fearlessly from the carriage and wrestled the man to the ground. He struck the villain hard across the face, causing him to drop his weapon. The man struggled to his feet and ran off."

"With your purse in his possession?"

"Yes, but I am a wealthy man, and the sum wasn't much to me, though I am sure it was considerable to such a wretch."

"And did you report this attack to the police?'

"Yes, but there was little they could do to find out the scoundrel."

Soon we were in Hornsey, a burgeoning part of the city where handsome brick houses stood in row after row, and in those few empty spaces where no house yet stood, men were busy laying the foundations for more. At the end of a row lay a house nearly twice the size of any of those that surrounded it. It was a lovely structure of orange-and-tan brick, with a small garden wrapping around two sides.

"Here we are," said Douglas P. Stillwell, Jr. "Welcome, gentlemen, to Perfect House."

We were greeted at the door by the footman.

"Ah, Rodger!" said Stillwell, "This is Mr. Sherlock Holmes, the renowned detective, and this is his associate, Dr. Watson."

The footman gave us a long bow.

"I am glad you have come, gentleman," said he. "There is something that has been weighing on my mind all day, Mr. Stillwell, and I feel it is best that I should share it now with both you and Mr. Holmes."

"By all means."

He was an attractive youth, built like a dancer with narrow shoulders and long limbs, his stance a conscious poise.

"Well, sir," he said, "the business of last night got me thinking. I have sometimes in the evening, when using the servant's entrance on the side of the house, noticed a fellow standing in the road round the corner, by the garden. He doesn't seem to do much else but stand there, as though he was waiting for something. He doesn't appear every night, mind you, but once or twice within a week."

"How would you describe the gentlemen?" asked Holmes.

"A great bush of grey hair and whiskers with round spectacles. Dressed humbly, nothing much to note there. Usually had a cigarette in his mouth."

"That's the man!" cried Stillwell. "Bushy grey whiskers and round glasses? That's how the man who tried to rob me in the woods looked!"

"When is the earliest you can recall seeing the fellow?" Holmes asked the footman.

"I cannot say for sure, sir. But I don't recall seeing him before the attack Mr. Stillwell just mentioned."

"And you have never addressed him?"

"No, sir."

"Thank you. You were very wise to bring this to our attention. Now, Mr. Stillwell, I should like to make my way directly to the study."

"As you wish, Mr. Holmes," our client replied. "Rodger, lead the way."

289

The footman led us upstairs and down the hallway to the study. Outside the door stood a short constable with a small, neat moustache.

"Ah, Dolman!" said Holmes as we approached. "Why must Lestrade always relegate such promising officers to be nothing more than glorified doormen?"

"That is kind of you to say, Mr. Holmes," said Constable Dolman. "The inspector said I should expect you. No one has been in the room since he left."

"Very good. Why don't you take a break, Dolman? You have been standing guard for hours. We will watch over the room."

"Thank you, sir. Much appreciated."

"Rodger," said Stillwell, "take this good officer to the kitchen and see that he gets something to eat."

"Thank you kindly, sir," said the constable with a nod and a grin.

He followed the footman downstairs. Holmes examined the study door.

"This lock certainly wasn't forced," he said. He leaned into the room without his feet crossing the threshold.

"Ah, dust! No one appreciates it other than the criminal expert. I promise you, I would solve every single case brought before me were it not for the diligence of London's housemaids. There is a layer of dust upon every surface of this room a sixteenth-of-an-inch thick. The floor isn't of help to us. We would have been able to tell much from it, but Lestrade and his men have stomped through and obliterated anything that would have been of use. All may not be lost, however. Stay here."

Stillwell and I remained in the hallway as Holmes entered the study. From what I could see, it was a beautifully furnished room, anchored by a massive desk of ornately carved walnut which stood in the center of the room, placed upon a dark-green Oriental carpet. Holmes made his way gingerly round the desk and to the window behind it.

"The fellow your footman described would certainly have been able to view this room from where he stood in the street," he said, looking out the window. "This tree might possibly provide a way to the window from below, but it wouldn't be an easy climb in either direction."

He then glanced at the floor.

"Not too many people have stepped here. I can clearly see the inward twist of Lestrade's left foot. These bare feet must be yours, Mr. Stillwell – you said you came to the window to try and spot the thief. There is one more set of footprints here." He didn't elaborate, however, but stared at the ground in silence for a moment, and then moved on to the desk.

290

"The picture that was stolen rested here, by this small bust of Byron. The dust makes that clear. It was quite small. Five-inches-by-seven, I would say."

"That is so," said Stillwell.

"The bust itself has been picked up and then placed back down. Did you see Lestrade or any other officer do this?"

"No. Mr. Lestrade gave strict orders to leave everything just as it was."

"Someone has sat in the chair for some time and placed something on the desk. I must thank you, Mr. Stillwell, for your refusal to let the maid enter this room. Watson, come here."

I entered gingerly, leaving Stillwell in the hallway. The heat of the humid air and the smell of dust combined were suffocating.

"That mark there is most intriguing," said Holmes. "Do you see?"

He pointed to a spot on the top of the desk, in the center of the front edge.

"Certainly something has cleared away the dust here," I said, "but I couldn't tell you what was the cause."

"Had it been wiped away," replied Holmes, "there would be a defined edge between where there was dust and where there wasn't. Again, had something been there when the dust fell and was then removed, it would result in a hard edge, such as we have over here where the picture frame stood. But the edge of this oblong shape is soft, there is a gradual progression between where dust is and isn't. That is most instructive." He turned to Stillwell. "This dark lantern on the corner – it belongs to the thief?"

"Indeed. I have never seen it before in the house."

"Was there any other light when you entered the room? A candle, perhaps?"

"No, sir."

"That is curious. As is this!"

Holmes walked round the desk and faced a matching walnut cabinet that stood against the opposite wall.

"Look at the floor here," he said, indicating the space before the cabinet, and gesturing to Stillwell to enter the room. "The dust is practically cleared away. Someone has stood here often before now. And see here: The handles of the cabinet doors are clean, as is the waist molding directly underneath the doors. Clearly, someone has been opening this cabinet regularly."

"But that is impossible!" cried Stillwell. "Though someone may have been able to access this room via the window, they wouldn't be able to open this cabinet without the key."

"I assume there is only one and it, too, is in your possession?"

"Yes, it and the key to the room are on the same ring."

"But you don't always keep them on your person?"

"No, they are usually kept in my bureau, beneath a secret panel in one of my drawers."

"Does anyone know of this secret panel?"

"Only me and the manufacturer."

"Do you have the keys on you now?"

"Certainly."

"May I see them?"

Stillwell handed Holmes the keys. Holmes examined both minutely, gliding his finger along each one. He rubbed his finger against his thumb, then examined both. This done, he took the cabinet key and unlocked the cabinet. Inside were shelves lined with titleless volumes and stacks of papers.

"My father's private papers," said Stillwell. "He was a prodigious diary-keeper, from boyhood until his final days."

"Have you ever read them?" asked Holmes.

"Goodness, no! My father kept them locked up for a reason. I couldn't bring myself to break his trust, not even in death. But wait a moment!" Our client's eyes went wide. "There was a fellow who was asking after the papers."

Holmes raised his eyebrows. "Oh? Who was it?"

"John Octavian was the name, I believe. Shortly after my father's death, he wrote to me expressing his condolences and explaining that he and my father were boyhood friends from school and as young men had kept a lively correspondence. He wished to have his letters back, as a way to better remember his friend and asked if he could visit the house and look through my father's papers to see if they were among them. I remember speaking to Urwin about it at the time. He said he had never heard of the gentlemen and was suspicious that it might have been some sort of ruse to gain access to the papers. I asked him why anyone would desire to do so, but he couldn't say."

"Did you write back to the gentlemen?"

"I did and informed him that such a thing would be impossible. I didn't hear from him again."

"Perhaps," I ventured, "he is the grey-haired fellow that has been seen so often by the footman?"

Holmes looked at me with an amused expression and was about to reply when the footman appeared at the door.

"Pardon me, gentlemen," he said, "but is Dr. Watson available to come downstairs? I am worried for Augustus. The doctor this morning said he would be quite all right, but I think a second opinion is needed."

"Has his condition worsened?" I asked.

"It seemed to have been improving. I was visiting with him and he was finally conversant. He ate a small cup of soup that the cook had brought up for him and asked if he could have more. I went to fetch it for him, but when I came back, he had vomited his previous helping and was quite faint once more."

"Well, with those symptoms," I said, "it certainly would seem that his head injury is worse than originally thought. I apologize, Holmes, but I must leave you for the moment."

I expected him to be annoyed by this development, but the tilt of his head told me that he was curious about it instead.

"No apologies necessary," he said. "I think I've gleaned all I need from this room at present. Let us all go together and see what we can do for this ill young butler."

Augustus Coburn was lying in his bed asleep, but he woke as soon as we arrived. He was a striking young man, with features more akin to feminine beauty than masculine handsomeness. His eyes, an arresting sea blue, peered at us from beneath a substantial bandage.

"You must be Mr. Holmes and Dr. Watson," he said in a voice so soft it was barely audible. "Rodger said you had joined the investigation. Thank you for helping Mr. Stillwell."

"From what I understand," I said, "it is you who are deserving of thanks. It was quite the brave thing you did."

"To speak the truth," he said with a slight grin, "had I known what was waiting for me in the master's study, I'm not sure I would have entered."

I examined his eyes for signs of concussion but saw none. I then removed his bandage and examined his wound. It was a large, wide bump in the middle of his forehead. It was swollen but didn't appear to me to be so formidable a wound as to cause vomiting and blurred vision. As I checked his pulse, the young man turned to Stillwell.

"Rodger told me, sir, that that scoundrel who tried to rob you in the Highgate Woods has been spotted outside the house. Though, as I said to the inspector earlier, I didn't get a good look at last night's burglar, he may well have been the same man. He wore glasses, of that I am sure."

"Well, then," said Stillwell, "he is certainly our man. Have you any idea who he might be, Mr. Holmes?"

"I wouldn't venture to answer that quite yet," replied Holmes. "Mr. Coburn – "

"Please, call me Augustus."

Holmes smiled.

"Augustus. Why did you not have a candle?"

The young butler glanced up at Holmes.

"Whatever do you mean?" he said with a weak voice.

"It was quite dark last night, as you observed," said Holmes, "There was no moon, and the street lamps are too far from this side of the house to provide much light. As such, I am curious why you did not have a candle with you when you went upstairs to see what was going on in the study."

The young butler considered a moment.

"I was eager to find out what was going on," he said, "and so didn't take the time to light one. I am more than familiar with the house and can make my way through it in the dark without difficulty."

"I see. You took the time to slip on your trousers and dressing gown, however."

"I didn't think it was an emergency, and didn't feel it appropriate to move about the house undressed."

"Though Mr. Stillwell didn't mention it, I assume you wore these slippers by the bed here?"

"Yes."

Holmes lifted one of the slippers and looked over it. Coburn watched with curiosity.

"And the dressing gown," said Holmes, putting down the slipper. "Was it this one hanging here?"

"Yes, sir."

Holmes walked over to the robe hanging on the wall by the head of the bed. He reached out and squeezed both pockets. I was confused by this action, but Coburn seemed alarmed.

"Is there anything wrong with my dressing gown, Mr. Holmes?"

"Not at all. In fact, it is quite lovely. Chapman's of Goodge Street – a fine tailor, more suited to the master of a house than a servant."

"Quite so, Mr. Holmes. When I received my inheritance, I admit I used some of the funds to buy a few comforts I would otherwise have been unable to afford."

"Of course, of course," said Holmes, quietly, his mind apparently focused on something other than the conversation. He turned to Stillwell. "There was a boy on the landing just down the hall. Is that his usual station?"

"Geoffrey. Yes."

Holmes moved to the door and called down the hallway, "Geoffrey! Come here!"

He pulled out a notebook and pencil from inside his jacket and began to scribble a note. A young boy appeared at the door.

"If you need a message delivered, Mr. Holmes," said Rodger the footman, "I would be happy to take it for you."

"No, no," replied Holmes, "I will need you here."

"I do have my duties to attend to."

"I am sure that on such a day as today, Mr. Stillwell will understand if not all of your daily responsibilities are fulfilled."

"Certainly, Mr. Holmes," said Stillwell. "The case above all today. We owe that to young Augustus here."

"Here, lad," said Holmes, folding his note and handing it to the hall boy. "This is a message for Constable Dolman. He's down in the kitchen. Deliver it straight into his hands. Thank you."

The boy disappeared down the hall.

"Now," said Holmes, moving to the center of the room, "I believe we can begin to bring this business to a close before the constable joins us. Rodger, if you would be so kind as to stand in that corner there, to the right of the bed? Good. Mr. Stillwell if you would go to the left there, by the window. Thank you. Finally, Watson, please, block the door."

I had become so used to following Holmes's orders, I moved to the door before the implications of this request entered my mind. As I placed myself before the door, it dawned upon me what Holmes had done. The butler was trapped, with men on three sides and a fourth blocking the exit. I saw this thought enter Coburn's mind as well. He had been limp and supine, but now he sat up, his whole form on alert.

"What is this, Mr. Holmes?" the butler asked with a nervous voice, his eyes darting from one to the other of us.

"Come now, Mr. Coburn," Holmes replied. "You have proven yourself to be an intelligent and capable man. Surely you can recognize when the game is up?"

"If you are suggesting I had anything to do with this business – "

"I am asserting that you have everything to do with this business. The fact is, Mr. Stillwell, that no one broke into your home last night, and that it was Butler Coburn himself who took your mother's bridal portrait from your father's study."

Stillwell was taken aback.

"How do you know it, Mr. Holmes? And why?"

"We will get to *why* in due time. As to how I know it, there were a number of indications that made the case fairly obvious to me from the beginning, and I shall be happy to share them with you. It must first be noted that on the evening of the burglary, no one saw the supposed burglar other than Coburn. The next thing that raised my suspicions was that the door to the study was unlocked. It could be, as you suggested, that the burglar entered through the window and then unlocked it from the inside. But why would he do this? The only item taken came from the study, and there was no evidence he had been anywhere else in the house. It was far more likely that the door had been opened by a duplicate key.

"You stated, Mr. Stillwell, you heard the burglar's supposed final blow to the butler's head the moment before you opened the door and that by the time you reached the window, there was no one to be seen in the street below. It would have been a remarkably fast and agile man who could climb out the window, clamber down a tree, and race all the way down the street and out of sight so quickly. Already it seemed to me far more likely that Coburn was up to some scheme and the burglar was a mere fiction.

"This was confirmed upon an inspection of the study. There were footprints all over the floor, but only three sets beneath the window: Yours, Mr. Stillwell, Inspector Lestrade's, and another pair that were clearly made by someone in slippers, which could be explained by Coburn himself going to the window and throwing it open. There were certainly no marks to indicate that someone had entered or left through the window.

"Then, of course, there was the matter of Coburn's head injury. Watson, you examined the mark the blow left behind. Would you say it was hard enough a blow as to render the man unconscious?"

"It is possible," I replied, "but unlikely."

"Now, Watson, considering the wound once again, does it strike you as the sort of injury that a man with a stick might deliver?"

I looked over at the young man on the bed and recalled my close examination of his injury.

"No," I said after a moment's contemplation. "Not only is it an odd angle for a blow delivered by someone in close quarters, but it is too broad to have been made by a stick. Such bruising would come from hitting a large, flat surface."

"Like the top of a desk, for instance?"

"Exactly!"

"Which brings me to that spot upon the desktop that I drew your attention to earlier. The center of the spot was clear of dust, but there was no defined edge. This indicated that something had struck the spot, causing the surrounding dust to fly into the air. Clearly, this is how the butler received his injury."

Augustus Coburn turned his wide blue eyes to his master.

"Mr. Stillwell!" he cried. "Surely you don't believe this nonsense! I have been nothing but loyal to you. Would you believe this stranger's wild accusations over my word? He couldn't even make it as a real police inspector, but has been relegated to begging for clients as an amateur!"

Stillwell, who was now wiping his brow constantly, opened his mouth to respond, but Holmes held up a hand to silence him.

"It will be clear quite soon," said Holmes, "who in this room are the professionals and who are the amateurs. A professional criminal would know, for instance, that when making an impression of a key, clay or putty is the preferred medium. Certainly not soft wax, which will leave a thin waxy residue on the original. As it happens, when I inspected your keys, Mr. Stillwell, I found a waxy residue on both. Now, if your keys were kept in a secret panel in your bureau, who but your most trusted servant would spend enough time alone in your room to find them and make impressions of them?"

Stillwell seemed flummoxed.

"I – I still don't quite understand, Mr. Holmes."

"I'll walk you through what happened and see if we can make things clearer for you. Coburn made a wax impression of both the key to the study and to your father's cabinet therein, in order to make duplicate keys. Night after night, he would sneak out of his room with a dark lantern, enter the study, open the cabinet, remove a volume of your father's diary, sit at the desk, and read. Last night, after his nightly reading had concluded, he moved to put the volume back into the cabinet, when he accidentally knocked the small bust of Byron off the corner of the desk. It landed with a thud. Coburn was certain the sound was loud enough to wake you, perhaps he heard you as you woke with a start. He had to move quickly. He began shouting at an invisible burglar, and to make all manner of gasps and grunts while he closed the cabinet, threw open the window, replaced the bust, and, as it was the only item small enough for him to conceal in the pockets of his dressing-gown, snatch up the sketch of your mother on her wedding day. And finally, in an attempt to gain your sympathy and to throw off suspicion, he slammed his head down on the edge of the desk and fell to the ground, feigning unconsciousness."

"This is absurd!" cried Coburn. "I had already put my life at risk to protect Mr. Stillwell and his property last month, and now that I have done so again, wild accusations and lies are the thanks I get!"

There was a knock on the door, and in stepped Constable Dolman.

"Mr. Holmes, sir," said the constable.

"Ah, Dolman, did you find it?"

"Yes, sir, where you said I would."

The constable handed Holmes a small picture frame. Inside was a drawing of a beautiful young bride, sitting with a bouquet of flowers in her arms. Though it was only a sketch, it was a captivating image. The small smile on her round lips and the glow of her large eyes clearly portrayed the excitement a bride feels upon her wedding day.

"My mother!" cried Stillwell. "But where was it?"

"As you saw earlier," said Holmes, "I checked the pockets of Coburn's dressing gown, to see if he still kept the picture in one of them, but they were empty. As he has been confined to his bed since the time of the incident, I assumed that he enlisted his accomplice to carry it away."

"His accomplice?"

"Yes, the man who wore a grey wig and glasses last month and acted the part of a robber so that Coburn could gain your trust: Rodger the footman."

All eyes turned to the footman in the corner, who burst out in tears.

"He paid me," he cried through pathetic sobs, "and promised me more when he was done!"

"Shut your trap, you fool!" cried Augustus Coburn. The footman collapsed in the corner, his face buried in his hands.

"Your mother's portrait," said Holmes to Stillwell, "was in Rodger's room. After learning that I had begun to investigate the case, he and Coburn knew that it would be dangerous to keep it in this room, so he took it to his. Upon meeting me, he became nervous and quickly invented a story about seeing the very man he himself had portrayed last month standing in the street, hoping that it would throw suspicion away from him. He told these developments to Coburn while we were engaged in the study upstairs, so when we came down and spoke with him, Coburn could confirm this new fiction by saying the burglar he fought was bespectacled."

There were six of us stuffed into that small room, the sun shining bright and hot through the window. Not since my time in Afghanistan had perspiration flowed so freely down my face. Across the room, Stillwell was sweating so profusely that he looked as though buckets of water had been poured over his head. The young merchant stepped toward his butler with shaking knees.

"But – *Why?*" he stammered. "Why would you betray my trust when I had come to rely so thoroughly upon you? Why would you betray the honour of your father, who served mine so faithfully, and disgrace his good name?"

The butler glanced up at his master with cold eyes.

"My father soiled his own honour," he said through clenched teeth, "and I will do everything within my power to reveal his dishonor to all of England and America too – to soil his 'good name'!"

Stillwell took a moment to steady himself.

"No!" he cried, some strength returning to his voice. "No! I cannot – I *will* not! – believe that so good a man as Hugh Urwin could have committed any misdeed that would warrant this behavior!"

Augustus smiled.

"I am not speaking of Hugh Urwin, little brother. I am speaking our father: *Douglas Stillwell Sr.*"

The reactions in the room to this last statement were varied. The constable and I both gasped in surprise, the footman sighed in defeat, and Holmes exhaled in that satisfied way of his, showing that he wasn't surprised at all. Douglas Stillwell Jr, however, seemed to stop breathing altogether. He stood frozen for a moment, then fainted to the floor.

I dashed to the man, while Holmes and the constable moved to keep the two conspirators in place. I removed Stillwell's tight cravat and searched for a pulse beneath his fleshy throat. I found it, but it was faint and slow.

Holmes moved to the door and called out for the hall boy. He then bade the constable to handcuff the butler and footman to the bed and stand guard over them while he, the hall boy, and I carried Stillwell out of the bedroom and to a nearby parlour.

"How will he fare?" asked Holmes after Stillwell was situated on a sofa, his head and shoulders propped up with cushions and pillows to make his breathing easier.

"It's a simple case of exhaustion, due no doubt to the combination of emotional stress and this terrible heat," I answered. "With rest and nourishment, I think he will recover without difficulty."

Douglas P. Stillwell Jr.'s return to health would take longer than I had predicted, however. He remained unconscious and senseless all day and developed a terrible fever that night. I handed his care over to his own physician. For three days, it was feared that the young merchant wouldn't recover. On the fourth day, however, the heat that had been griping London finally broke, as did Stillwell's fever.

The following day, on a cool and pleasant morning, Holmes and I sat in our rooms on Baker Street when Stillwell's carriage appeared in front of our door.

"I would ask after your health, Mr. Stillwell," said Holmes as we three sat down together, "but your colour tells me all. I think I can speak for both Watson and myself in saying it is good to see you so well recovered."

"Thank you, Mr. Holmes," replied Stillwell, "and you, Dr. Watson, for all your assistance to me. I have yet to be informed about what has happened to Augustus and Rodger since the day you came to Perfect

House. I have an appointment with Inspector Lestrade later today to discuss the case, but I feel I cannot wait until then. No one has explained to me Augustus' shocking claim – that he isn't the son of Hugh Urwin, but is, in fact, my brother. Can you tell me?"

"I had the chance to interview Mr. Coburn at Scotland Yard," said Holmes as he lit a cigarette. "He made his confession, which followed my description of events perfectly. As to his motivation, that was soon made plain. I have here a copy of his verbatim statement as he made it before myself and Inspector Lestrade. Watson, would you be so kind as to read it, starting from the paragraph that begins '*My mother*'?"

I took the document and began . . . .

> *My mother was Lettie Coburn, and never has there been a woman so hard-working, so caring of her son, and so wronged by the man she loved. She came from the states. Charleston, to be precise. She came from a poor family, and at sixteen was told that she must leave home and find her own way to survive. She signed on with a maid service. The first job she was offered was to work for Douglas Stillwell, a wealthy gentleman from England who was renting a home by the waterfront for a few months' time.*
>
> *She was at once impressed by this handsome, charming Englishman, so unlike the rough-talking South Carolinians with whom she was familiar. Soon she was more than his maid – she was his mistress, though slave may be a better word, for her devotion to him became so strong that she would do anything that he asked of her.*
>
> *When the war broke out and Stillwell felt the need to make a hasty return to England, he brought her with him, promising that he would make her into a proper English lady and wed her. He bought a lavish home, but still he made her work as his servant, swearing that he would soon elevate her to his station. I believe, however, he never had any intention of doing so. A few months later he announced his engagement to Josephine Westphail, the only daughter of a fellow wealthy merchant who stood to inherit a fortune. Mother was heartbroken, yet her devotion to her master continued. Even after his marriage, she continued to serve him in every way that he desired.*
>
> *Then she became with child. The instant that Stillwell learned of this, he turned on her, accusing her of doing so on purpose in an attempt to destroy his perfect life in his perfect*

300

*house with his perfect wife. He refused to speak with her
again, instructing his butler, Hugh Urwin, to send her away.
Urwin was a good man and had known Mother since
Charleston. She was in an incredible state of distress, going
so far as to threaten to take her own life. Urwin comforted
her, however, and found her work in the home of Captain
Mumford, a retired officer living in Dorset. It was in the
Captain's home that I was born.*

*Though Stillwell would never communicate with my
mother again, Urwin kept up a regular correspondence,
checking to see that both she and I were well cared for. On a
few occasions, he even sent her money so she could buy me
gifts. Over time, the letters became less and less frequent, until
the last few years, when none came at all. I knew none of this
as I was growing up. Mother refused to tell me anything about
my father.*

*To reach our quarters at Captain Mumford's, one had to
walk down a narrow and steep flight of stairs. When mother's
health declined, this was no longer possible for her, so the
Captain allowed her a sunny room on the ground floor. One
night, I went to her old room and searched it for evidence of
who my father might be. It was then that I found the letters she
had exchanged with Urwin over the years. It didn't give me a
complete story, however, so I taxed her with them. It was
wrong for me to make her relive the pains of the past when
she was so close to the end. Yet even then she defended
Stillwell, unable to accept that his love for her was false. She
no longer had the strength to lift her head, so her tears flowed
freely down her temples as she spoke.*

*She died the next day. Sick as she was, I couldn't help but
feel responsible, as though my demands of the night before
had been too much for her heart to bear. Lettie Coburn died
with nothing to her name and only a son to mourn her. I vowed
that I would make Douglas Stillwell pay for the wrongs he had
done to her.*

*I made my way to London. The first thing I did upon
arriving in the city was call upon Hugh Urwin, to let him know
of mother's passing. I remember approaching Perfect House
for the first time, feeling the rage swell inside me with each
step I took toward it. Once there, I was met with two
developments I hadn't foreseen: Douglas Stillwell was dead
and his son, my half-brother, Douglas Jr. had inherited all.*

Furthermore, Urwin himself was near death. He was delighted to meet me. We spent many hours together over the next few weeks, telling each other the stories of our lives. When I finally told him my purpose in coming to London, to have my revenge on my father, Urwin said, "Ah, but he is gone now. There is nothing to be done."

"Nothing to be done?" I replied. "On the contrary, my plans have changed very little. I may not be able to disgrace Douglas Stillwell Sr. by revealing myself to the world, but I can disgrace his memory!"

"Please don't, my boy!" Urwin pleaded. "He may have had his faults, but Master Stillwell was a good man. He always treated me with kindness and respect."

"What of me?" I threw back at him. "What of my mother? What kindness and respect did he show us? I will inform my half-brother of who I am and demand I receive the inheritance that is due to me!"

"If it is money you want," said Urwin, his eyes wide, "there is another way. Please, let me help you as I helped your mother."

He then offered all he had. His wife had passed, and they had had no children. If I wanted to be the sole inheritor of all he had, he would make it so, as long as I promised not to reveal his late master's secret. I agreed, but I never for a moment intended to keep the bargain. For all his talk of helping my mother and me, the fact remained that he only did so to hide his master's shame, and therefore was just as guilty.

Urwin died, but not before issuing a new will naming me the sole inheritor of his estate. It was a respectable sum. I could have lived a decent life off of it for some time, but it wasn't enough. I was the first born son of Douglas Stillwell. I deserved all he had left. So I began to plot my next move.

Urwin had made mention of my father's prolific journal writing. He wrote for an hour or more each night of his life, creating a record of all he did. I knew those writings were the key to proving my mother's story. The very evening Urwin told me this, I wrote to Douglas Jr. in the person of John Octavian, an old friend of his father, seeking access to the papers. It was a clumsy effort and I regretted it the moment the letter was sent. Not knowing who Octavian was, Douglas Jr. took the message straight to Urwin, who, to my good fortune, felt compelled to pretend he knew nothing about the matter.

302

More good fortune was to come, it seemed, for before I had thought of a way to get inside Perfect House after Urwin's death, I received word from Douglas Jr. inviting me to visit. I didn't know why he wanted to see me. I was fearful that he had in some way discovered the truth of who I was. To my delight, however, he wasn't only ignorant in that regard, but was in all regards an utter fool, who hung onto every word of the false story I invented in that very moment: That it was Urwin who made false oaths of love to my mother and fathered me, that we had been reconciled, and that that was why he changed his will so close to the end. The imbecile was so trusting that after a single meeting, he offered to make me the head of his household staff!

The job wasn't difficult. Most of the staff has been here for years and were trained well, so they did their work without much input from me. I spent most of my time in the company of Douglas Jr. The fool was in such desperate need of a friend and confidant he made me both instantly, and so long as he was paying me handsomely, I was happy to play the part. Within two months, he was regularly inviting me to sit with him in the evening to drink, calling in Rodger or Susan to serve me right alongside him. It amused me to earn his trust, to make him evermore reliant on me for happiness, knowing that one day I would strip everything he had from him.

Some of the staff resented me, I suppose. Most treated me quite coolly. But Rodger? Rodger understood me from the start. He didn't know my secret, but he knew I was playing Douglas Jr. "for a sap", as my mother used to say, and found amusement in it as well. While I pretended to become close to Douglas Jr., I was in truth doing so with Rodger. The fellow wasn't smart, but smarter than my brother and much more pleasant to look at.

The handsome dullard has one major fault, however: He is a terrible gambler. One night he gambled away every penny he had, and a few that he didn't. When he brought his dilemma to me, I knew what to do. I got him a wig, fake whiskers, and spectacles. Douglas Jr. always rode through Highgate Woods on Saturdays with me accompanying him. There is a quiet spot along the path that passes under a small stone bridge, the perfect place for an ambush. That Saturday as we rode along, Rodger leapt out from behind the bridge, wearing his disguise and demanding our money. Douglas Jr. had tossed him the *bag before he had even finished asking for it! I leapt down from the carriage and Rodger and I pretended to wrestle for a moment before he slipped my grasp and ran back to Perfect House. He got the money he needed, and I secured Douglas Jr.'s absolute trust and respect.*

As I spent my days gaining the trust of both men, by night I was attempting to access my father's papers. On my first day as butler, I learned of the locked study and the cabinet in which all his writings were kept. It took me three months before I could trick Douglas Jr. into mentioning where he kept the keys for both and into drinking enough wine to forget the conversation. The next day, I took wax impressions of both keys, from which I had copies made.

Each night, well after the rest of the house had gone to bed, I took my dark lantern, tip-toed upstairs to the study, unlocked the cabinet, took a volume of my father's diary, sat at the desk, and read. I began earlier than the age at which he met my mother. I felt comfortable in my position and had no problem taking my time. And as I never knew my father in person, I found this window into his mind, that likely no one else had ever read, to be insightful. I was surprised at how similar his ways of thinking were to my own. His ambition, his doubts, his perception all rang true in my mind. There were passages that I could have easily written myself.

But when, after weeks of reading, I reached his time in America, I was shocked to find he made no mention of my mother. He wrote of everything in his life – of his business, of all the Americans he met, of his conversations with Urwin, of the doings of his little spaniel – but never mentioned Lettie Coburn. Her name didn't appear during the recounting of his flight from South Carolina, of his courting of wife, or of his early days in Perfect House. He wrote of other servants from time to time, but never of her. I was perplexed and frustrated.

Then last night, I entered the study some time past one and began to read, as usual. I had only been reading for a few minutes when I came to a passage that made my blood run cold. He wrote: The bitch has got a litter in her. Told Urwin to get rid of her.

Suddenly I understood. The villain never had a dog. Every passage he had written about his "little spaniel" had been about my mother! That is what she was to him. That is what he thought of her – as a beast whose only purpose was to amuse and serve him.

As quickly as my blood had frozen, it now began to boil. I, having lost my senses for a moment, leapt from the chair. In doing so, I bumped hard against the desk. I saw the bust of Byron tip and fall over the edge. Before it even hit the ground, my mind became perfectly clear again. I knew that the sound would awaken Douglas Jr. I had played out what I would do in such an eventuality in my mind many times. I cried out to an invisible intruder, then began to grunt and gasp as though in a struggle. As I made these sounds, I threw open the window, put the diary back in the cabinet, and closed it. I knew that the burglar should steal something, but the only thing that would fit into the pocket of my dressing gown was the picture of my father's bride on the desk. I took some delight in stealing it, knowing how much it would distress Douglas Jr. to find it missing. Finally, as I heard Douglas at the door, I took a deep breath and slammed my head down onto the desk. It was certainly painful, but never as bad as I let on.

You have stated yourself, Mr. Holmes, what happened next and I won't deny anything you have said. It was exactly as you described. There is only one thing more I have to say: Charge me with whatever crimes you see fit, so long as I can tell my story before a court and let the world know that Douglas Stillwell was my father and as vile a fiend as ever seduced an innocent young maid.

"My Lord," said Stillwell once I had finished. "The poor man! I had no idea!"

Holmes raised his eyebrows at this, as did I.

"Do you mean to say," I asked, "that despite all he has done against you, you still take pity on the scoundrel?"

Stillwell looked at me with a confidence that I had hitherto not seen from him.

"Despite his protestations to the contrary," he said, "I refuse to believe that the pleasant hours Augustus and I spent together were all an act on his part. He was understandably bitter when he made that confession, so his words against me were perhaps harsher than they would have been, were he in a calmer state of mind. In the end, whatever his machinations may have been, no real harm has been done to me. As both the robbery in the park and the burglary were mere performances, I was in

305

no way ever in danger. I am disappointed in Rodger, of course. It saddens me that he didn't bring his financial woes to me, I would have gladly given him the sum he thought he must steal. My mother's bridal portrait has been returned to me. When all is accounted for, no real damage has been done. I must see Inspector Lestrade and tell him that I don't desire to press any charges against either man. Thank you, gentlemen, for your assistance in this case."

Stillwell rose to his feet.

"But what of Hugh Urwin?" I pressed. "Coburn clearly coaxed the man into granting him his inheritance. Do you forgive that, too? You will have no say whether he faces that charge."

"Ah," said Holmes, "but Lestrade will know that there's no use in charging him for that alone. Augustus was quite careful in his confession to point out that Urwin offered him the estate, that it was the old man's idea, and there are no witnesses to present a contrary view. Between this and the fact that there is no apparent relative of Urwin's who would stand to benefit from a challenge to the will, I doubt the matter will ever make it to court."

"Perhaps it is all for the best," said Stillwell. "Hugh Urwin was a good man who undoubtedly cared for Lettie Coburn's well-being. I am sure he was glad to give what he had to her son. If you will excuse me, gentlemen, I will be off to Scotland Yard to inform Inspector Lestrade of my decision. Here is a check for you, Mr. Holmes, covering your quoted rate with an additional token of my appreciation. Thank you for your assistance. Good-bye."

With that, the young merchant gave a small bow and walked out of the room.

"It cannot be helped, Watson," said Holmes as our client's carriage made its way down Baker Street. "We are merely investigators, not solicitors or judges. How often have we presented a client with the truth, only to see them deny it, excuse it, or take an utterly wrong lesson from it? All we can do is hope for the best and then forget the matter entirely. Our time will be better spent focusing on what new clients await us rather than dwelling on what follies our old clients have made."

At the end of my notes for this case, there is a brief account of a conversation I had with Douglas Stillwell Jr. some years later, when we met by chance on a train. He did not, in fact, press charges against his half-brother, and although he was certainly unwilling to give up his rights of inheritance, he did gift a generous portion of his wealth to Augustus, who took the small fortune to America. Stillwell didn't hear from his brother until a year later when he received a letter asking for yet more money. Stillwell wrote back to refuse and never heard from his brother again.

"A result," Holmes said at the time, "that would surprise no one other than Stillwell himself."

The Adventure of the
Downing Street Demise
by Brett Fawcett

"[T]he general election swept Lord Salisbury, disguised by Watson as Lord Bellinger, into his second premiership. Salisbury promptly named Lord Iddesleigh, formerly Sir Stafford Northcote, as his Foreign Secretary, the post for which the 'Secretary for European Affairs' in 'The Second Stain' is an obvious blind. Towards the close of that year — 1886 — occurred a series of startling Ministerial changes for which English historians have heretofore never been able fully to account . . . Lord Iddesleigh was then literally ousted from the post of Foreign Secretary . . . ."

– Felix Morley, "The Significance of the Second Stain"

"Lord Iddlesleigh . . . was, perhaps, not unreasonably, offended to read the first news of it in the daily papers of January 12, [1887] . . . Tragedy, never very far behind the curtain, came forward swiftly on the heels of this. That same afternoon Lord Iddesleigh called upon Lord Salisbury at Downing Street, and, being overtaken in the anteroom by the heart disease from which he had been so long afflicted, he expired in the presence of the Prime Minister."

– Sir Winston Churchill, *Lord Randolph Churchill*

"As I looked upon the dead body stretched before me I felt that politics was a cursed profession."

– Lord Salisbury, Letter to Lord Randolph Churchill
January 14, 1887

As a recorder of the remarkable exploits of Sherlock Holmes, I confess to being committed not only to accurately reporting the facts of any given case, but also to providing a satisfying literary experience to my readers. To give an hour of joy to those who read my chronicles is nearly as important to me as it is to be a truthful historian.

Consequently, there are episodes in Holmes's career that may have included thrilling moments and striking demonstrations of my friend's remarkable gifts, but which I have chosen not to share with the public because of the effect I predict they would have on my audience. One such case was that of the death at Downing Street. Despite being one of the most significant and stirring cases of my friend's career, I decided not to publish an account of it, not only because of the scandal that would result if the facts were made known, but also, and perhaps just as importantly to me, because it would undermine the ending of one of the most effective and well-received stories that I *have* chosen to publish. Nevertheless, I have included an account of that case in this dispatch box so that intrepid students of Holmes's methods may have access to it for their personal research.

The published story to which I refer is "The Adventure of the Second Stain". The reader will recall the events of that tale, which took place while Lord Bellinger was Prime Minister: A European potentate (whom I will not identify) wrote an unfortunate letter complaining about British colonial expansion. He later regretted writing that missive, which could have caused war between his country and ours had it been leaked to the public and its contents made widely known. The letter was entrusted to Trelawney Hope, the Secretary for European Affairs, and its existence was to be kept a secret. However, a spy in Hope's office informed Eduardo Lucas, an international secret agent (as well as man-about-town and amateur tenor), about the existence of the letter. Lucas blackmailed Hope's wife, Lady Hilda Hope, to steal the letter for him. However, Lucas was murdered by his jealous Parisian wife, allowing Lady Hilda to recover the letter from his home. Holmes was able to restore the letter to Hope without him ever learning about his wife's involvement – or, for that matter, about Lucas, or the spy in his office.

The adventure ended perfectly: The situation was fully resolved, the villain was slain, and the protagonists were left happy and with bright futures before them. At that time, Hope was one of the most promising statesmen in Britain, and Holmes had saved his career. After putting the final period at the end of that story, any sensible author would set down their pen with contentment.

But alas, "The Second Stain" has a sad sequel.

Those events took place in autumn. On a dreary winter morning a few months later, the second page of *The Times* carried the news that the Prime Minister had unexpectedly removed Hope from his position as Secretary for Europe Affairs, despite him having been in the middle of treaty negotiations with ambassadors from Scandinavia. The consensus in the opinion columns was that Lord Bellinger had behaved inexplicably and that Hope had been treated most unjustly. I, too, was naturally surprised and wondered aloud at the time if this dismissal could have been the consequence of Hope having temporarily lost such an important letter, but Holmes dismissed this. Why would Lord Bellinger have waited so long to punish Hope for that perceived misstep? I shrugged it off, content to assume that internal cabinet politics which would forever remain beyond my ken were responsible for this development.

The following morning, the front page of *The Times* carried this even more startling article:

> *The death of Trelawney Hope occurred with painful abruptness on Wednesday at the official residence of the Prime Minister in 10 Downing Street. For many years past, the noble politician had suffered from an affliction of the heart, and the possibility of a sudden termination of his life was not unforeseen by medical attendants. Nevertheless, there has been no time for years past when so mournful an event was less to be anticipated, particularly since his death came only a few hours after the world became aware that he had lost his post as European Secretary.*
>
> *According to various witness testimonies, Hope left his house in Whitehall Terrace at half-past-two and was taken by carriage directly to the Foreign Office in King Charles Street. He was met there by his Private Secretaries, Messrs. Eric Saumarez and Arthur Dorrington, and subsequently, just before leaving, saw Cathcart Soames, the Under-Secretary for European Affairs, with whom he had an animated conversation lasting several minutes. He then walked to Downing Street to see Lord Bellinger, and arrived at nearly seven-minutes-past-three.*
>
> *Probably the change from the warm atmosphere of the Foreign Office to the cold air outside had an immediate effect upon Mr. Hope, for the usher at Downing Street who opened the door for him, Mr. Foote, noticed that he looked ill. Mr. Hope waited in the antechamber outside the Prime Minister's office while Mr. Foote went in to announce his arrival to Lord Bellinger, but when Mr. Foote returned, he found Mr. Hope sitting in a chair and gasping for breath. When he entered the office, he collapsed next to a sofa and had to be helped onto it by Lord Bellinger and Mr. Foote. Dr. Wirst, who maintains a nearby practice, was sent for and arrived a minute or two later, but by then Mr. Hope had lost consciousness which he would never recover. Mr. Hope breathed his last at ten-minutes-past-three.*

It is needless to add that the Prime Minister was profoundly affected by the painful event. Currently, Mr. Soames is working as the acting Secretary for European Affairs until Lord Bellinger can determine who will permanently succeed Mr. Hope.

Our deepest sympathies are with the widow, Lady Hilda Trelawney Hope.

That two such devastating tragedies should befall Hope in quick succession was as striking as it was heartbreaking, but, despite the dramatic circumstances of his death, there was no obvious reason to suspect anything nefarious about it. The shock of his demotion, coupled with the already weakened condition of his heart, seemed a sufficient explanation for his death. Holmes barely remarked on this, complaining instead that he had been enduring a recent dry spell of stimulating crime in the news and that Hope's death did nothing to interrupt that suffering. I, however, could not help but grieve Hope. It felt as though we had rescued him from infamy for nothing.

The following morning, Holmes was still listless and annoyed at the lack of any intriguing problems on the horizon, and had begun to hint that he was prepared to use cocaine or morphine to fill the time until something more stimulating presented itself. As we argued, I glanced out our window to the pavement below.

"Hold off, Holmes," I interjected. "It looks as though you have a new client."

Holmes perked up and joined me at the window. Through it, we could see a young woman standing below us in front of our building, seemingly hesitant about whether or not to knock at the door. Before she could make a decision, however, a man suddenly appeared before her, as if from thin air. He had golden, curly hair, wore a long grey coat covered with pockets (each of which seemed to be filled), and carried a Gladstone bag. Even from our height and distance, there was something intense about this strange figure.

He had a conversation with the lady in which, to judge by the way in which she carried herself, he confirmed that she intended to call upon us. He then talked to her without interruption for some time. Whatever he was saying seemed to practically mesmerize her, for she looked at him blankly and quietly as he spoke. At the end of his monologue, he handed her an envelope. She gasped as she opened it and discovered it was stuffed with money. She thanked him profusely and took off, leaving him alone at our door.

"Well!" remarked Holmes, obviously impressed. "Someone is *very* eager to speak to us before anyone else can – someone with considerable powers of persuasion, or perhaps simply of considerable financial means."

"Is anything more persuasive than being of considerable financial means?" I asked.

Holmes grinned. "*Touché*, Watson. Perhaps not. In any event, this is quite encouraging. Perhaps I will not need morphine today, after all."

Moments later, the man was in our room, his steely eyes boring holes into both of us. He was not tall, but his presence seemed somehow imposing. He turned his focus to my friend.

"Mr. Sherlock Holmes," he stated in what sounded like a Swedish accent.

"It is I," replied Holmes airily, lighting a cigarette.

"I know." Each word was as sharp, cold, and pointed as an icicle. "I am Theo Eckerman. I am here to hire you. But not for myself."

"For who, then?"

"The King of Scandinavia."

If this impressed Holmes, he didn't show it.

"Are you one of the Scandinavian ambassadors here for the treaty discussions?" I asked.

Eckerman's mouth stretched into a smile that was as tight and humourless as a garrote wire.

"I am the opposite of a diplomat, Dr. Watson. I am part of the Scandinavian Secret Service."

My eyes widened. It seemed shocking that a spy would so openly admit his profession to two men he had just met. Nevertheless, everything about this strange and vaguely dangerous figure suggested that he was telling us the truth.

"And what need has the King of Scandinavia, or his intelligence service, for me?" asked Holmes.

"To investigate the death of Mr. Trelawney Hope."

Without asking permission, Eckerman sat in a chair across from us.

"Is this related to his negotiations with your country?" I asked, taking out my notebook. Eckerman glanced at it with what appeared to be displeasure, but didn't remark on it.

"Mr. Holmes," he said, turning to him and ignoring me, "we are aware of your involvement with Mr. Hope and the missing letter."

"But the facts of that case weren't publicized!" I protested. Eckerman continued to ignore me.

"As you surely inferred, the author of that letter was the King of Scandinavia. He has been irritated by the British Empire's expansion into the Caribbean last summer to try to monopolize sugar production there.

That intrudes on Scandinavian colonies, as you know. Mr. Hope recognized the necessity of keeping the letter secret, but also took its contents seriously. He was hoping to include terms in this in which Britain would agree to withdraw from much of the Caribbean and allow Scandinavia to continue to reign over those areas, so as to avoid further conflict."

"I can appreciate why his removal and subsequent death would be disappointing to you."

"It is more than this, Mr. Holmes. A war between England and Scandinavia would be very welcome to many officials in Austria-Hungary. You may know there is some tension between that empire and ours of late. There have been various attempts to smooth this over. There are even talks of marrying the King of Bohemia to the King of Scandinavia's daughter in order to strengthen ties between the two empires. But many within that regime would be pleased to see Scandinavia humbled so that Austria-Hungary can rise, and would have no problem if that humbling were done by England."

He leaned forward towards us. "Mr. Holmes, we think Austria-Hungary may have agents within the British government willing to help them achieve this goal. Those agents may have been responsible for having Mr. Hope removed."

"Even if this were true, by all accounts, there was nothing suspicious about Hope's death."

Eckerman snapped open his Gladstone bag and pulled out a large envelope, which he handed to me. Inside, I discovered large photographs of a cadaver in a morgue. I soon realized whose corpse I was looking at.

"These are the remains of Trelawney Hope!" I exclaimed. "How in blazes did you acquire these?"

"Dr. Watson, everyone has their skills. Mine is knowing how to make the right friends. In this case, I had a friend who was able to procure these for me. Do you notice anything in these images? One might miss it if he isn't looking for it, or chooses not to look for it, but you might find something on Mr. Hope's forearm, just under his wrist."

I felt slightly sickened, but looked at the images closely until I noticed a small hole in the skin where Eckerman has described. "Why, that looks like the mark of a hypodermic injection!"

"Perhaps." Eckerman took a ring with a large stone out of his bag and slipped it on his right finger. "But not necessarily."

Eckerman held up his right palm so the bottom of the ring was visible. He put his left hand behind it and pressed down on the stone. A small needle poked out of the bottom of the ring.

313

"The stone of this ring contains concentrated foxglove poison," he explained dryly. "A single injection of this is equivalent to an entire syringe of digitalis."

"That could kill a man in less than five minutes!" I cried.

Eckerman nodded slightly. "Suppose you are an assassin with this on your finger. All you must do is shake your victim's hand a certain way, and he will walk away from you dying, with nothing but a slight pricking in his palm to warn him of this. And, if you find the ring too gaudy, you have other options: Lapel pins, pens, umbrellas . . . Bump into someone in a crowd, or brush across them at a party, and you have assassinated them as surely as if you had used a bomb or a dagger."

I wondered with bewilderment what the wars of the future would be like, if they were to be waged with weapons such as these.

"Why don't *you* investigate?" asked Holmes, puffing at his cigarette.

"As a foreigner, even with my . . . *friends* . . . I have certain limitations that you do not. Besides, the King of Scandinavia had a feeling you might find this an interesting problem. If it isn't, however, money is available that might make it more interesting to you."

"And should I choose to pursue this, how will I relay my findings to my . . . client?"

Eckerman set a card on the table. "Wire me here. Whatever you report will be passed on immediately to His Majesty. But don't seek me at this address. You will not find me there."

With that, and with no further farewell, Eckerman disappeared out the door. It felt as though he left a gust of frigid wind in his wake. Holmes exhaled a large cloud of smoke and stared into it.

"A fascinating problem in its own right, made even more alluring by the fact that we know something that Mr. Eckerman and His Majesty do not: Lady Hilda informed us that Eduardo Lucas had a spy in her husband's office. This lends independent credibility to their suspicions of foreign presence, if not control, in the British government."

I shuddered.

"If that is so, it isn't only your job as a detective to find the spy, but your patriotic duty!"

"True – though that is a slightly different task than the one the Scandinavian monarch recruited me for." Holmes rose. He threw his cigarette in the fireplace and then stared into the flames.

"I had Lucas pegged as a free agent, not a tool of Austria-Hungary," Holmes murmured. He turned from the fireplace towards me. "When he first approached us, Hope assured us that only two, possibly three, officials in his office knew about the letter. Presumably, the spy was one of this small number." Holmes pointed at the mess of paper on our table. "Would you fetch yesterday's *Times*?"

I did so.

"Does it not mention him conversing with three people at the Foreign Office?"

I scanned the article. "His two personal secretaries and the Under-Secretary."

"Hmm. That sounds like two or three officials. Come, Watson. Before we poke around Downing Street, we'd best start by doing some reconnaissance work at King Charles Street."

A few minutes later, a hansom cab had brought us to the ornate and stately Foreign Office building. The Office of European Affairs was near the front of the building. We entered it to find a long antechamber filled with chairs, sofas, and other pieces of furniture meant to facilitate conversation. Three desks were visible, each of which had a large nameplate to identify the man who sat at it. Eric Saumarez had noble, aquiline features, while Arthur Dorrington had a fiery red but close-cropped mustache. The third desk, that of the Honourable Cathcart Soames, was empty, though a hat and jacket hung on the wall behind it. Beyond that desk was an office door which still bore a nameplate reading "*The Hon. Trelawney Hope*".

Both men rose to greet us. I felt myself grow tense, knowing that one of them was likely an Austro-Hungarian spy and could be wearing any number of weapons invisible to myself. I bowed stiffly rather than offering either of them my hand. Holmes looked around Soames' desk.

"Where is the Under-Secretary now?" he asked.

"He's in Mr. Hope's office, cleaning up," answered Dorrington, perhaps a little awkwardly.

"Ah – making himself comfortable there." Holmes knocked at the office door, which opened to reveal an immaculately dressed young man with jet-black hair. Behind him, a stack of disorganized papers sat on the desk that had once been Hope's. Soames smiled artificially at us.

"How may I help you gentlemen?" he asked, not a little pompously.

"We have been asked to clear up a few questions regarding the sad demise of the Honourable Mr. Hope," announced Holmes.

"Ah. Well, I don't think there is much left for you to discover that hasn't already been publicly reported, so perhaps you could content yourself with reading – "

"Did you get your hair coloured while you were in Saint Barthélemy," Holmes interrupted, "or did you have it done on Lower Burke Street? You really ought to avoid that shop, you know – respectable as it looks, it's a

315

front for all sorts of crime. An intrepid journalist could easily tarnish your name if they discovered you patronized it."

Soames' eyes bulged, as did those of Dorrington and Suamarez.

"How did you – "

"I can discover things no one else has found in sights that many other eyes have seen. Now that you know this, perhaps you will be more obliging."

Soames sat down at his proper desk with the wordless humility of a chastened schoolboy.

For the next hour or so, Holmes conducted interviews with the three men, both individually and as a group. We confirmed that Hope had arrived at around 2:35 and spent fifteen minutes discussing various administrative issues with his two secretaries, both of whom had been recently hired by him and both of whom spoke glowingly of him. At 2:50, he went into his office with Soames to discuss the Scandinavian treaty. Soames admitted a bit sheepishly that he differed from Hope on this issue. His visit to the Caribbean had convinced Soames that Britain should push on with her presence there, not withdraw and yield it to Scandinavia. Hope, however, was insistent that this treaty be completed so as to avoid a Continental war.

The two argued for ten minutes until Hope, more agitated than Soames had ever seen him before, ordered Soames to leave the office, with a parting shot that implied he expected it to be his office again before long. Soames returned to his desk in the antechamber. At almost exactly 3:06, Hope stormed out of his office and left without saying a word to any of his three assistants, presumably intent on meeting Lord Bellinger. After Holmes had a thorough look around Hope's office and the antechamber, we left our three suspects and headed on foot for his home in Whitehall, the address of which was still fresh in our mind from the last adventure that brought us there.

"Do you know which of them is the spy?" I asked as we walked.

"I know what each of them looks like. For now, that is all I need. Would you care to explain my deductions about Mr. Soames to me?"

"I presume you noticed hairs on Soames' hat and jacket that weren't black."

"Grey, and too short to be a woman's. You saw how carefully his clothes are cared for. He must have them regularly cleaned. The fact that grey hairs are still found on them means he must have changed their colour to black very recently."

"I also noticed his tan, but how did you know it was from being in Saint Barthélemy?"

316

"Soames is the Under-Secretary for *European* Affairs. If he has traveled recently, it must have been to a location under a European government. Do you know anywhere on the Continent one could achieve that skin tone in winter? He must have been in a tropical European colony. We know the Caribbean is currently a point of contention between a European power and ourselves, and, since Saint Barthélemy is the center of sugar farming in that region, it seemed reasonable to assume that was where he had been."

"And Lower Burke Street?"

"His jacket had the unmistakable fragrance of Firebrand Blend, an American brand of tobacco which is illicitly manufactured there, illegitimately imported here, and illegally sold at only one location, a criminally owned specialty store on Lower Burke Street. It isn't their only forbidden ware. Hopefully, it is the only one Mr. Soames purchases. Keep those observational powers sharp. We will have much need of them today."

We arrived at the Hope estate and were met at the door by Jacobs, the butler who had also served as Hope's valet. He was the very model of professional aloofness and courtesy, but a palpable melancholy hung about him like a cape. The soft but unmistakable sound of weeping could be heard from deep within the house.

Without waiting for an explanation for our visit, Jacobs silently showed us into the sitting room before disappearing down a hallway. A few minutes later, he returned with Lady Hilda at his side. Her clothes were black and her eyes were red. She still carried herself with some of the strength and self-assurance she had displayed to us before, but it was clear she was also beginning to crumple under the weight of the two great emotional blows she had just suffered.

"We are so sorry to trouble you at this time, Lady Hilda," apologized Holmes.

She shook her head. "Thanks to you, my husband went to his grave never knowing of my crime against him. Seeing you today is the least I can do to thank you, though I cannot promise I am fit to usefully answer any questions. You don't . . . suspect anything, do you?"

"Your husband was known to be a thorough man," answered Holmes smoothly. "He would have wished for us to examine everything about his death, even if there were nothing to find."

Lady Hilda closed her teary eyes and breathed deeply. "I say that, Mr. Holmes, because I must frankly admit that his manner *had* changed of late. He seemed distracted and troubled over the last week, though he refused to tell me what was bothering him – something related to his work, I presume. I was concerned, of course, especially because of his history of

317

heart problems. We had been looking desperately for any treatment that might have helped him. Jacobs had been up and down Harley Street seeking some sort of cure. When Trelawney read in the paper that morning that Lord Bellinger had sacked him, I truly feared the shock was going to kill him right there at our breakfast table. He took the rest of the morning to rest, to think, and to prepare some papers – papers he refused to show me, of course."

"Do you know what has become of those papers?"

Lady Hilda shook her head again. "I have tried looking for them in his dispatch-box, but they seem to have disappeared."

"Hmm. What did he do for the rest of the day?"

"He sent Jacobs out to do some errands while the two of us lunched together."

"Grocery shopping," explained Jacobs, his voice distant and empty.

"As we ate, Trelawney . . . Well, he assured me that everything would be fine. He headed out shortly after Jacobs returned, and . . . ."

Her shaky composure gave way at this point, and her face collapsed into a tortured wail of grief. Jacobs' demeanour also changed: The calm, unemotional servant gave way to a consoling, avuncular figure who clasped her hand and whispered soothingly to her, entreating her not to despair. It said a great deal about Lady Hilda, I observed, that she could have this effect on as stolid a personality as Jacobs.

The doorbell rang. Jacobs apologetically slipped away and returned moments later with a tall, handsome older man with grand military mustaches and a shiny black walking stick topped with a silver lion's head. If any doubt remained that this was Alastair Farrer, better known to the public as the Duke of Belminster, it was erased when Lady Hilda threw herself around his shoulders crying, "Oh, Papa!"

"There, there, child," he cooed in the deep, velvety voice that had made him such an effective diplomat and military commander in his younger days. She stepped back and clasped his free hand with both of hers. Her smile was like the sun breaking through a storm cloud. Her father's touch and presence seemed to have restored something of the self that would otherwise have died with her husband, and to have brought out a latent and hitherto unseen childlikeness.

He turned to us. "You men are here about Trelawney, I suppose. I must tell you that, from the first moment Hilda introduced me to him, I believed in him absolutely. Not only did I do my best to mentor him, but I always took his side whenever anyone doubted him, right from the beginning. I even endorsed him to the Prime Minister – Lord Bellinger and I are old friends, you see – although I think he got by on his merits far more than he ever did by my recommendation. I have known great men, sirs, and he was a great man."

Hilda made a sound that was somehow both a laugh and a sob at once. "Oh, Papa, please do come again this time tomorrow!"

"You can always depend on me, child."

Holmes and I took this as our cue to thank them both and to slip out.

"What did you observe?" Holmes asked as he scribbled on a piece of paper.

"She is distraught, obviously – "

"Yes. Even I, who lack your talents of decoding the feminine, detected that," sighed Holmes with some exasperation as he hailed a cab. "I was asking what you noticed about her father, the Duke."

I thought for a moment. "His walking stick was obviously expensive. Its sheen was still fresh, and it had no scuff or scratch marks on it, so it must have been purchased recently. I would deduce he has been able to maintain his wealth in his retirement."

Holmes had stopped a cab and handed his note to the driver before we climbed in. "You have an amusing but destructive habit of correctly reasoning yourself halfway to the truth before allowing yourself to be derailed," he chuckled as we sat down. "The stick was expensive and new, but his clothes are old. He has unsuccessfully attempted to rub a food stain off his shirt collar with soap, and his shoes have been re-soled. Always look closely at the shoes of those who wish to impress you. The Duke of Belminster has been in financial straits for some time, but has recently come back into wealth. As I said before, you will need all your observational acumen for the job I have for you tonight."

"Oh? And what am I to do?"

Holmes leaned back and looked at me with a serious expression. "We will need some insight into the inner workings of the cabinet, and the facts of these matters are always better ascertained through indirect channels than direct ones. I will be dropping you off for a few hours in an institution known as the Rahab. It is something in between a hotel, a club, a public house, and a secret society. Its clientele can make you privy to the sort of gossip about government which is most likely to be accurate. Do your best to find out what people are saying about why Trelawney Hope was demoted, and what they are expecting to happen next. But take care. No one will trust you until you make them, and no one there who distrusts you can fail to be a danger to you."

I felt my heart beating faster as he explained this. "And how am I to make them trust me?"

"By introducing yourself – not with your name, but with the phrase 'I hear that Jupiter has orbited out from behind the sun.' Don't trouble yourself with its meaning, but never hesitate to use it if you don't feel safe. And do leave as soon as you think you've learned everything you need – and come directly home when you do."

It takes a great deal to make me sweat from nervousness, but Holmes's words were having this effect on me. "Why won't you be there with me?"

"For two reasons: One is that I have every confidence in you. You know I wouldn't send you anywhere from which I thought there was any real risk you wouldn't come back. The other is that I have a task of equal importance to complete which must be accomplished tonight. Ah, here we are: Lord Street in Brixton. Head to that office building and use the side door. Have faith. You will be well, and all will be well."

With these words as my only spur and comfort, I dismounted the cab and walked around the drab structure Holmes had pointed out until I found a plain wooden side door. I knocked, and a man in black tie attire answered the door and looked me over with narrowed eyes.

"I hear Jupiter has orbited out from behind the sun," I offered, trying to sound confident and casual.

Looking no less suspicious of me than before, the porter admitted me, though not before patting down my clothing to ensure no weapons were concealed on my person. I found myself in something like a private restaurant. There was a long, well-stocked bar, several tables, and, most strikingly, several rooms from which patrons circulated in and out. Although the large chandelier hanging in the center of the room shone brightly, there was also an oil lamp on each table. No darkness was permitted to exist anywhere in this establishment. As I entered this strange place, I felt the same nervous thrill that I experienced in Afghanistan whenever my duties would take me near, or even into, enemy territory.

The patrons themselves, many of whom had expensively and revealing dressed women hanging on their arms, were drinking, eating, gambling, and generally engaging in predictable postprandial recreations. Yet a cautious unease hung in the atmosphere. Each of these men had a shiftiness and seriousness about them that reminded me of Mr. Eckerman. Although I presumed each had been checked for weapons, I still found my eyes roving from table to table looking warily at every umbrella or cigarette case or other everyday item that could potentially conceal a poisonous pinprick.

Summoning my courage, and keeping my hands firmly in my pockets, I drifted from table to table, from the bar to the cards table, in search of the information I needed, taking care that the *shibboleth* Holmes had taught me was the first thing I said to every new stranger I encountered. It always loosened their tongues, even if it never removed

320

their distrustful frowns. Only years later would realize that this was a coded way of telling these men that I was an ally of Mycroft Holmes (of whose existence I was still unaware at the time) and therefore worthy of their confidence. Despite this, there wasn't a single moment where I didn't feel as though a host of eyes were glaring at me, like so many hunter's rifles pointed at my back. Even on the cab ride home, I felt as if their stares had somehow followed me out the door and were still aimed at me from across the city. I shivered when I finally closed the flat door behind me, as if shaking their gazes off my shoulders. Holmes was already there and was in the process of donning his dressing gown.

"What on earth is that place?" I demanded.

Holmes smiled at me. "Is your Biblical knowledge even rustier than mine? You will find the meaning of *Rahab* in *The Book of Joshua*. What have you discovered?"

"According to those gentlemen," I answered, perhaps a little tartly, "Lord Bellinger had been considering revoking Hope's cabinet position for the last two weeks. What exactly prompted this remains a mystery, but apparently the Premier even met privately with the Duke of Belminster to discuss this decision and, despite the Duke presumably advocating for Hope, the Prime Minister obviously chose to go ahead with the demotion. People find this surprising, since Lord Bellinger is known to typically take the Duke's advice on these sorts of matters, which has led to all sorts of speculation about what could have caused him to break from that advice on this occasion. As for what's next, Lord Bellinger is said to be deliberating between giving the job to Cathcart Soames or to Lord Holdhurst. Holdhurst was known to be sympathetic to Hope's views on issues like the Caribbean question, and would almost certainly continue his policies and initiatives – such as, for example, the Scandinavian treaty – while Soames, as we've seen, absolutely disagreed with Hope's priorities, and his appointment would represent an utter sea change in England's Continental policies."

Holmes clapped his hands loudly, his face beaming. "Outstanding! You have more than met my expectations. This provides us with fresh and valuable evidence and confirms certain key intuitions I've had about this case. I shall have to send you on more of these fact-finding missions."

This hearty appreciation of me caused some of my testiness at having been sent into that environment to melt away. "And what have *you* been doing?" I asked.

"Ah, Watson, it has been a most valuable evening! I have finally been able to attend a performance of the amateur choir at Orsino Theatre and Concert Hall on Howe Street, who put on the most marvelous rendition of Verdi's *Requiem*. They have a lovely custom of allowing the choir

321

members, still carrying their sheet music, to mingle with the audience at the intermission. The programs have a page reserved entirely for autographs. Very considerate!" He held up one such program proudly. "As I told you: I had a task of equal importance."

My bitterness resurfaced. "You mean you have been relaxing in a comfortable music hall while I have been out doing difficult and perhaps life-threatening work to solve this case?"

"Well, not *only* relaxing. I also communicated to the Prime Minister's office that I must stop in tomorrow for some unobtrusive observations, and sent a telegram to Mr. Eckerman requesting a small but potentially pivotal piece of information."

"I am glad you found time for something other than frivolity," I muttered as I went up to my bedroom. As I shut the door, I glanced at my shelf and noticed my old pocket Bible from the war sitting there. I took it down and flipped through the Book of Joshua until I came across the name "*Rahab*" in the second chapter. A realization dawned on me when I read that Rahab was a harlot who hid spies in her home.

I awoke the next morning to find Holmes, having already breakfasted, fully dressed and smoking his pipe. His face was a mask of focus, but it was a different expression than he normally wore when contemplating a case. This looked more as if he were ruminating on a moral dilemma. A paper with a list on it lay on the table before him.

"Mr. Eckerman is as prompt in responding to me as he promised," Holmes remarked absently, "and his friends seem to be every bit as knowledgeable as he implies they are." He looked at me with an expression of concern. "It was good that you didn't have your gun yesterday. You wouldn't have been admitted to the Rahab if you were carrying it. But you may wish to bring it today, my friend."

My irritation with him evaporated. "Do you expect danger in Downing Street?"

"Danger takes many forms," he answered, his voice distant again. It was clear he would say nothing more for now, so I sat down to eat while he puffed at his pipe. Less than an hour later, I was with him in a cab. In his pocket was the list from Eckerman. In my pocket was my service revolver.

The cab stopped, not at Downing Street, but at St. Charles Street. Without an explanation, Holmes led me into the Office for European Affairs. Soames, Dorrington, and Saumarez were each working at their desks, but rose as Holmes entered.

"Pardon me, gentlemen," he said, gesturing for them to sit back down, "but I need to look quickly at Mr. Hope's office again. I won't be a minute." He entered the main office, glanced around it perfunctorily, and came out again. "Thank you – I'll not trouble you again."

Holmes turned to Saumarez's desk. The secretary looked at him with a neutral expression.

"I say, Saumarez," remarked Holmes airily, "have you ever been to Orsino's?"

The bland expression wavered as a look of panic came into Saumarez's eyes.

"I cannot recommend it strongly enough," Holmes continued. "Here is the program from last night's performance, to give you some idea of what to expect." He produced the brochure and tossed it on the desk. Saumarez grabbed the pamphlet and opened it to the middle page. His face drained entirely of blood.

Holmes smiled and turned to me. "To Downing Street!" As we left, it was clear Saumarez was attempting not to tremble.

"Holmes," I whispered excitedly as we left the building, "is Saumarez the spy? How on earth did you gather that? And why are we not apprehending him now?"

"Because he will deliver himself into our power in ten minutes," Holmes replied, "and we have work to do in the meantime."

The walk from the Foreign Office to the Prime Minister's residence takes only a minute, so it was but a moment later that we were at 10 Downing Street. We were met at the door by a short, amiable usher who introduced himself as Mr. Foote, the same attendant who had admitted Mr. Hope before his death. Foote explained to us that Lord Bellinger was at the Scandinavian Embassy that day, but that he had explicitly ordered that Holmes was to be granted full cooperation and access to any part of the building, so long as nothing involving national security was compromised. Holmes assured Foote that he was only interested in seeing the spot where Hope passed away.

Holmes discussed the case briefly with Foote as we headed to the Premier's office. He couldn't tell us much more than we had learned from the papers, but confirmed that Hope already looked sick when he opened the door. Once we were in the office, Foote brought us to the florally patterned sofa where Hope had collapsed and ultimately died. Holmes politely but firmly asked Foote to step outside for a few minutes. Foote hesitated but, perhaps remembering Lord Bellinger's instruction, left the office, closing the door behind him.

The moment it clicked shut, Holmes leapt upon the sofa, yanking off its pillows and cushions. When this yielded nothing, he cursed under his breath and threw himself on the floor, sticking his arm under the couch and rummaging around. The next moment, he stifled a cry of joy and pulled a small box out from under the sofa. I immediately recognized what it must have been, but Holmes nevertheless opened the container to confirm what was inside: It was a small hypodermic syringe.

"Quick, Watson, help!" he whispered harshly, putting the container in his breast pocket. We hurriedly returned the pillows and cushions to the sofa and adjusted them so that no disturbance could be detected. Holmes then checked his watch and waited a few minutes before casually strolling out the office door, thanking Foote for his help, and heading out of the building.

"How on earth did you know that was there?" I asked excitedly.

"You are missing the bigger question: What did Hope intend to speak to Lord Bellinger about on the day he died?"

"He intended to demand an explanation for his sacking, surely, and perhaps to ask for his position back."

"To hear Soames describe him, Hope wasn't *confused* that he had been sacked. Rather, he was indignant, and confident that he would soon be back in his role. He knew something that he needed to tell Lord Bellinger. Think on that. As for your other questions, some of their answers await us at The Red Lion pub."

The Red Lion is a brief walk from Downing Street, though my impatience to understand the meaning of what I had seen today made the time seem twice as long. Inside, we found Saumarez, who was nearly trembling, seated at a table upon which the concert program was lying open. My blood turned to ice at the sight of him. As we sat down across from him at the table, I slipped my hand into my pocket and clutched my revolver. I glanced at the program and saw that it was opened to the autograph page. Holmes had written:

All is known re: Lucas. Only hope: Red Lion, 10 minutes.

"Must we meet here?" grumbled Saumarez.

"An open forum such as this prevents you from attempting anything foolhardy. It puts you at our mercy, rather than us at yours."

"How did you know it was me?"

"Very easily." Holmes seemed almost irritated to have to explain this, like a professor expounding upon material to a student that should have been mastered in boarding school.

"I knew a man like Eduardo Lucas wouldn't communicate with any of his operatives by the post. He knew perfectly well the risks of having someone stealing and reading his mail. He must have used some other outlet to gather information and relay instructions. It would need to be a regular channel, since there would be no way to safely communicate any changes in protocol to his lackeys. But Lucas was always on the move, whether within the city or between London and Paris. There was nothing consistent about his schedule – except for one thing."

Holmes flashed a look at me. "You remember that Lucas was an amateur tenor, yes? He often performed at Orsino's with their choir. Those concerts are regularly and publicly scheduled, so his agents would have known exactly when and where to see him. Last night, I attended one of these concerts with an eye towards ascertaining Lucas' communication methods. As I mentioned: During the intermission, the performers mingle with the audience and sign their programs. All his spies would need to do is write their messages for him on the autograph page and offer the program for him to sign. He could write his instructions for them at the bottom of the page, a rather direct way to issue orders. Once I realized this must have been his *modus operandi*, I simply asked the staff if they had seen anyone matching the descriptions of Soames, Dorrington, or yourself regularly attending the concerts and interacting with Lucas. Yours was the only physical description they recognized. To confirm that it really was you at those concerts, I wrote you this message on the autograph page of *my* program. When I gave it to you, you not only recognized what that document was – The look on his face was quite eloquent, was it not? – but turned immediately to the autograph page to find my message. All perfectly elementary."

Saumarez grinned mockingly. "I'm not sure that's enough to convict me."

"Would this evidence be enough to persuade a grand jury to hang you? That is hard to predict. But would it be enough to persuade English spies to garrote you on your way to work one morning and hide your corpse where it would never be found? That, Mr. Saumarez, is much more likely."

Saumarez's smug expression disappeared. He looked down at the table. I tightened my grip on my gun.

"You are right, Mr. Holmes. You must understand, he blackmailed me – "

"None of this matters and none of it will save you," Holmes interrupted sharply. "Your only chance now is to answer my questions quickly and honestly. Did Lucas recruit you before or after you worked for Hope?"

"Before, sir. Lucas told me he was going to get me a job in that office and to pass him on any information that could be used to cause conflict with Scandinavia. He said he had a connection who would have no trouble ensuring I would be hired at the European office."

"When was this?"

"Last summer, sir . . . ."

"And who procured the European Affairs position for you?"

"Well, I applied for the job, but when I went in for an interview, Mr. Hope told me he wasn't going to bother vetting me. He would hire me on the spot since I had such a credible reference endorsing me."

"*Who* endorsed you?" I demanded.

"Mr. Hope told me it was the Duke of Belminster."

I almost dropped the revolver in my pocket. Had the table before me sprung into flames, I wouldn't have been more surprised. Holmes, on the other hand, seemed unphased.

"When you leave here and return to the Foreign Office," he ordered Saumarez, "you will resign your position immediately and destroy anything incriminating in your possession. By the end of this week, you will have left England, never to return. I cannot promise your treachery will not be exposed. All I can promise you is a head start you do not deserve. You can infer what will happen to you if you deviate one hair's breadth from these instructions. Now – *Go!*"

Holmes shouted this last word. Everyone else in The Red Lion turned to look at us. Saumarez looked around frantically and darted out of the pub. With all eyes on us, Holmes took the opportunity to order two pints of beer for our table.

"The Duke of Belminster a foreign agent?" I sputtered, trying to keep my voice as low as possible. "Influencing our national Premier? This goes deeper than we could have imagined!"

Holmes simply sipped his beer in response.

"But," I continued, the flood of my thoughts spilling out in my words, "there's no evidence the Duke was anywhere near the Foreign Office or Downing Street! Was Hope killed by another agent, then? And – and how the devil did you know what to look for under that sofa?"

Holmes smiled without mirth into his beer. "My dear Watson, you solved the case before we finished our conversation with Eckerman. You grasped the essentials then, perhaps faster than I did. Now you are distracted. But we must indeed speak to the Duke, and we know where he will be within the hour. Come, let us finish our drinks before we confront him. It is unhappy work that lies before us."

We finished our glasses in silence, though for me it was a restless silence as my mind worked furiously to interpret all the facts of the case.

We walked to Whitehall Terrace again and Jacobs showed us in once more. Lady Hilda greeted us in her sitting room again, still mournful but seeming less distraught than before.

"You are back, sirs! Have you learned something? My father is just about to arrive . . . ."

326

"Lady Hilda," Holmes interrupted in a strong but solemn voice, "we did you a great favour once. Now I just ask you to repay it. You must leave us alone with your father. You must take your leave and stay as far from your father and us as possible until we are finished speaking. I was willing to conceal some information for your sake once. You must now allow me to conceal some things to you. You have my word it is for your good, just as my earlier discretion was also for your good."

Lady Hilda looked curious and ambivalent all at once, but finally nodded.

"What you say is fair, Mr. Holmes. I will wait in my room until you give me leave."

Moments after she left, Jacobs escorted the Duke of Belminster into the sitting room before disappearing down the hallway again. The Duke looked around the room before resting his gaze on us, leaning heavily upon his walking stick. He opened his mouth, but Holmes spoke first, his voice drenched in contempt.

"When did your wealth and prestige become more important than your son-in-law?"

The Duke's expression darkened, and the room seemed to darken with it.

"Would you care to explain – ?"

"When we saw you yesterday, I deduced you had lapsed into a long season of poverty. A gambling addiction, perhaps? In any event, you were too proud to confess your situation or to seek help. Of course, that affliction has recently lifted. Your clothes are practically rags now, but your new walking stick is a great indulgence. Why have you not yet updated your wardrobe? Perhaps because you aren't sure whether your good fortunes are here to stay."

Holmes seemed to relish in describing the Duke's financial plight.

"What, then, could be the miraculous source of these fresh funds, so plentiful at one point but now so uncertain? As it happens, Britain's sugar production in the Caribbean has also recently improved, but is at risk of being severely curtailed if a particular treaty is passed. I made inquiries."

He whipped the paper from his pocket and thrust it in the Duke's face.

"This was delivered to me today: A list of the major investors in British sugar companies operating in the Caribbean."

"How do you have this information?" the Duke demanded angrily.

"Anything can be obtained with the right friends. I notice one particular name near the top of the list. Do you happen to know an 'Alastair Farrer', sir?"

The Duke stared viciously at Holmes before snatching the paper from him. "This proves nothing," he snarled. That such a composed and stately

327

figure was reduced to this display was already a kind of self-incrimination. "What of it if I am profiting from the success of our empire?"

"You *were*. But Scandinavia's complaints threatened British sugar farming, and thus threatened your newfound wealth. How, then, to stop Scandinavia? You concluded that the only way to conclusively stop them from thwarting your profits was to crush them – through war."

The Duke's hands tightened around the lion's head at the top of his stick.

"But how to start a war? One has an ace up his sleeve when his son-in-law is in charge of European Affairs. You knew he might have access to something that could be used as a *casus belli*. But how to get that information and use it without incriminating yourself? You found a way: You reached out to a spy – to Eduardo Lucas. You helped him plant one of his men in Hope's office. You were willing to let an enemy of the state have classified information if the final result was a war that would lead to your profit. There is no use denying it. Suamarez has told all. Need I remind you of the legal definition of treason?"

"I am no traitor," the Duke hissed. "I wanted a war with Scandinavia, but only because I knew we would win."

Rage flared up within me as I remembered the mangled bodies, the unrecognizable corpses, and the cries of the suffering wounded I had seen in my days as a medic. "And many brave and noble men would die for your pocket book!" I yelled. The Duke looked away from me. Holmes gestured at me to calm myself, though his face showed complete agreement with my sentiment.

"Your plan failed – thanks to Lucas' jealous wife and the efforts of Watson and myself. Things got worse for you when you learned that Hope was negotiating a treaty with Scandinavia that would eradicate your new source of income. You tried to persuade him against it, I'm sure, but to no avail. Finally, you resorted to trying to be rid of him. Observers noted your private meetings with the Prime Minister about Hope, but you weren't attempting to *save* his career in those audiences, but to *destroy* it, and probably trying to replace him with Soames, whose views on the Caribbean were more congenial to your economic interests. I assume you made false claims about Hope's competence in hopes that Lord Bellinger would believe your lies and remove Hope as secretary. Hope discovered this, and found out about the craven motivation for your backstabbing. When he learned he had been sacked, he knew it was your work. That is why he was heading over to Downing Street: To tell Lord Bellinger the facts about you. He knew this would prove you were untrustworthy, and would almost certainly lead to his reinstatement."

"But he died before he could manage to do so," I growled, looking at the Duke's stick and imagining what might poke out of its tip.

For the first time, the Duke looked worried. "Everything you have said about me is true," he protested, sounding defeated, "but I didn't kill Trelawney. Hard as this may be to believe, I truly did love him as a son."

"God have mercy on your real children," I muttered.

The Duke turned on me savagely. "How dare you, fiend!" He raised his stick as if to strike me, but I had already drawn my revolver from my pocket and leveled it at his chest.

"Settle yourselves!" snapped Holmes. The Duke's eyes and mine remained locked in a mutual death glare as we lowered our weapons.

"I am offering you a single lifeline, Mr. Farrer," Holmes announced, nearly spitting the nobleman's legal name. "Before tomorrow's end, you will use every power of persuasion at your disposal to move Lord Bellinger to make Lord Holdhurst the new European Affairs Secretary. Should you fail to achieve this, your financial ruin, your manipulation, and your treacherous behaviour will fill the front page of every paper on Fleet Street. If I ever learn of any further chicanery from you – and, if you attempt any, I *shall* learn of it – you will be exposed and lose not only your reputation but also potentially your life. Lady Hilda will be informed that you have taken ill and had to return home early. You will depart from our presence – *Now!*"

The Duke sneered fiercely at us, but slowly backed away without taking his eyes off us until he had turned the corner to the hallway to the front door. We waited until we heard it open and close before either of us spoke.

"Holmes, you have now let a second traitor and potential murderer go free!" I protested.

"Neither Saumarez nor Farrer is Hope's killer," said Holmes, who seemed to be growing tired. "Remember the syringe at Downing Street. Don't you see what it indicates? It suggests the person who made the fatal injection was in the room when Hope died."

"What – who – Foote? Or Dr. Wirst? With a name like that, he could be Austrian . . . wait . . . Holmes, you don't mean . . . Not the Prime Minister himself – !"

He sighed and smiled at me with transcendent patience. "I told you: You solved the murder within moments of our learning of it. You said to Eckerman that an entire hypodermic needle of digitalis would kill a man in about five minutes. Yet Hope was alone in his office from 3:00 to the end of 3:05. Had Suamarez, or even Soames, poisoned him before that period of solitude, he would never have left that room alive. Yet he not only survived his time in the office, but proceeded to live for another four to five minutes after he left. Remember also that didn't interact with anyone in the European Affairs antechamber when he left, meaning no one had any opportunity to poison him before he left the Foreign Office."

"True, but – "

"Could he have been injected by Foote when he met him at the door? Unlikely. After one minute's walk from the Foreign Office, Hope arrived right before 3:07 and died at 3:10. Just over three minutes falls rather short of the five minutes of survival you diagnosed. No, the most likely scenario is that Foote was telling the truth and that Hope was already dying when he arrived. Indeed, working backwards five minutes from Hope's death brings us to the period when he was alone in his office. All of which points to one unmistakable conclusion: Hope injected himself."

"Good Lord!"

"That was why he needed to be alone: So he could take a drug. And if that is the case, there would be no need for hidden poisoned pinpricks – those are for injecting people without their knowledge and are rather unnecessary for anything self-administered. Most people injecting themselves with anything would prefer to use a syringe. And didn't you also tell Eckerman that the hole in Hope's arm looked like a normal needle mark?"

I nodded in awe and confusion.

"However, Soames didn't mention finding a needle in the European Affairs office after Hope left, nor did I find one, and no syringe was reported as having been found on Hope's body after he died. Where could it have gone? The most likely scenario was that it had fallen out of Hope's pocket and into or under the sofa when he collapsed. As you saw, I was able to verify that hypothesis."

I inhaled deeply, trying to process all I was hearing. "So . . . did Hope commit suicide?"

Holmes looked in my direction with a deadly intensity.

"Hope didn't prepare that syringe. *You* did."

I started, but realized that he was now looking past me. I turned to see a forlorn Jacobs standing in the doorway.

"Remember," Holmes continued, his piercing gaze still directed at Jacobs, "that Hope didn't leave his home until Jacobs returned from his errands. Lady Hilda told us Jacobs had been looking for treatments for Hope's heart. That heart was under great strain that day. Surely Hope would have asked his valet to prepare something potent for him before he went out. *You* ensured it was a deadly amount, didn't you?"

Jacobs trembled almost imperceptibly.

"But," I said to Jacobs, "Hope told us you were a loyal servant for years. Surely you aren't *also* a traitor!'

Jacobs walked into the room with the careful steps and hushed silence of a mourner walking through a graveyard. He sat down near us, folded his hands in his lap, and hung his head like a penitent making his confession.

"A few days ago," he began, "on an evening when Lady Hilda was out with friends, Mr. Hope called on the Duke of Belminster. He returned in a state of agitation and frustration, with a look on his face I'd never seen before, and made me swear I wouldn't tell Lady Hilda where he had been. I didn't ask him to explain anything. That is not my place. But that Wednesday morning, after his breakfast, he prepared some papers at his desk. Just before lunch, he gave them to me in an envelope and told me to mail them to Lord Flowers, the Secretary of Justice. He also said he would be going to clear up some business at the Foreign Office and tell Lord Bellinger something important, and asked me to pick up something for him that could help him sustain his heart. After ensuring he and Lady Hilda had lunch prepared, I set out on those two tasks.

"There was something about the look Mr. Hope had when he was instructing me, sirs. It was the same look he was wearing when he came back from his father-in-law's. I knew, somehow, that this had something to do with the Duke, so I did something I've never done before in all my years: I read Mr. Hope's mail. It was an accusation against the Duke of Belminster, saying he was trying to steer government policy into a war for personal gain. It even implied Mr. Hope suspected the Duke of having planted a spy in his office who was stealing his personal documents, though he admitted he couldn't prove this."

Holmes and I exchanged a knowing look which Jacobs didn't seem to notice.

"Sirs, you have seen how Lady Hilda draws strength from her father, particularly in times of great difficulty. She's always been very close to him. She *is* his youngest daughter, you know. Having her father's lifetime of goodwill with the British public be shattered – to see him publicly denounced, shamed, who knows what else . . . It would crush her."

"More than the death of her husband would?" I asked incredulously.

"We had been aware of Mr. Hope's heart troubles for quite some time, Dr. Watson. As dejected as she is about this loss, it's a loss for which we have all been preparing ourselves. From everything I had observed and everything I had read, I was sure that Mr. Hope wasn't long for this world anyways. That means Lady Hilda could have seen her father being destroyed in the eyes of the world, knowing full well her husband was the cause of this, and then, perhaps only a few days later, lost her husband, too."

He looked up for the first time, his expression plaintive. "She didn't deserve that, sirs. I realized there was another possibility which would protect her father's reputation and allow her husband to die in a way that won the sympathy of the whole nation. I destroyed Mr. Hope's mail and got a full syringe of digitalis at the pharmacist's. I had studied heart medicine enough to know what would happen if Mr. Hope injected the whole needle at once. And when I returned to the estate, that's exactly what I told him to do."

His eyes welled with tears. "I loved Mr. Hope. My hand trembled when I purchased the digitalis for him, and I have been wracked with guilt ever since the moment I gave him that counsel. What have I done to my soul . . . ? All I can console myself with is the fact that I have saved a good woman."

"By killing a great man!" I protested.

Tears began to stream down Jacobs' cheeks. "God forgive me!" he wept, covering his face with his hands.

Holmes walked over to Jacobs. "Go and care for Lady Hilda," he quietly commanded him. Sniffling, Jacobs recovered his composure and left the sitting room. Without waiting for me, Holmes headed for the front door. I hurried after him and found him hailing a cab.

"You aren't apprehending Jacobs, either?" I said as we climbed into the carriage.

"What would arresting him accomplish?" said Holmes as we settled into our seats. "At the trial, Lady Hilda, and the rest of the world, will learn that her father had essentially betrayed his country for personal gain, that her husband was murdered, and that her loyal servant is the killer. And for what end? To send Jacobs to the gallows? Do you think Jacobs is likely to murder anyone else? And even if he were, despite his confession to us, a reasonably skilled barrister could easily make the case that the overdose of digitalis was an accident."

"We have unearthed many crimes in this investigation, Holmes. Is no one to face justice for any of them?" I asked sourly.

Holmes looked thoughtful. "I recently had a discussion with a young Roman Catholic seminarian named Brown on the topic of justice," * he began to answer. "He reminded me that its classical definition is 'giving to each man what he is due.' What do you think Lady Hilda is due? Do you disagree with Jacobs? Does she deserve utter emotional devastation?"

"But what about what Trelawney Hope deserves? What is he due?"

"A spy has been removed from the Foreign Office. Lady Hilda will be cared for in the presence of those she loves, and will never know the crimes of her father, which Hope was obviously trying to shield her from as long as he could. The treaty with Scandinavia will be completed and war will be avoided – which is the extent of what I will tell Mr. Eckerman. Is there anything else Trelawney Hope would want? And as for our culprits: Saumarez will spend the rest of his life a fugitive from his homeland, Farrer will return to a state of impoverishment, and Jacobs' conscience has inflicted a worse punishment upon him than all the hangmen of Tyburn ever could. So where has there been a failure of justice? Where has anyone involved in this case failed to receive their deserts?"

We were both silent. Finally, Holmes made the final comment he would ever utter to me about this adventure.

"There is one outcome of this case that should be agreeable to you."

"Oh?"

"For the time being, it has erased any desire for me to inject anything into *my* body."

For the first time since our investigation began, I felt myself smile.

NOTES

* This conversation between Holmes and the young seminarian (and future Father) Brown can be found in "The Adventure of the Uncommitted Murder", (*The Detective and the Clergyman: The Adventures of Sherlock Holmes and Father Brown*, Belanger Books, 2023)

Notes on Chronology

Though Watson never mentions this fact to maintain the vagueness he used in "The Second Stain" (SECO), the Trelawney Hope death occurs on January 12, 1887, the historical date of the death of Stafford Northcote *a.k.a.* Lord Iddlesleigh. [1] This takes for granted that "The Second Stain" took place from October 12 to 13 of 1886. Both the identification of Hope with Northcote and the 1886 dating of SECO are well justified by Felix Morley and William S. Baring-Gould.

What follows is a justification for dating "The Second Stain" in 1886, for identifying Hope with Northcote rather than any other politician (Leslie Klinger mentions two other options which I will refute), and for dating my own story, in which the King of Scandinavia hires Holmes, in January of 1887.

Date of "The Adventure of The Second Stain"

I find Felix Morley and William S. Baring-Gould's contention that "The Second Stain" must have occurred in 1886 persuasive, not only because Lord Bellinger could only be the twice-elected Lord Salisbury, but also because two of the three spies mentioned, La Rothiere and Oberstein, re-appear in "The Bruce-Partington Plans" (BRUC) (set in November of 1895), but Lucas is not mentioned there, strongly suggesting that BRUC occurred after his death. Since Watson is living with Holmes in SECO, this means it must have either occurred during the first year and a half after The Great Hiatus (spring of 1894-November 1895) or sometime between 1881-1886. (1887 is off the table because SECO occurs in autumn, and Watson was married in September of '87, according to "The Five Orange Pips").

But I cannot imagine Holmes would not have included Mycroft in a gambit involving secret agents (as Holmes was intending to do before learning of Lucas' death) unless he was still shielding the extent of Mycroft's influence from Watson (as he admits to doing in "The Bruce-Partington Plans"). But after The Great Hiatus, Holmes knew Watson well enough to let him know about Mycroft's status and his connection to espionage (which is exactly what happens in BRUC). Yet Mycroft is not mentioned in SECO. This suggests to me it must have occurred in the earlier window of time, in the 1880's. If we accept Baring-Gould's date of GREE as being 1888, then Watson would not even know of Mycroft's existence yet if SECO occurred between 1882 and 1886.

Further evidence is found in "The Naval Treaty." In that tale, Lord Holdhurst seems to hold the same position in the cabinet that Trelawney Hope did, and he states that Holmes's name is "very familiar" to him. This suggests to me that Holmes is already well-known within the cabinet, suggesting he has already been involved with them. The only case we know of where this could apply is SECO. This would not only place NAVA after SECO, but would also raise the question of why Holdhurst was doing Hope's job, a question my story answers. NAVA is set in the July after Watson's marriage. This could be July of 1888 (leaving two months before the death or divorce that left Watson open to meeting Mary Morstan in September of 1888) or in July of 1889, either of which fits comfortably after 1886 (and after January of '87).

Moreover, Holmes seems to already be a well-established celebrity in SECO, which suggests it occurred later in the 1880's.

All of this not only proves that 1886 is the most likely date for SECO, but also that Stafford Northcote is the strongest candidate for the identity of Trelawney Hope. Joseph Chamberlain, who has also been proposed, did not become Secretary of State for the Colonies until 1895. Lord Randolph Churchill has also been suggested, but in 1886, he was Chancellor of the Exchequer and there is no clear reason why he would be entrusted with a foreign potentate's letter. Northcote, as Secretary of State for Foreign Affairs in 1886, is far and away the best candidate to be Hope. [2]

Date of "The Adventure of the Downing Street Demise"

In "The Noble Bachelor" (NOBL), Holmes says his most recent aristocratic client was the King of Scandinavia. Watson says NOBL occurred "*a few weeks before my own marriage*" and in autumn. There are two scenarios here, and I think I have an explanation for either of them.

If this is a reference to Constance Adams, then there are two possibilities. One is that the conventional dating is correct: Watson married Adams in late autumn/early winter of 1886. This would obviously place NOBL before January of 1887. (Indeed, Baring-Gould dates it to four days before SECO.) However, I have intentionally left it vague whether or not this case is the first time that the King of Scandinavia has hired Holmes. Holmes is indifferent when he hears who his client is, and it may be that he has rendered previous services to that monarch (which would also explain why the King of Scandinavia knew to hire Holmes for this case: Holmes had already proven himself to him). Thus, even if one accepts the Baring-Gould chronology, my story still works.

Another possibility that I would suggest is that the conventional dating is wrong and Watson actually married Adams in autumn of 1887. This would also explain why, in "The Reigate Squire", which says it takes place in April of 1887, Watson seems to still be living with Holmes. [3] FIVE purports to take place late September of 1887. This is tight, but could fit (NOBL could be early September or even late August, the wedding occurred mid-September, FIVE occurred late September of 1887), and the chronology of the King of Scandinavia hiring Holmes in January of '87 would be fine. This is my own personal interpretation of the facts. It may mean that the Constance Adams marriage was even more tragically short than chronologists recognize, but this would explain Watson's longing in *The Sign of Four*.

On the other hand, if the marriage in NOBL refers to Mary Morstan, my own head canon has their wedding in early 1889 (incorporated into my own Father Brown crossover pastiche, "The Adventure of the Uncommitted Murder"). This still leaves the problem that in March of 1888, Holmes had the King of Bohemia as a client. My explanation for this (should the reader choose to see this as an allusion to the Morstan marriage) is that the King of Scandinavia was a higher-ranking king than the King of Bohemia. Bohemia was part of the Austro-Hungarian kingdom, while, in this version of history, Scandinavia is a similar hybrid kingdom including Denmark, Norway, and Sweden (as in the Kalmar Union). Holmes is thus invoking the higher of the two monarchs who has hired him as a way of humbling Lord St. Simon further: Not only has a nobility hired him in the past, but the highest possible monarch outside of England has hired him (which is more impressive than being consulted by a regional monarch like the Grand Duke of Cassel-Felstein).

Also speaking of "A Scandal in Bohemia", when the King tells Holmes, "*I am to be married*" to the daughter of the King of Scandinavia, Holmes replies, "*So I have heard.*" I would suggest he has heard about this from the King of Scandinavia himself, which makes me want to place the case where the Scandinavian king consulted him prior to SCAN, *i.e.* before March of 1888. (Also, I have tried to provide a reason in this story why the Bohemian-Scandinavian marriage was so important. The cancellation of the wedding would have not just been an embarrassment but potentially a geopolitical risk. This is why, in my mind, Holmes was awarded the snuffbox of gold in "A Case of Identity", despite declining a gift in SCAN. The snuffbox was a reward, not for the specific job of saving the Adler papers, but more generally for helping avert a war.)

Miscellanea

Although this does not deal with chronology, I want to point out that Trelawney Hope states that the only people with access to his bedroom, and the dispatch-box inside it, during the day are two maids and his valet. Yet at the end of the story, Jacobs, the butler, is sent by Hope to fetch the dispatch-box. I can only conclude from this that Jacobs is both the butler and Hope's valet, and I have depicted this in the story. *An Encyclopedia of Domestic Economy* from 1852 states, "*The butler in establishments of second and third rate undertakes some of the duties of the house-steward and valet*" (page 332), so it isn't unheard of.

Sir Cathcart Soames is mentioned in "The Priory School", which occurs between 1900 and 1904. Because my tale occurs a decade-and-a-half before this, I have presumed he was much less accomplished at this time and would not yet have been knighted.

Footnotes

1. Large portions of the newspaper report of Hope's death are taken verbatim, or nearly so, from an actual news report of Northcote's death:
    https://newspapers.library.wales/view/3044463/3044466

2. Historians have mistakenly claimed that Northcote's wife's father was a mere solicitor and that her son with Northcote, the 1st Baron Northcote, was the first in their family to be raised to the peerage. This is an error due to omissions in the historical records, and Dr. Watson has recorded the facts more accurately. My story gives some indication of why the Duke of Belminster's noble status may have been forgotten.

3. Baring-Gould tries to explain this away by noting that Watson says he was "together" with Holmes in Baker Street rather than in "our rooms", or by claiming it is unusual that Holmes would not invite Watson to join him on his investigations that year. But while Constance Adams may be the reason for this latter fact, it could simply be that Watson was spending more time with his fiancée and was less available for adventures. Moreover, Watson is not just "together" with Holmes in Baker Street for an afternoon. The implication is that they remain in Baker Street together until going off to Reigate. (And notice that Watson never alludes to getting permission from his wife or even mentioning such a trip to her. Typically, Watson includes those kinds of marital details.) Also note the language: After fetching Holmes from Lyons, "*we were* back *in Baker Street together.*" Watson is "back" in Baker Street, and in apparently the same way that Holmes is *back* in Baker Street (*i.e.* not just back visiting his old stomping grounds, but back home).

The Continental Conspiracy
by Martin Daley

Chapter I

Sherlock Holmes became involved in many political cases during his long and illustrious career, many of which could not be related at the time because of their sensitive nature. Perhaps the most sensitive of all was the case that took him to the Continent in the spring of '87. The investigation would have significant ramifications for the government in London and its counterparts in virtually all the capitals of Europe.

After many years, and given that most of those involved are no longer living, I feel as though I am now on safe ground laying out part of the narrative regarding this incredibly complex and intricate case. I would stress that what I am about to relate is only one thread of a tangled skein in which Holmes found himself embroiled. The particular loose end that my friend discovered eventually led to the unravelling of the whole conspiracy and resulted in Holmes becoming the toast of Europe. Such acknowledgement however, almost came at the highest possible cost to his own well-being.

The early months of the particular year in question proved physically and mentally draining for both Holmes and myself, but for very different reasons. I had caught a chill during the preceding Christmas holidays that gradually worsened and developed into a nasty bout of pneumonia. I knew that I would need complete rest and specialized treatment, so I therefore made some enquiries and received permission to return to the Royal Victoria at Netley for a short period of recuperation.

Little did I know at the time that the period would be one of several weeks, as my condition initially showed little sign of improvement, and then finally, when I did begin to recover, it was at a glacial pace.

During my convalescence I was unable to keep in touch with Holmes, and was therefore unaware of any adventure in which he may have found himself. It was only when I returned to London in early April that I learned he had left for the Continent and had been gone for several weeks. Feeling much better myself, it was on the morning of the 14th, when I was reading the newspaper full of the resignation of the Secretary of State for Foreign Affairs, that I received the telegram informing me that Holmes was ill and needed my assistance in Lyon. I made arrangements to catch the Continental Express later that night.

338

I have previously described the desperate condition in which I found him, * and I was keen to get him back to London. I gathered up the carpet of congratulatory telegrams and stuffed them into a bag, bundled Holmes into a cab, and headed for the station, intent on getting us back to London as soon as possible.

No sooner had we arrived than it occurred to me to accept the open invitation from my old comrade, Colonel Hayter, to stay with him in his home in Reigate. I convinced Holmes that it would do us both the world of good and – drained as he was after his mammoth investigation – he reluctantly agreed with a gesture. I emptied the bag of telegrams and crammed them into my old dispatch box, fully intending to read them upon our return. Returning the bag to Holmes and packing one for myself, off we went. Little did I know, however, that our trip would result in yet another case for Holmes, but thankfully, it turned out to be a blessing in disguise as it proved once again that the best stimulant for the consulting detective was *work*.

We returned to London invigorated by our sojourn to Surrey, and again I tried to ask Holmes about his investigations in France.

"Not right now," he replied darkly. "Let's leave that for another day."

Through long experience I had learned the wisdom of obedience, and I respected his comment by never mentioning it again. Imagine my surprise when Holmes himself raised the matter a year-and-a-half later, following the investigation into the unfortunate Mr. Melas. ** That case had been brought to Holmes by his brother Mycroft, whom I met then for the first time. As if the revelation in learning of Holmes's brother wasn't enough, when we were back in our sitting room, I was further surprised when Sherlock Holmes informed me that he had regular contact with Mycroft over the years, and the two had discussed many a case together.

"Take the Continental affair last year," he remarked casually.

"The one that took you to France?"

"Not only to France, but also to Amsterdam and Geneva."

He explained that a few days after I had left to convalesce at Netley, Mycroft summoned him to the Diogenes Club and demanded that he investigate "'a matter of national importance'." Holmes lit a pipe and waved an arm as he imitated his brother with a flourish. Sir Richard Rosendale, the British Ambassador to France, had been assassinated while at an official function in a Paris hotel.

"I had read of the killing in the newspaper and asked my brother why it wasn't a matter for the French police and Scotland Yard."

"'That is just the point,' was his reply, 'The French authorities are refusing to involve Scotland Yard, claiming the poor man's demise is strictly a domestic matter. The Prime Minister doesn't want to kick up a fuss and cause an international scandal in his first twelve months in office, but equally, he is deeply mistrustful of the French and wants someone from this side of the Channel to look into the ambassador's death. He wants the matter dealt with as discreetly as possible, Sherlock, and I know that you are just the man!'"

"So that was me," said Holmes, as he prepared to tell me of his adventure, "bags packed and off to Paris. Little did I know at the time that the case would take me into three countries."

"Apparently, the killing took place when the ambassador excused himself from his table during the function. When the alarm was raised, people rushed to the cloakroom to find him lying in a pool of blood, dead from gunshot wounds. There were no apparent witnesses, and a Moroccan waiter was quickly arrested and charged with the murder."

"On what grounds?" I asked.

"Basically, on the grounds that he was a Moroccan waiter." Holmes was not being facetious. "He lived on his own in a modest dwelling. He had no family in Paris, and certainly had no motive to murder a British diplomat – or anyone else for that matter.

"The staff in the hotel had a little area where they kept their personal possessions. When our man's belongings were searched, a gun was found among them. He claimed to know nothing about it, but that didn't stop the enthusiastic – if easily led – *Sûreté* from arresting him and charging him immediately with the murder. Fortunately for him, the detective assigned to the case was Francois Le Villard, who I subsequently met for the first time. Of equal good fortune to the poor immigrant was the appointment of Monsieur Duclos to represent him as his lawyer – one of the few honest and decent men of that profession in Paris.

"Mycroft had wired ahead to Duclos through the British Embassy and he had managed to delay any thought of a hasty trial – and presumably conviction – pending further investigation. By the time I arrived there, almost a week after the assassination, Le Villard and Duclos had virtually unpicked the allegation against our Moroccan friend. The case fell apart within days. Not only was it proven that he didn't own the gun that was found amongst his things, but the gun itself still had a full chamber and showed no signs of being fired – hardly the work of a master criminal. Inference? It was planted by some incompetent buffoon who was seeking to set up an innocent, vulnerable bystander. The prosecutor quite rightly dismissed the case."

I contemplated this fantastic adventure I had missed. It seemed that – at the time – political assassinations had become a scourge around the world and, on the face of it, Sir Richard had simply been the latest victim of some anarchist or disgruntled extremist. But there was another line of enquiry that interested the British Government: Prior to Holmes's departure, Mycroft had appraised his brother of a letter written by Sir Richard's personal aide – a man called Winterburn – to a friend of his in the Home Office.

In it, Winterburn expressed his concerns for Sir Richard's safety. The ambassador had apparently discovered some unusual activity involving a shipping company based in Amsterdam who had major trade routes to the Far East. Without elaborating on his thoughts, and before Sir Richard could make his findings official – After all, why would the ambassador to France be concerned with a shipping company in the Netherlands? – he was murdered. The letter from Winterburn had been brought to the attention of the Prime Minister, who wanted to know if the ambassador's findings and his murder were connected in any way.

This had all taken place while I was in my hospital bed at Netley, and I was completely oblivious to the complexities of the matter. I was full of curiosity. "So what happened next?"

"Duclos' work was done, but I then formed an interesting working relationship with Le Villard. I must say I was impressed by the young man's enthusiasm. His observational and deductive skills are excellent. This, coupled with a basic common sense and a willingness to learn, makes me believe there are the makings of a fine detective there.

"It was obvious that the Moroccan didn't murder the ambassador, but who did? By the time I arrived in Paris, Le Villard already had the guest list of those attending the dinner waiting for me. The event was an annual gala hosted by the French Government to which officials from all the foreign consulates and embassies in Paris were invited."

"Who discovered the body of Sir Richard?" I asked.

"Excellent, Watson!"

It was one of those occasions when I could never quite work out if Holmes was being complimentary or condescending. I ignored his exclamation however and encouraged him to continue.

"It was an official from the French Foreign Ministry who discovered the body."

"What did this official report to the police?"

"He stated that he was just passing the cloakroom when he discovered the body."

"*Passing* the cloakroom, and yet the body was *inside* the cloakroom."

"All a little too convenient, wouldn't you say? It was the same man who suggested the waiter may have been the assassin."

"Despite him not witnessing the incident."

"Indeed."

"Did anyone else hear shots fired?"

"You are in scintillating form today! No, they did not, and that is a very distinctive point. By acting with such enthusiastic haste, the French official only succeeded in attracting attention to himself. It seems thereafter that poor Le Villard was warned off from digging too deeply into the individual by some of his superiors."

"But that didn't stop *you*."

Holmes glanced across at me and smiled. "It would have been a pity to go all that way for nothing."

Chapter II

Holmes's Continental investigation would eventually lead to the arrest and conviction of one of the most notorious criminals in Europe. Neither he, nor anyone else, could have predicted such an eventuality when the detective set out from London on that late winter morning.

It would be the vague letter sent by the ambassador's aid – and shared with Holmes by his brother Mycroft – that would provide my friend with a thread to pick, and one which would ultimately unravel numerous illicit schemes and plots around Europe, where the lines between officialdom and crime organisations became so blurred that they became almost indecipherable.

The public is now aware that, following Holmes's work, the Netherland-Sumatra Company was established by the Germanic-Franco-Dutch nobleman, Baron Maupertuis. He took advantage of the confusion caused by the war between the Dutch and their colony in the East Indies to start his own illicit trade route between the Far East and Europe. Illegal goods were shipped between the two continents. War and a lack of regulation at one end, bribery and corruption at the other, each created a perfect channel for the villain to exploit. With his status and initial reputation for success, Maupertuis had no difficulty attracting backers for the venture and, within five years of its launch, the vast profits being made by the company for its *shareholders*, as he called them, began to attract the attention of governments around the Continent.

However, instead of performing even the most rudimentary of checks into the practices of the company, and instead of carrying out any robust audit of the accounts, the profits being generated for the benefits of the investors sadly created a wilful blindness amongst the authorities of Europe.

Although he had heard of Maupertuis, Holmes was completely unaware of the extent of the wrong-doing perpetrated by the villain and his network of activity when he set out for the Continent to investigate the killing of the British Ambassador. But as history teaches us – regardless of duration – such schemes only have a finite period, and inevitably in the case of Maupertuis, the time came when the wrongdoing and malpractice generated by those associated with the Netherland-Sumatra Company couldn't be concealed any longer. That time came with the killing of Sir Richard Rosendale.

Once in Paris – thanks to Mycroft's influence – Holmes gained access to the ambassador's residence within the British Embassy.

"I questioned Winterburn, the aide, and asked him about the letter he wrote."

"'Well sir, I don't really know. Sir Richard confided in me that he had come by some information that could have some consequences for the Foreign Office.' The man was frightened, Watson.

"'Consequences?' I asked.

"Winterburn was hesitant. 'Well, I don't really know the details, sir. I would regularly join him in his study for a nightcap after the staff had all turned in. Over a drink, we would chat about various issues. I think he saw it as a kind of therapy – a way of unburdening himself from the troubles of the role.'

"'And what troubles was he dealing with?'

"'Well, that's just the thing, sir. In the week before he died – ' Winterburn had to pause for a moment and compose himself, his distress still evident. ' – I had the impression that he wanted to tell me something about the information he had obtained, but he dare not. It was most unlike him. Then, on the night of the gala dinner itself, he almost seemed reluctant to go. Perhaps I am reading too much into it with the benefit of hindsight, but I remember his wife was ready before he was, which was an extremely unusual occurrence.'

"'Almost as though he expected danger?'

"'Well, that's how it looks to me now, Mr. Holmes, but maybe I am guilty of fitting the question to the answer, rather than the other way around.'

"'Perhaps, Mr. Winterburn, but it seems a plausible hypothesis, given what we now know. Speaking of Lady Rosendale, where is she now?'

"'She returned to Berkshire, sir, to stay with family.' He reflected and shook his head. 'Poor woman, they were devoted to each other. I don't know what she will do now.'

"'Did anyone visit the embassy shortly after the assassination?'

"Winterburn's demeanour changed markedly. He snapped out of his reverie thinking about Lady Rosendale, and a saturnine expression came over him.

"'Yes, sir. The morning following the murder – just as we were all learning of the killing – officials claiming to be from the French Government came to the embassy and asked to see Sir Richard's office and apartment. We were all in a state of shock and confusion as to what was happening and looking back, I must confess that I mistakenly allowed them free reign. I never thought anything of it at the time. I didn't know what was going on, but now I think about it, it was if they knew exactly what they were looking for. They weren't here very long, and left with a box full of papers. I was surprised when Inspector Le Villard came along later that morning. I told him of the officials' earlier visit, and it seemed clear to me that he hadn't authorised it. When the inspector and I entered Sir Richard's study, it was obvious that it had been thoroughly searched, as the drawers were all open and papers were strewn across his desk. I couldn't be sure exactly what they had seized, but after the inspector left, I went up to Sir Richard's sitting room and was relieved to find that his personal journal was still there. I couldn't bring myself to read it, but it may be of some use.'

"'I think that will be extremely useful, Mr. Winterburn,' I said as he handed it to me. 'Thank you for your time and assistance.'"

Holmes left Winterburn and went to speak with Le Villard. When he asked the French detective about the matter, he confirmed Winterburn's story and said he knew nothing about the confiscation. The local man questioned his colleagues and confirmed to Holmes that no one connected with the investigation into the murder had removed anything from the ambassador's quarters.

"This was suggestive," said Holmes, re-filling his pipe. "If it wasn't the police who removed the items, it could only have been someone from the French diplomatic service. The items removed would have been of no interest to common thieves, and no one else other than government officials could ever wish to gain access to the embassy."

I followed Holmes's train of thought. "The suggestion being that there was something among Sir Richard's papers that someone wanted kept hidden. And you obviously suspected these characters of carrying out the brazen sequestration? Did Winterburn get any names or give you any description of the men?" Holmes looked at me with an expression of abject disappointment. No words were necessary. "Well, he would no doubt be in a terrible state of shock that morning," I said in Winterburn's defence, having myself been the subject of the detective's discontentment in the past.

"No doubt," he mumbled. "The only word he used to describe them was '*menacing*', which I thought was interesting."

"It sounds as though poor Winterburn was frightened for his own safety," I commented.

Holmes affirmed my supposition with an "Mmm. I immediately notified Mycroft at this point and appraised him of my findings." He broke off from his narrative and chuckled to himself as he reflected on his brother for a moment. "I sometimes wonder if Mycroft's influence is somewhat greater than he would have others believe.

"After reporting my discoveries to him, he in turn approached the Prime Minister, who summoned the French Ambassador to Downing Street. It was then that Le Villard in Paris who told me that the ramifications of the London meeting were being felt all over the French capital. Every station and government office had been briefed about the 'theft', as it had been termed from the British Government, and searches were ordered. This was a significant development, as it confirmed that the French Government weren't involved in any wrongdoing on an official level."

"But unofficially?" I asked.

Holmes smiled. "Exactly – *unofficially*. It suggested that rogue diplomats or politicians were acting independently, presumably for their own personal advantage. Returning to the murder itself, the interesting point was this question about the noise – or should I say, *lack* of noise – made by the gun."

"*Lack* of noise?" I repeated.

"Yes – apparent silence, in fact. You yourself commented that it was unusual that no one had heard any gunshots. When questioned, even the waiter and the other hotel staff swore that they didn't hear anything."

"How can that be explained?"

Holmes looked intensely at me. "I had previously heard of a man called Von Herder – he is a blind German mechanic who turned his skills to gun-making some years ago. It is said that his touch and feel is like that of the most skilled watchmaker. Appropriate perhaps, as although he learned his skills in Berlin, he has spent that last ten years living in Geneva."

"What has *he* got to do with all of this?"

"The reason I knew about Von Herder was because I discovered he had been developing and experimenting with a noiseless device that is fitted to the end of a pistol, thus rendering it virtually silent when fired."

"That's surely too fanciful to be believed!" As a former army man and someone who had handled weapons most of his adult life, I couldn't see how such a contraption could be possible.

"With imagination and skill, nothing is beyond the cleverest minds and hands. Sadly, too often, those skills are used for nefarious purposes. If it were true that Von Herder had been successful with his development, it could change the course of firearms development in the future. Just think of the damage such silent devices could do when fitted to different kinds of pistols and rifles. It seems the more modern the world develops, the crueller it becomes."

"So if this silent gun was used," I asked, "where is it now?"

"If such a weapon existed, it would almost certainly be used by a skilled assassin. This would be no random killing. Therefore, it would have been planned to the point where the killer would be admitted to the event and aided in his escape."

"So he must have had an accomplice." I was being drawn into Holmes's narrative with every revelation. "Who could it be?"

"I immediately suspected the French official, Monsieur Lionel Brossard. He was either an innocent guest himself who was simply unfortunate enough to make the gruesome discovery, or he participated in the assassination in some way. I suspected the latter of the two alternatives before pausing to reconsider. You'll recall my hasty conclusions in the case at the Munro household."

"Norbury," I said with a chuckle, remembering Holmes's request to whisper the word to him when I thought he was getting a little overconfident in his powers.

"Norbury, indeed. I asked Le Villard what he thought of the individual concerned. He informed me that Monsieur Brossard was an aid in the French Foreign Office. He had been in his current position for over five years. Le Villard amusingly described him as 'a person of interest'." Holmes laughed at his recollection.

"It's plausible that he may have been disgruntled," I commented, "but could such a feeling of injustice extend to murder?"

"That is what I had to find out, but given the lack of material evidence, I used it as a working hypothesis.

"Undoubtedly, the most interesting characteristic of the murder – given that it was carried out with a gun – was this apparent lack of a sound. When Le Villard informed me of this oddity, I immediately thought of Von Herder. Unfortunately, my French colleague couldn't leave his duties in Paris, but *I* was free to travel the length and breadth of France and beyond its borders in search of answers to the assassination."

This was made all the easier for my friend as he was fluent in the language. He informed me that he left Le Villard in Paris and made the long journey across the border into Switzerland. Some discreet inquiries in Geneva eventually took him to the door of the afore-mentioned Von Herder.

346

"I appeared in the guise of an assassin based in southern France with connections in Corsica. I was gambling that if he *had* successfully manufactured the noiseless appendage, it would be such a character who he would be manufacturing it for. My assumption proved accurate.

"'Are you connected to Bardet?' he asked when I explained the purpose of my visit. Before I could answer, he added, "He came here last month and took the only one that has been a success so far.'

"'It was Bardet that put me on to you. He obviously didn't realise that you had only made the one to date.'

"'He told me he had a job in Paris,' said the craftsman, 'but was reluctant to tell me who his client was. Mind you, not that I was much interested. I'm only interested in my work and the money it makes for me.'

"'Yes, of course, that's where I saw him. I came straight here from there. He said it had been an enormous success.'

"'No doubt he will be back in Marseilles by now,' commented Von Herder, thus giving me the information I was looking for – a name and where I might find him.

"I travelled back across the border and headed south to the port city. It's a dangerous place. Seldom have I been so concerned for my own safety, for those dark alleys and taverns along the waterfront must constitute the vilest murder-trap in the whole of France."

Rarely had I heard Holmes speak with such gravity regarding the dangers involved in his chosen profession, and I kept having to remind myself that this had all taken place while I was incapacitated in my hospital bed. My dearest friend could have been murdered in that far off place and I would never have known. "What did you do?" I asked.

"You have complimented me on my acting skills in the past – they were certainly required on this occasion." He continued in response to my questioning expression. "Still in the guise of a dangerous ruffian myself, I made some discreet enquiries as to the whereabouts of this Bardet character. He didn't take a lot of finding in such a cesspool of villainy. He lodged in a small garret above a dingy barber's shop on the waterfront."

"Surely you didn't confront him?"

"No." Holmes paused, I'm sure for dramatic effect. "I waited and watched until he left and broke into his lodgings."

I was incredulous. "Holmes, that was d----d irresponsible! Had he caught you, your life wouldn't have been worth a farthing!"

"Calm yourself, my dear fellow. It was a calculated risk, and I've always found that the bigger the risk, the greater the reward."

"Your venture was successful then?" I asked after composing myself once more.

"It was indeed. Amongst the detritus in Bardet's room, I found a telegram from none other than Monsieur Brossard."

"The Foreign Office official?"

"The very same. And he was advising Bardet of the date, time, and location of the event at which Sir Richard Rosendale was subsequently shot and killed. So there you had it – within ten days of being in France, I had established the probable assassin and the likely weapon he used to carry out the killing. The next step was to establish the motive for murdering the British Ambassador.

Chapter III

While I was still taking in Holmes's incredible tale, our landlady knocked and entered with our afternoon refreshment.

"I thought you might like some coffee and crumpets, gentlemen."

"That's wonderful, Mrs. Hudson," I said, taking the tray and setting it down. Pouring the coffee for us both and retaking my seat with a plate swimming in warm butter, I steered Holmes back to his Continental investigation.

"By good fortune, I arrived back in Paris from Marseilles on the morning the box of papers taken from Sir Richard's study were found."

"Where were they found?"

Holmes smiled and replaced his cup on its saucer. "In a box in a small office of the *Gendarmerie*, hidden away in an obscure suburb in southwest Paris."

"How was that explained?"

"The finding had all the clumsy, amateurish hallmarks of the individuals who planted the gun among the Moroccan waiter's belongings. Upon being met by Le Villard at the Gare de Lyon, he informed me of the finding and we went straight to the site. I discovered that a window to the office had been forced from the outside – they had actually broken *in* to plant the box of papers, apparently in an attempt to implicate the local *Gendarmerie* and distance themselves from the potential scandal!"

"How ridiculous!" I cried. "Why on earth would the local *Gendarmerie* have stolen the papers?"

"Precisely. Such incompetence on the part of my adversaries gradually succeeded in making my investigation simpler. It was clear that the officers at the station knew nothing about the papers, as they reported the incident upon discovering the box when they opened the station the following morning."

"Did you see the contents?"

348

"Indeed, I did, and this proved a significant episode of that enormous investigation."

Sir Richard had somehow obtained details of British Government dealings with the now infamous Netherland-Sumatra Company. Among the papers were trading accounts, with Sir Richard's annotations pointing out various discrepancies. There were false balance sheets, and evidence of dividends being drawn by individuals from what appeared to be capital investment. Losses had been written down as profits, and unaudited references had been made to dubious expenses and use of petty cash.

"The ambassador's journal, given to me by Winterburn, was perhaps the most damning of all," continued Holmes. "In it, he mused over how deep into the heart of government this suspected wrongdoing ran. He expressed his uncertainty as to whether he should raise the matter, and further questioned himself as to whom he should raise it *with*."

"Poor chap," I said. "He must have been in emotional turmoil. This was obviously what was on his mind when he spoke to Winterburn. Why didn't the thieves simply destroy the papers?"

I was taken aback by Holmes bursting into a roar of laughter. "I pride myself on my own detective skills," he said after composing himself, "and I must say I am impressed by the work of the young Le Villard, but I must concede that in this line of work, one does need to have a little luck at times. Fortunately, on this occasion, I was dealing with a gang of villains whose incompetence appeared to know no bounds. You will recall that the chamber of the gun planted to implicate the Moroccan was full for some bizarre reason, indicating that it couldn't have been the gun the killed the ambassador.

"Regarding the papers, the British Government protested in the strongest possible terms to the French that they considered the removal of documents from the Embassy as theft. Failure to recover them would result in an international incident. Therefore, rather than destroy the documents, those responsible decided to dispose of the evidence by breaking into the small suburban station in order to shift the attention of the investigation elsewhere and away from themselves."

"Without much success, it would appear," I added, joining in Holmes's amusement. I thought for a while and then asked, "How did Sir Richard come by these incriminating documents in the first place?"

Holmes laughed again. "The ridiculous act of trying to secrete the box took place during the night when there was no one on duty. Such buffoonery was preceded and surpassed, however, by the original act of misplacing the papers in the first instance. Whoever gathered the documents together presumably employed one of their lackeys to take the papers to the German Embassy for the attention of *their* ambassador.

Instead, the imbecile took them to the *British* Embassy, where they naturally – if unintentionally – came into the possession of Sir Richard."

"The German Ambassador was involved in the conspiracy?"

Holmes took a drink of coffee. "Conspiracy is the word. He and his chief advisor were guilty of channelling funds from the German Government into the coffers of Maupertuis to invest in his nefarious activities. Not only German but Italian officials were also ultimately exposed as being involved in funding the Neapolitan Camorra and the Sicilian Mafia through their dealings with the Baron. Governments and royal houses from virtually every country in Europe had indirectly been drawn into the villain's web. Once he had his claws in individuals connected to these great institutions, blackmail, embezzlement, and any other heinous act you care to think of became reasonably straight-forward.

"In effect, they all became agents of Maupertuis – initially blinded by greed, but then snared to the point where it was impossible to extricate themselves from his vast international crime empire. As a result, the countries they represented became unknowingly drawn into the conspiracy."

I paused, reluctant to ask the obvious question. Holmes shot a glance at me without moving his head and read my thoughts. "Yes, sadly the tentacles of Maupertuis spread to these shores also. Before Sir Richard could expose the wrongdoing in London, he was murdered.

"Of course, Maupertuis never got his own hands dirty with such activity. But his world of crime grew to such an extent that it became unwieldy, and ultimately spiralled out of control. It was poetic justice that this proved to be his downfall. As we have discovered, he developed many allegiances and generated various illicit schemes around the world, but they became so vast that it was impossible to control and oversee all the activity that was taking place. As a result, individuals were left to their own devices. When Brossard realised that evidence relating to an illegitimate alliance between government officials in London, Berlin, Amsterdam, and Paris had fallen into the hands of the innocent Sir Richard Rosendale, he took matters into his own hand and had him killed by the Marseilles assassin, Bardet.

"The evidence against Bardet included the telegram received from Brossard, and was sufficient for our friend Le Villard to approach the prosecutor in charge of the case and have the Marseilles man arrested. I provided his address, and he was taken into custody and transported to Paris for questioning. It was under this scrutiny that he implicated Brossard, telling Le Villard that he had been hired to kill the Englishman. Brossard let Bardet into the hotel on the night of the murder, and then helped him make his escape before the body of Sir Richard was properly discovered.

"Following the questioning of the killer, Brossard was arrested – " Holmes broke off in more laughter. "The effrontery of the man! He tried to claim diplomatic immunity from any criminal investigation!

"Upon further study of Sir Richard's papers, his annotations included several references to '*LB*' and his involvement with two British officials in the Foreign Office – Small and Featherstone. They had been responsible for what appeared to be a legitimate British investment in this Netherland-Sumatra Company. What was unknown to investors, however, was that, far from making profits through lawful means, the profits made by the company came from embezzling, smuggling, and piracy. Shareholders were paid their return, while other monies were used to set up phantom companies in Switzerland. These *companies* – " Holmes spat out the word. " – would then use various accounts in Geneva banks which would, in effect, make the money appear quite unsullied. That money was then re-invested into companies in Britain."

"For what purpose?" I asked, struggling to keep up with the incredible scheme.

Holmes smiled. "For the purpose of lining the pockets of the British officials who had invested other people's money in the first place. It was no surprise to learn that they were major shareholders in the companies involved."

I sat and pondered the villainy for a few moments. "Remarkable."

"The more complex these schemes were, the harder they were to detect. And when it is considered that government officials themselves were involved in some, it became virtually impossible to uncover some of the wrongdoing. The likelihood is that there will be other illegal ventures that remain, and will forever remain, unsolved."

Afternoon had turned to evening and Holmes informed me that he needed to go out. I remained in our rooms and, after dinner, spent the rest of the evening writing up the details of what Holmes had told me of his Continental adventure so far. I was determined to find out more the following day.

Chapter IV

It was a beautiful September morning as I opened the curtains in my room. I had struggled to get to sleep the previous night. My mind had raced with what Holmes had told me of his case from more than twelve months earlier. I looked forward to pressing him on its *denouement*. I was to be initially disappointed, however, when I went downstairs and found our sitting room empty. Mrs. Hudson informed me that my companion had left earlier that morning. It would be shortly after lunch before he returned.

"Where have you been?" I asked. "If Mrs. Hudson hadn't told me of your early departure, I would have believed you had been out all night."

Holmes chuckled. "No, two separate matters. Nothing that you need worry with." He removed his hat and coat and rubbed his hands together. "I must say I am starving."

"I will make a deal with you: I'll go and ask Mrs. Hudson to make you a sandwich, and you must tell me the rest of your tale from yesterday."

"Very well."

I believed Holmes was enjoying teasing me with his adventure. Mrs. Hudson duly arrived with a tray and I allowed him to eat his lunch unhindered. For my part, I sat in silence, reading and re-reading the front page of *The Times,* unable to concentrate, and tortured with impatience as I waited for him to resume his narrative. Finally, he did so.

"I alerted Mycroft to Small and Featherstone, the two government individuals in the Foreign Office, and he made arrangements with Scotland Yard to have them arrested. The matter would ultimately result in the resignation of the Foreign Secretary himself. Although not personally implicated in any wrongdoing, he did the honourable thing, as he had personally appointed the two diplomats."

"Yes, I remember reading about it in the newspaper. But why didn't you return to London?"

"As I had found the first chink in the armour of Maupertuis's empire, word began to circulate around the capitals of Europe about their own possible involvement. Representation was therefore made to London to see if the success the British had enjoyed could be replicated."

"So Mycroft commissioned you to stay and see whatever else you could uncover." Again, Holmes looked up and smiled at my perspicacity. "Although I would imagine you took little convincing, given such a challenge."

"You know me all too well."

"What *did* you uncover?"

"I first went to Amsterdam to see what I could find out about this so-called shipping company. I presented myself as a senior official of the British Maritime Association."

"I've never heard of such an organisation."

"That's because it doesn't exist! It is yet another example of the complacency that exists in this parallel world of crime. There a so many acts of wrongdoing perpetrated by so many different parties from so many countries, it has become almost impossible for one element to keep track of – or even be aware of – what is happening elsewhere. In my case, I simply mentioned the names of James Small and Ronald Featherstone from London, and this gave me free access to the records of the wretched Netherlands-Sumatra Company.

"The first thing I discovered was that Small and Featherston had invested tens of thousands of British monies in the company. I would later discover in Geneva that they were personally benefitting to the tune of several hundred-thousand pounds in return for their unlawful investments."

Holmes then learned that Maupertuis himself was looking to expand his empire still further and was currently in transit on his way home from the Americas, where no doubt he would have had his eye on the blends and spices of Columbia and Brazil.

"This gave me some time to investigate the various arms of his operation virtually unhindered. Because some of them had become so large and had been in existence for so long, there were little or no barriers required to hide the operation."

"And I suppose," I ventured, "if various branches of officialdom were themselves involved, there would be no incentive to monitor what was happening."

"You are correct." Holmes lit a post-lunch pipe and settled back into his chair. "Power and greed are a potent combination among those in positions of authority. Small and Featherstone in London proved to be the tip of an exceptionally large iceberg. The procurement of goods and services – with their ridiculously complex processes and high levels of interactions between public officials and private businesses – leaves any government vulnerable to corruption. And so it proved across Europe at the orchestration of the Baron.

"Those private companies meanwhile would simply misinform their shareholders as to their activities, and even go so far as to registering their dealings in another country. Any cursory investigation into such dealings could never hope to uncover the true extent of the wrongdoing.

"Even some of those in the various European insurance agencies weren't beyond temptation when it came to the giant conspiracy. The war between the Dutch and its colonies in the southern oceans also provided an ideal opportunity to distract and hide suspicious activity.

"Piracy is rife in the southern seas, and when raids weren't being perpetrated on legitimate vessels, they were being staged by vessels attached to the company in order to defraud the insurance companies of thousands. From what I could find out, this had been going on ever since the wretched company had been founded. One vessel – the *S.S. Zealand* – had been the subject of no fewer than twelve insurance claims over the past five years. In wandering around the port, I discovered the ship had been in dry dock for the past eighteen months! It appears as though anyone who took an overactive interest in the company and its subsidiaries' activities, a bribe could usually rectify their curiosity."

"And if it didn't?"

Holmes looked at me earnestly once more. "I discovered no fewer than forty-three murders, and more than a dozen kidnappings, running parallel to the innumerable financial crimes, could be traced back to, or connected with, the giant web created by Baron Maupertuis."

From Amsterdam, Holmes travelled to Lyon and took a suite at the Hotel Dulong. The city's proximity to the Swiss border, and Geneva just beyond it, gave him the perfect location from which he could carry out the remainder of his enquiries. It wasn't long before he discovered that it was the same city from where Maupertuis himself conducted much of his operation, presumably for the same geographical reason.

"Each time I conducted a line of enquiry," remarked Holmes, "the same name would invariably crop up – that of Lionel Brossard."

"The official from the French Foreign Ministry?"

"The very same. His clumsy handling of the ambassador's killing inadvertently led to the uncovering of the Maupertuis Empire. Brossard himself proved to be a man of great wealth, raking in thousands from his association with the Baron. His account in the Credit Lyonnais was worth a king's ransom alone. But invariably, complacency sets in with such individuals, and the trick is to follow the money. As this whole underworld of nefarious activity gradually became known over the following weeks, it transpired that Brossard had counterparts in Germany, Italy, Belgium, and Greece. And all the while, the giant financial houses of Europe – Deutsche Bank, Banca Monte dei Paschi di Siena, Banque Nagelmackers, the National Bank of Greece – all unknowingly had facilitated illegally-obtained money through their grand old institutions. Hundreds of accounts in scores of cities across the Continent provided the perfect cover for the giant operation. Those in authority who weren't part of the enormous conspiracy were simply oblivious to its workings, such was its vastness."

"It is incredible that the conspiracy lasted so long without detection," I said.

"Being entirely without any scruples or sense of loyalty," Holmes replied, "Maupertuis wouldn't hesitate to dispose of one of his generals if he believed him to be too careless and risking the exposure of his operations. Take Brossard for example. His bungling in the handling of the papers which led to the assassination of Sir Richard would certainly have led to his own killing had Maupertuis been in the country at the time."

"And so Brossard ended up in a prison cell as opposed to a coffin."

Holmes laughed. "It is as though you have adopted the language of the Continental villain! But yes, you are correct. And once Brossard was taken into custody – in an effort to save his own skin – he began to confess, not only to his part in planning the assassination, but also in the various schemes of which he was aware. His compliance with the investigation ultimately saved him from the *guillotine* as, one by one, his connections with his associates in various other countries led to each of their arrests. As each card began to fall, the evidence against Maupertuis ultimately became overwhelming. He was arrested and charged with hundreds of crimes for which, I am pleased to say, he has been convicted."

Suddenly, Holmes fell into a brown study and he silently stared into the fire. I was instantly reminded of the state I found my friend in when I travelled to Lyon to accompany him home. On that occasion, he was drawn and paler than usual, as if he hadn't eaten or slept for days. Over twelve months after the events described on that September afternoon, I finally plucked up the courage to ask him about his final days in France before Maupertuis's apprehension.

"I can't help feeling you are holding something back. I understand it had been a lengthy investigation, but its ultimate success and the adulation you received upon its completion seem to be at odds with the condition in which I found you, when I arrived at your hotel. You appeared not only exhausted but . . . *frightened*." I couldn't think of another word.

My friend looked up at me from the fire. "You aren't wrong. Danger is part of my trade, but rarely has a case presented so *much* intensity and danger over a prolonged period of time. The truth is that I had to endure not one but two attempts on my life towards the conclusion of the investigation."

"Holmes!" I exclaimed, unaware of what my friend had coped with. "Had anything happened to you, I would never have forgiven myself."

"My dear fellow, there is nothing you or anyone else could do. Living on one's wits in enemy territory will always be exhausting and hazardous. It wasn't only within his own organisation that Maupertuis demonstrated a ruthlessness. It also applied to those with whom he was in competition *and* opposition."

It was this latter category within which Holmes found himself, and he explained that when the Baron arrived back from the Americas, he began to discover that all wasn't well within his European empire. From Copenhagen to Athens, from Vienna to Lisbon, hairline cracks were starting to appear. Once those cracks developed into noticeable fissures, he suspected something was amiss. Through his network of agents, it wasn't long before he found out about a British agent who was dismantling areas of his organisation, following the debacle involving Sir Richard.

355

"It was at this point that I knew my life would be in danger. The Baron had rarely been questioned, let alone seriously opposed, regarding his activities, and I was aware that he wasn't about to begin at that moment.

"The first attempt to rid me from his world came when I was making one of the numerous journeys back to Lyon from Geneva. We were crossing the border and I was passing through one of the carriages. Suddenly, one of the doors was slid open with some force and two ruffians emerged into the narrow passageway. They managed to overpower me to the extent that I was bundled into the compartment from which they had sprung. I was thrown to the floor and had to act quickly from being completely incapacitated. I managed to roll away from a kick aimed by one of the ruffians and, at the same time, grab his foot and send him careering into his associate. This allowed me to regain my feet and even the contest somewhat by connecting with a straight left to the other flailing lout.

"I then had enough time to hastily exit the compartment and raise the alarm. The train was halted, but the two leapt from the external door within the compartment and fled into the night. Upon the recommencement of our journey, it became apparent why they had waited to make their assault – the train passed over a giant viaduct. Had I not extricated myself and made my escape when I did, I have no doubt that I would have been overpowered and thrown from the train at that very point."

"You said that wasn't the only attempt." I was still coming to terms with the thought of losing my friend without even knowing it.

Holmes sunk his chin into his chest, his voice almost becoming a lament. "Yes," he paused. "That is the saddest part of the whole tale. Once I arrived back in Lyon, Le Villard asked me to return to Paris in order to share my latest findings with the prosecutor who was, by this time, building the irrefutable case against Maupertuis. After our meeting with the prosecutor, Le Villard and I were leaving the *Palais de Justice* in the company of two young *Gendarmes.* At one point, Le Villard stumbled on the steps and I moved to assist him at the very moment a shot rang out from across the square. When we both regained our footing, I turned to see that one of the young officers who was standing behind me had been shot in the head. He died instantly and lay there bleeding on the steps of the highest court in the land."

"The bullet had been intended for you."

Holmes nodded sadly. "I later learned that the young man had recently become a father. His wife would be left to bring up their child alone – more victims of the web spun by this wretched creature. It made me even more determined to bring the matter to a swift end. I craved seeing Maupertuis' empire come crashing down and him being brought to justice.

"In light of the most recent atrocity, the prosecutor gave permission to use whatever resources were needed to apprehend the villain. Le Villard accompanied me back to Lyon where we intended to bring down the final curtain on the whole repugnant affair. Dozens of officers surrounded his chateau, south of the city. As it was, his apprehension proved much simpler than we had anticipated. As the order was given to rush the building, it was found that the Baron was virtually unguarded, save for the two characters I had encountered on the train some days earlier. They and their master were all taken into custody there and then. It was over."

"Did you get to speak with the villain?" I asked, knowing my friend's habitual liking for confronting his vanquished opponent.

"No words were exchanged," replied Holmes as his gaze returned to the fire and he brought his pipe back to life. "You are the military man, not I, but Wellington's quote after Waterloo came to mind, as Maupertuis was led away: *Nothing except a battle lost can be half so melancholy as a battle won.*

"I was completely exhausted after weeks of seemingly endless days of travelling, detection, and – at times – self-preservation." In recollection of his painful experience Holmes's voice lowered almost to a whisper. "As he was led towards the police vehicle, he paused and looked at me – clearly knowing who I was. He was a thick-set individual with thinning dark hair that was creamed heavily against his scalp. His complexion suggested more of a Mediterranean origin than northern European. But I'm sure I speak for all of his adversaries when I say it was his black, evil eyes that left a deep, unsettling impression. Clearly the man had no conscience.

"I didn't have the energy or the inclination to converse, and before *he* could do so, two of the Gendarmes – no doubt aware of their colleague's murder in the capital a few days earlier – bundled him unceremoniously into the back of the wagon. Le Villard then escorted me back to my hotel where I asked him to send a message to you."

He finally looked up and I – exhausted myself after listening to my friend's adventure – slumped back in my seat, on the edge of which I had been perched, transfixed for the best part of two days.

"Good Heavens! When I discovered the condition you were in upon my arrival in Lyon, I thought little of the cause – I was simply interested in getting you back home. Now that you explain the series of events that led to such a state, I am only surprised and thankful that medically, you weren't in a worse circumstance."

We sat in silence for a while longer before another thought occurred to me. "Holmes, I wasn't aware of any recognition from the government for your efforts regarding the matter?" My friend sneered his contempt at such a suggestion, but I persisted with my point. "Lesser men have received knighthoods for simply attending Parliament!"

"And they are welcome to their awards, and to telling each other how great they are and how they serve their country so well." Holmes made no effort to hide his cynicism. "No doubt, those same men will impose on my brother once more, who in turn will call on me the next time there is a difficult problem to solve."

NOTES

*   "The Adventure of the Reigate Squire"
**   "The Adventure of the Greek Interpreter"

The Belmore Street
Museum Affair
by Bob Byrne

"Watson, do be a good fellow and get the '*W*' volume down for me, please."

I had just returned from lunch and billiards at my club, and that was Holmes's greeting as I entered our sitting room at 221b Baker Street. Taking off my coat and hat, I crossed to the shelf where he kept what he called his "Good Old Index". It was a collection of clippings, notes, and other ephemera on any conceivable subject he might find of use.

"I see that you bested Thurston at billiards. That makes twice in as many weeks."

My hand stopped reaching for the book as I turned in amazement. "How could you possibly know that? I haven't said a single word since entering the room. And I didn't mention that I had gotten the better of Thurston last week either, for that matter. You are positively inhuman sometimes."

He sighed in disapproval at my clear lack of acknowledgement of his abilities. "Not at all, Doctor – merely observant. Though I was out when you departed this morning, I heard you tell Mrs. Hudson last night that you would be at your club and would eat lunch there. There is chalk on your wrists and cuff. Having played billiards with you, I know that though you roll up your sleeves, you still commonly get chalk on the edge of your cuffs."

I involuntarily glanced down. "But how could you possibly know that I won?"

"Recently, you mentioned that the horses have not been kind to you. I've thought of suggesting you return your check book to my drawer again, but of course, your finances are your own affair."

"Yes, yes. What of it?" I said testily. I still failed to see how he could have deduced that I had defeated Thurston.

"When you return from having won at billiards – or the ponies – there is a spring in your gait and a little extra swing in your arms. I attribute that to the gain in your financial situation. I admit that my identification of Thurston as your victim is just a probability, based on the frequency of your games with him."

Yet again, Holmes's impeccable logic made it all seem so simple once he explained things.

He spoke before I could give voice to that thought. "Observation, analysis, and deduction, Watson. It is a chain that can be forged with practice and effort."

I resumed my task and took my chair after giving him the requested volume from the shelf.

He began leafing through it. "Winthrop. Murdered by his brother's fiancé. Hidden beneath the veneer of some family legend."

He paged backwards. "Warburton. Colonel James. Strange case of madness there."

Apparently, he had gone too far. He went forward one page.

"Ah, here we are. Ward, Mortimer. Discovered a tomb in the Valley of the Kings. Two years there and around Thebes. Possibly found Cleopatra's mummy in the Temple of Horus. Recently appointed curator of the Belmore Street Museum, succeeding the famed Professor Andreas." He leaned forward to show me a sketch of the man that had appeared in the newspapers, and then shut the book.

"Why this interest in an archaeologist?"

"Because he sent a message by commissionaire, imploring me to see him at four o'clock. He couldn't get away from the museum any time sooner."

"'Implore', eh? What concerns him?" I asked as I lit my pipe.

"He didn't say, though his note, and desire to hurry here, implies great anxiety on his part. Perhaps it shall relieve my boredom."

I grunted noncommittally and turned my attention to the latest issue of *The Lancet*. As a practicing physician, I did my best to stay up on current issues and advancements in my field.

It was a few minutes before four when our long-suffering landlady, Mrs. Hudson, ushered our visitor into the room. As soon as he was seated, he turned to Holmes for assistance.

"I am at a loss, Mister Holmes."

Mortimer Ward was a moderately robust specimen. Some men, after years in the blistering heat and harsh conditions of the field, which are the hallmarks of so many digs, suffer deteriorated health. Such was not the case with Ward, who had acquired a deep tan during his time in Egypt. The constant wind had wrinkled the area around his eyes and his forehead, but he looked ruggedly handsome, not worn and weathered. It was as if the sun enervated him in the way mental stimuli recharged Sherlock Holmes. He was certainly less stocky than myself, but I suspected that he had some of the wiry strength that had so often well-served Holmes.

"Perhaps if you would tell us what troubles you?" I prompted.

He told us of his current position as a curator. "Each morning, I make the rounds of the museum before we open – a final check before the public is admitted."

Holmes nodded languidly. I could certainly see the sense of such a measure.

"Imagine my horror this morning to find that one of our rarest treasures had been tampered with!"

"Surely you mean stolen?" I interjected.

"No, no, Doctor Watson. Shamefully damaged, but not taken."

I saw a glint in Holmes's eyes and he leaned forward, interested now.

"Pray continue your story. What is this valuable item?"

Our visitor turned his attention back to Holmes. "It is the Queen of Sheba's necklace. The Bible tells that the Queen brought spices, gold, and precious jewels to King Solomon. Other texts talk of a great necklace that she wore in her court. It's believed that very necklace is on display at our museum."

"And what does this necklace look like?"

His face took on a glow of pleasure. "It's a work of marvelous craftsmanship. There are three beautiful green emeralds in a row, with three priceless blue sapphires in a row above them. As if that weren't enough, there are three fiery red rubies below. It's the finest necklace I've ever seen."

"It's kept under glass?" I asked.

Holmes shot me a disparaging look.

"Of course. And there's a warden assigned to every two rooms during the day. The necklace was most certainly untouched at close last night."

"What has happened to this rarest of necklaces?"

A look of anguish came over his face. "Someone must have broken into the museum last night, for they attempted to pry out the sapphires."

The boredom which Holmes had complained about earlier was now completely gone. His eyes shone as he leaned forward. "But they didn't secure any of the stones?"

"No, thank the Creator, they did not. They bent the settings, doing horrible damage, but they didn't remove any of the stones."

"How many settings were damaged?"

"All three with sapphires in them."

"But all the sapphires themselves are still intact?"

"Yes."

My friend smiled. "Most peculiar. Yes, very much so." He sat back in his chair and looked at me. "I think we should accompany Mister Ward to the museum. I am very interested in this case." He paused. "Do you not see the significance of the damaged settings?"

"Well, I'm not surprised. Surely the villain was in a hurry and damaged them while attempting to pry out the stones."

He gave me that smile which indicated I had missed something that he considered obvious. I had seen such a look many times in our association. "Yes. Surely." It was a tone of dismissal, rather than of wholehearted endorsement.

"And dash it, Mister Holmes, I had received a warning some three days past." He handed Holmes a piece of paper.

As was his wont, Holmes examined the paper thoroughly. He held it up to the light, looked at both sides, and studied the handwriting. I knew that every element was imprinted on his brain – at least for the duration of this case. He often shared his observations, but didn't do so this time.

After reading it, he carelessly handed it to me:

Sir,

I should strongly advise you to keep a very careful watch over the many valuable things which are committed to your charge. I do not think that the present system of a single night watchman is sufficient. Be upon your guard, or an irreparable misfortune may occur.

I stared at our visitor as Holmes spoke. "This says that you have just the one watchman."

He nodded his head. "Correct. He is a commissionaire, honorably discharged from Her Majesty's service. He seems adequate to his task."

"And his name?"

"Smithson."

Holmes internally made a decision and rose. I followed suit. He moved and took his coat from a peg by the door, reassuring our visitor, "We shall accompany you back to the museum. I shall do my best to aid you in this business."

Mortimer Ward looked relieved for the first time since arriving. He was quite pleased that Holmes was going to investigate. I called out to Mrs. Hudson as we went out the front door, and then we secured a cab.

Holmes watched the scenery pass by, apparently content to save his questions until we were at the museum. I asked a few unobtrusive questions about our client's experiences in the field, but he was quite distracted, and I quickly gave up.

We came to a stop in front of the museum. There are few such in the world that compare favorably with our own British Museum, but the one on Belmore Street had a sterling reputation. The Babylonian and Syrian

362

rooms were well-regarded, and several of the Egyptian and Jewish pieces in the Central Hall would be welcome at any museum in the world.

The museum was already closed when we arrived for the day. I noted mummies, papyri, some very impressive scarabs, and even a meticulous duplicate of the seven-branched candlestick of the Temple in Jerusalem. The actual item was said to be lying in the bed of the Tiber River. I often thought that if Holmes had turned his prodigious talents to the field of archaeology, many lost treasures would be found again.

We reached the middle of the Central Hall, where a glass case sat upon a pedestal – clearly the showpiece of the entire Museum. Inside the case, which was locked, was a stunning necklace. It was made of what looked to be filigree silver, with a both simple and ornate design. Somehow it looked both elegant and showy.

There were three rows of superb gems, just as Ward had described. These gems were simply stunning – the finest I had ever seen. I could well believe that this had adorned the very neck of the Queen of Sheba.

Ward actually wrung his hands, and was clearly upset. Looking at the row of sapphires along the top, I understood why. The settings, which held the brilliant blue stones, had been bent and scratched. It clearly contrasted with the excellent condition of settings for the other six gems.

"Mister Ward, would you please open the case so that I may inspect the necklace?"

The curator certainly wasn't going to argue with Holmes about bringing out the necklace – clearly, the damage had already been done, but Holmes stayed him when he began to pick it up. "No, this will suffice for the moment." With that, he whipped out the magnifying glass which had become so closely associated with him, though he didn't use it as often as is commonly supposed.

He examined the settings, the jewels, the rest of the necklace, the interior of the case, and even the exterior. Ward watched anxiously, while I roamed over and looked at a rather interesting vase. I had no part to play until Holmes asked for my assistance – if he did so at all – and I found it best to avoid being in his way.

Finally Holmes was finished with the necklace, which he hadn't touched. "Someone has obviously tried to remove the stones, in a quite unprofessional manner. But it does appear to me that these are the original sapphires, and they are undamaged."

I had rejoined them when Holmes began speaking. "So the would-be thief didn't succeed," I stated.

"As you say," he replied enigmatically. He turned to our host. "I would like to explore the museum, and hear of your security measures."

Before we left the room, I asked Mortimer Ward if he had called the police.

He looked a bit apprehensive. "No, Doctor Watson, I did not. The publicity resulting from the theft of jewels from the necklace would have damaged the museum's reputation." He paused and looked a bit abashed. "And it would certainly reflect poorly upon my administration. I am still establishing myself in my position."

My look must have betrayed some of my feelings regarding his failure to inform the authorities, for he added, "But I would certainly have gone to them if Mister Holmes had recommended it."

Holmes then suggested that the man bring in an expert jeweler to examine the gems. "It can certainly do no harm to have a professional pronounce them unharmed. I can suggest a name if you don't have one readily available."

Without waiting for an answer, he moved off and we went from room to room, with Holmes examining each one. "I haven't visited in many years, though there is much of interest to see." He critically eyed the layout of the room in which we had presently paused. "Are there monitors roaming the museum during the day?"

Ward beamed with pleasure at the compliment. "Thank you." His mind then turned to Holmes's question. "We are open to the public from ten until five. During that period, there is a guardian for every two rooms. He is stationed at the door between them."

Holmes nodded and admired a Roman sword – I believe it was called a *gladius*. "It would appear that you have sufficient staff to protect the necklace during your public hours." He moved on and we went to the next room.

"The warning note mentioned just one guard at night. How else is the museum protected after hours?"

Of course, I had wondered this myself, and I knew Holmes would ask about it. Mortimer pointed towards the front of the building. "We have iron shutters, as impregnable as can be, which cover the doors and windows. My predecessor cherished the antiquities under his care and took every precaution. Frankly, it was a bit of a surprise he retired so young." He looked thoughtful for a moment, and then continued.

"The building is secured from entry without. The watchman has a room near the main entrance, and he walks his round every three hours. We keep one electric light burning in each room all night. We take security very seriously here, Mister Holmes."

"Indeed."

We finished our tour, with Holmes continuing to look at various items. Each display had a card with information about it. Holmes

364

examined many of the cards and asked questions, which our host was more-than-happy to answer. It was clear that he was an expert on the treasures under his care.

Finally, we arrived at Ward's office, which wasn't as large as I would have expected, but it definitely had the look of a place where someone did a great deal of work. Documents and objects were on the desk, shelves, the guest chair – even the floor. It wasn't so much that it was untidy, like our lodgings were when Holmes ignored my entreaties to straighten things up. It was simply that there just wasn't enough space for all the things which it held.

"The person who sent this note is obviously aware that you only have the single watchman. Is that common knowledge?"

Ward gave this some thought. "I wouldn't think so, in general. The public wouldn't know."

"Might I again see that warning note which you received?"

Holmes studied it silently, then handed it back and asked that Smithson, the watchman, be summoned. After arriving, the man was adamant that no one could have gotten in through the windows or doors, and that there had been nothing amiss during his rounds. He had been at his post when not circulating through the rooms. It was a mystery to him. Holmes thanked and dismissed him.

My friend turned to our client. "I cannot yet definitively say what happened, but I do believe that no real harm has been done. Do you have someone in mind to examine the necklace?"

Ward was certainly feeling better than he had been when he came to Baker Street. He assured Holmes that a distinguished jeweler worked with the museum and would be summoned without delay.

"Well then, I believe that repairs can be made to the clasps. There are a few interesting aspects which I intend to look into, but I don't believe that you need worry about the gems being stolen."

The man's praise was effusive as he escorted us to the door. Holmes waved off offers of payment, saying it offered him a few of those curious elements that so interested him. He bade Ward to notify him if anything further untoward happened.

As we rode back to our rooms, Holmes lay back, eyes half-closed.

"That certainly could have been much worse," I said. "Apparently just some form of mischief."

"You really think so?"

Far too often I had found myself wading into these dangerous waters. "Don't you? You yourself said the gems weren't taken."

He eyed me as we bounced along London's streets. "You believe that someone simply damaged the fastenings intentionally? To what purpose?"

"Dash it, how should I know? The necklace was damaged. The jewels were unharmed. Nor were they taken. What else could it be?" He could be exasperatingly cryptic.

"I believe there is more to this affair than it appears. What if I were to tell you I know who wrote the warning note?"

I sat up straight. "Come now! How could you possibly know that already? We didn't see writing samples from Ward. Or even from Smithson."

Holmes chuckled. "No, we didn't. Nor did we need to. Did you happen to look at any of the cards associated with the exhibits?"

"Yes, I did. I read several of them. They were quite informative."

"Indeed they were. I daresay the man who wrote them is nearly as expert in his own field as I am in mine."

Other than for musicians who he admired greatly, Holmes rarely doled out such praise. "And who is that?"

"Why, Professor Andreas, of course. The former curator. He was certainly the most qualified to do so."

I reflected on that. "Well, yes, I suppose so. But what has that to do with anything?"

He sighed in the way that indicated he wondered how I could be so obtuse. "Watson, you might have inferred from this very conversation that the same man who wrote those cards also wrote the warning note."

"What?" I cried. "Professor Andreas?"

He smiled at my dismay. "As you may recall from that matter at Reigate, I have made a study of handwriting. It can be most distinctive. After again examining the warning letter, I found no less than five exact correlations. I have no doubt I could identify several more were I to subject the note to a more detailed study, opposite several of the information cards."

"But Holmes," I sputtered. "Why in the world would the professor send that warning? And even if he suspected that something might happen, why wouldn't he just tell Ward directly?"

He closed his eyes and sat back again. "That indeed is the question. I shall make some inquiries after we return. I don't yet know what game is afoot, but there is clearly more going on than it appears."

He said no more, and we rode the rest of the way in silence. Once home, he sent a flurry of messages, and then went out for well over an hour, but told me nothing. I napped and enjoyed Mrs. Hudson's plain but nourishing repast.

The fire comfortably warming our rooms, Holmes later interrupted my reading. "I have learned much today."

I put down my newspaper and urged him to continue.

366

"I visited Professor Andreas' lodgings. He wasn't home, but I did speak with his daughter, who lives with him. She has a fine bone structure, but appeared rather haggard."

I imagined that she was normally a pretty woman. Holmes would of course describe her beauty in terms of her bone structure. His common indifference to feminine beauty was most unusual.

"She said that her father was in Scotland, visiting his brother, the Reverend David Andreas. You know that I too sometimes have a way with what you call the fairer sex, Watson. She talked over tea, telling me that her father had been tired of late, and seemed to be carrying a great weight on his shoulders. He had brushed off her concerns, and said that he had to go talk with his brother. I deduced that her fatigued state was attributable to worry over her father."

"A Captain Wilson arrived not long before I left. He is her fiancé." He reached over to the table beside him and picked up some crumpled papers. "A word from certain sources was most helpful in determining that 'Wilson' isn't his name, and he is a scoundrel of some note."

I immediately saw the implications. "Why, the cad! He has won the young woman's affections as part of some dastardly ruse to steal the jewels." I all but rose out of my chair in indignation.

Holmes smiled in amusement. "He is quite possibly involved in this matter, but let us not call for the darbies just yet."

I was surprised by this and attempted to determine what our next step might be. "If you say so. Then we are off to Scotland?"

"No, I don't believe our answers lie in the land of Macbeth."

Trying to guess what Holmes was thinking was worthy of one of his three-pipe sessions. The obvious was rarely the most likely to be the case.

Other than to tell me that we would see what events held in the next few days, he didn't speak of the affair any further that night. I admit to being totally in the dark, but that wasn't unusual. And of course, the jewels hadn't actually been stolen: Things could certainly be much worse. I tried to dismiss the matter from my mind, though rather unsuccessfully.

Early the following morning, Holmes received a dispatch, summoning us to the museum. The would-be thief had struck again. There was a sparkle in his eyes as we returned to Belmore Street. He would say nothing, other than we would see what we would see when we arrived.

Smithson had been waiting for us at the entrance and ushered us to the Central Hall, where we found our client at the necklace display. A uniformed constable stood at the entrance to the Hall, and two men stood talking with Mortimer. One was our old friend Inspector Lestrade.

"I see the Yard has taken things in hand, Lestrade," Holmes greeted him as we approached.

We had crossed paths with Inspector Lestrade of Scotland Yard many times. He was honest and tenacious, but with a limited imagination. His determination to find a straight-forward solution consistently left him many steps behind Holmes.

He looked up at our approach, not overly glad to see us. "Well. Mister Ward here has told me that he sought your services yesterday, instead of coming to the proper authorities, as he should have done." He gave a sour look to our client.

But Holmes was looking at the other man, who was examining the necklace with a jeweler's magnifying glass.

Ward introduced him as Dennis Ladwick. He was an expert who had worked with the museum many times before. He looked up at the mention of his name, apparently finished with his examination.

He spoke in a dry, clipped tone. "These are definitely the original emeralds. They are certainly as priceless as the sapphires. The settings for the sapphires have also clearly been damaged, and in a fashion quite similar to the three that are holding the emeralds. While the fastenings have been damaged, these are most certainly valuable gems. I'm certain of that."

Holmes had moved beside the case and was looking at the sapphires. As I've mentioned, they were in a row of three, below the emeralds and above the rubies. I had to peer over his shoulder, as the space was rather crowded. The fastenings were definitely damaged, as if someone had attempted again to pry them open so that the gems could be removed. It sickened me to see such wonderful silverwork harmed in this way. I wondered if the damage could be repaired.

Lestrade spoke. "Surely the same thief broke in again, and attempted to steal the sapphires this time."

"You think so, Inspector?" Holmes didn't seem convinced, though I failed to see the reason for his doubt.

"Why, it's plain as a pikestaff! The thief failed to pry out the emeralds last night, and returned to try his luck with the sapphires."

A sardonic grin was on my friend's face. "And yet, here they are."

Lestrade often grew frustrated with Holmes's vague comments. I admit that they could bother me as well, but I had grown rather accustomed to simply enduring them. "Yes, there they are. Clearly, the thief heard the watchman coming, and had to abandon his work."

"This being a repeat of events the previous evening?"

"Well, Mister Sherlock Holmes, I wouldn't know what happened the first night, since he – " He nodded his head towards Ward. " – saw fit to go to you, instead of me."

"That is true. Our thief would seem to be both persistent and none too bright, to make the same failed attempt, two nights in a row. Does it not seem that you have a . . . simple solution, Lestrade?"

The rat-faced little man gave Holmes a condescending look. "You see, there's your problem, Mr. Holmes. You're always looking for some difficulty. Even when the solution is staring you straight in the face." He smiled. "I will admit, once or twice it has helped you solve some little problem, but you'll find there's no replacement for surveying the facts and coming to the obvious answer. Just good old-fashioned, honest police work."

"Really, Lestrade, I think our association has proven that the obvious answer isn't always where a dispassionate analysis of 'the facts' leads one."

He was unruffled. "If you say so, Mister Holmes. If you say so."

"Have you already explored the museum?"

He snorted. "Of course I did! Rather than playing one of your games, why don't you just tell me what I should have seen?"

"Come now, my good man. No need to be churlish. We're all after the same thing." Holmes looked up at the ceiling, and a dusty skylight. Lestrade followed his gaze.

"Yes, I saw the skylight. We went up there, and it's a lumber room. The dust on the floor was undisturbed, so no one lowered himself down from there. And before you bring it up, I also saw the trap-door from the cellars. It wasn't used either."

The inspector was clearly not pleased that Holmes was involved. He preferred to be the one to bring Holmes into a case.

"Well done, Lestrade. I agree that neither provided entry for the supposed thief."

It was obvious that the inspector had had enough of this. "It is of no real matter, anyway."

Holmes arched an eyebrow. "No?"

"Of course not. I have many important matters to attend to. Nothing was taken here. It was merely an attempted burglary. And a bungled one, at that. I suggest that the museum security be improved, and all can be forgotten."

"That is certainly one view. Perhaps you could assign a man to patrol the street more frequently for a week or so? Surely the presence of a constable would serve as a deterrent."

Lestrade stared at Holmes as if to determine whether he was exhibiting sarcasm. Detecting none, he nodded agreeably. "Mister Ward, I shall see that the patrol along Belmore Street is increased for a bit. You might consider adding a second night watchman for a time, just as a precaution."

He said goodbye to us all and left, taking the constable with him. The jeweler spoke with Holmes for a few minutes, confirming that the fastenings were not beyond repair, and again confirming that the gems were authentic. Then he too departed, to effusive thanks from the curator.

The three of us stood around the damaged necklace and Holmes turned to me. "Tell me, Watson: What do you think motivates our evil-doer?"

I often drew upon my medical training in attempting to divine the motivations of criminals in Holmes's cases. "It could well be a case of monomania."

"You think so? Can you put forward any theory?"

I was warming to the topic, encouraged by Holmes. "There are many Egyptians who are upset that we have forces there, assisting the Khedive against the oppression of the Turks. Could this not be the work of natives, protesting our presence? They are destroying this national treasure, held in our museum."

He raised an eyebrow, which meant he gravely doubted my speculation. "Surely merely stealing the necklace, and returning it to Egypt, while embarrassing the museum, and thus the nation, would be the more sensible approach? And certainly with less chance of being caught. Hmm?"

Holmes often had me looking for ways to salvage my position. "Perhaps defacing the necklace, and stealing the gems, is more insulting," I said, rather weakly. "Leaving the damaged remains."

Holmes shook his head. "Admittedly, the thief has avoided capture, but certainly the risk versus the reward isn't suitable. Surely just taking the necklace would suffice. If desired, the gems could be removed in relative safety. No, I think we must turn elsewhere for our motive."

I had learned not to try and quickly fashion a new theory after Holmes had demolished one. Done with me, he turned to our client.

"I believe that we might be able to put rest to your difficulties this very evening, Mister Ward. If Watson and I could stay in your rooms here at the museum after closing, I think that would be sufficient to bring this matter to a close."

I'm not sure who looked more puzzled – myself or the curator. "Why, yes, yes, of course," he stammered. "Happy to oblige."

"Very good. You will go about your business as usual, and Smithson should follow his routine. Watson and I will secrete ourselves in the museum. I daresay you will know if anything untoward occurs. I will certainly call for you to join us if appropriate."

With that, he assured the man that we would be back before closing, and we departed. "It will be a long night, I believe. Let us treat ourselves. I am craving some steak-and-oyster pie."

Over a tasty meal, I tried to work out matters. It was clear that Holmes had a solution, and expected to bring things to a close this very evening. But I was at a total loss as to who was behind the damaging of the necklace, as well as the why of things. He wouldn't speak of it, which was often the case at times such as this. Eventually I gave up and enjoyed the dessert pudding.

We returned to our rooms, where I took a nap, knowing there would likely be little sleep that night. Holmes, absolutely indefatigable when on the hunt, looked through the newspapers of the day and actually cleaned up some of his disorderly desktop. That surface was as likely to have a vial of a deadly poison, or a mummified foot, as a partially-eaten cake.

At Holmes's request, Mrs. Hudson packed a hamper with some food for both of us. I had her include something for Ward, who would certainly be anxious about the night's events. Holmes said that we would be able to eat in his rooms, but then we would have to remain quiet during our vigil. That was the extent of the information which he shared with me.

There were still a few visitors strolling about the museum when we arrived. Having deposited the hamper in Ward's rooms, we casually roamed about the museum, and saw the wardens standing between the two rooms, as had been described.

It really was an impressive museum. Our great British Museum truly is a marvel of the world, but the Realm has many others of note, and not just here in London. There were fascinating reliquaries to visit and learn from. Holmes having finally satisfied himself, we went to Ward's rooms and remained there.

He visited once, to make sure everything was well, and then went about his duties. Understandably, he definitely seemed a bit nervous. Or perhaps he was just intrigued to see an end to this mysterious affair. Finally, Holmes saw fit to inform me of the night's plan. "It is another nocturnal watch," he said as he led me down hallways and up back stairs, the museum having closed over two hours before. He stopped at the doorway to a room. "We shall keep our vigil in here. We must remain silent, as we have in the past. The museum will be very quiet, except for Smithson's rounds. It is imperative we not make any untoward sounds."

So saying, we went in, and I realized that this was the lumber room with the skylight over the Central Hall. And it looked down directly upon the case which held the Queen of Sheba's necklace. There on the floor was some sacking, laid out around the skylight.

"I had Ward put these out for us earlier today. It isn't as comfortable as your bed in Baker Street of course, but it offers some cushion and warmth."

Holmes used a rag he found in the room and wiped clear a space in two of the skylight's corners. Each gave a full view of the Hall below. The skylight was of frosted glass. No one in the room below would be able to see us. We would just need to be quiet, which would of course be no problem for Holmes. I had shared enough such watches with him to know I needed to resist the fidgeting that boredom could induce. He had no patience for my potential disruption of a cleverly laid trap.

As the curator had told us, one electric lamp was left burning in each room. There were actually two such in the Great Hall, owing to its size. They gave off a cold, white light, and I could see much more detail than I would have expected. With nothing else to do, I examined the contents of the room. Professor Andreas, who had assembled most of what was there, really was a most accomplished and respected man in his field, and the collection could rightfully be boasted about.

I wondered if there was an actual mummy in the ornate sarcophagus. A replica of a tomb entrance had some jackal-headed god guarding the entrance. I was no expert on the less-distinctive differences between Egyptian and Jewish antiquities, but I could appreciate the items on display. Some were obviously Jewish, such as menorahs, and other worship pieces. And others had similar Egyptian designs.

I studied the tomb pictures of Sicara, the friezes from Karnack, the statues of Memphis, and the inscriptions of Thebes, but my eyes were always drawn back to the radiant gems of the Queen's necklace, and my mind would try to solve the singular mystery which surrounded it.

The long hours of night crept past and Holmes was immobile as he lay at his post. I moved very little, though I could see that there was obviously no one in the room below. We saw Smithson making his rounds once, then again.

While I don't suffer to the extent that many of my fellow wounded veterans do, I still have unpleasant memories in the quiet dark. Being shot in the heat of battle leaves more than just physical scars. While I often feel an ache in the damp London weather, utter silence and surrounding darkness can trigger things I would rather forget. I have to make a conscious effort to not dwell upon them.

So my attention was grabbed when I thought I saw a movement below. Smithson wasn't in the room, and I gasped quietly as I realized that the lid of the sarcophagus was slowly opening! The long watch, the dark, the place – I thought briefly for a moment that a mummy was behind all of this.

I knew that Holmes's keen gaze was locked on the sarcophagus as gradually, gradually, it opened further. We couldn't hear any sound through the skylight glass as the black slit which marked the opening was becoming wider and wider. It was so slow that the movement was almost imperceptible.

A thin hand appeared now, pushing back the painted lid. Another hand, and finally a face. I was relieved that it wasn't wrapped in decaying bandages, feeling a bit foolish at my flight of fancy.

"I knew it!" whispered Holmes as we saw a face. It only took me a few seconds to realize that it was the former curator, Professor Andreas, as recently shown to me by Holmes in a newspaper sketch. The man who had sent the warning was the villain of this story? I was at a loss.

He stepped out of his hiding place, head constantly shifting left and right as he actually slunk to the central case. He was moving on tiptoe, listening for the slightest noise. He finally reached the case and took a bunch of keys from his pocket.

Holmes held up a hand, staying me from rushing downstairs. He wasn't yet ready to apprehend our miscreant. Andreas unlocked the case, took out the necklace, and, laying it upon the glass in front of him, he began working upon it with some small, glistening tool. From our angle, his bent head covered his work, but I could guess that he was finishing his strange mission of disfiguring the necklace.

Waiting for Holmes to spring into action, I wondered at the deep hatred that must have festered inside the professor's breast. Had he been forced to retire for some reason unknown to us, and harbored such ill feelings towards his successor? I had no ties to this lovely necklace, but it pained me to see such mutilation. Why such sinister malice from such a distinguished man?

Holmes silently arose and finally indicated that we were to go stop this travesty. We crept silently to the Central Hall, Holmes having already told me that we wouldn't be utilizing Smithson's aid. The two of us would be a more-than-sufficient force.

We reached the entrance of the Hall, and our quarry was still focused on his evil deed. I must have made some noise, for he looked up and turned, giving a startled cry which echoed throughout the deserted museum. Holmes was upon him and grabbed him firmly by the upper arm before he could flee. The necklace lay upon the case, and my friend pulled Andreas away from it, ensuring that the treasure wasn't accidentally knocked to the floor.

Attracted by the noise of the capture, Smithson had puffed into the room. He was shocked to see three unexpected people in the museum, but obediently went to bring our client at Holmes's command. Holmes had me

373

watch our prisoner, who was totally despondent and displayed no threat to flee. Nonetheless, I stood next to him, hand on his arm, as Holmes examined the necklace.

Mortimer Ward arrived, flushed, nightgown in disarray. He took the situation in quickly, though he was clearly in a state of disbelief. Andreas looked utterly defeated. "Professor Andreas! Surely you weren't attempting to steal the jewels. I can't believe it!" The very foundations of our client's world had come undone.

"Nor should you believe it," my friend said to Ward. "The professor wasn't, in fact, attempting to take the gems. Well, not exactly that," he added cryptically.

"Holmes, how can you say that?" I sputtered. "We both watched him trying to pry the gems out of the necklace."

"Indeed we did. But all isn't quite as it seems, is it, Professor?"

Without meeting Holmes's gaze, Andreas said, "Apparently you know my shame. Soon, all will."

I don't know who was more confused: Myself, or our client.

"Smithson," Holmes said, turning to the watchman. "I would be most grateful if you would stand guard just inside the entrance here, to ensure that any possible confederates don't attempt to finish the night's work." I knew that Holmes was giving the man an unnecessary task to remove him from our inner circle.

"And if you would kindly take the necklace," he said to the curator, "I believe explanations would be more comfortable in your rooms."

Totally confused, I escorted our prisoner to the same rooms we had been in before our late-night vigil. Andreas was sunk deeply into a padded chair, any will he'd shown had fled. Holmes and I stood, and I was ready in case action was needed – unlikely as that seemed. Ward sat behind a small work desk, still trying to put the scattered pieces of this affair into some kind of order.

"Allow me to explain some parts of this unfortunate matter," Holmes said. Andreas weakly waved him on.

"Watson, you'll recall that I wondered why someone would try to steal the gems during multiple visits, rather than simply take the necklace with them?" I nodded that I did remember.

"That was the curious factor that led me down the correct path. You didn't think more deeply on it. I doubt that it even occurred to Lestrade." He sighed.

"We knew that someone was surreptitiously entering the museum, apparently damaging the clasps as if to remove the gems, three at a time –

not simply taking the necklace, which indicated that it was important that the necklace itself remain in the museum."

I couldn't restrain myself. "Yes. That's why I said that perhaps it was some scheme to embarrass the museum. Or the nation." I paused. "And now that we know it is Professor Andreas, I find it even more probable that he did all this to cast a poor light on his successor."

"No!" cried the professor, rising in dismay.

Holmes moved forward and reassured him. "I assure you I know that such isn't the case. You supported his appointment as your successor, and you wouldn't intentionally embarrass him." Holmes's words brought the man some solace, though I confess I was more confused than ever.

Holmes looked at Ward, then me. "I take it neither of you has a theory to put forward, based on the situation as I have presented it?" Our client was certainly in no condition for rational thought, let alone adding to the conversation. I merely shook my head.

"I put it to you that the good professor wasn't attempting to steal the gems, or damage the necklace. He was, in fact, replacing the *fake* jewels in the necklace with the *original* gems."

I cannot imagine a more surprising pronouncement from my friend. A mix of horror, shame, and hope was on Professor Andreas' face. I was speechless. Frankly, after the earlier shock of the evening, I don't believe our client had any idea what to think.

"You do know my secret, Mister Holmes? Then all is lost."

"Perhaps if you were to explain the rest, we can decide upon our course. Captain Wilson is at the root of all, of course."

And so Professor Andreas, the respected historian and archaeologist, told us a story that Holmes would have called romantic claptrap had I written it. Andreas' daughter, Elise, had fallen completely under the spell of the dashing stranger. I knew of his sordid background from Holmes's earlier comments, but Andreas hadn't. He had inquired into the man's background and character, and what he could learn was satisfactory.

Wilson paid attention to Elise, while also spending a great deal of time in the museum. He was clearly knowledgeable about antiquities – especially those in the Great Hall.

Elise became more and more attached to him. After the two became engaged, he took to spending time alone in the museum. Andreas shook his head mournfully. "I realize now what an utter fool I was."

I could only silently agree that he had certainly fallen prey to the scoundrel's machinations.

"And after their engagement, you learned that Captain Wilson wasn't the man you had thought?" Holmes said.

He shook his head in resignation. "He most certainly wasn't. He had a reputation as a thief and a swindler. And the rogue had used my daughter to get inside the museum!"

"But there is more to the story than that, isn't there?"

"I don't know how you could have deduced all this, but you're entirely correct."

His complex story continued, as he now told us how he confronted the man, promising that Captain Wilson would never see his daughter again, as well as barring him from the museum, protecting the valuables inside. Wilson had listened patiently, then walked across the room and called in Elise.

"I stood stunned as they both revealed that she already knew his dark history – and she loved him anyway! She held his hand and vowed to remain with him, as he said she was the last good influence he could expect to come into his life."

Andrews looked helpless as he continued. "He stood before me and said that he loved her and would never again do something in his life which could bring shame to her. And then he walked over, opened a box, and dumped nine brilliant gems on the table."

"He said, 'I did have designs on your treasures, Professor. And I already took the gems from Sheba's necklace. I'm quite handy with my tools, and you didn't notice I had removed them.'

I slowly began to understand what had happened. The professor's continuing explanation helped me follow in Holmes's footsteps. Albeit, well behind them.

Holmes then continued the tale. "Having already had excellent reproductions made, he had replaced the originals with them, undetected. Now you held the nine original gems, a repentant thief was standing in front of you, and your daughter's future happiness was hanging by a thread."

The professor collapsed back into the chair. "What could I do, Mister Holmes? I had already warned young Ward that I suspected that the museum was in danger. Now if I went to him or the police, my daughter's life would be ruined! And certainly she would hate me for it. Are you a father?"

I had to cover my mouth and fake a cough. It would have been inappropriate to laugh out loud at that moment, but I don't know if I'd ever heard a more amusing question. Holmes glared at me and merely shook his head in the negative.

Andreas couldn't bring himself to turn Captain Wilson into the authorities, or to approach Ward. He had raised his daughter alone after his wife passed away of consumption, and to lose her affection was anathema to him.

Holmes took over the narrative again. "So you struck upon the idea of replacing the gems yourself. If you could, then no one need know your daughter's fiancé had stolen them. And you wouldn't alienate her."

He nodded his head vigorously. Mortimer Ward was listening to all this, dumbfounded. I don't know that he could have spoken if asked to do so.

"I still had museum keys, and I told my daughter I was off to Scotland, to see my brother. I took a room around the corner, and knew I could get in here at any time. I knew Smithson's schedule all too well, and was confident I could avoid him."

"And so you replaced the sapphires one night."

It had taken him all evening, hiding in the sarcophagus to avoid Smithson on his rounds. His skill was nowhere up to that of Wilson's, and it was obvious that someone had been at work on the fastenings. But he managed to successfully replace the sapphires.

He returned the next evening and repeated the process with the emeralds.

A thought occurred to me. "You had figured all this out. That's why we set this trap. You knew he was going to attempt to replace the rubies tonight."

"It was the most logical explanation. It would be madness to break in three nights in a row to unsuccessfully steal the gems. Since the fastenings for the rubies were untouched, I suspected that our expert jeweler didn't closely examine them, and he was completely correct in certifying the emerald and sapphires as genuine. The professor had already replaced them – thus, the damaged fastenings."

He looked levelly at Andreas. "I wasn't yet certain of the identity of our nocturnal visitor, but the warning, the letter, the knowledge of the security measures – and what I discovered of Captain Wilson, who was in the professor's orbit, and the refusal to simply take the necklace: I certainly had a prime suspect.

"Having determined that somebody was replacing the gems, it was a certainty that there would be a final attempt to switch out the rubies this evening."

Professor Andreas stood up, facing all of us, but specifically addressing our client. "Mortimer, I am so sorry. I wouldn't have done anything to harm you or the museum, were it not for my daughter's sake. As it is, now all will be known. Captain Wilson and I will surely go to prison. Poor Elise will lose both her future husband and her father. I cannot imagine what her life will hold. All is lost."

While I couldn't condone his actions, I understood them. I looked at Holmes, who was watching dispassionately. How he could maintain such cold, rational emotions in all circumstances remained an eternal mystery to me.

Finally casting off some of his state of shock, Mortimer Ward rose and moved over to Professor Andreas, grasping his shoulder. "You should have come to me. We could have found a way to solve this problem. I would never ruin your daughter's life, or your relationship with her. I'm hurt that you felt you had to resort to such measures."

My cheeks suffused with warmth at such a compassionate gesture.

"Mortimer – I don't know what to say. What of me now?"

Ward turned to Holmes. "Is there any way we can keep this from the police, now that they have already been called in?"

Holmes smiled a little. "I do believe that Inspector Lestrade will be somewhat overbearing regarding my failure to catch our non-thief, but I've endured worse jibes from him. Can you trust Ladwick to restore the original rubies, and then repair the fastenings?"

He gave this some thought. "It might be difficult not explaining how the fakes were placed in the necklace."

I could well see how that was the case. And the jeweler would certainly, if only casually, mention it to someone. Word would circulate.

"Yes, quite," said Holmes. "If you would be willing to leave the necklace in my care for a few days, I can guarantee a flawless and silent repair. You can tell the public that the necklace is being cleaned, if the need arises."

Ward hastily agreed, which left Andreas staring hopefully at Holmes.

"Professor, if Mister Ward is willing to overlook your actions, I believe we can keep all of this amongst ourselves." He paused. "And I will strongly suggest that you return *all* of your keys to the museum."

Andreas pulled the keys we had seen earlier out of his pocket and shoved them at Ward, who had no choice but to take them. Our client looked thoughtfully at the professor, and then at Holmes. "Yes, I think it's best for all concerned if we don't pursue the matter further."

It was some months later, in our Baker Street lodgings, that I informed Holmes we had both been invited to the wedding of Elise Andreas to Captain Wilson. Holmes snorted in reply. He did inform me that the Belmore had received a generous donation from Wilson, who truly had seemed to repent of his evil ways.

"Professor Andreas has led an expedition to Egypt, which should keep him from sneaking into museums here. Lestrade remains convinced that increasing the patrol on Belmore Street scared away the odd thief. Of course, I haven't corrected him. Let him have this little victory."

That seemed like a final coda to the matter of the Queen of Sheba's necklace. I would have to change the names, and the museum, if I ever published it – but I had done such in my notes before. I arose and went to my writing desk, sensing Holmes's frown. He didn't approve of my recountings of his cases. I just hoped he wouldn't begin that infernal sawing on his violin while I worked.

NOTE

"The Belmore Street Museum Affair" is an adaptation of Arthur Conan Doyle's "The Story of the Jew's Breastplate" (1899). The original story did not feature Holmes, Watson, or Lestrade. In the original story, the jeweled item was a Biblical relic worn by the Jewish High Priest, and not the Queen of Sheba's necklace. These were all added for the new story.

Doyle's story was also adapted by Edith Meiser for Basil Rathbone's radio show *The Adventures of Sherlock Holmes* as "The Hebraic Breastplate" (November 11th, 1934), but the author had not listened to that version, and it was not used.

– Bob Byrne

The Adventure of the
Furniture Collector
by Tracy J. Revels

"My husband, Mr. Holmes, is a fool. He cannot see that the fellow who visits our shop is a rascal. This is hardly a case for the police, for I cannot say that a crime has been committed, but clearly a man who would change his name and appearance three times in a single month is up to no good."

My friend smiled as he settled into his armchair. It was a bitterly cold winter morning, and the gray, muted sky held the promise of snow. I had rather selfishly hoped that no case or client would disturb us, for it was a day when a man wants nothing more than to sit with his feet toward the fire, enjoying a glowing pipe and an all-absorbing novel. I had been questing with a medieval knight for the previous hour and was irked to leave our fair damsel in distress while Holmes permitted this dragon to invade our domicile. The repellant lady was perhaps fifty years of age, extraordinarily tall and thin, dressed in a black frock and a gray fur coat that was worn to a greasy shine. Her features were too sharp for any pretense at beauty, and her small eyes shone with a ferocity unbecoming in her sex. As I reluctantly put aside my novel for my notebook, I marveled that such a hideous woman had somehow managed to acquire a husband – even one who was, in her words, a fool.

"Your spouse is certainly fortunate to possess a supremely intelligent wife," Holmes said, clearly working not to laugh. "Watson sometimes thinks me as a sullen misogynist – " Here my friend gave me a conspiratorial wink. " – but I assure you that I value the observations of the fair sex, who are often aware of subtle elements which elude the masculine gaze."

"Hmmph! I am aware that Horatio Thornbill was *nothing* before he married me," the woman answered, with a sharp nod. "My people have been in business since the Tudors ruled. I was the one who taught him the secrets of our trade."

"Which is?" Holmes inquired.

"The sale of used furniture. Or – as I have instructed Horatio to call it – the careful curating of exceptional furnishings. We read the newspapers, and when someone of note dies impoverished, I send Horatio out to speak with the relatives who are usually eager to sell off what they can to settle debts. The elite have more taste than ready cash, and we acquire fine pieces for a pittance, especially when wayward heirs do not know the value of what they have inherited. Our store on Pancras Road displays furniture once owned by counts and knights and baronets – even by the occasional embarrassed duke or duchess." The lady lifted her long, hawkish nose. "It is a wonder how much some people will pay for an unremarkable mirror or sideboard because it once graced an ancestorial hall."

"A fascinating trade," Holmes said dryly. "How much would Watson's old chair or my deal-topped table fetch?"

Mrs. Thornbill removed a small notebook from her purse, ignoring Holmes's jibe. "I felt you would want our experience presented to you in order. That is, if what I hear is about you is not mere fiction, but reflections of your interest in all that is strange and bizarre in our city's life?"

Holmes elevated an eyebrow. "Very well, Madame. Please proceed."

"It started in November – the tenth of the month, to be precise. Just an hour before closing time, a gentleman came into our business. He introduced himself as Mr. William Sherman, and from his accent I would guess him to be an American, or perhaps a Canadian. He was a memorable man – tall, with a great head of white hair and a silver goatee, very elegantly and tastefully dressed, and softly spoken. He seemed to have very particular tastes. He asked if it was true that we had recently acquired several hand-made items from a certain estate. He picked out two items from that collection – a sideboard and an armoire – and made a down payment on them. Horatio extended him our most favorable credit."

"I take it from the coolness of your tone that you did not agree with your husband's decision."

"I fear not. He should have asked for credentials! The gentleman was gracious and pleasant, and I will acknowledge that he put down five pounds easily enough from his pocketbook as he provided the address where the goods were to be delivered. But there was something about him I did not trust. However, we sent the items to him the next day, in our van, and I later asked Teddy and Morgan – they are the two stout lads who come by twice a week to make deliveries for us – about the situation they found. They said the gentleman tipped them well, and that he was clearly in need of furniture, for the flat was almost completely bare.

"I gave it no more thought, but a week later, Mr. Sherman reappeared in our shop. I noticed that he had a black armband on his sleeve. Horatio rather clumsily asked Mr. Sherman who he had lost, and he sighed and told us that his wife had perished. 'A sudden thing,' he said. 'Her doctors think an aneurysm in the brain.' But before either of us could express condolences, he gestured to the wall behind me and asked if the mirror there, in a very unusual octagon frame, was from the same suite as his other furnishings. When I confirmed that it was, he insisted upon purchasing it. Horatio – in a moment of sentimental weakness – let him have it at a discount, on account of his recent bereavement, and insisted on adding it to his credited account, rather than demanding so much as a shilling in down payment."

"Again," Holmes said, "I sense your disapproval."

"What kind of man suddenly needs a fancy mirror when his wife has just died?" Mrs. Thornbill snapped. "He hadn't even mentioned a spouse on his previous visit. He clearly cared nothing about her! Perhaps he only married her for her money."

"Horatio agreed with me that our customer hadn't appeared overly grief-stricken. And eight days later, while I was in our back room working on our accounts, Horatio came galloping in with the news that another gentleman was interested in the same ensemble Sherman had purchased from and was willing to pay handsomely for a writing desk and chair. This aroused my curiosity and I glanced through the curtain that separates our showroom from our storage.

"Mr. Holmes, this man – who had given his name as Mr. Philip Sheridan – had hair as black as coal and was clean-shaven. He wore a green and gold checkered coat, with a scarlet tie and a purple silk vest. His voice was booming, and his manner was gregarious and boastful.

"'A fine, beautiful piece. Such elegant craftsmanship. I must have. Let us add in that bookcase, which matches the desk. You can make me an excellent price, I presume?'

"Of course, Horatio – overwhelmed by the man's familiarity – did so. He extended generous credit. And once again – "

"You felt cheated," I guessed.

"Oh no – I was *infuriated*, for it was clearly Mr. Sherman, with his face shaved, and wearing a new set of garments and an altered attitude. I had almost burst through the curtain, but I wouldn't wish Horatio to be embarrassed before a customer, and so I held my peace, though the moment Mr. Sheridan strolled away, twirling his cane, I took Horatio by the ear and pulled him into the back room, where I gave him a piece of my mind for being so easily deceived.

"'Why would he come here in such a garb and pretend to be someone else?' I asked. And, Mr. Holmes, my husband answered with the most ridiculous words that have ever fallen from his silly lips.

"'Katey,' he said to me, 'if the man has just lost his wife, he is probably in search of a new one. Women are more easily drawn to a jolly man than a grim fellow, and perhaps the word in his neighborhood is that he is cursed, or even that he did away with his lady. That is why he must adopt a disguise and take a new name. Some men simply cannot exist without female companionship. Why, Katey, if you were to suddenly die, well, I would have to find myself a new partner, and I would waste no time in doing so.'"

"Ah," Holmes said. "And where did you hide the body?"

The woman glared at my friend. "It was difficult *not* to murder him."

"I would imagine. But please go on – your tale is intriguing."

"I warned Horatio that any man who feels the need to change his face and name isn't a man who will cover his debts. And just as I predicted, Mr. Sheridan's payment didn't arrive on time the next week! I wrote out a note and sent it round, and when that went unanswered, I dispatched Jeffrey, our new clerk, to see to the collection himself. He returned looking solemn."

"'He's dead,' Jeffrey told me.

"'What!'

"'Yes, Mrs. Thornbill, dead as Caesar. His landlady said so. Seems that he was in a terrible accident, thrown from a cab and trampled by horses, right near Trafalgar Square. I asked about the furniture, but the landlady had already sold it, because he was behind on his rent when he died.'"

"That was exactly five days ago. This very morning, another man came into the store and inquired about the rest of the stock Mr. Sherman-Sheridan had begun purchasing. This gentleman was stoop-shouldered, and shabbily dressed in a long black coat. He leaned heavily upon his cane, and his voice was a broken, raspy thing, barely able to escape through the tangle of his bushy white beard. When he removed his hat, his head was completely bald and dotted all over with painful-looking sores. I couldn't tell you the color of his eyes, for he wore heavy, green-tinted spectacles. He gave his name as Grant, and Horatio was about to make him a price for the remaining objects. I fear I rather lost my temper, for I was tired of this game."

"'What do you want with those items?' I demanded, thrusting myself between my husband and our customer.

"'Why, I am furnishing my house,' the man replied.

"'But why these particular items?' I asked. 'If you need a hat stand and a curio case, we have a dozen more, in better condition and for lower prices. Will you take them?'

"'I think I know what I want!' he snapped.

"'You may want the moon, for all I care, for we will not sell these pieces to you.'

"Horatio was, as you might imagine, about to die of embarrassment. After all, the gentleman was certainly offering to pay as much as the articles were worth. And at my words, he doubled his bid for them. Still, I ordered him to leave. He shook his fist at us, then turned away and departed.

"'Katey, are you mad?' Horatio whined.

"'Are you blind?' I snapped. 'That was Sherman! Or Sheridan! Didn't you notice that he walked to our window with his shoulders high, but when he came through the door he was suddenly bent and lame? And that outrageous beard and those hideous glasses – no one with any sense would be fooled. Don't you understand – he's trying to collect the ensemble, without being able to pay for it in full."

"'But why would a man go to such lengths to purchase a single set of furniture – and not pieces that belonged to anyone who was famous?'

"'I don't know, but I would wager Mr. Sherlock Holmes does! You will go to see him, right this minute!'

The lady shook her head. "But he wouldn't, sir. Horatio argued that if I was so certain of the man's criminality, I should be the one who consulted you. As much as it pains me to say it, my husband is a fool, and a coward in the bargain."

My friend's eyes were gleaming. I knew that a trip into the bitter cold was in our future.

"Mrs. Thornbill, you are to be commended for your astuteness," Holmes said. "I will endeavor to live up to your faith in my powers. But first let me put a few questions to you. You say the furniture is all a set. Where did it originate?"

Thornbill flipped through her notes and tore off a page, passing it to Holmes. "From the household of the late Agnus Parker. His daughter, who handled the sale, still resides at this address."

"Do you know what the gentleman's profession might have been? You have said he wasn't one of your persons of note, whose former possessions might tempt a collector."

Mrs. Thornbill shook her head. "He wasn't famous, but he was talented. He was a woodworker, one of the best carpenters in London, and he made furniture and cabinetry for discerning clients. His daughter informed me that her father had spent his youth in America, but that is all I know about him. The pieces were quite lovely. The man's skills far exceeded that of an ordinary craftsman."

"Did his daughter state the reason for selling the furniture?"

Mrs. Thornbill frowned. "I didn't handle the negotiations, but I recall that Horatio said Miss Parker seemed eager to leave London. I remember this only because he said her urgency to be freed of the city mirrored her Christian name – which is Emancipation."

384

Holmes rose, his hands clasped behind his back. "Just a few more inquiries if you please. When Sherman-Sheridan returned in disguise as Grant, were you able to take his address?"

"Horatio hadn't made it that far in their discussion."

"And your clerk – Jeffrey. How long has he been with you?"

"He came in November, just after the visit by Mr. Sheridan."

"Are his wages fair?"

Mrs. Thornbill sat up straighter, a bright flush of indignation staining her cheeks. "Sir, that is a rather impertinent question!"

Holmes held out a conciliatory hand. "I am only curious to learn if the young man might be tempted into wickedness."

Our guest blinked rapidly. "He's paid well enough, but he is new, and he must work for a year before he earns any commissions. He drinks more than he should. I have told him that if he returns once more smelling of liquor, he will be sacked." Mrs. Thornbill shook her head. "He's annoying at times, but rather harmless."

"Then here is my advice to you. Return home immediately and close your shop for the day. Find some petty tasks for your clerk to do, to make sure that he remains on the premises. Doctor Watson and I will pay a call upon your shop by five at the latest. I think, at that time, I should be able to answer your most intelligent question."

Mrs. Thornbill seemed poised to launch a dozen more inquiries, but Holmes caught her elbow, hoisted her from the chair, and rather brusquely led her to the doorway. He then turned to me and began issuing orders.

"There is no time to lose. Pull on your warmest coat, Watson, and let us see where this curious and delightful little problem will lead."

Our first call was upon the bereaved daughter. While in the vestibule of Baker Street and just before we stepped into the frigid air, Holmes had scribbled a note. At our destination, this was passed along by a young maid, who quickly returned to lead us into the lady's parlor.

There was no need for Holmes to draw my attention to the obvious as we entered, for the room was nearly empty. Dark patches on the wallpaper revealed where pictures and mirrors had once hung, and only a few scattered porcelain figurines remained as decoration on the mantel, along with a half-dozen photographs in tarnished frames. More remarkable than the impoverishment of the room, however, was the chamber's sole occupant – a gray and black dog, some hideous blending of a wolfhound and mastiff, which immediately raised itself up to its impressive height and issued a warning growl from deep within its massive chest. Just as we had begun to fear for our lives, the lady entered through the opposite doorway and spoke firmly to the beast.

"Down, Rex! These gentlemen are friends." The creature immediately sank to the sad, much-frayed carpet, but its eyes followed its mistress's progress, and a show of teeth made it clear to us that no impropriety would be tolerated. "Forgive him, sirs. Rex is quite jealous of me."

Holmes shook the lady's hand and offered a quick condolence on her father's passing. She was still clad in black, a color which ironically flattered her fair skin and beautiful swirl of ash-blonde hair. She was barely twenty years of age, with large, innocent blue eyes, and I suddenly felt the need to protect her and lighten her burden.

"Thank you for seeing us so unexpectedly, Miss Parker. I am sorry to intrude upon your grief, and to ask such bizarre questions, but I fear some greater issue may be at stake."

"I only hope that I can help you," the lady said, glancing briefly at Holmes's note, "and I am grateful that you came promptly, for in two days I begin the most unpleasant task of moving. I have decided to live with a maiden aunt in the Lake District."

"Did your relocation motivate the sale of your furniture?" Holmes asked.

"In part . . . though to be truthful, I hadn't intended to leave this home until my year of mourning was done, but now I am afraid to stay here, with just my maid and noble Rex to look after me."

Holmes insisted that she take the only seat remaining in the room. The dog curled around her feet, still maintaining a watchful gaze at the strangers in his lair.

"And what has provoked your fear, Miss Parker?"

"A most unpleasant incident that occurred in this very room, less than a week after Father's funeral. Had Rex not been so close, I fear I would have lost my honor, if not my life."

"Your house was burgled?" I asked.

"No, sir. I endured a very distressing visit from a man who introduced himself as Mr. George Thomas. His letter of introduction claimed that he had known my father in America, and that he had some information which would be of interest to me. I received him here, and at first he seemed pleasant enough, and his memories of Father appeared authentic."

Holmes's eyes had narrowed, and a troubled look passed across his face. "Can you describe this gentleman?"

The lady gave a sharp sneer. "He was no gentleman, for all of his fine coat and silver watch chain. He was tall, and handsome in the face, but both his hair and beard were dyed a rather vulgar shade of red, as if he were trying to pass himself off as a man half his age. He moved around the room restlessly, and kept touching and examining objects, as if

386

preparing to purchase them. It unnerved me, the way he caressed the furniture. There was a little writing desk just there, in the corner. Before my very eyes, Mr. Thomas opened every drawer and pilfered inside them! It was more than I could bear, so I rose and very curtly asked him to leave.

"'My dear,' he said, in a most forward manner, 'I cannot. Your Father, in his last days, wrote to me and begged me to come to London upon his passing and take care of you. I will love and cherish you forever.'

"It was nonsense, Mr. Holmes – foul and repulsive nonsense. I knew Father would never have sent such a letter, especially to a man of whom I had no prior knowledge, had never met before that hour. But the wretch wouldn't go away, even when I ordered him to depart. To my horror, he fell upon his knees, seized my hand in his paws, and begged me to marry him!

"I told him to leave that instant – he said he would not. I called for my maid, but he rose like a flash and threw his arms around me, begging me to kiss him. He tried to force himself upon me. I fought him like a tiger, I screamed for help – and suddenly Rex broke from where he had been tied in the next room and flew upon the man. The fellow shrieked as my dog's teeth clamped around his arm. He shook loose but Rex seized upon one leg. The last I saw of Mr. George Thomas, he was fleeing down the street in a most indecent state, for Rex had ripped away the entire seat of his trousers!

"I was so shaken I couldn't sleep that evening. I decided I would sell everything and leave London to live with my aunt. The furniture was easily dispensed with – sold to Mr. Thornbill, who understood how unique Father's handmade pieces were – but there were other details to arrange, including the sale of the house. Thank goodness I can depart soon."

Holmes nodded, then posed a strange question. "Do you know why your father gave you such a unique name? I have made the acquaintance of ladies named Temperance and Charity, as well as Europa and Americus, but never Emancipation."

The young woman smiled. "There is indeed a story, though of interest to none but me. Father was an American, born in the state of Wisconsin. He was twenty years old when the Civil War erupted, and he longed to enlist in the army, for he had a passionate hatred of slavery and believed that the southern rebels should be punished for their many crimes. But sadly, father had a club foot, and he was deemed unfit for military service. Eager to serve the nation's cause in some fashion, he moved to Washington, where he helped to build military hospitals and other necessary structures. He even met and worked for President Lincoln. Father so admired the president that he vowed, should he ever have a son, he would name the boy Lincoln, and if a daughter – " Here the lady smiled.

387

" – she would be Emancipation, for Father could think of no other feminine name that would better honor his hero."

Holmes thanked the lady and we exited her house. The moment we reached the sidewalk, Holmes flagged down a cab, giving the driver Mrs. Thornbill's address and promising a sovereign if the man could get us there in twenty minutes. The driver whipped the horse so enthusiastically that I was nearly pitched out of the vehicle.

"I say – Why the hurry?"

"Because," he answered, "I fear I have made a critical error. Watson, do you recall the sad fate of my client, Mr. John Openshaw?"

It took me a moment to sort through the vast cast of characters, the many people who had called upon my friend in their hour of need. At last, the young man's pale, worried face returned to my mind, but it was difficult to answer Holmes over the wild clattering of hooves. The pavement was slick and icy, and our driver was reckless to the point of homicidal.

"I do – but why should I?"

"Because I blundered. I sent him away when I should have kept him close, and he was murdered as a result. I fear I have made the same error. I should never have allowed Mrs. Thornbill to return to her shop."

"Good Heavens! What makes you think – ?"

"I didn't take the affair seriously. I was certain the clerk was involved, but I suspected a petty crime. Now, I realize a game of greater stakes is being played."

"Why are you accusing the clerk?"

"Because of the lie he told. There was no 'Mr. Sheridan' as we have learned – therefore there was no carriage accident or dispersal of the furnishings. And recall that the clerk joined the shopkeepers *after* the initial visit from the rascal in his first incarnation. He was brought into the plot – I am certain."

"Perhaps there is a female accomplice – she could have lied to the clerk."

"A possibility – but there is far more danger for the Thornbills if the clerk is dishonest or bears a grudge against them."

My head was spinning, and not just from the violent motion of the cab as we took yet another turn on a single wheel. "I still don't understand – what is the point in acquiring Parker's household goods?"

"Consider what we have learned! The man who visited Miss Parker is obviously the same man who appeared, in three different aliases, to the Thornbills. He went to Miss Parker first, he knew that her father was an American, and he made a rather sinister inspection of her parlor. Clearly, he is after something – some relic or treasure – that Parker had hidden. He

388

was so desperate he tried to compel Miss Parker to marry him, but his clumsiness only caused her to summon her hound. Shortly afterward, she sold the objects, and this man began to purchase them. He lacked funds to buy them outright, and so went after them on credit, in different personas." Despite our cab's rough passage, Holmes's expression was calm and deliberate. "Whatever Parker possessed is a relic of great value."

"What could it be?"

Holmes made a grab for his hat as our cab skidded around another corner.

"The carpentry is the essential element. It must be something that could be concealed in a secret compartment. Perhaps a jewel or some important document."

"If such a treasure existed, why was the lady ignorant of it?"

Our cab cut between a lumbering omnibus and a regal brougham bearing a coat of arms. We were assailed with curses on all sides.

"An excellent question, Watson. Perhaps the father acquired this prize illegally or felt shame for possessing it. Only Mr. Thomas-Sherman-Sheridan-Grant knows for sure."

"What a strange quartet of aliases."

"They have a meaning."

"But what?"

At just that moment, our driver pulled hard upon the reins, and we came to a skittering halt. Holmes tossed him an ample reward. We had arrived at the Thornbill shop, a converted warehouse that dominated a corner of the grim, unattractive block. I was relieved to see a '*Closed*' sign hanging in the window. Yet Holmes gave a cry of alarm.

The door was ever so slightly ajar.

We raced inside. The showroom was illuminated only by the wane winter light creeping through the windows. There was no movement in the space, a large, open area filled furnishings of every description, a vast forest of chairs, cabinets, armoires, and bookcases. Holmes struck a match, applying it to a lamp on a countertop. Even as he did, I heard a low groan.

"Here!" Holmes hissed.

A thin, pale gentleman, who I presumed to be Mr. Thornbill, was sprawled behind the counter. His face was covered in blood, but when I knelt beside him, I quickly determined that the wound was superficial, and his pulse and breathing were both strong. He had been knocked unconscious, leaving an ugly gash upon his forehead, but he would easily recover. Holmes's fingers clamped to my shoulder.

"Let him wait – his lady may be in true peril. Move silently and don't hesitate to strike the villains down."

I nodded, melting into Holmes's wake as we tiptoed toward the rear of the shop, where a heavy curtain was hung, dividing the area for more storage. We eased beside it stealthily, and Holmes parted the fabric, peering into the back quarter. I dared not press closer, but I suddenly heard a voice, deep and firm.

"It isn't in the curio case – it must be in the hat stand! Do you have a screwdriver?"

"There's one in a cabinet up front," an eager speaker said.

"Go and fetch it."

Holmes and I stepped back. A moment later, a young, fair-haired man shot through the drapes. My friend was on him in a flash. With a chopping movement of Holmes's hand to the side of the neck, the youth fell senseless to the floor.

"Jeffrey?" the deeper voice called. "Jeffrey, what is it?"

There was a clatter, followed by heavy footsteps. A tall, robust, man stepped through the curtain, his jaw dropping at the sight of his helper upon the floor.

"What in the blazes – ?"

It was all he had time to utter, as Holmes stepped forward and delivered a sharp right hook to the fellow's bare jaw. The man dropped like a stone. In an instant we had him restrained, with Holmes's handcuffs upon his wrists. Together, we dragged him to a chair and made him more secure. Holmes then stepped to the street and blew upon his police whistle, summoning a constable.

"Where is Mrs. Thornbill?" I demanded of our prisoner.

The man in the chair glared at me. He was clean-shaven, bald, perhaps fifty years of age, and strongly built. Despite Holmes's talents as a boxer, I was grateful that we had taken such a solid opponent by surprise.

"It's none of your business. Who are you to barge in here and assault us? I'll have you arrested!"

Holmes returned from summoning the official forces. He folded his arms and stared down at the man.

"I would advise you to reconsider, Mr. Sherman. Or is it Mr. Sheridan? Or Mr. Grant? Or Mr. Thomas?" Holmes shook his head. "Really, which general of the American Union army are you choosing to impersonate today?"

"I don't know what you are talking about! I'm innocent, I tell you!"

Holmes rolled his eyes. "So you intend to be wearisome. Very well, we shall place two murders to your credit – your wife as well as Mr. Thornbill."

"I have no wife! That was merely a tale, for sympathy, to acquire a discount and – !"

390

Holmes smiled. His prisoner suddenly blanched, realizing he had given away part of his game. Much of the bluster instantly went out of him. He dropped his shoulders, slumping forward with a moan.

"I've done nothing wrong," he whined. "I've committed no crime. True, I told a few fibs, but it was the lad who struck his master, not me. And the lady is locked upstairs, in a washroom. No harm has been done to her, I swear it."

"The inspector will be here soon," Holmes said, "and every word you speak then may be held against you. I would suggest – if you wish any sympathy from me – that you make a full confession now. Watson, will you see to the lady?"

I hurried upstairs, into the family apartments. I quickly spotted a door with several heavy chairs pushed against it. Weak calls for help originated from inside the room as I removed the barricade. Mrs. Thornbill was indeed unharmed, though ghostly pale, her hair in disarray.

"It was Jeffrey," she gasped. "He pulled a gun from his pocket and marched me up the stairs. Horatio had gone away to the market, but I knew he would come back soon, for he left his spectacles behind – My God, tell me he hasn't been killed!"

It was easy enough to trace the train of events. The couple had closed the store, as Holmes had ordered, but the clerk had taken advantage of the husband's absence to confine the lady and admit his confederate. Mr. Thornbill was extremely unlucky to have returned prematurely. I found him at the bottom of the stairs, staggering about in confusion, and left him to the care of his wife.

The vicious Jeffrey had recovered his senses by the time I returned and was huddled beside the older man's chair. Holmes handed me the youth's revolver.

"Pay careful attention to him, Watson. Any lad capable of pistol-whipping a frail old man will not hesitate to commit future mischief." With that, he turned back to the principal culprit, who now wore an expression of exhausted contrition on his face. "Let us have it from the start, beginning with your identity. I will not dishonor the four principal heroes of the Union army by applying their names to you."

"Why did you choose those aliases?" I asked. It seemed far too intentional. Surely there was some purpose.

"Because I followed them," our prisoner groaned. "Four long years, tramping along with the Federals . . . it makes an impression on a man. My real name, sirs, is Oliver Wilson, and Agnus Parker was my friend from boyhood. When the war came, he went to Washington, and I became a sutler for the Union armies, selling newspapers, food, and tobacco to the

391

soldiers. We chose different ways to serve our country, but we remained close, and during the war I often received letters from him.

"Agnus was master carpenter. One day, early in the war, President Lincoln came to view the construction being done at a hospital and struck up a conversation with Agnus. He admired my friend's skills and offered him a place in the executive mansion, to oversee all carpentry repairs for that house.

"Agnus was a good man, a hard worker, friendly and kind, and a great favorite of children. He made several toys for the president's youngest son, Tad – play-things which were a comfort to the boy following the death of his brother Willie. It was Tad who showed his father a wooden soldier Agnus made, one with little compartments inside, where a child could hide his foolish treasures. That very evening, Lincoln called Agnus to his office and asked if Agnus might construct something similar for him – not a toy, but a desk with secret compartments where items of great value might be stored.

"Agnus did as Lincoln requested. He wrote to me and told me that the president was pleased with his new possession and used it often.

"At last, the dreary war came to an end. April 14th, 1865, found me in Washington. By pure luck, I saw Agnus coming down Pennsylvania Avenue. We went to a saloon, where we began recounting our separate adventures. We talked for hours, until the sun went down, and the establishment became uncomfortably crowded with soldiers, newsmen, and various idlers.

"'And what shall we do now?' I asked, for both of us were in high spirits, and perhaps more intoxicated than was respectable.

"'Come – I will show you the president's home,' Agnus said. "I am known to all the guards, and the president and his lady are attending a play this evening. No one will mind, and I want you to see my marvelous desk.'

"And so we found ourselves inside the executive mansion. The residents had gone out for the evening, and the attendants were relaxed, the guards and servants smoking and playing cards together. Parker was a popular character among them, so none objected when he led me through the suites of rooms, pointing to the beautiful portraits and the gifts presented from foreign leaders. At last, we slipped into a little side chamber, a private office where the president retired when he wanted to be undisturbed. My friend's achievement was handsome and useful – for every obvious drawer there were two hidden ones, which could only be opened with deliberate precision of touch. Parker demonstrated one, and I noticed a small, red, leather-bound book within.

"'What is this?' I asked, picking it up.

"'Whatever it is, it is none of our business, Ollie! Put it back!'

"But curiosity had seized me, and I had already opened the little tome. It was a diary, such as soldiers carried, and it was filled with tiny, tight script. At the bottom of one page, I saw the president's distinctive signature – *A. Lincoln*. I was about to show it to Agnus when suddenly a loud cry went up in the house. People began shouting, there was a great tramping of running feet. Agnus went into the hallway, and was back a moment later, urging me to hurry, that the president had been shot. We dashed to 10th Street, and the humble boarding house where the nation's leader had been carried. Like so many others, we stood vigil all night, praying that God would spare him, and walking away in horror and sadness when the doctors came forth to announce that he had passed.

"'I must go.' Agnus said. 'They will want me to build a bier, perhaps even the coffin.' He turned and gave me a piercing stare. 'The book you found in Mr. Lincoln's desk – do you still have it?'

"I reached into my coat pocket and drew it forth. I hadn't realized I possessed it, as alarmed as we were when we ran from the mansion. Agnus snatched it from me, muttering that he would return the book before it was missed.

"I thought no more about that item. I moved to New York City, but Agnus met a young lady of British origin, and in 1867 he followed her to London, where they were wed. For years, I received the occasional note from him. He told me of his wife's early death, and the beauty of his little daughter, and how he was making a comfortable living building furniture for wealthy Londoners. Often, I wondered how many knights or nobles had a desk like Mr. Lincoln's, and whether those desks might be filled with documents containing state secrets or private disgraces.

"But in mid-October, I received a strange and disheartening letter from my friend. He informed me that he had a cancer, and his doctor had told him to make his peace with God and the world. The letter was something of a confession – he begged my forgiveness for several childish injustices he felt he had committed, small follies I had long since forgotten. And then, to my great astonishment, he wrote that he had never returned the President's diary. His admiration for Lincoln was so deep, and his desire to have some last relic of the great man so strong, that he had retained the little red book among his own possessions. Now, facing death, he was ashamed of his theft, but he was uncertain of how to proceed, for he had read through the diary and knew that it contained 'personal things' that might damage the late president's reputation. Above all, he wanted to shield his daughter from learning of it. He begged me for advice.

"My mind ran riot. Many people in our nation consider Lincoln a saint and collecting anything associated with him – his signature on a letter, one of his old coats or hats – is a mania. My current employer, who

393

I dare not name, only to say he is a hero of the war and a captain of industry, would part with thousands of dollars to own such a book. I sent a telegram begging Agnus to wait, that I would come to London to speak with him. Why shouldn't his fortune be made with this item? If not for himself, then to support his soon-to-be orphaned daughter? Agnus telegraphed back that he would place the diary in a 'secret compartment' in one of his creations and await my arrival.

"But when I reached England's shores, I learned a harrowing truth: Agnus had died while I was at sea. What was I to do? He hadn't revealed where the diary was hidden, nor had he told his girl about the book. A wiser man would have laid the case before the young woman, but greed overcame me. Why should she have a claim upon it greater than my own? I confess I tried, rather clumsily, to seduce her as an avenue to searching her home but was chased away by her dog. I considered burglary, but the dog had my scent. Then, a few days later, I learned the household furniture was being sold to the Thornbills. Now my scheme focused on getting my hands on those pieces Agnus had constructed. I had staked everything on this journey, and after my initial purchase I was running low on funds. That is why I pretended to be different men, to see what I could get on credit. Every article, I chopped up, destroyed, in search of the book. The only piece that remains is that hat rack, just behind the curtain."

Holmes pointed to the clerk. "And this man?"

"I know nothing!" the youth shouted. "This is crazy talk!"

"He came to collect my payment," Wilson sighed. "I had barely a penny left to my name, but I plied him with drink and promised him half the reward if he would help me. He had no love of his employers, especially the old lady, and he agreed to be my accomplice."

The bell at the door jangled. Inspector Lestrade came stamping inside, grumbling about the cold weather and tugging at his muffler.

"Attempted murder? Thievery? *Furniture*? What's this all about, Mr. Holmes?"

"I'm sure Mr. Wilson will be happy to tell you. And I would recommend some leniency for him – but none for his helper, who tried to knock out an old man's brains. Watson, perhaps we should go upstairs and see to the health of the victim."

I spent the next half-hour attending Mr. Thornbill, making sure the damage was, as I had initially diagnosed, more cosmetic than dangerous. His wife, who had been so quick to dismiss him as a fool, now hovered about him like Florence Nightingale, cooing over his wound and attending to his every need. Holmes took her aside and told her, in hushed tones, of her customer's confession.

394

"You may be in possession of an object of great historical value, hidden in a hat stand."

"Oh, please – take the awful thing with you! I don't want it in my house. Why, it almost cost *dear* Horatio his life. Oh, how horrible it would have been to have lost him . . . My brave, sweet husband! What do I care for a dead American's diary? Do away with it!"

"The hat stand is worth five pounds!" the old man on the bed croaked. Holmes smiled.

"Then I shall leave ten in your cash box. Come, Watson, I think we may depart."

The next morning, Miss Emancipation Parker arrived at Baker Street, a puzzled look upon her pretty face. Holmes explained the case to her, revealing the real intentions of Oliver Wilson, and his quest to own every possible item that might contain her Father's stolen treasure, the secret diary of Abraham Lincoln.

"I was loathe to involve you," Holmes said gently. "Clearly, your father was a protective man and didn't wish you to know about the book. But if charges are brought against Wilson, there is no hope you will be kept out of the case. Your testimony against him will be essential."

The lady stiffened her shoulders. "I understand, and I will do my best to be brave should that day arrive. What of the final piece, which you purchased from the Thornbills?"

"I have it here," Holmes said, removing a flimsy cloth that had covered the item. "I thought you might wish to witness the last element of my investigation."

"There is no need."

She spoke sharply. Holmes froze, one arm reaching for the stand, the other grasping a small screwdriver. Other tools were laid atop his table, ready to be used if he couldn't unlatch any hidden compartments.

"And why is that?" my friend asked.

The lady exhaled loudly. "Mr. Holmes, as much as I appreciate your detective work, and how swiftly you have brought two criminals to justice, I question whether you understand anything about a woman's nature. From childhood, I knew my father made furniture to keep secrets for wealthy and important people. Did it not occur to you that I would be curious, especially after Father had passed away, to find what secrets he might have kept from me? The day following his funeral, I explored every object he had made for hidden drawers and cubbyholes. Most contained sentimental items – love letters from my mother, a packet of my own baby hair, an old photograph of Father during the war. But then I discovered . . . *this!*"

The lady reached into her purse and removed a small, red, leather-bound book. Holmes and I were both shocked and, I admit, rather embarrassed.

"You have read it?" Holmes asked softly.

"Yes. And it is indeed filled with 'personal' things. Mr. Lincoln well deserves his reputation as the Great Emancipator and the savior of the American union. But I alone know how deeply human he was, and how – as a man – he loved and was loved, in ways he could never reveal." The lady considered the tiny volume in her hand. "I would never disrespect his privacy or his memory, nor would I sell this to any collector, not even for the fortune it might bring."

"What shall you do with it?" my much-humbled friend asked.

"For now, I shall keep it, but eventually I will have it returned to America, to a proper historical repository. Mr. Edwin Stanton, upon Lincoln's death, said that he belonged to the ages – This volume does as well. It should be read in some future world, when all who knew Mr. Lincoln personally are gone, and any prejudices of our time are banished." She rose with a sigh, glancing toward the final article of furniture that had caused such intense pursuit. "I did not sell all of Father's creations, of course. I retained several small, personal items to remember him by. Please keep that hat stand, Mr. Holmes and, I beg you, think kindly of me."

The Serpent's Tooth
by Matthew White

It was on a May afternoon in 1889, the rain beating ceaselessly upon the window, that, while visiting Holmes in Baker Street, I sat in my old chair before the hearth reading *The Lancet*, while across from me the thin, ascetic figure of Sherlock Holmes sat in a dreamy haze of tobacco smoke. I looked up at him and saw that his eyes were closed and his fingers were slowly, rhythmically tapping on the arm of his chair. I had learned that such behavior in my friend was indicative of either intense concentration or deep melancholy, and I watched his face, attempting to puzzle out which it was. After a moment, he smiled.

"You needn't worry, Watson," he said, keeping his eyes closed.

"Worry?"

"You are wondering if I am in a low mood. You are watching me."

"And you," I said, "are pretending your eyes are closed so you can spy on me."

"Not at all," he replied, and now his eyes opened and sparkled with amusement. "I could tell you were watching me instead of reading."

"How, if your eyes were closed?"

"You have certain habits when you are reading. You sometimes mumble the words softly to yourself, and you continually shift in your chair, because your wound makes it uncomfortable to sit in one position for too long."

"That much is true, but I don't know about the mumbling."

"I'm sure you don't realize you do it. A moment ago, the sounds from your chair stopped, and your breathing became quieter. *The Lancet* had lost your attention. Your breath was very quiet and you were completely still. You were watching me and wished me not to notice. Most people would not have, but I have trained myself to do so. I have a theory, based upon my own observations, that our senses are continually aware of the most minute details of our environment even if our minds are not, so that a slight change – a movement of the air, a flicker of light and shadow, a sudden, subtle sound – awakes our primitive instincts without our reason knowing quite why. Such reactions are the origin of what people sometimes call their 'sixth sense'."

"Ah," I said. "Like when you know you are being watched without seeing the watcher?"

"Precisely so. There is nothing supernatural in it. It only appears so because it happens outside our awareness."

"Someone is here to see us," I said.

"There is no need to make fun. It's a perfectly reasonable – "

"Not at all, dear fellow. I heard the door while you were talking."

I heard Mrs. Hudson fussing about the state of our visitor's wet coat. A moment later, footsteps ascended the stair and Inspector Davies of Scotland Yard appeared in our sitting room door.

"Come in, Inspector, and warm yourself by the fire," said Holmes. "You look, if I may say so, a little the worse for wear. Doctor, will you kindly provide a restorative?"

"Much obliged, gentlemen," returned the short, wiry Welshman as he settled into the basket chair. I poured him a brandy and Holmes produced a cigar from the coal scuttle.

"Now, once you are settled, tell us what has caused you to be washed up on our humble doorstep like flotsam in a flood?"

"I hope I shan't be a bother, Mr. Holmes," said the inspector. "No doubt you have something on hand already?"

"On the contrary. The last three weeks have been entirely uneventful."

"Oh, I see. And you, Doctor?"

"I cannot say the same. I am fairly inundated with respiratory complaints, no doubt due to this wet weather."

"It is awful, isn't it?" said Davies. "I was in Rotherhithe two days ago, and the mud was nearly up to my ankles."

"Come, come, Davies," said Holmes impatiently. "To what do we owe the pleasure of your visit? You have clearly had a very tiring day, and I cannot imagine you came so far out of your way only to inquire after Watson's schedule."

"I can see you're eager for a case, Mr. Holmes, so I'll get to the point. Have you heard anything about Howard Glenn?"

"The name means nothing to me," said Holmes, raising an eyebrow in my direction. I shook my head to indicate that I shared my friend's ignorance.

"I thought not. I'm sure it'll be in the newspapers tomorrow morning. Howard Glenn is, or *was*, a naturalist. He was found dead this morning at his home."

"A suspicious death, I presume, or else you would not be here."

"I'm inclined to think so, whatever the coroner may say."

Holmes leaned back into his chair and closed his eyes, steepling his fingers as was his custom when devoting himself to the facts of a case.

"Pray start from the beginning," he said, "and be precise as to the details."

The inspector cleared his throat.

"An inspector was called to the house because the death was, at first, deemed suspicious. At quarter-to-ten this morning, I arrived at the residence. The coroner was already waiting for me in the reptile room."

"The reptile room?" said I.

"Oh, yes. The fellow had his own little menagerie of snakes and lizards, which he kept in the warmest room in the house, in glass cabinets decorated to resemble their natural surroundings. He kept all kinds, even dangerous ones."

"He seems to have been quite dedicated to his chosen field," observed Holmes.

"It might have been better for him if he'd chosen a different one. For you see, it was one of his pets that killed him. It was a gila, a kind of venomous lizard from America. Glenn had the only live one in England, maybe in Europe. He was found on the floor by the gila's cabinet. There were two little punctures just above his right wrist, on the inner side where it bit him."

"Was he not wearing gloves?"

"No, and I thought that was queer, for I saw a pair of long, thick gloves hanging by the door."

"I see. Who found the body?"

"His daughter, Alice, was the first to see it, at about eight o'clock. She lives in the house, together with her brother Alec, and their stepmother. Four servants also live in the house. There's Mrs. Margaret Turner, the housekeeper, two maids, and a cook. Well, as I was saying, by the time I arrived, the coroner had concluded that Howard Glenn had died of a gila bite, and he said he was sorry I had wasted my time coming there. But I thought that, seeing as I was already at the scene, I'd not be doing my full duty if I didn't examine things for myself."

"Your diligence is commendable," said Holmes. "Describe the body, just as you saw it."

"Howard Glenn was an elderly man – nearly seventy, in fact," Davies said, "but he looked to be in good health, aside from some bagginess about the face. The body was quite stiff."

"Signs of injury?"

"Apart from the bite marks I mentioned before, the left side of his face was badly bruised, as though he had hit his head on the edge of the cabinet as he fell. He was wearing a smoking jacket and slippers. His cane was under him.

"After the coroner, Alice Glenn was the first person I talked to. The poor girl was badly shaken, but she's tougher than she looks, and she was more than willing to answer my questions.

"'When Father wasn't at breakfast,' she told me, 'I thought perhaps he had gone out on some early business. I asked Alec and Miss Margaret, our stepmother, but they hadn't seen or heard Father at all. Mrs. Turner likewise told me she hadn't seen him since last night.'

"'Would it be unusual for your father to leave the house without telling anyone?' I asked.

"'Extremely unusual,' she answered. 'He never goes anywhere without telling someone. I looked in every room, but when I couldn't find him, I went to Alec straightaway and told him I was afraid something had happened.'"

Holmes interrupted.

"Do I understand correctly," he asked, "that she didn't find the body in the reptile room during her first search?"

"Yes, Mr. Holmes," Davies said. "But that isn't surprising. There are two rows of cabinets in the room, so that someone only looking in through the door wouldn't see anything on the floor unless it were before the first row. The gila's cage was on the far side of the room, by the back wall."

"I see. Please continue."

"Alice told me how her brother had ordered the maids to search the entire house and grounds. 'Alec and I walked around outside the house,' she said. 'He was terribly nervous. Finally we came to the back of the house. I happened to glance through the window into the reptile room, and saw Father lying there on his back! Alec dashed back to the door, with Mrs. Turner and myself following. Miss Margaret heard the commotion and came flying down the stairs. I ran at once into the reptile room and knelt at Father's side. I grabbed his arm, but he was as stiff as a statue. His features were frozen in the most horrible expression of shock and fear I have ever seen on a human face.

"'Miss Margaret came with Mrs. Turner and started wailing when she saw Father. Alec stood outside the room by the door, and his face was blank – empty, as though the shock had driven all thought from his mind. Miss Margaret snapped at him to go at once for a doctor, and he hurried away.'

"That was all I could get out of her before she began to weep. I hadn't the heart to press her further."

"It seems unusual," remarked Holmes, "for Alice to refer to her stepmother as 'Miss Margaret'. Did you ask her why?"

"It hardly seemed important at the time."

"Anything unusual is usually important," Holmes returned. "Please, go on."

"After speaking to Miss Alice, I went to question the rest of the household, and that's where things began to seem queer. Could I trouble you for another drink?"

After I refilled Davies's glass, he sipped from it and resumed his story.

"The next witness I spoke to was Mrs. Margaret Glenn, the deceased's young wife."

"Young?" I asked.

"Yes, Doctor. She isn't yet thirty. Can you imagine? She was more composed than Alice, but still very nervous. She claims her husband got out of bed that morning, dressed, and left their room. She assumed he was merely going to check on the reptiles, as he often did before breakfast."

"What time was this?"

"She doesn't know exactly, for she was still very sleepy. She supposes it must have been six in the morning or so, which is the time at which he usually rises."

"I find that hard to believe," I interjected.

"Which part of it?"

"You said Howard Glenn's body was stiff when Alice found it at eight," said I, "but if he died shortly after six, it would be impossible for *rigor mortis* to set in so quickly."

Davies nodded.

"The same thought occurred to me."

"Did she see daylight in the windows?" Holmes asked.

"Their bedroom windows are quite closed up. She cannot sleep in less than complete darkness, she says. In any case, my interview with her went in this way:

"'Your husband was an early riser?' I asked her.

"'Oh yes,' she replied. 'He never slept for very long because of a chronic pain in his right leg which kept him awake.'

"'What did he do in the mornings?'

"'He looked after the animals, for the most part.'

"'Had he ever been injured before while handling them?'

"'Only once, years ago. This was before I met him.'

"'Does he wear gloves while tending to them?'

"'I don't know. I never go into that room, for I can't stand the things.'

"'Did your husband ever behave recklessly? Given to drink, perhaps?'

"'Certainly not!'

"She's a close one, Mr. Holmes, and no mistake. Answered all my questions, but never volunteered a scrap of information I hadn't asked for. When I had finished talking to Mrs. Glenn, I went to speak to the victim's son, Alec.

"'Mrs. Glenn tells me your father often rose early to care for the reptiles,' I said. The young man shook his head sadly.

"'Rose early to drink himself into a stupor, more like,' he said.

"'He was given to drink?'

"'The old man hardly knew himself by lunch time.'

"'Your stepmother said quite the opposite.'

"'She is – *was* – embarrassed about it. Not only for his sake, but because she rather feared it reflected poorly on her as a wife.'

"'Were there arguments between them?'

"'You must understand, Inspector. My father was a singularly difficult man to live with. Maggie – that is, my stepmother – was devoted to him, and as good a wife as a woman could be. Still, when Father drank, all reason and compassion left him. He could be quite cruel to her.'

"'Did your father ever drink before handling the reptiles?'

"'I see your suspicions are the same as mine,' he said sadly. 'I think that may be the cause of my unhappy father's death. He had handled creatures like these all his life, so I cannot imagine why he would be so careless as to get himself bitten unless he were impaired.'

"Finally, I asked him if his father had ever been injured by one of his reptiles before.

"'Years ago, he was bitten by a crocodile or some such blasted thing,' he said. 'He had to kill the creature to get it off him.'

"'And had your father been drinking when this happened?'

"'I'm sure I have no idea,' he answered. 'I was only a child at the time.'

"Well, to make a short end of it, my interviews with the family were concluded just as the body was being removed. The coroner's official opinion is that Howard Glenn died of a venomous bite, and that may well be. But, given the inconsistencies between the different statements . . . ."

"Quite so," said Holmes. "I am surprised, however, that you neglected to question Alice Glenn again after hearing these inconsistencies. Unless you have omitted anything, you also failed to question any of the household staff."

"As a matter of fact," said the inspector, looking uncomfortably into his glass, "that's why I came to you, Mr. Holmes. I've been an inspector only nine months now, and while I'm far from an expert, I know enough to know when I'm out of my depth."

"Believe me when I tell you that that insight alone puts you ahead of the majority of your colleagues. I presume you would like me to help you sound the bottom of this mystery?"

"I should be very grateful for your assistance."

"You shall have it. Are you game, Doctor?"

"Of course," said I.

"Capital! Let us fortify ourselves against the weather and be on our way."

Ten minutes later, the three of us were ensconced in a four-wheeler bound for the scene of the morning's tragedy. The going was slow, for the streets were slick and muddy and the rain torrential. During the journey, I conversed with Inspector Davies while Holmes sat back, eyes closed, as though he were asleep. Yet I knew that this expression belied the working of his keen mind, contemplating the mystery before us.

At last we passed the large, wrought-iron gate that marked the beginning of the property. The house was large, but not expansive, and it looked to be quite old. We alighted and hurried along the unkempt gravel drive toward the door. Inspector Davies knocked, and moments later the door was opened by a matronly yet handsome woman, a pair of *pince-nez* perched on her nose and her silver-flecked auburn hair pulled back into a severe bun held in place by an exquisite silver hair-pin.

"Why, Inspector Davies," she said with some surprise, "we weren't expecting you to return." I noticed that her hands were not still, but vibrated with what I recognized as a nervous tremor.

"Just following up a few things, Mrs. Turner," said Davies in a cheery voice. "No need to be concerned. These gentlemen are colleagues of mine – Mr. Sherlock Holmes and Doctor Watson."

"I see. Well, come in, gentleman. I'll tell Mrs, Glenn you're here."

"No need, Mrs. Turner," said a sweet, musical voice. A tall, slim woman, dressed all in mourning, appeared at the top of the stairs and descended in a slow, dignified way. As she got closer, I saw that she was quite a beautiful lady, with full lips and large, almond-shaped eyes. Her steady gaze lingered over the three of us.

"Why, your clothes are soaked through!" she exclaimed. "Mrs. Turner, dry our guest's coats. I will see to them."

"Yes, ma'am," replied the housekeeper. She collected our coats in her shaking hands and left us alone in the hall with our hostess.

"I'm sorry to inconvenience you, Mrs. Glenn," Inspector Davies said apologetically.

"You are only doing your duty, I'm sure. And these two gentlemen are – ?"

"Specialists, madam. I've asked them to help me verify the facts of the case."

"I wouldn't have thought the police needed help verifying such a plain set of facts," said Mrs. Glenn. There was a touch of irritation in her voice, but she seemed to realize it and her tone softened at once. "Forgive me. This has been a very trying day."

"Quite so, madam," said Holmes soothingly. "You and your family have been through a terrible ordeal. With your permission, then, we will waste no time finishing our work so that we may leave you in peace."

"I would be most grateful, sir."

"To begin with, I should like to speak to your stepdaughter, Miss Alice Glenn, in a room with a little more privacy."

Mrs. Glenn conducted us to a parlour before going to find Alice. A minute later, a young woman, also dressed in mourning, joined us. She had a slight, youthful figure which, together with her delicate facial features, gave one the impression of fragility, and the redness of her face showed that she had been crying only moments before. The poor creature looked so sorrowful that I was filled with pity.

"Miss," said the inspector, "thank you for speaking to me again. This is Mr. Sherlock Holmes and Doctor Watson."

"Forgive my appearance, gentlemen."

"Not at all," said I. "I'm sure this has been a terrible experience for you."

She nodded wordlessly, her eyes downcast.

"Miss Glenn," said Holmes, "I am sorry, but I shall have to ask you some difficult questions."

"I understand."

"Very well. Are you aware of any recent arguments between your father and stepmother?"

The young lady's expression curdled at the mention of the other woman.

"There were always little things, Mr. Holmes. Disagreements at the dinner table, domestic quarrels, and things like that."

"Forgive me for being indelicate," said Holmes, "but it has been suggested that your father would drink to excess and behave cruelly toward his wife."

Upon hearing this, the girl's cheeks grew red and her tone much harsher.

"Did she say so? I'll have you know, gentleman, that is a *lie*! She was the cause of every argument they ever had. That *woman* – for I shall never call her my mother – delights in manipulating people!"

404

The girl spoke rapidly now, pouring forth rage like the sudden flood of water through a burst dam.

"She married my father for his money, and not for love. You may be sure of that, and ever since the wedding, he had scarcely a moment of happiness in his life! My father used to have friends who would visit every week. That vile woman made him run them off, so she could have him all to herself. She would say things – just the right things to upset him – and then, when he became angry, she would pretend to be afraid of him, knowing that he would feel guilty and give her whatever she wanted to make amends. But he never laid a hand on her, whatever she says."

"Actually, it was your brother who said so."

"What? Alec? Well, I suppose I shouldn't be surprised. She has been digging her talons into him too."

"How so?"

"She has an unhealthy influence over him. We used to be very close, but now he hardly speaks to me, and I know it is her doing, because she knows I dislike her. Lately, she has convinced him to start arguing with Father about money. My brother has several debts in arrears, and Father has refused to give him money to pay them off – quite properly, I believe, for Alec never learned to be careful with money. He shouted at Father, calling him a miser and accusing him of not caring about his future. I know that woman has put him up to it, for he never used to behave that way. Both of them have been badgering Father to get rid of the reptiles, saying they cost too much, but he held firm. That enraged them even more."

"Then your father wasn't given to drink?" I asked.

"He drank no more than any other man, sir. Maybe a little more, sometimes, because of the pain in his leg, but he never hurt anyone."

"Was he ever around the reptiles after drinking?" asked Holmes.

"Not that I know of. It doesn't seem like something he would do, for he was always very careful with them. I saw it myself, because he would let me help him sometimes."

"Have they ever injured him?"

"Not his own animals, but many years ago he was bitten by an enormous Asian monitor lizard – the size of a dog, if you can believe it. That is why he had trouble with his leg."

"You told Inspector Davies that you became worried after your father wasn't present at breakfast. He was regular, then, in his habits? Rose at the same time every day, went to bed at the same time every night?"

"At around the same time, yes."

"Thank you very much," said Holmes. "You have been of immense assistance."

405

"Sirs, I don't pretend to understand the intricacies of police procedure," she said, "but it seems to me from your questions that you don't believe my father's death was an accident. Will you not tell me your suspicions?'

"For the moment, that is all they are," said Holmes. "It wouldn't do to say more before we're certain."

"I really would like to help,"

"Then I would be obliged if you would show us the reptile room."

The girl frowned at being so rebuffed, but nodded to indicate her acquiescence. I could see that my first impression of her was mistaken, and that her fragile appearance belied a strong nature and keen intelligence.

Together we rose and followed Miss Glenn into the hall. She and Inspector Davies led the way, while Holmes and I walked a little way behind.

"She's a perceptive young lady," Holmes remarked quietly.

"Yes," I agreed, "but her statement was certainly unexpected. The thing seems more complicated now than before,"

"I rather think the fog is lifting. But I don't have all my data yet."

Miss Glenn reached the far end of the hall, where a little hallway branched off toward the back of the house. At the end was a heavy paneled door, which our guide unlocked for us. The reptile room seemed indeed to have been made for the purpose. It had a low ceiling and was much warmer than the other rooms in the house, owing to a number of gas heaters spaced evenly about. Three rows of cabinets crossed the length of the room, atop which, behind panes of glass, such a collection of scaly beasts as would be the envy of the London Zoo reposed upon rocks or slithered into narrow hiding places. The roof's glass panels and the large windows, running the length of three of the walls, would have ordinarily made use of other lights unnecessary during the day, but so cloudy was the weather that Miss Glenn took up a lantern which sat on a table by the door.

"Oh dear," she said, and I noticed that the glass was broken in several places, held together only by the iron frame. "Father must have dropped it."

"Did your father always use these when tending to the animals?" Holmes asked, indicating a heavy pair of stiff leather gloves which hung above the table.

"I never knew him to forget them, until this morning."

"And this stick is for handling the dangerous reptiles, I assume?"

"Yes."

"Was it with him when he was found?"

"I cannot remember clearly. I don't think so."

406

Holmes examined the gloves inside and out and sniffed them. He turned his attention to a wooden strongbox which sat on the table. He attempted to open it, but it was locked quite tightly.

"What is in this locked box?"

"Father keeps – kept – vials of venom in it."

"What on earth did he want with venom?" asked the inspector.

"In recent years, he spent a great deal of time doing research, and performing experiments with different venoms, in the hope of discovering new medical applications. I don't know very much about the details, I'm afraid, but I did help him sometimes."

"The key?"

"He kept it in his bureau."

Holmes put on the gloves and picked up the stick.

"The gila, if you please."

Miss Glenn took us to see the lizard, a large, lazy-looking animal which struck me as seeming more like a fat Cumberland sausage than a dangerous killer of men. Holmes unlatched and lifted the top of the creature's enclosure and disturbed it with the stick. I was surprised to see that the gila seemed hardly to mind, merely shuffling away. After a little while, Holmes, to my astonishment, put down the stick and lifted the creature in his gloved hands, examining its mouth while the gila hissed and kicked its fat little legs in vain protest.

"Is it always so docile?" I asked Miss Glenn. She was watching Holmes intently with a troubled expression on her face.

"Yes," she said. "Always."

Holmes looked at her, and nodded as though he had shared her thought. He lowered the creature gentle back into its glass home, and we watched it waddle toward the far corner.

"It hardly seems capable of biting anybody," said Holmes as he removed the gloves from his hands, "unless it had a very obliging victim, willing to sit still and wait. How often is this room cleaned?"

"Every day Father would clean it himself, for he didn't like the servants near the reptiles."

She hadn't finished speaking when Holmes dropped to his hands and knees, his searching eyes to the floor, while Davies and I watched him work. I had come to understand my friend's methods, so that when I saw him examine the floor with his magnifying glass and scrape small flecks of dust into small paper envelopes, I had some idea of the purpose behind his actions. A glance at the inspector's bemused expression, however, told me that he was quite as mystified by Holmes's actions as if he were watching a necromantic ritual. After some time he stood up with a look of satisfaction on his face.

"Thank you, Miss Glenn. I wonder if you would be good enough to bring me the key to the venom box?"

"Certainly, Mr. Holmes."

After the young lady had left, Holmes held out his open palm, but it took a moment before I saw what was in it.

"A shard of glass!" said the inspector.

"From the lantern, no doubt," said I.

"Precisely. Howard Glenn met his end in this room last night, probably after dinner. Hence the need for a lantern. This much we suspected already, however, for it would take at least that long for *rigor mortis* to set in."

"And he can't have been alone," I said, "because someone put the lantern back after it was dropped."

"So Mrs. Glenn is caught in a lie. I'll arrest her at once."

"Hold a moment, Davies," said Holmes. "We cannot say yet whether she herself is the murderer. We need more exact data."

"And the true cause of death must be accounted for," I said.

"I'll question her at the Yard."

"That would be a mistake," said Holmes firmly.

"Why, for God's sake?"

"Because our evidence is here, Inspector, not at the Yard. There are as yet too many missing links in your chain of reasoning. Now think on it. Do you really suppose you could hold this woman on the mere suspicion of having told a lie? And if she isn't the murderer, would you not be giving the true villain ample opportunity to destroy evidence?"

"I suppose you're right, Mr. Holmes, as usual. I take it then you have some idea of where to look for additional evidence?"

"I do."

At that moment, the young Alice Glenn returned with the key and handed it to Holmes, who unlocked the box and carefully lifted the lid. Inside were four rows of slots not unlike test tube racks. Each vial, stopped with a cork, had a little label tied to it identifying which creature the venom had come from. Holmes took out his magnifying glass and examined each of the vials minutely, sometimes removing one from the box to look more closely at it.

"This vial," he pointed out, "has been placed rather hastily. Observe how it is misaligned with the bottom of the holder. Make a note of that, Inspector."

Holmes closed the box, locked it, and returned the key to Miss Glenn.

"I have seen enough here, I think," he said.

We left the reptile room and returned to the hall, where we found the housekeeper speaking to one of the maids. Holmes said some hurried words in a low voice to Davies before approaching the women.

"Forgive the interruption," said Holmes. "May we speak privately, Mrs. Turner?"

After a glance at Miss Glenn, who nodded her assent and turned to other business, we accompanied the housekeeper to the same parlour in which we had interviewed her young mistress.

"I presume, Mrs. Turner," said Holmes, closing the door behind us, "that since you keep the affairs of the house so well in hand, you would know about any small quarrels or arguments which might come up?"

"The staff are very disciplined, sir. I'd not abide any troublemakers."

"Of course, but I was referring to the family."

"It isn't for me to speak of, sir."

"I quite understand, and under normal circumstances you would be quite correct. But between us, there has been a murder done, and anything which you could tell us would be of immense help in clearing it up."

"I . . . I'm sure I couldn't . . . ."

"It would be best for you to cooperate, Mrs. Turner," said Inspector Davies, his Welsh accent bristling with impatience. "Otherwise, you may find yourself charged with impeding an investigation."

For the first time, the equanimity which prevailed over her features was broken and I saw the shadow of fear. Tears welled up in the corners of her eyes, and I would have had words with the inspector over his insensitivity, but I sensed that it would disrupt Holmes's questioning.

"There, there, dear lady," said Holmes, producing his handkerchief and offering it to the elderly lady, who took it gratefully and wiped her eyes with a trembling hand.

"Now, please, Mrs. Turner, will you answer some questions?"

She nodded.

"Was there much tension between your master and his wife?"

"They argued."

"Often."

She nodded again.

"Intensely?"

"Yes."

"I observe that you are a smoker of cigarettes. If it would soothe you, please have one."

"I am not permitted to smoke upstairs."

"Well, it is only us here now."

After a moment's hesitation, Mrs. Turner produced a cigarette case and withdrew a small, thin cigarette. Holmes lit it for her and, after taking a moment to savor the smoke, she said, "I am ready to answer more questions, sir, if you have them."

"Did Mr. Glenn have a contentious relationship with his former wife, the children's mother?"

"Never. They were a perfectly harmonious couple."

"And the children's relationship with their stepmother?"

"Mrs. Glenn – the present Mrs. Glenn – has always tried to be friendly with them. She and Master Alec have become quite close, but Miss Alice avoided her. Never spoke to her except at meals, so far as I know."

"And your own relationship with Mrs. Glenn?"

"She is . . . she is kind."

"I see. That is all, Mrs. Turner. Thank you."

Back in the hall, Holmes approached Miss Glenn, who it seemed had been waiting for our return.

"I think my case is complete," he told her. "Will you please ask your brother and stepmother to meet us in the parlour?" Once all were seated before him, Holmes said, "Thank you for coming." His hands were folded behind his back, and he looked down his thin nose at each of us in turn.

"This is a little irregular, isn't it?" said Alec Glenn in an irritable voice. "I'm not accustomed to being summoned by amateur detectives in my own house."

"I thought it best if everyone were together to hear me share my findings. I am very sorry to tell you that Howard Glenn didn't die of natural causes. He was murdered."

"That's ridiculous!" the young man ejaculated. "The coroner said – "

"The coroner overlooked some important evidence."

"What happened, Mr. Holmes?" asked Miss Glenn.

"Howard Glenn met his end last night, not early this morning, and he was killed with an improvised weapon used to mimic the bite of an animal – a weapon coated in snake venom."

"I don't see that it's anything more than a fanciful theory," Alec Glenn sneered. "If you're so sure of yourself, where is the murder weapon?"

In answer, Holmes reached behind Mrs. Turner's head and smoothly plucked away the silver hairpin. For the first time, I noticed that it had two long prongs.

"These," he intoned solemnly, "Are the fangs which delivered the fatal venom into the body of Mr. Howard Glenn."

For a long moment nobody spoke, but only stared amazed at Holmes. The housekeeper sat in shock, still as a statue except for the twitching of an eye, before bursting into tears.

"Are you saying – ?" began Davies.

"I am afraid so, Inspector. Mrs. Turner murdered her late employer."

"Is this true?" cried Alice Glenn. The old woman did not answer.

"Will you say nothing, Mrs. Turner? Well, well, most of what occurred I know already. I know that last night, you had arranged to meet Mr. Glenn in the reptile room. Before doing so, you had acquired the key to the venom chest and dipped both points of your hairpin in one of the vials, containing the venom of a species of adder which is particularly feared in Egypt. When your master arrived, the two of you stood talking for some time. When his guard was down, you seized your chance and stuck him with the deadly instrument. He was startled, and dropped the lantern on the floor before collapsing. He would have died almost instantly, without having the chance to cry out. Am I right?"

Mrs. Turner nodded.

"Why, Bettie?" Miss Alice asked. The housekeeper spoke so softly we could barely hear her.

"Because he betrayed me!"

"Betrayed you?"

"I loved him. For years. And he loved me, even though he would never admit as much to anyone else. After your mother died, God rest her soul, it was me he turned to, and I believed he would . . . It was foolish, impossible . . . but he told me, and I believed him, he told me he would marry me. Instead, he married that beast!"

Her thin finger pointed shakily at Mrs. Glenn, whose face seemed utterly devoid of emotion. Her stepson's face turned red, and he put a hand on her shoulder which she hastily shrugged away.

"He broke my heart! But for his sake, I didn't leave, for I knew he never really stopped loving me, because he begged me to stay on. But that woman, his new wife, is a witch if I ever saw one! A devil incarnate! She utterly controlled him from the moment she entered this house, and anything she wanted she got, or made the one who denied her to suffer. You gentlemen – you never witnessed her cruelty. You thing from Hell! May God strike you dead!"

For an instant it seemed she would leap from her seat and attack Mrs. Glenn, but she composed herself and went on.

"She knew his feelings for me – our feelings for each other. One day, he told me he had to let me go, because of her – because she was jealous. At that moment I felt sick – not with love, but with contempt, for I loved him and was always good to him, but he would throw me out for this fiendish creature who tortured him. He cared nothing for the years I had spent by his side, while he gave me gifts and whispered idle promises in my ear. I am an old woman, and I have lived my whole life for him and he, the coward, would throw me out. My love turned to hate. I convinced

411

him to meet me one last time, last night, and the rest you know. If you ask me what I hoped to gain, the answer is nothing. I wanted vengeance, restitution for my broken heart. He cared nothing for me!"

Mrs. Turner buried her face in her hands.

"Well," said the inspector, once the four-wheeler arrived and his prisoner was secure within, "it seems you have done it, Mr. Holmes, but for the life of me I can't imagine how."

"In detection," he said, as though lecturing a pupil, "it is of the utmost importance to concentrate on what is essential, and not to allow yourself to be led astray by distractions. The statements of the family were hopelessly incompatible. We could get nothing useful from them. Therefore, I turned my attention to observing the scene of the death itself.

"The lantern in the reptile room proved that Glenn hadn't been alone when he died. The amount of broken glass on the floor showed it had not been swept since last night, and yet the lantern was returned to the table."

"To hide that it had been used," I said.

"The ash on the floor also confirmed that there were two people, for there were two different kinds of tobacco ash present. One kind was near the place where Glenn must have stood, and belonged to a cigar of Indian manufacture. The other kind had fallen a few feet away, and came from an inexpensive sort of cigarette. The amount of cigarette ash present indicated they had been standing there at least twenty minutes."

"Very well, Mr. Holmes, but how did you know it was Mrs. Turner?"

"I suspected she had an unusual relationship with her late master the moment I saw her hairpin. Now tell me, do you think even the most highly-paid servant could afford such an article as that? No, it was a gift, and I thought Howard Glenn was the most likely candidate for gift-giver. For this reason, I paid special attention to her. Your sharp medical eye no doubt observed, Watson, the intermittent tremor in her hands?"

"I did."

"I observed that one of the vials of venom had been hastily placed in the case, so that it didn't align properly in the holder. The person who replaced it had been either hasty, or trembling. It then occurred to me that Mrs. Turner's hairpin, coated in venom, might be used to imitate fangs. It would account nicely for the peculiar nature of the 'bite marks' on Mr. Glenn's wrist."

"Of course," exclaimed the inspector. "That's why they were only present on one side of his wrist."

"Exactly. If it were truly a bite, there would be tooth marks on both sides. Having noted that she possessed the peculiar yellowing of the teeth which is the near-universal sign of an inveterate smoker, I completed my chain of evidence by inducing her to smoke in the parlour, confirming that her cigarettes were those which had left behind the ash in the reptile room."

Davies laughed with delight.

"Well done, Mr. Holmes! It all seems so simple and straightforward, now that you've explained it, but by the Lord I couldn't have done it. I shall not forget you in my report."

"On the contrary," said my friend, "I wish you to omit my involvement altogether. That would be most agreeable to me, and most advantageous to you."

"Well, if you're certain, Mr. Holmes."

"I am. And allow me to congratulate you, Inspector, on a successful investigation. Your career, if you remember and practice such methods as I have demonstrated today, promises to be a long and notable one."

"What a bizarre household," I said as we rattled toward Baker Street in cab. "What a grotesque family."

Holmes smiled.

"The human mind, Watson, is unquantifiably complex, with numerous shadow recesses and unguessed hidden facets with no reasonable limits on how they might manifest. Affections may be twisted in unnatural directions. Love may be twisted into hate. Such is human nature."

"It isn't a very comforting thought."

"To you, perhaps not. As for me, it give me hope that there will always be new surprises, and new problems to solve. The day human nature is reduced to perfect predictability is the day I will find myself out of work."

About the Contributors

The following contributors appear in this volume:
The MX Book of New Sherlock Holmes Stories
Part XXXVII – 2023 Annual (1875-1889)

Hugh Ashton was born in the U.K., and moved to Japan in 1988, where he remained until 2016, living with his wife Yoshiko in the historic city of Kamakura, a little to the south of Yokohama. He and Yoshiko have now moved to Lichfield, a small cathedral city in the Midlands of the U.K., the birthplace of Samuel Johnson, and one-time home of Erasmus Darwin. In the past, he has worked in the technology and financial services industries, which have provided him with material for some of his books set in the 21st century. He currently works as a writer: Novelist, freelance editor, and copywriter, (his work for large Japanese corporations has appeared in international business journals), and journalist, as well as producing industry reports on various aspects of the financial services industry. However, his lifelong interest in Sherlock Holmes has developed into an acclaimed series of adventures featuring the world's most famous detective, written in the style of the originals. In addition to these, he has also published historical and alternate historical novels, short stories, and thrillers. Together with artist Andy Boerger, he has produced the *Sherlock Ferret* series of stories for children, featuring the world's cutest detective.

Donald I. Baxter has practiced medicine for over forty years. He resides in Erie Pennsylvania with his wife and their dog. His family and his friends are for the most part lawyers who have given him the ability to make stuff up just as they do.

Brian Belanger, PSI, is a publisher, illustrator, graphic designer, editor, and author. In 2015, he co-founded Belanger Books publishing company along with his brother, author Derrick Belanger. His illustrations have appeared in *The Essential Sherlock Holmes* and *Sherlock Holmes: A Three-Pipe Christmas*, and in children's books such as *The MacDougall Twins with Sherlock Holmes* series, *Dragonella*, and *Scones and Bones on Baker Street*. Brian has published a number of Sherlock Holmes anthologies and novels through Belanger Books, as well as new editions of August Derleth's classic Solar Pons mysteries. Brian continues to design all of the covers for Belanger Books, and since 2016 he has designed the majority of book covers for MX Publishing. In 2019, Brian received his investiture in the PSI as "Sir Ronald Duveen." More recently, he illustrated a comic book featuring the band The Moonlight Initiative, created the logo for the Arthur Conan Doyle Society and designed *The Great Game of Sherlock Holmes* card game. Find him online at:
www.belangerbooks.com and
www.redbubble.com/people/zhahadun and
zhahadun.wixsite.com/221b

Bob Byrne was a columnist for *Sherlock Magazine* and has contributed to *Sherlock Holmes Mystery Magazine* and the Sherlock Holmes short story collection *Curious Incidents*. He publishes two free online newsletters: *Baker Street Essays* and *The Solar Pons Gazette*, both of which can be found at *www.SolarPons.com*, the only website dedicated to August Derleth's successor to the Great Detective. Bob's column, *The Public Life of Sherlock Holmes*, appears at *www.BlackGate.com* and explores Holmes, hard boiled, and other mystery matters, and whatever other topics come to mind by the deadline. His mystery-themed blog is *Almost Holmes*.

Barry Clay is a graduate of Shippensburg University with a BA in English. He's dug ditches, stocked grocery shelves, tutored for room and board, cleaned restrooms, mopped floors, taught cartooning, worked in a bank, asked if you'd like fries with that (and cooked the fries to boot), ordered carpet for cars, and worked commission sales at Sears, and most recently a long-time veteran of the Federal employee workforce. He has been writing all his life, in different genres, and he has written thirteen books ranging from Christian theology, anthologies, speculative fiction, horror, science fiction, and humor. He volunteers as conductor of a local student orchestra and has been commissioned to write music. His first two musicals were locally produced. He is the husband of one wife, father of four children, and "Opa" to one granddaughter.

Martin Daley was born in Carlisle, Cumbria in 1964. His thirty-year writing career has seen over twenty books and numerous short stories published. Inevitably, Holmes and Watson remain his favourite literary characters, and they continue to inspire his own detective writing. In 2010, Martin created Inspector Cornelius Armstrong, who carries out his police work against the backdrop of Edwardian Carlisle. With the publication of the first Inspector Armstrong Casebook (published by MX Publishing), Martin became a member of the Crime Writers' Association. He lives with his wife Wendy, in Kirkcudbrightshire, in Southwest.

Sir Arthur Conan Doyle (1859-1930) *Holmes Chronicler Emeritus*. If not for him, this anthology would not exist. Author, physician, patriot, sportsman, spiritualist, husband and father, and advocate for the oppressed. He is remembered and honored for the purposes of this collection by being the man who introduced Sherlock Holmes to the world. Through fifty-six Holmes short stories, four novels, and additional Apocryphal entries, Doyle revolutionized mystery stories and also greatly influenced and improved police forensic methods and techniques for the betterment of all. *Steel True Blade Straight.*

Steve Emecz's main field is technology, in which he has been working for about twenty-five years. Steve is a regular speaker at trade shows and his tech career has taken him to more than fifty countries – so he's no stranger to planes and airports. In 2008, MX published its first Sherlock Holmes book, and MX has gone on to become the largest specialist Holmes publisher in the world with over 500 books. MX is a social enterprise and supports three main causes. The first is Happy Life, a children's rescue project in Nairobi, Kenya, where he and his wife, Sharon, spend every Christmas at the rescue centre in Kasarani. They have written two editions of a short book about the project, *The Happy Life Story*. The second is Undershaw, Sir Arthur Conan Doyle's former home, which is a school for children with learning disabilities for which Steve is a patron. Steve has been a mentor for the World Food Programme for several years, and was part of the Nobel Peace Prize winning team in 2020.

Brett Fawcett is a humanities and Latin teacher at the Chesterton Academy of St. Isidore in Sherwood Park, Alberta. He lives with his wife and son in Edmonton, where he is a member of The Wisteria Lodgers (The Sherlock Holmes Society of Edmonton). He vividly remembers the first time he finished reading the Sherlock Holmes stories in Grade 6, and has been a student of Holmesian literature and scholarship since then. He is also a frequent author of columns and articles on topics like theology, education, and mental health, as well as the occasional mystery story.

Mark A. Gagen BSI is co-founder of Wessex Press, sponsor of the popular *From Gillette to Brett* conferences, and publisher of *The Sherlock Holmes Reference Library* and many other fine Sherlockian titles. A life-long Holmes enthusiast, he is a member of *The Baker Street Irregulars* and *The Illustrious Clients of Indianapolis*. A graphic artist by profession, his work is often seen on the covers of *The Baker Street Journal* and various BSI books.

James Gelter is a director and playwright living in Brattleboro, VT. His produced written works for the stage include adaptations of *Frankenstein* and *A Christmas Carol*, several children's plays for the New England Youth Theatre, as well as seven outdoor plays co-written with his wife, Jessica, in their *Forest of Mystery* series. In 2018, he founded The Baker Street Readers, a group of performers that present dramatic readings of Arthur Conan Doyle's original Canon of Sherlock Holmes stories, featuring Gelter as Holmes, his longtime collaborator Tony Grobe as Dr. Watson, and a rotating list of guests. When the COVID-19 pandemic stopped their live performances, Gelter transformed the show into The Baker Street Readers Podcast. Some episodes are available for free on Apple Podcasts and Stitcher, with many more available to patrons at *patreon.com/bakerstreetreaders*.

John Atkinson Grimshaw (1836-1893) was born in Leeds, England. His amazing paintings, usually featuring twilight or night scenes illuminated by gas-lamps or moonlight, are easily recognizable, and are often used on the covers of books about The Great Detective to set the mood, as shadowy figures move in the distance through misty mysterious settings and over rain-slicked streets.

Arthur Hall was born in Aston, Birmingham, UK, in 1944. He discovered his interest in writing during his schooldays, along with a love of fictional adventure and suspense. His first novel, *Sole Contact*, was an espionage story about an ultra-secret government department known as "Sector Three", and was followed, to date, by three sequels. Other works include seven Sherlock Holmes novels, *The Demon of the Dusk*, *The One Hundred Percent Society*, *The Secret Assassin*, *The Phantom Killer*, *In Pursuit of the Dead*, *The Justice Master*, and *The Experience Club* as well as three collections of Holmes *Further Little-Known Cases of Sherlock* Holmes, *Tales from the Annals of Sherlock* Holmes, and *The Additional Investigations of Sherlock Holmes.* He has also written other short stories and a modern detective novel. He lives in the West Midlands, United Kingdom.

Paul Hiscock is an author of crime, fantasy, horror, and science fiction tales. His short stories have appeared in a variety of anthologies, and include a seventeenth-century whodunnit, a science fiction western, a clockpunk fairytale, and numerous Sherlock Holmes pastiches. He lives with his family in Kent (England) and spends his days taking care of his two children. He mainly does his writing in coffee shops with members of the local NaNoWriMo group, or in the middle of the night when his family has gone to sleep. Consequently, his stories tend to be fuelled by large amounts of black coffee. You can find out more about Paul's writing at *www.detectivesanddragons.uk*.

Roger Johnson, BSI, ASH, PSI, etc, is a member of more Holmesian societies than he can remember, thanks to his (so far) 16 years as editor of *The Sherlock Holmes Journal*, and thirty-two years as editor of *The District Messenger*. The latter, the newsletter of *The Sherlock Holmes Society of London*, is now in the safe hands of Jean Upton, with whom he collaborated on the well-received book, *The Sherlock Holmes Miscellany*. Roger is resigned to the fact that he will never match the Du
ke of Holdernesse, whose name was followed by "*half the alphabet*".

417

Steven Philip Jones has written fiction novels for adults and young adults, comic books, graphic novels, radio scripts, non-fiction, and advertising pieces. His Sherlock Holmes pastiches include the novel *The Adventure of the Coal-Tar Derivative* from MX Publishing and the radio dramas "The Adventure of the Petty Curses" and "A Case of Unfinished Business" for Jim French Productions' *Imagination Theatre*. He currently makes his home with his family in northern Utah.

Sonya Kudei is a writer, illustrator and former web developer with degrees in English Literature and Cognitive Linguistics. Originally from Croatia, she lived in London for over twelve years and currently resides in the Netherlands.

David Marcum plays *The Game* with deadly seriousness. He first discovered Sherlock Holmes in 1975 at the age of ten, and since that time, he has collected, read, and chronologicized literally thousands of traditional Holmes pastiches in the form of novels, short stories, radio and television episodes, movies and scripts, comics, fan-fiction, and unpublished manuscripts. He is the author of over one-hundred Sherlockian pastiches, some published in anthologies and magazines such as *The Best Mystery Stories of the Year 2021* and *The Strand*, and others collected in his own books, *The Papers of Sherlock Holmes*, *Sherlock Holmes and A Quantity of Debt*, *Sherlock Holmes – Tangled Skeins*, *Sherlock Holmes and The Eye of Heka*, and *The Collected Papers of Sherlock Holmes*. He has won first place fiction awards from *The Arthur Conan Doyle Society* and the Nero Wolfe *Wolfe Pack*. He has edited over eighty books, including several dozen traditional Sherlockian anthologies, such as the ongoing series *The MX Book of New Sherlock Holmes Stories*, which he created in 2015. This collection is now at thirty-nine volumes, with more in preparation. He was responsible for bringing back August Derleth's Solar Pons for a new generation with his collection of authorized Pons stories, *The Papers of Solar Pons* and *The Further Papers of Solar Pons*. Pons's return was further assisted by his editing of the reissued authorized versions of the original Pons books, and then several volumes of new Pons adventures. He has done the same for the adventures of Dr. Thorndyke, and has plans for similar projects in the future. He has contributed numerous essays to various publications, and is a member of a number of Sherlockian groups and Scions, as well as *The Mystery Writers of America*. His irregular Sherlockian blog, *A Seventeen Step Program*, addresses various topics related to his favorite book friends (as his son used to call them when he was small), and can be found at *http://17stepprogram.blogspot.com/* He is a licensed Civil Engineer, living in Tennessee with his wife and son. Since the age of nineteen, he has worn a deerstalker as his regular-and-only hat. In 2013, he and his deerstalker were finally able make his first trip-of-a-lifetime Holmes Pilgrimage to England, with return Pilgrimages in 2015 and 2016, where you may have spotted him. If you ever run into him and his deerstalker out and about, feel free to say hello!

Kevin Patrick McCann has published eight collections of poems for adults, one for children (*Diary of a Shapeshifter*, Beul Aithris), a book of ghost stories (*It's Gone Dark*, The Otherside Books), *Teach Yourself Self-Publishing* (Hodder) co-written with the playwright Tom Green, and *Ov* (Beul Aithris Publications) a fantasy novel for children.

Will Murray has built a career on writing classic pulp characters, ranging from Tarzan of the Apes to Doc Savage. He has penned several milestone crossover novels in his acclaimed *Wild Adventures* series. *Skull Island* pitted Doc Savage against King Kong, which was followed by *King Kong Vs. Tarzan*. *Tarzan, Conquerer of Mars* costarred John Carter of Mars. His 2015 Doc Savage novel, *The Sinister Shadow*, revived the famous radio and pulp mystery man. Murray reunited them for *Empire of Doom*. His first Spider novel, *The Doom Legion*, resurrected that infamous crime buster, as well as James Christopher, AKA Operator 5, and the renowned G-8. His second Spider, *Fury in Steel*, guest-stars the FBI's Suicide Squad. The Spider clashed with The Skull Killer and his Nemesis, the Scorpion, in Scourge of the Scorpion. Twenty of Murray's Sherlock Holmes short stories have been collected as *The Wild Adventures of Sherlock Holmes*, Volumes 1 and 2. He is the author of the non-fiction book, *Master of Mystery: The Rise of The Shadow*, which is an exploration of the famous radio and magazine character, and a sequel, *Dark Avenger: The Strange Saga of The Shadow*. *The Wild Adventures of Cthulhu* Volumes 1 & 2 collect Murray's Lovecraftian short stories.

Sidney Paget (1860-1908), a few of whose illustrations are used within this anthology, was born in London, and like his two older brothers, became a famed illustrator and painter. He completed over three-hundred-and-fifty drawings for the Sherlock Holmes stories that were first published in *The Strand* magazine, defining Holmes's image forever after in the public mind.

Tracy J. Revels, a Sherlockian from the age of eleven, is a professor of history at Wofford College in Spartanburg, South Carolina. She is a member of *The Survivors of the Gloria Scott* and *The Studious Scarlets Society*, and is a past recipient of the Beacon Society Award. Almost every semester, she teaches a class that covers The Canon, either to college students or to senior citizens. She is also the author of three supernatural Sherlockian pastiches with MX (*Shadowfall*, *Shadowblood*, and *Shadowwraith*), and a regular contributor to her scion's newsletter. She also has some notoriety as an author of very silly skits: For proof, see "The Adventure of the Adversarial Adventuress" and "Occupy Baker Street" on YouTube. When not studying Sherlock, she can be found researching the history of her native state, and has written books on Florida in the Civil War and on the development of Florida's tourism industry.

Dan Rowley practiced law for over forty years in private practice and with a large international corporation. He is retired and lives in Erie, Pennsylvania, with his wife Judy, who puts her artistic eye to his transcription of Watson's manuscripts. He inherited his writing ability and creativity from his children, Jim and Katy, and his love of mysteries from his parents, Jim and Ruth.

Fifteen of **Brenda Seabrooke**'s Sherlock Holmes pastiches have been anthologized in MX Publishing and Belanger Books, six in *Best Crime Stories of New England*, one in *Destination: Mystery* and *Mystery Tribune*, and twelve in literary reviews such as *Yemassee*, *Confrontation*, and one in *Redbook*. Twenty-two of her books for young readers have been published at Penguin, Clarion, etc., and won awards such as a Notable from the National Council of Social Studies, Junior Literary Guild, Hornbook Honor, an Edgar finalist, etc. She received a grant from the National Endowment for the Arts, and The Robie Macauley Award from Emerson College. In 2022, MX published her collection, *Sherlock Holmes: The Persian Slipper and Other Stories*.

Michael Sims's nonfiction books include *Arthur and Sherlock*, which was a finalist for the Edgar of the *Mystery Writers of America*, the Gold Dagger of the *Crime Writers Association of Great Britain*, and the H. R. F. Keating Award of *the International Crime Writers Association*; *Adam's Navel*, which was a *New York Times* Notable Book; and *The Story of Charlotte's Web*, which was chosen by the *Washington Post, Boston Globe*, and other venues as a *Best Book of the Year*. His many anthologies include *The Penguin Book of Murder Mysteries*. His Sherlockian pastiche "The Memoirs of Silver Blaze" appears in the Anthony-winning anthology *In the Footsteps of Sherlock Holmes*, edited by Leslie Klinger and Laurie King. His work is widely translated around the world.

Thomas A. (Tom) Turley has been "hooked on Holmes" since finishing *The Hound of the Baskervilles* at about the age of twelve. However, his interest in Sherlockian pastiches didn't take off until he wrote one. *Sherlock Holmes and the Adventure of the Tainted Canister* (2014) is available as an e-book and an audiobook from MX Publishing. It also appeared in *The Art of Sherlock Holmes – USA Edition 1*. Tom's collection of historical pastiches entitled *Sherlock Holmes and the Crowned Heads of Europe*, was published in 2021. Although he has a Ph.D. in British history, Tom spent most of his professional career as an archivist with the State of Alabama. He and his wife Paula (an aspiring science fiction novelist) live in Montgomery, Alabama. Interested readers may contact Tom through MX Publishing or his Goodreads author's page.

DJ Tyrer is the person behind Atlantean Publishing and has had fiction featuring Sherlock Holmes published in volumes from MX Publishing and Belanger Books, and an issue of *Awesome Tales*, and has a forthcoming story in *Sherlock Holmes Mystery Magazine*. DJ's non-Sherlockian mysteries can be found in anthologies such as *Mardi Gras Mysteries* (Mystery and Horror LLC) and *The Trench Coat Chronicles* (Celestial Echo Press), and on *Mystery Tribune.*
DJ Tyrer's website is at *https://djtyrer.blogspot.co.uk/*
DJ's Facebook page is at *https://www.facebook.com/DJTyrerwriter/*
The Atlantean Publishing website is at *https://atlanteanpublishing.wordpress.com/*

Mark Wardecker has contributed Sherlockian pastiches to *Sherlock Holmes Mystery Magazine* and the *MX Book of New Sherlock Holmes Stories – Parts XIII* and *XXXIII,* and has contributed Solar Pons pastiches to *The New Adventures of Solar Pons*. These stories and others can be found in his book, *The Endeavours of Sherlock Holmes* (MX Publishing, 2022). He is also the editor and annotator of *The Arrival of Solar Pons: Early Manuscripts and Pulp Magazine Appearances of the Sherlock Holmes of Praed Street* (Belanger Books, 2023) and has contributed articles to *The Baker Street Journal* and *The Sherlock Holmes Journal* (forthcoming). He is an instructional technologist at Colby College.

Emma West joined Undershaw in April 2021 as the Director of Education with a brief to ensure that qualifications formed the bedrock of our provision, whilst facilitating a positive balance between academia, pastoral care, and well-being. She quickly took on the role of Acting Headteacher from early summer 2021. Under her leadership, Undershaw has embraced its new name, new vision, and consequently we have seen an exponential increase in demand for places. There is a buzz in the air as we invite prospective students and families through the doors. Emma has overseen a strategic review, re-cemented relationships with Local Authorities, and positioned Undershaw at the helm of SEND education in Surrey and beyond. Undershaw has a wide appeal: Our students present to us with mild to moderate learning needs and therefore may have some very recent memories of poor experiences in their previous schools. Emma's background as a senior leader within the independent school sector has meant she is well-versed in brokering relationships between the key stakeholders, our many interdependences, local businesses, families, and staff, and all this whilst ensuring Undershaw remains relentlessly child-centric in its approach. Emma's energetic smile and boundless enthusiasm for Undershaw is inspiring.

Matthew White is an up-and-coming author from Richmond, Virginia in the USA. He has been a passionate devotee of Sherlock Holmes since childhood. He can be reached at *matthewwhite.writer@gmail.com*

The following contributors appear
in the companion volumes:
The MX Book of New Sherlock Holmes Stories
Part XXXVIII – 2023 Annual (1890-1896)
Part XXXIX – 2023 Annual (1897-1823)

Ian Ableson is an ecologist by training and a writer by choice. When not reading or writing, he can reliably be found scowling at a clipboard while ankle-deep in a marsh somewhere in Michigan. His love for the stories of Arthur Conan Doyle started when his grandfather gave him a copy of *The Original Illustrated Sherlock Holmes* when he was in high school, and he's proud to have been able to contribute to the continuation of the tales of Sherlock Holmes and Dr. Watson.

Tim Newton Anderson is a former senior daily newspaper journalist and PR manager who has recently started writing fiction. In the past six months, he has placed fourteen stories in publications including *Parsec Magazine, Tales of the Shadowmen, SF Writers Guild, Zoetic Press, Dark Lane Books, Dark Horses Magazine, Emanations,* and *Planet Bizarro*.

Donald I. Baxter *also has a story in Part XXXIX*

Chris Chan is a writer, educator, and historian. He works as a researcher and "International Goodwill Ambassador" for Agatha Christie Ltd. His true crime articles, reviews, and short fiction have appeared (or will soon appear) in *The Strand, The Wisconsin Magazine of History, Mystery Weekly, Gilbert!, Nerd HQ,* Akashic Books' *Mondays are Murder* web series, *The Baker Street Journal, The MX Book of New Sherlock Holmes Stories, Masthead: The Best New England Crime Stories, Sherlock Holmes Mystery Magazine,* and multiple Belanger Books anthologies. He is the creator of the Funderburke mysteries, a series featuring a private investigator who works for a school and helps students during times of crisis. The Funderburke short story "The Six-Year-Old Serial Killer" was nominated for a Derringer Award. His first book, *Sherlock & Irene: The Secret Truth Behind "A Scandal in Bohemia"*, was published in 2020 by MX Publishing. His second book, *Murder Most Grotesque: The Comedic Crime Fiction of Joyce Porter* will be released by Level Best Books in 2021, and his first novel, *Sherlock's Secretary*, was published by MX Publishing in 2021. *Murder Most Grotesque* was nominated for the Agatha and Silver Falchion Awards for Nonfiction Writing, and *Sherlock's Secretary* was nominated for the Silver Falchion for Best Comedy. He is also the author of the anthology of Sherlock Holmes stories *Of Course He Pushed Him*.

Leslie Charteris was born in Singapore on May 12th, 1907. With his mother and brother, he moved to England in 1919 and attended Rossall School in Lancashire before moving on to Cambridge University to study law. His studies there came to a halt when a publisher accepted his first novel. His third one, entitled *Meet the Tiger*, was written when he was twenty years old and published in September 1928. It introduced the world to Simon Templar, *aka* The Saint. He continued to write about The Saint until 1983 when the last book, *Salvage for The Saint*, was published. The books, which have been translated into over thirty languages, number nearly a hundred and have sold over forty-million copies

421

around the world. They've inspired, to date, fifteen feature films, three television series, ten radio series, and a comic strip that was written by Charteris and syndicated around the world for over a decade. He enjoyed travelling, but settled for long periods in Hollywood, Florida, and finally in Surrey, England. He was awarded the Cartier Diamond Dagger by the *Crime Writers' Association* in 1992, in recognition of a lifetime of achievement. He died the following year.

Ian Dickerson was just nine years old when he discovered The Saint. Shortly after that, he discovered Sherlock Holmes. The Saint won, for a while anyway. He struck up a friendship with The Saint's creator, Leslie Charteris, and his family. With their permission, he spent six weeks studying the Leslie Charteris collection at Boston University and went on to write, direct, and produce documentaries on the making of *The Saint* and *Return of The Saint,* which have been released on DVD. He oversaw the recent reprints of almost fifty of the original Saint books in both the US and UK, and was a co-producer on the 2017 TV movie of *The Saint*. When he discovered that Charteris had written Sherlock Holmes stories as well – well, there was the excuse he needed to revisit The Canon. He's consequently written and edited three books on Holmes' radio adventures. For the sake of what little sanity he has, Ian has also written about a wide range of subjects, none of which come with a halo, including talking mashed potatoes, Lord Grade, and satellite links. Ian lives in Hampshire with his wife and two children. And an awful lot of books by Leslie Charteris. Not quite so many by Conan Doyle, though.

Alan Dimes was born in Northwest London and graduated from Sussex University with a BA in English Literature. He has spent most of his working life teaching English. Living in the Czech Republic since 2003, he is now semi-retired and divides his time between Prague and his country cottage. He has also written some fifty stories of horror and fantasy and thirty stories about his husband-and-wife detectives, Peter and Deirdre Creighton, set in the 1930's.

Danica Dvorak is a multimedia freelance artist and first year architecture student. This is her first commissioned work, though she is now currently hard at work on new projects. She enjoys visiting museums, traveling, and reading

Anna Elliott is an author of historical fiction and fantasy. Her first series, *The Twilight of Avalon* trilogy, is a retelling of the Trystan and Isolde legend. She wrote her second series, *The Pride and Prejudice Chronicles*, chiefly to satisfy her own curiosity about what might have happened to Elizabeth Bennet, Mr. Darcy, and all the other wonderful cast of characters after the official end of Jane Austen's classic work. She enjoys stories about strong women, and loves exploring the multitude of ways women can find their unique strengths. She was delighted to lend a hand with the "Sherlock and Lucy" series, and this story, firstly because she loves Sherlock Holmes as much as her father, co-author Charles Veley, does, and second because it almost never happens that someone with a dilemma shouts, "Quick, we need an author of historical fiction!" Anna lives in the Washington, D.C. area with her husband and three children.

Denis Green was born in London, England in April 1905. He grew up mostly in London's Savoy Theatre where his father, Richard Green, was a principal in many Gilbert and Sullivan productions, A Flying Officer with RAF until 1924, he then spent four years managing a tea estate in North India before making his stage debut in *Hamlet* with Leslie Howard in 1928. He made his first visit to America in 1931 and established a respectable stage career before appearing in films – including minor roles in the first two Rathbone and

Bruce Holmes films – and developing a career in front of and behind the microphone during the golden age of radio. Green and Leslie Charteris met in 1938 and struck up a lifelong friendship. Always busy, be it on stage, radio, film or television, Green passed away at the age of fifty in New York.

Arthur Hall *also has stories in Parts XXXVIII and XXXIX*

Paula Hammond has written over sixty fiction and non-fiction books, as well as short stories, comics, poetry, and scripts for educational DVD's. When not glued to the keyboard, she can usually be found prowling round second-hand books shops or hunkered down in a hide, soaking up the joys of the natural world.

In the year 1998 **Craig Janacek** took his degree of Doctor of Medicine at Vanderbilt University, and proceeded to Stanford to go through the training prescribed for pediatricians in practice. Having completed his studies there, he was duly attached to the University of California, San Francisco as a Professor. The author of over two-hundred medical monographs upon a variety of obscure lesions, his travel-worn and battered tin dispatch-box is crammed with papers, most of which are records of his fictional works. These include several collections of *The Further Adventures of Sherlock Holmes*: *Light in the Darkness*, *The Gathering Gloom*, *The Treasury of Sherlock Holmes*, *The Travels of Sherlock Holmes*, *The Chronicles of Sherlock Holmes*, *The Histories of Sherlock Holmes*, *The Acts of Sherlock Holmes*, and *The Assassination of Sherlock Holmes* – as well as two Dr. Watson novels (*The Isle of Devils* and *The Gate of Gold*), the complete and expanded *Adventures* and *Exploits of Brigadier Gerard* (*Set Europe Shaking* and *A Mighty Shadow*), and two non-Holmes novels (*The Oxford Deception* and *The Anger of Achilles Peterson*). His short stories have been published in several editions of *The MX Book of New Sherlock Holmes Stories, Part I: 1881-1889* (2015), *Part IV: 2016 Annual* (2016), *Part VI: 2017 Annual* (2017), *Part VIII: Eliminate the Impossible* (2017), *Part XI: Some Untold Cases* (2018), *Part XVIII: Whatever Remains Must be the Truth* (2019), *Part XXIII: Some More Untold Cases* (2020), *Part XXV: 2021 Annual* (2021), *Part XXXII: 2022 Annual* (2022), *Part XXXVI: However Improbable . . . .* (2022), and *Part XXXVIII: 2023 Annual* (2023). Other stories have appeared in *Holmes Away From Home: Tales of the Great Hiatus* (2016), *Tales from the Stranger's Room 3* (2017), *Sherlock Holmes: Adventures Beyond the Canon* (2018), *Sherlock Holmes, A Year of Mysteries – 1881* (2021), and *Sherlock Holmes: Stranger than Fiction* (2021). He lives near San Francisco, California with his wife and two children, where he is at work on his next story. Craig Janacek is a *nom-de-plume*.

Kelvin I. Jones is the author of six books about Sherlock Holmes and the definitive biography of Conan Doyle as a spiritualist, *Conan Doyle and The Spirits*. A member of *The Sherlock Holmes Society of London*, he has published numerous short occult and ghost stories in British anthologies over the last thirty years. His work has appeared on BBC Radio, and in 1984 he won the Mason Hall Literary Award for his poem cycle about the survivors of Hiroshima and Nagasaki, recently reprinted as "Omega". (Oakmagic Publications) A one-time teacher of creative writing at the University of East Anglia, he is also the author of four crime novels featuring his ex-met sleuth John Bottrell, who first appeared in *Stone Dead*. He has over fifty titles on Kindle, and is also the author of several novellas and short story collections featuring a Norwich based detective, DCI Ketch, an intrepid sleuth who investigates East Anglian murder cases. He also published a series of short stories about an Edwardian psychic detective, Dr. John Carter (*Carter's Occult Casebook*). Ramsey Campbell, the British horror writer, and Francis King, the renowned novelist, have both compared his supernatural stories to those of M. R. James. He has also published children's fiction, namely *Odin's Eye*, and, in collaboration with his wife Debbie, *The Dark Entry*. Since 1995, he has been the proprietor of Oakmagic Publications, publishers of British folklore and of his fiction titles.

Naching T. Kassa is a wife, mother, and writer. She's created short stories, novellas, poems, and co-created three children. She resides in Eastern Washington State with her husband, Dan Kassa. Naching is a member of *The Horror Writers Association, Mystery Writers of America, The Sound of the Baskervilles, The ACD Society, The Crew of the Barque Lone Star*, and *The Sherlock Holmes Society of London*. She works in Talent Relations at Crystal Lake Publishing and was a recipient of the 2022 HWA Diversity Grant. You can find her work on Amazon.
https://www.amazon.com/Naching-T-Kassa/e/B005ZGHTI0

Susan Knight's newest novel, *Death in the Garden of England*, from MX publishing, is the latest in a series which began with her collection of stories, *Mrs. Hudson Investigates* (2019), the novel *Mrs. Hudson goes to Ireland* (2020), and *Mrs. Hudson goes to Paris* (2022). She has contributed to several of the MX anthologies of new Sherlock Holmes short stories and enjoys writing as Dr. Watson as much as she does Mrs. Hudson. Susan is the author of two other non-Sherlockian story collections, as well as three novels, a book of non-fiction, and several plays, and has won several prizes for her writing. Susan lives in Dublin.

Sonya Kudei *also has a story in Part XXXVIII*

John Lawrence served for thirty-eight years on personal, committee, and leadership staffs in the U.S. House of Representatives. A visiting professor at the University of California's Washington Center since 2013, he is the author of *The Class of '74: Congress After Watergate and the Roots of Partisanship* (Johns-Hopkins, 2018) and *Arc of Power: Inside the Pelosi Speakership 2005-2010* (Kansas, 2022). His collected "history mystery" Sherlock Holmes pastiches have been published in *The Undiscovered Archives of Sherlock Holmes* (MX Publishing, 2022), in numerous volumes of *The MX Book of New Sherlock Holmes Stories*, and in Belanger Books' *After the East Wind Blows. Sherlock Holmes: The Affair at Mayerling Lodge* will be published in 2023. He blogs at DOMEocracy (johnalawrence.wordpress.com). He is a graduate of Oberlin College and has a Ph.D. in history from the University of California (Berkeley).

Gordon Linzner is founder and former editor of *Space and Time Magazine*, and author of four published novels and dozens of short stories in *F&SF, Twilight Zone, Sherlock Holmes Mystery Magazine*, and numerous other magazines and anthologies. He is a full member of the *Horror Writers Association* and a lifetime member of *Science Fiction and Fantasy Writers Association*.

David MacGregor is a playwright, screenwriter, novelist, and nonfiction writer. He is a resident artist at The Purple Rose Theatre in Michigan, where a number of his plays have been produced. His plays have been performed from New York to Tasmania, and his work has been published by Dramatic Publishing, Playscripts, Smith & Kraus, Applause, Heuer Publishing, and Theatrical Rights Worldwide (TRW). He adapted his dark comedy, *Vino Veritas*, for the silver screen, and it stars Carrie Preston (Emmy-winner for *The Good Wife*). Several of his short plays have also been adapted into films. He is the author of three Sherlock Holmes plays: *Sherlock Holmes and the Adventure of the Elusive Ear, Sherlock*

Holmes and the Adventure of the Fallen Soufflé, and *Sherlock Holmes and the Adventure of the Ghost Machine*. He adapted all three plays into novels for Orange Pip Books, and also wrote the two-volume nonfiction *Sherlock Holmes: The Hero with a Thousand Faces* for MX Publishing. He teaches writing at Wayne State University in Detroit and is inordinately fond of cheese and terriers.

Michael Mallory is the author of the *Amelia Watson* series and twenty other books, both fiction and nonfiction. His story "What the Cat Dragged In," published in *The Strand Magazine*, has been selected for inclusion in *The Best Mystery Stories of the Year*, 2023 edition. By day he is a Los Angeles-based entertainment journalist who works with the Academy of Motion Picture Arts and Sciences' Visual History Program as a researcher and interviewer. He can also tell you where to find the best British pubs in Southern California.

David Marcum *also has stories in Parts XXXVIII and XXXIX*

Jen Matteis is a professional writer and editor who lives in Silicon Valley. Her writing has appeared in a dozen community and alt-weekly newspapers on both coasts of the U.S., magazines, fiction anthologies, and countless other publications. When not writing for work, she writes for fun: mystery, sci-fi, horror, and fantasy. Find her online at: *www.jenmatteis.com*

Carlos Orsi is a Brazilian writer of mystery, science fiction, and fantasy, and an award-winning science journalist. He coedited the first anthology of original Sherlock Holmes stories by Brazilian authors, Aventuras Secretas, in 2012. His mystery stories have appeared in Ellery Queen Mystery Magazine, Mystery Weekly, and Needle. His Sherlockian musings have been published in The Baker Street Journal and The Watsonian.

Ember Pepper was born and raised in San Diego, CA. She has an M.F.A. degree in Creative Fiction Writing. She has been a fan of The Great Detective since she was a pre-teen and her greatest artistic enjoyment is challenging herself to write quality pastiches of Sherlock Holmes and his stalwart biographer and friend, John Watson.

Tracy J. Revels *also has stories in Parts XXXVIII and XXXIX*

Roger Riccard's family history has Scottish roots, which trace his lineage back to Highland Scotland. This British Isles ancestry encouraged his interest in the writings of Sir Arthur Conan Doyle at an early age. He has authored the novels, *Sherlock Holmes & The Case of the Poisoned Lilly*, and *Sherlock Holmes & The Case of the Twain Papers.* In addition he has produced several short stories in *Sherlock Holmes Adventures for the Twelve Days of Christmas* and the series *A Sherlock Holmes Alphabet of Cases.* A new series will begin publishing in the Autumn of 2022, and his has another novel in the works. All of his books have been published by Baker Street Studios. His Bachelor of Arts Degrees in both Journalism and History from California State University, Northridge, have proven valuable to his writing historical fiction, as well as the encouragement of his wife/editor/inspiration and Sherlock Holmes fan, Rosilyn. She passed in 2021, and it is in her memory that he continues to contribute to the legacy of the *"man who never lived and will never die"*.

Dan Rowley *also has a story in Part XXXIX*

Jane Rubino is the author of *A Jersey Shore* mystery series, featuring a Jane Austen-loving amateur sleuth and a Sherlock Holmes-quoting detective, *Knight Errant, Lady Vernon and Her Daughter*, (a novel-length adaptation of Jane Austen's novella *Lady Susan*, co-authored with her daughter Caitlen Rubino-Bradway, *What Would Austen Do?*, also co-authored with her daughter, a short story in the anthology *Jane Austen Made Me Do It*, *The Rucastles' Pawn, The Copper Beeches from Violet Turner's POV*, and, of course, there's the Sherlockian novel in the drawer – who doesn't have one? Jane lives on a barrier island at the New Jersey shore.

Geri Schear is a novelist and short story writer. Her work has been published in literary journals in the U.S. and Ireland. Her first novel, *A Biased Judgement: The Diaries of Sherlock Holmes 1897* was released to critical acclaim in 2014. The sequel, *Sherlock Holmes and the Other Woman* was published in 2015, and *Return to Reichenbach* in 2016. She lives in Kells, Ireland.

Shane Simmons is the author of the occult detective novels *Necropolis* and *Epitaph*, and the crime collection *Raw and Other Stories*. An award-winning screenwriter and graphic novelist, his work has appeared in international film festivals, museums, and lectures about design and structure. He was born in Lachine, a suburb of Montreal best known for being massacred in 1689 and having a joke name. Visit Shane's homepage at *eyestrainproductions.com* for more.

Award winning poet and author **Joseph W. Svec III** enjoys writing, poetry, and stories, and creating new adventures for Holmes and Watson that take them into the worlds of famous literary authors and scientists. His *Missing Authors* trilogy introduced Holmes to Lewis Carroll, Jules Verne, H.G. Wells, and Alfred Lord Tennyson, as well as many of their characters. His transitional story *Sherlock Holmes and the Mystery of the First Unicorn* involved several historical figures, besides a Unicorn or two. He has also written the rhymed and metered Sherlock Holmes Christmas adventure, *The Night Before Christmas in 221b*, sure to be a delight for Sherlock Holmes enthusiasts of all ages. Joseph won the Amador Arts Council 2021 Original Poetry Contest, with his Rhymed and metered story poem, "The Homecoming". Joseph has presented a literary paper on Sherlock Holmes/Alice in Wonderland crossover literature to the Lewis Carroll Society of North America, as well as given several presentations to the Amador County Holmes Hounds, Sherlockian Society. He is currently working on his first book in the *Missing Scientist Trilogy, Sherlock Holmes and the Adventure of the Demonstrative Dinosaur*, in which Sherlock meets Professor George Edward Challenger. Joseph has Masters Degrees in Systems Engineering and Human Organization Management, and has written numerous technical papers on Aerospace Testing. In addition to writing, Joseph enjoys creating miniature dioramas based on music, literature, and history from many different eras. His dioramas have been featured in magazine articles and many different blogs, including the North American Jules Verne society newsletter. He currently has 57 dioramas set up in his display area, and has written a reference book on toy castles and knights from around the world. An avid tea enthusiast, his tea cabinet contains over five-hundred different varieties, and he delights in sharing afternoon tea with his childhood sweetheart and wonderful wife, who has inspired and coauthored several books with him.

Kevin P. Thornton was shortlisted six times for the Crime Writers of Canada best unpublished novel. He never won – they are all still unpublished, and now he writes short stories. He lives in Canada, north enough that ringing Santa Claus is a local call and winter is a way of life. He has contributed numerous short stories to The MX Book of New

Sherlock Holmes Stories. By the time you next hear from him, he hopes to have written more.

William Todd has been a Holmes fan his entire life, and credits *The Hound of the Baskervilles* as the impetus for his love of both reading and writing. He began to delve into fan fiction a few years ago when he decided to take a break from writing his usual Victorian/Gothic horror stories. He was surprised how well-received they were, and has tried to put out a couple of Holmes stories a year since then. When not writing, Mr. Todd is a pathology supervisor at a local hospital in Northwestern Pennsylvania. He is the husband of a terrific lady and father to two great kids, one with special needs, so the benefactor of these anthologies is close to his heart.

Tom Turley *also has a story in Part XXXIX*

Charles Veley has loved Sherlock Holmes since boyhood. As a father, he read the entire Canon to his then-ten-year-old daughter at evening story time. Now, this very same daughter, grown up to become acclaimed historical novelist Anna Elliott, has worked with him to develop new adventures in the *Sherlock Holmes and Lucy James Mystery Series*. Charles is also a fan of Gilbert & Sullivan, and wrote *The Pirates of Finance*, a new musical in the G&S tradition that won an award at the New York Musical Theatre Festival in 2013. Other than the Sherlock and Lucy series, all of the books on his Amazon Author Page were written when he was a full-time author during the late Seventies and early Eighties. He currently works for United Technologies Corporation, where his main focus is on creating sustainability and value for the company's large real estate development projects.

Peter Coe Verbica grew up on a commercial cattle ranch in Northern California, where he learned the value of a strong work ethic. He works for the Wealth Management Group of a global investment bank, and is an Adjunct Professor in the Economics Department at SJSU. He is the author of numerous books, including *Left at the Gate and Other Poems*, *Hard-Won Cowboy Wisdom (Not Necessarily in Order of Importance)*, *A Key to the Grove and Other Poems*, and two volumes of *The Missing Tales of Sherlock Holmes* (as Compiled by Peter Coe Verbica, JD). Mr. Verbica obtained a JD from Santa Clara University School of Law, an MS from Massachusetts Institute of Technology, and a BA in English from Santa Clara University. He is the co-inventor on a number of patents, has served as a Managing Member of three venture capital firms, and the CFO of one of the portfolio companies. He is an unabashed advocate of cowboy culture and enjoys creative writing, hiking, and tennis. He is married with four daughters. For more information, or to contact the author, please go to *www.hardwoncowboywisdom.com*

Margaret Walsh was born Auckland, New Zealand and now lives in Melbourne, Australia. She is the author of *Sherlock Holmes and the Molly-Boy Murders*, *Sherlock Holmes and the Case of the Perplexed Politician*, *Sherlock Holmes and the Case of the London Dock Deaths*, *The Adventure of the Bloody Duck and Other Tales of Sherlock Holmes* and *Sherlock Holmes and the Curse of Neb-Heka-Ra*, all published by MX Publishing. She is currently working on her sixth book, *Sherlock Holmes and the Hellfire Heirs*. Margaret has been a devotee of Sherlock Holmes since childhood and has had several Holmesian related essays printed in anthologies, and is a member of the online society *Doyle's Rotary Coffin, as well as being a member of Sisters of Crime Australia.* She has an ongoing love affair with the city of London. When she's not working or planning trips to London. Margaret can be found frequenting the many and varied bookshops of Melbourne.

I.A. Watson, great-grand-nephew of Dr. John H. Watson, has been intrigued by the notorious "black sheep" of the family since childhood, and was fascinated to inherit from his grandmother a number of unedited manuscripts removed circa 1956 from a rather larger collection reposing at Lloyds Bank Ltd (which acquired Cox & Co Bank in 1923). Upon discovering the published corpus of accounts regarding the detective Sherlock Holmes from which a censorious upbringing had shielded him, he felt obliged to allow an interested public access to these additional memoranda, and is gradually undertaking the task of transcribing them for admirers of Mr. Holmes and Dr. Watson's works. In the meantime, I.A. Watson continues to pen other books, the latest of which is *The Incunabulum of Sherlock Holmes*. A full list of his seventy or so published works are available at: *http://www.chillwater.org.uk/writing/iawatsonhome.htm*

The MX Book of New Sherlock Holmes Stories
Edited by David Marcum
((MX Publishing, 2015-   )

"This is the finest volume of Sherlockian fiction I have ever read, and I have read, literally, thousands." – Philip K. Jones

"Beyond Impressive . . . This is a splendid venture for a great cause!"
– Roger Johnson, Editor, *The Sherlock Holmes Journal,*
The Sherlock Holmes Society of London

Part I: 1881-1889; Part II: 1890-1895; Part III: 1896-1929

Part IV: 2016 Annual

Part V: Christmas Adventures

Part VI: 2017 Annual

Eliminate the Impossible
Part VII: (1880-1891); Part VIII: (1892-1905)

2018 Annual
Part IX: (1879-1895); Part X: (1896-1916)

Some Untold Cases
Part XI: (1880-1891); Part XII: (1894-1902)

2019 Annual
Part XIII: (1881-1890); Part XIV: (1891-1897); Part XV: (1898-1917)

Whatever Remains . . . Must be the Truth
Part XVI: (1881-1890); Part XVII: (1891-1898); Part XVIII: (1898-1925)

2020 Annual
Part XIX: (1882-1890); Part XX: (1891-1897); Part XXI: (1898-1923).

Some More Untold Cases
Part XXII: (1877-1887); Part XXIII: (1888-1894); Part XXIV: (1895-1903)

2021 Annual
Part XXV: (1881-1888); Part XXVI: (1889-1897); Part XXVII: (1898-1928)

More Christmas Adventures
Part XXVIII: (1869-1888); Part XXIX: (1889-1896); Part XXX: (1897-1928)

2022 Annual
Part XXXI: (1875-1887); Part XXXII: (1888-1895); Part XXXIII: (1896-1919)

"However Improbable . . . ."
Part XXXIV: (1878-1888); Part XXXV: (1889-1896); Part XXXVI: (1897-1919)

2023 Annual
Parts XXXVII (1875-1889), XXXVIII (1889-1896), and XXXIX (1897-1923)

<u>In Preparation</u>
Further Untold Cases (Part XL – and XLI and XLII as well?)
. . . and more to come!

The MX Book of New Sherlock Holmes Stories
Edited by David Marcum
(MX Publishing, 2015-)

431

The MX Book of New Sherlock Holmes Stories
Edited by David Marcum
(MX Publishing, 2015-   )

An Investees' Anthology
Edited by David Marcum
(MX Publishing, 2022   )

Selected Contributions to
The MX Book of New Sherlock Holmes Stories
by Members of
The Baker Street Irregulars

*All royalties from this collection are being donated
for the benefit of the preservation of Undershaw,
a school for special needs students located at
one of the former homes of Sir Arthur Conan Doyle*

Stories, Forewords, and Poems in this volume
have previously appeared in Parts I – XXXVI of
The MX Book of New Sherlock Holmes Stories

Featuring Contributions by:

Mark Alberstat, Marino C. Alvarez, Peter Calamai, Catherine Cooke, Carla Coupe, David Stuart Davies, John Farrell, Lyndsay Faye, Sonia Fetherston, Jayantika Ganguly, Jeffrey Hatcher, Roger Johnson, Leslie S. Klinger, Ann Margaret Lewis, Bonnie MacBird, Stephen Mason, Julie McKuras Nicholas Meyer, Jacquelynn Morris, Otto Penzler, Christopher Redmond, Tracy J. Revels, Steven Rothman, Nancy Holder, Mark Levy (and Arlene Mantin Levy), Nicholas Utechin, and Sean M. Wright (and DeForeest B. Wright, III)

MX Publishing

MX Publishing is the world's largest specialist Sherlock Holmes publisher, with over five-hundred titles and over two-hundred authors creating the latest in Sherlock Holmes fiction and non-fiction

The catalogue includes several award winning books, and over two-hundred-and-fifty have been converted into audio.

MX Publishing also has one of the largest communities of Holmes fans on Facebook, with regular contributions from dozens of authors.

www.mxpublishing.com

@mxpublishing on Facebook, Twitter, and Instagram

www.ingramcontent.com/pod-product-compliance
Lightning Source LLC
Chambersburg PA
CBHW020920020726
47495CB00002B/267